Born

Melissa A Geary

This book is a work of fiction. Names, characters, places, and dialogue are products of the author's imagination and are not to be construed as real. Any resemblance to actual events, organizations, or persons, living or dead, is entirely coincidental.

Copyright © 2019 Melissa A Geary

Cover Photograph by Melissa A Geary

Co-Editor Jacob Ryan Rodriguez

Interior Map Art by Jonathan Mui

Author Photograph by Jess Dalton

ISBN: 978-1979567374

DEDICATION

This book is for my loving husband, Tom. Thank you for understanding my constant babbling about this book and this world. I hope you know it's only going to get worse as I move on to book two!

ACKNOWLEDGMENTS

This book could not have been a possibility without two very important people. Thank you Olivia for being my voice of reason. I would not have even started this adventure without the little push and pep talk you gave me all those years ago. You might not believe me when I say this, but you are the reason this world even exists. Jake, you know that I am forever indebted to you. Without your enthusiasm I would have given up on this story a long time ago. Thank you for pushing me as a writer and allowing me to watch your journey as you fell in love with my work as I was still creating it. That is a gift that I will always cherish. I also want to thank my brother, Jonathan, for making the map of this world. He put my creation to paper in a way that I never could and I'm so grateful for his hard work.

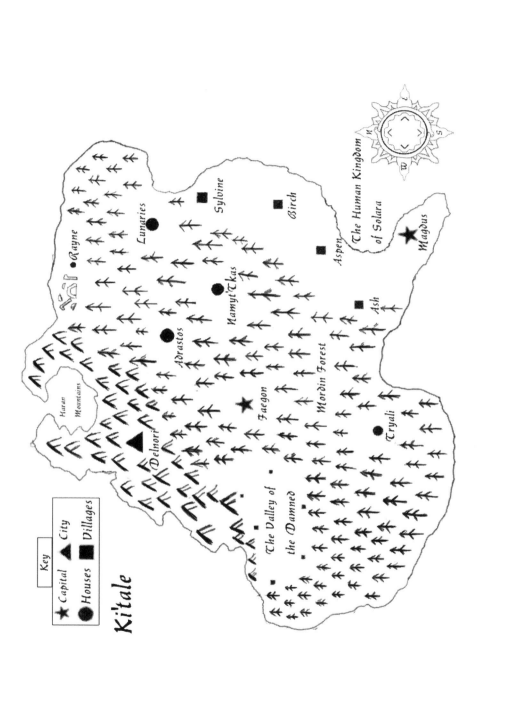

Ki'tale

Key
★ Capital
▲ City
● Houses
■ Villages

The Human Kingdom of Solara

Magdus

Sylvine
Birch
Aspen
Lunaries
Rayne
Namyt'Ckas
Ash
Adrastos
Mordin Forest
Faegon
Huran Mountains
Delnore
Cryali
The Valley of the Damned

GWYNDOLYN

Gwyndolyn, of the great vampire House Faegon, sat in the corner of the run-down pub surveying her surroundings with unabashed distaste. The air was thick with humidity, causing her travel warn linens to stick to her skin, constricting her every movement. Fresh mud clung to her boots, and to many of the pub's patrons, causing an unpleasant aroma of decay to permeate the overcrowded room. It was mixed with the sour smell of human sweat and greasy pub food, a noxious scent that had her feeling rather fortunate that she couldn't become sick off the fumes. The rain in the Valley of the Damned hadn't subsided in nearly a week and Gwyndolyn would have been happy enough for shelter if it didn't include being surrounded by so many people. Humans and vampires alike were partaking in wine, blood, and other vices all around her while Gwyndolyn sat still as stone, waiting for her partner to return from the bar.

Cody Gilhart had the face of a child to match his charming personality. It was no surprise that he fared better at the bar, teasing information from the patrons without raising any alarm, than she. They had learned a long time ago that his warm blue eyes and beautiful smile made for a better conversationalist than her own dark gaze. It mattered not to the woman. She had taken the job as a bounty hunter for a reason; she didn't have to be charismatic to hunt thieves, murderers, and any others who committed treason under the purview of the Crown. Save for Cody, she rather detested all people, humans and vampires alike, and she would be happy to never have to hold a proper conversation for the rest of her existence if she could.

"You look lonely, m'lady. Care for some companionship?" An ill dressed man, with dirt in his matted black hair, crooned from the end of the table. His odor was particularly foul and his eyes were glassy; it was obvious he had consumed too much spirits.

"No."

It was clear that the man was not accustomed to hearing the word, or possibly he was more inebriated than she had originally assumed, but his eyes squinted and his brow furrowed. "What do you mean, no?"

"I believe even a simple man such as yourself should understand the word no." Gwyndolyn was hardly in any mood. She and Cody had been trailing the elusive vampire named Decker for weeks. He was rumored to be part of the traitor's court and a high bounty had been placed on his head. There weren't many who evaded her's and Cody's capture, but this Decker fellow was good, she would give him that. His ability to keep multiple steps ahead of them spoke to his intelligence, something that most of their marks lacked, which was both refreshing and infuriating.

"A Lady such as yourself shouldn't turn down a man like me." His words were becoming harder to understand as his face colored an ugly purple. He was angry, that was an emotion that the female bounty hunter could understand all too well.

"Well then, it's lucky I am no Lady." The man looked as if to move toward her and she rose to her feet in one graceful movement. A vampire of her age and training had little need for weapons, but she kept a sharp dagger on her belt to deal with the thick foliage of Mordin Forest and she let it slide from its sheath until the cold steel reflected off of the dim candlelight.

"You don't scare me," his words were louder this time and the unwanted attention of others bored down on her in swift, judgmental fury.

Gwyndolyn took a moment to compose herself and think of her next steps. She was normally not so quick to rash actions, but she was exhausted and rather looking forward to a cool glass of blood and a dreamless sleep. Seeing Cody eye her from over the brute's shoulder was enough to remind her to keep her emotions in check. Without a word, she sheathed her dagger and took her seat. The eyes that had instantly trained themselves on her seemed to slowly lose interest.

"That's right, you dirty whore," the man aimed to spit at her, but he was drunk enough that he missed and got it on himself. Whatever satisfaction she may have felt was robbed of her as the man seemed to believe the sickening glob of spittle trailing down his chin had come from her. He advanced on her with deceiving speed for a man of his size and inebriation.

There were no eyes on her then, Gwyndolyn was careful to brush the longer strands of brunette hair from her cool grey eyes. Drunk or not, this man would know the look of a vampire in bloodlust and she intended on making her point clear. She felt her fangs descend and she knew her eyes were glowing brighter than usual. It had the desired effect. The human backed up with such speed and force that he knocked into the table behind him. She was quick to draw back her bloodlust and appear normal and the patrons who had begun to pay them no mind looked back toward them again, though this time their judgmental eyes were trained on the stumbling man.

"Careful there, Gwyn, you don't want to draw any attention to us." Cody said by way of greeting as he placed a goblet of blood before her. There was a teasing glint his eyes that nearly made Gwyn snap in response before she remembered with whom it was she was speaking. The boy merely laughed under his breath, turning his attention back to the drink in hand. His own mug was letting off small puffs of steam and a weak scent. It most likely a thick broth that had very little taste and even less nutritional value, but they took what they could get on the road and Cody never complained.

"What did you find out?" She asked, her voice sounding harsh even to her own ears. To his credit, the boy hardly seemed bothered by it. Cody had been in her care from the tender age of fifteen and now, a decade later the boy showed her no fear, not even on her worst days. She had never decided if that was bravery or stupidity on his part, but she knew he could certainly be both in equal measure. It was endearing, though she would never admit it to the boy.

"He's nearby." Cody sipped the sludge in his cup without complaint. It was one of his best qualities. Being a bounty hunter was not an easy job and most found that the rewards were very little in comparison to the sacrifices made, but Cody never seemed to mind. He was very grounded, so much so that sometimes Gwyn was sure that the fates had sought it fit that she find him when she did. She may have taught him everything he knew, but he helped remind her of what was most important in life, she often wondered where she would be had he not insisted on joining her a decade before.

"Do we know that for sure? We've had a lot of false leads." They had been on this bounty longer than most in large thanks to the fact that most of their leads had come up short. There was no shortage of rogue vampires wreaking havoc in the Valley of the Damned. The fact that Decker was a direct childe of Cassandra, and thus bore her mark, seemed to escape most first hand accounts. Cody had been the one to remind her that most humans were too busy running in terror and were less likely to have the training in observation that they had, but Gwyn still found it no excuse for leading them astray.

"Well the wounds are all consistent, though the person I spoke to this time did accurately describe Cassandra's mark on him and that was not a detail your average human would know."

The wounds that Cody referred to were the crudely carved 'C' in the foreheads of Decker's victims. It was the maniac's way of tributing his kills to his sire and queen.

"Then we should go now," Gwyn was just about to rise from her seat again, but the look in Cody's eyes stopped her.

"You're tired," before she could argue, the man grimaced and corrected himself, "we're both tired. I for one would like a few hours of sleep with a real roof over my head before we chase after a madman."

"This is the first time we've gotten an accurate description of him, paired with the wounds we cannot let him get away. We can't afford creature comforts until we've found him."

"Well it's a shame that I've already spent the money on a room then, we've only got so much to sustain us for this bounty and we really ought not to waste it." Cody's tone was serious, but his eyes shone with mirth. She knew that she had been played and while she was upset with the boy, she was also thankful; rest would do them both good.

"Fine." Gwyn lifted the goblet of blood to her lips to fight the smile that involuntarily slid on her face at the sight of Cody's triumphant grin. Their extended time together had allowed the boy's carefree attitude to grow on the austere huntress and she found herself indulging him more and more.

A shrill scream from the street brought the two from their relaxed posture to their feet in moments. For all of his talk of rest, Cody looked alert as he unsheathed his dagger and Gwyn allowed the bloodlust to take over once more. Her eyes glowed and her fangs protruded past her lips as her senses became intensely heightened. There were more desperate screams in the distance, and the sounds of feet sloshing through the muddy streets toward the pub were growing louder.

"Let's go," Cody said, echoing her own thoughts. He took the lead, never once allowing his humanity to slow him down.

The two left the pub, pushing past confused and scared patrons as they made their way to the door. The rain was pelting down hard and Cody pulled his hood up over his messy blond mop, shielding his eyes from the worst of it. Gwyn motioned to the right with a subtle gesture and Cody fell into step with ease allowing her to lead, since she had keener senses, especially in such weather. Unlike Cody, Gwyn didn't bother to cover up from the storm; it would only serve to slow her down and a little rain had never bothered her. They moved along the wall of the pub in complete synchronization. The huntress felt her partner at her back like a shadow, as if he was an extension of her own body.

The pub was in the center of the village and was lined on either side with other such buildings that held other businesses. It only took them a few minutes before they left the center behind and found themselves surrounded by small huts that made up the residences of the villagers. The village itself was pitifully small; only a few hundred people lived in tightly settled huts forming a circle around the village square. They were one of the poorer groups of people that the pair had seen on their journey, though it wasn't uncommon this far from the protection of House Faegon to be treated with such poverty.

The few people who had been milling about when they first arrived to the village, were nowhere to be found. Rogue attacks must have been common, as the windows of many of the structures they passed were boarded up with old, rotting wood and every door was shut tight, not even the flicker of a candle peeking through the cracks. It seemed that the people who had been running toward the village center had already found shelter and the loud echo of wood barriers slotting into locks could be heard in nearly every hut they passed. Over each thud Gwyn could hear the steady beat of Cody's heart and it brought her comfort. There was nothing more valuable than having a reliable partner in their field of work and Cody was just that.

"To the left, there is a clearing that lies right along the edge of the woods." Cody whispered, tapping her left shoulder and sliding up to take the lead. Cody had taken the task of scouting the village earlier that day while Gwyn had gone ahead to the center and had tried her hand at questioning the locals. She trusted that he would take them in the right direction and was not disappointed when the closely packed buildings gave way to a small clearing directly leading to the thickly settled Mordin Forest.

The rain was coming down harder with nothing to shelter them and Gwyn thanked her naturally enhanced eyesight for not failing her now. Right at the tree line there was a mass that appeared to be a stack of bodies while a single figure loomed over them, thrashing about and spraying blood into the air. Even from such a far distance, Gwyn could see the vampire's glowing purple eyes. They had finally made their mark.

"That must be him," Cody vocalized unnecessarily. "We need to take him down with minimal damage, remember the orders were to take him in alive."

"I don't need you to remind me of our orders, brat." Gwyn said, though there was no malice in her voice.

She had nearly forgotten that the directive had been for the rogue to be brought back alive. Normally killing the scoundrels and returning with their heads was enough to claim the bounty, but this one was special. Decker was not only a direct childe of the traitor Cassandra, but he was rumored to be one of her closest confidants as well as being close to her husband, Logan, the self proclaimed king and leader of the rogues. His potential knowledge of their plans was more valuable to the Crown than the possible damage it would cause to capture and bring him in alive. It seemed foolish to Gwyn, they could easily bottle his blood and have an elder on the council drink it to gain his memories, but she was not paid to make such decisions.

"Check on the humans if you can, but we must capture the rogue first."

Cody nodded his understanding, before hunching down, ready to spring into action on her command. Decker no doubt already knew that they were watching him, so there was no hope for the element of surprise, but they would need to move together if they had any hope to take down one of the most notorious members of Logan's inner circle. Gwyn watched as her partner breathed in and out, listening to his steady heartbeat and it reminded her just how much this human, her human, trusted her. She counted the beats to twenty, they were steady and that was all she needed to know that he was ready.

"Now." Gwyn whispered and Cody sprang into action.

Gwyn allowed him a moment head start before surging forward herself. She was faster and wouldn't take long to make the distance. She watched as Decker stopped from carving a 'C' into his latest victim's forehead to focus on the human and Gwyn was disturbed to see a chilling smile settle on his face. The purple glow to his eyes only added to the crazed look.

Cody was a seasoned hunter, but he wasn't a fool and she could practically taste his fear as he also recognized the crazed rogue honing in on him. The huntress could hear Cody's heartbeat even clearer now as it danced in an uneven pattern. It was so loud to her ears that she almost missed the faint heartbeats coming from the pile of bodies. There were survivors.

It was impossible to track time when her bloodlust took over. The wind whipped past her and she was thankful that running through the rain had slicked her long hair back, away from her eyes, instead of obstructing her view of the sick monster. Decker seemed to be waiting for them as he simply stood and watched. Gwyn realized too late that the rogue was not going to move from his spot and she could not stop herself as she slammed into the other vampire head on. The impact would have killed a human, as it was she could feel as her collarbone cracked. The hiss of pain that left her lips could have woken the very dead at her feet, her normal composure gone as she reeled from the impact. Decker, for his part, seemed less frazzled as he undoubtedly had prepared himself for the impending crash. It would seem that he had in fact been waiting for them and he was even more willing to be taken.

"Ouch, that sounded like it hurt," Decker smirked from above. It was only then that Gwyn realized she must have fallen as she was looking up at him.

"That's enough," Cody was standing behind their mark, his blade poised and dangerously close to the vampire's jugular. If it hadn't been a magically enhanced weapon, it might not have subdued him.

"Sunspears are a dirty trick." Decker spat, eyes narrowed. His fingers twitched, but with the weapon so close to his throat, he would not dare try anything. "Where would a human even get one of those? You must be very important to carry such a *prize*."

Cody was someone special. It was a gift from the Council given to him after his first big bounty. Forged in the heart of Faegon, the spears were dangerously sharp and the hilt was delicately shaped so it could be sheathed in a holster meant to be hidden and close to the body. It was no longer than six centimeters, but it's size and ability to conceal was not the reason why they were so dangerous. Sunspears were soaked in sunlight for half a moon's turn throughout the forging process. Only elder vampires could make them and even then it was hard to forge such a weapon. For that reason there were few in existence.

"I would say that the fangs and unnatural strength are a dirty trick, but I understand those are not always a choice." Cody, for all of his normal cheery composure, could be serious when he needed to be. He was smart too, too smart to fall for such bait. The less Decker knew about them the better.

"It was my choice," Decker growled.

That was a curious thing. Most of the people turned by Logan and Cassandra were rumored to be forced and then carefully brainwashed to become loyal to their cause, but Gwyn could to tell that he was not lying.

"Enough," Gwyn sighed as she got to her feet. "Cody check the victims, there are still a few alive. I can handle him."

"I wouldn't bother, the ones that are still breathing will soon stop. I gave them a sample of my blood." To prove his point, Decker turned his wrist and showed the thin line where he had cut himself to bleed. It was healed, all save for a small scratch.

"Gwyn we cannot leave them."

"You know what has to be done." Gwyn stood at her full height, ignoring the sharp pain in her collarbone. It would heal quickly enough. "I"ll put the irons on him, you take care of the rest."

Gwyn had seen many despicable things in her time as a huntress; she would be the first to admit that she had also done many horrible things, but the carnage Decker had created on his own and in such little time was both impressive and terrifying. The bodies of at least a dozen humans lay about the field, some were so badly mutilated she couldn't be sure if they were men or women, adults or children. He hadn't drained the blood from every body and the sweet smell clung to the air making Gwyn dizzy. She had just fed and she had an iron will over her hunger, but such a display was hard even for her to ignore. There were few still breathing and she watched as Cody made quick work of slitting their throats. They may have drank vampire's blood, but killing them before the change would insure that it never happened. The human did the work quickly without hesitation, but not without remorse. Gwyn had seen a lot of death, had caused a lot of it too, but this was senseless and despicable. Decker, for his part, seemed to looked quite pleased with himself even with his hands bound behind him in sun-soaked iron shackles.

"I would say I was sorry for the mess, but of course that would be a lie." The lazy comment from the rogue brought Gwyn from her thoughts and her critical gaze fell on him again.

"You're fortunate that our orders are to bring you in alive. I wouldn't hesitate to skin you alive myself."

"Do you always follow your orders? I'm sure your *Crown* would not be pleased to know you killed innocent humans." Gwyn did not like the smug look he gave her or the disgust he infused into the word Crown.

"We spared them the fate of a forced turning, I doubt the Crown would be upset."

"Isn't it odd that you demonize me for not giving them the choice of taking the gift, but you justify your own actions when you take the very same choice away from them? You are no better than we are."

"Enough," Cody cut in. Gwyn and Decker would have argued in circles for hours had he not stopped them, of this the huntress was sure. Throwing a wary look to the rogue first, Cody continued. "We should get some rest, Gwyn, the shackles will hold him through the day."

"Even if they did, we couldn't go back into the village, there is no way they would allow it."

"I can't image why they'd be upset to see me." Decker drawled. Gwyn ignored the comment and Cody seemed more than happy to follow her lead.

"But the rooms—"

"We will make the money back and then some when we turn in this bounty."

"I think there is something simply abhorrent about people profiting from the capture and slaughter of other people." Decker continued as if he wasn't being ignored.

"That's rich coming from you," Cody motioned to the corpses around them.

"That? That's what I do for fun! I'm not asking anyone to pay me for partaking in my own pleasure."

"We need to get back on the road, before I change my mind about killing him." The human spoke casually, poking at the rogue's back with the tip of his sunspear toward the direction of the road.

"A wise choice," Decker nodded sagely and Gwyn closed her eyes sending a prayer up to gods she did not believe in, that their journey back to Faegon would not be a long one.

In response, if only to spite her, the weather responded to her prayer with a crack of thunder loud enough to echo and shake the trees. The only thing louder was the mad laughter from their bounty. Uncharacteristic dread pooled in the pit of her stomach.

"We should stop wasting time and get out of the rain," Gwyn said finally. Cody nodded and began toward the road keeping Decker between them; all the while the rogue continued his constant stream of antagonizing speech. If they didn't make good time to Faegon, Gwyn wasn't sure if all three of them would make it intact.

CODY

It was still raining in the Valley of the Damned. Cody was sure that it was the same storm brewing that had been present the night that he and his partner Gwyndolyn had captured their prisoner. Like the rogue's never-ending diatribe, the deluge would not let up. The heavy droplets stung at Cody's eyes, weighing down his long lashes, but he did his best to ignore it just as he had been ignoring Decker's constant chatter. Despite the gloom and Decker's generally annoying nature, the young hunter did his best to see the bright side of the situation. At least he was not in the predicament of their captive.

"We should be under the cover of Mordin Forest soon. I think we can afford to stop and rest then." Cody said, ending whatever Decker had been prattling on about, he honestly hadn't been listening.

"The more stops we take the longer it will be before we reach Faegon." Gwyn reminded him without taking her eyes off the road ahead.

"That may be the case, but a little rest would do us both good." Cody reasoned, knowing he had won even before she responded.

Gwyn was an elder vampire and Cody knew she could survive a lot more than most vampires could, but even she had a breaking point. The break she had suffered to her collar was very nearly healed, but she was still carrying her pack on one shoulder so it had to be causing her some level of discomfort, though he knew she would never admit it. He didn't need to rest right then, but he worried about his partner and was not above pretending that he was tired to force her to stop for her own good.

"Fine," Gwyn growled.

Cody did his best to hide his smile, he had known that would work. He had spent nearly half his life on the road with the vampire huntress. Originally he had been living in a small village in the Valley, but that had all changed when he met Gwyn. She had come to his village when he was fifteen, just on the cusp of being a man, in search of a rogue vampire. He'd known the woods nearby better than most, having always felt more at home amongst the trees, and he had provided invaluable information that had led her to a quick capture, which had increased the initial bounty. She'd offered him an opportunity to hunt with her on the spot and he hadn't looked back.

"If you don't wipe that grin off of your face, Cody, I will do it for you." The harsh bite in her tone did little to deter the brunet who often laughed off her threats, they were always empty. The fact that she had known he was smiling without even looking was telling of just how close they truly were.

"Let the human be happy. It will just make killing him that much sweeter." Decker spoke up sounding rather put out that he had been ignored while the two spoke.

"If you think that I would let you lay a hand on the boy then you are dumber then you look." Gwyn's ice cold glare should have instilled fear in the rogue, but he looked wholly unaffected.

"I doubt you could stop me even if you tried."

"That's rather rich coming from the one who is in irons right now." Cody thoughtfully pointed out.

"Did you ever consider that I simply let you *put me in irons* as you so graciously put it?" Decker leered and this time Gwyn did stop and turn. She ignored Decker and locked eyes with Cody. He had thought that capturing the rogue had been too easy and it seemed Gwyn had come to the same conclusion, though Cody was not surprised.

"We're wasting time, keep walking."

Cody watched as Decker smirked before following after Gwyn. He kept his eyes focused on the road ahead, checking on the rogue to make sure he wasn't attempting anything. The early morning rain was doing wonders to cover up the sun, making it dark enough for the vampires to travel in the open with little discomfort. Gwyn was old enough that the sun wouldn't have hurt her, much, but he was unsure how Decker would react and bringing him back alive and well enough to stand trial was their number one priority. The journey would take longer than most missions, and while it was more dangerous, Cody wasn't bothered by it. He hated having to kill their targets. For a moment he spared a thought to the innocent lives he had been forced to end due to Decker's gruesome actions and it made hatred boil in him in a way that he had never felt before. The irony that he was not allowed to kill the only bounty that he ever thought worthy of death was not lost on him. It was rather a blessing that he could not act on his anger. He was a seasoned hunter with far too much blood on his hands and he rather not add more to them if he didn't have to. Bringing on death never brought him any joy and he knew that should he kill Decker, it would be the same. Gwyn treated killing like a byproduct of their job and nothing more and she said it would happen to him one day too. He hoped that it never did, his resistance to killing reminded him that he was human.

Cody pulled himself from his thoughts to pay attention to the road. They were still out in the open on Smuggler's Road and so there were other humans and vampires around them, though they were giving their small group a wide berth. Despite the name, many honest farmers and merchants used Smuggler's Road to travel around the valley to push their wares.

"Get out of the way, blood suckers." An angry voice bellowed as a man on a cart, pulled by two aged horses, shot past them down the road. If he kicked more mud up at them then was necessary he certainly didn't seem sorry.

"Humans that can sniff out a vampire? Well, I'll be damned." The mockery in Decker's voice was clear.

"The humans around here have seen more than their fair share of rogues, they know to at least give all strange looking folk plenty of space. Most of them want no trouble and many and more willingly make the journey to Faegon. There are worse alternatives" Cody supplied, although the way his voice tapered off seemed to pique the rogue's interest.

"They *sacrifice* themselves?" Decker said the word as if it was a poison. He turned his accusatory look toward his fellow vampire. "Where is the fun in that? Where is the rush of the hunt? How can you even stomach blood you didn't fight for?"

"Simple, I spend my time hunting scum like you." Gwyn sneered. "It's time we get off the road."

Dawn was beginning to creep upon them and the sun was starting its climb up the horizon, through the clouds. The rain was so heavy that Cody had hardly noticed, but it seemed that his companions had. She might not be affected by the sun right away, but Gwyn would rather be in the shadow of the forest than vulnerable in the open during the day. Gwyndolyn took them off the path and to the right, through the thinning trees. The branches were far enough apart to let the three through with little trouble. The roots grew on top of each other, twisted and joined until it seemed like every tree was just an extension of the other. They had always been a great fascination to Cody, ever since he was a child playing with the few other children his own age. He had grown up not far from where they were, in a part of the Valley called the Deadlands by most. Many of the villagers where he was born were known for willingly becoming food for the vampires in Faegon and the other surrounding vampire houses. Many of the other humans looked down on them, but the protection it brought Cody's people was better than the alternative. There were far worse things beyond the Valley and in the vast mountain range to the North.

Cody knew little of what lived beyond in the mountains, his attention always drawn east to the trees. When Cody had been a child, Mordin Forest had been a second home to him. In some ways it had been his only home, the place where he had been able to escape the cruelty of the children in his

village. Even then he had been different, nothing like the other children his age. He had loved the trees and held no fear toward Mordin Forest despite his mother's warnings. In those times he had pretended that the trees had faces and spoke to them as he imagined other children had spoken to each other. Each had a name and a story that Cody still remembered.

"Follow me," Cody said, pushing thoughts of the past in the back of his mind where they belonged. Gwyn stepped aside for him to take the lead with ease. The tension that had existed between them on the road dissolved and Cody could feel the eyes focused on him as Decker looked on in mild fascination. Where once stood a young boy, teeming with energy, now stood a man, sure in his steps. They continued on the winding path, Cody leading the way through the most treacherous parts. While Gwyndolyn had been hunting longer than he'd been alive, Cody still knew the lands closest to the Deadlands and the Marsh better. Despite the thick canvas of leaves above, the ground below was still covered in patches of grass and weeds. Very few animals lived in the thickest part of the woods, but it didn't stop the crows from watching them from above.

Caw. Caw.

The sound brought the party to a halt. The baby hairs on the back of Cody's neck stood on end as he listened around for other noises. When it seemed silent enough, Gwyn gave the command to push on. They would need to move fast to make it to Faegon within a few days and that was only if Cody did not slow them down. While having a human liaison helping to enforce Faegon's rule was helpful, when it came to travel he often slowed down the operations. It would have been easy for two vampires to make the trip quickly, but with their slower pace, they would have to do their best to avoid any trouble. Trouble was not something that they could afford.

Naked branches reached out to Cody like long lost friends. He had climbed many a tree like them in his younger days and while he normally found their presence comforting, they did little to set him at ease. Their bare arms gave little shelter and the hunter could not help but feel that he was being watched. He knew that Decker was keeping a careful eye on him, but he still felt as if there were more eyes surrounding him, tracking his every move. He dared not voice his paranoia however, any sign of weakness in front of their captive and they could lose what little leverage they had over him. Despite his usually bright demeanor, Cody did in fact know when to keep silent and be serious. Placing each step with the utmost precision, he continued to lead the group through a winding path. Even though he made little noise, he could feel more than hear Gwyndolyn wince at his every step. If there were rogues in the forest they would be able to hear his movements too. Carefully, he adjusted his footing, hoping to lighten his steps. Their captive took a deliberate step on a twig, as if sensing his caution. The loud crack made both bounty hunters jump and the huntress shot her kin a cold look.

"You will stop that this instant." Her tone was soft and low, so much so that Cody nearly missed the threat, but he had no doubt that Decker heard the command. They weren't very far into the woods, but Cody could already tell that something was wrong. It wasn't uncommon to pass by other vampires even so close to the forest's border. There were vampires everywhere this close to the valley due to the proximity of the humans who gladly gave up their necks for the blood drinkers. Cody was accustomed to knowing that a friend or an enemy could be just around every bend, but the tension in the air felt different somehow. In his experience different often meant death.

"Or what?" Decker's grin was harsh, his voice loud. It bounced through the trees and a nest of birds flew off, upset by the sudden noise.

"Enough," Gwyn hissed just loud enough to be heard. She had her sunspear to Decker's throat before the other could react. Carefully she nicked his neck, making sure to leave a long, shallow cut. The second the steal touched his skin, Decker cried out in pain. "Before you think to threaten me again, remember that you are talking to someone who holds your life in the balance. I may have my orders, but say I forget them?" she let the threat hang in the air between them and moved out of his range.

"I know who you are Gwyndolyn of House Faegon, but does your human friend?" The rogue paused for dramatic effect, though Cody did not fall for the bait. "You think you're stronger than me, but don't forget there will always be someone older and stronger than you. I might not be your equal, but my Queen is always watching."

"Queen? If you could even refer to her as such. She would never endanger herself for the likes of you." Gwyn's tone was downright sadistic. Cody found he was rather enamored by it. She was always beautiful, but even more so when she had her prey cornered right where she wanted them.

"You know nothing of my Queen." Decker spit back. He made a move for her before remembering his wrists were still in irons. The slight stumble detracted from the fearsome air he was attempting to exude.

"I know more about her than you could ever hope to. You might think you're important to her, but Cassandra only cares about herself. If she cared for you at all don't you think she would have come for you? She has spies all around these woods, we may have just picked you up yesterday, but a vampire of her considerable power could have made to recuse you by now."

If the jibe stung, Decker didn't showed it. The tension had mounted to strangling heights, but no one dared to make a move. When it became obvious that the moment had passed, they pushed on, ignoring the crackling energy that had settled between them.

Water dripped down the leaves of the upper canopy, slowing the rain, though the path was still covered in mud. It was moments like this that made Cody wish he had accepted Gwyndolyn's offer of the Bite. She had only asked once, not that the offer had an expiration, but he had said no and he had meant it, even now. They were making their way through the thicket slowly on his account and the thought always made Cody feel as if there was a weight in his stomach, weighing him down. A soft sound came from their right, causing Gwyndolyn to stop, her head up and neck craned toward the direction of the sound.

"What's wrong, hunter?" Decker sneered, but Cody hushed him. The female's eyes had turned their telltale shining grey, which meant she was allowing her bloodlust to take over and her fangs grew out, instantly putting Cody on alert. The human reached for the sunspear at his hip. His weak human eyes took the best scan of the surroundings that they could, but he did not detect anything.

"We are being followed." Gwyn whispered confirming Cody's fears. Unlike his escorts, Decker's grin grew as if to welcome the intruder. All cheer from Cody's demeanor dissipated and his nerves frayed like torn cloth.

"There's nothing out there. Perhaps you're getting too old for this," Decker taunted.

For the first time since they had picked the rouge up, Cody actually saw Decker extend his fangs and stand tall. When they found him he had been crazed, exuding raw energy, but now he could actually feel the power radiating off of him. Cody had doubted that he might be one of Cassandra's inner circle, but now he wasn't as sure. He could tell now that Decker was a dangerous vampire, but not just because of his penchant for destruction, but because he was truly a force and Cody was only just starting to understand that. Before Cody could react, Gwyndolyn moved from the front of the pack to stand behind the rouge, her claws grazing his throat. The tension in the small enclosure mounted and the human was helpless to do anything, but watch.

"Well if I'd known you felt like that—" The leer broke whatever spell was over the three and the female vampire shoved their captive along.

"We're wasting time." Her fangs were out again. Cody could see that the lack of rest was starting to take its toll on her. Normally put together, Gwyn's silky brown hair had come undone in the their brief struggle and for the first time in a while, she looked wild to the human. She pushed the strands out of her eyes with more vigor than necessary as if she was pushing Decker out of her mind with the same motion.

"I have all of the time in the world." Decker smirked. Gwyn ignored him, turning back to the path and Cody took up the rear, keeping the rogue between them.

The further they walked into the dense woods, the more lively Decker seemed to get. Any tension that had been clinging to him seemed to evaporate with every step. Even Cody was left feeling uneasy with how cheerful the vampire seemed to become with every second that passed. The trees seemed to be more alive as well. There were more birds and small critters now that they were further removed from the human villages. It seemed to Cody as if Mordin Forest was singing a song, the noise drowning out all others. He did his best to listen to the woods, they had never let him down before, and the tune they played now sounded like a warning to the man. The branches reached out toward him as if to draw him in and protect him. Cody wished it were that easy.

Focusing his attention from the immediate sounds Cody did his best to pick out the sounds from further out. They were still sticking to a relatively well constructed dirt path so the trees that lined them on either side acted as a wall against the noises beyond. Human limitations were always a struggle, but Gwyn had spent the past decade teaching him to overcome them with intense focus and practice. With Gwyn leading them he could put all of his focus on listening out for any possible attack, trusting his partner to steer them in the right direction. There was a small creek that ran from a much larger river not far from them. Cody had played in those waters and he concentrated on hearing the soothing trickle again. There was a small animal to their left. The light step of paws on the mud made sloshing sounds that reminded him of the dog that had lived on a neighboring farm who had loved to jump in puddles.

The rain was tapering off and the silence became all encompassing. Instead of easing the growing unease in Cody's chest it only served to irritate it. Leaves were falling from the trees and landing heavy and wet mimicking soft footsteps. There was a village not a mile from their current position and Cody wondered if it was its inhabitants that he heard passing by or if it was someone with a more nefarious purpose. He very nearly suggested they stop there to rest, but he knew that bringing Decker near anyone else would only end in disaster.

By Cody's calculations, it was about midday when another sound brought their party to a halt. This time even he had heard the crack of a twig about a league off. He drew his sun spear at the same time that Gwyn did. Mercifully, Decker stayed silent and even he seemed wary of the possibility of an outsider. Taking a stilling breath, Cody moved to cover their captive, locking eyes with his partner in the process. They had worked together for a decade, it was almost like working with an extension of themselves. His partner looked calm as ever and it was enough to calm his erratically beating heart. There was no sense in losing his nerves over a simple transport. Taking the lead, Gwyndolyn moved toward the direction of the noise, sniffing out the air. Her fangs were showing and there was a hunger in her charcoal eyes that Cody had long learned to equate with safety.

"I know you're out there." Gwyndolyn growled. The gravel in her tone always caused Cody to pause. It was imbued with such strength and ferocity that it was both comforting and scary.

Leaves were disturbed from the same direction, but it was much closer than before. Gwyndolyn dropped into a crouch, sensing the impending attack. A figure with long brown hair and impossibly pale skin shot out from the trees. The impact she made was enough to send Gwyndolyn flying and he swore he heard a hiss of pain as Gwyn's collar was undoubtedly re-injured. Cody had little time to think about what to do when he threw himself at Decker, sending them both well out of the direction of the fight. When Cody looked up to see what was happening, the two were on their feet again as if nothing had happened. They attacked swiftly and Cody had difficulties following the movement. Decker tracked the actions with no problem and Cody almost wished the vampire would describe it to him.

"Vestera?" Decker shouted in surprise. "What the hell are you doing here?"

"Decker," her voice was cold as ice and just as smooth. Her eyes glowed a sick lilac and her fangs dripped with Gwyn's blood, "how nice of you to bring them to me." The sneer was evident on both her face and in her tone.

"Bring them to you? Do you honestly think she'll believe that?" Decker glared.

"She'll believe it when I return without you."

By then Gwyndolyn was back on her feet, slowly inching closer to her. Cody dared not even look at her lest he give up her intent. Vestera seemed to sense her, however, and Cody physically reeled when focused purple eyes turned to land on the vampire huntress. Her claws dug even deeper into her pale white neck holding her in place before her sharp fangs made their mark. Cody stood watching in horror as the woman began to drink from his partner. The sight of blood forced the bloodlust in Decker out and his pupils dilated, watching as the brunette greedily fed off of Gwyndolyn.

"I swear, Vestera, you are not leaving me here to rot! Cassandra will hear about this!" Decker struggled with the irons binding his wrists, but Cody knew that they would hold. He was an elder and stronger than the human had anticipated, but he would not be able to escape the shackles.

"It doesn't look like you have a choice." Vestera laughed before turning back to Gwyn who lay limp in her arms.

Cody knew that he should have tried to fight back, but fear kept him rooted in place. A decade's worth of training and experience flew from his mind as he was forced to watch his teacher and partner become drained. Gwyn did her best to fight off the other vampire, but exhaustion and her wounds were making it impossible. Cody had seen death many times, but he had never seen a vampire dry out another vampire. It was cruel and the sound of Gwyn's whimpers were seared into Cody's brain. Even when the brunette was done and Gwyn's body slumped to the dirt, Cody swore that he could still hear her cries, ringing in his ears.

The power that rolled off of Vestera in waves was enough to make even Decker shake as she advanced on the rogue, her co-conspirator. Using her sharp claws, Vestera made quick work of slashing at Decker's throat, laughing as his blood soared through the air, dripping down into the soft forest floor.

Cody felt dizzy then, losing his breakfast at his feet. The sound of his retching and the smell of the bile drew the dangerous vampire's attention.

"And who is this? A human amongst vampires? You must be one of those foolish Free Riders. That's what you in the Deadlands call yourselves right? You certainly picked the wrong day to come out for a stroll."

Dark brunette hair rushed at him at a blur. In a moment of sheer panic, Cody regained use of his limbs and made a frenzied attempt at an attack. He was not nearly as fast or as strong as the vampire, but he meant to put up a fight. Decker had said that sunspears were an unfair advantage, but Cody could hardly see his weapon scratching the surface of power that the elder possessed. Gripping the hilt hard, Cody made feeble slashing attempts at the air around him. His first few wild strokes cut through empty air, but his fourth try garnered him a gasp.

"So the human likes to play? Too bad sunspears won't hurt me like the others."

Before Cody could blink, he was knocked on his back by an unseen force. Brunette hair whirled around him making Cody dizzy. When he felt cold hands clawing at his body, he abandoned all hope. The last thing he saw before the world went black was cold were lilac eyes and a feral grin.

ARTHUR

Arthur Grahame never thought that he would find himself heading back home. The last time he had crossed this stretch of the Beggar's Trail he had been heading in the opposite direction in the early morning. Love had taken him away nearly two decades past and now love would bring him back. The uneven dirt path was familiar and yet new like a long lost friend. It was midday this time, just one of the many differences in the two journeys. The company had also been much better when he had left, though he could hardly blame his companion.

"We must stop for food. The path beyond this point is more treacherous." If the young girl walking ahead of him had heard, she made no indication. Sighing, Arthur quickly caught up to his companion. Reaching out with a gentleness that only a father could know he wrapped his large arm around her slender shoulder forcing her to stop. "I said we must stop." His frustration was as evident as her indifference. With an aggressive shake of her shoulder, Natalya Grahame broke free from her father, her short brown hair grazing his fingers in the process. Slight as she was, there was no mistaking the strength in the glare she gave him. Bold brown eyes met their reflection as daughter attempted to stare down father.

"I thought I lost you old man." Like it often did, the cool gaze on Natalya's face cut Arthur deeper than any knife could. Even at a young age, Natalya resembled her mother down to just about every chilling detail and the cold look had no place on that face.

"If you think that's how you lose someone tracking you, then obviously, nothing I've taught you has sunk in." Arthur couldn't help but bark out his frustration. Regret gripped at his heart as soon as the words left his lips, but he could tell by the look that remained on her face that it was too late to retract. He understood little of the mind of a teenage girl and there wasn't a day that went by he didn't wish his wife was still with them to help. Natalya's mother, Elizabeth, died when she was still so young. It had been just the two of them for over half of Natalya's life and yet he was still no better at getting her to see things his way.

"And what exactly were you teaching me? How to get us properly kicked out of our home? I lived my whole life there! I was going to get married and start my own family and you ruined it!" Before Arthur could react Natalya ran off the path near the dense thicket. She was much faster than he remembered and when he reached the overgrown brush, she had already disappeared into the trees completely out of his viewpoint. He would have been impressed by her speed if panic hadn't set in first. As a child he had many dealings with Mordin Forest as it sat flush against the Beggar's Trail, none were good. He ran as fast as he could, the weaker twigs bending easily as he pushed headlong into them. He could hear Natalya not far in front of him and while his height gave him an advantage on normal ground, the branches were getting thicker and slowing him down. Natalya's slight frame was easily allowing her to weave in and out of them and get too far ahead for him to catch up.

"Natalya! Natalya!" Getting more and more frustrated by the minute, Arthur yanked his dagger from his belt, cutting his way through the thicker branches. The forest floor was becoming as thick as the branches above and he easily found himself losing his footing. Trying to not let anger and fear upset his movements was difficult and when the woods suddenly ended in a small clearing Arthur nearly fell forwarded, just catching himself on the nearest tree. Natalya was standing in the center looking just as cut up as Arthur knew he must be. Dirt decorated her cheek and twigs tangled in her thick brown curls. "Don't you dare run away from me again." The words came out louder and more harsh than Arthur had meant and the look of remorse that had been on Natalya's face vanished. Relief pounded through Arthur so fast that it hurt, but it didn't stop his mounting anger at the teenager's defiance.

The mid morning sun hung over them through the small hole in the skyline that the clearing allowed. The heat blanketed the two, making both of their frustrations heighten. The breeze that had been a calming grace on the trail earlier was gone now and the stillness only served to irritate the two more.

"She is an idiot. How could she put herself in such danger and just to prove a point? Why can she not just admit that I am right about these things and save us both the trouble?" He thought to himself. Natalya was wrong even if she didn't see it and he would just have to keep telling her so until she understood.

Honestly my love she's sixteen. She has every right to sulk. You're going to have to be the adult and talk to her. You should always be the adult. How could you expect someone so young to understand?

Even after eleven years, Elizabeth was still his voice of reason and

Arthur did his best to let go of his anger. Taking a deep breath to release the tension trapped in his body, he did his best to find the words that would get through to his young daughter. Before he had the chance, she reached out to him and took his large hand in her small one.

"I'm sorry, Papa." The words were so quiet that Arthur had nearly missed them. He hadn't heard his little girl call him that in nearly a year. The anger that still burned in his chest and threatened to twist and disfigure his heart slowly burned out until it was but a small, flickering flame. It was always lit, it had been since he lost the love of his life, but he had long since learned to keep the fire at bay. Protecting his daughter was too important to let anger take control of his actions.

"I know, Nat. I am too." He drew the girl into his arms, secure and tight. He took his time to appreciate the moment since ones so tender happened so few and far between. He hardly ever allowed such indulgences, but he knew more than ever that Natalya needed him and admitting to such weakness was worth keeping her safe.

A noise from the woods beside them made both jump and instantly Arthur put his daughter behind him. He had spent most of his adult life suspicious of Mordin Forest and his long harbored obsession was what drove him to train Natalya to be able to defend herself. It was also that obsession that forced them from the only home that Natalya had known. She was silent behind him, controlling her breathing like he had taught her. The only sign of her fear was in the form of her small slender hands tightly wound in his worn linen tunic. The noises from the woods surrounding them were getting louder and they echoed off of the trees making both father and daughter feel trapped, as if they were surrounded on all sides. More afraid than he would admit, Arthur steeled himself for an attack.

"Papa," Natalya whimpered as the sound got closer and closer, her grip getting strong enough to hurt. The feeling grounded him and reminded him that he had his little girl to protect and that he could not possibly fail.

The noises continued and as they got closer it was obvious that it was coming from the right. Arthur moved toward the sound and timed his attack until the last second. With quick reflexes he jumped forward, thrusting the blade in the direction of the noises, at the same time that a small brown rabbit appeared in the clearing. Adrenaline was pounding hard in Arthur's head to the point where he nearly missed his daughter's cursing.

"A rabbit? That's what you've been training me to defend myself from? You honestly ruined our lives because you are so afraid that every sound in Mordin Forest will do us harm. Your obsession had me scared at a rabbit! I hope you're happy with yourself." She turned her back on him and picked her way back through the trees from the direction that she came in.

Stunned, Arthur hardly had the time to catch up to her. Fear mixed with anger once again, both at himself and at his young daughter. The flame burned a bit brighter once more before Arthur forced it to return to the dull ache that kept him warm. They had little time left to make it before nightfall and spending it on anger was more foolish than he could afford. This new start was to prove that his anger did not rule him.

The people in the village said that he thrived off of anger. They had said it made him wicked. There was a time when Natalya had defended him from accusations, but even in the end she started to doubt his sanity. It was only the fear of the village folk that forced the girl to run from everything she once knew. He just wanted to keep his little girl safe and protect her from the monsters that surely lurked around every corner, but she just despised him. She blamed him for ruining her comfortable life. If only she knew about the things that lived just beyond their line of sight in the dark forest Mordin, but no. He would never talk about them, not to her, not to anyone. Talking had already done enough damage, it would seem, and so silence would have to be Arthur's new armor.

They made it back to the path with little incident, though every little sound from the surrounding woods made Arthur pause and kept him on edge. "We should stop for food," he said again.

"I'm not hungry." Natalya led the way, refusing to see reason and so Arthur went on hungry. The sun was slowly starting to make its descent when they finally emerged from the trees. They found themselves roughly where they had been before their excursion and Arthur cursed his daughter's foolishness. He could only hope that they would make it to their destination in time.

They were making their way back to his childhood home in Sylvine Village and while Natalya seemed to hate the very idea, Arthur rather thought that having the girl's paternal grandparents there to help would do her wonders. He hadn't seen his parents since he'd left home all those years ago, chasing after the love of his life. It had been a foolish act, even he could admit that, but he had loved Elizabeth more than he cared about his reputation. It wasn't until he was older that he'd realized that his actions might have negatively affected his parents as well. When he'd first left he would get a letter from his mother at least once a season, but after the first year they had mysteriously stopped. He thought harm had befallen them, but Elizabeth had always feared another evil had taken place. He had left his family and Mary Rose Cooper, the girl with which he had been betrothed to, and it was very likely that his parents had been forced from their home in shame, much the way he was now. He couldn't bare to think of the pain he caused them and often denied the possibility that his childish actions had in fact done more harm than good. The past was best left as such in this case and he fortified his mind against the troubling thoughts. He had bigger concerns to tend to.

If his calculations were correct, and they usually where, they would be arriving at their destination within the day if they moved quickly. They were running low on supplies; the pack that Natalya was carrying was all that remained of their provisions. They would have to make haste, there was no room for any more stops if they intended to make it before nightfall. It was nearly the end of the harvest months and the sun would still hang in the sky for a few hours, even when it looked to dip below the horizon.

Picking up speed, Arthur shot another cautious look at the woods beyond the brush beside him before catching up to Natalya and ushering her along. They would have more time to argue when they were safely at his old village. Thankfully, Natalya sensed his urgency and picked up the pace, keeping her scathing comments to herself. There wasn't much more ground to cover, but camping against the forest was not an option in Arthur's mind. He'd never had enough evidence that Elizabeth's disappearance and assumed death was because she had gone into Mordin Forest without protection, but his suspicious nature would not let the possibility go. There had been strange disappearances involving Mordin Forest in his youth and he would not allow them to fall to a similar fate.

They were coming up to a point on the road that Arthur knew too well and yet it looked so very different from the last time that he had seen it. Birds called out to each other as they flew from tree to tree settling in for the night. When he had come up the path from the opposite direction with Elizabeth and her family, they had stopped where the road forked to admire the sheer beauty of the trail. Arthur distinctly remembered a gentle deer had walked right up to Elizabeth and she had laughed without a care. It was the first time he had heard the noise and he very quickly became addicted to it. He stood back in awe of the beautiful girl, he knew he would call his bride, as she made friends with the many creatures in the meadow. He had thought then that he had been blessed by the gods. He knew now that the blessing had come with the curse of losing her just as quickly as she'd come.

They made it past the fork in the road and were coming up to the meadow where traders would set up tents to push their wares. Arthur had expected that the area would be sparsely occupied, but when they rounded the bend he was shocked to find it empty. The tall, wild grass was indicative of just how long it had been since someone had tended to the field. There were patches of brown grass, coarse and dead under the late summer sun. Even the gypsy camps that had once been a sore on the eye were gone. As a child, Arthur had played in the grass here with his friends. His parents had always warned him to keep clear of the queer folk. He and one boy, Ivan Duane who had been his closest friend, often would be found dancing around the encampments, daring the other to see who would get the closest.

The times that he had come from would have found the way to Sylvine crowded with market carts and other odd travelers. The harvest had always brought the most interesting traders with rare goods. He would sit in the meadow with Ivan sipping on sweet honey wine, that their parents hadn't caught them with, talking about girls. He had never been in love with Mary Rose, but he also hadn't ever considered a life where he wouldn't be marrying her until Elizabeth had come along. Sometimes Mary Rose would join them, during those times Ivan's presence had been necessary as a chaperone, though her mother had always been close by to keep an eye on them.

Arthur had led them to the left, the right fork would have taken them toward the capitol and into the heart of the kingdom. They had taken the last turn off the main road. They were heading down the path that would take them straight to Sylvine Village. There were no other outlets from this point. In his youth he had felt safe being so secluded from the rest of the kingdom, but now it set him on edge just as many things seemed to do. The more they walked down the path, the more obvious it was that no one had been around to maintain it. Arthur couldn't help but wonder if people had stopped traveling to the village because of this, or if it had been the lack of travelers that allowed the weeds to grow past the fields and into the road. Even the trees seemed to be reaching out to obstruct the way. New, thin tree roots were creeping up along the dirt. In many cases they blended so well with the terrain that they would have tripped him had he not been looking out for them. Natalya seemed to not fare as well as he heard her grunts of pain when her foot was snagged on a root or two.

In the time that Arthur had grown up, it would have been beyond question that anyone would let wild plants take over the only way in and out of the village and seeing it then concerned the older man to no end. Worry and angst grew in the pit of his stomach, feeding him to push on. Suddenly he wasn't so sure if bringing his daughter so far from her home had been the right idea. Even Natalya seemed to understand that something was amiss and she had moved closer until she was nearly walking on him. All of his fears from not hearing from his parents resurfaced until he wondered if anyone still lived in his old village.

Sylvine had once been a strong farming town that had provided for the kingdom Solara and all of its people. That time had been before Arthur had been born, but his parents had been alive at the tail end of that age and often told him and the other children stories. There had been a time when the ports on the edge of the village had been in great use and Sylvine had actually been as large as the capital city. People had traveled far and wide to go to market and hear news from far off lands beyond the Great Sea. Even when he had left, Arthur had known that the small remains of the great city was declining. The docks had all been closed when he had last been home. The people who still stayed had moved their homes closer to the village center for protection and before he had followed Elizabeth to Ash, Arthur had been one of the many signed up to build a large fence to meet up with the gate protecting the city from the road in order to completely seal off the village with a wall that covered them on all sides.

Arthur was walking in front of Natalya when they made it to a small outpost tower just miles outside of Sylvine. What was once a tall, proud structure now barely stood on its own. The flag of Solara, which hung limp from the tower rails, was torn to shreds. What was left of it hung forgotten from the splintered rafters. The depressing sight made the man stop, Natalya coming to stand beside him in silence, nearly tripping over him at her close proximity. Arthur was so consumed in his grief that he hardly noticed. He felt as Natalya gently took his larger hand in her own. She held her silence for which he was eternally grateful.

"I used to take the watch here." Arthur's voice broke with the effort of speaking. He held onto his daughter's small hand, wondering at what point he stopped being the protective father and instead needed her comfort to hold himself together. "This was where I was standing the first time I met your Mum."

He hadn't been much older than Natalya on that warm summer day. The heat of the sun had bore down on him, much as it did to them today, as he stood watch. All the young men of Sylvine were once forced to do so as long as they weren't tending to their farms. He had been ready to abandon his post and find Ivan to take a dip in the ocean when the three outsiders on horseback came racing down the dusty path.

"Halt in the name of the King." He remembered saying. It had been nearly a century since any king of Solara had called Sylvine home, but it had been the customary greeting of the proud people and Arthur had not been exempt from such pride.

"You wouldn't know the King even if he stood here before you, boy." The man of the party did the speaking. Only a naive boy then, Arthur hadn't noticed the way the man held himself. He had been in the presence of nobles and he had only had eyes for the pretty girl of the party. She'd been paler than any of the people of his modest working village, dressed in rich looking fabrics that he could never hope to afford in his lifetime. He should have known then that there would be a price to pay for pursuing someone so obviously out of his station, but he had been blinded by her beauty.

"Be that as it may, state your name and your purpose here." He'd tried to sound older, more important if only to impress the girl.

"We are here to see Master Adair Lanson. My wife is his sister. Our business here is none of yours." Only then did he notice that there was another woman in their party. She sat on a steed that bore the crest of the King. He had finally become aware of their standing and decided it was best to simply obey their request. Irritating nobles would not do well and he'd hoped to see the pretty girl again.

"Very well. I will see you to the gate." Arthur had descended then to meet them. The girl was even prettier when they were on level ground and he could see the shine in her chocolate eyes. "My name is Arthur Grahame, son of Aldrin and Lana Grahame," he found himself speaking without meaning to.

"Pleasure, I'm sure. But you would do well to bring us to the gate and keep your eyes off of my daughter."

Even when they had wed, Elizabeth's father had never much liked Arthur. The bitter memory of the old man was enough to bring him out of his trance and back into the world where he was left with only his daughter and the ruins of a life lived far too long ago. Despite this, Arthur could not bring himself to look away from the monstrosity. No matter how much pain it caused him there was a warm tenderness that lingered like the thoughts of his long passed love. He had hoped beyond hope that at least some of his and Elizabeth's memories would remain where it had all begun, but he felt hope fleeting him then. He hadn't even noticed that Natalya's hand was still in his, or that he was shaking, until her voice brought him back to the present.

"You never told me how you met." Natalya spoke gently as if not to spook a small animal. She was drawing circles on the back of his hand with the hand that was not holding his and he dropped it quickly as if it had burned him. He continued walking, not even glancing back to see if she was following. He could not afford such sentimentalities. He would not show weakness in front of his daughter and they were losing time. He hoped to never tell her the stories of his life with Elizabeth before Natalya had been born. He had loved his wife dearly, but there was too much darkness in that past to burden Natalya with.

There were no sounds of footsteps behind him which only served to irritate him further. "It's getting late, I want to get there before dark."

The sun was beginning to set just beyond the tree line and the wind started to pick up, making the shadows dance on the old watchtower. There would be very little light to walk by and Arthur hoped to avoid taking time to make and light a torch. Food and talk would have to wait until they were safely inside his parent's home. The mounting anxiety from earlier returned threatening to overtake him. He hoped that he still had a home to take his daughter to. They had run so quickly that there hadn't been time to write ahead and now he saw the folly in his plans. It mattered not what lay ahead of them now. Arthur had committed them to this and he would be damned if they had to change course now. He would have to continue to hold on to blind hope that there was something for them ahead because there was nothing but pain behind them. They continued their journey in silence, both stuck in their own thoughts. They were moving farther away from the forest and closer to Sylvine Village where Arthur hoped that their new life awaited.

NATALYA

There was a chill in the air as the sun set completely. The thin tunic, which had seemed enough in the morning heat, did little to shield Natalya as they came to an imposing wooden gate. She hid her shivers, as gooseflesh decorated her exposed arms, refusing to show her father any weakness. Focusing back on the gate in front of them, Natalya did her best to ignore her discomfort. Unlike the watchtower they had come upon in the road, the three-story wooden fence looked to be in good condition. The wood was chipping at parts, but it was well kept and seemed to be put to good use. It looked to wrap around the village, for it seemed to reach until it was out of sight in the fading sun. The large gate swung inwards and the opening was the most ornate of the structure; the symbol of Solara was carved into both doors, the sun surrounded by two snakes, both heads eating the tail of the other to form a perfect circle. The design was painted in with a faded gold lacquer, but it was still obvious that the markings were a point of pride to this remote village. Two men stood posted just beyond the threshold, their eyes trained on them and the open road.

"Halt in the name of the King. What is your business here?"

The older of the two guardsmen addressed them. He looked to be around an age with her father, but where her father had deep wrinkles setting in around his mouth and eyes this man still had a smooth face. His age showed in the tall gnarled stick that he leaned heavily on. His face was carefully blank as if he did not even see them and Natalya remind herself to be brave. It would not do to show fear in front of a stranger. The boy who stood beside him was much younger, though he looked no less weary. He was a whole head taller than her and looked like many of the farmer boys that came to call on her when she had come of age. They both wore linen tunics, much like the ones that Arthur had purchased for them to travel in. They were obviously of a lower class and the fear that had been building in the pit of her stomach turned to annoyance. How dare those of the lower class threaten her and her father? Natalya could have taken them both out if she had wanted to, but her father's hand on her shoulder held her and her temper in place.

"My name is Arthur Grahame of Ash Village, formerly of Sylvine Village. This is my daughter, Natalya." Arthur walked forward, squinting in the dimming light. When he got closer a sudden look of recognition crossed his face. "Ivan, is that you?"

"Arthur Grahame? Is that really you? It's been far too long old friend." A smile broke out on the man's face. Wrinkle lines became ever more prominent on the once smooth face making him seem that much older.

Natalya watched, confused as her father moved forward to embrace the man. She could see then that they were the same height and of similar build. She knew that before her father had met her mother he had been a simple farmer's son. It was obvious that these two knew each other from a time before her mother had been around. They could have worked the fields together. This man probably knew more about her tight lipped father than she did and the thought left a sour taste in her mouth.

When they parted, the man motioned for the boy to come forward and meet them. "This is my son Baldwin."

"It's an honor to meet you, sir." The boy stuck his hand out to grasp Arthur's.

He looked to be no older than herself and his easy way with her father only further irked her. She moved to stand beside her father to assert her place. This was *her* father and the boy had no right to act so familiar with him. She was surprised when the boy took her hand in his own, kissing it gently.

"And you, it is a pleasure to meet you." There was a twinge of humor in his eyes and she knew her jealousy had been found out. Her lack of reaction did not seem to faze the boy and he kept his gaze locked with hers until she snatched her hand back.

She was accustomed to such treatment from her suitors in Ash Village. She had been the only girl of an age to marry who was not part of the lower class. While her father had always been regarded as a crazy old man, she had been seen as the beauty of Ash Village. Coming from parents of two different classes, it had made bridging the gap between herself and farmers' sons easier as boys and young men had flocked to her side on her sixteenth birthday. She had been set to marry, before they had left. A young man by the name of Edward Donne had been lucky enough not only to win her favor, but also her father's. He was a handsome young man of twenty-two and had been one of many sons blessed to a rather large farming clan. He himself did not work the fields often and instead was in charge of inventorying stock before taking it to the markets of Magdus. It had been a smart match and while she had never loved him, she could have certainly grown to. Of course then her father had to go and make another public spectacle of himself and gone and gotten himself kicked out. The Donnes were smart enough to cut ties with her as soon as the hearing had ended and she had been forced to flee with her father rather than face persecution for being his daughter.

"You seem to know me boy, but I know nothing of you." Arthur regarded the boy with his stern eyes. A small smile graced the boy's face and Natalya fought back the urge to slap him.

"My father has told us much of you and your childhood adventures."

"Yes, well we have a lot to catch up on. Mary Rose and I wed not long after you left. She will no doubt be happy to see you again." Ivan drew the conversation back to him effectively cutting off the many angry comments on Natalya's tongue.

"I always wondered what had happened to our dear Mary Rose. I am glad she was not put to shame as I feared."

"She did not, my friend. But enough of such dour talk, Mary Rose is home with the younger ones. You remember her father's house, don't you? We will meet you there when we're done with our guard. I'm sure that she will be more than happy to make up two beds for you for the night."

"Thank you. Will you be back on the hour? I assume guard times have not changed since I left."

Natalya had never seen this side of her father before. She could not help but wonder how very little she knew her father, suddenly the man before her seemed even more of a stranger than Ivan and Baldwin. In the short time since they had left she had seen so many sides of him that her head was dizzy with the effort to keep all of the strange personas straight.

"A lot has changed, my friend, but some things have stayed the same," father and son stepped to the side allowing them entrance to the village.

The roads within the wall were much better kept than the one that led to the quaint village. There were lanterns lining the paths, illuminating the vast farming lands and sturdy houses. Off in the distance must have been the town center and Natalya noticed a grouping of eight trees that made a perfect circle. They looked old, as their trunks were easily twice as wide as any tree she had ever seen, and were clearly planted there purposefully, though for what reason she had no idea. On the other side of the road, there were cattle settling in for the night in the fields. To the left of the entrance a large community barn of horses sat further back, men and women tending to their steeds before turning in for the night. Arthur paid them no mind and turned to the right, where the buildings stood closer together. Each home seemed to have its own small plot of land where the families could grow their own crop, but it was obvious that most of the village came together in the larger fields.

The houses were made of thick logs, no doubt cut from Mordin Forest. They, like the fence, looked to be well lived in, most seeming to be at least three or four rooms in size. Few stood two stories tall, but there were some scattered throughout. Natalya did her best to memorize the way in the flickering lantern light, but she knew that by morning the village would look completely different. She kept her eyes ahead making sure not to lose her father. Upset as she may be with him, he was all she had and it would not do to lose him especially when they had finally seemed to make it to safety.

The two made their way through the streets with ease. It would seem that her father's memory was making up for the lack of light. They continued on the path, turning left, then right, and then another sharp left until there were only two buildings standing before them. One stood proud and welcoming, many candles shining in every window. Shadows moved within, at least three people seemed to be home, the second level more lively than the first. Across the way stood the skeleton of a home. It was only one story, but it sat on a large plot of land. There had been a time when it had been the home of a farmer, the old tracks of land still vast, though what once would have been well manicured fields now were overgrown and forgotten.

"This was my home." The broken sound in her father's voice brought sorrow and fear back into the girl's heart. She watched as tears fell down his dark face and the pain she had seen in his eyes at the watchtower returned. Everything from his past only seemed to bring her father pain.

"Who's out there?" A voice from behind them made Natalya turn quickly, though her father hardly seemed to notice.

In the door of the large, well kept home, stood a woman in her thirties. She was not what Natalya would have considered pretty, but there was a welcoming quality about the woman's dark face and bright eyes. She was heavy set, though her arms gave away that she was a farmer's wife accustomed to working the field. Her dark hair was piled high on top of her head and she wore an apron, old stains proving it was put to good use. Squinting in the light, the woman moved closer to them as if she was seeing Natalya, but not quite seeing her.

"You must be Elizabeth and Arthur's daughter, I would know her face anywhere. That must mean," The woman walked right past the stunned girl to her father, physically turning the man around to see him for herself. "Well I would have never guessed I'd live to see this day! Arthur Grahame now you tell me what's the matter?"

"What happened to my family?" His voice broke with emotion, something Natalya would have never thought her father possible of.

"You must have never gotten the letters, oh you poor dear. Well then, we'll have to fix a pot of tea, it's going to be a long night. Come in, come in." Wrapping her arms around both father and daughter, she rushed them into the home. "Slaven get a kettle on, honestly can't you do anything to help your mother?"

A young boy stood at the door watching the three of them and Natalya instantly recognized him. He was identical to the boy who they met at the gate, though she knew that was impossible. He looked at them strangely and it was obvious that he had been listening the whole time, despite his efforts to hide it. Natalya walked into the large common room before her father and the woman, shaking the arm off of her. She never liked being touched by people she knew, much less strangers.

The first sight to greet her was the crackling fire in the large hearth and instantly Natalya remembered just how much she missed her own home. She had spent many a night sitting by the fire with her father as he told her stories of the warriors of old and of the many magical beasts that lived in Mordin in the ancient times. This place was nothing like her home though. The kitchen was connected to the main room without any wall dividing the two. It was the mark of a commoner's home, something that Natalya wasn't used to. Her father had by no means been a wealthy man, but they had at least had a cook and a maid in their employment until recently when they had left them thanks to her father's reputation. Their kitchens had been set in the back of their home with the maid's quarters. She could not imagine anyone in this small village having a cook or a maid. There was a small pile of shoes to the right of the door and Natalya toed her warn traveling boots off as to not track in any dirt. When her bare feet touched the well worn rug she was surprised to feel how soft it was, the hand woven pattern was fashioned into the sigil of Solara by a well trained hand, though it was obvious that it had seen better days.

The large oak table in the center of what seemed to be the kitchen was the next thing to draw Natalya's eye. A young girl was sitting at the table, watching her curiously. She looked to be no older than ten, but she was at the very least a splitting image of her mother, though much scrawnier than the woman. Her dark hair sat in tight curls around her waist, though they were swept back by a large section of cloth. Her skin was not nearly as dark, clearly she was not sent to work in the fields. Her clothes were plain, but new and she hardly looked like she had worked a day of hard labor in her life. If she had met the girl out in the village she might even have assumed that she was born to the middle class, as Natalya herself had been. Another girl was working the fire, setting the kettle on that her mother had told Slaven to do. By comparison to the young girl, she looked much more like her brothers. Her hair was dark brown and cut short, even shorter than Natalya's and the girls coiled tight, not heavy enough to fall the way her younger sister's did. Though Natalya had to assume that they were about the same age, she was much more developed and Natalya instantly felt the stab of jealousy roll through her before she squashed the feeling down. Both girls, however, had the sharp blue eyes of their mother, like their brothers did and Natalya wondered for a moment if it was just their color that made it seem like each member of the household could see straight through her, or if maybe the long days on the road were just making her overly paranoid. Blinking away her thoughts, she focused in on the ongoing conversation.

"We tried to send you letters, but before long messengers stopped coming and going. It's been a tough twenty-three years. Your parents passed not long after you left. A fire consumed the home. Luckily your mother was visiting down by the church, but your father died that night. Your mother, poor dear, had little else and she was horribly sick, but you knew that. She died not long after. They're both out in the cemetery by my parents. Ivan can take you there on the morrow if you'd like."

"I would like that immensely," Arthur sighed, doing his best to hide his tears. Natalya wanted to reach for him, to offer some comfort, but she was beat to it.

"Here, take a cup of tea," Mary Rose patted his hand as her daughter handed her an old tea cup, "Thank you Maureen dear. Can you put some food on for our guests?" The girl nodded without word and began to serve supper at the table. Her father took a seat near the head of the table and motioned for Natalya to sit beside him. Maureen set a bowl before Arthur first before returning with another to place a cup of tea before Natalya.

"Here you go, Miss." Maureen's voice was soft as a song.

"I'm sorry dear, where are my manners? I haven't caught your name."

All eyes were on Natalya then.

"My name's Natalya." Extending her hand, she was surprised when she was pulled from the bench into a hug instead.

"My name is Mary Rose dear. I know it's not much of a home, but you and your father are welcome here for as long as you need. I assume you met my husband and son at the gate? This is Baldwin's twin, Slaven, and this here is my youngest, Kathleen. I have two older children, too. Emeline and Art live out by Rosewood Farms, but that's another story." Turning to her father again, a tender look crossed her face. "Where is Elizabeth, dear?"

"With my parents now I suppose."

The heaviness in his tone nearly made Natalya cry and she moved over to take a seat next to her father, wrapping her arm in his and resting her head on his arm. She knew she could never take the pain from her father, but she hopped that her presence would help. They had lost her mother when she was five and while she missed her everyday, she had been so young, she could hardly remember. It was so different for her father. He always said that she looked so much like her mother, whenever he looked at her Natalya always wondered if the sadness in his eyes was because he saw Elizabeth instead of his own daughter. Maureen came back to the table with the last serving of stew before Mary Rose could offer condolences. Taking her arm back, Natalya instantly dove for her food.

"Manners, Nat. Thank Mary Rose for her hospitality. I didn't raise you without common courtesies." Despite his grief, her father still found it in himself to tell her how to behave. Glaring up at him, she was about to respond with her own thoughts on the matter, but the motherly woman in front of her defused the situation with a casual laugh.

"Not a word of thanks from you my girl." The cheerful motherly affection sent resentment through Natalya and she stayed silent again. Turning back to her food, she fumed at her father and the woman who reminded her so painfully that she didn't have a mother. She hardly ever allowed herself any self-pity when it came to her mother, but she couldn't help it in the face of this woman. This happy woman acted as if she had known Natalya all her life and it unsettled the cautious girl. Not used to the doting of a female, her actions were strange and set all of Natalya's nerves afire. She vowed to hold her tongue lest she fight more with her father, or worse be forced to make pleasant conversation with anyone.

Ivan and Baldwin arrived near the end of supper and the two sat with their food, speaking quietly with Arthur and Slaven. Kathleen took care of the rest of the dishes and Mary Rose and Maureen took seats by the fire, needlework in hand.

"Would you like some dear?"

"I would, thank you."

Natalya settled herself in with the women and took the offered items from her. Needlework was one of the feminine activities that her father had actually allowed her to learn and even encouraged. She had been forced to embroider her own clothing in the past year. The estate had begun to decline with there being so little work left, they were often forced to purchase plain pieces from the local market to fashion into clothing. Edward had promised to bring her dresses that fit her status at the next market that he set out on, but that had been before the exile. Kathleen joined them before long and Natalya was grateful that the three seemed happy to work in silence. They kept at the needle until the fire began to die and Mary Rose collected their work to put away for the night.

"If you're ready I can show you up to the washroom." The offer of a tub was enticing enough to bring Natalya out of her brooding silence. Nodding eagerly, she followed the woman up to the second level to a smaller room. There was already a fire going in the hearth and the large iron tub was the most welcoming sight that Natalya had seen since she left home. Maureen and Kathleen were bringing in pails of water and Mary Rose busied herself starting the fire for the tub.

While there had been the cook at home and the maid that had often helped her fill the tub, they had all left long before she undressed. When Mary Rose looked at her expectantly, Natalya was at a loss for what the older woman was waiting for. Arthur, even before he had gotten older and earned the reputation for being overly paranoid, had never let the help near his daughter and so the last time someone helped her bathe had been when her mother had still been alive.

"Well don't just stand there dearie, you'll have the first bath." Without invitation, Mary Rose began to help Natalya undress. Red with embarrassment, Natalya did little to hide her body because she was in such shock. The woman hardly noticed, stripping her down to her small clothes before tending to the fire again. The girls had since finished filling the tub and made a quick retreat. "The girls will just have to bathe in the morning, your hair alone will take hours."

Natalya allowed herself to be moved closer to the water, she slid from her small clothes herself, accepting the inevitable. Gingerly she braced herself at the edge of the basin, testing her hand first. The steam rising did wonders to hide her blush and she gently stepped over the high side into the water. When she finally let her body sink into the water the stress of the journey seemed to melt right off. For the first time since she had left her home, Natalya relaxed and let her guard down.

"You must not be used to having someone help bathe you." Natalya's eyes snapped open, not realizing that she was not yet alone. "The thought of you all alone just breaks my heart. Arthur is a good man, but a hard one, there is no room with him for nurturing a young lady."

Squirming under the watchful eyes, Natalya reached for the washcloth hanging by her head trying to keep her hands busy. "How do you know my father?" It was obvious that she was not going to be left alone, but she would not be forced to suffer idle small talk if she was to be tortured already. This woman seemed to know so much about her father and the thought of another woman being so close to the man both intrigued and infuriated the young girl.

"Well surely you knew that this village was his childhood home." When Natalya nodded, the woman reached for the soap and began to lather her hair. Natalya was ashamed at the amount of dirt that floated in the water around her. "Well I'm sure that he would have never told you this, but there was once a time where we were betrothed."

"That's not possible, my father was always in love with my mother." Anger took over Natalya and she pulled away, blinking soap from her eyes. How could this woman let them into her home and then lie to her like that? Her father only ever talked about one woman, if he ever even spoke of her, and that had always been her mother.

"Settle down child. Betrothed doesn't mean that we actually did marry."

"Of course I knew that, I'm not stupid."

"Well I never suggested that, now did I? Now settle back down, those knots in your hair are not going to undo themselves." She waited for Natalya to relax back into the tub before starting again. "There, that's better. He wasn't always in love with your mother. There was a time before they ever met when he had eyes only for me and I for him. But that was a long time ago, nearly a lifetime now. There was a time when I was so very angry with your father and your mother. At first, when Ivan asked for my hand I refused. It all seems very silly now."

"What happened?" Natalya relaxed slightly allowing for her hair to be thoroughly washed out. Curiosity outweighed anger and she itched to know more.

"Well that is quite the story and maybe one for another night. I forgave them both, over time. Your father never meant me any harm and after a time I realized that he wasn't going to come back to me. When he left with your mother I knew that it was time that I moved on. Ivan and your father were boyhood friends, and first when I wed Ivan my mother had a fit. She had called it an insult. Your father's family wasn't wealthy but he was their only son. Ivan had three brothers, all older, that the family money would go to before he or I ever saw it. My mother was more interested in the money than in what I thought of the matter. She had seen it as me being passed over, you see, but even then I knew that Ivan would make a good husband. I was right, I have lived a very happy life here with him and our children. But listen to me prattling on. I'm sure you're not interested in love stories from a different life."

"Tomorrow I will have Ivan take you and your father to your new home. I know he had been hoping to live in his parent's old home, but the fire consumed it so long ago and no one thought he would be back so we never went about fixing it. My daughter is living with my second oldest and they will be needing help bringing in the harvest. For now, you and your father can live with her and help her out. Once the harvest is over if you two want to move out then we can look into fixing up his old home, otherwise I know that Emeline would love the company of another woman and I'm sure you'd like her."

Natalya had never worked on a farm, but she didn't find it prudent to mention that. While she had always trained in the art of hunting with her father, that had been the closest to hard work that she had ever had to do. With a cook and a maid, she had never really learned to cook or clean much and while it did not help her chances in finding a husband, it never seemed to stop the suitors and she never really thought that she would have to work to live one day. The very prospect frightened and disgusted her, but it would not do to further insult the woman who was gently untangling the last of the knots in her hair. By the time they were done, the fire had nearly run out and the water was a cloudy gray. Giving her a large towel and borrowed night clothes, Mary Rose left the room allowing her to dress herself.

After her bath, Mary Rose led her to the girls' room. Despite the size of the home, the girls still shared a room, though unlike the poorer houses, they were able to each have their own beds, a small hearth kept the room plenty warm and the sight was welcoming. Kathleen was asleep in the far corner, her small frame wrapped firmly around a stuffed rabbit toy. Maureen was in the middle bed, still awake with a book in her lap. She looked up to smile at them before returning to her reading. Natalya crawled into the empty bed in the corner, the one that had once belonged to the daughter that she would be meeting in the morning.

"Get some rest, my dear, I'm just down the hall should you need anything. Go to sleep, Maureen. Reading in this light will destroy your eyes."

"Yes, mother. Goodnight."

Natalya settled into the mattress, welcoming the comfort that it brought. Nights of sleeping on dirt had forced her to accept that her old life was far behind and now it seemed that any bed would feel like heaven. She had a distant memory of the incredibly soft mattress that she had back in Ash, but even that paled in comparison to feeling full, clean, and comfortable again. Sleep came faster than it had on the road and Natalya fell asleep with thoughts of her mother on her mind.

She dreamt of a large grassy field and a young boy. He was tall with midnight black hair and mischief in his eyes. He took her hand and they went off running. Laughter filled the air until she felt ready to burst from happiness.

CODY

It seemed too dark when Cody first gained consciousness, so much so that he wasn't sure if he'd truly opened his eyes at all. His body felt like lead had replaced his bones and the effort it took to move his limbs was excruciating. He nearly gave in to exhaustion and fell back into the blissful darkness, but something in his subconscious urged him to keep his wits about him. His hunter's instincts screamed in his foggy mind and forced himself to wake up. Air shot through his lungs in short, raspy breaths. Each pull in he took felt like less air was actually entering his lungs, leaving his head feeling even lighter than before. He was sure he would pass out again soon. The pain coursed in his veins as naturally as blood; the only saving grace was it served as a good reason to stay awake. Each second that passed only brought him more agony, but he fought through it.

With difficulty, Cody turned his head, realizing that it wasn't as dark as he had thought, but instead he had woken with his face pressed firmly into blood soaked dirt. The confrontation with the vampire who called herself Vestera came back to him like a shock through his system. Suddenly, Cody found himself very much awake. He had a job to do and lying in the dirt in a puddle of his own blood and self-pity would get him nowhere. Cody strained his muscles to push himself up, relying entirely on adrenaline to stay upright. Immediately there was a rushing sound in his ears as the blood in his head did its best to circulate to where it needed to be. He nearly passed out again from the effort, but he was eventually able to sit up without needing to vomit. He waited for his brain to settle before slowly opening his eyes.

It was much brighter than he had originally assumed and he shut his eyes quickly, bringing his protesting arms up to shield his sensitive eyes from the light. He had to slowly talk himself into dropping his hands and it took what felt like hours before he braved opening his eyes to the harsh sunlight again. When he was sure he would not go blind from it, Cody blinked until his eyes fully adjusted. By then the rushing sound in his ears had subsided, allowing him to clear his mind further and take in his surroundings. It was then that he noticed how unnaturally quiet it was.

Fear and adrenaline took his body the rest of the way until he was standing. The clearing was hardly as dark as he had first thought nor as bright as when he'd first opened his eyes. His vision had finally begun to adjust and the edges of the clearing no longer looked gray and abstract. It was nearly midday, judging from the height of the sun. He had somehow landed near the edge of the clearing pushed against the bushes. He was honestly surprised that he had even survived the attack. It was pretty obvious from where he had been dumped that the vampire who had attacked them had intended to leave him for dead. It seemed that being underestimated had more advantages than he had previously believed and he thanked the Gods above that he had been spared. He was not without injury, of course. Various cuts and bruises littered the parts of his body that he could see and his shirt had been ripped and tattered to the point where he was surprised it still clung to his body. He did his best to take quick inventory of the damages as he tried to remember where each injury had come from. Memories of the fight came back to him in flashes. They had been attacked by an elder, no doubt, she had come out of nowhere just as Decker had warned. Gwyndolyn had been her first target.

Gwyn.

Eyes wide, Cody scanned the clearing. He turned quickly in his haste and his knees gave out beneath him from the strain. He found himself on the dirt floor once more, clutching his aching head. The rush that had fueled him, forced up the poor excuse for a stew that he had eaten the night before. Had it really been less than a day since they had found Decker? Time swam around him with his vision and he was forced to wipe the bile from his chapped lips blind. Blinking rapidly, he made himself focus, taking care to look around slowly this time, though he was sure there was nothing left in his stomach to lose. A careful scan found Decker, who was slumped over across the clearing from him. He was propped against a tree in the direct path of the sun and even from such a distance, Cody was already able to see severe burn marks on his face and arms. He was pale, even for one of his kind. It was impossible to tell if he was truly dead or not. Pushing thoughts of the rogue aside, Cody continued to survey the area. Gwyn had to be his first priority. Everything in his nature was telling him that she would be fine. It was not the first time that they had been attacked and it would surely not be the last. Despite everything he was trying to convince himself, an uncharacteristic feeling of doubt was clouding his brain. It could have only been the pain, he could hardly tell the difference.

The clearing was covered in cut branches and fallen leaves. The fight left obvious marks in the terrain like cuts into skin. Grass was torn from the dirt leaving small mounds of disturbed ground in a dance like pattern. Even the trees wore battle wounds. As a child, Cody had made stories up for every tree he crossed. They each had names, a life, and a story. He imagined that each tree had their own feelings and emotions. He did not have the heart to consider what they were thinking just then. There was very little time to dwell on his childhood fantasies, he had his very real partner to find and care for.

His body protested as he carefully scanned the clearing again, just to be sure. Turning his head slowly was his only option as his vision swam with each passing second. It took much longer than it should have, but Cody was sure that his partner was not immediately within sight. He refused to allow himself to succumb to panic upon the realization. They had been separated a time or two in the past, this was nothing new. It happened more often the longer their missions dragged on and he was more than capable of handling himself. His self assurances did little to quell the unnatural fear settling in his gut. Something didn't quite feel right. A third look told him his eyes had not deceived him. He was truly alone with their charge.

Cody got back on his feet gingerly, looking for any clue as to where his partner could have gone. Gwyn had always told him that he was too optimistic considering their line of work, but maybe now she would allow him to gloat when he found her.

If I find her. The words danced around in his mind, sounding suspiciously like the taunts and jibes the children of his village would throw at him.

Pushing away the negative thoughts took too much effort and soon Cody was starting to believe the ominous words floating around his brain. He would have to focus if he was going to find his partner, though his head was hurting so much it made thinking clearly nearly impossible. He would have to tend to his own wounds before he attempted to move any farther. It would do no good to pass out again while trying to find Gwyn all because he'd let his own body go. There was still blood dripping from one of the deeper cuts in his arm. The slow warm track of liquid slid down his forearms and off of his fingertips, making it look much worse than it felt. His shirt was already torn up and it took little effort for him to obtain a strip of cloth to bandage himself up. He did his best to clot the bleeding with one hand, wishing again for the fast healing that vampires were blessed with. It wasn't until his makeshift bandage was in place that he noticed that there was more blood decorating the clearing than could have come from him. Judging from the injuries that he could catalog on his own body and the pool of blood he had woken up in, he would be dead if he had lost that much.

Contrary to popular belief, vampires bled just as humans did. Their body's rate of healing was simply so fast that you would never even see a cut before it healed unless you were trained to look for it. Cody had been with Gwyn more than once when she was injured and most times she wouldn't even flinch. Once, on a particularly nasty chase, she had gotten cut deep enough that she had needed human blood to heal. It wasn't the first time that she had relied on Cody for such things. They were always careful to bleed him into a vessel first. The act of taking blood from his body would have been too intimate, overstepping the bounds of their relationship and Gwyn was nothing if not proper. Still, a vampire could lose enough blood to become too weak to protect themselves. They would not die from it, of course. Eventually their bodies would heal, but without available blood or another person there to protect them it would be easy for them to be hunted down or succumb to the heat of the sun.

It wasn't until he made it a quarter of the way around the clearing that he saw a second patch of wet dirt, though this one was covered in coppery flakes, the liquid having long since dried. It may have appeared to be enough to kill a human, but Cody knew far more about vampire biology than most, having been trained by one to fight beside her. It had been important for him to know the lengths a vampire's body could be pushed both for hunting their targets and tending to Gwyn if need be. If the drying blood was Gwyn's she could still easily be okay, possibly even healed and simply off in the trees hunting down their attacker. The small spark of hope was enough to help Cody push the dread from his mind. He would have to assume that Gwyn was okay until logic proved otherwise. He knew that jumping ahead of any situation and assuming the worst would only cause more complications for himself. He had been a hunter long enough to know that without all of the facts present he had no hope of truly understanding the story. Cody hunched down close to the dirt looking for the splatter pattern. It was soon clear that a trail of blood lead out of the clearing. He looked behind himself to check on the rogue. He was still slumped against the tree, out cold. The voice in his mind that often reminded him of his job and position in the empire told him that looking after their captive took precedence, but the part of him that cared deeply for his partner won out. After taking a deep, stealing breath the hunter began to push back the branches and follow the trail. The Crown and his captive could wait.

A few yards away from the clearing something glistening under the fallen leaves caught Cody's eye. Brushing the coverings aside with the toe of his shoe a gold chain and pendant stared back at him. There was no denying that the charm he had found was Gwyn's. He had never seen the vampire without the sigil of Faegon, her home and the capitol of her people, hanging around her neck. The single snake wrapping around the crescent moon was bold and distinctive. It wasn't broken, and he couldn't help but hope that dropping it had been deliberate. Slipping the ice cold chain into his pocket, he continued to follow the trail. The snarling roots were becoming thicker and even with his hunting knife, Cody was having difficulty cutting through the maze and his earlier headache did little to help the matter as he felt the drumming in his skull grow more intense.

Caw. Caw. Caw.

The crows were sounding overhead again. They could smell death in the air and Cody knew that hoping for Gwyn's survival seemed a moot point. Twisting through the overgrown trees, Cody felt hope drain from him as the small splatter pattern seemed to diminish until it was gone. The complete disappearance of blood could mean two things. Gwyn could have found an animal to drink from, at least enough to allow herself to heal. If that was the case however, she was nowhere to be seen, nor was the dead animal she would have had to drain. The other option was that the mystery attacker had likely dragged her away and taken her prisoner. Without a body, there was no way for Cody to tell.

Cody had been hunting for nearly a decade and Gwyn had been his partner for the entire time. He had always thought that he would have been able to tell if she ever died, but there, in the middle of the crowded woods, he felt nothing. He had always thought that there was a strong emotional bond which existed between himself and the huntress. He had thought, or at least hoped, that it would alert him if she were in dire conditions. He had tried to explain it once to one of the boys back home, back when humans had still bothered to talk to him, but he had been told quite forcefully that there was no way he could understand monsters like the vampires. But that had never been true. Cody had always felt most at home in Mordin Forest and even more so when he was working with Gwyn. She had to be alive, he would not believe any other possibility. He had to believe that if she was dead he would feel it on a spiritual level. Their lives were so interconnected, they relied on each other for protection and companionship and something as big as her death would have had some effect on him instantaneously. He had to believe so in order to believe that she was still alive. Gwyn being dead simply was not an option.

Even now he could hear her voice in his head, *"you're always so trusting, so naive. Trust your gut and nothing else."*

Grief would do him no good. He couldn't even allow himself to think of what had become of his partner. His gut was telling him that she was still alive, but maybe she had always been right. Becoming a hunter so young should have jaded him, but Cody was always able to see the good in everyone, both human and vampire. He often felt that he had been given to Gwyn because her constant cynicism always grounded him while he had always hoped that his optimism gave her a little perspective.

He was on assignment though, and couldn't afford to bury himself in sentiment. Gwyn had risked her life for this mission, he could not bring himself to think that she could have died for it, but he had to face the reality of the matter. He would not disappoint her by abandoning their work and all for sentiment that she always chastised him for. They were only a few days walk from Faegon, but he would have to find a way to contain their prisoner without having the protection of another vampire nearby. It would also help to know if his prisoner was even alive. Filled with new drive, Cody forced his tired body to retrace his steps. Wiping a single tear from his eyes, the hunter took the pendent from his pocket and clasped it around his neck. It held no magic or protection spells, but just having something so personal of Gwyn's against his breast gave him all the strength he needed.

Mordin Forest had a mind of its own and Cody found himself back in the clearing much faster than he would have thought. He often felt like his old friends were guiding him with their outstretched branches. He had only wished that they could have warned him about the dangers that had been lurking around them.

When he returned to the clearing it was obvious that Decker was just as he had left him, giving Cody little hope that the vampire was still alive. He needed to bring the vampire in no matter if he was alive or dead. The High Council would still be able to see his memories from his blood so long as it was relatively fresh. He would have to bring the traitor's corpse to Faegon, along with word of Gwyndolyn's disappearance, but it would be difficult to move quickly if Decker was unconscious, or dead. Gingerly, Cody knelt beside the vampire, inspecting the deep gashes that were visible around his neck and face. The sun was higher in the sky and even if Decker was still alive, he would die soon if Cody didn't move him to shade. Scooping him up, Cody was surprised at just how light the rouge was. The rough, dirty clothes that he wore were extremely deceiving as they made him look much bigger than he was. The hunter would have thought that his captive would have been harder to carry. Standing with relative ease, Cody was further surprised when Decker stirred slightly. A deep, pained moan cut through the silence of the forest, and the injured vampire's head dropped to the side, falling on the human's shoulder. Unconscious and silent, Decker seemed much less of a threat than he projected himself to be. Cody almost let himself feel bad for the creature.

"Remember what he did to us." Gwyn's sharp voice rang through his brain though they were his own thoughts. It was not in her nature to be vindictive or vengeful. Cody was much more likely to succumb to those very human emotions, though it took a lot for him to feel such hate-filled things. Even when it was very clearly his own thoughts, his mind spoke them as if they came from Gwyn. The vampire had shaped so much of who he was that he even thought in her voice. Thinking of her served as both a distraction and as a grounding force and he willed himself to refocus.

Decker was little threat while drained of energy and sun-sick, but awake and unhurt he was more than Cody could handle on his own. He would have to heal the vampire enough to revive him, but keep him weak enough to still subdue him. Controlling anyone's fate so directly made him feel uneasy, but it was no use, he would have to do whatever was required of him to see this through for his missing partner.

There was a natural nook in a tree hidden in the shadows near where they were attacked. He could put Decker down there without needing to prop him up, it was not ideal, but it would work. Vampires could not die from infections, but they could still feel the discomfort as their wounds healed sick flesh over and over again until their body eventually dispelled the toxins. Cody was lacking any water to clean out Decker's wounds and there were no running streams nearby. There would have been water at any of the nearby villages, but Cody could not justify putting any others at risk even if it meant saving his prisoner and fulfilling his mission. There was very little water left in his deerskin sack but he would have to work with his meager supplies. There would be time later to find a running stream to get water and properly wash his own wounds. Decker might survive from the infections, but Cody would not and he needed to tend to his own wounds soon. Cody took the little water they had and allowed droplets to run down the largest cuts on Decker's body. He might not like the rogue, but he wasn't about to put him through more pain than was needed. Gwyn would probably have let him suffer and the thought brought a thin smile to his lips. He made quick work of the wounds before settling himself in next to the vampire, prepared to help him heal.

The only way to heal Decker would be to give him blood, preferably human especially considering how severe his wounds were. It was not ideal for the hunter to give him his own blood considering how much of it he had lost, but Cody saw no other options. Taking out his sunspear, he drove it into the dirt first to clean it. Cleanliness mattered little when used as a weapon, but his human body would react poorly to being cut by a dirty blade. He could barely contain his captive now, giving himself an infection would only further cripple him and his own odds. He would not feel the effects of the sunshine locked into the blade by magic, but it would need to be close at hand to control Decker if he regained his senses quickly. Tipping back the vampire's head, Cody made sure that his lips were parted just enough to receive the blood that would ultimately save him.

In one swift, careful stroke, Cody made a shallow cut on his forearm, angling it so blood dripped from him directly into Decker's mouth. Instinct took over and Decker's mouth opened to reveal his sharp fangs. The first few drops of blood hit his tongue and seemed to make little difference. Cody only allowed himself a moment of self pity before Decker began to stir. Eventually he reacted to the blood, moving his body slowly while the shallow cuts and bruises healed. Suddenly his eyes flew open and his hands grabbed for Cody's arm, his fangs fully extended with the intent of sinking into his arm. Cody pushed back with the blade of the sunspear and the hiss that erupted from Decker's mouth made a chill run down the hunter's spine.

The combination of blood and pain seemed to wake Decker up and the rogue eyed him wearily as he drank the offered blood with little protest. It seemed that even a proud rogue could take given blood if it meant survival. Cody nearly snorted at the sight, but kept his composure. Whether it was for show or because it was in his nature, Decker made another foolhardy attempt for Cody's arm, but the hunter held him at bay with ease. Cody had heard from humans in the villages that they had visited what it felt like to be fed on by a vampire. They had told him that it was addicting to have your life in their hands and the adrenaline boiled in your skin until you began to crave the experience more than the pleasures of the flesh. He had once felt curious about the rush they described, but seeing the crazy look in Decker's eyes easily put him off such curiosities. When Gwyn had delicately cut him for his blood she had been as gentle as possible, making sure to seal his wound with her saliva which had set his body on fire and left him feeling spent. He had been tempted then to ask for her to drink from him, though he knew she would never fulfill his request. Now he was glad he had never asked. The thought of becoming addicted enough on the feeling to allow a creature like Decker to feed from him made him feel sick. The blood loss was enough to make him wonder if his stomach would try to lose what little it had left in it and he knew that Decker had had enough. He pricked the vampire's skin slightly with the point of the sunspear and the vampire shot back as if he had been stabbed. The energy it took to heal his body drained him and Decker slumped back against the tree as his eyes closed once more.

Cody carefully wrapped up his arm wishing for Gwyn once more. She would have closed his wounds for him instead of leaving his wound open and bleeding. His efforts were rewarded when he watched as the burned skin on Decker's face healed. It was slower than he would have expected and the pink skin that was left still looked painful to the touch, but he no longer looked like he was at death's door which was an improvement, no matter how slight. Once the deeper cuts began to close Cody finally allowed himself to feel relief. He knew enough about vampires to know that his captive would be asleep for at least a day. His body would be strained from rejuvenating so quickly and at least for the first twenty-four hours Cody would not have to keep constant watch over him.

With a shaky sense of security, Cody finally allowed himself to feel his own pain. His muscles cried as he allowed himself to fall next to the tree that was holding up the vampire. He knew that he should at least bind the rogue to the tree. Some of their supplies had survived the attack and he knew that the sun-soaked ropes were still at the bottom of his shredded pack. It might not stop him from escaping, but it might give Cody enough time to spring into action if needed. The more he thought about it, however, the more tired he became. The irons would have to be enough for now. Despite all of his training, the hunter could not outrun sleep. His heavy lids seemed to shut in slow motion as the world around him began to blur. The last thing that Cody remembered before he drifted into a deep sleep was the smell of blood and the cold gold chain weighing down on his chest.

REAGAN

A harsh banging on her chamber door woke Queen Reagan from a deep sleep. The sun must have just set because she could still feel its lingering warmth in the heavy velvet curtains that hung around her bed. The cool body that wrapped around her was a luxurious contrast.

"What's going on?" The muffled female voice traveled up from the pillows besides the blonde. A mop of brown curls could be seen amidst the silk, but little else.

"I know not, my sweet. Go back to bed. The sun has only just set and you can sleep for another hour yet."

Reagan couldn't help but smile when her paramour nodded and retreated back into the pillows. The banging brought her from her pleasant thoughts and she accepted the inevitable. She would have to answer the door before Anya did. Slipping from the silk she wrapped her lithe body into a simple pale blue dress. It was not befitting of her title as a vampire Queen, but it would do for an early evening visit. Normally she would have had Anya or a handmaiden help her but she managed on her own with relative ease. Centuries of aristocracy did not erase her humble beginnings. Often, she wondered what the girl she used to be would think of all of this. That girl would have never been able to afford such lavish things. The silver embroidery swirled on the edges of the long open sleeves and along the bottom hem and they glowed with the protective magic that had been infused in it. The dress gathered at her slim waist before flowing around her legs in a pool. Her personal seamstress and also her most trusted handmaid Nicolette had done well in designing this piece for her.

The banging continued as she tied the final knot at her waist that would keep the fabric close to her body. "Alright then, I'll be right there."

Moving to open the door the blue-eyed queen was greeted to the sight of Commander Darius the head of her Queensguard. Deep worry lines creased in his brow. Normally his long brown hair was swept back at the nape of his neck, but it lay disheveled around his face. Young for a vampire, he still looked older than Reagan. The queen often wondered if it was because he bore the larger burden. She fought, when necessary, but her duty was to her people, to guide and protect them with her words. It was Darius' duty to protect them with his fangs.

"I'm sorry Your Grace, but it's urgent." Despite his four decades of service to his queen, Darius still remained mindful of his social graces, even when she had reminded him time and again that in privacy she was just Reagan.

"It better be, have you no notion of what time it is?" Anya's voice traveled from her place in the sheets and still her tone bore no niceties. Darius flinched from her words, reeling back as if he had been physically struck.

"After all this time and she still scares you. Honestly Darius," Reagan laughed gently. "What news have you?" Polar opposites, Reagan's smile was disarming and her nature gentle while her lover was honest to a fault. Reagan had often asked why she was so harsh towards Darius, but she never received a satisfying answer.

"We have a report. Rogues are on the move. Some say *she* walks Mordin Forest. The whispers are of an elder with long brown hair and purple eyes." Darius paused, his normal composure crumbling as fear clouded his face. "The Council has been called and court is being assembled."

All humor dropped from Reagan's eyes. "Wait outside, we will be ready momentarily."

Anya was by her queen's side in a blur of pale skin. She began to do Reagan's hair without preamble, not the least bit embarrassed by her nudity. Practiced fingers found Reagan's hair in a plaited bun secured by gem studded hair pins that matched the rich silk of her dress before she spoke again.

"If the Council is gathering and the people are already flocking to the throne room then we must be the last to know."

"The thought had crossed my mind. It is a slight, no doubt, but if the news is enough to wake the entire castle I am more interested in what has upset our people, the rest can be dealt with later." Reagan turned to watch as her lover as she dressed.

"You cannot let such slights go, do you suppose Darius took his time getting to us? How could he let the castle stir before knowing that you were aware of the distress?" Anya slid into her leather britches, lacing them up first before working on her boots. Her light tunic went on next, obscuring Reagan from eying her further. The pout she shot the girl did nothing to slow her actions. Next came her leather vest, the attached hood made a mess of her short curls and the girl huffed, moving to the vanity, ignoring the glittering pins in favor of her simple wooden ones. Anya swept her own hair back with a stick, twirling it in her short curls until they made an artful mess at the top of her head.

Since her lover was now fully clothed and there was nothing else to distract her, Reagan sighed and chose to answer her question. "I doubt Darius did anything beside coming to us as fast as possible. You know he can hear you, there is no need to provoke him"

"Fine." Anya held her hand out to Reagan, drawing her to her feet. She did a quick walk around, making sure that everything was in place before nodding to herself. Appearance was important to her paramour more than to Reagan. She was the Queen of her House. There would be no question of her power whether she arrived in her sleeping robes or a lavish gown. She had earned her rite by being named successor by Lunaries' late king, and her sire, King Gareth much to the protest of many of his own court. She of course still answered to the King of all vampire Kings, though he never dared soil his feet on their land. Governed as they may be by their benevolent King and his archaic High Council, she was the sole matriarch to her people and with them her word was law. Anya still believed that she should keep up appearances as if a coup would start due to her wardrobe, but Lunaries did have a tenuous history involving coups and Reagan often felt Anya's theory was best left not tested. When she seemed satisfied that they both looked the part, Reagan led the way back out into the hall. They were met by Darius, dutifully standing as guard, and the three made haste for the throne room.

The royal tower was set back in the farthest part of the castle. The large tower had been maid quarters at one time and many hidden staircases connected it to the rest of the main parts of the castle. They used the hidden door just outside of her own bedchambers that stood behind a large tapestry of a pale maiden standing in the light of a full moon. The staircase behind it led down three flights, torches lighting their way as they passed each door that led to other parts of the Royal Tower before they landed on the ground floor. From there, Darius slipped to the front, a practiced habit of protecting his Queen even within the depths of her own castle. Fresh air from the open garden was a welcome change to the stiflingly stale air of the hidden passageway and the queen silently mourned that they could not stop to appreciate it. They made their way through the inner gardens, Reagan noting that the usual guards were not at their posts.

"Where are the men and women stationed here?" She demanded of the Queensguard Commander.

"They should be at the throne room already, I believe."

How many of my people knew before me? "We mustn't keep them then." Reagan noticed that Anya was keeping silent, a blessing she was immensely thankful for.

They emerged from the inner gardens on the far end which led them to the heart of the castle. It was then that she saw her subjects gathered, humans and vampires alike, and they made way for their Queen with ease, though their whispers did not subside and Reagan held her own anxiety at bay.

Reagan swept through the back entrance of the hall awaiting the appearance of the rest of her Council. The small waiting room already held all but one of the members of the Royal Council. It seemed that they had all heard the news before her. Typical.

"We are just waiting for Lord Basil, Your Grace." Lord Cohen, her successor and heir to the throne bowed at her entrance.

"We will start without him, these are important matters and we best not delay." Reagan did her best to hide her annoyance, but Cohen knew her well. The smirk he gave her only irked her more.

"Of course, Your Majesty." Lord Nirosh was their Master at Arms. He was a silent man who was gentle in nature, but his talents with weapons was feared amongst the Empire as a whole. He was not the type of man you would want to cross. Reagan was grateful to have him by her side.

Lady Arinessa made her way through the door first, her full hips swaying in seduction as she threw a coy smile over her shoulder to Cohen who simply rolled his mirth-filled eyes. They each made their way to their place on the dais until only Reagan was left. She heard the hush fall upon her subjects as they anticipated her arrival. A cough behind her alerted her to Lord Basil's entrance and he canted his head to her before leaving again to take his place. She never expected explanations from her Council, their lives beyond the Council room were not hers to govern, though she felt a bit as if his dismissal was a purposeful slap the face. He would be dealt with at another time. Her people awaited her.

The Queen's Hall was large enough to admit her entire court and then some. The large arching windows let in the bright shine of the moon, though sconces were set into the wall between to hold the torches. There were long seats like benches that filled the front of the hall while the poorer stood in the back. When the people of the surrounding villages came to see their queen it often found the hall bursting beyond capacity, though at such short notice only half of the seats were taken. There was a draft in the air as the servants were only able to light two of the twenty hearths before their arrival. As a result only the high council would know the comfort of the fire. Reagan would have to speak with her serving staff to insure that such an oversight, even on such sudden occasions would never be repeated again.

"All Rise for Queen Reagan of Lunaries." A hush fell over the crowd and Reagan took the seat upon the throne. "Come forth, those who wish to bring these ill tidings to our Queen."

A young vampire moved away from the crowd, shuffling forward with his eyes cast toward the ground. His clothing marked him a commoner, the rough spun wool was dark from use. He wore a dark cloak with its hood drawn over his head, hiding his face from view. Long strands of blond hair fell out, masking his face further. The hall fell into complete silence as the youth fell to his knees.

"Rise, childe. How do suppose your Queen will listen if you do not look upon her?" Lord Basil's harsh words echoed off of the cold stone walls and yet it did not move the boy.

"Show your face, childe, or you will be forced to do so." Anya stood to the other side of Reagan, calculating eyes boring holes into the trembling figure.

"He's scared." Lady Arinessa chided the girl and Anya began to growl in response.

Reagan stood from her throne to end their squabble. She descended the stone steps, stopping before the boy and gently removed the hood. Pale green eyes looked up at her, but not with fear; instead he seemed annoyed. A large gash had been drawn into his face and while it had mostly healed, he was still too young to heal properly. "Who did this to you?"

"I know not, Your Grace." Gently, Reagan lifted the youth's arm, merely pricking his wrist with her fang, sampling his blood.

Visions of the forest swam to the forefront of Reagan's mind. It was night and many of the animals were awake and moving. It was hard to distinguish the different sounds, the boy's hearing was not as sharp as a fully grown vampire and so Reagan struggled to decipher the sounds in his memories. A distinctively loud sound came from the left and the vampire Queen followed the memory toward the sound. A blur of brown hair flew from the trees before searing pain racked through Reagan's face. The intensity of the pain was one that Reagan had not felt since she was a youth and it propelled her from the memory.

"My Queen." Panicked voices greeted her as she came to. Anya was standing to one side of her while Lord Cohen was on her other side. The rest of the Council seemed to have their hands full keeping the rest of the hall calm.

"We will continue this hearing later. Until further notice the Queen's Hall is off limits." Lord Nirosh was commanding from the dais as two sets of strong arms looped around her to lift her to her feet. Lord Cohen and Commander Darius were doing fine work of causing a greater scene.

"I'm alright, unhand me." As a Queen she knew how it must look, sprawled on the floor with all of the court looking on. It was not often that memories were powerful enough for her to feel pain so acutely, but this one had been strong. The youth's fear had been part of the reason that the feeling still resonated, but there was more than that. "Childe you must stay. We have much to discuss."

"You need to rest, Reagan." Lord Cohen began to hover as the doors closed and only the Royal Council and their informant remained. He was

Reagan's second in command and had been since she had become Queen of Lunaries centuries ago and thus could take liberties such as use her given name. Of all of her subjects, he was the only one who was not afraid to treat her like a friend behind closed doors.

"She does not need rest, she needs to put this childe to the sun. He's a spy, how else would his memory hurt her?" Anya bit back, shoving Cohen's arm off of Reagan.

"Your Grace must at least question the boy." Darius agreed as he often did to escape Anya's wrath.

"No one should presume what I need." Her council always meant well, but they often forgot their place. Their advice was not without value, but she was their queen and she would always have the final say. "Let us retire to the Council Chamber."

The Council made way for their Queen. Commander Darius and Lord Nirosh flanked the childe while Lady Arinessa took to the queen's side that Lady Anya had not plastered herself against. They made their way back through the waiting chamber and toward the council room which sat just behind it. There was one such room in the Royal Tower where she much preferred to do her business, though there would be no way to convince the Council to bring a vampire of questionable intent that far into the castle. The last meeting held left scrolls of confidential information scattered and Lord Basil did his best to scurry them away while a serving girl tended to the dying embers. When Lord Basil had seen to it that the House's secrets were kept as such the map of Mordin Forest was revealed. There were markers indicating where the current vampire houses stood while the names and locations of fallen houses were indicated with black stones. They situated themselves around the solid oak table with the boy to her right.

Reagan took his small hands in her own, squeezing them in encouragement. "What is your name, childe?"

"Clayton of House Namyt'tkas." The cut on the youth's face was nearly healed and it seemed his bravery had returned. He was no longer shaking and it seemed to pull back from her touch. She released his hands as if she had meant to all along and watched as he retreated further back.

"You will come to no harm here, Clayton. Now tell me where were you in Mordin Forest and when?"

"I was just outside of Namyt'Tkas' boarders on my way to the Capitol," he pointed out the spot on the map, indicating approximately where he had been. The spot was well out of any House's territory in unprotected land.

"Why were you there, childe?"

"I am a childe of House Namyt'tkas, it is my birthright to make the voyage. The King of Kings has called upon subjects from all of the houses and it coincided with my cluster's rite of passage. My King expects at least half of my cluster to fail, though I hoped not to be amongst those ill fated few."

"Why is King Zentarion asking for representatives? We never heard of such summons. How do we know that you're not lying?" Lady Arinessa spoke, an uncharacteristic sneer on her pretty face. She was the Lady of Inter-House and Kingdom Communications. She was a right sly girl and knew every secret that was worth knowing. It didn't look good on her to have missed such a large summons.

"You're losing your touch, Nessa," Anya sang and the women shared a glare before the annoyed cough of Lord Basil ended the impending argument.

"He's not lying." Darius said solemnly, nodding to himself as he watched the childe. Gifted with the Sight, Darius had been the obvious choice to lead her guard. There were varying levels and kinds of the Sight and Darius' gift was simple at best. All he could feel was energy fields around any being. Its primary use was to catch those who would dare try to lie, but he could also gauge moods and health if he focused intently.

"How do we know you're not lying to us?" Arinessa demanded, turning on Darius.

"That's enough, Nessa. We have larger worries at hand. We will speak of this oversight in time, but now we have more important matters to discuss. Darius, please see Clayton to a bedchamber near my own. See that he is given fresh blood and that he is not harmed. Post two guards outside his room. No one is to enter or exit without my leave."

Lord Basil waited for the door to shut soundly before launching his assault. "Well that was quite a show, Nessa. Are you holding out on us?"

"Don't be absurd. He was clearly lying." Arinessa glared back.

"Not according to Darius," Anya chimed in, her tone full of mirth.

"Because you're such an advocate for our great Commander." Arinessa growled, her hackles thoroughly raised.

"You're just upset that you've been outshone, Nessa. Honestly it doesn't suit your pretty round face."

"Alright that is quite enough, Anya. I am more concerned with our Queen's reaction to his blood." Nirosh rationed his words well and used them to bring the petty Council back to the point.

"Clayton was ripe with fear. That wound was more severe than it looks and that is part of the reason that I felt it," Reagan sighed, already tired of the spectacle.

"I still don't believe he's not involved-"

"I am not finished Nessa." The happy laugh that escaped her paramour brought the Queen's strict graze upon her. "And you, Anya, sometimes it would do you good to remember your place. You might take some lessons from Commander Darius in proprietary. The point that I have been trying to make is that his fear and the identity of his attacker made it so the memory was strong enough to lash back at me. She wanted him to be found. He was a message."

"She? You can't mean Cassandra?" Cohen near whispered, fear clear in his voice. "Do you think Logan could be near as well?"

The question gave her pause and it took Reagan a moment to gain back her voice to respond. "No, it seems Cassandra has let her pet Vestera loose on Mordin Forest."

"Can you be sure it is her?" Lord Basil cut in. She could see the wheels behind his eyes turning. No doubt he was thinking of what possible strategy there was in letting the wild vampire out, but Reagan was not interested in the intricacies of Cassandra's strategies.

"I saw the memory, did I not? I know the difference between Cassandra and her wretched pet better than most. You would be careful to question me, Lord Basil."

"Of course, Your Grace."

"Don't we have more important matters to discuss? The mad woman is a concern, that is true, but what of the slight from the High Council and the King of All?" Anya asked, shifting focus back onto the task at hand. If Reagan hadn't been so annoyed by the general happenings of things she might have been proud.

"I have no idea what business King Zentarion is planning, especially if Namyt'tkas felt it was something that they could send a childe to accomplish, but that cannot be our worry right now. If Vestera is so close to Faegon then something must be done. Anya you're going to have to lead a few men into Mordin Forest to find out what's going on. With that psychopath out there the bodies will start piling up before we can figure out her next move. If what I fear is true then we will send word to King Zentarion."

"How could you ask me to leave? Our people are still in danger. Don't think we've been forgiven by Zentarion so swiftly. That must be why we never got our summons!" Anya demanded.

"This is not up for debate. I can protect our people on my own, I am Queen or have you forgotten?" Reagan stood, aware that all eyes were trained on her.

"I will be here to protect the House as well," Cohen supplied to help ease her worries.

"No, you will be joining Anya. I don't want any accidents on this mission. You two are to go, find any possible survivors and come back."

"But-" Cohen stood then too, clearly ready to start a lengthy protest that they simply had no time for.

"This is not up for debate. Lord Nirosh and Commander Darius will accompany you as well. Lord Basil and Lady Arinessa along with the rest of the Queensguard will remain." Reagan squared her shoulders, her voice even. Both Cohen and Anya shrank back into their chairs. "I am your Queen and you will respect my commands. You are to see to any urgent assignments under your watch tonight and will be ready to leave before the end of tomorrow night. Do not mention a word of this outside of these walls." When she was sure that her words had set in, Reagan swept from the room, the silk of her dress dancing across the stone floors in her wake. She had not time to spare to see her Council's reactions. It was for the best, she was nearing the end of her patients with them for the night.

Ruling Lunaries had never come easily to Reagan. There had been a time when she would have gladly allowed Cohen the rite, but the option had not been hers to give. Gareth had trusted her enough to leave his House in her hands, so she found herself burdened with the responsibility. She knew that many questioned her abilities and even still whispers traveled through the castle walls, never quite escaping her ears. She paid them little mind. Her subjects had the right to their own opinions, but none of them had the strength to make the decisions that she was faced with.

Lunaries hadn't always been a weak house. Three full centuries of exile had brought a once great house to her knees. If it weren't for that, Gareth would most likely have still sat upon the throne and the building rebellion against Faegon would be but a dream. It was an exile Reagan had single handedly caused, but she never allowed herself to dwell on the past. It had been nearly two centuries since the Kingdom had brought House Lunaries back into the fold, not much less than the time that Reagan had become queen, but their alliance was still tenuous as best. If Faegon was making moves without Lunaries it would not surprise the Queen. The way she had come into her throne had been called into question by the High Council many times and since her last summons her House had been largely left alone.

Reagan made her way through the inner chambers of the castle knowing full well that Anya was not far behind. Outside of their chambers they were forced to watch their words with care. Walls in Lunaries were not nearly as thick as they would seem. The rest who had refused to kneel to her had fled when she assumed the throne.

Guards were posted at every entrance, even deep within the castle upon Anya's insistence. While Reagan had felt that her lover was over cautious, she had somehow persuaded Cohen to agree and that feat alone had forced her hand. At the heart of the keep was a small Royal garden. The days where human sovereigns had roamed the stone halls had long passed, but the garden remained. There were no flowers and little foliage, but there was a calming aura about the place that always seemed to draw Reagan to it. There, the Queen took a seat on the only marble bench still standing and looked up to the sky.

"You always look best bathed in moonlight." Anya spoke softly from the castle door.

The two guards posted just on the other side shuffled awkwardly, pretending to not listen to the intimate conversation. Anya did well instilling fear in nearly everyone but Reagan and Cohen and even the guards gave her a wide berth when she was in a mood. It was not often that she exhibited any tender emotions outside of their bedroom and Reagan suspected that it scared her guards more than her angry threats.

"Dreanna, Vessa you may leave us." Even with her back turned, Reagan could feel the relief wash over the two women before they closed the heavy wooden doors and made their exit. "You mustn't do that to the guards, we will have no people to protect and no one to protect them with if you keep acting like that." Her tone was kind despite the words, Reagan knew chastising her lover would do no good. Even she could not control the wild vampire.

"You have been telling me the same thing ever since you took me to be your paramour and we have yet to lose anyone." Anya sat down, resting her back against her Queen's. "Why are you sending me from your side? Have I done something wrong? I am so very sorry if I have." At the word sorry, Anya's voice broke and Reagan's heart along with it.

"You have done nothing wrong, my sweet." Reagan turned in her seat to cup her hands around the pale face. Tortured brown eyes met hers and she knew then that she was making the right choice. "You and Cohen are the most capable scouts there are. Promoting the two of you up in your ranks was the best thing that I could do, though I selfishly wish I hadn't. The two of you make it so no one can compare and thus must be the ones to head this mission. If I could have my way, I would never see either of you leave my side, but I need answers not more lost children."

And you have grown too attached to me. Cohen was right and I've been too blind by love to see it.

"You're sure this not a punishment? I swear I will right any wrong I have caused. I will work harder and I won't even fight with Cohen anymore." When Reagan leveled her with a knowing look, Anya quickly amended herself. "I won't fight with Cohen anymore in front of anyone else."

"Well at least I could believe you in that." Sighing, Reagan moved to wrap her arms around the shaking girl. "You are not being punished. I need answers and this is how it must be done. Besides, I have the rest of the Queensguard here. Nothing bad will befall us. You will go with Cohen, Nirosh, and Darius and get me that information."

"Why do you trust Darius?" The calming spell that had subdued Anya broke and Reagan knew that she had misspoken. There would be no getting through to her any longer.

"Because he is trustworthy. I give you many and more liberties as my paramour, but remember this, you are my subject and I your Queen. When I give you an order you are to obey and I am ordering you to stand down. Darius has served us well for the past four decades, he's been with us for nearly five. I will not have you question him or me at every turn. Be sure you and Cohen have your party ready and out on time." Gathering up her skirts to keep her hands from slapping the brunette, Reagan made for the castle doors. "And Anya," turning to insure she had her attention, "do make sure you come back unharmed. And leave your attitude in Mordin Forest because I will have none of it when you return." The hurt in the girl's eyes was near enough to break the soft hearted Queen, but Cohen's words swam in her mind once more.

You are too soft on her. She will be your downfall, mark my words she will see Lunaries burn before she would let go of her grasp on you.

CLAYTON

The hallways surrounding the Queen's Hall were packed with Lunarians of varying classes, making it very difficult for Clayton and his silent guard to navigate toward the back of the castle. Whispers followed the pair, eyes stuck on the childe, but he paid them no mind. He was small for a vampire and he knew it. Namyt'tkas had a strict policy on whom they granted the bite to. He had just made the cut, something that stung whenever he thought about it, and even after a decade of training he was still just a skinny boy trying to be strong. He had been the one least favored to make it to the capital. It would seem, much to his disgust, that his peers had been correct in their assessment.

Commander Darius, the guard assigned to escort him, inclined his head toward a much narrower path to the left and he followed with no protest. They were traveling through what was obviously servant's quarters and soon the judgmental looks of the Lunarian nobility staved off to make way for the chatter of servant gossip. The happy giggles of two young looking human girls echoed giving the otherwise deserted passageway a warm feeling. The youthful glee sounded foreign to his ears and when Clayton turned to discover the origin of such a pleasant noise he was met with matching azure eyes. They looked to be sisters, though not quite twins. Both girls wore their hair up in stylish braids which would have no place in the halls of Namyt'tkas and yet the Commander seemed not to notice. The servants curtsied to them and the older vampire bowed his head in return. It had always been said that Lunaries was a house far removed from the ancient ways and it seemed that the gossip of his elders had not been false.

The further into the Royal Tower they went, the fewer people, human and vampire alike, there seemed to be. There were guards posted, scattered throughout, but not near enough to stop an attack if there were one. The people of Namyt'tkas were born and bred fighters and it was not uncommon for there to be disagreements settled through fangs and steel rather than through words. It was a way of life that this lesser house seemed not to follow.

"You are being awfully silent, childe. Pray tell what is on your mind?" Darius' calm voice held the magic to settle his nerves which only served to raise his hackles higher.

"The walls in Namyt'tkas have ears, certainly not much is different between such old houses," Clayton responded in clipped tones, shaking away the lingering feeling of Darius' magic.

"True and yet in these walls the ears are treated well and have too high a regard of their Queen to repeat what they may or may not hear." If Darius knew his magic had no effect, he did not show it. His face was kind, but neutral.

"You place an alarming amount of faith in your people." It was not meant as an insult, but Clayton knew his words cut deep when the aura changed dramatically and what was once warm and comforting became cold and harsh.

"These people took me in, a stranger from the forest, a prisoner of a war that they could have avoided and yet they did not. They placed more trust in me than I dared to place in myself and from it I have grown to love the only true home I have ever known. You are an outsider here with a chance to find a true home. Your King sent you, a mere boy out to take on the task of a man. You will be safe here, childe. It's a right blessing you were found by one of ours." The conviction on the commander's face was almost endearing and if Clayton didn't believe so strongly in his own convictions he may have been swayed.

"I am capable of defending myself," Clayton paused to gather his thoughts before continuing. It would not due to anger a precarious ally further. "I am grateful for the help of you and your people, but my loyalties lie with my King and my House."

They passed a set of doors where two guards stood with purpose. They were adorned with glittering gold chains from which hung Faegon's sigil. It had been many long centuries past since Lunaries had been seen in the good graces of the Highest House, even Clayton knew that, and still their Queen's Guard honored them with its symbols in rich metals. Clayton had never seen so much opulence outside of the ruling class in his life. In his own House everyone wore the same, simple clothes and did the same tasks. Their King and his Council ruled from the shadows and where almost never seen. Inside these castle walls it seemed like everything he was taught was being mocked.

"Good evening," Darius greeted the two and the guards nodded to Darius, their eyes only momentarily stopping on him. The Commander made as if to stop and speak with them, but a glance back at his charge changed his mind. He placed a firm arm on Clayton's slim shoulder and continued to direct him further into the tower.

"Are you taking me so deep within the castle that I can't escape? I see no other reason for such pomp and circumstance," Clayton's peers in his cluster often said his mouth had no leash and would result in his demise. He wondered momentarily if they were right, before dispelling the thought.

"These walls have ears, as you said before. The Queen's Tower is a safe place in which no spy nor man of questionable intent may enter, I have seen to the aura warding magic myself, but I cannot say for those who dwell beyond its protection. This is a good House filled with good people, but to have good people, bad ones must exist to be made examples out of. You are to stay here until Our Queen decides what must be done."

"Your Queen. She is a Lady in her own right, but I will not recognize a ruler who is not my own."

"And thus is the root of the problem. The war of the six houses will come when no one man nor woman could name their true King."

"That is an old wives tale. There will be no war of the six houses, there are only five and King Zentarion has seen to keep it so."

"So you recognize him as King above your own?" Clayton saw the trap for what is was and shook his head.

"You speak more than a commander should be allowed. Take me to my room and then leave me. I will agree to council with your Queen, but until then I wish to be given peace."

Darius stopped and leveled him with a cool gaze. It was an unnatural look on the man's face to be sure. "And you speak above your post, childe. I would remember that when Queen Reagan sees it fit to grace you with her time."

Feeling thoroughly chastised, Clayton merely nodded. Satisfied, Darius continued to take him through the winding corridors, this time in silence. The general noise of the castle seemed to fade as they made their way up flights of stairs until it seemed that their journey was finally over.

A female vampire stood aside for them in front of a nondescript door, "Commander Darius."

"Lady Esmy, this is Clayton of House Namyt'tkas. He is to be under your protection for the remainder of his stay."

The vampire was pretty in a plain way. By the look of her face she appeared very young. There were no lines marring her face and her blonde locks were as white as a child's, not yet darkened with age. She was short, though Clayton held no illusions that she was weak. Anyone with eyes could see that she was more muscular than anyone of her stature should be. Clayton was sure that in a fight she would win. Her hair was cropped short allowing just the fringe to fall in her dark grey eyes, a woman of practicality more than fashion. She was far older than himself and Darius, of that he was sure. Her eyes were old, older than such a young face should hold and yet they bore through him with all of the wisdom held only by one much older than he.

"Lady Esmy," Clayton knew better than to insult a lady much less one who may be an elder and he dropped into a deep bow.

"So you will be polite to her and not me?" He could not be certain, but it almost seemed as if the man's tone was teasing.

"She is a Lady and you're just a commander, not even a Lord Commander." He was beginning to sound childish and he knew it, but there was something in the air around this Darius that put him on edge.

"I am the Queen's chosen guard, boy, that should be enough of a title to earn your respect." The humor fell from his tone. His eyes turned a sick lilac, eerily similar to the eyes that hunted him in the woods. Clayton should have known not to press, but his tongue was not obeying his mind.

"And what have you done to earn it?"

"Clearly the boy has some sense," Lady Esmy spoke with a forced calm that had the odd color bleeding from Darius' eyes until he looked upon the two with careful indifference. "Come along now, Clayton you should find all of the accommodations to your liking, anything amiss and we will right it for you." Lady Esmy opened the door and put herself between them, shielding him from the angry commander.

The room was smaller than the barracks he was accustomed to, but they seemed much too large for a single person. Being so close to the Queen's own quarters it was lavishly furnished with a large bed and a dresser that could have fit all the belongings of his fellow brothers and sisters. There had been a total of ten humans turned in his troop and he could not imagine that the other nine were in such an odd predicament as he.

There was a fire already set in the grate and the shutters were locked tight to keep the warmth in. A nightshirt and robe were hanging for him at the foot of the bed and one touch from his hand revealed it to be the softest material he had ever felt.

"That is silk. I'm sure you've never felt it before. Only the nobles of your house wear it no doubt." Her words were soft, not kind, but not judgmental either.

"And I suppose even the servants here are allowed fine treasures such as these?" He lashed out, not unlike a scared animal.

"Allowed? Yes, though their work keeps them from such attire. Queen Reagan is good to her people, however, and we have many feasts and formal occasions for all to wear their best and enjoy such treasures as you say." Lady Esmy didn't seem very bothered by his attitude.

"My people would never allow such frivolity."

"I can't say that we know much of the Namyt'tkan culture. We are very secluded here. Tell me, what must your people be like? You are quite capable, but far too young to be traveling across Mordin Forest to see the King."

Lady Esmy took a seat in the armchair by the fire. There was another opposite it, upholstered in the same rich green fabric with golden leaves embroidered throughout which she motioned to with one wave of her hand.

He sat before he realized he had obeyed her so quickly. "Honor is our shield."

"Yes I know the words, but that can only say so much about a House. What are the people like? What are your values?"

"You ask many questions for a guardswoman." It was a poor deflection.

A hint of a smile returned at his comment. "You refuse to answer a question directed at you from your superior, for one so adherent to honor that is very rude."

Clayton bowed his head in shame. His superiors would be furious with him had they heard his mouth. "You are too right, Lady Esmy. Forgive me."

"You will be forgiven if you answer my questions. The Queen will no doubt wish to speak with you soon, but until then I will be her eyes and ears. Commander Darius did not lie when he said that I was meant to guard you from those who might oppose the Queen's will, but I am also here to guard the House from whatever ill will you might possess."

"I possess no ill will." The thought was preposterous. There was no reason to wish ill on any house no matter how backwards their beliefs might be. Every house in existence had every right to operate in their own way so long as the King of Kings allowed them to do so.

"Alright then, why were you sent to see the King of Kings?" She sat further back in her seat and Clayton knew that avoiding her questions would not gain him anything. She intended to stay until he spoke and he saw no reason to delay her further.

"I wasn't the only one sent. Ten of us were reborn together. We learned and trained for a decade as a troop with little contact outside of us besides the instructors and our King. We were told that our task was to make it to Faegon alone where an elder from our House would wait to taste our blood and prove that we were worthy to serve our House. We were not permitted to leave together. I was the last of my troop to depart. Since your scouts found me and I am here, I will never be accepted back into my house. I have failed my task."

"That's absurd." The voice of the Queen was unmistakable and Lady Esmy was on her feet in an instant. Clayton reluctantly followed, bowing to someone else's Queen despite every fiber in his being screaming not to. "We might train our people to fight, human and vampire alike, but we would never subject a childe to such torment."

"It was not torment, we are the superior race. We are meant to be strong."

"We have no superiority to humans. That is the old way. If you were not born of human flesh you would never have been given the honor of taking the bite. It is a lesson many of our kind must be reminded of." The Queen's voice was soft. She relied on her people's respect and desire to hear her words to be heard and Clayton could understand why. She took Lady Esmy's seat, but not before pulling over the stool from the vanity for her.

"That may be true, but we were taught that the bite was given to man to help them evolve into a better form, one that would allow them protection from those meaning to bring them harm. Does that not make us better?" Clayton could not fathom this train of thought.

"Do the soldiers who fight in the name of the King of Kings become more important than the man himself? We might have advantages over the human race, but we owe them much and more. If we as a whole people were to understand this there would be no reason for the likes of a false King, and for their people to rally behind the name of a failed House. They say that House Rayne disappeared from the map because of King Zentarion's fanatical fear of the old legend, but I have always believe differently. They were a House built on hate, their words alone were evidence of this. *Death to the opposition.* What type of life did they support? We must learn to live in harmony with our human brothers and sisters. We cannot survive without them."

"You speak with passion, no doubt, but such radical thoughts would receive only laughter and a walk to the dungeons in my house."

"I thought I heard you say that you would have no place in your house now that you have received help from another. If you are meant to succeed without help, is the Crown and the High Council meant to maintain peace without the alliances between all of the houses?"

As queer as her ideals were, the Lunarian Queen was right in that regard. He would never be allowed home and while he might not be comfortable with such an odd house, it was likely the only one that would let him in after his failure. The Adrastosian people were too stubborn and Tryali was a House of cowards. He would never set foot in Faegon, not so long as a representative of House Namyt'tkas resided in her walls.

"I may no longer have a House, this is true."

"If you wish to reside in this one, you will refer to your queen with respect." Lady Esmy spoke for the first time in her Queen's presence.

"Enough, Esmylara, he has yet to decide if he wishes to stay. Until then, Lady Reagan will do. I must leave you now. Take your time to settle in, Lady Esmy will be at your door should you need anything. I will insure that Commander Darius is the one to relieve her. You are not our prisoner, but until you have made your decision you will be required to move about the castle with an escort. That is not up for negotiation." She stood from her seat with grace, not giving him the opportunity to respond even if he'd had one ready. "If you should need me for anything you must only ask your guard."

Both women left then, Lady Esmy's face was closed off, not giving away any emotions toward the easy dismissal of her Queen. On the contrary, Queen Reagan wore an easy smile. He had yet to agree to any of her terms and yet she carried herself as if he had already done as she expected. He had only met his own King once and that had been the day he had taken the bite, but it was obvious that the people of Lunaries knew and loved their Queen well. The mere idea was so strange that he felt his head begin to ache in a way that it hadn't since he had left his life for the regimented one that Namyt'tkas had provided him. There had been a time when Clayton had been convinced that the structure provided to him by such an honorable house was his savior, but now he began to question all that he believed he knew.

He sorely wished one of his brothers or sisters from his troop were there with him. He had grown close to them and greatly longed for advice from any one of them, even from Urien no matter how much he despised the boy. While independence had been the point of their training it had been impossible not to create attachments with the nine others that he had spent all of his time with. He had wanted to be alone, strike out and prove his worth, but now he realized how foolish that had been. He missed them, despite his best efforts. How he wished for their comfort now.

Frustrated by his own thoughts, Clayton stood from his seat, the heat of the fire suddenly very oppressive. He moved to throw open the shades on the window, overlooking a barren castle grounds. The moon hung high above and while there should have been much noise and movement from the castle below, he saw only empty stone courtyards and the tops of trees for miles. He was completely alone.

He should not wish for the comfort of others. He was taught that he had come into the world alone, he would most likely die alone, why should he rely on others to fill his time for the centuries in between? The need to rely on his troop went against everything he had been taught. He was meant to be a strong independent force against the rogue scourge. He would have to prove that by leaving this place in the night. He would accept their bed for the day and then strike out on his own. With his mind made, Clayton lay down on the plush mattress, much too soft for his tastes, and resigned himself to a sleepless morning with a heavy heart.

NATALYA

It was an uncharacteristically warm morning for the end of the harvest. Day had not yet broken and yet the stifling heat threatened to oppress those few unlucky to be traveling at the early hour.

"There is rain on the horizon," Ivan had remarked as the party of four made their way through the empty streets.

Natalya could see no evidence of this. The little clouds in sight were innocent enough, neither too dense nor graying. Moisture was thick in the air, though, and Mary Rose had made sure to supply her with an extra tunic to shield her from an impending storm. The fabric weighed her down almost as much as the heat and she cursed accepting the garment. She had felt so refreshed from her sleep, that sense had escaped her for a moment and now she shouldered the consequences.

The cemetery which had looked sullen and neglected by the cover of night only looked more so in the pale light of daybreak. Rows upon rows of cracked stone markers, all of various sizes, littered the uneven ground. They were sectioned off into clusters that upon further inspection seemed to be purposefully arranged. The largest of the group showed the surname while the smaller ones, littered throughout, held first names. Whole families were laid to rest on top of one another while richer families were set aside with the proper space to respectfully lay their dead.

Ivan and her father led them down a winding path in silence. Baldwin stayed beside her, blissfully keeping to himself. His initial attempts to engage her in conversation had only resulted in curt responses and so he chose to stand beside her as a silent shadow. What little she had conversed with Mary Rose the night before had exhausted her, as she was not accustomed to speaking with strangers. She had little to say by way of harvest patterns or predicting weather and she much preferred the company of her own thoughts to idle chatter. There was no need to waste energy.

The rougher disjointed plots fell away the further into the cemetery they went. Those plots that stood aside with room to spare which had looked rich in comparison were no contest to the statue markers in place for what must have been the wealthiest of families. There were few plots that clung to the gate that separated the richest of houses from the rest. The Duane plot set amongst those which, could only be classified as the upper working class, Ivan stopped to pay his own respects.

Her father continued on up ahead through the gate and toward a mausoleum in the very back. It was nearly as tall as many of the smaller house in the village and looked to be just about as big. Her father's family name was hard to miss as it was carved into the front of the large monument. Natalya could just remember the stories her father told her when she was much younger. He would gather her to him in the light of the evening fire and tell stories of the rich lands that his ancestors had farmed in the far off village of Sylvine. He had talked of the gypsy markets and the strange sails that came to port. Of course it wasn't until she was much older that Natalya had learned they were all tall tales. Her father hadn't even been born during those times and the once great village had already begun its steady decline when he was first born to the world.

Despite it having been generations since the golden age of Sylvine, the wealth of the Grahame's did not seem easily forgotten. There were dried flowers at the door. It took all of her father's considerable strength to coax the ill used door open though it was obvious that others had come and gone to pay their respects. Small wooden carvings lay about the grass, a tradition that those in Ash had also honored. Those spirits who were lucky enough to be loved in death as they were in life were gifted wooden carvings of the many things that they might need in the afterlife. It was common to burn them by their grave to insure the items were sent to them properly, but it seemed that whoever was willing enough to visit the Grahame's had not seen it important enough to open the doors and deliver their gifts.

Dust assaulted her eyes and nose as Natalya struggled to breath through the oppressive air that hung about the long forgotten tomb. Weak light poured in from the half open doors illuminating the coffins closest to the entrance. There were two that lay side by side and her father moved to them as if in a dream. Natalya stayed by the door, a stranger, as her father grieved alone. The sight became too much for her to bare and she pulled back from the stale air, gasping when the sun's light touched her skin and the taste of death no longer danced on her tongue.

There were other large structures littered about the grounds and Natalya moved around them, so out of touch with the world around her she felt like the dead wandering amongst the living. She stopped before a door marked Lanson, the building half eaten by strangling roots that stretched high until they wrapped around the slanted roof. She couldn't see far above from where she stood, but she imagined the vines intertwining at the top, tying the building up like a parcel from the market.

"Elizabeth's maternal grandparents lived in this village. They were the reason your mother and her family came here after leaving the Capitol. The Lanson name died out with your grandmother, but that hardly mattered. She was a well educated woman, your grandmother, and she was smart enough to marry a man from Magdus who took her away from this dying village to the Capitol." Ivan stood beside her, a look in his eye that Natalya could not place. "It's about time we get your father and head to Rosewood, it's not far from here, but it is still a walk and I want to make sure you have enough time to settle in before the storm."

Natalya simply nodded, not wanting to invite this man into conversation when she truly had no idea what to say. Ivan seemed more understanding than his son, and left her in silent search of her father. Not willing to wait, Natalya slowly made her way to the entrance of the cemetery. It was easy enough to follow the tombstones, this time watching as they went from large and opulent back to small and warn. Baldwin was standing at the entrance, but he was more concentred in throwing anxious looks up to the still clear sky to pay her any mind. When they were finally met by their fathers the group of four made their way, leaving the cemetery behind.

Rosewood Farm was the farthest building from the village center. Surrounded by miles of land and forest, Natalya found herself in awe of how open it was. The sun was just rising behind the small homestead and shadows were creeping up the front of the property as if to greet them. Out in the distance two ox were pulling large carts slowly being filled with what was left of the season's crop. Ash had not been a large scale farming village, especially not in comparison to Sylvine. Many of the people in Ash were trades people and very few farm lands were kept beyond small, personal plots. Natalya had never seen anything quite like a farm at this scale in her life.

"It was far too much land for Emeline and John to handle in the first place, but it was as generous a wedding gift that we could afford. They made do for a year, but near the end of the last harvest John went missing. Our oldest son, Art, is living out here with Emeline now. She's a brave girl, but I'm afraid for her. You two coming to live with her will settle some of my fears, selfish as it might seem." Ivan spoke softly to the girl though she still heard him. She was old enough to marry yet the two men still seemed hesitant to tell her anything that might upset her. It was only her preoccupation with the sheer size of the farm that kept Natalya from telling the two just what she thought of their coddling.

"I understand." Arthur nodded and Natalya could feel his eyes on her, boring into the back of her skull.

"I will go in a find Emeline. Art will be out to help you bring in your things I'm sure."

Thankful that she would no longer have to shoulder her heavy pack, Natalya let it drop to the ground with a heavy thud. The oppressive garment that Mary Rose had insisted she take slid off her shoulders and joined the pack in the dirt. Ignoring the dark look on her father's face, she walked toward the wooden fence marking the start of the Rosewood Farms. Where she was standing, the fields were farther out and only empty fields lay before her. Closing her eyes, Natalya turned her face upward allowing for the sun to soak into her skin. Dark for a girl who did not work in the sun, Natalya hated her complexion growing up as it had marked her as a commoner even though she was far from one, but here it made her look like she belonged. She might actually belong somewhere finally and the thought brought a small smile to her face.

"We will be happy here, you will see." The voice startled the girl and her smile vanished as she looked up at her father.

Her father was standing beside her, blocking the sun from her view and darkening her mood. Even though he had been a single parent for over ten years, Arthur still had no idea how to communicate with his daughter. Everything he said and did just seemed to annoy her and Arthur's first response was always to yell and then ask questions later, if at all.

"I haven't been happy since mom died. Why would I start now?" Natalya asked, familiar bitterness present in her voice.

"That's not true. You used to love training with me."

"That was before I found out what a freak it made me!" Tears stung at her eyes and she wiped them away refusing to admit weakness. Anger clouded her grief and Natalya continued to unleash all of her pent up rage at her father, neither mindful nor caring that Baldwin was witness to her outburst. "I never asked for you to raise me like a boy! I never asked for this life! Whatever it is in your delusional brain that makes you think we're in constant danger took away everything I had! I was going to be married! I was going to finally have a life where the death of my mother didn't hang over my head every waking moment of every day and you managed to strip that from me too!" Spinning around in a haze of dust and brown curls, Natalya pulled herself up and over the short fence and stormed off toward the fields without another word.

Wind whipped through her hair before she realized she had been running. Dried tears left tracks on her face and she stopped to catch her breath and scrub her face clean. Looking around, Natalya quickly realized that she had not run in a straight line and that she was entirely lost. All around her were tracks of open and empty land. Even the boy, ox, and plow were nowhere to be seen. Despite whatever grudges she held against her father, she had to admit that his constant lessons and training on how to best protect herself allowed her to focus on her surroundings, not allowing fear to take over her senses.

A cool autumn breeze carried through the field and the tall grass tickled at her skin. It was so far away from the rest of the village and Natalya took a moment to simply breath in the crisp air and enjoy the silence. Deep down, Natalya knew that her father meant well. The death of her mother had been hard on him. The man that he had been before had been open and caring. The shell of a man the devastating loss left was unrecognizable, but had become the normal she had been forced to live with. She loved her father, he was all she had, but she had her limits and he was fast approaching them.

Allowing the sun to wash over her, Natalya simply took in her surroundings, trying to decide what she would say to her father when she returned. She knew that she would have to talk to him again, even if she didn't want to. As hard as he was on himself she was even harder on him. Part of her truly felt guilty for all of the stress that she put her father through, but every time she tried to tell him that, he would do something else that set her off, leaving her in the same place as she found herself then.

In the distance a woman was making her way through the field. Her golden blonde hair shown in the sunlight, blinding Natalya, forcing the girl to shield her eyes with one hand, the other hovering just above the dagger that stayed secured to her hip. As the woman drew closer, it became obvious that it was the daughter that Mary Rose had told her about the night before. While she was much younger than the motherly woman who had soothed Natalya's nerves the night before, there was no mistaking that the girl taking her time to meet her was the woman, Emeline, that Ivan had said would be their host until the harvest was over. Where Mary Rose had been the very image of a hardworking woman, Emeline looked like a girl of the upper class. She was paler than most working folk with a slight body that hardly looked like it could lift more than a few pounds and bright blue eyes. She was smiling, putting Natalya in an instantly sour mood.

"I often find it comforting to get lost in these fields when I have trouble navigating my thoughts. Of course it helps that I know the way back to the farm." Emeline's voice was calm and even verging on teasing, making the young girl squirm under her gaze.

"I could find my way back if I wanted." Natalya bit back, not allowing the woman to see through her lie.

"I'm sure you could." The comment was neither belittling nor antagonistic and it threw the careful girl. She had little to no experience dealing with other people, yet she felt comfortable around the stranger and it unnerved her, leaving her at a loss for words.

The two stood in the middle of the field not exchanging a word. Natalya would steal a glance toward the blonde whenever she dared, but she just stared off toward Mordin Forest with a look of loss and longing in her eyes. It was a look that the girl had often seen on her father's face back when the hurt of losing his wife had still been fresh. At times Natalya would catch that look on her own face before pushing the sadness away. She had no time to dwell on anguish and it had no time for her. The pained look on such a beautiful face was enough to move the girl and she was about to ask what would cause the woman grief, but she was given the answer without needing to pry.

"My mother might have mentioned it, but this farm was once home to myself and my husband. He has been gone for nearly a year now." There was neither sadness nor anger in the woman's voice and Natalya felt as if she might actually understand this stranger she only just met.

"I'm sorry, how did he die?"

"He didn't, or I don't believe he did. He went hunting in Mordin Forest one day and never returned. At first the villagers thought he had merely gotten lost. They sent out a search party day and night for weeks. I sat by the back door of our home every day, just waiting. When the weeks turned to months they stopped looking. They took care not to talk in my presence, but I still heard the whispers. Many thought that he must have left me, run through the forest and made it to the main road. When winter hit, everyone gave up hope. Everyone but me." Cool blue eyes met Natalya's hard brown and very suddenly the girl saw the pain that Emeline did so well to hide. "More than ghosts haunt this land, but I have always suspected that I am one of them."

Lost for words, the hunter's daughter watched as her hostess turned back toward the direction of the farmstead. Without a word she started to head back and Natalya followed just as silently. As if the Gods had been listening to their conversation, the sky suddenly seemed to grow dark and a crack of thunder was the only warning they had before a sudden storm came upon them. Natalya instantly regretting leaving the tunic behind. Emeline seemed not to be effected by the rain, however, and Natalya resolved to be as unmoved as the beautiful blonde. When the girls made it back to the homestead, the sudden storm has subsided and the sun was doing a good job of peaking through the clouds, high in the sky. The land closest to the home was filled with prospering crops, large ears of corn shielded most of the view from the West side, but a smaller cabbage patch and other greeneries wrapped the East side in a lush, vibrant blanket.

"Art cares for most of the land and the larger crop fields, but the East side is mine. I also care for most of the animals. If you would like I can show you the barn after dinner. We have mostly chickens and two sows. I have a mare if you like to ride." Emeline tried for conversation, her voice more level than it had been when she had spoken of her husband, of that Natalya was sure.

"I would like that very much. Riding was always my favorite, but my father would not let us take our horses." He had said that it was because the noise would have alerted those in the village that meant them harm that they were attempting to leave. She hadn't believed him though, she suspected that it was because he enjoyed taking away the things that she enjoyed.

"Then we will go down to the stables as soon as we can. Now come along, we'll want to get out of these wet clothes before either of us catch a cold." The kind smile was once again so disarming that it made the young girl falter and even smile back. Normally, Natalya would have come back with a defensive remark, but something about Emeline's gentle nature made all of her comments catch in her throat.

"Thank you."

The first thing that Natalya noticed when she entered the homestead was how neat everything seemed. Unlike her mother's home, Emeline seemed to enjoy a more organized space, though having no small children to look after surely helped with keeping a pristine home possible. The hearth was set up to make up a stew, vegetables washed and waiting on the polished wood table. The men were nowhere to be found, though Natalya was sure she heard Ivan's voice not too far away.

Emeline silently showed her up the stairs to a small washroom. "Your things were put in your room, I will go and get you something dry if you'd like to freshen up."

Natalya was thankful that the woman left, not knowing how she would have reacted if she had tired to assist as Mary Rose had the night before. Natalya made quick work of drying her hair with a clean towel that had been left out. She walked to the small basin and pitcher on the far way, pouring just enough water in for her to clean the sweat from her face. A knock at the door was the only warning before Emeline returned with one of Natalya's plain shirts and a pair of pants.

"I think father and Baldwin are staying for dinner, would you mind giving me a hand when you are done? I know you must want to settle in."

"No, I wouldn't mind helping at all. It was my favorite thing to do as a child with my mom. After, father just let the maids do the cooking." Natalya's voice tapered off and Emeline had the grace to ignore her tone.

"My mother was never short of help when we were young. I think she found it rather overwhelming." Emeline's smile was kind and Natalya knew that the moment had passed.

"After mother died, father hired a nanny for me. She never liked it when I was in the kitchen and so it's been a very long time."

"Not to worry, I'll give you small tasks and if you have any questions don't hesitate to ask." Emeline took her leave then and Natalya made quick work of changing, not wanting to leave the other woman waiting. She left her dirty clothes in the wash basket and hurried back to the kitchen. She could not explain what drew her to the blonde, but talking with her made her feel the most normal she had in a very long time and she was not about to ruin their budding camaraderie by being rude.

"Where would you like me to start?"

"Perfect timing," Emeline smiled as if she really had arrived just in time. "If you can start with the corn? Please let me know if you have any questions."

Natalya set up by the door husking corn while Emeline prepared the chicken. It was awkward at first, but she was thankful that Emeline was patient and soon enough she fell into an easy rhythm. They worked in silence, though Emeline would occasionally hum when she seemed in deep concentration. The sun was pouring through the open door now, as if the sudden and quick storm had never happened, and only the autumn wind was keeping the stifling heat at bay.

Loud footsteps interrupted the calm and soon the small kitchen was over crowded as the men entered from the front of the house.

"We are going to work in the corn fields now that some of the humidity has died down. Let us know when dinner is ready." Ivan spoke for the group, kissing his daughter on the forehead before leading the way to the back door, his sons following close behind, finished by Natalya's father.

"I cannot say I've ever seen you husk corn before. Maybe this new life will do you more good than you originally thought." Arthur said, voice not unkind, looking down as his daughter continued her task without responding. Before she had a moment to argue, Emeline cut in.

"I think you living here will be best for me, I would love having another female to brighten up the farm, Art is a good brother, but he can be, well insensitive at times." Emeline leveled the older man with her gaze before dropping it to continue cooking. Natalya visibly relaxed at the girl's words.

"I see, well I will see you both for dinner."

The kitchen remained tense even after the men had left. Natalya continued to chuck the leftover husks into the compost pile, though she might have used more force than strictly necessary. The girls fell into a steady rhythm once more. The husks flew into the compost pile, each whistling through the air before landing with a soft 'plop', the corn banging in the wooden barrel beside the small girl. Emeline continued to break apart the chicken adding the gizzards to the stew and moving the breast and wings to the side to be salted and packed for the winter. It wasn't until a particular hard chuck that Emeline returned her knife to table and wiped her hands on the frayed cloth tied around her waist.

"Sweetie, slow down." Emeline placed her hands gently over Natalya's smaller ones. "Your father means well, but sometimes men don't understand how much their words can hurt."

"You don't know me or my father. Don't tell me what he means and don't call me sweetie." All thoughts of keeping the fragile peace long gone from Natalya's mind. However, the gentle smile that Emeline gave her was as bright as the sun. It seemed the woman was immune to any form of negativity.

"Come on, let's finish this up and after dinner I'll show you down to the barn and take you for a ride." They exchanged a small, conspiratorial smile before continuing their separate tasks and completing the meal.

The tranquil quiet which had settled over the kitchen while they cooked was abolished when the loud voices of the men barreled through the open door. Ivan was in the middle of a story which had his younger son nearly in stitches and even her father seemed to be holding back a smile. Art brought up the rear seeming much more reserved than his younger brother and even came to help the girls set the table. The others sat around the table giving no mind to the pair who were beginning to serve the soup and bread. Art proved to be quite the gentleman and he took the heavy pot from his sister before following her around the table as she ladled soup into every bowl. When they were done, the three sat just in time for the climax of what was seeming to be an epic story.

"You should have seen his face. The horse jumped so high and Arthur just fell off the back like a sack of potatoes!" Ivan roared splashing his tankard of ale, bumping his shoulder into his old friend.

"The horse was spooked! And if I remember correctly you were the one that ran shouting, afraid the thing would come after you!" Arthur shot back grinning just as wildly.

"So what spooked her?" Baldwin asked just as animated, bringing the two men back to their story.

"I've never seen my father act like this." Natalya whispered to Emeline, her eyes trained on her father. She was pushing her stew around with her spoon, hardly eating any of her food. Another loud laugh from the other end of the table made Natalya scowl and Emeline cringe.

"It'll be okay." The gentle squeeze of Emeline's hand on hers was the only thing that kept Natalya from hurtling her soup spoon down the table.

Dinner continued in much the same fashion and when the men returned to their work, the girls remained to clean up and store the leftovers for their supper that night.

The sun was just beginning its descent when the girls set out for the barn. It was to the east of the main home, beyond Emeline's lush gardens. Much of the vegetation looked to be harvested, sitting in baskets near the gate. Large, purple eggplants sat beside earthy potatoes and Natalya felt a much deeper appreciation for the meal she had just helped to create and consume. The tight ball of anger and resentment that had been festering within her for so long began to lessen and for the first time in a very long while she allowed herself a little peace. Suddenly living on a farm didn't sound like the punishment that she had once believed it would be. So long as she had Emeline to look out for her, her life would be much easier than it had been in some time.

The barn looked as new and well kept as everything else on the homestead. The large sliding doors made little complaint as Emeline's deceivingly strong arms flung them open wide. In comparison to the size of the main building, the barn looked like a palace. There was more than enough room for all of the animals that Emeline and Art cared for. The first sight and smell that assaulted Natalya's senses was the chicken coups. More than a dozen hens mingled amongst themselves, a few seemed to be off on their own, but the second they saw Emeline they came running, expecting to be fed. Shaking her head until her blonde curls fell from their careful knot at the nape of her neck, Emeline reached for the pail and scattered a handful of kernels for the pecking hens.

"I would warn you not to overfeed them, but then I would be a hypocrite." Despite her annoyed tone, the fond smile she reserved for the animals gave her away.

Further into the barn Natalya saw more sliding doors that opened into outdoor pens for pigs, sheep, and even cattle. It was obvious that Emeline and Art would be more indebted to Natalya and her father for the help they would provide than the two travelers looking for a home would be to them. The further into the barn they went, the more Natalya seemed to forget what had brought them there, until they came to a short stop beside some stalls.

The first few stalls held a calf and its mother as well as two other older looking mares. There were several empty stalls until the very last one which held a black stallion. It saw the girls first and eyed them wearily. After recognizing Emeline it gave a snort and kicked up at its stall door.

"That one back there is Kenta. He was my husband's' horse. He was with him the day that John disappeared. He came out of the woods alone and spooked. He used to be very tame, but ever since then he has been wild. I can't even get near him most days. Please just stay away from him. I don't want to see you get hurt."

Turning their attention to the mother and her calf, Emeline did her best to distract Natalya from the angry sounds of the stallion, but the girl could not help looking back toward the creature. He was beautiful and it seemed a shame for him to be left alone in the back. Natalya hadn't owned a stallion but there had been one in their village that she had often been allowed to take out since his owner was starting to get too old to ride. Emeline seemed to sense that something was on her mind because she took that moment to point her in the direction of a much calmer horse.

"This here is Cordelia, she's my mare, though I haven't taken her out in a while, not since she had Sophia. There are a few older mares down in those stalls and we can take two of those out today." Emeline walked them down to the mares in question, gathering the bridle, pad, and saddle before setting to work. It was clear that she had spent her whole life on a farm, the way her thin hands glided over its mane and Natalya found that she had more in common with this woman than she had initially thought.

"I know you've done this before, but I think we best take it slow for the horses. They're not really accustomed to anyone but myself, John, and Art. They can sometimes get skittish with strangers. Even my other siblings have a hard time with them."

Nodding slowly, Natalya brought her hand up to pat her snout. She emitted a whinnying sound and head butted her hand. Smiling, she felt her body relax and the mare leaned into her touch. "She doesn't seem to be reacting too badly."

"I'm surprised, she is normally one of the pickier ones. She seems to be having a good day." A loud snort from Kenta's stall made both girl's attention snap. A splintering crash was the only warning that they would soon be staring down the snout of a furious horse. Screaming, Emeline dove down. "Natalya get down now!"

Rooted by panic, Natalya felt her blood run cold as she turned to face the demon horse. She watched in horror as it galloped closer. Flinching back, Kenta's hooves grazed the air where her head had just been, the large stead rearing into the air to avoid hitting her. Its hooves came solidly back to the ground as he threw his head, sizing up the small girl. His black eyes bore into her and soon she felt like she was falling into an endless abyss, losing herself under his scrutinizing gaze. Overcome by the trance-like state, Nat felt her arm raise, slowly outstretching it toward the proud male. Tossing its head again, Kenta seemed to move away from her hand. Faintly, Natalya heard Emeline warning her to get back, but she pushed on, not even flinching when Kenta tried to take a nip at her finger. When he finally let her hand rest on the great horse's snout, he seemed to calm, allowing the young girl to stroke his mane.

Amazed, Emeline stood up from her spot on the floor and gingerly made her way to the pair. Slowly, she extended her own hand, though she only got about two feet away from his face before Kenta reacted. He pulled away from Natalya's hands and made to bite at Emeline, forcing the girl to jump back. Emeline shook her head mournfully, but Kenta was already bumping his head against Natalya's hand again looking for more comfort.

"I guess he likes you." The sad note to her voice went unnoticed by Natalya and the young girl smiled at Emeline. "Just be careful around him. Maybe next time he'll let you ride him."

"I hope so." Girl and horse continued in their own little world as Emeline watched on, her own hands tangled in her hay covered skirts, wrinkling and smoothing out the fabric in a well worn gesture of anxiety and helplessness.

"Please, be careful." The whisper perked Natalya's attention and she turned to face her new friend, a carefree smile stretching across her face.

"Don't worry about me, I'm always careful." The sentence hung between the two and made her smile falter. "What's wrong?"

"Oh nothing," Emeline forced a smile of her own. "Absolutely nothing."

CODY

Mordin Forest was most alive in the dying light of dusk. With the awakening of the forest's most dangerous residence came the scared chatter of the smaller prey looking for cover as they hunkered down for another night of avoiding becoming a vampire's meal. The birds chirped as they settled back into their nests overhead as if to turn their beaks down to the commotion below. It wouldn't be long before the night sang with the call of owls and fireflies would illuminate the well shrouded vampiric empire.

Dusk was not far off, but there was still an hour or so left of daylight with which to travel by. The ground was still warm. It was the first thing that Cody was acutely aware of when he awoke. From what he could tell a sudden noise had pulled him from sleep, but whatever it was he could not identify. His hunter's eyes adjusted to the fading light, the canopy overhead blocking most of the sun's light from him, and he blinked sleep from them as he got his bearings. So long as he had not overslept he calculated that it had only been a day since he had lost track of Gwyn, though it felt like a lifetime ago.

"You must be one of those foolish Free Riders."

Thinking about his partner brought thoughts of the wild vampire Vestera to his mind. Cody could still hear the cold, calculated, voice as if their attacker was there with them. Maybe she was. For all he knew she was lurking in the shadows. The shudder that rippled through Cody's tired body nearly made him lurch forward; the bile that followed it did. Before he could consider where he was, and in what company, Cody found himself heaving up whatever had rested itself in pit of his stomach. He didn't often indulge in feeling sorry for himself, but his situation seemed so dire he felt he might be allowed it.

"That is simply revolting."

The sarcastic voice shocked Cody from his self pity, his vision swimming as his head whipped up and his eyes landed on the vampire. Upon careful inspection, Cody noticed that the sun-soaked irons were still in place, which was mild reassurance. Despite being near death just that morning, Decker was already looking much better, the only evidence of his early injuries were the slight marks on his neck from where the sunspear had nicked him. Color was returning to his skin too, though Cody knew that most humans could not tell the difference. The rogue's skin had seem transparent just hours before and even just a tinge of color made the hunter relax. He would not lose his captive, not when keeping him had cost so much.

"I don't need opinions from a savage that hunts for sport," Cody replied, while using a stick he found on the ground to dig up dirt to cover his mess.

"You're a bounty hunter, how much better could you be than me?"

Cody paused for a moment, if only to make the rogue think he had bested him. "At least I get paid for what I do."

"Indeed." Decker snorted. Cody swore he heard him add, "that makes you worse in my book," but he didn't push the matter.

"How did you recover so quickly? I thought—" The rest of the words died on Cody's lips as a throbbing pain he hadn't noticed in his neck became suddenly apparent. Groping for the spot on his neck that hurt the most, Cody was stunned to feel two deep fang punctures. He began to feel dizzy, or the dizziness from vomiting hadn't subsided, he wasn't sure which. Even through his blurred vision, Cody could see the gaping grin on the rogue's face.

"Did you think I was going to run?" The crazed voice sent chills raking through the hunter and it took all of his remaining strength to not just pitch forward. "Why would I run when sticking around grants me a constant free meal? A pretty tasty one at that." The lewd smile might have bothered most humans, but Cody was accustomed to such tactics. He was also in far too much pain to care.

"There won't be a next time." Cody growled, the burning in his throat attributing to the tone. He mustered up enough strength to propel his body backward and into the tree he had been sleeping against. Dully it came to the forefront of his mind that the vampire had not only gotten the jump on him, but he had fed off of Cody and he had not even woken up. Cody was losing his touch.

"That's a shame. I suppose I will just have to die then. I'm sure you'd have a grand time explaining that to your council." Decker was nearly purring and Cody had half a mind to put him out of his misery, but reason won out.

The mention of the vicious vampire High Council was enough to make Cody pause. He had been in front of the elders more times than he would care to remember, but he had only ever been to see King Zentarion, the King of all vampires and of the High Council, once and that had been with Gwyndolyn at his side. Even with his vampire counterpart, the encounter had gone poorly. The High Council had never been warm in welcoming him even though he had helped bring down more dangerous vampires than any other human hunter to date, but the King of Kings hadn't even acknowledged that he was in the room for the hour long proceedings.

"Well I'll have to at least keep you alive until we get closer, what with me being a weak human and all, I'm not sure I'd be able to drag you." Cody did his best to fall back into his light hearted nature. Aggravating the rogue by verbally sparring would do no good, it would be better to keep him convinced that he was just a simple, harmless human.

"We both know that you're not weak human. You can pretend all you'd like, but I know exactly what you are, hunter." Decker taunted. Cody ignored him, he refused to give him the satisfaction.

The short encounter with his charge had given Cody enough time to find the energy to move. He hid his pain well, though not enough if the smirk on the rogue's face was anything to go by. Using the tree behind him as support, Cody gathered his pack, using the momentum of standing up to swing it onto his back.

"Get up, we're leaving."

Unlike the hunter, Decker stood easily. The blood he had taken from his captor had healed nearly all of his wounds and he looked much better, if only Cody felt as refreshed as the rogue. Beyond his injuries and blood loss, Cody was simply hungry and tired. He hadn't had a real meal or a decent night of sleep since he had left for this mission with Gwyn nearly two weeks ago. He wouldn't have more than the stale bread and cured meat that was in his pack until they returned to Faegon.

They were deep enough in the forest now that there was no vegetation to gather, no fruits, full and ripe, ready to pick. Many of the children in Cody's village had spent their childhood climbing tree branches, higher and higher to get to the sweet fruit. Even Cody, as a young boy, had taken to hiding in their outstretched arms on warm summer nights while his parents took to the fields, no longer bothering to force him down to help. He had grown bored of those trees before his tenth birthday, instead taking to the stranger looking trees just outside of the village lines. None of the children had understood him then, he remembered too clearly the names and taunts that they would spew, especially now without Gwyn there to support him. The trees had called to him then like old friends and soon he had spent more time climbing them than in his own home.

The thick roots had seemed huge to him as a child and they still seemed to dwarf him as an adult. He carefully picked his way through them, his respect for nature growing as it did every time he set forth into Mordin Forest. Most of the cedars and pines stood so tall that they surely reached the sky. Their trunks were wide enough that a family could have lived inside them. The scratching sound of claws on wood made him pause, but the sleek tale of a fox was enough to set him at ease. If there were animals still out they must not have sensed danger. Throwing a glance toward his bounty Cody wondered, not for the first time, just how dangerous the rogue must be. King Zentarion had asked for him personally. It was said that he was one of the traitor Cassandra's closest confidants, though Vestera was also said to hold the same sway and she clearly felt no love lost for Decker. Maybe the High Council hoped that capturing someone close to the false queen would get them closer the their real concern, the vampire named Logan who proclaimed himself the King of House Rayne and the leader of the brewing rebellion.

"I can hear you thinking, hunter," the melodic tone an obvious taunt.

"Cody."

"I'm sorry?" Decker sounded genuinely confused and Cody allowed himself to feel smug. Normally, pride reeked off of Decker like the soiled clothes he wore so any other emotion was like a breath of fresh air.

"Cody. That's my name. You've already taken blood from me, the least you can do is call me by my given name."

"Well then, I didn't think we were taking our relationship to that level, but I am more than okay with that."

"I'm sure you are," Cody snorted in spite of the weird situation he found himself in. Decker had quite the mouth on him, but he could handle him like this.

"I bet you wouldn't know what to do with someone like me," Decker continued, seeming to enjoying himself immensely.

"What? Someone who is allergic to bathing and enjoys terrorizing helpless villages?"

"Well no, I more meant a vampire. I know humans like you. You spend more time with vampires because you don't fit in with the humans, but you lack the guts to take the bite. I bet you've pined after your bitch of a partner all this time and she has never once looked at you. Or is it that she has looked at you? Maybe she just keeps you around for some sweet blood and a nice piece of—"

Cody moved quickly to pin Decker to the nearest tree. He used the surprise evident in the rouge's face to press his sunspear against the bared throat once more. "Taunt me all you'd like, but remember who is in irons right now and who has a means to put an end to you."

"I like you, Cody." Decker grinned back, the hunter kept his arm steady, not breaking eye contact or lessening his grip. "You're just full of surprises." A hiss of surprise was pulled from his lips as the searing hot kiss of the sunspear made a clean, shallow cut on his neck. Struggling away from the tight grasp of the lean human, Decker had to settle for the scrape of the harsh bark to keep from getting further slashed by the furious hunter.

"If I were you I would start shutting up." Giving the point of the blade one more quick thrust, Cody made another slash parallel to the first, higher up and right across the delicate Adams apple.

The rogue crumpled to the ground when Cody released him, the tension building between them even more as he looked up at the hunter with clouded eyes. It wasn't often that the young man felt it necessary to prove his strength, when Gwyn had been there he would have had no problem letting her take over, but there was only so much he could bare. There may have been a time when he would have let Decker's words go unchallenged, when he would have allowed them to sit in his mind and fester until they became a poison in his brain. He had always been more prone to letting others do the fighting for him when he had been young, many of the boys he had played with made fun of him for it, but his time with Gwyn had taught him everything he needed to know about fighting and defending himself. "Get up, we still have a long walk ahead of us."

Cody watched as Decker stood, the trail of blood on his neck the only reminder of their brief altercation. The rogue started back on the path first, leaving the hunter to keep a watchful eye on him from behind. Decker had made a good point earlier, Cody was the vampire's only reliable food source and so he had no fear that the monster would run, but it put him at ease to keep the vampire within his sights. Decker ambled along with ease as if he hadn't just been pinned to a tree moments ago. Cody imagined the grin that never seemed far from his lips was also present, though Cody couldn't be bothered enough to find out.

They continued for most of the night in silence. Silence was a natural soundtrack to Cody, disturbed only the sounds of the nightlife around them. Gwyn had never been much for idle chatter and Cody never minded, finding comfort in her presence while on a hunt. Silence had often meant safety. With Decker all of the normal rules seemed not to apply. Very early on into his capture the sharp tongued rogue had kept a steady, droning monologue of insults and filth. His sudden and complete silence was almost enough to make Cody loose his composure. Besides the occasional quiet murmur, Decker kept to himself, walking ahead of the human without complaint. It was unnerving to say the least, but Cody accepted the small gift for what it was and vowed to keep the remaining journey as peaceful as possible. The thought did cross his mind that this was just another game of Decker's. Since meeting him it was obvious that he enjoyed taunting and teasing for results. While it would seem impossible that he might be able to keep silent for so long, Cody wondered if it was another elaborate way to needle under his skin.

It wasn't the first time that a prisoner had tried to test him. It had always been because they perceived him as weak, not only for his humanity, but for his nature. He never saw reason to correct them of that assumption.

In fact, it proved an advantage to seem like the ill trained sidekick to the monosyllabic vampire huntress. They had made quite the pair and had even created a healthy reputation. Even with such a large reputation preceding them, many vampires still fell for his act, though Decker was obviously smarter than most of Cody's past targets.

"How much longer to Faegon?"

The first clear words from his prisoner in hours and already Cody felt the claws of determined annoyance digging through his skull. He would not succumb to the trying tactics of a mad, bloodthirsty killer. He knew that the rogue was purposely pushing his patience. He would not give him the satisfaction.

"You know the answer to that."

"I can see why blondie would want to partner with you now. I'd always heard she had no personality, she probably loved not having to have any form of conversation and kept you around."

"Stall all you want, rogue, we will make it to Faegon and then you will have to answer for your crimes."

"Decker." Caught off guard by his own words thrown back in his face, Cody remained silent, pushing through his mounting annoyance as he picked his way through the thick foliage.

"Decker. So be it."

"You are a rare breed," Decker said. This time he stopped to watch Cody, his calculating eyes unnerving.

Cody had little time or interest in understanding what that look could mean. "Indeed."

The silence was nearly tolerable then. They took their first break for sustenance near the outskirts of the Faegon territory. They were close to a village which meant that they were close not only to bleeders, but also to warm food for himself. The thought of keeping Decker from fighting back with an audience was enough for him to choose the seclusion of Mordin Forest and forgo a hot meal.

Cody ate his mix of nuts and dried fruits while ignoring the stale loaf and meat, aware that they were long past edible, dreaming of hot cooked meals. There was no doubt that a well prepared meal would be there to meet the travel worn hunter at their destination and it only served as further motivation to push on. Faegon was the largest house as well as the capital of the vampiric empire. The castle was home to two Kings and would welcome him with open doors as it often did when he returned from long stints in Mordin Forest. His last meal there, which had been at the conclusion of a particularly nasty hunt, had been filled with large helpings of boar, slow cooked in a heavenly sweet glaze that had been farmed from honeycomb found back in the valley. That trip had been to bring down three fugitives and acquire fresh vials of their blood for the High Council. Their memories had been vital, but it seemed that their lives had not. By all accounts it had been a good mission, but even then Cody had been shunned from the High Council meetings. He was still only a human in their eyes, though Gwyn often reminded him that meetings were long and boring and she wasn't allowed to eat or relax until afterward, something that he should not feel jealous over. The sentiment, while full of pity, had always made him feel better. The thought of eating in the castle, knowing that Gwyn would not be turning in their report just down the hall made his stomach drop. If he had just been stronger he would not be forced to return to their home without his partner. He didn't often wish so, but there were times when the hunter wished he had taken the bite when it was offered to him. Then at least he would have the unnatural strength and speed to contain his bounties.

"If you're going to eat then I should be allowed sustenance." Decker was looking worse for wear again even though he had fed only hours before.

"Okay." Cody only agreed because he was impressed at Decker's control. It went against the very nature of the rogues to ask for blood. Their entire belief system revolved around them being the apex predator. They never had to ask to feed. They could simply take what they wanted as it was their given right. To his kind, drinking offered blood was as good as a human eating twice cooked meat. It did the job, but tasted less than desirable. He took out his sunspear and cut a shallow line in his arm and motioned for Decker to come forward.

"What, only the arm?" Eyeing the blood wearily, Decker moved in to take the offer, not in the least surprised when he felt the hot kiss of steel against his throat.

"You didn't think I would let you near my neck did you?" It was a question posed with a tone of indifference and the vampire made to grab for his wrist. Using the knife as a guide, Cody directed Decker until his upturned head was positioned right below his tilted writs. It would be humiliating for the rogue to be fed like this and Cody watched as the vampire continued to eye his arm through half lidded eyes. "That's plenty to get you through the day."

Cody shoved him away with the sunspear and wrapped a scrap of his shirt around the wound matching the one he had from his cut earlier. It would clot soon and the bloodlust in the vampire's eyes would eventually fade once the fresh smell subsided.

The first time Cody had seen the bloodlust take over Gwyn's eyes he had been fascinated. Never before had he been close enough to see a vampire take blood and when her normally steel blue eyes had flashed until they shone brilliantly he had felt his breath stop. Vampires all have a sire, something that any human worth their salt would know, but the knowledge that Gwyn had imparted on him then had been a shock. When the bloodlust took over, whenever a vampire fed, their eyes would flash to the color of their sire's.

"In the end, we are all animals and when we feed, our baser instincts are at their peak. We feed to survive and we survive to serve our sire."

He had been young then, full of questions with little caution toward decorum. *"Then why do your eyes only glow? Does your sire share the same color eyes as you?"*

"No. If your sire is dead then your eyes do not change color anymore. Then you're free and your eyes are your own."

He had half expected to see lilac eyes still staring back at him when he refocused from the memory, but it appeared that Decker's control was better than he had expected. Instead, Decker was standing back, hazel eyes watching him curiously. The lilac eyes were queer and off-putting, but Cody found himself wondering what Decker would look like in bloodlust when his sire was gone. He imagined he would look captivating. Shaking the odd thought from his head, Cody cleared his throat.

"We are wasting time. Let's get moving." He tried to sound forceful, though he hardly believed himself. Watching him with the same thoughtful gaze, Decker followed with little complaint.

Time passed with little changes after their meal. The silence from earlier returned, but this time the tension from before seemed to subside. Cody was letting his guard down unintentionally and it seem that every time he tried to repair the cracks in his walls the cocksure vampire found another pressure point to push.

You must be stronger than the human that you are and the vampires that we fight. You doubt yourself and that alone will be your downfall. Gwyn's words from their earlier hunts still stuck with him, reminding him of who he was and what he needed to be in order to make his partner proud.

Cody was so lost in his thoughts he nearly missed the shout and responding snarl from behind him. Turning with his weapon raised, Cody was shocked to find a wild wolf stalking them from the side. Decker had his fangs showing, the cold lilac creeping back into his vision. Normally the animals left vampires alone, though the wolf facing them down then looked sick. It was crazed around the eyes in a way that made Cody feel fear rising through his body where it seemed to be taking permanent residence.

"Back up." The shout was Cody's only warning before Decker moved, attempting to rush the wolf and scare it off. As he sped forward, he yanked at his irons, effortlessly breaking the chain and freeing himself. Cody should have been more worried at the display of strength, but he was grateful for the help. If the wolf was rabid then Decker had a much better chance of healing from it than he could.

The wolf fought a fierce battle, but Decker fought harder. The grace and expertise that he had lacked in the surprise attack from the female rogue was on full display and it filled Cody with a mix of fear and awe. The wolf was sick with madness and it snapped out attempting to meet with any flesh that Decker dare let near it, not even reacting as Decker's claws dug into its flesh. Cody watched, helpless, as the wolf was forcefully pinned down by the rogue. As Decker moved in for the kill, Cody saw the snapping jaws of the beast reach up. Instinct finally seemed to roar to life and the hunter rushed to his aid. With all of the strength he could gather, Cody drove his dagger into the neck of the angry beast. The bloody scream that erupted as its life bubbled from the jagged cut was nothing compared to the searing pain that the hunter felt when the his arm was pierced by the sharp canines of the dying wolf.

A forceful grip pulled on Cody's arm and he blinked back the tears as he felt a second set of fangs sink into his arm. Before he could process what was happening, Decker was sucking on the original bite, stopping to spit out the bad blood before continuing to clean the wound. The pain from the wolf's bite did plenty to block out any euphoric feelings that a vampire's bite was meant to bring. He almost wished for the supposed bliss to replace the agonizing pain, but Gwyn's words rang in his ears once more and he was reminded of the strength he was meant to possess.

"Stop." Cody mumbled weakly swatting at the vampire.

"Don't be stupid, I'm trying to save you." Decker said in between spitting. "This is absolutely disgusting, I will have you know, and I get no joy from this."

"That's comforting." Cody bit back, raising his head enough to glare at the vampire, baring his human teeth in a perfect mockery of a vampire's warning.

"That's the pain talking." The two lay on the forest floor for what felt like hours, Decker cleaning out the blood until Cody was nearly passed out.

"What are you doing?" Cody jumped when he felt the vampire's wet tongue gliding over his open wound.

"Vampire saliva has some healing properties, otherwise when we drink from a willing human the blood lust can often be too much. We can close wounds quickly, it's beneficial to both parties."

The answer came to Cody in a haze and he wasn't sure if he had heard Decker answer or if the voice floating in his subconscious had been a memory from Gwyn.

"Sleep, I'll carry you the rest of the way." Cody knew for certain that it was Decker's voice then when he felt cold arms wrap around his tired body. He was lifted from the ground with ease and a gentleness that he had not been expecting. "Sleep now and I'll wake you when we get to Faegon."

Cody couldn't even summon the energy to respond, instead he let his heavy head fall against his once prisoner's shoulder, no longer fighting to stay alert. He was trusting a killer to care for him, the absurdity would have made him laugh, had he had the energy.

"It's been a pleasant surprise meeting you, Cody. If only the world was filled with more people like you, maybe it wouldn't be such a horrible place." The soft words lulled the battered hunter into a fitful sleep in which he dreamed of sharp fangs and purple eyes.

REAGAN

The Lunarian royal library was a mere shell of what it once was, much like the house itself. Nestled deep into the royal tower it once housed a myriad of beautiful and rare texts for the personal browsing of the Kings and Queens of the house and for their most trusted advisors. There would have been meetings held by the roaring fireplace and gossip shared between peers in one of the many small nooks, plush chairs left for that very purpose. There would have been a time when laughter and joy filled the room, a time when life was breathed into the very pages on the shelves by curious minds. Those times were long gone, however, and the royal library left a lot to be desired.

Centuries had passed since the coup, which had brought fire to the King's Tower, and yet the library was still left in ruins. As much as it had pained her, there had been higher priorities then rebuilding this room; the room in which all of her fondest memories with Gareth were housed. Every step amongst the fire-wrecked bookshelves was a knife in her heart; every laugh and secret between her and her sire lay like dust on the burnt surfaces. They swam in the air and stung the Queen's eyes as she blinked away the tears. The library was off limits to all those who inhabited her house, it still held many of the house's secrets, many of them her own, and she found solace in the empty room when her thoughts became too heavy to bear.

It was in this library that Gareth had told her that he meant to name her his heir. She had been just barely three centuries reborn then, still considered by many a childe in her own right.

"You are the only one I trust, my dear Reagan. You must take over when the day comes. I fear it will come sooner than you or I might like." The words whispered through the air as if they had just been spoken. She had protested, insisted that she was not ready nor worthy of the honor. They had sat in plush

chairs facing each other in front of the fire on that late spring night and Reagan knew then that only horror would befall them when the House at large knew his plan.

She had been right, of course. Gareth's original heir, the Lady Cassandra, had thrown a fit of grand proportions. No matter how much she detested the woman she had felt bad for her. She had been the heir to Lunaries for nearly five centuries and it seemed in poor taste to throw aside such a promise. Gareth had never come outright to tell her that he mistrusted Cassandra, but she had been his lover for longer than she'd been his heir and Reagan could see no reason for him to shame her so.

"Keep your enemies close, Reagan. You might just find that your worst adversary is one and the same as your bedmate. Do not panic, instead keep them close until you unravel their true desires." He had warned her of strange bedfellows and the like when she had been a childe. She had thought little of it then and even as she sat with him alone in his sacred library she thought little of his strange warning. Even on the night that Cassandra had set fire to the tower and attacked Gareth she had felt pity for the woman. She, a simple girl from a farming town, had ruined everything that was meant to belong to the Lady of the House. She nearly felt sorry for the woman until she learned the horrors the sadistic vampire had showered on Reagan's own brother. He had been a shy boy, easy to anger and easier to manipulate. Reagan would never forgive the bitch after all she had done to destroy her family.

A quick rapt at the door forced the memories to fade from Reagan's mind. She hardly remembered what thoughts had brought her to the moth infested room to begin with and she brushed the lingering dust from her plain gray robes. Anya had not been beside her when she woke and she had dismissed her handmaidens without fuss. She could manage to pull her long hair into a simple bun on her own and it only took two hands to tie the knots on her silk shift. She had no intention of taking any audiences and if Cohen or any of her personal guard saw her so underdressed they'd easily turn a blind eye. For how often they saw it fit to bother her while she slept in her own personal quarters it was a wonder that half of her personal staff had not seen her bare as the day she had been born. Not that it mattered much to her. She hardly cared how she looked. She could rule her House in her nightgown just as well as she could in the oppressively heavy royal gowns, but it seemed that those that sat her Council believed in insuring their Queen be a royal sight at least when appropriate. With that thought in mind, Reagan gathered her skirts and went to open the door.

"My Queen, I am terribly sorry to bother you. The childe Clayton wishes to speak to you." Commander Darius was there to greet her. His eyes were averted and she felt the shift in the air.

"There is no need for you to adjust my aura. Sometimes a bit of melancholy does the soul good." Reagan smiled gently appreciating the gesture.

"As you wish, My Queen. He awaits you in the Small Council room."

"Very well. Thank you Darius. I am not in need of an escort. Please see to it that you and the others report to the Small Council room when I am done with the boy."

"Yes, My Queen." The man bowed deeply before leaving her to walk alone.

The halls in the Queen's Tower were quiet for the early hour and Reagan enjoyed a peaceful stroll without the hindrances that came with ruling a House. She loved her people and ensuring their safety was little hardship, but the political nonsense that accompanied it often left a sour taste in her mouth. Faegon had left them well enough alone since Lunaries had been officially reinstated into the empire. They had never darkened their doorstep and any official summons had been sent without a proper escort, forcing Reagan to bring her own guardsmen with her and leave her House less protected in her wake. The slight it was meant to show her and her house was not lost on the Kingdom's youngest Queen. In the days of old the King of Kings would travel to bless a new House, King, or Queen personally, or at least those had been the tales. The need for such an occurrence had not happened since the houses Namytar and Tkasar had merged to form Namyt'tkas during the Great War. The offspring of which house sat waiting for her. Naturally her own crowning had gone ignored by King Zentarion.

Lilliana, one of Darius' new recruits was standing guard outside the Small Council door. She stood proud with one hand curled loosely around a six-foot spear. She was petite, standing at just short of five feet. It would seem comical to most, a girl so slight with a weapon so large, but Reagan had watched the girl in the practice rooms and she was more than skilled with her weapon. She moved with it as if it were an extension of her own arm, the talismans that hung from the spear only adding to the dance which she performed every time she worked through the steps of her craft. Similar talismans and even dark crow's feathers were woven into the shocking orange mane that sat atop Liliana's head. Today it was swept back with a simple ribbon. She wore the customary guard's uniform, though her normally worn leathers were replaced with clean ones. No doubt she only wore them when on duty as to appear presentable for her Queen.

"Your Grace." The gentle voice that fell from her lips often sounded like music. It was truly a wonder that such a sweet looking girl was their fiercest fighter of the new recruits. "Lady Esmylara tasked me to stand guard. She awaits you within along with the childe."

"Thank you Lilliana, you are relieved. Lady Esmy and I will be fine with Clayton."

"As you wish, Your Grace. Shall I return to the practice rooms?"

"If you desire. You have the night off," Reagan smiled as the woman visibly relaxed. She bowed quickly before dashing off.

Lady Esmy sat across from Clayton, her eyes darting between the doors and her charge. The boy was sitting slumped over the table, his eyes trained in his lap, he looked as if he were being taken to the gallows. It seemed that the boy had no intent of staying with their house and Reagan felt her heart tighten. The boy had put up a fight with Esmy the night before about silliness over ancient cultural differences. He was too young to even understand the words that he had been taught to recite and yet it seemed he was going to stick to his people's beliefs. She could hardly fault him for that. He was loyal and would have been a great asset.

"When do you plan on departing?" Reagan asked as soon as she took her seat at the head of the table.

Clayton jumped as soon as the words left her mouth and looked up to Lady Esmy as if she had been the one to sell him out. "Right away, if it pleases you, Lady Reagan."

"It would please me more to see you stay." She had a mothering streak longer than was healthy. She knew Cohen would have words with her about it later. For now she had to try and persuade the childe to stay where he was safe.

"I cannot do that. I must venture on to Faegon. It was my task and I must complete it."

"And if everything you spoke to me was true? What if your people really do shun you for taking our help?" Lady Esmy asked. She always spoke the truth even when those she spoke to would rather not hear it.

"I must risk it. If I leave now they will at least know that I only faltered in the beginning. Honor is our shield. They should see the honor in my taking help when I needed it."

"That is true. I believe they would see even more honor in your remaining with us for a time. We wish to have you as our guest and it would be best for your injuries to heal. There is no shame in allowing us to see that you are cared for."

"That is very well and kind of you to care, Lady Reagan, but I really must be off. I cannot delay further. I was the last of my troop to leave and am already horribly behind. I mean no offense, but I must be off."

Reagan studied the boy as he dared to stare her in the eye. His green eyes looked sure, not even wavering in the slightest. "Alright. You have my leave to go as soon as you have taken your meal and packed provisions. All of your supplies and your knapsack were lost when our scout found you. You will at least take these, no?"

"I will. Thank you Lady Reagan, Lady Esmy." The boy nodded to both women before hastily excusing himself from the room.

As soon as the latch in the door shut Lady Esmy leveled her with a cool glare. "Why let the boy go? He is still weak and I doubt he will make it to Faegon now. Namyt'tkas is much closer to Faegon and he is bound to be even less sure of himself after this ordeal. You are sending him out to slaughter."

"He was going to leave with or without my blessing. At least this way the poor childe has a hope to not upset the elders of his house. Also he will not be alone entirely. I want you to follow him. You must give him at least a day to gain some ground, but I want you to make sure he makes it safe."

"I am not a nursemaid. I am a fighter and one of your sworn guards. This is a task better suited to Lilliana or one of the newer guards." Lady Esmy scoffed. Reagan wondered when her people had grown so bold.

"You mistake this for an option. It is was an order, Lady Esmylara, one that I know you will follow. Besides, I want you to journey to Faegon for a far greater cause than to watch the boy. I need someone I can trust to be my eyes in the capitol. Something is happening and we will not be left out of any great decisions because of a mistake made four hundred years ago." It mattered not that it was her mistake. Many of those that were alive during that time had left Lunaries in the wake of Cassandra's coup. Very few still remained from the times before the exile and even still less knew the real reason that the once favored House had nearly fallen off of the map.

"You are right, Your Grace. I meant no offense. I am honored you would seek me out to protect our home. I hope you forgive my oversight." Esmy bowed her head diverting her eyes as a sign of respect.

"There is nothing to forgive. Go now. I believe Darius and the others are arriving and I still have many matters to attend to before the sun begins to rise."

The small council room that sat joined to the Queen's Hall housed most of the confidential information that they spent their meeting discussing. The room in the Queen's Tower was meant more for use in debating internal affairs. It was often called the war room by her council, though the name had little to do with war plans and more to do with the miniature wars that sprouted in the room when the many different voices clashed and their opinions came to a head. In this room they discussed things of merit to the House as a whole because as Reagan had seen it, her people meant more to her than the troubles of the empire. The empire had never cared much for her personally and she saw little reason to bring those troubles directly into her own chambers. The other room was kept locked and guarded at all times while this one was open for use amongst her personal staff. It wasn't uncommon for vampires and humans alike to use the space to settle personal disputes like who had stolen the new gear from the practice room or who was on morning watch duty.

The room itself was rather plain. The meeting table and the chairs around it were the only furniture. There was a modest fireplace set against the far wall and the windows were flanked by thick, black curtains. The only decoration of sort was the tapestry on the wall behind the head seat that depicted the Kings and Queens of Lunaries. It was made by one of the seamstresses within the castle long before Reagan had been born. It had been there before Gareth had ruled and before King Lamont before him. Near the very bottom of the tapestry, Reagan found her name in glittering gold letters. Broken lines attached her to Anya, a matter that had caused quite a fight between the two. It indicated that they were lovers, but they would never be joined by marriage. Cohen had distrusted the girl from the start and it was his constant warnings that solidified in Reagan's mind that she would never wed the girl. She could not see why Cohen disliked her so, but she owed him much and she allowed him to sway her mind at least in one way regarding the girl.

When Reagan's name had been added to the tapestry she had made comment that it seemed that there would be no room for Cohen. Something he had not taken well to. *"Pray to the gods, human or otherwise that that day never comes."* She had mistaken his comment for fear of his own abilities at first. It wasn't until weeks later when she had returned from a hunt injured that he had shed tears in front of her for the first time since the day he had taken the bite. *"I could never lose you. You are all I have."*

The door opened, signaling the entrance of her elite scouting party. Cohen was in the lead with Anya, Darius, and Nirosh not far behind. Her heir seemed relaxed as if the previous night had never happened. Nirosh looked much as he always did, passive but alert to any possible threats. Darius seemed wary of Anya who for her part looked as if she hadn't slept. Reagan could hardly remember if she had felt the dip of the bed as Anya had retired for the day. She could hardly remember since her return from a much needed hunt had put her into a strange headspace. It seemed that her lover easily remembered the events from the night previous and was not ready to forgive them.

"Were you looking to have us depart now, Your Grace?" The formality in Darius' voice served only to grate on Reagan's nerves as she motioned for everyone to take their seats.

"No. I have no intention of calling this mission off, but it has come to my attention that it must be delayed. Clayton wishes not to remain in the castle and is hoping to leave very soon. I think it would be best that you do not happen upon him. He wants little to do with us or this House as it is, so I believe allowing him some space will do him and us some good."

"Is it wise to allow someone so young out there alone?" Darius looked worried and Reagan was reminded of the big heart that her commander possessed.

"He will be fine. I have plans for him, be sure of that. There is nothing else to say about the matter."

"What of Faegon? I suspect still that this boy is not heading there just for a rite of passage. We have been getting reports of a gatherings at Faegon for over a month now. We have waited for such summons and yet none has come." Nirosh did not often speak during meetings. He much preferred to allow the others to speak the thoughts on his mind and simply observe, so it was odd to hear him now.

"That is also being seen to. I would not worry."

"Is that all or is there another reason you called us?" Anya was very clearly bored with their talk. She had been fidgeting in her chair since she'd first sat down and Reagan was tired of having her eyes automatically turn to her with every movement.

"That is all, Anya. You are all dismissed. Cohen may I have a word with you in my chambers?" The glare Anya threw the man was burning with unchecked rage, but she smartly stood and left rather than get into another row with the man.

For a brief moment Reagan wondered if she would send the two out on this mission and either only one or neither would return, but she dismissed the notion. Anya's mood changed as frequently and predictably as the moon's phases. She would calm down again by night's end and ramp right back up to unbridled anger in a few days, just in time for them to depart. There was little hope for the girl it seemed at times. Reagan often wondered if Darius' magic was to blame. She never would think the man to anger her on purpose, but his presence had been the beginning of her lover's odd behavior. He had come into their home fifty years ago and since then Anya's mood had soured dramatically. She had hoped that it would have evened out in time, but it seemed that luck was not on her side.

"Reagan? Are you lost in thought over there?" Cohen was the only one left in the room and his easy demeanor fell to show just how worried he was about her.

"Yes, sorry. I was just thinking about the past. I should know by now that there is nothing good there worth thinking of." Reagan sighed.

"That's not true. There were times when you were happy, were there not?" Cohen asked, concern evident in his eyes.

"Of course there were, it's just there are times when all of the bad seems to outweigh those small moments of good." He took her hand in his for a moment and squeezed it tight before letting their hands drop, the small moment of affection more than they could risk out in the open. "Let's retire to my quarters. There are matters of business that I wish to discuss with you and Lady Arinessa and if I know that woman half as well as I believe I do she will be waiting for us there."

They walked in companionable silence. The tower was empty, save for the few servants that went about their nightly tasks. No dignitaries from other Houses were scheduled to arrive within the next few weeks and the general upkeep that Reagan required of her staff was minimal at best. Many of those on her staff both human and vampire were given slow nights off. Her generosity was not without purpose. While many of the other vampire Kings and Queen ruled their Houses with fear and age alone, Reagan was by far the youngest and kindest of the vampire royalty. Her people genuinely loved her and it was their love that she cherished most of all.

There was no guard at her door when the two arrived, though Lady Arinessa stood waiting just as she suspected. "I dismissed the guard. I presumed this conversation was meant to remain secret."

"You presumed correctly, though I hope you will give me the chance to make that decision for myself next time."

"Yes, Your Grace." Nessa bowed low and opened the door for her in one graceful motion. She wore one of the tight corseted dresses that she favored mostly because of how they accented her chest and left most individuals regardless of sex or race hypnotized. Of course Reagan and Cohen had no such reaction, but it did little to stop the slightly disappointed look that crossed her face at their indifference.

"The childe Clayton is departing tonight. I will be sending Lady Esmy to follow him to insure his safety. I hope that with this show of good faith she can make contact with the representative from Namyt'tkas and we might be able to start a relationship with that house."

"I have reached out to their King more than once and I've had no response. At least Queen Libba has the common decency to tell me just what she thinks of me in her blunt refusal of my company. If we weren't nearly on their border I would have thought that all of our messages were getting lost on the way to Namyt'tkas."

"We always knew that building any relationship with Adrastos would be difficult and possibly not worth it. Queen Libba has ruled her House for too long and her ways are the old ways. Her house will fall behind before long." Cohen dismissed her aggravation.

"Little good that does me. How can I continue to do my job if no other house will speak to us?" Nessa pouted.

"I would ask if we've made any contact with Tryali, but I'm sure any attempt has been hopeless." Reagan sighed. Of the five vampire houses, Tryali was the most removed. If it hadn't been for Lunaries' exile it would have been easy to say that Tryali was the most isolated of the empire.

"We all know that signing a treaty with Logan's lot seems more plausible than contact with Tryali," Lady Arinessa scoffed, "I might as well retire my post if Lady Esmy is doing my work for me."

"Don't be so dramatic," Cohen chided, "she is simply going to pave the way. Should she be successful, you know that you will be our Queen's liaison with whichever King or Queen is willing to speak to us."

"That sounds terribly promising, Cohen, thank you for saving my job." Nessa's snide remark went without comment from the man and Reagan was grateful for a reprieve from the bickering, however short.

"Cohen is right, we must wait for Esmy to make the first move, but I have high hopes that we should have promising results within the month. Time moves slowly in the empire; a product of having the elders rule with no fresh blood on the High Council."

"You speak blasphemy," Nessa teased, though Reagan knew exactly her opinion of the High Council and their beliefs.

"I suppose I do. One could also say that I speak the way of the future, something this empire is severely lacking."

Nessa rolled her eyes and gave an exaggerated stretch, "I've had enough talk of anarchy and unrest for the night. I will retire to my quarters now if it pleases Your Grace."

"Go on, I wouldn't want to keep you." Reagan smiled as the woman rose from her seat and let herself out without another thought.

Cohen watched her leave, his eyes calculating and full of doubt. Reagan waited patiently for the man to speak his mind. It took no coaxing. As soon as he seemed satisfied that the Lady of Whispers was gone he leveled her with a somber gaze. "It was smart to send Esmy. She is a much better diplomat."

"That is not kind. Nessa does her job very well. Sometimes I think she enjoys it more than she should, but I have had no reason to doubt her skills."

"Skills? Reagan she's a whore who uses her title to sleep her way through half of the empire all in your name."

"Now Cohen, if you were allowed such a luxury you would do the same thing. There is no need for name calling because you must have a bit more decorum as an heir."

"That is absolutely not true and you know it." Reagan laughed and the man simply glared, his mouth pressed into a thin line. "If that is how you intend to act then I will see myself out, Your Grace."

"Oh stop it, Cohen. You have been far too stressed as of late. I think you should take the next few days off and relax before your mission. It will do you some good."

The man rolled his bright blue eyes and Reagan suppressed another laugh. Only when they were alone did she see evidence of the young man he had been before taking the bite. They had both been through much in their time at Lunaries and it often saddened her to think of the boy he had been before. She had been blessed to watch him grow into the strong man that he was, but she often thought of the shy boy who had come to Lunaries with stars in his eyes and hope in his soul.

"Would it be alright if I took the rest of the night off?" He sounded like the lost little boy that she remembered and it nearly broke her heart.

"Of course. In fact I know that I sent Lilliana off early and she said she wanted to train in the practice rooms. Maybe you should join her and work off some of that stress."

"Thank you." Cohen stood and Reagan followed, wrapping him in a tight hug. They didn't often have time to spend alone together without the regular company or their duties as a hindrance. It felt nice to hold him like she did before, but as always it never lasted. Reluctantly, Reagan let go and watched as Cohen walked out the door leaving her alone once more.

ARTHUR

The sun hung high overhead causing great drops of sweat to roll down Arthur's forehead. He and Art had been hard at work in the field since dawn and they had many baskets of crops lined up against the fence waiting to be brought back to the house. The sweat had been getting in his eye since mid-morning, but he didn't bother to wipe it away; his arms were covered in dirt and he remembered the consequence of smearing dirt in his eyes from his childhood on his parent's farm. The once dry rag that Emeline had provided him did not look any better and he knew that it was soon time to take a break. Working on his parents farm had been all he'd known before he'd met Elizabeth. He felt at home with Art hard at work by his side. He hadn't known the feeling of home in quite some time; since the days when his smiling wife and daughter filled their home with their laughter. But that had been a long time ago.

Life on a farm never quite left you. His sore and protesting muscles did not seem to agree, but his spirit felt free for the first time since Elizabeth's disappearance. Making a home with Emeline and Art was easier than he felt anything had right to be, but he loved every minute of it. It brought back good memories from his childhood which he had not often allowed himself to do. Working the field and bringing in the harvest made Arthur remember a time when he had stood with his father in their own farm. They had worked from dusk until dawn while his mother and younger sisters worked in the barn collecting eggs and milking the cows. He had had two younger sisters. Anna had been just two years his junior and Kelsi had been five years his junior. The last he had heard Anna was married and living in Magdus, the Solarian Capitol. She had stopped returning his letters when she had heard that he had left home to pursue his wife and broken the courtship between himself and Mary Rose. Kelsi had gone with Anna to find a husband and a good life as well. In the last letter that Anna had sent had told him how life in Magdus was perfect for her and she had high hopes for finding a good man. He had never really missed them before, only because he had never allowed himself think of them. Since returning to his birth village his sisters were nearly all he thought of.

When his time was not spent mourning the loss of his family, he worried after his daughter. Emeline seemed to be a good influence on the girl. The two spent their days in the barn tending to the animals and in the kitchen preparing meals. Natalya's cooking skills were growing by the day and he had even seen her genuinely smiling for the first time in many months. At night he often found them sitting by the fire as Emeline taught her to knit. Natalya took to the art about as well as he had expected her to, but she was determined to master the craft. She was as stubborn as he was which meant she would not give up until she could knit as well as Emeline. It was obvious that the older girl had been knitting most of her life, but he had no doubt that Natalya would catch up fast; it was how he had raised her after her mother's death. For his many wrongdoings, Arthur was at least proud of making his daughter strong. They fought often because of her stubborn nature, but he would not trade her determination for any other trait. Natalya might not see all of the good that came from the lifestyle he raised her to lead, but he knew that when the day came for him to reunite with Elizabeth, their little girl would continue to fight and survive without him.

Seeing how well the girls took to each other eased Arthur's worries that his little girl had missed out not having siblings growing up. The sting of his sisters refusing to speak to him still sat heavy in his heart, but having had them beside him throughout his childhood was enough to outweigh the heartache. He knew that the relationship that he had cherished with his sisters was forming between the girls when he found them cuddled in Emeline's large bed for warmth, something Arthur remembered too well from being young and sharing a bed with his own sisters to keep warm when there was not enough wood to light the night fires.

Emeline was a blessing for his little girl, but in some regards he wondered if the older woman was also a poor influence. He knew that her husband had disappeared in Mordin Forest and her longing looks towards the trees filled him with unease. He wondered if Emeline would see the potential in Natalya to help her search the wooded area around the farm. Emeline would not be strong enough to protect herself, but it was without doubt that Natalya was hard-headed enough to believe herself capable. He wasn't able to be by his daughter's side as he had before and he feared the ideas such freedom could give her. It was possible that Emeline was unraveling all of the careful fear of Mordin Forest that he had instilled in Natalya. She was quickly coming to respect the woman and Arthur knew that soon she would listen to her over anything that he had to say and that day seemed fast approaching.

"Tell me Art, does anyone still search for Emeline's husband?" He knew the answer for sure, though he dreaded it all the same. They were too young to have known such a loss, nearly as young as he had been when his own love had been taken from him and he knew the devastation it had caused.

"No, not truthfully," Art clearly chose his words with care, "of course my sister still hopes, but it has been too long, even our mother has called her a fool."

"Surely you have reasoned with your sister, she could marry again, yes? There is no reason for her to stay a widow when she could still bare a good man children."

"I fear she hardly sees it so simply. Before you came I often found her looking for him alone" He bore the tone of a man who had this conversation one too many times.

"You mustn't be serious." The loud clang of the plow hitting the ground signaled Art pausing in his work and Arthur felt the weight of his concerned looks. "There are many dangers in that forest. I would think such was apparent by his disappearance." Arthur knew the look the boy wore well. Concern slowly turned to pity, marring the young face. He halted his work as well to face Arthur fully.

"It is sad for certain whatever fate befell my dear brother-in-law, but you must be mad. There is not much out there besides harmless hares and smaller critters."

"Then what would you suggest took a young man from his new bride?" The silence that fell between them then seemed to spook the boy back to work. The sound of dirt over metal plows filled in where conversation could not. Eventually the boy seemed to find his voice.

"If something did take my good brother... What could it have been?" The question was honest. Arthur knew then that Art could be reasoned with. There was hope yet that he and his daughter could make a home of the farm without worrying about the motivations of their hosts.

"What indeed, lad," Arthur fell into deep thought. "I cannot say what, but I do know that something took my Elizabeth. When Natalya was just a child of five she and her mother were playing by the stretch of Mordin Forest that was near our village. I know not what happened, but Nat returned at night alone, covered in blood and so terrified it took her nearly a year to speak again. There was a search party sent out, but we could not find her. The blood on Nat had not been her own and we had found more blood in the forest, but no body. If it had been an animal they would have taken their fill of food and left her corpse when they were done, but she was simply gone. What could have parted a mother from her child in such a fashion?"

"I cannot say. If you speak the truth and I do not doubt that you do, then are you saying that we could be in serious danger living here?" The terror on Art's face made him seem even younger and Arthur felt for the boy.

"It is possible." Life with such a regular pattern had dulled his sense. He was no more safe here than on the road and it was long past time that he end this hibernation of his good sense. "Tonight, after supper, would you like to join Natalya and I for a training session?"

"Training? What for?" His interest was piqued and a look of unease rippled across his face, though he did not back down from the offer. Arthur could work with such an attitude.

"Survival." Understanding washed over the boy and he nodded in agreement. If only reasoning with Natalya could be so easy. Not for the first time, Arthur found himself wishing that his daughter had been just a bit more docile like the other young girls her age. He often wondered if she had always been a free spirit or if it had been his conditioning and the way he raised her that now fought against him.

"Dinner's on!" Emeline's voice carried from the house, rousing the men from their task.

The farm was by no means small in size and nor was the harvest, and Arthur knew no one on Rosewood Farm would be hungry come winter. He hefted two baskets of carrots and turnips on his shoulders to take back to the house. There would be more to bring back and they needed the baskets empty. He watched as the young man struggled with his single load. Farm life had not toughened him as one would expect. He knew that Ivan's craft had always been woodwork so it seemed safe to assume that before John had vanished, Art had never worked a day on a farm in his life. While it would do Natalya good to continue her training, it seemed that Art was in more dire need.

The trek back was short. The end of harvest was fast approaching and already the sun appeared low in the sky. Summer days would soon be behind them, but with the extra hands on the farm they would be able to haul in enough food to survive their first winter together. The storehouse was accessible by a small hatch located directly next to the backdoor. Arthur let them down the hatch, bringing his baskets down one at a time to empty them before having Art hand him his through the opening. It was dark in the cellar and the air was thick, but it was plenty cool and the food would easily keep through the winter. He carefully stacked their newly harvested goods to the side for the girls to sort and prepare. Much of the food stored below would be jarred and jammed, pickled and salted within the coming weeks. Just yesterday, the girls had been hard at work doing their part to prepare for the harsh months ahead. Satisfied that they had done their part, Arthur carefully resurfaced from the darkness, allowing his eyes to adjust before following Art back into the house.

Laughter trickled through the doorway and put Arthur at ease. The girls had since finished setting the table and the cozy kitchen was filled with the savory smell of honeyed chicken and boiled vegetables. Emeline was always able to put hearty meals on the table for the working men and Arthur knew that she took pride in her ability to provide. It was a shame she would never have a family of her own. She would have made a wonderful young bride. Even though she was young enough to wed again, Arthur knew too well the heartache of losing love so young and he doubted that she would allow herself to try again. He had certainly not afforded himself or his daughter that luxury.

"No silly, you want to hold it like this. Here let me show you," Emeline laughed as she took the yarn and needles from Natalya. Her sure hands corrected his daughter's error before returning it to her.

"I'm telling you I will never understand this. I'm just not meant to be a proper wife." The exasperation in her voice was a knife to Arthur's heart. He had done this to his daughter. "It's probably best that I never married Edward."

"Nonsense." Emeline brushed the comment away with ease. "He would have been a lucky man to have called you his wife. It's his loss really because you will find a great man here and he will have the honor instead. Now, if you just hold the yarn this way and the needle in your hand like so then it will be much easier."

"She always mothered us, being the eldest it seemed like her job." Art whispered as he made way to the running tap to wash up lest Emeline send them from the table before they even ate their fill. "It's a right shame she doesn't have any children of her own yet," he added, echoing Arthur's own thoughts.

"Alright you two, tuck in, you're going to need your strength out there." Setting their knitting supplies aside, Emeline began to serve up the chicken first, while Natalya began to scoop steaming carrots and onions onto their plates. The meat was sweet to smell and juicy when cut into. The fresh rolls from that morning were wrapped up in cloth, holding in their warmth. All that was missing was the milk and butter, but even still it seemed to Arthur like a meal fit for a king. All discussion ceased, though the room was filled with sounds of smacking lips and tin utensils hitting tin platters. The honey was fresh from a farm on the other side of the village. It was the most luxury that the village could afford. There were times when money and produce used to flow through the streets of Sylvine, though those times were long gone. The villagers now were forced to turn into a strictly bartering society and any of the fresh butter that would have accompanied their meal had been jarred in exchange for the one delicacy that the siblings could afford.

"What time are we going to begin training tonight?" The man's food lay forgotten then as he looked to his namesake for an answer.

"What is he talking about? I thought we were done with that!" Natalya abandoned her food too, leveling her father with an accusatory glare. "You already got us kicked out of our old home, are you going to try again so soon?"

"What is does she mean, kicked out?" Emeline asked. Her normally calm tone was tinged with anxiety. She was a strong woman and it took a lot to unsettle her, but she seemed upset by Natalya's words.

"All he goes on about is how there are things living in the forest, he ranted and raved about it until the men in our old village told him we had to leave because he was scaring the woman and children."

"Natalya Elizabeth Grahame you will not take that tone with me." As she always had, his daughter all too easily stared him down. Most girls her age would have listened to their fathers and then later their husbands without question. Natalya had never been like most girls, but then neither had been Elizabeth. Sometimes he wondered if she had learned her strength from him or inherited it from her mother.

"Why would you think that there is something out there?" Emeline eyed him wearily.

"Because whatever it is, it took your husband. It took my wife, too." Arthur responded without letting his emotion through. It would not do to break down now.

"What do you mean someone took John?" Emeline seemed to latch on to the idea, clearly hoping that it could mean that her husband was still out there.

"Not someone, something," Arthur stressed, glaring at his daughter to cut off her protests. "Why else would he not return? He loved you Emeline, I'm sure you know that. I know Elizabeth loved me there is no other explanation!"

"Natalya, I think your father's right. Maybe we should all train, the forest isn't that far from the house. If there is something out there then we should be ready." Emeline smiled and wrapped her hand around the younger girl's, reassuring her with a gentle squeeze that everything would be fine. "I've been teaching you everything I can, I think it's time you start teaching me some of those hunting techniques of yours. I bet you're quite the expert."

"Sure, I guess it wouldn't hurt." Natalya agreed with little difficulty, something that Arthur would have never believed before meeting Emeline.

"It's settled then, we'll start as soon as we've finished supper."

After taking their fill of dinner, Arthur and Art went back out to the field in silence. There was an air of determination about the young boy and Arthur hoped that he would take to training as well as Natalya had done in the beginning. When she had been young, and the trauma still fresh, Nat had been very easy to persuade to train with him. He had posed it like a game and she had been willing to play along. It wasn't until she had gotten older and the girls from her school began to avoid her and the boys to tease her, that Natalya's attitude began to sour towards him. Things were different now, though, and Emeline seemed to be mastering the art of handling his daughter, something he had never quite learned. He worked the remainder of the day with hope festering in him.

Supper was a quiet affair, Art and Emeline seemed excited while Natalya sat silently, brimming with anger, though she kept her comments to herself. The sun was just beginning to set when supper was cleared and Arthur brought out the weathered training gear. Back in their home in Ash, he'd had old bags made of non dyed wool and stuffed with dried hay marked up as targets. They would have to wait for daylight to practice archery, and so he still had time to make them here, but Natalya was skilled at both close quarter combat and with a bow. She had never quite mastered the crossbow, but he had high hopes that Art would gain the strength that his daughter lacked. Art wore the clothes that he had worked in that day and Natalya donned her traveling attire. Emeline lacked anything less than feminine and instead wore a strange combination of Natalya's pants which were much too short and Art's shirt which was much too long.

"Those will not do, it would be best for you to make some new clothes if you intend to continue practicing." Arthur demanded as soon as he saw the girl.

"You can't just tell her what she can and cannot wear." Always looking for a fight, Natalya seemed to deem it necessary to speak for the woman.

"It's alright, Nat, your father means well. Of course I can make new clothes, Mister Grahame."

"Come then, Nat will you please show these two a basic set?"

At his command, Natalya transformed from a stubborn young girl into a determined and calculated predator. Arthur brought two of the smaller targets up and held them before the girl. Natalya threw a quick left jab followed by a right, continuing in a pattern until she had easily walked her father to the edge of what they had deemed training ground.

"Good, now when you get better at this then we'll work with weapons. Would you like to show them what you can do?"

Natalya gave him a brief nod as her only acknowledgement before throwing another right, not in the least surprised when her father dropped the targets. They had spared before without any padding and while it normally ended in the girl walking away with at least one bruise, it was well worth it for the experience. She swung in low for a left hook using her short stature to her advantage. Arthur blocked the pass with ease. He noted that she didn't seem surprised and used the momentum she had gained to fuel her next hit and he felt pride for how far she had come. The two danced around the other, their hits raining down in a blur though neither were able to stop the other for long. Natalya was younger and thus was able to move quicker, but her exuberance was always what brought her downfall. Arthur knew that he only had to wait just long enough for the girl to tire before he could make his last move. As soon as the girl faltered in her step

Arthur reached out with his right hand grabbing her arm and twisting her around until she was tangled in her own arms. She was pressed against his chest with one of his dull knives leveled under her chin before she could protest.

"Yield." Natalya said when it was obvious that there was no escape.

"You're getting better," Arthur conceded when he let her go, "but what have I told you about getting ahead of yourself?"

"I know, don't." Natalya glared. They were both breathing heavily, though he seemed to have broken a sweat where Nat looked like she could have easily gone another around. The sound of clapping stopped the possibility of another fight.

"That was incredible! I'm not sure you're ever going to be able to teach me that." The laughter in Emeline's voice seemed to calm the girl and Natalya blushed at the compliment.

"Don't be silly, I'm sure you'll be great." Natalya's eyes softened and the frustration that had been present before melted away. Arthur ached to have such a calming effect on her, but settled for allowing Emeline the task of calming the wildfire that was his little girl.

"Good, Nat you and Emeline start on form and the basic set, I'm going to start working with Art."

The boy looked apprehensive to work with him after their display so Arthur did his best to put his worries to rest. "Now remember that Natalya and I have been training for going on ten years now, so I don't expect you to be at that level any time soon. I would like to work with you on throwing punches today. How does that sound?"

"Alright, I suppose." Art was not nearly as confident as Nat. He hoped that it was something that the boy would grow out of since working with him would otherwise become exhausting quickly.

"I am going to hold my hands out, I want you to punch first with your left, across your body, then with your right. Remember to always keep your other fist up to block any possible attack."

Arthur stood stationary as Art tentatively went through a set of punches. From his vantage point Arthur could see Emeline faring nearly the same as her brother. Natalya looked to be getting frustrated with Emeline as she continued to drop her blocking hand, but it seemed that she was doing her best to keep her feelings at bay. Before he could wonder if partnering the girls had been a good idea, Art seemed to find a rhythm and was hitting him in rapid succession.

"Good, we're going to continue this, but I might gently swing at you with my arm on the side which you are meant to be blocking. I won't actually hit you, but remember to keep your arms up."

They continued in the same fashion and much to his delight, Art seemed to grow more confident with each hit. He did manage to lightly cuff the boy a few times, but it only drove him to try harder and soon

Arthur was seeing real promise in the boy's perseverance. Even Emeline and Natalya looked to be working better together which made the anxiety that had crawled into his chest before finally loosen. The two pairs continued training until the sun had fully set and the stars began to shine. Soon exhaustion overtook them and the prospects of a full day harvesting on the horizon forced all four back to the house and straight to bed. As they filed into the house, sweaty and tired, all three young faces wore smiles and Arthur felt content.

CLAYTON

When Clayton was a child he had been terrified of Mordin Forest. Growing up on the West side of the valley had meant little exposure to vampires as a whole. It had also put the creatures rather high on the list of things that caused him nightmares that lasted until his early adulthood. The closest House to his village had been Tryali and everyone knew them to be a house of cowards, as they never bothered to leave their own borders much less pay the humans in the valley any mind. It also meant that they were never there to help protect the humans from the terrible ogres that lived in the mountains. It was something that neither he nor his people would soon forget, and yet here he was.

Clayton had never intended to become a vampire. His mother had cried the day he had left their small hut with nothing but a sack of food on his shoulder. The Namyt'tkan recruiters hardly ever ventured as far as their village but when they had, on the eve of his nineteenth birthday, it seemed to be the best of many terrible life paths that awaited him. His village had been so small that they hadn't even had a proper name. They simply referred to their little home as Misery because there was no better way to describe it. They were always able to produce just enough crops to survive, but no one in Misery lived comfortable lives. Added to that, the ogre attacks were more frequent since they had no vampire protectors and most children did not live to see their thirteenth birthday. There were hardly any children around Clayton's age when it came time to consider marriage; the only girl who had been eligible had been twice made a widow at the young age of sixteen and many in Misery thought her to be cursed. Going with the recruiter was the only option that seemed to end in survival, though Clayton had viewed it as an admission of defeat. He had seen becoming a vampire as just one step above living and dying in Misery. It hadn't taken very long for him to see the error in his beliefs. He could hardly remember a time without his brothers and sisters in his House. The time before Namyt'tkas seemed like a lifetime ago.

Before going through the training to take the bite Clayton had been a scared boy; years after with his training and the bite a distant memory he finally considered himself to be a man. All his life he had been taught not to rely on others and that same mindset followed him into his rebirth. He was above such weakness, though he knew that offering help to those less fortunate was as important. Honor was his shield and preserving the King's Peace was his duty. Despite this, it had saddened him to leave Lunaries. Their queen had been so accommodating and the people were welcoming as any others, but it was not his home. Staying longer would only jeopardize his mission which was something he could not afford. They had the good grace to let him go without complaint and he knew that after the completion of his mission he would have to return to properly thank them for their hospitality. He was already the last of his brothers and sisters to leave for Faegon and he could not make them wait for him any longer.

Of all of his brothers and sisters he knew that he could not let down Lenore. Lenore was the most beautiful woman he had ever met. She had been from the valley same as he, but she had come from a village that had been far less secluded than Misery. She had come to Namyt'tkas of her own volition and had taken to their training faster than any of the others. If he stopped and closed his eyes he could still see the sun as it reflected from her pale blonde hair, happiness dancing in her jade eyes. He had loved watching her practice with weapons in the yard before they took the bite. It had been a privilege to see her so alive then; he was proud to know that he was the last person to simply enjoy the sun with her before their ceremony had taken place.

If Lenore was the person he'd least like to let down then Urien would be the one he could least afford to appear weak in front. Urien had also taken a liking to Lenore. He was one of the boys who had come from the outer villages of Namyt'tkas. Those who had lived their entire lives under the careful eye of their King saw themselves as above simple people like Clayton. They walked with an air as if they knew better than those who came from the Valley or other villages outside of the empire simply based on where they were born. Lenore had been lucky enough to have a decent education and thus easily fit in with those who had lived amongst vampires their whole lives which made her an obvious match for the self-assured Urien who was the top male of their class. Clayton hated him for the presumptuous manner in which he treated Lenore like his own; his right. Lenore had confided in him one night that she hated the way he sought reasons to touch her. He was always giving her hugs and he would run his hands across her back during practice when she made a particularly daring move. Outwardly you would never know that the otherwise joyful and polite girl detested the attention, but Clayton knew better. He hated to think what Urien might do to Lenore without him there to help and that thought alone made him push on.

He had been going at a good pace for seven nights and had cleared the Lunarian border just three nights before. He was making good time, though he knew that it would take him a few more hours until he had even reached the point that he had originally been attacked at and he felt his body tense at the thought. He was strong for a vampire of his age. He might not be on the same level as Lenore or Urien, but he had good instincts and it hurt his pride to know how easily the strange attacker had come upon him and taken him out. If the rumors were to be believed; it had been the Lady Vestera that had attacked him. She was the loyal pet to the Lady Cassandra, who was once the heir to Lunaries and had helped to raise a coup to overthrow Lady Reagan. She was the wife of Lord Logan, another Lunarian vampire who rallied the rogues under the name of the long since dead House Rayne and who sought it fit to falsely present himself as King of that dead House. Of course if those rumors were true and furthermore the rumors of the Lady Vestera's age, then he had survived an ambush from a very old and powerful vampire.

Clayton was not one for rumors and he knew better than to believe in the idle gossip that had been tossed carelessly around the compound that had been his home, but he hoped that the ones about Vestera were true. If she was as powerful as many believed than her taking him by such surprise made a lot of sense. There was no shame in admitting defeat in the face of such an ill matched competitor.

Thinking of the terrible encounter wound up Clayton's nerves and he stopped walking to carefully take in his surroundings. He had felt as if there were eyes on him for nights, though he was sure that it was lingering paranoia as he was coming up to the very spot which he had nearly lost his life. Mordin Forest was as lively as it was most nights. There was a stream not far beyond the trees that he had swam in with the rest of his troop. The trickle of the water was calming and yet it brought with it melancholy as he remembered how simple life had been. Shaking unwanted memories from his mind he continued to focus on his surroundings. He could hear an owl calling out to others in the trees high above his head. There was a wolf tearing apart prey for its pups and Clayton knew that he could not take his thirst from the mom of three helpless pups. Beyond all of the noise that he had grown accustomed to there was an underlying feeling of eyes always watching that Clayton could not seem to lose.

The trees were dense where he had stopped and it seemed like a good place if any to take a break and drink from the small amount of blood that he still had left. He hadn't wanted to take from the Lunarian people, but he had refused their hospitality already and he could not bring himself to turn aside their kindness, especially when it came to much needed resources. He sat in the dirt, his legs crossed before him, though he was ready to jump into action if need be. He swung the light sack from his back in front of him and pushed aside the second change of clothes he had been given to find the last vial of blood that they had gifted him. The rest of the vials lay empty at the bottom of the pack for when he took the time to hunt and fill them again. They had provided him with fresh human blood, something of a delicacy as he had only been given it on rare, special occasions on the compound. He mourned the loss of his supply as he uncorked the vial and tipped it back to his lips. The liquid flowed down his throat and filled the aching hunger that had built up since his last meal. He was so consumed in enjoying the feast that a noise from the trees startled him enough to drop the vial. He watched in horror as the glass fell from his hands and shattered, the remaining blood spilling out into the dirt.

"What a waste of a good gift," the soft voice of Lady Esmy sighed. She moved fully into his view her gaze more indignant than angry.

"What are you doing here?" The interruption of his meal put him in a foul mood and his normal manners were instantly forgotten. "Why have you been following me?"

"Well, I was sent to Faegon as ambassador for my good Queen, but keeping an eye on you was an easy enough task to accomplish as well. My Queen wishes you no harm nor ill intent. I was merely meant to be sure you arrived to your destination without incident. I had been content to stay behind to simply keep an eye on you without being seen, but your perceptive skills are impressive. I thought it best to show myself so we might make faster time together,"

"I don't need your help." The retort sounded petulant even to his own ears. Lady Esmy leveled him with a look that clearly showed she felt the same.

"I suppose you don't. I suppose you also are not in need of the fresh supply of blood that I am carrying as you obviously have taken care with the one that we gave you." She turned her back to him then, moving back into the trees toward the Southwest were Faegon lay in the distance.

There would be no sense in sitting in the dirt pretending that she was not now a part of his journey. Lady Esmy was as stubborn as they come and as much as he was loathed to share the road with another at least she would help to fill the silence and also his aching belly. He had drank enough of the blood to satisfy his need until the next night, but the prospect of hunting versus taking the offered human blood was not worth considering and he lifted himself up with ease. Lady Esmy was not far ahead. She was much faster than he was and it was obvious that she had deliberately slowed her pace to allow him to catch up.

"How long have you been following me, Lady Esmy?" Clayton was curious to know how long his paranoia could be justified for.

"I left Lunaries two nights after you and Esmy will do just fine."

"You mean to say you have covered the ground that took me nearly seven nights in five?"

"Speed will come with time. I was not nearly so fast at your age, though I was faster still. I feared that you kept checking for me behind your back and it was slowing your progress. We both must reach Faegon eventually and showing myself seemed the smarter choice."

They fell into an easy silence as the night wore on. Esmy kept up a brisk pace which forced Clayton to keep up. With her pushing him on they would easily make it to Faegon within the week. He might still be the last of his brothers and sisters to arrive, but at least he would not be so far behind. Lenore was not the only one he missed. There was a younger girl named Orchid, whom he had grown very fond of. She had been nearly too young to enroll when her parents had dropped her off to the recruiters, but they had taken pity on her and taken her in as the story went. At the tender age of nine she had trained with the group before Clayton's though she was still far too young at the end to take the bite. It was because of this that she had gone through the training again with his troop. At first most of the members had made the mistake of underestimating her because of her size and age, but she fought just as well as most if not better and was smarter by far. She had been the reason that the oddly matched group finally agreed to work together as a unit as opposed to fighting each other at every turn. While Clayton hated Urien for how he acted around Lenore, he could at least admit that even the callous and self-centered man looked at Orchid with all the pride of a brotherly figure. When Orchid had been allowed to take the bite with them each and every one of her brothers and sisters had celebrated her graduation with such fanfare that even the trainers discarded their tough exteriors for a night to join in the festivities. Ten years was the longest time that any human had gone through the training, normally the training was five years, and she had only been allowed the bite because keeping her from it any longer would have seemed too cruel.

"You miss them." It was a statement and Clayton nearly didn't respond.

"Of course I do. Would you not miss your kin?"

"I suppose. We do not train our young as you do. There is no isolation, human or otherwise. We believe that integration is key to successful adjusting."

"The bite is an honor. My people go through rigorous training to insure that they are ready for such an honor. To mix them with those already bit would only cause relationships that might be detrimental to either party. To take the bite is only the first part of our honor. To be truly accepted into the House you must also pass the test of journeying to Faegon alone."

"Spare me your mindless recitation, you speak as if the words were forced upon you." Clayton flinched at her words, but Esmy forged on. "You were never exposed to the House at large. You have no understanding of how those who are truly part of Namyt'tkas live, what their individual beliefs may be. They are grooming easily manipulated soldiers. In Lunaries, we are concerned with raising bright minds that bring new possibilities to the table. We work with many different minds because it is our differences that make us stronger."

Her words seemed to affect him as much as they had while they spoke the night he'd spent in Lunaries. He had never been given the opportunity to compare his people's ways to any others. Questioning their teachings had never been something that Clayton could have imagined himself doing and yet he found himself doubting the integrity of those who had led him to believe that their way was the only true way of the vampiric empire.

They were making their way through his people's territory and while the trees were so familiar in their odd formations they all looked different now that he had been given the ability to see the world around him anew. It was unsettling and Clayton promptly decided that he had no desire to continue to view the world with such new and open eyes. The transition from what he had felt he had known while living in Misery versus the life he had been leading for the last combined fifteen years at Namyt'tkas had been hard enough on his psyche. He could not accept that the world might be so drastically different again. He would not stand for it.

"You're wrong." As soon as the words left his mouth it seemed as if the world around him shifted. He spotted a grouping of trees that he and Orchid had often climbed when they had first begun training. It was something he knew and seeing how it was not changed at all only helped solidify the facts in his mind. "You have many strange beliefs, Esmy, and while you are free to see the world in such a bizarre fashion I will continue to understand this world for the way it most obviously is."

Ignoring the disgusted sigh that escaped her thinly pursed lips was childish, but of course her reaction was equally without class so Clayton felt he was quite justified. He nearly felt pride for being the bigger person, for not rising to her bait, but of course Esmy was not done.

"I just feel so much sadness for a new generation of this empire that lacks the intelligence to push us into a new age. Being immortal means very little if we cannot learn from our mistakes and brainwashing our children to ignore the errors of our past will be the empire's downfall."

"You speak blasphemy," Clayton looked around them as if to be sure that there were no members of the crown lurking behind the trees.

"I speak the truth. Your inability to see that is proof that the fate of the empire is hardly promising."

"You mock me for being a childe, but I know better, you know not the fate of our people. You are no seer and I am no fool to believe your words."

Esmy stopped walking to face him and her grave look made him feel even more like a child. "My intent is never to mock you. You are a smart childe. You were able to sense my presence even though I was more than careful to hide myself from you. I believe you will go far in this world, but I fear that the things you have been taught to believe will take you far from the right path. What reason could I have to wish harm on you?"

Her words made sense and yet it was that which caused Clayton's head to ache. She could not be right, if she was then those who had taught him all that he believed he knew had lied to him and the thought squeezed his heart until he felt tears push at the back of his eyes. He would not respond to Esmy. There would be no good to come from furthering the conversation and he turned to continue at the pace she had set. They were already too far from Faegon for his liking and such talk would only cause them to lag even farther. His brothers and sisters were waiting for him and he could not allow Lenore a moment longer alone with Urien. He knew the man believed himself to be the perfect match for the beautiful warrior. She might never see him as a companion as he wished, but it was his duty as her friend to keep her from the likes of Urien.

Esmy seemed to respect his need for silence and she neglected to return to their prior conversation. He much enjoyed the silence to her confusing questions. He knew she was invaluable as a companion, though he could do without. Esmy was very skilled, there was no doubt that as one of the Lunarian Queen's own personal guards-women that she was a good ally to have by his side. He knew she would fight alongside him without complaint and would even come to his aid despite his own feelings on the matter. She was a good person, one he would normally have no issue traveling with, but it was her troubling views on the world that left him feeling as if the eyes of Namyt'tkas and, by extension, Faegon were on him. The Lady Reagan was well loved by her people, but she bit and raised strange folk. He would not want an association with them to taint his reputation.

Being a child from Misery, he had already had a bit of a poor reputation when he first arrived in Namyt'tkas. Most of the people had never heard of his little village, only of the people who lived so far out of reach that they were not quite human and certainly not fit to be vampires. He had done everything possible to prove them wrong. He had excelled in his practical lessons; spacial awareness had been key to his survival as a child and he had amazed even the most unmoved instructors with his sharp human senses. The books had always been a struggle for him. There had only been a few members of his village who could read and write and even fewer who would pay a poor boy enough mind to teach him. He had learned his numbers as they had been important on the few times he had been sent to market. Those had been four day long treks just to the Village Marketplace. It was really the largest trading post in the Valley accommodating the many people from all of the villages which sat between the mountains and the woods, though the simple name did it little justice.

Even knowing his numbers had not proven useful as the others had proved that reading had been very much a part of their upbringing.

He had never once believed in giving up, but there had been a time when Clayton had really wondered if he had made the right choice in leaving his mother and his only home to live in a strange land with its even stranger people. Of course Lenore had seen his struggles then and had promised to teach him his letters in secret. She would leave him notes to decipher and respond to. The system had been rough at first, but with the training in their classes and her determination Clayton had learned to read and even to write, though the latter had taken even longer to accomplish. He could never forget the kindness and sacrifice that she had made to help him. She had often given up her time, which she was meant to be relaxing between their studies and tests, to write him silly notes and teach him the proper way to hold a feather quill without smudging the ink. Had it been any other person Clayton would have refused their help. He could not afford to look weak around anyone, but Lenore had always looked right through his dented armor and seen the lost boy for who he was. She had never treated him differently for his lack of education and had deftly ignored the others when they attempted to pry into what they got up to while the others ran about the trees in play. He owed her a debt so large he wasn't sure he had room to owe debts to any other. He would spend the rest of his life making sure that Lenore wanted for nothing and that no harm would ever befall her. It was still not enough to give for all that she had given him, but it would have to be.

First and foremost he would have to protect her from Urien and his lustful advances. Urien was a pitiful man whose pride was second only to his ego and he would do harm to Lenore before long. She was much too sweet to tell the man that she did not share his feelings and Clayton knew that it would not be long before he forced himself on her. Lenore was strong and smart, but she was still a woman and weak to the ways of men. He often felt ill as she and Orchid would laugh about the male trainers that had come and gone in their fifteen years together. Orchid was young, but not without eyes and she had often encouraged Lenore to look at the men as they trained, commenting on which one seemed stronger or which one might be gentle to his lover. Lenore had always humored the girl and often played along forgetting that Clayton sat with them. Orchid had always favored Urien's looks over all others and Lenore had only agreed to seem polite, Clayton was sure of it.

The trees were beginning to look gnarled and bathed in shadows the further they walked. It was nearly sunrise and Clayton could feel as his tired legs protested any movement. Another night or two of good walking and they would be leaving the Namyt'tkan border. It wouldn't be long before they were deep within Faegon's land. He could feel the change in the air as well as see the difference in the foliage around them. There was a taste that sparked on this tongue with every step and it filled him with unease. Faegon was the cultural hub of the empire and thus many magical folk gathered there. The elders told them that the magic that lived within the core of all humans and vampires seeped into the land around them, changing all living things both for the better and for the worse. There had been no one possessed with magic in Misery to explain the bleak living conditions that he had been exposed to, but Clayton had seen first hand the way a tree would twist and curl away from magic from his time in the empire. He had a hard time believing that magic could have any good effect on nature as every tree and every field touched by it seemed void of life. Of course he had been told he was wrong by nearly every teacher that he had asked and he had decided not to bother again. They seemed to believe that there were those special few who had nothing but pure, good magic at their core that could heal the lands scarred by millennia of magic being wielded in the many wars that plagued the empire's history.

Esmy did not seem to be bothered by the grotesquely disfigured trees and Clayton chose to keep his thoughts to himself. There was no sense in asking the woman her opinion as he'd had quite enough of her opinions to last himself a vampire's lifetime and then possibly another afterwards. As it seemed that there was no immediate reason to worry about the horrifying change in scenery, Clayton allowed his eyes to wander over the gnarled wood. The trees were leaning as if toward the direction of Faegon to point the way. The air was thicker and the taste of pure power hung around his head making him dizzy with the potential. Faegon was the empire's capital which meant that all kinds lived within her walls. Humans and vampires mingled in harmony and it held the highest level of ambient magic from its inhabitants. The idea of such cohesion still made little sense to a man born in seclusion. Going from Misery to Namyt'tkas had hardly been a change in terms of his exposure to the world around him. The training had taken place in a small compound that lay within the Namyt'tkan borders and he had only ever left it and been to the main castle once. That had been the day he had begun his trials. It was larger than Lunaries, though not by much, and from the stories it wasn't comparable to the greatest vampiric House.

Dawn would be upon them soon and Clayton wished he was alone so he might take a rest. Esmy seemed determined to push forward to gain lost ground. They were traveling through a wooded area which had a canopy dense enough to protect them from the sun, though it did little in regard to his depleted energy. He hadn't slept well while traveling alone and the toll of his recent stress was beginning to settle into his bones and take up residence in his core. The silent guards-woman was either ignorant of his struggles or impassive. She was built with a sturdy frame, her body more muscular than lean and she seemed at home with dirt beneath her boots. Her gray eyes held little clue to her emotions as she pushed forward without a glance back. Her traveling clothes were much plainer than those she had worn at the castle and he noted that they seemed to be wearing thin. The brown dyed wool hung loose from her upper body, but it was still obviously fraying in parts especially around her elbows and around her neck. She seemed almost more comfortable in her worn clothes on the desolate road than in the halls of Lunaries. He had no wish to share the road, but his traveling partner could be worse. The thought of being subjected to Lady Arinessa, the supposed Lady of inner and outer house affairs, made him feel uneasy in more than his mind. She was a dangerous woman, using her looks and charm to needle her way into the business of others and he suddenly felt very grateful in the Lady Reagan's choice of ambassador.

It wasn't long until Esmy's sure stride began to slow and they came to a stop just off the path in a small, open grouping of trees. "I will take first watch. Sleep now and I will wake you at midday."

It seemed that their earlier conversations had exhausted his companion and he was eternally grateful. There would be a time and place to evaluate the troubling questions raised by the sharp-eyed blonde, but now was not it. He was tired and the thought of sleep was enough for him to unroll his musty pack and settle in against the nearest tree. He would have plenty of time to think as soon as he made it to Faegon and was with his troop. Lenore would know what to say, she always did, and the thought of her pretty jade eyes lulled Clayton into a deep sleep.

CODY

The overgrown trees seemed to part instantly when they reached the edge of the Faegon grounds. Their scarred trunks leaned forward, guiding their way to the capitol city. They were moving at a good pace that took them around the edge of the grounds where there would be few villages or other people to pass. Moving with little interruption was the hunter's top priority even if it meant taking a slightly longer route. Cody had stopped leaning on Decker to walk just the night before and arriving at the outskirts of Faegon with his own strength did wonders to improve his dampened cheer. He was grateful for all that the rogue had been willing to do to keep him not just alive, but well enough to move on his own. He had no desire to show undue weakness in front of the vampires of the Crown. It did not escape him that he did not mind showing such weakness in front of the rogue, but he ignored that. There would be time to analyze his thoughts after they reached the safety of Faegon.

Decker had been remarkable in the past five nights since the wolf attack, though his intentions had always been clear; he needed Cody alive to be his readily available blood source and an ambassador in Faegon. The vampire went through great lengths to insure he never let his fondness for the human show, though Cody was much more attentive than given credit for. As they were beginning to come up on the meager camps which lay scattered around Faegon's great walls, the rogue seemed to be distancing himself from Cody. He stood with his back painfully straight and his eyes were determined, glaring holes in the dirt before them. Where easy conversation had been before a cold silence lay between them and widen the ocean of tension.

Decker looked as if he belonged with many of the inhabitants of the first campground that they passed. Most of the people who were out of their dilapidated huts looked gaunt. Their faces hung low and their eyes looked nearly dead. They paid the odd pair no mind, though their glances paused on Cody longer than the hunter felt comfortable with. Even with the dirt of the road beginning to cake on his skin he still looked far better than those around him. Decker moved closer to him instinctively and it wasn't until they nearly brushed arms did he realize his mistake before backing up a few paces. They walked quickly, doing their best to pass the sad excuses of shelter in favor for the empty road.

The following nights passed in much the same fashion. They passed a total of four camps, each looking richer than the last until they came upon the last which nearly looked like a proper village, though the people still looked half dead. The last few hours of their journey found them through more thick woods with no more sightings of other humans or vampires. The silence remained and Cody found it unsettling. There had been a time when he would have been happy to have silence, there often was with Gwyn at his side, but since meeting Decker he found he had grown to enjoy the noise. Despite his efforts, he had grown fond of the rogue. Logically he knew that the rogue should be held accountable for his crimes, but he could not bring himself to feel happy about it. If Gwyn had been with them he had no doubt that she would see his feelings clear on his face and set his mind straight, but she was not and so he was alone with these dangerous thoughts.

The trees were beginning to thin out alerting Cody that they were nearing their destination. They were heading to a little used gate on the far side of the wall which separated Faegon from the rest of the forest. Before long the parted trees made way for an imposing stone wall. It stood nearly thirty feet tall and was easily thick enough to house hundreds of guards who stood watch in the wall with arrows notched and at the ready. Cody could see the eyes of a few of them as they stared them down, not bothering to lower their weapons. They came to a halt at the large gates. Of course those were mostly for show, beyond the towering metal gates stood a thick stone wall which would be opened for them if the guards saw fit.

"This looks to be the end of it then." Decker whispered. He didn't say what *it* was, but he also didn't need to. Cody ignored the words for fear he might turn back on the promise he'd made to himself. He knew how unfair the High Council could be. He could not deny the fear he felt when thinking of the punishment Decker had to face, but his duty was to Gwyn, and to House Faegon. He would not go against his oath to save one rogue. He was a good person, but he was not soft.

"We will be there soon. When we enter the gates you are no longer my charge, but I will do whatever is in my power to assure you are fairly treated. Rogues who are convicted by the High Council can see the inside of a cell for anywhere between ten years to a few centuries depending on their crime, though I know not what crimes they will see you convicted of. I will tell them of your courage in the act of saving my life. It could reduce your sentence."

"Your council will do whatever they see fit to, as they always have," Decker spat. It was the first true sentence he had uttered since they reached Faegon's border. "Nothing you have to say will sway them, though I think it sweet of you to try." He punctuated the last statement with a wink and for a moment all felt right to the hunter. "Plus if they kill me I won't be your problem anymore."

The words were said in jest and yet they still felt like an ax digging into the hunter's ears. They mixed with the dread he'd been feeling and settled heavy in his heart. He wanted to assure the man that a trial hardly ever meant death, but the words would not come. Most times prisoners were allowed to live out as slaves if they behaved and even so they were given adequate food and shelter to sustain them, yet Cody could not find it in himself to lie. He knew whatever fate befell Decker, it would not be pleasant.

"Everything will be fine," Cody finally spoke. The words felt too loud when they came tumbling from his clumsy mouth. Birds that had been sleeping soundly in a nearby tree flew off, but not without proclaiming their displeasure. He made himself come up astride Decker to look him in the eyes. Suddenly feeling that it was extremely important for Decker to trust in his sincerity. "I promise."

"You truly are a rare breed, Cody Gilhart," The words were soft, but he heard them nonetheless. "It was good to know you in the short time that I did."

There seemed to be nothing left to say and Cody took a breath before turning to face the wrought iron before them. Together they pushed and the gate creaked open loudly, detesting its use before clanging shut behind them. Inside stood two guards with stone-like façades to meet them as soon as they passed through. They spoke no words, but stepped aside when Cody showed them his sunspear, a mark of a High Council sanctioned hunter, as well as the pendant that hung heavily against his breast. Though she was not there, Gwyn still remained with him and guided him in his mission. The stone door took longer to open than the wrought iron and the deafening sound of stone grating on stone inflamed his nerves until the hunter was nearly shaking with stress as they finally passed through into Faegon.

The gate they had crossed through took them to the poorest part of the city known only as the slums. Humans and vampires of the lowest cast moved in and out of the squatting huts which looked nearly as bad as those in the first few camps they had passed only nights before. A plump man, not more than thirty, stood outside one in particular with the door ajar giving the two a clear view of the nine other occupants of the small quarters. The stench of human filth was strong and Cody resisted the temptation to plug up his nose. Further down the narrow pathway scantily clad women called out for male patrons.

"Spend the night with a woman who actually wants to be in your bed!" A pale vampire cackled as her pink skirt curled around her body. Her breasts hung out of the front of her top and another woman, darker in skin and wider around the hips, draped herself over the skinny woman.

"Women and men welcomed!" To emphasize her point the rounder girl squeezed the vampire's small, tight chest and it only caused her cackling to grow.

"What about you, boys? Looking for a good time?"

"If only my handler would allow it ladies, I am sure I could find no love better." Decker jeered and Cody knocked him in the shoulder, forcing him along. The rogues nerves were beginning to show and Cody selfishly felt glad that he wasn't the only one affected. Decker brushed his hand against Cody's in a clear contradiction of his words. He had no intent of attempting to outrun his fate and Cody was glad for that.

"Maybe your handler just wants to keep you for himself." The vampire smirked as they narrowed on the slight contact between them. Cody gripped Decker's arm with more force than necessary to drag him along.

"Not now ladies, I'm sure I will see you again." Cody pushed past them ignoring as the other girl called out to them.

"It was good to see you Cody, maybe when you leave that bitch of a vampire you call a partner we'll actually see you around here." The woman laughed as if she'd told a joke and Cody ignored them as he always did. The whores that worked behind the gate were known to learn the names of every passing man and trick them into their beds before charging them more fees than seemed possible to create. It was the scam of their profession, one that Cody had only fallen for once, before Gwyn had heard and given him a firm talking to.

"Were those ladies familiar with your rare breed of charm?" Decker leered as soon as they were far enough away to not be hassled again.

"If we make it to Commoner's Market now there should be less people. It's more direct than walking along the wall and up through the Royal Bazar." Cody replied, moving too far and too fast for Decker to both keep up and taunt him at the same time. He was glad that the man had found an outlet for his pent up anxiety. He could only suffer its oppressive nature for so long, but he was no fool and he would not rise to the bait.

It was nearing dawn by the time they made it through the slums to the Commoner's Market and yet it was still well and awake. As the capital of the vampire kingdom, Faegon had the best markets and trading posts in all of Mordin Forest. The market allowed vampires and humans of all castes to barter their goods and services in the closest to social equality that Cody believed the empire would ever see. The Commoner's Market was always fuller and louder by far then the Royal Bazar as it catered to all. Moving through it could prove challenging though it had its advantages. It sat back farther from the castle and allowed the pair to travel without being stopped by guards every few paces. Decker looked just as seedy as some of the vampires pawning their wares and in a sea of other poor, dirty folk no one would look twice at them. Cody was also using the extra time to strategize what he was going to say to King Pa'ari. Faegon's King was the opposite of King Zentarion, the King of Kings, in every way imaginable. He was kind and fair with a reputation of listening to all those who came to him before passing judgement. Speaking to him before seeing the High Council or the High King might improve Decker's already slim chances. Thinking was impossible in the noise of the market and Cody wondered if a more direct path would have been better.

"Fresh blood here, straight from the source! When was the last time you drank blood that had been farmed less than an hour before? Drink like the kings for only five hundred zentarions!"

"Fish from the Great Sea sold here! Our fishermen are trained to only take in the best and are transported by the fastest horses in Mordin! Come get your fresh fish for two hundred zentarions or in exchange for blood!"

"Does your woman want to wear the finest silks? Pay half of what the royals do with these pieces made by apprentice tailors! She will ignore the mismatched threads when she slips on the softest dress she has ever felt! Tunics starting at seventy-nine hundred zentarions!"

Cody grasped Decker by the arm and dragged him through the noisy crowd. If he'd been with Gwyn he might have taken the royal's route as she would have been there to smooth over their arrival. Much to his surprise, Decker took his arm in hand as well allowing the man to bring him through the confusing market and through to the other end without complaint. From there it was easy to cut through the working class's tidier streets until they made it to one of the castle's many servant entrances.

"No matter what you hear or see in there you must remain quiet and follow my lead. Do you understand?" Cody saw Decker nod before passing through the doors into one of the castle towers. There were five large towers that branched off of the main castle, one of which housed King Pa'ari and his personal servants and council. Another tower was dedicated to King Zentarion and the High Council which governed over all of the empire's people. Cody was not intimately familiar with all of the castle; Gwyndolyn would often receive their orders and come find him in his home in the city below. He only knew the way to King Pa'ari's quarters by heart from the many times the King had personally treated with them. Beyond that his only knowledge of the castle came from those who worked in it, but lived near him. Cody lived a modest life in a small home between the Commoner's Market and the upper city. There were barracks set up for Faegon's city guard and also for the bounty hunters both human and vampire employed by the crown. Cody had been working with Gwyn, a master bounty huntress, for long enough that he was given his own quarters in a house not far from her own.

They were left alone as they walked through the servant's doors. Dusk was not far off and the last of the night's chores had the staff running about which meant that no one had time to pay them any mind. The walk toward King Pa'ari's receiving room left them unmolested until they actually reached the room in question. Two guards stood by the door, who looked much like the ones who had guarded the outer gate. They were both vampires, armed with true sunspears that stood crossed in front of the doorway, their expressions stone-still.

"Halt. King Pa'ari will not be seeing you at this time. You were to report to the Great King Zentarion personally." The guard on the left spoke, although his eyes never met their gaze. "Gwyndolyn would have known this. Where is she?"

"We were attacked, I must speak to King Pa'ari at once." Cody demanded, ignoring the guard's pointed words.

"You will speak with more respect, human." The second guard scolded. "Where is our sister? You are to tell us."

"There is no need to yell, gentlemen. If this man is on the business of the Great King and the High Council then surely anything he has to say is for their ears only." Another guard spoke as she made her way down the hall. She was nearly as pretty as Gwyn, although her eyes were a much warmer sapphire and her dark hair sat in a halo of curls around her heart-shaped face. She wore rich garments that marked her as a lady of King Pa'ari's court.

"Lady Jayne, it is a pleasure as always." Cody regarded his savior warmly. It was only then that he realized that he'd put himself between the guards and Decker. He moved then to allow the sapphire-eyed vampire the chance to better see the rogue.

"Of course, Cody. You both may come with me. The High Council is waiting." Lady Jayne threw one more contemptuous look at the two guards standing before King Pa'ari's tower. Satisfied that the lowly guards looked thoroughly chastised she turned around to lead them to the opposite side of the large castle. "You will have to excuse those two, they take their jobs very seriously."

"Do you know why the High Council wanted to speak to us directly? I was hoping to speak to King Pa'ari first." Cody pressed on. He had genuinely believed that Decker would be given a shorter sentence with his testimony, but the High Council's demands made him feel like a child facing their parents after acting particularly naughty.

"I wish I had an answer for you, though you must know this. They are not happy and without Gwyndolyn I doubt their moods will be improved."

"We were attacked, I'm not sure—" Cody began, but Jayne stopped walking altogether and turned to face him. Her arms came up to grasp him by the shoulders. She looked as if she was at an age with him, but Cody knew that she'd been reborn just shy of two centuries before and she held more wisdom than her young body suggested.

"I believe that no matter what happened to my sister you did everything in your power to keep her from harm. Be that as it may, I am not on the High Council, dear Cody. Please remember that they know naught of you or how hard you work for the Crown. They know only of the wishes of their King and that it is their upholding of our laws that keeps the fragile balance of this world to the next. They care not for your pretty face or your nice words, no matter if the story is true. Whatever they wish of this rogue, they will make it abundantly clear. Please, just be careful in there."

"I will, m'lady." Jayne placed a simple kiss to Cody's cheek, despite the dirt that lingered there, and turned around to lead them the rest of the way in silence.

Lady Jayne led them past the guards at the front of King Zentarion's wing and straight through to the private royal quarters. Few servants ventured this far into the castle unless explicitly requested and Cody felt as if he was trespassing. They did their work during the day when all were asleep as their presence offended the King, or so went he rumors. Cody had many friends who worked in the castle that lived near the barracks and so he heard many a strange story from the Great Royal Wing. They passed the open High Council room; much to Cody's surprise, but Lady Jayne raised a hand to silence all questions. It wasn't until they reached the doors of the King's private council room that dread really began to settle in his abdomen.

"You did not tell me this was where we were meant to go." Cody whispered hurt that she would keep important information from him.

"I am truly sorry, Cody. Please remember what I told you." Her parting words cut like a dagger and she swept into the room, announcing their presence to the High Council and the King. "I have brought the bounty hunter and rogue as you asked of me, Your Grace."

"So you have, you are dismissed." The cold voice of the King slithered down Cody's spine. He felt like a mark that had been captured when blood-red eyes landed on him and Decker. The King sat in the center of the long table facing the door while the seven members of the Council sat flanking him. "You may enter and kneel before me, Your King."

Cody understood then as he knelt that no words of his would have any meaning to the King. Decker stood back, away from the red eyes and Cody's obedience with disdain.

"You are not my King." Decker spat. A guard came forward and hit the dirty rogue about his neck with a spear and Cody winced when he heard the vampire's bony knees crash to the stone floor.

"I am everyone's King." King Zentarion's voice was low and dangerous. It carried from his strong frame to permeate the air, winding its way into every crack and crevice until it echoed back at them, bouncing off Cody's ears until he found himself unsure of how many people had spoken. "Where is the vampire you were sent with? Where is your handler?"

"We were attacked by a rogue named Vestera, servant to the vampire calling herself Queen Cassandra, of House Rayne. Gwyndolyn was taken." Cody tried to reason, but to no avail.

"Impossible, there is no queen of such filth." The King dismissed the truth as if his word alone made it a lie. "How could you have let your vampire handler be taken?"

"My Lord there have been reports of such rogues posing as King and Queen to the animals." One council member bravely spoke.

"Such reports are market gossip Lord Aaron, you should know better. I want to know why this human was allowed to walk through the town languidly, without his handler, without being brought right to me." Cody knew that in the eyes of the Crown, Gwyn was seen as a babysitter to her human liaison, it was how every human liaison was viewed and Cody had been lucky that Gwyn was kind where it counted. The King's accusations that he needed a handler were beyond appalling to anyone who actually knew the man, but of course the King would never give him the chance to prove himself.

"We did not want to disturb the Royal Bazar, we came as quickly as possible. There is a vampire out there who either killed or took Gwyndolyn. We must find her and stop her."

"You are a mere human living in my walls, do not dare tell me what needs to be done. As far as I can tell you returned with a wanted criminal and claim that this wild vampire exists and she took your handler. How am I to know that this is not a scheme born of your sick human mind? This thing you are protecting is a wanted fugitive needed for questioning and now we will add the death of our own to his long list of crimes."

"Decker had nothing to do with it! He saved me." Cody fought passionately. He knew that Decker was a killer, that he deserved to be brought to justice, but Cody would not see him stand trial for crimes that he had no part in.

"And you feel you owe him for that? I can see now that he has manipulated your mind and twisted you to his purpose. Now he will be questioned and when we are done he will be strung up in the sun for killing Gwyndolyn." The King waved to the guards and Decker was seized.

"You can't do this, he didn't kill her. Take my blood, you will see the truth!"

"That is quite enough from you. Put him in a cell." More guards swarmed Cody and they hauled him off of his feet and toward the door. He was hardly surprised when Decker was pulled in the opposite direction, closer to the King to face their judgment.

"I will see to it that you are not strung up to the sun." Cody whispered as he struggled against his guards. If they heard him they ignored him and Decker stopped his own fight to give the human a sad smile.

"You are truly one of a kind, Cody Gilhart. It was good to know you in the short time that I did." Cody watched as Decker hung his head, ready to accept his fate.

"No! Let me go!" Cody kicked out, attempting to catch on to anything that would give him proper leverage.

"Get him out of my sight. Now, vermin, tell me of your connection to the false king, Logan."

Cody could barely fight off Gwyndolyn when she used to practice with him much less two vampires, but he needed to hear what the King was talking about. Struggling against them would only make it worse and he knew it, but any information was worth it. A swift punch to his gut made Cody see spots and it immobilized him long enough for the two vampires to haul him from the room with no problem. The stunt rewarded him with one last comment from the King.

"You will remain my prisoner until you have told me everything." Cody risked looking over his shoulder to catch Decker's eye. The vampire was slumped on the floor with his head turned down. He looked up to nod toward Cody, a stubborn glint in his eyes, before returning to his sullen state, admitting to nothing. If nothing else, Decker would play weak and refuse them everything until there was no strength left in him and that gave Cody some strange comfort. "If you want to make this more difficult than so be it. I want this thing to be taught a lesson. Leave the neck and mouth alone. I want to be sure that he can still talk. He's going to want to after you're through with him."

The King needed Decker's knowledge more than he could afford to allow his bloodlust to take over and just kill the rogue. If the two of them were smart, Cody would be able to devise a plan to get them both free before Decker was beaten beyond repair. The sensible part of Cody knew that aiding Decker might be the biggest mistake he could possibly make, but the greater part of him that believed in true justice knew that seeing him to a fair trial was what needed to be done.

As soon as he was taken out of earshot of the council chamber, Cody allowed his body to slump forward. There was no longer a reason to fight. He was only human and he would not heal quite as easily as his two guards. He would need all of his strength and cunning to make an escape.

"Open the damn door." The skinnier vampire bellowed while the taller, bulkier one stayed silent. They were at the top of a set of stairs that lead to the dungeons, a place that he was very familiar with considering his job.

"You're not going to the main cells, human. You know them too well." The skinnier vampire whispered when they were let through and they were halfway down the stairs. "It's maximum-security for you and your little friend."

At least they would be put in the same location, it made Cody's job much easier. He had never been in the maximum-security cells before. It was considered too dangerous for humans to even go near the door so it was a little concerning that they intended to leave him there. There were nasty rumors about the vampires that they kept in those cells, ones that Gwyn had never confirmed or denied when he'd asked. That had been when he'd first signed on as her liaison. It had been when he was still an over eager child and Gwyn had been reluctant to take him on. She had never told him why she'd been called down to the inner dungeon and it had been the only time she had been in their time together.

At the end of the stairs they continued to drag him along a dark hallway. There was very little light and it took a long time for Cody's eyes to adjust well enough for him to take in his surroundings. By the time his tired eyes were able to convert the gray masses to stone cells it became clear that he would not be finding his way out of the dungeons soon. The cells that ran along the wall in that section were all empty. The bars were thick wrought iron and the hinges were built on the outside allowing the stone to cover them from behind. There would be no way to gain the leverage to pull the pins out. Even if Cody attempted to chisel away at the stone it would take too long and a guard would notice before he even got close enough to think the word escape.

The hallway gave way to a fork which split into two more rows of cells. The guards took him down the one on the right though Cody had little hope such information would be put to use. That short hall branched into four more directions and with every turn and empty cell that passed Cody found even his sharp mind could not keep up. It was a labyrinth designed to confuse even the best trackers. The click of the vampires' boots should have echoed, but there was a magic in the air that prevented it. It felt as if an unseen force was literally sucking the sound out of the space, disorienting the human and setting him on edge. There was no doubt that the magic altering his hearing was also altering his eyes since there was no way that such a vast dungeon would be built to remain so empty. He could easily see how someone could go insane in the inner cells. He'd heard that the guards that worked down in the depths were given a decade rotation before they resurfaced. From there they were scattered into the city guard and royal guard depending on their performance. King Zentarion personally employed the ones that knew the castle too well. The rumors were that they were placed in his personal guard or even in the bounty hunters ranks where they could be controlled. The ones that were put into the barracks with the rest of the hunters were there to gather intelligence and were allowed to kill in the King's name without question from the High Council. Of course those were all just rumors and there was no way to prove it.

Another round of twists and turns lead Cody toward a group of cells that were actually occupied. Old, dirty vampires slept in old, dirty cells. They were kept so there were at least three empty cells between them, far enough that they could see each other, but not near enough to talk. Cody had noticed by then that the air worked as a sound bubble of sorts, if they wanted to talk they would have to yell and that would alert the nearest guard. When they reached an empty cell four doors down and across from a scrawny vampire with glassy eyes, Cody was roughly shoved in.

"Welcome to your new home, human." The quiet vampire whispered, the magic modifying the air making it sound like he was being spoken to through a tunnel. "I wouldn't make yourself too comfortable, I'm sure you won't be here too long."

"Lock him up!" The skinner vampire yelled and Cody stumbled back, covering his ears. The ringing was just beginning to fade as the two guards walked off, a silent jailer taking his spot just down the row. The chances of escaping were looking even slimmer, but Cody knew that he would have to try. If he didn't he just might die a prisoner and then no one would be left to try and find Gwyn, alive or dead, and bring her attacker to justice.

GWYNDOLYN

The overwhelming scent of mold and smoke curled up Gwyndolyn's nose. It choked her senses and forced her eyes to water. The offending smell nearly caused her to retch. It burned worse than sunlight on her skin. She blinked the tears away, too tired to move her limbs to brush them aside. She was lying on well compacted dirt of which she was sure was mixing well with the dirt and blood no doubt already caked into her clothing and hair. The dull pain of her broken collarbone was gone so she knew she must have been unconscious for quite some time. Instead, another more painful sensation pulsed through her limbs making her dizzy. It took her eyes a moment to adjust beyond the drying tears and exhaustion but when they did she was met with bleak surroundings. The stone walls that made up her cell were painted with soot and grime. The pungent smell of lingering fear knotted in her abdomen and she turned her face, eyes shut tight to push it out.

Heavy shackles kept her tied to the ground. They were tight around her thin wrists and bit into her ankles. The painful heat of the sun soaked steel made Gwyn want to claw her own limbs off, but she lacked the insanity and mobility to do so. She was intimately familiar with the castles and dungeons of every house and yet she lacked knowledge of her whereabouts. Knowing her exact location was not a necessity. A good bounty hunter should be able to work in an unknown environment and use the provided resources to get free, but Gwyn could feel her remaining strength fading. It would be ignorant to say that she was unaccustomed to fear. While she showed little emotions outwardly, she felt them burn within her possibly with more strength than most. As a woman, it was taught to her at a young age that her emotions were her curse. Only through hard truths did Gwyn come to find that it was the perception of emotion that made you weak. She felt fear, but never let it show. Only a fool lived without fear and a fool she was not.

It would not do to allow herself to be consumed by emotion. Setting her mind to the task at hand, Gwyn scanned her cell searching from her position to gather what little information was given to her. She could tell time of day by the way her body yearned to bath in the light of the moon. There was no doubt in her mind who her captor was or in whose name it had been done. There had been no mistaking those sickly purple eyes as the mark of the rogue Cassandra. She had never met the rogue before, but the stories of her rage during the coup at House Lunaries had traveled through the empire and every hunter and huntress had been trained to know her or her children on sight. Vestera was well known by the elite hunters to be her crazed supporter, willing to endanger herself and those around her in the name of her Queen and her King, the rogue named Logan. The very idea was preposterous, of course. To be a house, to have a King or Queen, went against the very ideology of being a rogue and yet the vampires had sweet-talked their way into organizing what had not long before been pure chaos. What could be worse than organized chaos?

If it weren't for their twisted sense of justice and lack of morals, Gwyn could almost respect the kind of power that Logan and Cassandra held.

Unlike their titles would suggest, the King and Queen of the Rogues held no court, at least none that Faegon had ever been able to discover. Knowing her captors shed no light on her whereabouts and Gwyn let her head fall back, exhaustion taking over. She would have to conserve all of her remaining energy to attempt her escape. Any information she could gain before would be preferable, but such information would be of little use if she couldn't make it out alive. The knowledge that her people and the Crown had need of her yet, forced Gwyn to close her eyes and gain what little rest her constraints would afford her.

With her eyes closed she was able to focus on the varying myriad of noises echoing out of the empty cells around her. There were no heartbeats within the whole facility. Every great vampire house had humans that lived within the walls. They acted as liaisons to their respective villages as well as useful scouts, protecting the house during the day when many if not all of the royal guard were forced to retreat indoors. Of course they also acted as a willing food source which kept the kingdoms alive and thriving. The absence of humans spoke volumes of her captors and was all the proof that Gwyn needed to confirm that she was being held by rogues. She could hear low voices from floors above. The wood directly above her had been blackened by flames, she'd taken note before her eyes had become too heavy to keep open and she had to assume that not all of the castle had taken the same abuse. She could hardly make out the words that were being spoken, something that she could only infer to be due to her tired body and the sturdy flooring and stone walls that separated her from the speakers.

I'll only rest a minute. Her thoughts were muddled and it wasn't long before her senses dulled and the world around her faded into nothingness.

When Gwyndolyn awoke again it was to the sound of angry voices hovering just above her head. They had moved her, if the hard rock beneath her back was any indication, though she could still feel the burn of her sun soaked shackles. She kept her eyes closed, making sure to hold her body impossibly still. Her senses began to waken and the noises around her slowly began to sound like actual words that she could follow. The voices were quiet, but precise. There were three people standing around her, but her senses told her there was a fourth person off in the background not speaking. She might not have any magic of her own, but all of the training she had been put through as a girl had taught her enough to trust her instincts and learn how to identify auras. She might not ever be able to alter an aura or tell people apart by small characteristics that made every aura different, but she could always sense when there were others present. The fourth, silent figure worried her because she could feel a wrath emanating from them that was stronger than that which she had felt from other rogues in the past. Pushing the unease from her mind she did her best to listen to the voices in the hope of learning more about her captors.

"I say we skin the bitch." The voice nearest to her left spoke. His tone was gravelly and his laughter harsh. He was older, there was a quality to his voice that spoke of ages long since passed and sights that should have never been seen. He might have been an elder of one of the great houses before he defected to the rogues. It was obvious in the way he spoke that he was used to giving orders and having them obeyed.

"Our Queen would not be pleased with that at all." A slimier voice spoke from her feet. The way it crawled up her skin and assaulted her ears made Gwyn want to curl her toes and draw her legs up to get away from the man. It took all of her self-control to keep still as he continued on the sickly, coy tone. "I'd shudder to think what would happen to anyone who opposed My Lady."

"I would hold your tongue if I were you." A woman's voice responded then. She was standing at Gwyn's head. She spoke as if in song and her tone was wicked in a way that made Gwyn sick. There was no mistaking that the voice belonged to Vestera, the woman who had attacked her to begin with. "I would never presume to understand the many wants and wishes of Our Lady."

"Are you three stupid enough to not realize that our guest is awake?" The fourth voice was soft and young in a way that revealed the boy's age and status easily. The childe sounded both short-tempered and timid in the way his question had started out strong before it ended in uncertainty. Her game was up and Gwyn saw no reason to pretend any longer. She opened her eyes to look straight into the eyes of the woman above her.

"Nobody asked you, Leon," Vestera hissed. Her eyes were an eerie purple, something that hardly surprised the bounty huntress. It had been rumored that the rogue would often maintain a state of bloodlust, although the theories as to why were varied. It was no less unnerving seeing them a second time and Gwyn wondered how seeing those eyes would feel when she finally met Cassandra. It was unsettling to see a small sample of the power the twisted vampire had over her people, she wondered what kind of woman she must be to have such power. She turned her head to glance at the boy in question, in order to escape the piercing gaze.

She had been right about the boy's age. He didn't look to be more than seventeen, though it was hard to judge how old he truly was. His short brown hair stood up at odd ends as if he had just been running his hands through it in frustration. His eyes were the color of warm honey, though they held nothing but the fire of pure unadulterated anger. He was lanky with thin limbs, though she suspected there was strength in the boy which could easily be overlooked. Gwyn was still held down by the sun soaked chains and while the other three seemed to hardly mind standing so near them, Leon was careful to stand back. At first Gwyn believed it to be a show of respect from a childe to an elder, but the sneer set on the boy's face spoke volumes on his idea of respect.

"Queen Cassandra will be asking me as soon as she arrives." It was a poor comeback and Gwyn flinched when the large man beside her reached over the table and struck the childe.

"You will not speak the Queen's name as if you have the right." The deep tone felt like a physical weight above Gwyn.

"And you will not strike the Queen's favorite childe." A voice from the door signaled another man entering. He was porcelain white in a way that only elders were. He had clear blue eyes that swept over Gwyn's body both admiring and assessing for danger. All four of the vampires around the stone table that Gwyn was affixed to bowed to the man. "Lord Jarrod you will apologize to Leon and to your Queen when she arrives." His words were chosen carefully and his steps were just as punctuated.

"My Lord." The woman moved from her spot at the head of the table to bend the knee before the man. She dipped her head to kiss his bare feet, her eyes never quite meeting his gaze.

"Oh get up, Vestera." The man rolled his eyes, kicking his foot out to catch her under the chin. She had enough sense to keep any protests to herself and she slid back to her feet with grace. "And you Wyndell, of course you'd be here." The distaste was obvious and the slippery man in question simply bowed his head toward the man.

"My place is always to be where my King and Queen cannot be." There was a hidden message in those words one that no one seemed to miss. It only angered the man further.

"Is that your newest excuse?" The King, as he would seem, asked. He held his temper in check though not very well. Lord Wyndell didn't seem to mind, however, and kept his gaze even in a blatant show of disrespect. "Well then you are dismissed, you snake of a man."

"As you wish." Lord Wyndell bowed out, his dark eyes lingering longer on the King than strictly polite before his slight body slipped between the heavy iron door and the stone frame.

"Come here, Leon." The King beckoned and boy walked forward with his head bowed, though even Gwyn could see the grin on his face. He came before the man and waited for his praise. Instead he was shocked when the swift, solid hand of his King came in contact with the still blushing cheek.

"My King!" He cried and the look of distaste on the King's face only grew. "Learn your place Leon and maybe you will receive less punishment. Now off with you." The boy fled the chamber with tears stinging down his eyes.

"It would be in poor form for me to apologize to the Queen for striking the boy while you have gone and committed the same crime and consider it just punishment." Lord Jarrod advised though he seemed not to care what his king did. His hard eyes were nearing a shade of black that matched the tone with which he spoke. His hair had silvered with time and the slight wrinkles around his eyes spoke of just how old he must be. Gwyn thought it a miracle a man of his age and power would take orders from the likes of a king who would only be a childe in his eyes.

"You will understand, Lord Jarrod, that I don't give a damn what you think. Now come, what kind of show are we putting on for our guest?" All eyes fell on Gwyn again. "I would hate for her to tell Queen Cassandra about the cruelty she saw here."

"She's seen nothing of cruelty." Lady Vestera's face was hovering over her again. Her eyes were wide, cold, and calculated. The grin that spread across her face was sickening and Gwyn turned her head to look the King in the eye. She had been silent for too long. The window to assert herself was thinning until all she would become was a sullen prisoner.

"I know everyone else's name. What's yours?" It was bold, possibly bordering on too bold, but she hardly cared. There seemed like very little for her to lose at this point and she was willing to put all of her cards on the table as it were. She was already strapped to a table of sorts so there was nothing left for her to give.

"You will speak to King Logan with respect." The vampire above her moved her sharp nails against Gwyn's throat. Strands of her brown hair had fallen from its haphazard up do and hung in her eyes only making her look even less stable than before.

"That's enough Vestera." The King moved further into the room and the two vampires shadowing Gwyn instantly fell back. They might not like their King as much as they obviously liked their Queen, but they feared him. "Un-cuff her."

Lord Jarrod came forward, his large hands circling around each cuff without flinching. He made easy work of her bound ankles and moved to her wrists with little discomfort. He was older than anyone in the room, turned millennia ago if Gwyn was a good judge. Even the so called King was standing with enough distance from the cuffs to avoid being hurt. The possible motives of an elder following these children, while interesting, was not high on Gwyn's list of necessary information to commit an escape. The reason for her capture and the motives of the rogues were more interesting to Faegon and would help her wiggle her way back into the good graces of her employer.

"Thank you Lord Jarrod. Now the two of you may leave us." The Queen's men eyed the pair, though they made no move to dispute his order. When the two were alone, Logan extended his hand with a coy smile twisted on his pale face. She took it with little hesitation and allowed him to pull her up until she was sitting near the edge of the stone slab. Playing a role in order to make her mark was not a new concept to the bounty hunter. Before she had met Cody she had spent much of her time parading as people she was not to gain the information needed by the Crown. Changing her demeanor for the sake of a mark came to her easily, even if she personally hated doing so.

"Now, let's begin again, shall we?" Gwyn allowed her eyes to start at the fine blond locks that fell into cool blue eyes all the way down to the bare feet planted into the dirt. "My name is Logan, you can leave the title it's a bit much, don't you think?"

"I don't know, that depends on if you think flirting with me is going to get you anywhere." Gwyn returned the soft look. Their hands were still joined and Gwyn used the leverage to pull her body closer to the man's. She never much enjoyed playing games like this, but she was good at her job and her job was to take down rogues in any way she deemed fit, so long as she got the information she was sent in for.

"Where do you think I want to get?" The words were soft, just a whisper on the shell of her ear. It was sweet, the way a lover might speak to one he'd known for a lifetime. If she'd been another woman, a gentler, more naive one, Gwyn could see herself falling for his charm. As it was it wouldn't take much to dig deep inside of her and convince him then that she was enjoying his attention, a testament to his skills and the lack of amorous affection in her lifetime.

"I would never suppose that I understand the mind of a King." The words were true, she had no idea what motivated the dangerous man before her, but she knew that she could at least try.

"What is your name, my dear. You know mine, it only seems fair." Agile fingers danced from Gwyn's hand and up her arm, pulling her even closer to his solid body. They met hip to hip, the swell of her breasts pressed into his toned chest. Logan's lips hovered over hers and each second that ticked by waiting on her response brought their lips ever closer.

"Gwyndolyn of House Faegon."

Both of his hands came up to grip her shoulders, the shift made their bodies align and Gwyn rocked her hips knowing full well the dangerous game she was beginning and their lips crashed together in a practiced motion. It had been quite some time since Gwyn had taken a lover and still her hands found purchase on Logan's sides as if she'd done this all her life. A stranger's hands were sliding under her shirt and yet her traitorous body gave in while her mind did it's best to remember what to do next. Wooing men for information had been part of her repertoire before Cody, in some ways this felt like a homecoming as strange as it might seem.

His large, strong fingers circled on her ribcage like weights anchoring her to the stone slab below her, grounding her and returning her mind to the task at hand. She gasped at the contact allowing Logan to take control of the kiss. He dipped her low into the slab, the angle changing entirely and pulling a dirty moan from them both. Logan pulled away to mouth at the base of her neck, moving up until his mouth was ghosting over her ear again.

"Well Gwyndolyn of House Faegon, welcome to my humble castle."

The words sounded like a challenge to her ears and the wicked glint in his eyes seemed to back the unspoken taunt. If this king wanted to play games then who was she, as a lowly huntress, to deny him? Gwyn unlaced the man's trousers as easily as she sharpened her blades. She drew him from his trousers and coaxed another deep moan from the vampire king feeling smug for her efforts. He did not give her long to gloat before he pulled at the rest of her clothing. His actions were stunted and demanding and she lifted her hips from the table to allow him to rip her dirty linens from her body. His savage movements only encouraged her to reciprocate in kind and her hands tightened around his manhood, roughly pulling strangled groans from his thin lips. He was a king, thus not accustomed to being denied the things he desired, so Gwyn found herself on her back without warning as he pushed forward, forcing her hand to fall away from him. She encircled him with her legs, drawing him closer until they slipped together and became one. She knew better than to continue to dangle herself in front of such a dangerous man for too long without giving him what he wanted. She fully intended to make this man divulge all of his people's secrets and if that meant letting him take control then she could allow him to think he was the one guiding the show.

"I find nothing humble about this." Gwyn moaned, playing up her enjoyment to feed into the man's ego. His movements were becoming rough with increased pace and she knew that she had him.

"I'm glad we can come to an understanding." Logan sang in her ear when another harsh thrust brought him to completion. He pulled away from her with little finesse and wiped himself off on her pants. "Clean up, Gwyndolyn. If you think you're going to get information from me that quickly, you're sorely mistaken."

There was a draft in the room and Gwyn slid from the table not bothering to hide her nudity. He knew that she was a well trained huntress from Faegon and it hardly surprised her that he would see through such a transparent game. Sex didn't always get her the information she needed, but it never hurt to try. It seemed that this king was playing a similar game with her and she made note of the calculating gaze on his face that she was sure her own was mirroring. They were distracted from their contest of wills when a noise above signaled the arrival of the House's Queen.

"It seems my dear wife is home. Come I will bring you to a clean cell where you may bathe and dress. There is no doubt that my wife will want to speak with you."

Gwyn left the room before the king with her head held high. Her clothes were left in ruins behind her and she could still feel the ghost of his hands on her body, but there was no reason for her to back down now. He might know the game she was playing, but he was playing the same game as well and that put them on even ground. He was a man, and a proud one at that, so outsmarting him would be easy in time. She threw a coy smile over her shoulder to show him just how much she cared at being found out.

"I've heard of your wife before; a bit crazed and with a vendetta against the empire, or so I've been told. She seems like the type I wouldn't much like to cross. Think of what she will say when word of what we did reaches her." It was a risky move to put herself out in the open so boldly. Her sleeping with the Queen's own husband could end in her death just as easily as it could in his suffering. The king regarded her a moment before nodding to himself.

"You are a far better matched opponent than I thought." Logan's smile was more genuine than any she had seen before. In that moment she thought she might be seeing a glimpse of the man he could have been before whatever madness had led him down the path that he now walked. It was clear to her by how the others treated their king that they had no respect for him which led her to believe that he was just another follower of the rogue Queen. Could he have been a good man before? Would he be so again when the empire removed the stain of Cassandra from the map? She had been part of the select few which had been made privy of the fact that the High Council believed Cassandra to be the true and sole leader of the rogues. What had simply been a game before suddenly seemed much bigger and more important than anything she had done in her life. He had been handsome, if not cold before, but with warmth lighting up his eyes he was devastating.

"I do hope you can keep up." Gwyn responded, confidence filling her as she felt more sure of her task at hand. She turned her back on him in a clear sign of what she thought of his show of power and led the way from the lower cells toward the only door.

The two moved in silence from the lower cells. The heavy wooden door had given way to drafty stairs. The walls surrounding them were cracked and there were sizable holes throughout the stairwell until they made it to the landing which stood exposed by a missing outer wall. There was another door at the top which Logan leaned over her to open. He draped his body over her own, being careful to let his unoccupied hand to brush over her naked hip.

"Right this way, My Lady." Logan teased, moving to take the lead as they walked toward a row of cells that were closer to small bedchambers than prison cells.

"I am no Lady." Gwyn laughed outwardly though she could barely cover her annoyance. It would figure that a noble man would think it funny to call her by a title. Another weaker girl might find it flattering, but she was not any other girl.

"I suppose that is what is most intriguing about you." Logan's teeth were sharp and the moonlight shone from them. "I shall leave you here. A servant will come with hot water soon, though I am afraid they lack the manners of a proper royal house. You will have to bathe alone."

"A shame that you won't be joining me." Gwyn heard herself say. She hardly recognized herself when she put on airs for a mark. This time was no different, though this time she was risking more than she had ever done before.

"Maybe next time." Logan leaned in for a single kiss. "Though when my wife is done with you I fear there might not be a next time."

It was a clear challenge, one that Gwyn knew she would rise to with ease. Torture had been part of her rigorous training and she had no doubt that the vampire elder would do her best to break her, but nothing would compare to the things that had been done to her by her own people to train her for such occasions.

"Until next time then." Gwyn smiled before slipping past the door. Logan's eyes raked over her body until she was securely in the room and every one of her nerves sang under his scrutiny. She felt in that moment that this was what all of her training had led her to and she was more than ready to face it.

CASSANDRA

Shadows were beginning to form at the corners of the front entrance hall. Moonlight shone through the holes in the wall which only helped to sour Cassandra's mood. The rebuilding effort was slow going, though the fault never seemed to stick to one individual for long. Set a bunch of unorganized vampires to an organized task and it was no wonder that barely anything had gotten repaired in her absence. Naturally her husband couldn't be bothered to see to anything, but of course a king had other duties to attend to, as he often enjoyed reminding her. The past two centuries had been rough more often than not, but she was patient and had the advantage of immortality on her side. Together, they had done what many considered impossible, they had united the untamed rogues in one common desire; to see the Crown fall. It hadn't been hard to convince them that Crown was repressing them and keeping them from their true nature. Vampires shouldn't be bowing down to humans. They should be taking blood from the weak, not protecting them and begging them for the meal that they deserved. The difficult part had been to convince them that their rebellion could only be made possible if they united under the rule of a King and Queen.

She would have to remind the miscreants that worked for them of what they were working so hard to achieve, though the words would have to come for her husband's mouth. She had worked tirelessly to make him the figurehead of her uprising, it wouldn't do to ruin that image now. It was not all a lost cause, however. Things had begun to shape up in the fallen castle that once belonged to the original House Rayne. The rogues, who were once a mindless group of delinquents, now answered to the combined forces of their King and Queen after over a century of manipulation. The rebellion that had been brewing under the surface of the empire was finally coming to a boil and it would be on her terms, something Cassandra had always dreamed about. The road ahead would prove to be more treacherous even, but she had come too far to consider the alternative.

Servants lined every hall as the Queen swept through the corridors. They bowed at her presence and continued on their business in her wake. It might not look the same as the days when she had walked Rayne's halls as a childe, but the improvements could not be ignored. Cassandra had spent many sleepless nights to bring order to the chaos that she had helped instigate and there was only so much she could expect. Those that she kept company with hardly had an appreciation for the finer details, but she could forsake the comforts she once had if it meant finally seeing the world brought down to its knees, as had been done to her. That being said, there was a certain level of order that Cassandra required from her servants and she knew that in her absence things were not kept to those standards, but then again Logan was never quite the iron fisted ruler that she'd hope to groom him to be.

"My Queen." Leon, her favorite pet stood in wait at the end of the hall that led to her council room. She noticed the marks on his cheek immediately and the sullen look that settled on his already grim face spoke of the punishment he had received in her absence.

"What happened my dear?" Cassandra cooed, sweeping down on her prey with a false gentleness that the childe ate up. Her cold hands cupped at the boy's face to better examine the damage. "Who would dare strike you?"

"My Lord, the King." The response was fast, without hesitation and Cassandra glowered at his lack of manners.

"That would be m'lord to you, and that is more than one mark on your face." The boy must have thought himself crafty and he kept his mouth shut, refusing to name the second culprit. "If you are this disobedient when I'm not here it's no wonder that you're not struck more."

She let him pull from her grasp. His eyes were downcast in defeat, but she knew that if she had gotten a look in his eyes she would see the burning fire of defiance. That would just not do, but she had deeper concerns at the moment.

They made their way toward her private council chambers in silence. She would have to deal with the childe when her kingdom was in less jeopardy. As she expected the doors were closed. Her guardsmen lay in wait and allowed her entrance. Beyond the door King Logan sat at the head of the table, Lady Vestera and Lord Jarrod on his left while Lord Wynn waited impatiently just on the other side. Word of Queen Cassandra's return had come just moments before and already her trusted council waited like well-trained dogs. At least some of her reign stood ground in her absence. They were one short, though none dared mention Decker's absence. She'd had Logan send him on a mission, it's intent only known to her, and she was more than pleased to keep it that way.

"My Queen, I fear to tell you of such terrible happenings during your absence." Lord Wynn was at his Lady's side as soon as she swept into the room.

Cassandra wondered if a moment's peace might be granted to her before she was burdened with the no doubt petty drama that had unraveled in her wake, but it seemed that it was too much to ask. She held back her anger, instead focusing on shedding her traveling garb. Her long dark hair was knotted at the base of her neck and she undid the pin before handing it to her man of secrets. He took the piece in stride. Her traveling cloak came next revealing the state of her traveling clothes. They were dirt stained, covered in patches of dried blood. Wynn turned the articles over to Leon without sparing the boy a glance.

"I'm sure you would be delighted to tell me all about it, but there are more important matters for me to attend to." The pale vampire scanned the room until her gaze landed on Logan. "I have a report to share from my travels. I trust that idle gossip can wait until after the real business is taken care of."

"Of course, my dear. Please, tell us of your travels." Her husband looked at her passively, though there was a smug aura radiating from him that absolutely would not do. It would seem that whatever had occurred in her absence would certainly need to be dealt with, and fast.

"I have just returned from speaking without brothers and sisters that we have placed in deep undercover roles throughout the forest and I have some good and some troubling news."

"Are we concerned about their loyalties?" Vestera asked, sounding all too eager to hear the answer.

"Not as such, the girl we placed in Adrastos is fairing well, from the scouts that we left on their border we know that she has risen in the ranks, I am more concerned about the people we have in Faegon."

"Suffice to say we are working hard on that." Wynn responded, sounding put out. Faegon was his responsibility. Each of them was in charge or infiltrating a house with their spies, though they all reported back to anyone on House Rayne's council. Vestera has been put in charge of Adrastos, but in her absence, Cassandra had taken the report.

"Well, I suggest you work harder." Jarrod comment, seemingly bored of the trivial conversation.

"And what of Tryali? Lord Jarod how are you faring with your spies?" Wynn asked, his tone reeking of confidence.

"House Tryali was always a stretch, we knew that infiltrating them was not going to be easy, but also not necessary. Faegon is the key to our success. Without it, we will not dismantle the Crown and bring on the true era of vampires" Cassandra dismissed the jibe before a true argument could ensue.

"It would be easier to control if someone did not go about attacking and kidnapping their huntress." Wynn shot a dirty glare at Vestera and the woman sneered in return.

"She had Decker and we had reason to believe that he was going to betray us," The pretty vampire snarled, her gentle features hardening.

"What reason? I have heard no such talk," Wynn spat back, affronted. As a man of whispers it did not look good for others to have knowledge that he did not.

"That would be my fault," Cassandra spoke calmly, bringing the attention back on herself. "I had suspicions for some time now, but I was not sure. I sent Vestera to discover for me if they were true. She had my permission to use any force necessary."

"What of House Lunaries?" Logan asked from the head of the table, finally breaking his silence.

"What of House Lunaries?" Wynn asked perplexed, echoing the thoughts of Cassandra as well.

"How are the spies in House Lunaries?"

"They are fine," Cassandra dismissed, though Logan seemed determined to continue the conversation. With a pointed look from her husband, Cassandra knew that it would be impossible to avoid him much longer. "I am truly sorry, my dear council, but I grow tired from my long journey. I'm sure you will all understand that I wish to speak to my husband alone."

"Of course, your grace. We should have let you rest before conducting this meeting," Wynn was gracious enough to pretend that he did not notice the looks between his King and Queen, but Leon did not have such manners.

Almost as one, the Lords and Lady bowed out without protest, though her page lingered. Wynn slipped a small scroll into the fold of Cassandra's traveling cloak which was still in her page's grasp and Cassandra knew that Logan was merely pretending to turn a blind eye.

"Leon can you not hear? The stain on your face should not impact your ability to abide by my orders." Cassandra glanced at the vampire next to her. It was true that he was one of her favorites, though she could do without the occasional insubordination. He was turned by another rogue only one decade before, but he'd shown great potential as her page and she'd taken to him immediately. "I assure you with my husband present there is no further need for you."

"As you wish My Queen. My apologies, My Queen." The page bowed out of the room without further protest.

Once the room was cleared, Cassandra took moment to study the man before her. He was younger than she was, though he was still considered an elder by their people's standards. He'd been by her side since the beginning, something she did appreciate him for, but the potential that she had seen in him had never come to fruition and more often than not simply looking at him caused her disappointment. Despite that, she trusted him and his discretion because he had never given her a reason to doubt them. She held her secrets just as she suspected him to hold his own.

"You speak far too freely of House Lunaries, you will draw suspicion to yourself."

"That was long ago, my dear, and all those who would even remember it are either dead or not here. You are being paranoid."

She thought of responding, but thought better of it. "Come, let us retire for the night."

The door to the meeting room was shut tight, but the main wall was still crumbling in spots and it left the two no illusion of privacy. The only rooms that were completely rebuilt were in the royal's quarters. Without preamble, Cassandra moved from the room toward the back exit that made way directly to her own chambers. She knew that Logan would follow without question. They kept separate quarters, though it wasn't uncommon for him to spend lonely days in her bed before retiring to his own. There was no love lost between the two. There was too much history to ignore their passion, but it didn't lend itself to a full functioning marriage, though she had never wanted that from him so it suited her just fine.

"You look tired my dear, did your travels not go as planned?" Logan asked in what passed as small talk in the open halls. There were servants every twelve paces and all of their words would be heard, catalogued, and spread through the compound.

"Not as such, but it wasn't anything that couldn't be dealt with." They often spoke with room for the silent words that the other understood. Even in council meetings they spoke in one language, but communicated in another built from four centuries of moving within the other's space.

"Will there be any repercussions?" Logan looked to her sideways without concern for the many ears that lived within their walls. Some were his own, she was sure. Some were employed by Wynn in her name, though he knew not of all of them. There was no doubt in Cassandra's mind that he was suspicions of her, he would not have lasted at her side as long as he had otherwise.

"What do you take me for? Of course not." Cassandra scoffed, nodding to the guard who opened her door. "That will be all, you are dismissed."

"As you wish, M'Lady." The guard bowed them in. They both listened for the click of his boot heels to signify that they were finally alone.

"Tell me about your troubles, my dear, together we can solve anything." Logan's voice was sweet as honey, but it hardly fooled her. She'd taught him the art of deception well, though the student had yet to outsmart the master.

"Why don't you first tell me of the woman in the dungeons?" She had heard the whispers even before entering the castle. She should have to speak to Vestera to gauge the success of her mission.

"Her? A prisoner from Faegon, she is nothing more." The dismissive tone was light, lending little for the Queen to work with.

"Don't lie to me, Logan, it's exhausting." Her demanding tone had the desired effect. The pretty face before her morphed to one of disgust. She eyed him carefully as she disrobed with little shame. The tight leathers rolled down her thighs with ease and she kicked them to the side. Her tunic fell with it and she unwrapped her underclothes, walking through the room bare.

"If you think that your nudity could will truth from me then you've grown soft." Logan countered and it pulled a sharp laugh from the Queen's lips. She turned and was on him before he could react. His silk garments felt cool to the touch. Not a wrinkle blemished his court attire, he'd just changed then, and she ran her hands down the front of his robes until they landed comfortably in his lap.

"Are you sure you haven't spoken too soon?" Her fingers teased into the flesh hidden underneath the robe and her King gasped. "Are you sure you want to lie to me?" She captured his lips in a daring kiss, the taste of another woman was all of the proof she needed.

"She could give us information." Logan gasped, moving his body in time with her own. He was smart, a decent King, but still a man. From Cassandra's experience men, especially those who fashion themselves kings, think with their heads until a beautiful woman arrives. The high that comes with having power clouds their judgment and they become animals. They believe that they can have anyone that they pleased just because of their title.

"Did you need to put your cock in her to get that information?" It was best to get to the point. Logan wasn't any good at being subtle with her and Cassandra had little patients to chase him down for the answers that she sought.

"It certainly couldn't have hurt," was the cocky reply and Cassandra scoffed, pushing herself off her unfaithful husband. "How did you know?"

"The castle talks."

"Already? You just got home." Logan laughed as if his infidelity and their people's knowledge of it mattered little to him. Cassandra was almost certain that it didn't matter at all.

"We will have to use this." Plans were already forming in her mind. Her dear husband was an idiot at times, but it was her duty to clean up his messes and set things right. "We can use your inability to keep your hands to yourself to our advantage."

"And what of yours?" Cassandra flinched when she felt his strong body align to her back. His hands danced up her sides and cupped her breast with abandon. His mouth was at the base of her neck, leaving a wet trail up to her ear in a move that was so practiced in their bed that it almost seemed droll.

"What of mine?" There was no use in denying that she was unfaithful, though she was much more discreet than her King.

"Leon, your page. He's young and easy to mold. Just your type."

"I've never heard you complain before." Cassandra punctuated the words by turning in his arms and pushing him away. "I am going to have to see what I can salvage from this, you left her in the dungeons I hope."

"As opposed to in my bed?" The cheeky grin set her nerves ablaze, but she was much too old to be falling for such childish taunts.

"Precisely. Hand me my travel clothes."

It gave the vampire satisfaction giving her husband orders. It distracted her as his words did hold truth. He had been her page once when she'd been another man's lover, but that had been another time. She pushed the old thoughts into the darkest depths of her mind to settle with the thoughts of her humanity rested and were left untouched. She hardly remembered those days and it would do her no good to begin down that path again. She took the clothing Logan had handed her and dressed with little fanfare. If Logan was curious as to her plans he did not ask.

"I will be in the dungeons for the rest of the night should anyone ask."

"Be gentle with her, all I did was slap yours," He smiled at her, though the taunting in his tone didn't quite meet his eyes. If she hadn't known better she would have thought he looked a bit sad. "Did you ever love me?" Cassandra had thought the words had come from her own lips for a moment. They were ones she's thought often when it came to the man before her. It seemed the thought had been on his mind as well.

"Did you?" Her response was telling enough. She knew that Logan had always known. There was no love lost between them because there never had been any. "I'm looking forward to meeting your whore," she said, just for something cutting to say.

"Prisoner, my dear. Remember I call yours your page." It was a low blow, but she felt he deserved it and she let it pass. "Remember also that your pet brought her home."

There was no reason to respond to the comment and Cassandra made for the door, Logan close behind. As she suspected, there was a guard stationed at her door. The woman bowed to her Queen, never raising her eyes. "Anything you heard is not to be repeated, to anyone."

"As you command, m'lady." She was one of Wynn's then, he only ever employed those of lower rank and she wouldn't have been standing guard if he hadn't orchestrated it himself.

"Even to the keeper of secrets, am I clear?"

"Clear as the river's water, m'lady."

"The river is dry as bone, childe, I'll take that to mean that you've already told him." She didn't give the girl a chance to answer as she turned toward the dungeons, Logan keeping stride with her.

"She's one of Wynn's, where is the trouble in that? Haven't you got the man in your pocket?" They often played blind to the other's affairs, but there were times when conversations could not be avoided, though Cassandra hardly felt that this was one of the occasions.

"I'm sure I have no idea what you speak of, it also seems I have no pockets to speak of."

"She slipped that parchment from Wynn in your pocket, don't think I didn't see that." Logan eyed the hidden pocket in her pants that only she and Wynn should have known of. "That is the second secret he had brought you in under an hour. It seems our slimy snake is earning his keep after all."

"Is that so? If you put this much energy in covering your own deceit then we wouldn't have had to have our early conversation."

"I put my energy into every important task that I do. Including beautiful women." Logan leered and Cassandra had enough decorum to keep a straight face.

"There is no need for you escort me to the dungeons."

"Yes, but perhaps I enjoy the company of my dear wife and wish to spend a few fleeting moments with her."

"I am not going to let you stay with me while I talk to her."

"Talk? That's a funny way of pronouncing torture." This time a pretenses were lost and Logan wore a full smirk as his eyes danced with mirth.

They had arrived at the iron gate of the girl's cell. Even from outside, Cassandra could feel the power of the elder before her. She could not be as old than Cassandra herself, but she must be an of an age with Logan, that alone intrigued the queen.

"Leave us, Logan, I'd like some time alone with our guest."

Cassandra dismissed her lover like she would dismiss a servant. He left her side without a complaint, though she knew him well. She would have to have another talk with him after she took her time with the whore. When she was sure that he was gone, she opened the gate and stepped into the cell, letting the heavy iron swing shut behind her. Despite looking like it had been weeks since she had seen a bath or a good meal, the huntress stared her down with defiant eyes. She was seated on a small cot looking incredibly bored and not nearly miserable enough for a captive of war. Someone would have to rectify that.

"I see my husband took good care of you," Cassandra sneered, though her captive did not seem bothered by her comments.

"Your husband? I'm sorry, who are you?" She had a passive look on her face and Cassandra wasn't sure if she was being genuine. "I have only ever heard of King Logan I didn't realize he had a Queen."

Cassandra held her tongue. The huntress was obviously trying to garner a reaction from her and she would not give her the satisfaction. She wanted the world to see Logan as the leader of their cause, there was too much at stake for her name to be associated with the cause just yet, but she knew that someone of the huntress' caliber would be more knowledgeable than the average vampire. She had to find out what the woman knew. "We both know that you know more about this House than you will admit. I imagine your precious King Zentarion has trained all of his hunters and huntresses to be on the lookout for evil rogues."

"If you think I've ever had a conversation with the Great King then you must think I am a far more important than I am."

"Don't be coy," Cassandra sneered, bored of the conversation already. "I know just who you are, Gwyndolyn of House Faegon." It wasn't entirely true, but she had her suspicions. There was far more to this vampire than she let on.

"Oh you do? I wasn't aware I was more than an accomplished vampire huntress, tell me what else I am." The smug expression she wore had no place on her face.

Cassandra was through listening to her lies. She slid a small dagger from the hidden pocket in her pants, feeling the warmth of the sunspear in her hand. She moved into her captive's space and used her own body to keep her caged. She pressed the edge of the blade against the soft skin of her throat leaving a shallow cut. She was not surprised when she hardly flinched. She knew that Vestera had shackled her with sun soaked irons, but the wounds that they should have caused had already healed. Even Logan would still be sporting marks of such confines for at least a night or two had he been in her place and he was a strong vampire. It was clear that she had been trained to withstand the sun and it's harmful effects beyond what a vampire of her age could normally handle. Carefully Cassandra pushed the blade forward again, taking care to deepen the cut without doing damage to her vocal cords. She was rewarded for her efforts with the pained hiss that escaped Gwyndolyn's lips. She pulled the blade back, not willing to admit that she was impressed with the rate that the wound healed.

"Tell me what you know about this House. Tell me what your foolish King is planning." She punctuated each demand with another cut, infuriated as the gashes bled slowly before they closed and only thin, red lines remained.

"I know nothing of your house or the King's plans."

Cassandra was done toying with her prisoner. She shifted and grabbed for her hand, pulling until she had the underside of the woman's arm was exposed. Making swift cuts, Cassandra gouged jagged lines into her forearm, carving her own name deep enough that it would take nights to heal. If she wasn't going to get any information from her then she would at least inflict as much damage as she could so her husband would have to face the consequences of her wrath the next time he chose to take pleasure from the girl. This time, Gwyndolyn graced her with a blood curdling scream. She tried to wrench her arm free, not concerned that it may do further damage it, but Cassandra was already holding her in place, angling her body until it covered Gwyndolyn's, not allowing the grime on the huntress' clothes to disturb her. If she wasn't going to get any information from her she would at least take the opportunity to take her mounting aggravation out on the woman. She might not be able to get her claws on Zentarion, yet, but she would take her time with one of his own, before sending her back as warning to the cocky, power-hungry king. She was going to dismantle his empire and everything it stood for, even if she had to do it by taking out one vampire at a time.

NATALYA

The late morning sun beat down on Natalya and Emeline as they circled each other in the practice field. Nearly two weeks had passed since their post supper training with her father and not for the first time Natalya found herself sparring with Emeline after their morning chores were completed. True to her word, Emeline did not take to the art of combat quickly, though she never stepped away from the training field discouraged. Natalya threw another right jab as slowly as her patience would allow, yet Emeline still managed to seem surprised when her open palm gently smacked her cheek. They had learned in the beginning that Natalya actually forming a fist was not a good idea and the bruise on the older girl's cheek had only just healed. The fight that had followed between Natalya and her father had left the air in the farmhouse sparking with tension for nearly a week.

Archery had not been much different, though that had more to do with her weak grip. It had taken Natalya a long time to build the muscle necessary to skillfully retract and release an arrow and she hadn't expected Emeline to take to it any quicker. Often she would draw the arrow nearly half of the necessary distance before her arms would give way and the arrow would launch toward the ground. On a few occasions the arrow head would pierce the ground, but often times it lacked the force and would instead clatter to the dirt. After a particularly frustrating shooting session, Natalya had decided that they would focus on defense first and return to the bow only after the blonde could successfully protect herself.

"Remember to keep your arms up and guard your face." Natalya barked as she extended her arm in a slow right punch. Emeline's attempted block made contact for the first time and she let out a cry of startled joy, completely dropping her stance.

"Did you see that?"

Natalya couldn't help the smile that slipped passed her lips as pride swelled in her breast. "Good job Emeline, but stay focused."

Emeline simply grinned back, falling back into a defensive stance without needing to be prompted. Natalya watched carefully as the gleam in those blue eyes become more focused. Noticing the difference in concentration of her student, Natalya prepared to throw another right. Emeline blocked it again with little difficulty. While her excitement was still clear on her face she held her stance this time. They continued much in the same way; Natalya's calculated movements becoming quicker by the fraction of a second and Emeline keeping up with every other punch. They were so engrossed in their exercise that the two nearly forgot about dinner and the men. It was only when the heard the murmur of voices from the nearby field that they dropped their sparring stances and noticed the high hanging sun.

"Come on then we'd better go in. Father will be mad if we don't have dinner on the table." Natalya broke her stance first. They were practicing without weapons so they had little cleanup to worry about and Natalya ran ahead into the house to wash up quickly before heading straight to the fire. Emeline was not far behind her and she threw the leftover pork from the night before into the large soup pot. Nat made sure to add the broth she had help make that morning and the vegetables Emeline had been in charge of cutting. They worked quickly in silence as they danced around each other with a level of comfort as if they'd been doing this their whole lives. Natalya took the heavy cast iron pot from Emeline when the fire was set and began to stir. They traded places once again as Emeline handed her the bowls to set the table. They continued to work around the other until the peaceful atmosphere was broken by the men returning from the field.

"In late again?" Arthur's booming voice cut through their comfortable silence making the hairs on Natalya's neck stand up. All of the carefully chosen retorts waiting to spew from her mouth were for naught when Emeline responded for her.

"Now quit your complaining and wash up. I will not have you tracking dirt into this house. By the time you lot get that dirt off your faces dinner will be set." Emeline spoke without turning from the fire. Natalya smiled gratefully to her before fetching the water jug to fill the glasses. When she passed her father he gave her a disapproving look that clearly stated that their conversation was not over. There was simply no pleasing the man.

"How is your training going Em?" Art asked cheerfully attempting to cut the tension. "We saw you from the field, it looked like you might have even gotten a hit in on Nat."

"She's doing a great job. She's even got blocking down after today." Emeline blushed at the compliment, but nodded her agreement. The beam her brother gave her lit up her face. "If we keep working on it I'm sure she will be able to defend herself in no time."

"Well, we'll just have to hope that none of you need to." Arthur's words were final and it was obvious that the subject was closed.

"But even if the need should arise Nat has been making sure that I will be ready. She's even begun to show me how she handle her knives." Emeline, in all her optimism did not see the error in her words, but Natalya knew as soon as she spoke them that trouble was headed her way.

"Natalya Elizabeth Grahame! She is not ready for that. Nor are you skilled enough to teach her." His face was purple as all the blood rushed to it in his displeasure. It had been some time since she'd seen such anger from her father, but Natalya knew this side of him well.

"I never let her touch them! You ought to give me more credit than that! I showed her how I handle them so she might remember for when she is ready. You're always telling me how I need to be prepared and so I'm just preparing them!"

"What you teach them is not for you to decide!" Arthur yelled, his fists hitting the table as the plates and utensils clattered every which way.

"Then why don't you work with her? Obviously nothing I do is good enough!" Anger boiled in the girl's veins and it took all of her self control not to throw her water at her father.

"You will stop that right now!" Her father's mounting anger made the room feel stifling raising the temperature higher than the cook fire. Emeline tried to place a gentle hand on her shoulder, but Natalya roughly shrugged it off. Glaring at her father she fled the room for the field.

"Natalya!" Emeline's raised voice didn't even cause her to pause.

"Let the girl go," Arthur sat with his back to the door waiting for Emeline to spoon out their dinner, "if she will not act like an adult she will not eat."

Natalya had not quite been far enough from the door and she heard his last comment which only added to her rage. Natalya let her instincts take her to the archery practice field, blind rage dulling her senses. Picking up her favorite bow, she strung the arrow with the ease of drawing breath. Aiming for the heart of the target, Natalya let the arrow go, allowing the ripple of the string vibrate through her stiff body. She hardly allowed herself the time to check if she had made her mark before yanking another arrow from the ground beside her and firing off again. A dozen arrows found their mark, two hitting dead center, the latter splintering the former. The aching in Natalya's muscles slowed her down and it wasn't until she let her bow slip from her grasp and fall to the dirt that she noticed her vision was blurred by tears. She hated how her father treated her like a complete child, but even more so she hated how weak it made her feel.

"Nat!" Emeline's voice brought her out of her haze, the blonde looked ethereal in the high noon sun. The loving expression made memories of her mother's kindness flood the girl, causing the tears of anger to burst and turn into tears of sadness. "What's wrong?"

Natalya threw herself into waiting arms. The force of her impact sent them sinking to the ground, Emeline's embrace never faltering. Sobs racked through the smaller girl leaving her shaking and shivering. The girls sat until the warmth of the sun faded and the ground became cold. Natalya's tears had long since dried, but exhaustion had kept her from moving and Emeline was content to sit with her. While she would periodically rub her back and comb her fingers through the short brown hair, she remained silent.

"They'll be wanting supper soon. Would you like me to take your food up to you?" Emeline leaned in to catch her response. Nat's mop of curls a mess, pressed into her shoulder.

"Yes, please."

"Go on then, I'll start up the hot water and draw you a bath."

"Thank you," and after a moment she added, "you have been nothing, but kind and I've been acting like a spoiled child."

"Nonsense, you're a joy to have here, now go on." Natalya let herself be picked up and pushed toward the house. "Now go up and get the fire in the washroom going and I'll be there before you know it."

Natalya lacked the words to thank the woman who was steadily becoming like a mother figure to her. As she busied herself at the hearth, Natalya vowed to do everything in her power to show Emeline just how much her kindness meant.

She set to work setting up the fire in the cozy washroom. Setting up the logs was hard work and she had worked up a sweat by the time she had a roaring fire sitting below the empty caldron in the hearth. A knock at the door signaled Emeline with a bucket of water and between the two of them they were able to heat up enough water to fill the tub. She was soaking in the hot water before the sun began to set. Natalya sank back into the suds as Emeline's thin fingers massaged through her scalp.

"I know he might not act like it, but your father does really love you." Emeline spoke in her calming tone which meant that she was in for a lecture. She loved the girl dearly, but she had heard enough about how her father supposedly loved her and how Emeline thought him training her to protect herself was sweet. If she had to listen to one more of those talks she knew that she would lose her composure and Emeline did not deserve that.

Searching for a distraction, Natalya asked the first question that came to her mind. "Emeline, what really happened to your husband?"

"I'm sorry?" The hands in her hair pulled away and she instantly wished she could take back the words.

"I'm sorry, I just wanted to learn more about him. You never talk about him and I thought it would be nice to do something to remember him by." Emeline's eyes narrowed but her hands returned to massaging her scalp.

"He was a good man. You would have liked him. He was tall and handsome. He had the clearest blue eyes, he was perfect. He would spend his days in the farm and still come home energized and committed to me. I would wake up to breakfast on the weekends and last summer we would sleep under the stars in the meadow."

"It sounds like you really loved him."

"I still do. It's crazy, but I know he's still out there. Everyone says he must be dead, but wouldn't I feel it?"

"I'm sure you would." Natalya watched as her best friend stood and began pacing the small room. The relaxing atmosphere was gone for the night.

Emeline was the nicest person she had ever met. She had opened up her door to them and never asked them for anything in return beyond helping to harvest the food that would sustain them through the winter. Natalya knew then that she had to do everything in her power to make Emeline happy. She deserved so much and all life ever gave her was struggle and heartache. Natalya thought that she'd had a rough life, but she could not imagine losing a love as true as Emeline's. She had lost the opportunity to find that love, but there would be others for her. She was still young, as was Emeline, but she feared that the woman would never allow herself to find happiness again. She knew that her friend would never truly heal from this, she had seen how broken it had made her father and she would not let that happen to the girl who had given her so much. Emeline had lost the love of her life and no one believed her that he was still alive, but Emeline herself. For the first time Natalya felt that she had a purpose in life. She loved Emeline, she was like family and she was going to do everything in her power to show her just how much the kindness she had shown her truly meant. She was going to find her husband and bring happiness back into Emeline's life.

"The water is still hot if you want to soak for a bit. I can take care of the kitchen." Emeline stopped pacing to give her one of her sweet smiles.

"Thank you, you are too kind." Natalya stepped out of the water and took the offered towel that Emeline had left to warm by the fire. She dried off quickly and slid into the nightdress that Emeline had thoughtfully left out for her. She made sure to set a new one down before going to the kitchen to tidy up. Emeline had left the cleaning to be finished later in order to take care of her.

She worked tirelessly to scrub the large pot that held their supper. They were going to be roasting pig in the morning so they would need the hearth set with the spit over readied logs. The utensils from supper were soaking in a bucket and Natalya worked on them next. She scrubbed until her fingers were raw and she'd worked up such a good sweat that her bath hadn't been necessary. She worked in the kitchen until the sun had fully set and the sounds of the animals on the farm settling down filled the empty space. She trudged up the stairs feeling bone tired to find Emeline sound asleep in their bed. Working in the kitchen had been exhausting and she was sure that as soon her head hit the pillow she would fall asleep and yet as soon as she settled down sleep evaded her.

She spent the next hour laying awake awash in moonlight devising a timetable to look for Emeline's husband. She would need time to gather information and starting in the place where he had been last scene would be the best way to begin. According to what she knew, John had gone into the forest to hunt and forage for food and had never returned home. Knowing all too well her father's feelings on Mordin Forest, she saw the only way to accomplish this task was to do so in dead of the night. The soft rise and fall of Emeline's breathing was enough to give Natalya the notion to start then. She wouldn't want to tell her friend of her plan. If she did not succeed that would bring unnecessary strife on her already delicate heart. Steeling herself to commit to the decision, Natalya slipped from the warmth of the bed into the brisk autumn air. Her dagger and bow and arrows were still on the field with the rest of the duller practice equipment, it would be easy enough to collect them without waking the house.

Donning her travel garb, Natalya tied her wayward curls as tightly to her scalp as she could manage. She would only be gone for a few hours so there was no reason to pack any provisions. She looked back to check on Emeline, noting the easy rise and fall of her sleeping form. Her nerves would cause her to talk herself out of leaving and that would not do. She carefully opened their bedroom door, using her training to move without sound. The latch for the door was heavy and she gently released the handle, grateful when it barely made a sound. She passed her father's room next, making her steps light as air with little issue. More than comfortable with the layout of her new home, she missed every noisy step and eased open the old wood door. Even though she was doing her best to move silently the iron hinges complained louder than a drum call and Natalya stopped, paralyzed with fear. She was sure she and had been caught and she feared the worse. Minutes passed where the only noise was the crickets outside and Natalya's own heavy breathing. When no answering noise came, she fled to the field to snatch up her dagger and into the forest beyond.

The forest was thicker than those next to Ash and for a moment Natalya felt true fear. The rough bark of the thick trunks seemed to be patterned in the shapes of faces which watched the young girl crouch and skulk through the uneven terrain. A stray branch snagged at her shirt and Natalya a muffled her scream with her hand clapped firmly over her mouth. The many warnings of her overprotective father swam in her thoughts as she realized that she had no way of knowing where to start her search. Turning around slowly, she found that all of the trees looked the same. If it hadn't been night she could have tracked her own steps back, but she could hardly see in the dark. Panic set in then and she shut her eyes tight, allowing her breathing to slow. She would never find her way out if she let her fear overpower her senses.

"What's this?" The smooth sound of a cold male voice shocked Natalya and the girl whirled around to face a dirty looking man with strange green eyes. "A human out all alone?"

He circled her prone form and it took all of her strength for Natalya to stand up from the ground her hand twitching over her dagger.

"I wouldn't bother, child." The man hissed, his teeth bared revealing sharp fang like teeth.

"What are you?" Natalya asked awed, all thoughts of her weapons gone. Hypnotic green eyes drew her in making her lean closer to the strange individual. "You're not human."

"You're quite good at acting calm for such a scared little girl." The sneer made her snap out of the trance and her body instinctively reeled back.

"I'm not scared!" Even to her own ears it was a lie. She sounded like a child, quivering in her boots and the thought made her angry. Anger was something she could work with.

"Lie." A thin finger came up to stroke her cheek, wiping away a stray tear she hadn't known that she'd shed. Shivering, she shrank into herself trying to escape the touch. "Where do you think you're going?"

He grabbed her and held on. No noise escaped Natalya's mouth as strong hands wound around her throat. Natalya's hands clawed at the grip around her throat pulling at them and trying to draw in air. Natalya felt her will to fight draining like the air leaving her lungs. She thought she must be screaming, but no noise invaded her ears and panic was replaced by omission. The already dark forest became fuzzy and a blanket of pure black ate at her vision plummeting her into unconsciousness.

"Get away from her!" Emeline's voice rang out, pure as fresh fallen snow. The grip on Natalya's throat instantly disappeared. Air raced into her lungs filling them again and made the world spin. Gasping and struggling for air Natalya focused all of her energy to regaining her sight, surprised when she was met with an infuriated Emeline holding the man at the point of her dagger.

"What an interesting scent," the creature smirked, licking his lips in anticipation of his up and coming meal, "you will taste so much better than the brat."

"I said get away from her!" Emeline danced around him keeping him an arm's length away.

"Emeline get back, he's not human." Her voice sounded strangled to her own ears. The words seemed to startle the blonde, but her resolve was not shaken.

The creature moved too fast for Natalya to track. She watched horrified, her body immobile as her mind tried to process what she was seeing. The thing flew through the air at a speed that was certainly inhuman and crashed into Emeline, leaving them sprawled on the dirt. They were struggling before her eyes and she was too terrified to move. Emeline was crying out and Natalya watched as the creature's sharp fang-like teeth sank into the girl's pale skin. Emeline dropped the weapon in her hand and Natalya knew then that there was no hope. She hadn't really believed that Emeline would be able to fight off the beast, but there had been hopeful before the dagger fell to the ground.

Natalya watched in horror as she struggled to force her body into action. If she could just get to the dagger then she could help. As she reached forward she looked up and her eyes made contact with Emeline and she was shocked still once more. Those blue eyes which were normally so warm were wide as blood dripped from the creature's mouth and down her neck. Natalya's own cries fell on deaf ears and she found herself watching helplessly from the sidelines.

Emeline recovered from her shock quickly and finally began to fight back. Natalya watched as she angled her limbs to kick and punch at the horrifying creature and Natalya was absolutely no help. After all she'd been training for she couldn't even help her friend. Natalya watched as the small amount of training she'd given Emeline helped her lay glancing blows on unmoved flesh as the monster continued to cling to her neck. With one more frustrated yell Emeline caught her captors arm in her flailing hand doing her best to bite it back. Her teeth made contact and she viciously ripped at his skin. The shock of her retaliation forced the thing to gasp, effectively setting Emeline loose. Finally free, Emeline fell to the ground her body drained of energy and blood. The creature turned and ran without so much as a look behind him and Natalya was left to watch her dying friend in shock.

Finally she found it in herself to move and she scrambled to her friend's side. Emeline was barely breathing and Natalya feared the worst. She ripped part of her tunic to put pressure on the wound and the pained gasp that left her lips made her wish she could do more. Instead she sat in the blood drenched dirt silently sobbing over her dying friend.

COHEN

Cohen absolutely hated being away from his queen for so long. Normally two weeks was nothing to vampire, but Cohen hadn't left Reagan for this long in decades. That last trip hadn't been terrible, but he wasn't as lucky this time. Between avoiding Anya and her incessant remarks towards Darius, and Nirosh's perpetual silence it was a wonder that they could be trusted to accomplish anything. The party that Queen Reagan had dispatched was small, though not without power. They were the most elite of her Council and Queensguard and while she had many loyal to her Cohen felt that his Queen was in danger without them by her side.

He wasn't the only one who felt that way. Cohen knew that Anya had greatly disapproved of leaving her paramour's side with arguably two of the most important people, entrusted with guarding the queen. It was the only thing they could agree on, but Reagan's word was law. Cohen had taken his orders graciously, from the irritated looks Reagan had given Anya before they left, she had not. He might have felt better about the whole thing if they had turned something up, but so far their jaunt in the woods had supplied them with no new information about the rogue queen. Reagan would be far less than pleased.

They moved by day and moonlight. Anya was the youngest among them and even she, at just over eight decades, could withstand the sun for at least a few hours total a day and so the four were making good time, even if they had nothing to show for it.

"Should we not be heading back?" Anya asked, obviously trying for disinterested though her tone deceived no one.

"For the last time, Anya, we had our orders to scout the area for any signs of rogue activity. I will not return to my Queen with no new information." Cohen replied his tone even though the prickle of anger was hard to miss.

"And for the last time Cohen, Reagan put me in charge of this mission."

Anya was fast, but Cohen was faster. He had her pinned to a tree with his fangs dangerously close to her neck before she could escape him. He would not hurt her, of course. It was a show of dominance of, which he was sure the Queen's lover knew.

"I do not presume to understand why My Lady takes you to her bed, but know this, you will never gain by throwing your relationship in my face."

"Jealous?" Never one to back down, Anya baited him on.

"You could never understand." It was neither answer nor omission. Cohen shoved himself away from the woman using much more force than necessary. He distracted himself from her furious gaze by looking to the two men beside them who were waiting patiently. They had the manners to pretend they had not just been gawking at the scene before them. "We are not to return until we have news for the Queen. We should push on if we want to go home soon."

Cohen felt Darius fall into line beside him. Darius had once been a rogue, something Anya loved to remind anyone who would listen, and given her history with the rogues it was no wonder that the girl would not trust him. At first Cohen had agreed with the brunette. Having a rogue in their ranks had seemed too big of a risk to take. He had come along not long after Reagan's paramour had joined them and Reagan's rule, while absolute, had still been challenged by many of her people. He had proven his loyalties time and again, however, and Cohen considered Darius a good friend and a valued asset to their house.

"You seem troubled, m'lord." Darius' abilities often seemed invasive to most, but Cohen had always enjoyed the blunt way the dark vampire spoke. It certainly left for less drama, something any individual whom was forced to spend any amount of time with Anya could appreciate.

"Not so, Darius, only sick for home."

"It has been too long since you have left the Queen's side. And to think, what the good that came of the last time," he said with a private smile.

"You speak out of turn, Darius." He was not a vampire turned by a king or queen. He did not have title nor cause to be so familiar with one of the vampire noble class. In private, Cohen wouldn't have minded the comment, but with Anya so close by it would be unbecoming.

"I speak as a friend, m'lord. I apologize if I have committed offense." There was no regret in his tone, it didn't take one gift with the art of reading auras to see that.

"Indeed. I believe others in our party could do without the Queen's company."

"Now who speaks out of turn?" His face was blank as the new moon's night though humor danced in his black eyes.

"You are too right." Cohen assented, his eyes never leaving the path ahead, though he nodded toward his companion, a true smile playing at his thin lips.

"I know the bond you share with our Queen is one of love, I don't need to hold magic to see it, but I have always told Anya that she has nothing to fear."

"You presume to understand things you know nothing of, my friend, I would be careful where you tread." Cohen warned, glancing back to Anya and Nirosh who seemed to be paying them no mind.

"I know whatever it is that you and m'lady share is deeper than blood." Darius had never feared speaking his mind, it was how he had risen through the ranks so quickly despite his low birth. Reagan always enjoyed a council filled with strong minds.

"Indeed, now must we continue this talk? I fear much more and we will insight further rage from the brat."

"Of course m'lord." Darius inclined his head in a slight bow and once more Cohen was left with his own thoughts.

The last time Cohen had been sent from his Queen's side had been days after Anya's rebirth. There had been reports of rogues in their land and Cohen had gone with Nirosh and a small group of vampires that now made up the Queen's personal guard. That had been the night that they had found Darius. Just a boy in size and demeanor, he had been left by the other rogues for dead. It had been Cohen's word that had spared him for questioning. He hardly knew if Darius remembered much of his rescue and transport. He had been a beaten mess. It had taken his blood to reveal to Reagan that he had been a servant to a rich merchant, who was ambushed and turned against his will by Cassandra, herself. Reagan had worked with him personally, absolving him of sin and welcoming him into their home.

"Do you smell that, m'lord?" Cohen heard the question just as his sense were assaulted with the smell of pure, human fear.

"It's this way!" Anya hissed, pointing even farther from the direction of the castle, toward the edge of the forest. They were well out of their land by then and completely in the right if they chose to turn around for home, but Cohen had never been that kind of person.

"Everyone be careful, we don't know how many there are," Nirosh cautioned. He spoke very little and Cohen knew better than to dismiss his warnings. Even Anya seemed to understand the severity of the situation and nodded, squaring her shoulders preparing for a fight.

In any case of a human being attacked the protocol was always the same; save the human, but capture or kill the rogues at all cost. Normally it helped to have a human hunter with them, though Lunaries lacked in many strong allies and those that worked out of the Capitol were strictly for hire. Even if they'd had the money or persuasive power to higher a human liaison, they were expected to drop any and all jobs not related to the high King's command and return to Faegon when necessary. Reagan had spent many a night with the council discussing the benefits of acquiring a hired human, but they all agreed that it was an option which the benefits did not outweigh the risks. They had no coin nor bartering power to hire one of Faegon's human hunters and they had so few allies that none of the other houses would come to their aid. There were humans in their House whose children showed interest in becoming human liaisons; they were beginning their training with Lord Nirosh and Darius, but it would be years until they were ready. Even if they were strong enough, their House still didn't have the sway to give them any power in the hunter community.

Despite their differences, Cohen and Anya fell into line side-by-side as they'd practiced since the girl had first been turned. Nirosh had a hand in training every vampire who the Queen deemed necessary, but Reagan had seen to it that her lover had been trained by Cohen personally. Whatever animosity they felt for each other instantly melted in the face of a shared threat. Darius and Nirosh brought up the rear. Together the four moved as one. They swept through the trees at such a speed that they cut through the brush, spearheading the way toward the overwhelming scent. Cohen could only smell one vampire, though there seemed to be a second human that hadn't been there moments before. They were only fifty meters off at most and Cohen was sure they would make it in time. A shift in the breeze nearly made the strong vampire become sick with the scent of pure agony. One of the human's was being bit and drained and if the sudden, harsh cries were any indicator, the vampire inflicting the torture was being purposefully cruel, dampening any aphrodisiac that could have eased her pain. Breaking form, Cohen raced toward the smell, letting sharp branches scratch at his thin skin, ignoring the pain as cuts formed and healed.

A quick look told him that Anya had followed his lead, running in an arch in the other direction. She would be prepared to ambush the vampire from the other side while the last of their party would come at them from the middle. All four broke through the last of the trees and landed in the clearing just in time to hear the piercing scream that ripped through the still night. The overwhelming mix of the sharp noise, and the flickering of the human's scent until it disappeared entirely, shocked the group into paralysis. Before them lay a very pale woman with hair that shone bright like the sun fanned about her. It was soaked in her own blood making a grisly scene. Her thin face was laying in a younger girl's lap, as shaking hands fluttered over her closed eyes. The younger girl seemed to be in shock. Her own appearance wasn't much better. Her clothes were streaked with blood though it wasn't clear whose it was. She was shaking, though it seemed as if she was forcing her body to hold together as her thin fingers traced any pulse point that she could reach. She was so consumed by her futile search for life that she hardly seemed to notice the vampires that surrounded her.

Anya and Nirosh were the first to move, taking off in the direction of the rogue's stench. It was only then that the human seemed to notice her audience.

The younger girl moved her friend's head gently before jumping to her feet. She moved with such speed and agility that a human could only posses in times of great fear and stress and Cohen took the offensive instinct in stride. Whomever she was, she was well trained despite her age. Her eyes were cold. The look was harder than one any child her age should know. She'd known great loss before this moment, of that Cohen was sure. There was no immediate danger and the vampire took a risk, dropping his dagger and slowly raising his hand. The sharp steel echoed off the packed dirt and in the background he could hear Darius follow his lead.

"Get back." Her voice was strong, more imposing than Cohen expected and instantly he found respect bubble up in the pit of his abdomen, slowly rising up his chest and choking his throat.

"We mean you no harm." Darius' voice was deep, calm as always and the girl flinched back, not sure where to keep her focus. Her eyes darted back and forth between the men, her anger fueled facade of superiority wavered and Cohen found his voice again.

"We are nothing like the creature that attacked your friend." It wasn't a lie, entirely.

"Don't lie to me!" The anguished cry was Cohen's only warning before the brunette launched herself forward. She was fast, but nothing could beat the speed of a vampire. Cohen had her in his grasp and he disarmed her just as quickly. She was not about to relent, however, and he soon found her trying to wriggle loose from her prison between his chest and solid arms. "Let me go!"

"If you tell us what happened, we can help." Cohen tried to soothe this time, but it only managed to reward him with a swift kick in the shin. It stung more than he had expected and he was momentarily impressed before he was struck again and the dull pain turned to annoyance.

"Let me, m'lord." Darius moved forward toward the girl. The concentrated look that clouded his face when he began to use his magic made its home in his stance and Cohen felt confident that they would begin to get their answers.

"Get away from me," the girl shouted.

"It's not working." Darius flinched back as the girl made to jump at him, but Cohen firmed his grip. "My magic is being blocked."

Anya and Nirosh came through the trees then, the woman's eyes narrowed on the scene, though she managed to hold her tongue. Darius moved from their confusing charge to the pale body of the other girl. Her hand twitched, startling everyone in the clearing.

"She's alive?" The human gasped, stilling completely for the first time. Cohen's gripped slack just enough for her to break free and trip forward to her friend.

"Not alive, no." Anya sighed, rubbing hand over face with more agitation than strictly necessary. "Well, more alive than that rogue anyway."

"You killed him?" Darius asked, careful to keep his tone neutral as to not raise Anya's ire.

"Not on purpose, he struggled, but he was weak. I doubt he'd eaten anything for nights before now." Anya seemed more interested in the scene before them to argue with Darius and for that Cohen was glad.

"What do you mean, not alive? She's moving!" The girl cried, bringing full attention to herself again. She spoke with the air of one who was used to getting their way and Cohen briefly wondered if they were in the presence of human royalty, but he brushed the thought aside. No one from the human royal family had stepped foot in Mordin forest in centuries, not since long before Cohen had even been born.

"She is undead, child. She is one of us." Nirosh spoke, taking pity on the girl. "She must be an outsider from the West. The humans there know nothing of us. They have long since forgotten the vampires on their border."

"Vampires? What does that mean?" The whispered question floated between the reconnaissance team, though none offered up an explanation.

"We must head back, the Queen will understand." Cohen decided, leaning down to pick up the pale girl. She'd been turn by a rogue and they'd found her. She was his responsibility now. As soon as she woke she would go through the rights and be a sworn sister of House Lunaries. It would not due to allow more harm to come to his charge.

"And the human?" Darius deferred to him, ignoring the increasing glare spreading across Anya's pretty features.

"We leave her. She's not our concern," Anya's tone was cool, meant to brook no argument

"You're not taking Emeline without me!"

"Anya don't be so petty. She is under our care as well." Nirosh spoke and the Queen's lover had the sense to bow her head in respect. His pale eyes fell on the human and the girl flinched back.

"You are brave, for a human."

"Are you sure this is wise?" Anya asked, proving just how much she detested the idea. She could never willingly look to Cohen as an ally unless she was desperate.

"She will be needed for questioning," Cohen reminded. Anya's glare deepened, but she refrained from continuing. All the while, Cohen felt the young girls eyes on them. She was watching them, no doubt learning as much as she could about them just by observing. Whomever had taught this girl had done a very good job. Cohen wasn't sure if he ought to be impressed or annoyed. It would make their work all the more difficult if she fought and resisted at every turn.

He started toward their lands leaving the others to take control of the girl. There was some shuffling and grunts from the men, but when Cohen turned to look back at them, Nirosh and Darius flanked the girl while Anya took the rear. Both men had their hands on her arms, effectively keeping her in line. It would have been comical, had he not just had to hold the same small girl with most of his strength just moments before. No harm would befall the girl in their care, unless of course she hurt herself attempting to fight them. The angry human had no knowledge of them or their kind a such ignorance would get her killed.

"Where are you talking me?" The girl screamed, louder than Cohen would have liked. There still could be rogues nearby and it would best not to attract more. He was about to say so, but Darius spoke calmly.

"A safe place. What is your name? We can't keep calling you girl or human." Darius coaxed and she shied away from his gaze.

"You think I am giving you my name, you're not just a monster, you're an insane one."

"If you continue to yell, more of those monsters will show up and they will actually hurt you," Anya stated casually.

"Leave the human alone," Nirosh sighed, sounding rather bored of their verbal sparring. Sometimes Cohen wondered why an elder of his age and caliber bothered himself with them, even Cohen was merely a childe in his eyes, but he was loyal to Reagan and for that he was grateful.

"She's a human, a stupid one at that," Anya snorted, "why else would she be in the woods."

"You know I can hear you, right? And stop calling me human."

"Well, we could call you by your name, if we knew it," Cohen threw out conversationally, hoping it push the girl into talking.

"Natalya," the girl bit out. "Now where are you taking me?"

"Well, Natalya, my name is Lord Cohen, that would be Lord Nirosh to your left and Commander Darius to your right. The cranky one behind you is Lady Anya. We are taking you to our home, to our queen."

"Enough talk, we'll only attracted more rogues." Anya hissed.

Cohen adjusted his grip on the frail body in his arms. Emeline, as she'd been called, was no longer moving. While she held no pulse, her eyes were flickering beneath their shuttered lids and she seemed to be fast asleep. Rebirth took a large toll on the body and while it was rare for one to not make it, the girl did not seem to be faring well. Her best hope would be for their swift return, one that Cohen was certain to provide. It was not often that rogues turned humans, the girl's own ordeal was bizarre at best and Cohen knew Reagan would be expecting answers.

Anya was blessedly silent and even the other girl, Natalya, seemed to understand the gravity of the situation. She was obviously displeased with him holding her friend, but it seemed that she accepted that she was safer with them than without them and she trudged along silently. Nirosh kept behind them to keep an eye on the skittish human and Darius kept to his side while Anya took the lead. They weren't terribly far from home, but with a human and a newly reborn childe it would take them at least four or five days to return.

The trees surrounding them had thick trunks and easily sheltered them from the oncoming sunlight overhead. It would be hours until daylight, but Cohen had a feeling that they would need to stop much sooner. They were trained to survive days without sleep, but the young human was obviously tired. It was late into the night and it was no wonder that her feet dragged and she seemed to fade in and out of sleep as she slowly shuffled along. Cohen could only keep watch over one girl at a time and he eased up on his pace until he came up along stride Nirosh.

"I will watch her, if you don't mind." Cohen nodded toward Natalya and the silent Master of Arms held out his arms to receive the childe. She was light and it was easy for Cohen to gently place her in his arms. Natalya seemed to notice the shift and she looked at Cohen with guarded curiosity as he moved to walk beside her. "When was the last time you slept?"

"Last night," Natalya said, pausing as if she was stopping herself from answering. Cohen let her think it over, not willing to push her this time. He was rewarded for his patients. "I came out here because I couldn't sleep. She wasn't supposed to follow."

"She will be alright. She is going through what my people call rebirth. When a human and a vampire share blood the human begins to change until they are no longer human. Your friend seems worse for wear now, but she will heal with time."

"How do I know you're not lying? How do you know that you won't hurt us?" She was strong even in the face of danger and Cohen could admire that about her.

"You don't, not really. I could tell you that you have nothing to fear. It would be the truth, but you are a smart girl. I can tell you're not the type to blindly believe everything you're told. You will either come to find that we mean you no harm and you are both safe in our care or you will fight us until you push it too far and then, well that's an outcome that I'd rather not consider."

"I can't tell if you're being brutally honest or if you're trying to lull me into trusting you to enact some darker plan," the sarcasm was hard to miss and Cohen had to keep himself from laughing, he didn't think Natalya would appreciate that much.

"Vampires might be immortal, but that doesn't mean I'm a patient man. I am not the type to play with my food, my dear. If I wanted something from you I would have already seen to it." He flashed her a smile with just enough fang to make the girl glare back. She was either idiotically stubborn or fearless. He couldn't quite tell which, but he found himself warming to the girl nonetheless.

"My father will be looking for us, and her brother. She lost her husband to these woods and I lost my mother. They will come for you with everything they have."

"I'm sorry for your losses. I have lost my own kin to these woods, I know the pain that comes with it, though I had more closure than I'm sure you had. All that aside, your father and her brother will not find us. It is the dead of night and before the sun rises we will be deep enough in the woods that they will never gain on us. When your friend is healed we can search for them and reunite you, but until we know that she will be safe then it is my duty to not only care for her, but for you as well."

"So you will let us go?" There was a lick of hope in her words and Cohen was struck with just how young this girl must be. She put on the face of a fearless adult, but she still had a child's heart.

"Yes. It might turn out that Emeline will stay. A vampire, especially one newly bit will not survive in the human world. The sun is lethal to our kind. The older you are and the more exposure you allow yourself to it then you might build a slight resistance, but it is still deadly. She will never be able to live as the humans do again."

"How could you call that a life? To never feel the sun again…" She became silent again and Cohen felt pity for her. She was a strong and stubborn girl, but it was clear that she did not believe that her friend was cut from the same cloth. She was clearly afraid that her friend would not be able to survive in their world and he felt personally responsible for reassuring her that he would protect them.

"You adapt and if you are strong you learn to savor the short moments which you are able to bask in the sun."

The answer seemed to end the girl's endless questions and she fell silent besides him. The others continued their march without word. Even Anya was being remarkably well behaved. It seemed that the presence of this strange human reminded her to maintain a certain level of decorum. If only she would remember that when they arrived home, then maybe the mounting tension in Lunaries' upper ranks would start to subside. Movement at his side brought his eyes back to the girl. She was glaring at the back of Darius' head as if the man had somehow offended her. The head guardsman turned to look at her, the queer look he got when he was using his magic clouding his face. Natalya stopped walking and flinched back as if he had struck her. Darius hardly seemed bothered by her reaction, his eyes more puzzled than concerned. Cohen would have to keep an eye on the two of them, and especially on Natalya. There was no doubt in his mind that the human girl held magic, whether she knew it was the question. Even if their mission seemingly ended in failure, Cohen wasn't so sure that he was returning to his queen as empty handed as he had first believed.

ARTHUR

The warm harvest sun poured through the windows reminding Arthur that he'd forgotten to close the drapes the night before. His body ached from the work of a life long behind him and he grunted as he rose from the bed. He stretched his limbs until a satisfying pop told him that he was ready to start his day. The house was silent despite the late hour. That in it of itself was something to cause worry, Nat didn't know how to be quiet even if it could kill her and Emeline often could be found humming as she did the morning chores.

Arthur grabbed for his underclothes and linen breeches like a blind man. He hurried to lace his pants and failed to do so twice before he became so irritated that he simply slipped on a tunic to hide the undone strings.

"Art!" The panic that invaded his senses felt like a long lost friend or a jilted lover as it tore through his body and suffocated his lungs forcing him to breath in short gasps. He hardly heard when Art came tumbling out of his own room sleepy-eyed and scared.

"What? What's wrong?" The boy's attire didn't seem to fare better than his own and Arthur's paternal instincts finally kicked in. With much steadier hands he was able to lace up his trousers and duck back into his room for his boots.

"Doesn't the house seem a little too quiet? Where are the girls?" Realization passed over Art's face as he went back into his own room to get on his outer clothes.

"We should search out the barn before we get too worked up, yes?" The boy asked and Arthur did his best to hold back his aggravation. He knew that the young man had lived a charmed life, that John's disappearance had been his first experience with losing a loved one to Mordin, but Arthur was more than certain that he knew what had happened to the girls.

"We check the woods first. Nat was mad at me last night and she would have known that the one way to get back at me to prove her stupid point would be to take Emeline into the woods to look for John." Art ran off ahead, followed by Arthur's heavier steps. He stopped in the kitchen to pick up a hard loaf of bread and a block of cheese. "Put that away, boy, we have no time for breakfast."

"If we are to go looking through the woods for my sister and your daughter I think it's best we pack provisions." Chin up, the boy looked older and younger in the same moment and Arthur sighed knowing he was right.

"Fine, but we make haste. I am not wasting any daylight."

"I'm sure they're fine. Maybe we should get some of the townspeople involved? A lot of them helped when John went missing."

Flashes of taunts and jeers from his past assaulted Arthur's memory without permission. When he'd lost Elizabeth he'd already been treated as an outsider in Ash. Like his own village it was hard for someone not born within the walls to fit in. Elizabeth's family ties were the only thing keeping them from being run out immediately on sight when they'd first arrived and when it was obvious that she wasn't coming back it was the only thing keeping Arthur and Natalia from being forced from their home. The village had tried to be tolerant of them. Arthur knew that they'd been at least cordial for the sake of his young daughter, but his insistence that the forest needed to be razed was what had really pushed them over the line. Arthur could see now where he had gone wrong he had relied on others and that had been his downfall.

"No, we will not be going into the village proper. We are wasting time!" The pitch of his voice set the young boy on edge. The tightness of his posture and the way his body leaned away from Arthur reminded him so much of Natalya in the old days that it hurt. He'd been drunk more often than not when her mother had first gone. She'd been unresponsive to just about anyone, including all of their household staff and she'd only smile with him. He'd been so consumed by his anger that he'd missed what his daughter had needed most and taken his rage out on her. "I'm sorry, I'm just worried."

"I know, I am too." Art relaxed, picking up the rest of the food. "Let's go."

The transformation he saw before his eyes made Arthur pause. Where a young scared reminder of his own child stood a strong man appeared. His jaw was set in a look that Arthur often saw reflected back at him and the hunch in his shoulders straightened until his posture looked almost painful. A curt nod jumpstarted Art and the two made from the house and into the field at a hurried pace. The sun was high in the sky and Arthur cursed the lost time. Just as he had suspected, a quick check of the cellar and the barn turned up nothing and the worried Art look had thrown him only fueled

Arthur to keep going.

They entered the forest with caution. Arthur took the lead, moving carefully to avoid roots underfoot and wide branches overhead. Art was fast in picking up the pace, moving like his namesake moved, mirroring each step. They worked in silence, Arthur's eyes trained ahead and on the ground. He could see his daughter's steps, small and barely there. He'd taught her well. It nearly made him proud to see, but it made it harder to track them. The prints beside her were much darker, obviously from someone who wasn't accustomed to hiding her own tracks. They were small as well, not suggesting that much weight was behind each step. It was more than enough proof for Arthur that Emeline had been with his daughter.

"I heard a noise. This way." Art motioned away from the path that they were tracking.

The boy was chasing a false lead. Arthur would have told him as much if the boy had given him the time, but it was obvious that he was already tuning out the rest of the forest, focusing on the sound. Cursing under his breath, Arthur took off after him. He kept enough distance between them should they get ambushed they couldn't be taken at once. Arthur pushed his aggravation behind him doing his best to focus on whatever it was that Art had heard. At first only the natural sounds of the forest seemed to drift past his ears in waves. He could hear a small animal to their left upsetting an overgrown patch of weeds. To the right a bird called out singing in time with another which must have been just above Arthur's head. If he listened close enough he thought he might be able to locate a thin stream just a little ways forward and to the right.

Whatever noise Art had heard was long gone, of that Arthur was sure. They were wasting precious time on the boy's foolish whims and he was prepared to say as such when he caught up to him. Despite her rebellious nature, Nat had always taken her father's lead in such situations. The man found himself sorely missing his daughter. Then he remembered that it was her childishness that had brought them into the forest in the first place and familiar anger returned. Cursing the ways of the youth, Arthur prepared himself to catch up with Art and give him a good telling off. A soft crack of a branch made every hair on Arthur's body stand on end. The boy in front paused then too, their collective focus settled toward the dense trees where the sound had originated.

"Keep back." Arthur warned. His knife slid from its holster with ease. He crouched low, his back bowed so to keep out of sight. He watched his footing and moved through the leaves in turn, dancing through the gnarled roots in a practiced motion. Arthur let his body move with the world around him. He placed each step deliberately and with a purpose solely meant to bring his daughter back to him.

He saw the creature before him through the trees. At first it looked like a woman, dirty and deranged. Clumps of her hair were missing like the sick people Arthur had seen in his youth when a monstrous plague had taken nearly half the lives of the people of Sylvine. Her skin was pale, her eyes empty, but when she turned to look at Arthur he knew she was not human. She was a monster. A gasp from behind signaled Art's entrance. The ugly woman had long fang like teeth protruding from her cracked lips. Art looked at her in pure horror and Arthur wished he had the chance to tell the boy that this was what was out there. This was the reason he trained Nat so hard and the same reason that he hated Mordin Forest with such a passion. All such sentiments were brushed to the side when the monster made to jump forward to attack them. Art's yell nearly distracted Arthur from the perfect strike and he felt the grime caked claw sink into his arm at the same moment that the tip of his blade made contact with the side of her other arm. Blood spilled free from both parties as Arthur made for another cut, this time higher up toward the creature's neck.

"Sever the head, stop the creature!" Arthur yelled through his struggle as Art continued to act as a bystander, helpless and alone. "Never let them bite you!"

The creature lunged again, as if the cuts to her arm had meant nothing to her. Her blood did not run quite as quickly as Arthur's and the man knew that the cut in his own arm would soon need attention. They danced the dance of predator and prey, as Arthur landed blow after blow. She was faster than him and obviously stronger, he was sure, but she was crazed and seemed more content to attempt to bite than to kill. Arthur's blade rained down on her paper thin skin revealing that her blood did in fact run red and deep. Each cut seemed to slow her more, though the creature didn't even seem to realize it was happening.

If Arthur was ever forced to admit his greatest weakness he would never pick pride. Perhaps he would say it was his judgment; many of his past choices seemed to point to his lack of foresight. Perhaps, in a truly desperate moment, he might admit that he was getting older. He wasn't quite old and done just yet, but certainly not the man he once was. So in the moment when he saw an opening, he took it, never once believing that he might fail. His dagger met with air when the creature dodged with a speed that had, until that point, seemed to be waning. Caught by surprise, Arthur was not prepared to feel the sting of fangs colliding with his already injured arm. The pain was extreme. He was not aware that he'd been crying out in pain until a swift hit to his throat ceased the loud screams. The deafening silence threatened to engulf him.

It was with great relief and confusion that Arthur was released from the strong jaws holding him captive. A cry that sounded as if it were meant for battle echoed off of the trees, filling Arthur's ears and quelling the roar of fear that had been pounding behind his eyes moments before. Art, despite his lack of training, was on the beast with a swiftness that Arthur envied. A dagger was in the boy's hand coming between him and the monster until it buried itself deep into her throat. Her wet screech sent shivers down Arthur's spine as Art's weak hands made a mangled wreck of her throat. He was forcing the blade in the wrong places, trying to push too far and not quite making it between the bones of her neck. The effort resulted in her endless cries until a lucky nick cut her vocal cord and instead she lay in a pool of her own blood convulsing as Art watch on, fear struck and covered in red.

The silence that settled was unnatural. Arthur could not decipher whether it was his ears acting up or his brain, but he knew there was no way that the heavy rise and fall of Art's chest was producing no noise. He strained his neck, turning to look at the boy more clearly and he realized then that he was lying the forest floor. He couldn't recall when he had fallen, or when the world had taken on a gray tinge, but he was sure that he could not move or else he may pass out. Even panic was slow to settle in his body. His eyes slid closed like a blanket being drawn over him. How long had it been since he'd felt the hands of another settling him into bed. Maybe not since Elizabeth. The thought made him sad and might have inspired tears if he hadn't been so very tired.

Hands wrapped around Arthur's shoulders, shaking his body. He had no notion of how long he lay there, but he knew that those hands were not ones he'd felt before. His eyes flew open and his namesake stared down at him. The sun shone down from high above, encompassing the boy's visage in a halo of light and forcing him to question if he'd finally met with his own demise.

"Arthur?" The voice was scared. He sounded too young by far and Arthur was jolted back to the present. Art wasn't much younger than Emeline, not quite old enough for marriage, but nearly so. The way he looked then made Arthur wonder if maybe he wasn't closer to Natalya in age. Fear turned the boy young, but the blood that colored his linen tunic spoke of the heroics he'd committed. That had been the action of a man, not a scared child.

"I am so proud of you." Arthur choked out. He felt the skin of water pressed again his lips and took greedy gulps. At the angle he was reclined in, more water found its way down his chin and soaked into his shirt, but it didn't matter. The cool liquid that managed to run down his throat tasted better than anything he'd had before. The feeling of the water flowing through him was enough to keep him coherent, focusing his eyes and his mind.

"I thought I was going to lose you." Art whispered and Arthur forced himself to move so his uninjured hand was grasping at the boy's arm.

"Stop that. You were a man when you saved me. Be a man now. Use the water to help me clean my wounds and then wrap them tight. Also give me bread the cheese. I will need my strength yet and so will you." Stunned, the boy stared back as if he hardly understood a word he'd been told. "Well, go on then." Arthur barked, his voice still raw from screaming.

Art scrambled into action. He made quick work of washing and wrapping the wounds. The bandages were too loose and Arthur knew he would have to teach the boy better, but his head still felt heavy and the effort it took to feed himself was almost too much to bare. He would be fine, he had to be. He forced himself to finish the meager meal, before willing his body to move the way it was meant to. Art steadied him into a sitting position before returning to the sack of food, having his own small portion. Arthur was impressed to see him scatter and bury the crumbs after, cleaning up their mess and hiding the evidence that they had been there at all. It would seem some of the lectures he had been giving Art while they had worked in the field had set in. There was still the matter of the blood and body to attend to, however.

"Cover the blood with dirt, smear it into the ground, it will attract less of them. I doubt there is much we can do with the corpse, but we can hopefully dampen the sent."

"Less of what, exactly?" Art demanded as his gaze flicked to the dead thing that he'd pushed as far away from them as he'd dared.

"Less of them," Arthur motioned around them lamely, "the reason why I told Nat to stay away from Mordin Forest in the first place." When Art seemed to want to protest for more information, Arthur silenced him with a glare. "Talking tires me out. We must get on the move. The girls mustn't be too far."

"But you're hurt!" Art complained, though he was doing as he was told, slowly turning up the earth and trying his best to hide the bloody scene before them.

"If we don't move from this place we could turn out worse for it." Arthur sighed and pushed up against the ground until Art came to his side easing him to his feet. He knew that without Art he wouldn't make it far in his condition, but it had been the boy's idiotic blind running that had gotten him hurt in the first place. He wondered if he'd been wrong to bring the boy along.

"Which way?" Art seemed resigned to follow his lead and Arthur sighed in relief.

"This way," he pointed back toward the way they came, "we track the trail we knew we had and we find the girls before another thing can find them first." Arthur let the words hang between them, hoping that his namesake would now understand why it was imperative that they find the girls.

"I understand now. Let's go find them and bring them home."

He could hardly waste precious energy arguing with the boy and he prayed to the gods he didn't believe in to bring him the strength necessary to find his daughter. Every step caused him pain and his body protested the strain as they forged on. Each branch that reached out to snag into his shirt managed to scrape past his wounds. He grit his teeth to push through the pain until the pressure began to travel to his skull; the pounding was near enough for him to forget the agony caused by the deep gashes in his arm. Art was staying blessedly silent and with a little more effort than Arthur would willingly admit, they returned to the main path that they had been tracking.

They continued on without stopping as Arthur did his best to track Emeline's sloppy steps, hoping that Art was watching their surroundings. His head was swimming with the strain to keep upright and he could hardly be expected to track the small steps and keep his ears open for any oncoming attacks. It seemed their luck would hold out as the sun moved high overhead and the oppressive heat of the end of the harvest beat down on them, much later into the season and they would have had no light with which to track by. He could feel Art's feet dragging behind him without stopping to look and he was reminded of Natalya as a small child. The villagers hadn't helped him look for Elizabeth for very long after her disappearance. He would go out for days at a time looking for his late wife and it didn't take long for Natalya to insist on coming with him. She never lasted more than a few hours before complaining of being tired and Arthur had been forced to carry her. It had irked him to no end that she was so stubborn about being with him, but ended up slowing down his search. Looking back it was easy to see that she had been a very young girl missing her mother and her father who had been present wasn't actually there for her either. By the time he had realized his mistake and attempted to repair it with training and spending more time with her it was obvious that the damage had been done. His daughter despised him. He had held out hope that they had worked past her refusal to adhere to his rules, now that they were in a new environment, but it was obvious that he had been wrong once more.

Emeline's neat steps had become hurried at a point and the smudged lines showed a rushed pace. Arthur dreaded what he might find at the end of the path, but he knew that there was no sense in putting off the inevitable. "This way."

Art moved closer to him as they departed from the main path once more. Emeline's steps were hard to find in the upturned dirt, but Arthur could see an opening in the brush beyond them and he hoped that the clearing ahead would give them more answers. Instead they found an empty patch of dirt. His eyes scanned for more tracks, but the dirt was covered in the footprints of at least seven different people and it made tracking whatever had happened impossible.

"Arthur!" Art called out. The panic in his voice sent Arthur into an adrenaline fueled rush as he lurched toward the center of the clearing where the boy stood.

There, under the harsh light of the sun, lay a patch of dirt saturated in a very large pool of dried blood. There was much too much blood for a human or animal to be alive and yet there was no body.

"This can't be them. They'd still be here if this came from one of them right?" Arthur didn't have the heart to tell the boy that if Natalya or Emeline had produced the blood that lay at their feet they would most certainly not be alive. It had to be Emeline, if it had belonged to one of the girls. His Natalya was much too strong and smart to have succumbed to one of those beasts. If she had gotten away, however, it still begged the question of where the blood had come from and where the girls had gone off to since.

Arthur ignored the boy's question and began to circle the clearing looking for more footsteps. There were more hurried prints that originated from the blood in the center and two cleaner sets of prints followed after them. They returned back to the clearing not far from where they had left and a group of five prints were obviously leaving at another point in the clearing close to where the two men had entered from. One of them certainly looked like his daughter's, but Emeline's distinct prints were not with them.

"We will find the girls, Art. But for now we rest." He could not tell the boy of his suspicions. It was obvious that a group of people had come and taken the girls. Natalya was smart and strong, but not enough to take on four adults, human or otherwise. He trusted that his daughter would try to escape from whomever the people were who had taken them when she could. He suspected that with Emeline incapacitated or worse it would slow down her escape, but Arthur trusted that she had a plan and with that assurance, he knew that his body could afford a little bit of rest.

"How can you be so sure?"

Arthur watched the boy as he made his way towards him, already reaching for the unraveling bandages. He knew that they would find the girls because he had never found his wife and he could not suffer another defeat. "Because we must. There is no other option."

Art looked like he was about to argue, but seemed to think better of it. He made quick work of unwrapping and cleaning the wounds before wrapping them tighter than before. It wasn't much progress, but Arthur knew that hoping for more would be folly. He would have to work with what he was given if he was to bring his daughter home and he knew in his heart that this time he would not fail. As he had said to Art, there was no other option. He would bring his daughter home or he would die trying.

CLAYTON

The knots in Clayton's stomach seemed to have doubled in size from anxiety as he and Esmylara came to the gates of Faegon. He had been tamping down the feelings of his own insecurities since the night before when he could feel just how close he was coming to the end of his mission. There was something undeniably intoxicating about the air around the well protected House, but it only served to set the vampire further on edge. For her part, Esmy had seemed just as tense over the past night. She was obviously more at home in the silence of the forest, and even in Lunaries the guard had walked as if on shards of glass, never once truly relaxing unless in the presence of her Queen. Lady Reagan had an enchanting quality about her and Clayton wondered for a mere moment if he had made a mistake in leaving her House and the protection it had offered.

They came to a halt at the closed gate as two impassive guards stood watch. "Speak your name and your business in the name of the great King Zentarion and in the name of his grace King Pa'ari of House Faegon."

"I am Lady Esmylara of House Lunaries. I come in the name of my Queen to answer the summons of our great King Zentarion." If the guards knew that no such summons had been made they made no indication. Both sets of cold eyes landed on Clayton then.

"I am Clayton a childe of the House Namyt'tkas here to complete my journey and report to a representative of my House."

"You are the last, childe, and very late. They await you in the tavern in the upper city. It is not far from the gate and owned by a woman named Adelina."

Clayton felt like a scolded childe and he knew that Esmy's eyes were boring into him the same as the others.

"I am familiar with the tavern. I will escort the boy before making my way to the castle. I do hope his Grace will understand." She bowed to both men and Clayton found his body doing the same though he hardly remembered commanding it to do so.

They walked through the large iron gate through the thick stone wall before coming out through the other side in the open moonlight. Clayton moved without seeing, relying on Esmy to guide him. He was surprised from his stupor when the woman addressed him sharply. "You will stop that this instant."

"Stop what?" It felt good to talk back despite knowing that Esmy hardly deserved his foul mood. It was not her fault he had been delayed. If anything she was the reason he had arrived as quickly as he did and he supposed she deserved some gratitude for that, though he could hardly find it in himself to provide her any.

"Stop acting like a child. You made it to the city as you were tasked. It matters not the time it took you. If you wish to be taken as an adult and a fully grown vampire then, when you meet with your House's representative, you will act the part."

She had a point. Her views of the world might be highly misguided, but Esmy was a woman of sound character and she would not lead him astray in this area. "Thank you."

"You are very welcome. Remember all that I've told you. You might not see it now, but there will come a day when you question the structure of your House. When that day comes House Lunaries will always welcome you back."

There was no proper response to her prodding and instead he simply nodded to acknowledge he'd heard her without damning himself with a verbal agreement. He moved to stand straighter as they walked and he held his head high with pride he wasn't sure he possessed. They made their way through the crowded cobblestone streets in silence. The buildings that littered the main street were made mostly of stone with thatched roofs, though some of the smaller structures were made of the strong wood of Mordin Forest. The tavern was obvious from the street, with its large wooden sign hanging out front. The name Adelina's was painted in bold script and there was a healthy crowd about its entrance.

"I suppose I will not be seeing you from this point forward," Clayton said in lieu of a goodbye. He hadn't much liked the conversations he'd had with the woman, but he could respect Esmy for her strength and her loyalty to her House.

"I would not be so sure. I will be at the castle tonight to report to King Zentarion and then I suspect that I will be staying within the city for some time. Queen Reagan has business for me to attend beyond the castle and I shall be stationed here until it is completed."

"Still I will be returning to Namyt'tkas soon and then I doubt I will have a reason to return here."

"Alas, then this must be goodbye." The words didn't seem to meet her eyes, but Clayton ignored her worried glance.

"Goodbye then." the words sounded much too little even to his own ears. Clayton turned toward the tavern to fight back all his feelings of uncertainty as the woman watched his retreating back.

It was easy to pretend that he forgot Esmy in the noise of the tavern. It was still early in the evening so many of the vampires of the higher class seemed to be out. Adelina's was obviously popular and it took Clayton longer than he would have liked to push his way through the crowd. The main tavern was littered with small round tables with four or so seats surrounding them. The main bar was attended to by a beautiful woman with sharp brown eyes and a head of curls so massive that it looked like a mane from a distance. There were stairs behind the bar which lead to rooms for rent and what appeared to be a back room from what the sheer cloth covering the door revealed.

"What can I do you for, my dear? We have blood from humans all across Mordin Forest and even from the Valley and the mountains beyond." The woman smiled with all of her teeth and Clayton reminded himself to act like the man he wished to be seen as.

"I am looking for the representative from House Namyt'tkas. I believe I am the last to arrive."

"Clayton, is it not? We were wondering when you might arrive. They're waiting for you through the back. Well on you go, no sense in keeping them waiting longer." He was waived into the direction of the covered door before he had time to process that it seemed like everyone in Faegon knew he was late in arriving.

Clayton passed through the light fabric dividing him from the back room as if he was passing into another world. The noise from the main tavern seemed to stop at the threshold and the calm air about the small room only sent his nerves farther on edge. Only a few members of his troop were present in the room. Lenore and Orchid were sitting at a table in the corner deep in conversation. Thankfully Urien was nowhere to be seen though Ketevan and Kleio, the strange twins from the even stranger Delnori mountain town from the far east, stood by the fire. They seemed to both be deep in thought as no words passed between them. Two sets of calculating slate eyes trapped him at the entrance as both girls surveyed him as if they were seeing in for the very first time. They had been seventeen when they had arrived at Namyt'tkas. Their upbringing couldn't have been more different from his own, though they also were seen as outcasts. If he had thought that it would have brought them closer due to their common ground he could not have been more wrong. They were identical, both with straight brown hair and pointed chins that always seemed to be held above the others around them. They spoke little to each other when there were others around and even less to the troop as a whole. Even Orchid hadn't been able to crack their hard exteriors and there had been a time when

Clayton was sure that they would not make it through the training, but there they stood eyeing him as if he were a rodent beneath their feet.

"Clayton I presume." The only person he did not recognize in the room stood behind the nearest table watching him with interest. His neatly cropped red hair stood out against his pale skin and azure eyes. He was shorter than Clayton, though the man himself stood fairly tall a few inches over six feet, so it hardly seemed a comparison. He could not be considered an imposing figure and yet Clayton felt trepidation at the sight of him. "I am Lord Tory. I am the representative from our great House tasked with welcoming your troop to the capital."

"Lord Tory." Clayton bowed low before the man. He was dressed in fine silks of the upper-class which were adorned with gold disks lining the many intricate folds in the delicate robes. He wore deep green, the colors of their House and his fingers were glittering with emerald encrusted rings.

"You are late boy. Sit. We will discuss the reasons and then I shall see to setting you up with a room for the night."

Clayton held back the glare that dared to shadow his face as he took the offered seat. His legs ached from the pace Esmy had kept and it felt good to sink into chair and take the pressure off of his sore feet. "I was attacked, M'lord. I apologize for keeping you and my brothers and sisters."

"Attacked you say? Not on our land I hope." His tone dared Clayton to prove him wrong and the boy wished to do just that.

"It was on our territory, to tell the truth. I was attacked by an elder with long brown hair and piercing lavender eyes."

"I know of no elder with such eyes. You will provide me with your blood to see that this is true."

Clayton pulled his sleeve up roughly, shoving his bare arm across the table without hesitation. "Would you prefer the edge of a blade or will your fangs suffice, m'lord."

"Don't be barbaric, I can collect it from you later. Now tell me, being attacked by an elder would surely have left you worse for it, how did you come out from this supposed encounter and heal fully to arrive to us in the time that you did?"

As loath as he was to admit to a weakness, Clayton knew that lying would afford him no advantages. "I was taken in for the night by House Lunaries."

"They turned you out after just a night? You must have still been healing then. I have heard strange things about that House ever since the death of King Gareth, though I hardly believed them."

"No, their people were more than kind. Their Queen, the Lady Reagan was more than willing to allow me to stay, but I had to refuse. I could not disappoint my people further by making them wait."

"That would be Queen Reagan, please tell me you called her by her title." The guilt in Clayton's face must had spoke for him for Lord Tory sighed, "You caused your House a great dishonor, Clayton. You would not call the great King Zentarion Lord would you? And to turn away their hospitality? What are our words?"

"*Honor is our shield,*" Clayton spoke through a clenched jaw. He was no childe, not truly. Had he not taken the bite he would be thirty-four in human years and he deserved more respect than this.

"It is. There is nothing in this world more important than honor. When you go out into the empire you represent our House and you have done it a great injustice these past weeks."

"How? Staying in another House's company, taking their blood and their shelter when I hardly saw the need is not honorable! We are trained to be strong a help the poor! Acting weak and taking the handouts from another House hardly seems the honorable way."

"And this is where you are gravely mistaken, young Clayton. We are not better than other Houses and their people simply for being stronger. We are better because we are wiser, able to assist the lesser Houses even when others might not take the risk. You mistake our kindness for superiority. There is no dishonor in admitting that you too might need help. You dishonor yourself and our people by denying it."

"I hardly see the honor in being reliant on those who are not our own."

"Even if they had been our people, would you have taken their help?"

It was a question worth asking. Clayton hardly accepted help from anyone, Lenore being the only exception to that and his debt owed to her ran too deep for him to hope to return on it in his lifetime. No, he would not have accepted help from one of his own House either, but it hardly seemed prudent to admit to that. "I would have sought the help of my own, of course."

"Lie." Lord Tory looked at him with such distaste that Clayton could feel the weight of his disappointment as a physical burden on his chest. "It pains me to do this, but you have left me with no choice. We do believe in chances at House Namyt'tkas, but there is no way for you to return from such a catastrophe. Clayton it is with great sadness that I, Lord Tory, ambassador of the great House Namyt'tkas strip you from your title as brother to our House. You will henceforth have no sire and no class in our society."

Clayton nearly missed the gasps from the girls in the room above the dull roar in his ears. It couldn't be possible. He had not heard Lord Tory right, of that he was implicitly sure. House Namyt'tkas was his home, his only home. He could not have been removed from it for something as small as calling a Queen by the wrong title and refusing to use her for her kindness. It made no sense.

"This cannot be." He heard someone say from the back of the small room and he realized too late the girls had been witness to his shame. He looked up to meet the jade eyes of Lenore, her face betraying just how upset she was by Lord Tory's proclamation.

"It can and is." Lord Tory rose from his seat with the air of a royal, his eyes never once sweeping over Clayton. "Clayton please leave all affects granted to you by House Namyt'tkas, the table will be fine for now. I will send another to collect them."

Clayton grasped for his blade with hands that suddenly felt much too large for his body. The heavy copper chain around his neck which held a shiny iron shield was next to go as he lifted it up and over his head, completely numb to his surroundings. The last piece on his person to go was the clasp that sat at his breast. It was not from Namyt'tkas, but was a gift from Lenore when he had learned his letters well enough to keep up with the rest of their troop. It had been fashioned to look like a feather quill and had been the best present he had ever received.

"Oh do keep that, Lord Tory would not expect you to return a gift from a friend." Lenore's quiet words brought him back to the present as he realized he had pricked his thumb on the end of the pin in his carelessness. Orchid and the twins were gone and the two sat alone at the small table. "Clayton."

He didn't understand how she managed to say his name laced with such sorrow and pity, but sound so sincere. It made him sick. "I'd really rather not have this conversation now."

"You should have taken more care in Lunaries. I cannot hope to help you return to Namyt'tkas, but if you return to them this Queen Reagan might take you in again."

Clayton's mind returned to Esmy's warning and invitation. She had seen this coming. She had known that he would fail and instead of saving him from such a fate she had simply stood by and placed the seed in his mind to think of Lunaries should the worst happen. Lady Reagan might be kind and just, but it was only because she allowed her subjects to do her dirty work for her.

"Clayton? Are you listening to me?"

"I must return with you to Namyt'tkas." He said without hesitation as if she had never spoken.

"And how do you suppose you will manage that? And for what purpose? Lord Tory made it very clear that you were denounced of your rank and birthright. You cannot come back."

"If I do not then who will protect you?" She flinched back from him as if he had struck her, her beautiful eyes wide with disgust.

"Protect me? From what? If anything I should think that your presence would tarnish my reputation."

She did not mean those words. No, he had been gone from her for too long. The others had always thought their relationship odd and had sought to break them away from each other. Only Orchid would spend time with them and seemed to understand the special bond that existed between them. He had been gone too long and they had poisoned his one true friend against him. "From those who could mean you harm."

"Who could mean me harm? Are you sure you're not still hurt from the attack? You're starting to frighten me."

"Don't be absurd. I'm fully healed. Don't act like a fool, Lenore. If I was not here then no one would be able to keep Urien and his sickening looks away from you. It is the least that I could do for all of the help that you have offered me. I will forever be in your debt, but at least at your side I could make it right."

A dark look formed over Lenore's pretty face and Clayton hardly had a moment to consider how his words might have affected the girl. "How dare you!"

"Beg your pardon?" His mouth, it seemed, hardly knew when enough was enough and it ran away without his permission.

"First of all I helped you because you are my friend and that is what friends do! To think that I might expect a debt in repayment? How could you think that of me?" Before Clayton could respond she stood abruptly with her slender finger pointed between his eyes. "And furthermore I do not need your protection from anyone, much less Urien! That slimy idiot may continue to try making advances at me as much as he likes and I will continue to handle it by telling him off on my own. I am no damsel in distress and of all of people in our troop I would have thought that you understood that! And to think that I felt sorry for you for being banished! You ought to be! You're just a bad as Urien, in fact I think you might be worse!"

Her voice had risen to painful decibels and Clayton sat there in total shock. Her words had made perfect sense and yet he had no notion of where her anger stemmed from. She might think that her handling of Urien's advances were enough and yet the boy still came around unless he was there. She was hopelessly in denial about her own skills and she was even more ignorant if she thought that without him Urien would stay away for long. It seemed that whatever fire that had fueled her anger was beginning to die as Clayton took longer to respond. In the end her stiff posture softened and her strong shoulders hunched until she stood withdrawn.

"Here. I made some extra coin from arriving first despite not being the first to leave. I was going to offer it to you for a room for the night, but I'm sure that you will just see it as pity and refuse it." She threw the coins on the table with more force than necessary and one bounced off the dark wood, rolling underneath them until Clayton felt the pang on his boot.

"I can't take that."

"Of course you can't," Lenore sighed. "I hope that you find yourself out there, Clayton. I really do. You are too lost, I fear, for anyone else to."

She left him then, though he could feel her eyes on him every few seconds as if she couldn't leave without looking at him one last time. It felt like an age had past before she was gone and Clayton found himself well and truly alone. He would not take her money. Charity from her tasted bitter on his tongue. He fingered the pin attached to his breast, as if to remove it, before thinking better of it. It had been a gift and even if he was sure that Lenore would hate him for the rest of her life he knew that throwing away the one good thing that had come from his time at Namyt'tkas would be a mistake.

With no coin and no prospects it seemed pointless to sit about in the back room of a tavern. He stood slowly as if in a haze and made his way through the door into the din of the main tavern. He didn't know whether the eyes that followed him were his imagination, but he refused to meet any of them to see. He felt as if the room became quieter with every step he took through it, though he was sure that was a trick of his ears. No one cared about him; not anymore.

It had begun to rain while he had been in Adelina's and he rather felt that it was only right that the weather reflected his mood. He began to walk with no true idea of where his feet were taking him. He had never been in such a big city before and it was easy to imagine getting lost. The great hulking mass of stone in the distance was obviously the main castle shrouded in rain and fog and Clayton turned his back on it. Esmy would be there and he had little energy left to listen to another person tell him how wrong he was. Even with Lenore's anger, Tory's dismissal, and Esmy's judgement he still saw no fault in his logic. He held onto his decisions like a lifeline. He supposed they were, in a sense. It was all he had left and his choices might have led him to this very moment, but it could also be said that his choices were the only ones that mattered. He had never needed anyone to survive before and he certainly didn't need anyone now.

With his mind firmly set Clayton set off down to the lower city. He would put distance between himself and the so called upper-class, who only deigned to snub him and spit in his face, and make a place for himself amongst the common folk as he always had. He had been a fool to think that he could belong with the likes of his troop in such a prestigious house such as Namyt'tkas. His former troop, his mind supplied and he felt his mood worsen. He had never truly belonged amongst them and it was time that he remembered just who he was. He had come too far and worked too hard to allow others to bring him down and now was his time to rise above them and survive on his own. If his finger absently brushed against the feather pin and a pang of of guilt danced across his heart that it was his secret to keep. No one would have to know because there was no one left in his life to tell.

NATALYA

The trip with the vampires was long, more than a week had passed, though it was surprisingly without incident. Natalya was thankful that the quiet allowed her enough time to plan an escape, but with little to work with the chances seemed slim at best. There was little chatter between the group and the tension that ran through the party of six seemed like something she could manipulate to her advantage, but she didn't know how. Her father would have known. Thinking of her father brought her nothing but pain and regret. He had been right all along and she might never be able to tell him. Monsters really did exist and the chances were good that her father hadn't been crazy in thinking that a monster had been what had taken her mother away. When she did find her father again she would have to apologize. *If you ever find him,* the nagging voice in her head supplied without her consent. Natalya shook her head to rid the thought. She wouldn't be able to get away from the monsters if she continued to think about such things. All of her energy would have to be focused on watching the strange group around her and preparing for the right time to make her escape.

Anya was at the front of the party, her face stony and closed off. Cohen was carrying Emeline while Nirosh stood at his elbow. They spoke in low voices, sounding agitated, though she couldn't decipher the words being said. She could probably understand them if she'd tried, but it would have taken more effort than she wanted to expend. She needed to reserve all of her energy to escape and details as insignificant as the worries of her captors did not warrant wasting her skills. Darius walked beside her with a firm grip on her arm. He had remained silent for most of their journey, though he kept stealing glances at her every few minutes and it was setting the girl on edge.

"What do you know about vampires?" Darius' tone was conversational despite the unsettled air about it. The grip of his hand tightened and was the only indication that the man was on edge.

"You're monsters." Natalya responded just as evenly. Logic told her to keep her mouth shut, but she couldn't help herself. It was always how she'd gotten herself in trouble with her father, though her father's punishments might have been tame in comparison.

"We have been called that, yes." Cohen spoke then, his face turned to address the girl, though he kept a trained eye on Anya. The woman in front walked with a stiff back, her whole posture speaking of her thoughts on the situation.

"Not all vampires are bad, just like not all humans are good." Nirosh spoke his piece of wisdom and turned to the blond vampire. "My Lord."

Cohen nodded and handed Emeline to the older man. He fell back with Darius and Natalya, gently taking her arm in his hand. Natalya allowed her captors to change her guard easily, noting that Cohen was gentler then Darius, but she knew he was stronger by far. He would not bruise her in his hold, but he would be harder to escape from. As if he read her mind, Cohen looked down at her, disapproving.

"If you ran, where would you go?" She searched for the threat behind the words and only found passive honesty staring back at her. "We do not wish to hold you against your will. If you promise not to run, I will unhand you."

"I promise." Natalya spoke without a second to think about the consequences of lying to vampire.

"Lie." Cohen remarked easily and he continued to talk as if she'd never spoken. "If you are going to be spending anytime with my people there are things you are going to have to learn. As Lord Nirosh said, not all vampires are bad. The thing that hurt your friend is what we call a rogue. They are not welcomed in our home and are the reason we have hidden our society from humans. They are vermin." Cohen spoke with more passion and emotion than Natalya had heard from him since their brief encounter and she found herself drawn to the words as if she were in a trance.

"We are from an old vampire house called Lunaries." Darius spoke from behind them and Natalya felt all of the hair on the back of her neck stand on edge. "Think of the Houses like small kingdoms, we run well on our own, but we all answer to one House when it comes to big decisions."

"House Faegon, home of the Kings of Kings." Anya spat and Natalya eyed the strange vampire wearily.

"What does that mean?"

"Well, like Lord Nirosh said, we are independent. Each head of House is our King or Queen. In our case our leader is Queen Reagan." Cohen brought the human's attention back to him, also sparing a glance to the female vampire before them. "Then there is the vampire High Council and the King who resides on the Throne of All."

"Queen Reagan's word is final in our House, but if she were ever called to the High Council she would still have to answer to the King of Kings." Darius slid up to stand beside Natalya, his tone soft and his gaze far away. "I hear the horns, we're close."

Natalya's weak human ears could hardly pick up the low thrum of horns in the far distance. They were drawing close to the castle and if she were to run there would be little chance left. Her focus fled their conversation and shifted to Emeline. She was still lying limp in the older vampire's arms and she had little hope for her friend's recovery. She noted that Cohen would spend most of his time watching her, but he would spare a worried glance for the girl. Natalya quietly counted the seconds that his gaze would leave her, when his grip seemed to slack for just a moment and waited. She felt horrible leaving Emeline behind, but it could not be helped. The girl was most likely dead and there was no sense in throwing away her own life. She hoped that Emeline would have understood.

The perfect moment arrived when Darius moved to the front of their party to address a concern with Anya and Nirosh shifted his grip on Emeline. Cohen reflexively loosened his grip on Natalya and leaned away from her and closer to Nirosh to assist if necessary. Natalya broke free from his relaxed grip with a twist of her arm with practiced ease. She bolted in the direction that she hoped would lead her home faster than Cohen's strong grasp could close back around her. The thrill of escape thrummed through her body and Natalya let the high take her as far as her legs could carry her. The high didn't last long. She felt the press of a body behind her and the tackle sent her and the assailant tumbling to the ground. Anya's slim figure was deceivingly strong and Natalya found herself pinned to the dirt with her face pressed painfully into a pile of twigs before she could make a move to right herself.

"That's it," Anya growled in her ear. Her thin fingers trailed from Natalya's shoulders up to her neck. Despite the gentle caress of the thin fingers, terror seized Natalya into a shocked stillness. For the first time she saw that her rebellion had darker consequences than she could talk her way out of. "You stupid humans are nothing but trouble. I should have known better than to allow you to come with us."

"That's enough Lady Anya." Cohen barked the order somewhere to the left of Natalya's head and she did her best to raise her head. Her gaze fell on the man's boots and the strain on her neck forced her to fall back onto the ground. "Let the girl go."

"I don't have to listen to you." Anya spat back. Her fingers dug into the warm flesh beneath her and Natalya struggled for air.

"Yes, you do. You know better. If you don't unhand her I will make you and then you will have to explain to our Queen why you disobeyed a direct order from your superior." Cohen stepped closer and Anya's grip relaxed until Natalya was able to pull breath into her lungs in burning gasps. "Good. Let her up."

"*Yes, My Lord.*" Anya hissed as she moved off of Natalya, making no move to help the girl. Cohen audibly sighed and moved to Natalya. She lay panting on her stomach, her face cut from the branches. She flinched when he came too close to her and the shadow of disappointment colored his face before it was gone.

"I will not hurt you child, have no fear." Cohen knelt and tucked his hand under her chin. He licked the thumb that wasn't holding her face and slid the wet digit over her cut. Natalya felt the pain fade away instantly. Only the blood on his thumb gave any indication that she'd been cut. "Our saliva has healing properties, it helps clot the blood and close the wounds when we feed," he said by way of explanation. "We just want to help you, Natalya, please let us." The look in his eyes was earnest, causing Natalya to trust him despite the situation.

"Okay." She let him lift her up and inspect her to ensure she wasn't cut elsewhere. When he was satisfied he took her hand in his own. It was intimate and kind and it put her nerves to ease. It seemed obvious to her now that Cohen meant it when he said he would not allow harm to befall her. He was clearly much stronger than Anya and with the display that the female vampire had just put on, Natalya had no doubt that the blond man beside her could do anything he pleased to her and she would be powerless to stop him. She might not have wanted to make an ally out of one of these strange creatures, but Cohen was the obvious choice and there seemed no sense in angering the only person who seemed to care about her safety. "When do we meet your Queen?"

"Soon, home is close." Cohen replied, taking up the lead.

As if on cue, a woman emerged from the woods dressed in plain travel clothes. When she saw the group, she fell into a well practiced bow, her eyes flashing brown before becoming a cloudy gray once more. "M'Lords, m'lady, Commander Darius, I have been sent by Queen Reagan to scout for you and to inform her of your arrival."

"Thank you Dreanna," Cohen smiled, nothing in his tone or demeanor spoke to the tussle that had just occurred. "Please alert the healers that we have a charge who needs their attention immediately and also have the washroom nearest the castle entrance prepared."

"M'Lord," Dreanna bowed once more before turning and making haste back to the castle.

They walked for an hour more before the thick woods made way to a breathtaking structure. A castle sat nestled in a modest clearing with trees growing in at all sides. Thick vines grew up the grey stone wrapping around its walls in an artistic pattern. The vines looked like they belonged to the castle or possibly that the castle belonged to the forest. The way the trees grew overhead made it so very little of the sun's light permeated through. There was a sense of magic about the forest and the ancient trees only helped to enforce the feeling. There were two guards standing at the gate, their eyes fixed on Emeline and Natalya. They stood aside without question when Cohen came forward, Natalya beside him with the rest bringing up the rear.

The grounds within the stone walls were crawling with people. Tent like structures littered the ground and hearths were built where people were gathered to partake in food and gossip. They were human from what Natalya could tell, their skin healthy with color. They didn't seem like slaves as they moved freely around the property along with other monsters. The hustle of the common grounds mesmerized Natalya and it took Cohen's gentle tugging to get her moving in the direction of the castle doors.

"Where are you taking me?" Natalya whispered as they made their way through the shadowed entrance way. She noticed as Nirosh took Emeline toward the back of the entranceway while Cohen was leading her to the right. "Where is he taking her?"

"I will be taking you to a washroom where two of Queen Reagan's handmaidens will assist you. Nirosh is taking your friend to be looked after. When you are finished you will be taken to meet the Queen. If all goes well then I will bring you to see Emeline when our healers say it is okay."

Natalya searched the pale blue eyes for a lie. Instead she saw a soft smile that caused slight wrinkles around the man's eyes. The slight change in his face gave away age and experience that the girl could never comprehend. Cohen nodded toward the hall and Natalya sighed. He had given her no reason to distrust him and the sourness in her throat from her terrible escape attempt was reminder enough to go along with his request. She followed him into a small, but grand washroom allowing the vampire to take the lead. Two young girls were already in the room and they stopped their fussing about to drop into low curtsies for their Lord. They already had a hot tub filled and a beautiful yet simple dress hung on a partition in the back corner of the room.

"M'lord it is a pleasure as always." The younger of the two girls spoke first. She looked young, yet her eyes seemed to belong in the face of a person who had seen at least a lifetime or two. Her long brown hair was fastened at the nape of her neck though a few shorter strands fell into her sharp honey eyes. She flashed her fangs for a moment and her eyes turned a much brighter hyacinth before her features reverted to human again.

The girl beside her was older. She looked to be in her late twenties while the vampire beside her looked nearly of an age with Emeline. She had short black hair that shone in the firelight. There were no fangs or flashes of queer eyes so Natalya could assume she was human. "Lord Cohen," she inclined her head in a respectful gesture before returning to her task.

"I will leave you to it. I will return soon to escort you to Queen Reagan."

Cohen left and the girls made quick work of disrobing Natalya, gently easing her into the tub. Neither spoke while they scrubbed the dirt of the hike and the fight with Anya from her skin. The younger looking of the two girls combed through her hair while the older made quick work of her body.

"You've never met a vampire before." It was a statement. The vampire continued to work out the knots in her hair as if they were discussing the latest trade routes.

"I didn't know about them at all."

"You must be an Eastern girl then. My name is Freya, that's Islara." The human smiled up at her when she was introduced. "The rogues are nasty, but we live a civilized life here."

"Why are humans here? Why don't I know about vampires?"

"I live here because it's safer." Freya spoke up. "Turn please Miss so I might clean your back."

"Safer? What do you mean?" Natalya turned and allowed Freya to adjust her posture so the girl could reach her back.

"I lived in the Valley of the Damned, it's to the West, past Mordin Forest. It was a hard life and my parents had many children. We did not have enough food to put on the table and then there were the wild things that live in the mountains. They are worse than any treacherous rogue. They are pure beasts and cannot be reasoned with. A man and woman from the vampire house Faegon visited once, bounty hunters and they offered us a proposition. Anyone who wished could return with them with the offer of food, shelter, and complete protection. I chose to follow and found myself being sent to House Lunaries. That was in the days when the Crown had taken in humans and saw them placed in any House that would have them."

"And the price?" Natalya was young, but not naive.

"The humans who live under our care are a compliant food source." Islara replied. She was towel drying Natalya's hair while Freya helped the girl stand and move toward the fire.

"Food source?"

"Vampires drink blood, Miss." Freya moved for the dress while Islara pinned up Natalya's hair in an intricate knot at the top of her head. Natalya did her best to keep still and not flinch away from the vampire at her back.

"Not to worry, Miss. There are very strict laws in place protecting humans from vampires. They are only allowed to drink from the willing, hence why we come to live with them. We get protection and they are allowed the food they need." Freya took Natalya's wrists in her own and drew her closer. "Not to worry Miss, you're safe here. Queen Reagan is a gentle queen with a soft heart, but a strong sense of morality. She will be cross with the filth that attacked your friend, but if you fight with her she will not hesitate to put you in the cells."

"We know of your fight with the Lady Anya." Islara eyed her carefully.

"She started it." The comment sounded petulant even to her ears.

"The Lady Anya is Queen Reagan's paramour." A knock on the door stalled Natalya from a reaction and Freya rushed to answer the door.

"Be careful Miss," Islara's last warning sent a shiver down Natalya's spine before Cohen's blue eyes fell on her again.

"You look lovely, Natalya. Come we mustn't keep the Queen."

The large oak doors of the throne room stood closed as Natalya and Cohen approached. The guards bowed and allowed them to pass into an open and airy room. Every few feet an elaborate sconce, lit with tall white candles, set a calm mood to the room. Forty or so well-dressed vampires mingled about at the front of the room, while humans and vampires of a lower caste stood in the back. The chatter was light and it put Natalya on edge. Her father's view of the monsters and her own experience with the thing that attacked Emeline conflicted with the scene before her. She had never been to the human capitol, much less in its castle, yet she imagined it would look something like what she was seeing now.

Cohen led her to the front of the hall. The sea of onlookers parted for them without protest. Natalya felt her skin crawl under the scrutinizing gaze of humans and vampires alike and she felt her nerves flair and her temper rise. The budding need to scream was struck from her as quickly as it appeared as a surprising sight greeted her. Emeline was sitting on the steps that led up to the dais. She was paler then Natalya remembered. Her eyes seemed vacant and she looked at Natalya as if she'd never seen her before. Nirosh stood behind her keeping her under his protective gaze. Darius was nowhere within sight.

Cohen left her side to take his spot on the smaller of the two thrones, a stoic expression slipping onto his face. Anya was already there. She stood beside the other throne. A beautiful woman occupied the larger, more ornate seat. She looked at Natalya with a concentrated, calculating gaze, but there was a soft edge to her and Natalya instantly felt drawn to the woman. Her eyes were a blank, cool blue that seemed to be looking beyond Natalya and into her very soul. She wore her blonde hair in a similar fashion to the one that her handmaidens had swept Natalya's short hair into. Her rich green dress draped over her thin frame and hugged at her waist and breasts displaying her beauty in a confident way only a royal would dare. The Queen continued to survey the room and soon the chatter turned silent, all eyes on the dais. Everyone in the room seemed just as drawn to the Queen. While their eyes were focused on Natalya their bodies seemed to lean toward their leader.

"You have brought our sister home to us, you mustn't fear. No one will harm you here." When she spoke, it felt like honey washed over her, soothed her into a bath of sweet comfort and lulled her racing heart. "My name is Reagan, Queen of House Lunaries, protector of its people and property. Come here child. Tell me, what is your name?"

"This is Natalya of the village Ash, of the human kingdom Solara. If it pleases My Lady." Cohen spoke for her. His eyes shifted between the

Queen and his charge.

"An Easterner," Lady Anya interjected and Natalya found herself biting her tongue hard, heeding the warning from Islara.

"I know where the kingdom Solara is, Lady Anya." A titter of laughter ran through the hall and a hard scowl fell across the paramour's face.

"My apologies, My Lady, I meant no offense."

"No, you never do. Come now, Natalya. What would you have of me in thanks for the safe return of our sister?"

"Let me take Emeline home, she belongs with her family." Natalya demanded, passion lacing her voice. She was met with the same passive stare.

"We cannot allow her to leave just yet. She is sick and is not taking the bite well. If all goes accordingly then she will regain herself in a few nights. The longer we care for her, the quicker she will have full capacity of her facilities and memories."

"How do I know you're not hurting her?" Natalya glared at Anya.

"You are very protective of someone who is not even your kin. Pray tell why." Anya spoke over her Queen. "How can we be sure you did not have her turned to gain access to our home?"

"I didn't even know your kind existed until they attacked her! How dare you accuse me of putting her at risk!"

"You still haven't answered my question." Anya all but commanded.

"That is none of your concern." Natalya's shoulders squared and she unconsciously took a step forward toward the dais.

"You are in my home, it is my concern!"

"Enough." Reagan was on her feet, her slight body effectively placed between Anya and Natalya. Cohen was on his feet just as quickly. He stood beside the Queen with his hand on the paramour's wrist. His sharp teeth showed faintly under the curl of his upper lip. Nirosh's hand hovered over the blade he kept holstered to his side and even Emeline turned her body to take in the scene. "Lady Anya you will not speak to our guest in such a way. Natalya, we cannot release you or Emeline until she is well. If you must, we will allow you to visit her when convenient to the healers. After you are educated in our ways."

"I will not become one of you." Natalya spat and Anya tried to break free of Cohen's hold. There was a brief struggle and the Queen separated herself from it, moving down the dais until she stood in front of the scared girl.

"No one will ask that of you. All humans who live within these walls are first put to schooling on the history and customs of our people. Should you wish to stay and see your friend through her full recovery then you must do the same. If you wish to receive such lessons then we may call an end to this meeting and see you to your rooms."

Natalya looked into the eyes of the Queen and then back to her friend.

Emeline seemed to have slipped back into the trance like state that she'd been in when Natalya had first entered the hall and dread filled her lungs until she found it hard to breath properly. She would not leave without the girl and she would not let the monsters hurt her. Lessons had never been her favorite at home, but suffering through them seemed a small price to pay for their freedom.

"I will take your lessons," Natalya agreed before glaring over the Queen's shoulder at the still struggling female vampire in Cohen's grasp, "so long as they are not taught by her."

"Whatever she may or may not be, you will address her as m'lady or Lady Anya. Respect is important in my court."

"Does she know that?" Natalya whispered and was met with another reproachful look from the beautiful queen.

"Your first lesson is that vampires have extremely good hearing." The advice was whispered as well and Natalya colored. "Now I believe we can adjourn this meeting. I have a court to oversee and Cohen will show you to your new rooms."

"With me, Miss Natalya." Cohen released the unruly vampire and his fangs reseeded until he looked almost human again. The room made way for the two once more and Cohen gently led her from the room without a word. The heavy doors opened and banged shut, the echo filling the dull halls. There were a few people still crowding the entranceway when they passed through. Most of the house was either tending to their duties or attending court. When they seemed to be truly alone, Natalya spoke again.

"Why does she hate me?"

"The Lady Anya is a tough creature. You might soon find that she loves no one, but our Queen and is often brash with others." Cohen spoke lightly as if her attitude was perfectly normal. "Of course not many can withstand her character. We often find the small council of the Queen rotating members."

"Why are you telling me this? I'm sure the Queen would not want you speaking ill of her paramour." Natalya paid little attention to where he was taking her. The castle was far larger than any structure she had ever seen and she was grateful that she would be taken to and from her lessons until they felt she could be trusted. It made perfect sense, but also meant that she wouldn't have to worry about getting lost often.

"You asked." Cohen shrugged, as if the simple statement was obvious. "If you wish to stay until your friend is truly well there is no sense in lying to you or omitting the truth. You would come to the conclusions yourself, in time." The respect that she was being afforded was curious and enough to make her want to stay to understand the strange creatures better. "Your room, Miss, Queen Reagan will send a handmaiden for you and she will see to you personally when you have settled."

"Thank you, Lord Cohen." Natalya bowed her head respectfully. If he would show her dignity she owed it to him to return it.

"When there is no court to impress you may call me by my given name." Cohen gave her a small smile. "We will speak again soon, I am sure of it."

Natalya waited for him to leave the room before fully taking in her new quarters. The room was large enough for her, but sparsely furnished. A large bed stood in the center with soft bedding and smooth sheets. A large fire was already set in the fireplace to the right while a wardrobe stood to the left. After quick inspection Natalya found several of the same simple dresses as the one that she currently wore as well as underthings and two dresses that looked fit for entertaining or an important dinner both of which she had no experience with. Beside the wardrobe sat a vanity with more hairpieces than Natalya had ever owned. Many were plain, with multiple teeth to catch and hold her hair she assumed. She had never owned such things and lacked the imagination to guess at how they were meant to be fastened. Other pieces still were decorated in shining gold and colored stones and surely worth more than all of the belongings that she'd had to her name in her old home. There were pieces of deep red rubies and breathtaking sapphires in the shape of tears. One pin in particular was shaped like a snake and its body was comprised of emeralds with onyxes for eyes. She let her fingers glide over every piece with care and felt her heart race at the thought of wearing them. She had never dreamt to see such beauty and yet here it lay for her to try and wear to his heart's content.

Above the vanity was a window that overlooked the front grounds. The disadvantage would seem to be the smell from the over inhabited camp like settlements, but it was still more than Natalya had ever been given and her short time on the farm had built her immunity to odors and sights best not mentioned in polite conversation.

A knock at the door drew Natalya from the inspection of her room and she moved to answer it, surprised to see Freya at the other side.

"M'lady has requested I stay with you during your time until you complete your lessons." The girl smiled warmly and Natalya graciously let her in. "M'lady understands that you know little of her people and she had hoped another human presence might calm your nerves."

"That was very thoughtful of her." Natalya mused and allowed the handmaiden to bustle about, kindling the fire and pulling back the sheets on the bed.

"M'lady is kind, you will see. Now come to bed Miss. I know you are accustomed to sleeping when the sun is down, but here we abide by their sleeping patterns. You will be given a night to grow accustomed to this and then Lord Nirosh will take you for your first lesson."

Natalya allowed Freya to unlace and hang her dress and unpin her hair before crawling into the bed. It was softer than any she'd slept in before. She had been forced to keep the creature's schedule on the road, and while she still found it odd to sleep while the sun shone, it was easy enough to find sleep in the comfort of a warm bed. It hardly even mattered to Natalya that she found herself with another strange bed warmer to keep her through the morning. Her father would have been horrified to see her let her guard down like this, but she hadn't enough energy to care. Natalya allowed sleep to claim her then, comforted by the soft inhale and exhale of the woman beside her.

COHEN

The tension that had been building in Cohen's chest since they found the girls in Morden released as he shut the door to Natalya's room behind himself. Natalya was safe in her room and he knew that one of the handmaidens would stay the night with her. He had expressed to Reagan that the girl might take better to a human and he knew that she would be in good hands with Freya. In the short time it had taken him to make sure the girl was all set a guard had taken her place at the door. She had been one of Nirosh's students and while he trusted Darius and his judgement, it made him feel better to know that their newest human ward was being protected by one of the best guards in Lunaries. They were in the deepest part of the castle, so there should be no need for a guard, but Cohen was overly cautions and it seemed Nirosh had felt the same. They had agreed to place Natalya in a room right outside of the Royal Tower so she would be close enough to them and they could check in on her frequently.

He had agreed to meet with Reagan after seeing to the girl and he began to walk further through the corridor toward the inner council room. He knew that after finishing with the court that Reagan would wish to retire to the relative peace of her own tower. She was a good ruler who spent much of her time among her people, but when she could afford to slip away she often did. Reagan had never been much of a person to enjoy large groups and it had seemed funny to Cohen when she had first taken the throne, but she took to it well and enjoyed solitude when she could.

The doors to the small council room were closed and no guards were posted. It should have seemed strange enough for him to question, but Cohen pushed the door open without thought and swept into the room without a care. Inside he found Reagan and Anya at opposite sides of the council table and the air between them seemed to spark. Anya was leaning over the table with her arms outstretched as her hands steadied her. A deep-set glare was marring her face. Reagan was sitting, her hands folded neatly in her lap. She had a passive, unreadable expression on her face. It was obvious that he had walked in on a fight. He immediately wished that he had paid more attention to the atmosphere of the room before entering. He loved and respected his queen more than any other, but he had no tolerance for Anya. He had told Reagan more than once that he saw little need for her in their court. She could be her paramour without sitting on the council, but Reagan was too soft. She did not see the path of destruction the angry vampire had set course for. She did not see that she was dragging the whole House down. *How could she be blind to her poison, even now?*

"If I may, My Lady," Cohen bowed himself into the room. He kept his eyes trained on his queen ignoring the penetrating glare he felt from Anya. It would do the girl some good to hold her tongue in front of her elders, no matter what her imagined superiority granted her.

"There is no need for such formalities, you know that." Reagan brushed her skirts aside and stood, moving to embrace him. When her slender arms wrapped around him he felt Anya's eyes burn into his back. "How has our new human ward settled in?"

"As well as can be expected for an Easterner. She seems to be in shock, but if we give her some time. I'm sure she will come around." Cohen relinquished himself from her grasp and pulled out the seat at the head of the table for her before taking her vacated one across from her still furious paramour.

"I still see no reason to keep her here. Her people refuse to even acknowledge that we exist. What good could come from her alliance?" Anya growled. She was still standing, though the tension in her shoulders and back was beginning to lessen. Cohen noticed that as soon as he was no longer in their Queen's close proximity she had calmed down significantly.

"Must we argue about this again?" Reagan sounded tired as she gazed reproachfully toward the youngest vampire. "An ally is better than an enemy and she might just prove value yet. Darius believes she might hold some magic. His calming aura had no effect on her."

"Is it possible that Darius is just not as good as you once believed?"

"I've had enough of this, childe." Reagan's sharp gaze fell on the girl and Cohen winced. Reagan was never hard on either of them, they were her favorites and she often took their opinions into high esteem. She would rather have them speak their mind than to sit in silence and watch her rule, but this time she seemed to have had enough. Her lover was still young, too young to truly grasp the art of politics and war. She had no knowledge of how to conduct herself in a dignified manner and Cohen hoped that Reagan would see her mistakes for what they were. "You will leave us, we will discuss your behavior in our rooms later. Wait for me there."

"You cannot mean to dismiss me! How could you take the side of that traitor Darius and this brown-noser over me!" Anya looked to Cohen with disgust making him bristle. He did not need to speak to put the childe in her place, Reagan might favor them both, but even Anya knew that he had been with their Queen since the very beginning. Reagan valued him more than her and that was the main point of contention between the two.

"There is truly no contest between you and I. Our Lady must see to the protection of this House and I am far better fit to help in that regard." Cohen spoke out of turn and he knew it. He was only making matters worse, but watching this little girl be so brazen in front of the woman he loved and respected made his bloodlust cloud his better judgment.

"Enough, both of you." Reagan commanded and Cohen hung his head in shame. He did not mean to stoop to the brat's level, but it was hard at times to remember that he could not just give her a good tongue lashing as if she were the childe she acted as. "Anya, to our quarters, now."

The girl turned on her heel without another word. The loud clack of her boots echoed through the hall and acted as a metronome to calm Cohen's racing thoughts. He did not bother to look up and face the enraged queen beside him. He knew her anger toward him was justified. Being as old as she, he knew better than to become involved in the petty fights of the children vampires that made up most of their House. The air in the room seemed to be set ablaze and Reagan stood to pace, an act very unlike her normally composed self. Cohen listened for the light whisper of her skirts as she made several circuits of the room. When it seemed that an eternity had passed she spoke again, her voice even once more.

"Morale would drastically increase if you only stopped baiting her." The words were light, even playful and Cohen was reminded of the girl that he remember Reagan to be. She had been so gentle. He remembered how, even then, her passion for those that she cared for had gotten her into trouble.

"It would help even more if she stopped being an idiot. You must remind her again that I am no threat to whatever it is you two have."

"Be that if it were true." Reagan stopped pacing to watch his reaction carefully. "I believe you might have been right all along."

"That must pain you to say," Cohen grinned with his fangs drawn, "what exactly do you think I was right about?"

"You know exactly what I mean. I ask you to not make me admit it aloud." Reagan leveled him with a pointed gaze, but Cohen saw no reason to relent. This easier side of her was one that he did not get to see often. She was usually flanked by her guards or her lover and never seemed to have time for him. He once wished that things were just the way they had been before she had become queen, maybe even before they had been reborn, but it was foolish to think such things. *I will never have my sweet Reagan to myself again, I should have known that long ago.*

"What will we do about Cassandra and Logan? Surly even Anya must see that something will need to be done. We cannot allow them to run free."

"Cassandra has always been the concern. Her little House of rogues will crumble as soon as she does. It will not matter in the end if we take them down, but it will matter that we dismantle her hold on them and show just how much of a poison she is. I know that Anya does not see that now, but in time I'm sure she will see what needs to be done." Cohen noticed that even now she refused to speak his name and it only caused him to feel more grief.

"I'm tired of you making excuses for her! It is critical that we move to stop Cassandra now, unless you have forgotten what kind of woman she is." Cohen hated the excuses that he always heard. Ever since Reagan had taken the girl in and given her the bite she was a thorn in his side. He found it ironic that she could see Cassandra as a poison, but not Anya.

"Forgotten? How could you even believe that I have forgotten? After everything she did to our family how could you even consider that there isn't a day that doesn't go by that I don't want her dead?" Her steady voice broke and she fell back into her chair. Cohen had never regretted words more than he did when watching such as strong woman break down. He leaned across the table to take her hands in his hands.

"You are right, sister mine, you could never forget what she is. I am so very sorry." Cohen's heart broke to hear his strong sister sound so broken. Before they had gotten the bite, before Cassandra had torn their world apart, they had been happy. Reagan had been the oldest of the three of them, back when their brother had been with them. Not a day went by that he didn't think of how his family had once been, but it would have been worse for Reagan. She had been the oldest and the one who felt responsible for keeping them all safe.

"Sh, speak not of that now." Reagan brushed her fingers against his to soothe him. Even when he meant to offer her comfort she managed to see to his needs before her own. It was what made her such a great ruler. Everything she had taken from her time as a human, from their life before as being brother and sister, she used to help her see to the care of their people. "You know what dangers lie ahead if anyone knew. We mustn't speak of this here. The walls have ears."

"You fear a spy?" It was the first that Cohen was hearing of this. It was unlike Reagan to keep anything from him. It was true that only one person in their court knew the true nature of their relationship and their shared history with the rogue queen, but she had never once told him she feared a betrayer in their midst.

"I am not sure and so you must keep this to yourself. I hope to find out soon and I don't want suspicions roused until I have more proof."

"What proof do you speak of?" Cohen whispered, his eyes darting around the room as if there was someone watching.

"Hush now, baby brother. I will speak to you about this again in time, until then I need you to keep an eye on our two new wards."

"The two girls? Do you think they are hiding something? I thought they were both innocent humans, well before the bite they were both innocent humans." It never occurred to him that the two girls that they had found could be part of Cassandra's game. Of course Anya had suggested it, but that had made the idea even more ludicrous. Now that Reagan seemed to think that a rogue was infiltrating the House it seemed more realistic that the girls would be part of some game.

"Not quite, but I think we should leave them wanting for nothing and be sure they are never alone." Cohen knew that she was keeping something from him, but he would have to let it go for now.

"Should we allow them to see each other? Are you afraid that they might be working together?" Cohen asked. He didn't often receive direct orders from his queen and even less often were they so vague. Whatever she was playing at he knew that he would have to do everything in his power to have her back. She would never admit to him, of all people, that she needed help and it was his responsibility as her second in command to protect her, even from herself.

"I think they should be separated for a time, but not because I fear them. They will both need time to adapt to their new lives here and it would be best that they are forced to do so alone. Too many reminders of their past could keep them from moving forward."

"Is that why you replaced me by your side with that childe?" Cohen couldn't help the hurt that appeared in his voice then. Centuries old or not, he still felt that as her one and only true relative he belonged by her side on the throne.

"I will not have this conversation again. I need to see to my testy paramour, I would like you to check on Emeline." Reagan's word was always final and Cohen learned long ago to let her be.

"Yes, My Lady." Cohen stood and bowed, knowing that the formalities would set the woman on edge.

"Don't test me, Cohen, I will see you soon." Cohen nodded to her before leaving. Emeline was staying in the Royal Quarters despite not being made by a vampire of high blood. Reagan's personal healers, per the queen's orders, would be seeing to her.

The halls of the castle were bustling with servants and guards as they always were. Since the eventful court that had been held it was obvious that the people of Lunaries were teeming with excitement. It was not often that they welcomed new brothers and sisters into their home, but three visitors within the span of a moon's turn was unprecedented. The arrival of a former human and her companion from the East was nearly as big of news as the day that Reagan had come home with her new paramour on her arm. Then it had been cause for joy and celebration, now it was the marking of a new era. Their land was already too close to the humans of Solara. It had been a major concern during their council meetings, but there wasn't much that they could do. It would be impossible for them to move their home further into Mordin Forest because of their tenuous relationship with Faegon. If it was possible for two girls from a nearby village to stumble so close to their territory then it was certainly possible for the humans who had left them alone for centuries to remember them. As it was, they could hardly afford to wage a war against the rogues; they would not be able to fight two wars on all fronts.

Cohen moved through the halls with little issue. The servants parted way for him as he glided with each step. The fires in each sconce were meant for the humans who were in their service, whose eyesight were not as strong as vampires, and the flames left shadows licking up the walls. Cohen paid little mind to everything around him until he stopped in front of a heavily guarded door. Two of the younger royal guards stood watch, their faces solemn and unyielding. Darius had picked them himself, promising that they were two of his brightest and best. The men stepped aside instantly for him and Cohen nodded before entering.

The large fire warmed the room and the heat felt stifling to Cohen's skin. Emeline was still recovering from her rebirth and chills would consume her body until her heart completely stopped. It would take nights for her to fully recover. They would have no way of knowing if she would survive, until then. The girl lay in the middle of a large bed. Silk sheets wrapped around her slim form, pillowing her and holding her close. The room was sparsely furnished except for a single, stiff, high backed chair. Nirosh was sitting perfectly still, his gaze never leaving the girl. It was hard not to see that he was already forming a soft spot for her.

"She's strong, I'm sure she will be fine." While he made no indication that he had known that Cohen had entered the room Nirosh didn't seem the least bit surprised to hear him.

"Did our lovely Queen send you to check up on me?" The response was tired, as if he already knew the answer.

"Do you need to be checked up on?" Nirosh was the oldest member of their House. He was the only one who Reagan had professed absolute trust in besides himself. He had been part of Lunaries before even he and Reagan had and he was the only one who knew everything about the queen and her brother. He was the only one who remembered the things that Cassandra had done. He had supported them through the uprising, when all hope seemed to be lost and then had stood beside Reagan and supported her rule. He had never once asked for anything in return.

"No, you know that boy." Nirosh scoffed and turned back to face Emeline. "She looks like my daughter. My human daughter."

"You've been one of us so long, I'm surprised that you remember." Cohen remarked and took to the other side of the girl's bed. He sat against the footboard so he could watch the man and the girl carefully.

"Would you forget? Don't you remember your brother?" Nirosh knew the answer and Cohen didn't see fit to give him one. The two sat in silence, simply watching as the girl slept.

"She will wake up, Nirosh. When she does we'll teach her how to protect herself so nothing will harm her again."

"You don't need to reassure me of that, boy." Nirosh growled, his hand coming to lie on hers. "I would not allow anything else to befall her, but first we wait."

"How long do the healers believe it will take her to recover? I was surprised to see her awake and sitting at court."

"They had given her some potion to waken her especially for that. It seemed that others on the council had thought it best to have her visible for the people."

The other lords and ladies that sat on the council hadn't been present for court that night and it seemed odd to Cohen that their decision had made any matter. He might not know much about the magic of healing, but he knew that it was dangerous to use potions on a sick childe just going through the change.

"I find it hard to believe that Reagan would have allowed that."

"She seems to believe that playing the safe route with her subjects will serve her better than pushing them to act rashly."

The two shared a knowing look. It seemed that Nirosh also knew of the suspicions which Reagan had just made him privy to. If it had been any other then he might have been jealous, but the man brushed his fleeting anger aside. Nirosh did not threaten his place in the House or his place at their Queen's side. If anything he was the only vampire in the castle's walls that was the least threat.

"Do you share her beliefs?"

"I find it hard to disagree. Our Queen is a smart woman. She has her reasons for keeping secrets, you of all people should know that."

When the coup had first occurred many of the people of Lunaries had fled. While it was difficult to say if they had joined rank with Cassandra or simply looked to find shelter in a non disgraced House, there were very few who stayed. The years following had been brutal, as most of the noble class had been eradicated, and the House had to be rebuilt from the ground up. Even when Gareth had been the King of Lunaries, there had been few who knew the true nature of their relationship. It had seemed like dangerous knowledge, as their entrance into the House had caused the banishment to begin with. It had been Gareth's idea to keep the secret and it had been Reagan's idea to honor it even after his death. Nirosh had been one of the advisors on Gareth's council and thus was one of the few still alive who knew the true reason for Lunaries' banishment. Even centuries later if the truth came out then there would certainly be a rebellion among their people. Of course it had seemed odd that Cassandra hadn't spread the news of his sweet sister's shame, but it seemed that she gained from keeping secrets too. He had been of the opinion that killing Cassandra as quickly as possible would end the danger for Reagan as well as the stupid rebellion that the rogue queen was attempting to start, but again Anya's insistence kept his sister from thinking or acting.

"Secrets are necessary, yes, but at what price? When does it become too rich to continue?"

"Careful, those who might misunderstand you would consider your words treason," Nirosh warned. There was no heat behind his words which told Cohen all he needed to know that the elder meant him no ill will. He understood where his frustrations stemmed from.

"It is very good that you do not misunderstand me then."

"Indeed." Nirosh broke eye contact with him and turned to gaze upon Emeline once more.

The moment was over and Cohen knew a dismissal when he was handed one. Quietly, the queen's brother let himself from the room to leave the elder with his thoughts as his own haunted his mind. Change had been lingering in the air for some time and the man feared what lay on the horizon. He could not help but feel as if the scale that their lives had been balancing on had just tipped. There was nothing to be done except ride the downhill slope if he hoped to see it to the end. Reagan had her suspicions and it was his duty to investigate them and see his House through to the end of the oncoming uprising even if it meant that he was not standing when the dust finally settled.

REAGAN

It seemed that the night of a queen never truly came to an end. Reagan loved her people and most of all she loved her heir and her paramour, but there were nights that they completely exhausted her, and it seemed that this night would be no different. Cohen truly meant well and normally his distrust of someone would send her instincts into a fury, but with Anya she could not concede. There had been a time when her lover had suspected that Cohen was jealous of their relationship, though if she truly thought about it, Reagan was sure that Anya still held that fear. Of course she hadn't believed a word of it for she knew that Cohen would never love her in the way that Anya expected, but to explain that would be to admit to secrets which had been held for too long to give up now. Anya was a beautiful woman and smart, despite how she might carry herself, but even some things slipped her notice. No, Reagan's secret would remain one for as long as she might live.

Cohen had hated Anya from the day that they had met, but Reagan had never understood why. It was true that Anya had been wild when they first took her in. She had been a lost child in the woods running from the terror that Cassandra wrought. She had been angrier then, but also scared. It was hard to believe in the aftermath from another one of her outbursts, but she had been much worse when Reagan had first brought her home. Cohen had spent many nights questioning her sanity. Even Nirosh had asked her privately of her intentions for the girl, but Reagan would not allow them to force her hand. She was their Queen and they were going to respect her decision. They had come around, after sometime. Anya was a product of the terror of Cassandra; a terror that Reagan felt partially responsible for. It was her duty to mend the wounds that the evil woman caused across their world. Anya had calmed down considerably and things had begun to settle for the first time since she had come into their lives. Of course that had changed when Darius had arrived.

Reagan often wondered if she was too kind and trusting. She admitted that she had brought Anya into their circle without consulting the others, but when it came to Darius, everyone had liked him; everyone, but Anya. It was jealousy, of course. Reagan had taken to him quickly and worked hard to make him feel at home with herself and their people. There had been a time when she and Anya would stay up late, arguing about whether or not Darius should be allowed to take a rank in the guard, if he could be trusted enough to become part of her council. The fighting and her attitude had escalated to a point where Reagan had seriously considered casting her aside as Cohen had insisted, but Anya did eventually relent and a tentative peace had been mostly maintained. Cohen often asked her what it was that Reagan saw in the girl that allowed her to forgive her every wrongdoing. If she were being honest with herself it was the fire that raged in Anya that made her so attractive to begin with.

Cohen had always said that she was crazy. She was half convinced to agree with him. Anya brought trouble wherever she went and yet she would look at her with such expressive eyes and Reagan would find herself forgiving her again. Whether it was how old the arguments had become or if it was just because of the stressful past few weeks that the House had suffered, Reagan had reached her limit. She knew that Anya would be fuming when she returned to their chambers and a very small part of her desired to run away instead of facing her. Of course she did not give into those very cowardly thoughts. She was a Queen and in the end if anyone should be running it should be Anya. She didn't want that, not truly, but the girl would have to learn her place or be removed from that place until she proved that she could conduct herself in a way that was expected of any ruler's paramour. With her mind made on how to handle the situation, Reagan made her way through the emptying halls at a brisk pace.

Her subjects hardly ever saw her in one of the moods she now found herself. She suspected that if she had the chance to glance at her reflection that she would find a grim, determined shadow marring her face. She hated to feel the way that she did and hated more that her people might see it cracking through her smooth exterior. Cohen would chide her if he was still beside her, but he was not. She had seen to it that he was busy about the castle doing a job she should have been doing had she not had to deal with her disquieted lover. She cursed the way things had become under her breath as she stilled before the door that led to her chambers. For the first time since she had taken these chambers as the Queen of Lunaries she felt as if they didn't belong to her. They hadn't been her chambers when she had first arrived to this House, then they had belonged to King Gareth and his own troubled lover. On long nights when Anya was sleeping soundly and her thoughts kept her awake she thought of the life she would have lead had Gareth not fallen to the wicked ways of that woman, but it was folly to travel down that road as much as it was folly to hope that the conversation awaiting her could be anything more than an argument.

She knocked on the door as a courtesy to Anya. She had every right to burst through the heavy wooden doors with the fury that burned in her chest, but she had more respect for the woman and more regard for her position than that. The door was heavy, a reflection of the burdens she carried and she felt the anger flee from her as she caught sight of her distraught lover. Anya sat in the middle of their large bed. She had long since shed the clothes she had worn to court and instead was hunched over herself. Her bare arms were wrapped around her naked legs and were the only thing covering her thin form. The tears staining her face were what caught and held Reagan's attention and it took all of the willpower she believed she possessed to not rush to the woman's side.

"Why are you crying, childe?" The words tumbled from her mouth lacking grace or compassion.

Anya was stubborn by nature and she sneered at her, the tears ending abruptly. Reagan almost wondered if they had all been a lie. "You ought to know, *Your Grace*."

"If you insist on taking such a tone with me you may see yourself out." The conversation was quickly spiraling out of her control and she found it hard to care.

"Would you really so easily cast me from your side? After all we have been through I would think I mean more to you than that," she spat and removed her arms from their tight grip.

Whether she meant to hide her weakness or tempt Reagan with her body, the queen was not sure, but either way the action had remarkably failed. It would do them both good to put distance between them and Reagan turned her back to compose herself. She took the time to carefully undo her hair as a mindless distraction. Freya had seen to her before going to the new human and had twisted and teased her hair until it was painful, but she did admit to liking the outcome. It would irritate Anya for her to take her time now and it would help to calm her own nerves.

She took one pin out at a time, being more than careful as they snagged and pulled at her fine hairs and made her wince. The twist in her hair began to unwind and it settled around her shoulders like a blanket. She wished she would wrap herself up in it and hide from the impending fight. Her hair was done so her dress came next. The ties that bound the heavy dress were undone with shaking fingers. The knots held the fabric together at her collar and at her waist. They were tight and it became obvious that she wouldn't be undoing them on her own. Anya was beside her in a second, her callous hands moved to the ties at her collar first before pushing aside the fabric to reveal Reagan's naked breasts.

"My Queen." Anya's tone was trying for demure, but Reagan knew better.

"Don't start with that. Speak your mind or be done with it."

"You're tired from the activity of these past few weeks, come to bed and let me help you forget it."

Reagan watched the brown eyes she had fallen in love with and regretted the need to bring the false calm to an end. "I'm tired of your behavior. If it was the House that tired me then I wouldn't have made it this long into my reign."

"How dare you," her voice was as sharp as her fangs that protruded from her mouth and slurred her words. "I love you! All I want to do is protect you!"

"Protect me from what, exactly?" Reagan kept her voice soft in an attempt to calm her lover.

"From any who wishes you harm."

"And who in these walls wishes me harm?"

"I don't know." Her eyes were downcast and Reagan gently brought her face up until she could look into her eyes. The blue had cleared with her anger and her fangs had receded. "I just don't trust them."

"Them who? Tell me, childe, and I can investigate them. I want to put these silly thoughts of yours to rest. Maybe then you will begin to behave like a Lady."

"Will you reconsider then?" Anya was only her paramour because of Cohen's request. Reagan had never told her, she believed the reason that they never married was because Reagan would not marry her until she saw the woman mature and be worthy of the title.

"It would not hurt your case." Reagan hated lying to Anya, but it was the only thing that Cohen requested of her and she could not refuse him that. "Tell me names and I will do what I can to ease your fears."

"Darius."

"Not this again, Anya. What proof do you have?" She swatted Anya's distracting hands away and undid the rest of her dress, the green fabric slid down her body and pooled at their feet.

"Why must we have this conversation now? You're tired, come to bed we can rest and then we can talk about this tomorrow."

"No. I will not put this conversation off any longer. You will tell me now why you hate Darius so and what could possibly make you think that he would betray us."

Reagan watched her lover for any signs of a lie. She could not count how many times she'd had this conversation with the woman and every time her answers had been evasive and less than helpful. She had hated him since the day that he had arrived and that had put the Queen on edge. Her Commander of the Guard had been forced to go through a more rigorous training and scrutiny than many others, but he had passed all of his tests with flying colors. Anya had grumbled through it all, but she had relented when he joined the Council. She had known then that there was no sense in pushing the matter, but that never stopped her from restarting the age old argument whenever a mood overtook her.

Anya was biting her lip in a tell tale sign that a half truth was about to pass her lips. Reagan was tired of these games, but she would allow the woman a chance to speak. Anya had retreated to their bed and Reagan sat back against her vanity, putting the required distance between them. They would have this conversation no matter how much Anya wished to distract her from it.

"I don't trust him."

"Anya," Reagan warned, "I am going to need more than that to go behind the back of one of my most trusted men."

"Does my trust mean nothing to you?"

"You know that I value your opinion, but you need to give me proof. I will not tell you again. Give me proof or let this argument rest. I am tired and we have guests in the House."

"I believe he might be a spy." Anya spoke the words like an eruption of fire from her chest. The words surprised her nearly as much as they surprised her Queen and she looked more uncomfortable than she had when she had first been found in the woods nearly a century ago.

"That is a dangerous accusation."

"He slips off at night, I've heard the maids talk about it when they work."

"What maids? My people do not hide such secrets from me only to gossip about them carelessly where anyone else might hear them." Reagan could feel the anger which lay deep in her veins rise as she stood to get closer to Anya as if it would bring her closer to answers.

"No, they do not, My Queen, I have misspoken," Anya whispered. She shrank back in fear, her eyes wide with it until it seemed like they might stick like that. "I merely meant that I have heard these things and I worry."

"Who has told you these things? Are you keeping spies in my halls?"

Lady Arinessa employed spies, but it was her job. Reagan hated the thought of people who lived in her House and did not report to her, but she knew that it was important to have a mistress of secrets. She could not be in control of every detail of her House and Lady Arinessa was a necessary evil. If Anya had her own spies, however, it might explain the feeling she'd had of being watched.

"No one, My Queen. Please forgive me."

"Stop groveling. Who is feeding you this information."

"No one. I have seen him sneaking off. No one else has given me this information."

Reagan watched the woman carefully. It was possible that she was telling the truth. She and Anya spent little time together when they were not in bed or in Council meetings. Reagan had a House to run and Anya did whatever it was that pleased her. She had never been given a proper title as

Cohen did not trust her enough to see to it that she was given a task. It meant that the woman had a startlingly large amount of free time and Reagan wondered if that had been a mistake. Clearly the woman had taken to using her free time on pointless endeavors like following around respected members of the Council.

"What have you seen when you follow him?"

"Admittedly not much. He goes beyond the walls often and I dare not follow him there."

"There are no laws that prohibit leaving these walls. There is no reason that he should not be allowed to leave. Maybe he is seeking solitude from a place where he is needlessly harassed and followed by someone who is meant to be his peer."

Anya had the decency to look guilty at her words, or at least she did a fine job of acting like she felt something more than rage. "Be that as it may, I still do not trust him. Why don't you have one of Arinessa's people follow him? Or one of yours?"

It was a poorly kept secret from the Council that Reagan employed her own spies separate from the mistress of whispers. No one knew who they were, or at least Reagan hoped that was the case. Freya and Islara were among the small group that she trusted to find out information for her. It was part of the reason she had sent them to the human. She was glad that the girl had taken to Freya. She didn't believe the girl to be a spy, but she was not a friend to be sure. It hurt no one to have a pair of eyes on her at all times. Islara and Freya might be noticed if absent from the castle to follow Darius, but she might have the right person for the job. It felt wrong to send a friend to follow a friend, but if it would ease Anya's worries and help to calm the girl then it would be well worth the guilt.

"I have few people who would be suited for the job and fewer still who are available, but I will see to it if only to ease your fears."

"Why are your spies not available? Is something going on?"

Cohen's worry echoed in her mind, but Reagan pushed it aside. Anya put her trust in her and told her about following Darius. Truth should be honored with truth, it was something that she had always believed. "I have felt the eyes of others on me and this House for some time. I think there might be a spy in our midsts, but I know not who."

"It is Darius, I am certain of it. How could you not tell me that you feared someone amongst us?" The silence was telling and Anya's face hardened. "You suspected me?"

"A good Queen can never be too careful," even Reagan knew how vague her answer was.

"So you suspected me, but I'm sure you never once suspected Cohen." Again her silence damned her. "Why him? Why does it always come down to him?"

Truth should be honored with truth and yet this secret was too big to tell. Anya would never understand, no one would ever understand what had happened. Those who had been there, who had lived through it had turned from her; all except Cohen and Nirosh. She wanted to believe that Anya would understand too, but she knew that the risk was not worth the reward.

"I know Cohen would never do anything to harm me."

"And I would?" There was hurt in her brown eyes. It swam through them and spilled down her cheeks. For a moment she looked like the scared girl she had found in the woods, but anger took over her before long and the stubborn woman she had kept by her side was back.

"I don't think you would, not truly. I am very sorry."

Torn between hurt and anger, Anya lashed out. "You're sorry? You doubt me and humiliate me and you're sorry?"

She let the words hang between them in the air. She knew that she should speak up. Anya was a master at stewing in her own anger until it boiled over and erupted causing havoc to anyone who was unfortunate enough to be within the vicinity to be scalded by the overflow. Reagan knew from experience that it was only a matter of minutes before the tight control that Anya held on her mounting anger broke and she was faced with the ferocity of her rage bearing down on her. Pride was not a vice she believed she suffered from, but Reagan bit back what little she had left to make peace with her lover.

"Anya, please. You must understand the stress of being watched by one of my own has addled my brains. Forgive me, my sweet, and I promise I will look further in your own suspicions. I should not have turned aside your advice so carelessly. Now please, will you forgive me? It has been a long night and all I wish for now is to find some peace in the arms of the woman I love."

Anya watched her with her naturally guarded face until a small smile from the queen broke her icy exterior. "Of course I will forgive you, what kind of lover would I be if I didn't?"

Reagan could have imagined the pause at use of the word lover and she chose to ignore it. Anya was finally listening to sense and there was no reason to cause another fight. With a satisfied sigh, she walked to the bed and slid underneath the sheets that Anya already had draped around her own body. The curtains were tightly drawn in anticipation of the rising sun and Reagan felt the pull of sleep calling to her as she opened her arms for Anya to turn into. The mop of brown curls nestled deeper into her chest, fanning around her shoulders and neck as they always did and Reagan allowed herself to finally relax. Whether it was because she was tired or because she genuinely forgave her queen, Anya was silent and asleep in a matter of moments.

Cohen would be mad to know that she had told Anya of her suspicions, but she could not bring herself to care what with the girl sleeping soundly in her arms. It seemed impossible that Darius might be the spy in her court, but she owed it to Anya to at least look into the possibility. She would have to speak with Cohen about it when the moon rose, but she would worry about it then. For now she would enjoy a moment of peace in the midsts of chaos.

ARTHUR

Despite having grown up exploring the woods just outside of his village, enough time had passed that Arthur felt like a stranger as they carefully picked their way through the trees to find the old trail. He was a good hunter and his difficulty could be directly contributed to the pain in his arm and the haze that seemed to have invaded his mind. Art was blessedly quiet beside him as he followed his lead through the tangled branches. They were far enough into harvest that the leaves were beginning to slowly change and soon they would fall to blanket the ground. Arthur did his best to keep his focus on the trail, Art's hurried steps in the background keeping him from slowing down. Everything else around them became white noise as Arthur refused to allow anything to distract him from his mission. It was a slow effort since Arthur's wounds prevented him from moving quickly and Art was just as lost as he was, but the man was determined to make do with what he was given.

Using his good arm to apply constant pressure to the gash on his left arm, Arthur had to blink through each moment of searing pain. Every breath hurt and he was more than a little concerned that any moment could find him passed out in the dirt. He shuddered to think how Art would react. The boy's idea of an adventure before now had been a ride outside of his village's walls, this certainly was far more than he could navigate on his own. With that in mind, Arthur turned his attention back to the task at hand, Art was relying on him as were the girls. Because his focus was solely placed on their previous steps he paid little attention to the wayward branches which stretched out to kiss his skin and catch on his clothes. From the sounds Art emitted beside him the boy seemed to fare even worse and Arthur had no doubt that they would be decorated in new scrapes and cuts before the day was done.

"Are you certain we're not lost?" Art asked. Fear clouded his voice and

Arthur was reminded of a young Natalya. He had stayed by Arthur's side since the incident in the clearing, huddling close to him like Natalya used to when she was still young and afraid.

"We would have been fine if you had just stuck to the trail." Arthur growled. It was getting later and the fading light made it even harder to find their way.

"I thought I'd heard something, I'm sorry!" Art hissed back.

"Sorry isn't going to fix my arm is it?" Arthur sighed. He was tired of fighting with the boy, but it seemed that fighting was what they did best. They were truly lost, loath as he was to admit it, and there seemed to be little hope for them to regain the time they had wasted.

"Well, pushing on like this in the woods with no direction isn't going to help either!" Art grabbed at his good arm and forced him to stop. "It's getting late, we really need to rest."

Arthur hated nothing more than admitting defeat, but the boy was right. He wasn't sure how much longer he would be able to stand much less move. If they took the time to rest now then his body would have more time to heal and he would be ready for the next attack. They were getting nowhere and he was sure that the tracks that he was following were beginning to cross as if they had managed to walk in circles. Some rest would really do the both of them good. When he'd fought with Natalya in the past it always seemed like a good night's rest made both he and his daughter forget their differences. Of course the last time he'd tried such a method she'd run away and managed to get them into the mess they were currently in, but he couldn't think of that, not now. He would get her back and then there would be time to argue about how she had left. He never believed he would look forward to arguing with his daughter again as much as he did in that moment.

"We will spend the rest of the daylight looking for shelter. I will not hear another word from you unless it is a matter of life or death. Are. We. Clear?"

"As clear as water," Art glared back before adding under his breath, "I can see why Natalya left now."

Arthur had enough sense to pretend that he hadn't heard the last part. He knew that getting mad at the boy would do no good. Despite knowing this, he couldn't help the rise in his blood that he felt when Natalya and he fought. He was older, wiser. If she had seen reason then she would still be at home safe. He knew that if things continued, Art would follow down the same road as Natalya. He just had to make sure that the boy didn't end up the same way.

Thankfully the boy kept quiet as they continued their search. Thick brush and overgrown trees gave little shelter when monsters lurked in the woods. If they were truly to feel safe they would need a natural structure that afforded them coverage on all but one side. At least then if they were attacked he would have less ground to cover. The boy had proven himself under pressure, but Arthur had significant doubts on whether he would survive another attack. He was trailing behind in the same manner that Natalya had and the thought made the older man grimace. He was going to lose the boy at the rate that he was walking and it put him even further on edge.

"Pick up the pace, we can't get separated." Arthur demanded. No matter how he intended his words they always seemed to come out harsh, colder than he meant.

"Yes, sir." If Art was anything like his daughter he was rolling his eyes while Arthur wasn't looking.

"If you'd rather get killed then be my guest." It was an empty threat and Natalya would have known it, but it seemed that where she had understood her father's moods, Art took his words literally.

"If you care so little for me why are you trying to find my sister? Or are you only looking for her thinking it will lead you to your daughter?" It was a fair point. Arthur's only loyalty to the two was through his friendship in Ivan, which was strained at best. His pause seemed answer enough for the boy, who promptly turned on his heel and began in the opposite direction.

"Where do think you're going," Arthur bellowed far too loud.

Birds flew high above, squawking in protest to the noise and a rabbit ran across the trail, back into the trees. He was exhausted and the thought of chasing after the boy was enough to make him begin to see the fog edge into his vision again. He did his best to run and track at the same time, but the forest began to blur after his first dozen paces. The blood loss was taking its toll and it took all of his strength to keep upright as he crashed through the woods blind. He could hear Art ahead, moving even faster and louder and he hoped that the boy would stop soon. If he kept up this pace he would collapse and he doubted the boy would stop to aid him. As if he had heard Arthur's thoughts the boy came to an abrupt stop not far ahead and Arthur pushed his aching body to meet him. The scratches of stray branches felt like kisses in comparison to the fire burning from his arm to his lungs. With each breath he dragged into his lungs, water sprang to Arthur's eyes and his vision swam dangerously until he could barely see beyond the threatening blanket of oppressive silence and nothingness. He had to slow down or he would lose his balance. When he was finally able to keep his body from swaying and the forest around him began to come into view once more he was relieved to see that Art stood beside him. The boy looked haunted and Arthur understood why when he followed his line of sight to the ruins that lay before them.

Nestled between the gnarled, overgrown trees sat what might have been a small village. There were collapsed structures scattered throughout what was obviously once a clearing. Now it looked as if the trees were the only ones living there as they grew through the walls of house, stretching through their roofs and tangling with other trees as if to greet them and bring their foliage even deeper into the homes. There were thick vines growing on every surface where the trees seemed to grow unscathed and the nearest hut had a curtain of vines covering it, shielding the inside from view.

The space was eerily quiet. Even the normal sounds of animals running through the forest was missing from the odd enclosure. Arthur stood still to listen for any movement, but could only hear the air being drawn in and out of their lungs. There were no people within the encampment. If he'd had the energy he might have stopped to think about what had caused the village to become desolate. He would have thought that whatever had drawn these people from their homes and made it so they never returned could also cause them trouble, but he was tired and such thoughts would have sapped the last of his energy. In that moment it seem that, while not ideal, the structures would provide them the shelter that they needed. They were completely alone and with any luck it would stay that way as they took their rest.

"You're not seriously considering this place," Art said and Arthur couldn't quite tell if it had meant to be a question or a command.

"Would you rather carry me elsewhere?" Arthur felt the boy turn to place a steadying hand on his arm just before his legs collapsed.

His vision went briefly white then black again and the forest swam in and out of view. The pounding in his head was deafening and prevented him from hearing anything else. His arm felt as if it was truly on fire and the air in his lungs tasted acrid on his tongue. He felt the bile in his stomach make its way up his throat, but the effort it would have taken to vomit was too much and instead he was left with a heavy feeling in his chest. He closed his eyes to block out any additional sensations and he felt Art tug at his arm. Arthur knew that the boy was strong enough to take him the rest of the way. Despite his many flaws, he had worked hard on his sister's farm with little aid for a full year and had done quite well for himself. With that thought in mind, Arthur allowed his body to sag under the stress of the day and Art was left with the brunt of the work.

Branches and fallen leaves crackled under his weight as he was dragged toward the huts. He felt as each piercing cut dug into his back, effectively distracting him from the pain in his arm and lessening the drumming in his head. It was a blessing, though he knew he would regret the tears in his only shirt and unnecessary cuts in his back in the morning. The noises began to fade like his vision and even the pain seemed to ebb away until it seemed to disappear and Arthur felt nothing. Art would take care of him just like Natalya would have. He would have to believe that. It was his final thought before the world blissfully melted away into darkness which Arthur greeted like an old friend.

Heat was the first thing that Arthur became aware of as he slowly roused from the nothingness that had consumed him. Not the same kind that had burned from within, but a warm heat that emanated from somewhere in front of his prone form. Through his lidded eyes he could see the inconstant light moving like waves. Someone had built a fire. Slowly, Arthur allowed his eyes to open. They felt heavy, like a thin wool blanket that was wrapped too tight. When he finally blinked away the sleep, he was met with a low burning fire. He seemed to be inside one of the huts. Art had thoughtfully cut out a section in the vines and the smoke from the fire rose harmlessly through it. Arthur could see a sliver of the night sky from his vantage point. It was completely dark, and the slight thud in his head kept him from ascertaining the time. When he felt that he could move his head without losing consciousness again, he looked down to his arm to find fresh bandages. They were tied tighter than the last time and looked relatively clean and with very little blood coloring it. There was a small pitcher of water near his head and a spread of bread and cheese. Arthur felt his stomach protest and he wondered when the last time he'd had a proper meal had been. It hardly seemed possible that it had just been five days ago that he'd sat down to supper with his daughter, it seemed as if a lifetime had already passed and Arthur was sure that he was sporting the grey hairs to prove it.

Arthur was able to push himself up with a little more effort than it should have taken. Slowly he pulled himself closer to the food and drink and consumed them greedily. The water felt impossibly cool to his lips and rushed down his aching throat like an elixir. The cheese and bread tasted as if it were made for kings and Arthur felt his senses returning to him in such a rush, threatening to make him dizzy again. When all was gone, he took a better look at his surroundings. He was certainly in one of the huts; he could see the places where vines from the outside were making their way through every crack and crevice. It seemed that the structure that he was in was an old village hall, a place where everyone could meet and talk. It was smaller than most of the village halls that he'd seen in his travels, but the old wooden benches and the sizable fire pit were enough evidence for Arthur.

The boy was nowhere in sight, but the soft humming just audible outside of the doorway told Arthur that he hadn't gone far. Despite his lack of training, Art had shown immense bravery and he knew that the boy had done everything in his own power to take care of Arthur despite the cruel words they had exchanged. He waited for the guilt to wrap its bony hand around his heart, but it never came. He knew the boy had been hurt by his words, but he would be hurt worse by the monsters who lived in Mordin Forest and it was his job to protect the boy. With his mind made, Arthur doused the fire before limping out of the hall. Art sat with his back against the vines, eyes scanning back and forth lazily.

"You should get some rest," Arthur said by way of greeting. He had never been one to admit weakness and thanking the boy was more than he could bear. The least he could do was relieve him from watch. Art jumped at his words, obviously not aware that the older man had woken.

"Are you alright?" Art's voice was pitched high and it made Arthur wince.

"Be quiet, we have no idea what could be out there!" He hissed through gritted teeth.

"You're right, sorry. But you should go back to sleep, I'm alright out here." The dark cloud that had disappeared from worry returned to the boy's eyes.

"Don't be stupid, go in and sleep. If you're too tired to notice I'm up then you'd be no use if anyone had come into the area."

"That's a bit rude coming from the person that was unconscious minutes ago."

Arthur bit back any retort that might have come spilling out. He was well and done with fighting and the boy could not be reasoned with.

"Well, I'm going to be taking watch, if you want to stay out here with me, so be it."

Art pushed past him and into the hall as he had expected. Arthur waited to hear the boy settle in, making sure that he heard even breathing before he allowed himself to sit down in the same spot where Art had been.

The ghost village was silent as Arthur had expected. He was more alert than before and he wondered what had happened to the people, but it seemed of little concern then. They were safe, at least for the night, and would need to be on their way as soon as the sun rose. He was glad that there was no one there. He preferred to be alone versus the company of others. When he was a child he had enjoyed the company of peers, but much had changed and the man he was welcomed the silence. Of course silence meant that he had time to think and that brought on the ghosts.

Whenever he found himself alone, Arthur would think of his late wife. Elizabeth had been his life, she had been the reason that he'd gone to Ash and forsaken his family. If he closed his eyes he could still hear her laughter, but with the passing of time details of her were leaving him. He couldn't remember what it felt like to hold her. He imagined that the warmth of the sun was how her smile had looked. He often looked at their daughter and wished that she were more like her mother. In some ways, she was just like her; stubborn, defiant, and with a bit of a rebellious streak. Elizabeth had fled her home in Magdus, the capitol of their Kingdom because of her condition as her father had phrased it. She had become pregnant, though Arthur had never asked who the man had been. He had never cared, his love for her was so deep, and when she had lost the baby it didn't seem to matter any longer. He had let himself forget the whole ordeal after they had wed. It wasn't until he had overheard his wife talking to their daughter when she'd been an infant that he had begun to guess at what might have happened.

He could still remember coming home one evening to see his young wife cradling their baby to her chest. She was sitting by the hearth, rocking Natalya to sleep all while telling her a story of a young woman and her love for a prince. She'd told their infant daughter that the young woman was a fool and for her actions she'd been banned from her home. The story had ended with the prince marrying another and the woman doing the same. Arthur had always wanted to ask her if the story had been true, if that was the past his wife would never speak of, but she hadn't been talking to him and he couldn't bring himself to break her trust.

If the story had been true that it was only fitting that Natalya had been thrown from her own home because of love; his love for his wife. Natalya had never understood that it was his love for her and her late mother that caused him to push her so hard. Losing Elizabeth had been horrible, but losing their daughter, his only connection to her would certainly kill him. If the story had been true then Arthur knew without a doubt that Natalya had also gained her mother's rebellious streak, but then he couldn't see the woman that he'd loved going behind her King and Country on a childish whim. The woman he'd loved had been strong, proud, but most of all smart. She kept her emotions hidden and radiated confidence and beauty. He could not simply believe that she'd run from home, shamed, and he understood then how his daughter must feel even if he did not share the sentiment. While Ash was the place where he'd built a home with Elizabeth, his true home would always be in Sylvine.

Near the end of their time in Ash, Arthur had felt like a true outsider, intruding on the lives of the people. He had no connection to the village beyond his wife and it was obvious that no one took kindly to his obsession with Mordin Forest. He'd honestly been trying to push his daughter to train in the hopes that she would agree that the village was too dangerous and would want to move away. He had never counted on her having suitors from important families. No one had ever cared for him and he hadn't thought that anyone would want his or her son married to the daughter of a widowed loon. He had been very wrong. If he'd let her stay, been there long enough to see her wed, then he wouldn't be fearing for her life and his own in the one place he hated most. He could have returned home after the ceremony and lived with Ivan and his wife. He would have been able to help Emeline and Art and no one would have encouraged the girl into the forest. There would be no need to find them now. But thinking on the things that could never be would not do. Arthur sighed and scrubbed at his face as if the action would take his memories away.

The lack of sound and movement was disorienting. He was beginning to wonder if the snapping twigs were coming from his imagination or if there was someone or something watching him. He turned to look around trying to see beyond the darkness and into the woods. There was nothing there or at least nothing that his old eyes could see. The stillness was starting to play with his mind and he closed his eyes to block out the unreliable senses. There was a gentle wind that carried through the still night, carrying fallen leaves with it. There was nothing around them and yet it felt like eyes were on him then. He looked around to dispel the feeling and found nothingness stared back. It was unnerving and the feeling of being watched only mounted until it was too much.

He shut the world out once more and the aches and pains from the day were at the forefront of his mind once more. He would need more time to heal, but they had very little time left. Five days was already the longest time he had ever been parted from Natalya and he could not bear to allow his own weakness to lengthen that time. The thought nearly brought tears to his eyes and he had to push the thoughts away to deal with the more physical pains. The vines added a sort of cushion for his aching back and logically Arthur knew that he should get up and stretch. It wouldn't do to fall asleep just as he had accused Art of being on the verge of doing. Of course he also knew that standing would drain him of what little energy he had left. He wasn't nearly young enough to go off running in the woods any longer especially with his injury, Arthur was more than a little surprised that he was still awake and alert. He hadn't had to exert as much energy as he'd used on the farm and then in their search in a very long while and it seemed that he was paying the price. With the thought of getting up eventually at the forefront of his mind, Arthur fell asleep before the sun rose.

CODY

It was impossible to count the passage of time in the maximum-security cells. They were far too deep underground to track by light and tracking by meals would be no less accurate. It was obvious that the vampires were not accustomed to housing humans and the slop that they gave him was few and far in between. As a bounty hunter he was accustomed to not eating much, but even he had his limits. If pride were a trait Cody was guilty of, he might have even felt that he was faring better than most humans; he had pushed himself to become the top human hunter at Faegon and that had not come without sacrifices. When he'd first started there had been doubts from the Crown about his abilities. There was nothing odd about having a human liaison, but usually they were older and they were almost always already trained. The Crown wasted no time on weak humans. Cody was a child when Gwyndolyn had found him and she had done everything in her power to prepare him to be the best human bounty hunter this century. She'd risked everything for him and it had become its own reward; he was the most successful human liaison that the Crown employed. They had the highest success rate of any current partnership which made this failure sting even more. He was proud of the work that he did because it was all he had. Gwyn was all he had beside the next adventure and he had dedicated his life to the two.

Hunting was hard work, but Cody thrived in the reward it gave him. He never felt more powerful than when he and his partner were on a mission facing the latest rogue as an equal force. While they were out on a hunt all other obligations were pushed aside. Finding their mark and ending their reign of terror was more important than taking care of himself. Missing a meal then never seemed like a big deal. There were days where tracking the mark was more important than stopping for food or even for hunting down easy prey. He and Gwyn had learned very early on just how far they could push their bodies before it was time for a rest.

In contrast, food deprivation in the cells was worse than anything that Cody had been forced to endure in his life. The magic that was soaked into the cell bars played tricks with his senses. He had nothing to distract himself and his thoughts became consumed with two things; food and escape. He forced his mind to focus on half-planned schemes of seeing the world outside of his cell between meals. When the next meal came he felt the strength return to his body before it was stripped from him as the effects of the magic surrounding him took their toll. There were moments when his cell would feel cold as ice, only to heat to a scalding temperature that made him sick moments later. Vampires were immune to temperature as they were to human illnesses and the passage of time. It would seem that the security had been updated at least enough to accommodate him.

How sweet of them to think of me.

His thoughts were bitter and sounded like Decker. They were his only comfort.

While he sat alone, suffering, it was hard not to notice the lack of noise coming from the other prisoners, or prisoner. Since his arrival the only other captive he could see was the glassy-eyed man directly across from him. He never saw the original two guardsmen again and he also never saw Decker. The strange vampire housed across from him mostly slept and only appeared awake when the jailers would bring him old blood. It was just enough to keep him from going comatose and looked pretty disgusting if the old vampire's reaction was anything to go by. A small look of surprise passed the old face before it fell back into the unreadable mask that Cody had come to assume was the only expression he was capable of making. Even though he seemed to detest his meal it still warranted more attention than the lowly human. He made no effort to make contact with the hunter and Cody was more than a little put off by him.

There was little else to pass his time with and so Cody studied his cell and what little of the dungeons that he could see. He prided himself on being keenly aware of his surroundings. He could track the passage of time just as well as any hunter, but the magic was disorienting. There were moments where he felt tired beyond reason despite having just woken up and he wondered if they were drugging his food or if there was something in the air that lulled him to sleep. He had only been fed twice since he had arrived and he had eaten the slop with embarrassing quickness. The last time had been yesterday, or at least he thought it was yesterday. He had slept twice since then, though it could have been three times, he wasn't all too sure. His normally sharp mind seemed to permanently be blanketed by a thick fog that made all matters beyond eating and sleeping inconceivable.

He had spent the last time he'd remained awake studying the walls of his cell. Looking outside had proven difficult when with one touch of the bars he had been assaulted by the charms that replaced all other security measures. He had discovered through trial and error that the effects of the iron on his skin ranged from the feeling of being burnt without lasting damage to all of the air quickly escaping his lungs until he blacked out. He was pretty sure that one had happened more than once and would explain the ache in his head like horses galloping across his brain. He had learned to keep well away from the bars quickly enough and soon he kept to inventorying his cell. The stones that made the wall were old, though they were maintained well. There were few cracks scattered around which had been patched up wherever they could be. The moss that grew between the large cracks looked soft, but there was hardly enough for him to make anything with it to grant him any comfort. The floor was composed of packed dirt and had been swept clean of anything that could be used as a weapon. He spent a moment pacing a circle around his cell, looking for a means of escape or defense, but as always, found nothing.

It seemed that this day would be just the same as the last until a glance across the hall showed old eyes staring back at him. It took him a moment to remember that he was not entirely alone and his crazed actions had been on display for the creature across from him to see. The old vampire guarded him with a look that suggested he hadn't noticed Cody before, though the hunter found that doubtful. It was hard to believe that a vampire, even one kept in such an environment would have been able to ignore the sound of Cody's beating heart or the rush of blood that raced through his veins, though the magic could have been the cause. When their eyes met the vampire appraised him as if he was seeing him for the first time. He slunk closer to the bars without touching them. His body was hunched at an odd angle which looked excruciating. Cody could not be sure if it was because of the vampire's age or because of the magic, but every move seemed to cause him pain. He stopped just before the bars and began to make wild gestures. Cody tried to understand what the gestures could mean, but any amount of focus only caused his vision to blur.

At first it seemed that the man was waving about and moving his hands as if to sign out words, though they flexed and straightened at odd intervals which Cody could not track. It looked as if the movements were either exaggerated and slow or faster than human eyes could comprehend. It might have taken hours for Cody to find enough balance between concentration and spacing out before he could make out the man's gestures or it could have been minutes. When Cody finally nodded to acknowledge that he was beginning to follow the movements the vampire tapped his nose then point toward the direction opposite from where Cody had been dragged. He didn't understand what the man could mean by that and he shrugged to show that he wasn't following the charade. The vampire tried again, but the meaningless waving still meant nothing to him. There was some significance to the area beyond their cells, but Cody could not fathom what it could mean. The vampire threw his hands up in a sudden motion showing his pure disgust before he turned away and curled back into himself. Defeated, Cody turned his back to the old man knowing that his chances of escape were slimming.

It had never been in Cody's character before to feel self-pity and yet he felt the ugly emotion deep inside his bones. If Gwyn had been with them he would never have found himself in such a predicament. She had always been his shield from the Crown and he had never fully appreciated just how much her name alone could keep him from winding in the deepest depths of hell. Of course, things would have been different if he wasn't human. Gwyn had told him a long time ago that being turned would make his life easier. He had never really believed her, but now it seemed to make sense. Despite the occasional fleeting wish to be stronger and more capable like his partner, Cody had always relished his own humanity. Besides, had he taken the bite the one time Gwyn had offered his role as a human liaison would be over and then he would have just been another hunter. He wouldn't have been able to be Gwyn's partner, they would have found a new human to partner her with. Of course, if he had been a true member of the Crown than he and Decker would never have found themselves in this predicament, but then he might not have even been on the hunt for him in the first place.

When the guards came to throw him his sorry excuse for food Cody couldn't even muster the energy to get up. They refused to give him any utensils and the grey slop they passed off as food was served in a lightweight wooden bowl. The edges were filed down so there was no way to use it to break out of his cell. They came to remove the old bowl quickly the last time he'd been fed and he had been lucky to finishing it all. He felt much weaker now and he hoped that they would leave it long enough for him to find the strength to crawl to it and pretend it was worth being labeled as a meal.

"Eat, you might not get another meal for a while." The vampire across from him raised his eyes from the spot they normally remained attached to.

"Enough talk!" The booming voice from down the hall might have been one of the guards, but Cody could hardly remember what they'd sound like.

The vampire in the cell watched him closely as they waited for the sound of heavy boots to fade away. The grey sludge was already starting starting to cool and look even more unappetizing, though Cody hadn't thought that possible. It seemed the other prisoner felt that they were finally alone because he crawled closer to the bars and sat facing Cody. His eyes were dark as night and had certainly seen more than Cody could ever comprehend, but they softened when they landed on him. He began to make the same hand motions as before. Cody sat in front of the bars of his cell and did his best to follow along. He was pointing toward where the guard had come from and again toward the part of the hall where Cody had never been down. He repeated the same motions pointing to the left and then again to the right. Cody could understand the significance of being worried about where the guards came from, but there seemed to be little reason to worry about the area of the dungeons that no one seemed to ever visit.

Wait. No one ever goes past our cells.

It made no sense. How had he never realized that the guards never traveled past their cells. There hadn't been many prisoners in the long walk that they had taken before dumping Cody in his new home and unless they weren't being cared for, there were no more prisoners beyond himself and the nameless vampire. The more he thought about it, the more he wondered just how many enemies of the Crown were kept this far below ground. What warranted a prisoner being sent to the lowest point in the castle and what had he and Decker done to deserve being sent there? What had the vampire across from them done to be put in his cell?

He looked up to try to ask the man himself, but suddenly the atmosphere began to change. The air felt tight as he tried to draw it into his lungs. The dusty taste sat on his tongue and made his mouth dry until it felt like dirt was packed in between his teeth. The transition from feeling sane to choking on nothing was startling and he almost missed the sound of heavy boots returning from down the hall.

The two guards looked no different than before and yet Cody sensed that something wasn't quite right. With the wits that he still possessed, Cody tried to discern what was different. He quickly noted that their clothing was the same and their faces were still blank, showing little emotion. While he hadn't taken the time to commit their every detail to memory before, they seemed to be the same men that brought him down. Anger welled in the hunter's stomach, eating at him like a poison. He was better than this; he should be able to realize differences faster. His window of opportunity left when the guards moved away, taking his uneaten food with them.

Cody could see eye to eye with the vampire across from him again. His old eyes were narrowed, accusatory. He could see every wrinkle as the man so obviously attempted to glare the truth into Cody's mind. He looked impossibly old, much older than before. Suddenly Cody understood.

At some point during his realization the magic in the room had altered. The air felt less congested when he'd been thinking about the possibility that he and the old vampire across from him were the only captives considered dangerous enough to be kept this far in the maximum security cells. The temperature hadn't fluctuated then; instead it had felt nearly comfortable to the human's skin. The more he thought and his rising panic subsided the more he noticed that magic shifting again until it was no more than a low ache at the back of his mind. His mouth began to water again as he remembered that they had taken away his food. The dryness in his mouth was gone and his senses were beginning to return. His vision was becoming more precise; he had never noticed the small carvings that were dug into the iron bars which explained many of the magical security measures that his cell held. Gingerly Cody extended his hand to touch the bar. He braced his body for any impact and found himself both relieved and a bit disappointed when his shaking fingers met cool, un-animated metal. He had no way of knowing why the magic had ended, but it had.

Finally beginning to feel normal again, Cody thought over the possibility of escape. He knew that alone it would be impossible. The old vampire seemed like he would be little help, but then again he'd hunted vampires who had looked even less imposing and had given quite the chase, to his and Gwyn's surprise. Decker had attempted to fool them by hiding behind a wall of pointless talk, but his act hadn't lasted long. Thoughts of Decker suddenly exploded in his mind and Cody felt the serenity he had regained from the sudden absence of magic fray and unravel.

The temperature change was more subtle than the feeling of dry mouth and the mounting headache, but it was just as dangerous. Goosebumps scaled his arms and shivers racked his body. The tatters of his clothing did little to provide him warmth and he felt his body curl up instinctively. Sleep was calling out to him and despite all of the rest he had gotten in the past few days he still felt fatigued. Maybe closing his eyes for a bit wouldn't hurt. As his tired body slouched forward, his hand slipped from his lap to tap against his prison bars. The calm of falling into darkness was interrupted by the sudden feeling of drowning and it crushed Cody's lungs. He was forced into high alert again, his vision swimming once more as he clawed at his throat trying to breath. The harder he fought, the worse it became.

Stay calm you fool.

Gwyndolyn's voice crashed into his consciousness and Cody realized his mistake. The magic was tailored to his mental state. It would drag him down; force him into insanity, only to relieve him long enough for him to have a sane thought, before returning him to an even stronger state of panic. It was no wonder the cells were so empty. There were stronger men out there than Cody and he was sure they would fare just as well as he. Knowing that remaining calm would grant him just enough sanity to escape drove him to release his own throat. He dragged air into his lungs in gulps, realizing his vision was only swimming because of the tears in his eyes. When he tried to rub them away he smeared blood on his face. His own skin was caked under his nails; blood running down his throat from where he'd opened his own neck. The salty tears that traveled down from his eyes mixed with the fresh wounds. It stung but it also helped to flush out some of the dirt that mixed into the cuts and Cody welcomed the feeling. He blinked rapidly to produce more tears and was greeted by the sight of the old vampire plastered to the bars of his cell. He was hissing though Cody wasn't sure if it was because he was trying to get through the bars to get at the fresh blood before him or if the magic was hurting him in some way. Intellectually, Cody knew there was no way for the vampire to get to him and yet he felt fear like never before at the look of pure hunger he saw in the dead, black eyes.

Cody estimated that it took another good hour before the guards came to respond to his episode. The older looking guard wore thick leather gloves, a sun spear in his clenched fist. He pushed it through the bars of the adjacent cell, forcing the hungry vampire back into the shadows of his dank cell. After taking a cursory look over at Cody without getting too close the two must have deemed the situation handled because they left cloaked in the same silence in which they'd come. Cody began to relax again. The other prisoner was back in the shadows of his own cell and he could tend to his own wounds alone. His tunic was already torn and it was easy for him to take off another strip to clean his hands. There would be no point in rubbing the dirt from his shirt into his wounds, they would have to heal on their own until he was able to get to clean water and linen. He would have to escape for that and until he had a viable plan he would have to work with what he had. Focusing precious time on trying to tend to his superficial wounds would do no good.

The clang of the main dungeon door opening sent a shock down Cody's spine, interrupting the silence that had begun to settle. He hadn't noticed before just how much the sound deprivation was becoming a calming presence. Now, every sound seemed to pierce his skull and send him into a panic. The silence returned before the sound of boots rang out like drum calls. When the guards came and went they were quieter than death and the sudden sound sent all of the warning bells in the hunter's brain off. He couldn't gauge their distance from the sound. He forced himself to tear his eyes away from the adjacent cell and did his best to find the source of the noise. Due to the magic slowly increasing in presence once again he could only hear select noises, the volume waxing and waning making it so that Cody could catch syllables and not a single, full word. He didn't have to wait long to see the two guards that had originally brought him down walking past his cell. He couldn't help but feel like the walk he'd taken had been longer as if somehow they had created a shortcut through the maze. It occurred to him that maybe it had been magic that had caused the maze effect and there might be even less cells in the dungeon than he'd originally believed.

They were dragging a limp body between them and at first Cody was convinced he was dead, but the slight struggle that he man tried to exhibit proved otherwise. Both guards had their strong grasp locked on the arms of a man who looked like he'd been sent through a mill a few times and then given a good beating by every guard in the fortress. Cody got as close to the bars as he dared to get a better look at the beaten man. Both of his eyes were sealed shut, bruises upon bruises decorated around his sockets and it was clear that his nose had been broken in at least two different places. Cuts rained down his hollowed cheeks and ran down his neck until the tattered remains of his tunic. Cody wondered if the jagged gouges in his own neck looked as grotesque. Blood lined the top of the tunic, soaking into the odd stitching which looked awfully familiar. Cody knew that he'd seen it before. When he'd seen it last, it had covered the back of his own captive.

"Decker?"

Cody wasn't sure if he'd spoken out loud. The pressure in his ears was making him dizzy, coupled with the sight of the man who was supposed to be his responsibility he felt the panic from before return. Cody slumped to the floor of his cell, his body pitching forward until he came in sharp contact with the iron bars. It did little to heighten his mood when he realized that touching the bars had no adverse effects to his already battered psyche as Decker was pulled down beyond his line of vision. So consumed by his horror, Cody didn't see the boot until it made contact with the bars in front of his face. The rattle of leather on iron shook through the hunter and shocked him into falling backward, Decker quickly falling out of sight. He scrambled like a foul still learning to use its legs to see the vampire again. Peering out of the bars, Cody saw as Decker struggled in the guard's' grasp and twisted his body to catch Cody's eyes. He had been expecting to see the strength and defiance in those cold, dark eyes, but instead he saw acceptance and defeat. They had managed to do what Cody thought was impossible; they'd managed to break the rogues' spirit. That realization, more than anything, fueled Cody's anger and brought him from his debilitating fear. He would have to find a way out of the cells, if nothing else to get Decker free and to true justice. It did not escape him that the rogue was an asset to the vampire kingdoms, but he also knew that given the chance Decker would betray them all for the slight he had just been served. No amount of kindness from one frail human could turn him to the right side of justice, but Cody had seen a good in him that could not be ignored.

The moss that grew in his cell would have to be the first step in Cody's plan. He often used the plants in the forest to fashion any imaginable item needed. Whether it was bandages or bowls, Cody could work and weave together the necessary implements to see his plan to fruition. He would need the old vampire to help set him free. Quickly he began to fashion himself a patch with which to staunch his own blood. He would have to act fast and collect enough blood to give to the vampire in order to insure he would be strong enough to help aid his escape. He would need to wait for his wounds to heal first and for his own strength to return. There was no point in giving power to the other prisoner without making sure that he himself was fit enough to fight. Cody only hoped that he could collect enough blood to strengthen the vampire, have enough blood to heal

Decker, and still stay conscious. The guards passed his cell without incident. They had no idea of his plans or they would have stopped the way his shaking hands clawed at the moss. He would have to wait patiently for the best time to try and smuggle his only bartering tool to his single means of escape, but now that he knew where Decker was it seemed that time might very well be on his side. He had finally found the motivation he had been missing before and he would be damned if anyone tried to stop him. Decker was counting on someone to fight for him and it was clear no one else would. Decker wasn't the only one, Gwyn needed him too. Even if she was dead at the hands of the rogue queen her legacy would forever be tainted unless he avenged her and he could not do that from behind the bars of a cell.

CLAYTON

Nothing could be worse than living in Misery. It had been a belief that had resonated with Clayton for his entire life until he had accepted it as fact. He had thought that he would have lived his entire life, unnaturally permanent as a vampire's existence was, and never known a place worse, but that was before he had lived in the slums of Faegon. No matter how affluent a city it was, nor how prosperous the empire was, there could not be a poorer place to live then in its slums.

The first thing that had bothered the disgraced vampire had been the smell. The slums were made up of huts which were littered around the city's outer walls. They were pushed out of sight of the rest of the city and the castle, though Clayton was sure that the nobles sitting atop their high towers would be able to see the smoke that rose from the outer city. It was made for squatters, both human and vampire alike, and the stench of filth and excrement was enough to drive Clayton away for the first few nights. He hadn't a coin to his name and the good people of the upper city didn't take kindly to the fact that he wandered around their streets, with nothing to provide to them or the Crown. Clayton had been forced to the slums at the threat of being removed from the capitol all together by the third night. He had briefly considered looking for Esmy then, but he could not bring himself to it.

After he had learned to block out the smell, Clayton learned that sustenance would be hard to come by. While there were certainly humans living amongst the impoverished vampires he would never lower his standards enough to take their blood. He would rather die by lying out in the sun than drink from the dirty people around him. He might have come from poverty himself, but at least he and his people had the decency to care for themselves. In Misery they had been forced to trek far for fresh water during droughts and they could only spare a few men to hunt for their food and even fewer still when not all of them returned, but they had bathed and acted like civilized people. Here the people acted as if they truly were the trash that was thrown out by the upper city.

"You've been here a week now, love. You're going to need to feed soon you might as well take some from me while you can." One of the women who had taken up in the same hut that Clayton had found vacant when he'd first arrived coaxed.

"That's quite alright, ma'am." Clayton had refused to give her his name and had no desire to remember her's. "I've told you already, this is a temporary situation for me. I will be gone before the week is out."

"If you insist. I don't see the point in lying though. You only end up down here if you have no other place to go."

"Is that why you're here?" Clayton snapped and was faced with narrowed apricot eyes. He supposed that if she had a reason to smile they would shine and almost look pretty, but in the dying fire they looked pale and sickly.

"I was cast aside by my employer by request of his wife," she spoke with such venom and Clayton need not imagine why his wife could have taken such a disliking to her. "She was no saint either, mind you, but when you're a Lady of the upper class those things are easily forgotten I suppose."

"I suppose," he agreed more to distract her than to continue the conversation.

"You think you're better than me, don't you?"

Clayton held back an answer. The woman didn't seem the violent type, but at present he was sharing sleeping quarters with her and it wouldn't do to anger her further. She had arrived looking for a place to stay six nights ago. Then, she had been dressed in a clean purple dress made of rich cloth. Her hair had been fastened by a shining amethyst clip and the gold leaf that decorated it had glittered in the moonlight. She had since lost all of her treasures having traded them for food and for protection from the men who might find that she had not yet lost all of her value. She stood before Clayton now in a torn, brown dress that had most likely been owned by a maid. He hair was matted and looked more like a wet horse's tail than the bright raven locks they had been. Clayton took pity on her, but he was in no position to help himself, much less another. That and her constant nattering on was becoming quite tiresome and he almost wished one of the other men had taken her. It wasn't very honorable, of course, but neither were the actions that landed her in this predicament and his own sense of morality was pacified by that.

"Well, whatever you did to land yourself here, I'm sure it was no nobler than what I'd done."

Clayton watched as she turned back to the fire to tend to it, intent on ignoring him. She went through phases where she tried to talk to him as if they were friends and when that obviously was not going to work she would fall into moments of silence that Clayton found he rather enjoyed. He hadn't been lying to her, this was a temporary situation for him and he was going to find a way out of the slums, but it was hard to think about his options when she continued to pester him and the hunger was starting to take its toll. He needed to get out before he did drink from her. He needed to find his way out. The only option he had left was to find Lady Esmy and take shelter with her until he was well enough to be on his own. With his mind made, Clayton stood from his dirty cot and made for the door.

"Where are you going? It's almost morning!"

"I don't need to answer to you," he said, knowing how impolite he sounded. He was too tired to care what the girl might think of him and he needed to set some space between them before he snapped.

The sun would be up in an hour or so. He could see the beginning of its light creeping up in the sky on the horizon. He wouldn't have a lot of time, but he could at least try to get to the castle before then. He hated that he was about to go to Lady Esmy, but there were few other options that he could see. He knew that he would have a hard time making it through the city much less up to the gates in his current state, but it was worth the risk. He hadn't trained so hard and forsaken his family and his village just to be cast aside with the rest of the empire's garbage. Even if it meant putting aside his own pride, Clayton would need to rely on the only leverage that he had left if he was going to make it out of the shame his former House had placed him in.

Most of the people who wandered in and out of the slums were preparing to turn in for the morning and so the walkways were bare. Humans who were accustomed to living with vampires usually kept the same sleeping patterns unless they were part of the working class that maintained affairs while the sun was up. No one amongst this lot would be trusted enough or important enough to be awake and active during the mornings and so they dampened their fires the same as the lords and ladies. Those that remained on the streets spared him few looks as he made his way through the thinning crowd toward the wall that separated them from the rest of the city. There were armed guards posted on both sides of the opening watching to make sure no brawls that happened within the slums spilled out into the city proper where any member of polite society might see them.

"The sun is on the rise, vampire. See to it that you return to your place before then," a guard warned him, though Clayton knew better than fear him. There were too many lost souls wandering past these gates and in a few minutes his face would be forgotten just as any others would.

There were a few markets that were held in the lower city for the poorer folk who would still need to make purchases, but weren't allowed in any of the other city's marketplaces. Most of them were empty, the peddlers retiring as most of their clientele would be in their homes preparing for morning. There was one stall in particular that had been vacated already, but some of the merchandise remained. With a quick look around, Clayton made sure that there were no onlookers before slipping into the stall. There was a rough-spun tunic that had been dyed an ashy coal color. It wasn't pretty, but it was better than his own soiled clothes. With little regret, Clayton slipped the tunic, a plain pair of pants, and a heavy black cloak off the rack and darted into the nearest ally. If the merchant had really not wanted the items taken than he wouldn't have left them out. He changed into his newly acquired garments, using his own dirty clothes to wipe away as much of the dirt from his body as he could. He was not clean by any means, but with his hood up he at least looked more presentable which would allow him to make it further into the city than before. He was careful to remove the pin from his cloak and fix it to his new garb before turning his attention back to the street.

He watched from the mouth of the alley to insure that no one was watching him before walking back onto the street as normally as possible. There were hardly any people out with the sun just beginning to show on the horizon. He adjusted the hood to cover his face from the weak rays and turned his back on the slums toward the main city. He hardly made it three steps before a hand clasped on his shoulder and stopped him.

"You will come with me if you don't want to be taken to the authorities." The voice was low and rough like the sound of loose stones grinding under heavy boots.

"Under what grounds?" Clayton contemplated using Lady Esmy's name to get him out of this trouble, but he stored the thought away. He would not give up his only form of currency to a coward who would not even face him.

"Don't play stupid, boy." The man was strong and he tugged him toward the city where Clayton had been heading. There was no sense in fighting with his body as weak as it was, especially if they were heading in the direction that he had been planning to go all along. He could find a way to use this to his advantage.

Clayton allowed himself to be lead through the empty streets. He dared not look behind him not for fear of his companion, but to avoid the shine of the sun. Even with his hood up and the light rising at his back he could still feel the fatigue from its heat creep through his muscles and burn through his veins. He was much too young to be out this late. He should have waited for the following night to make his move, but spending his remaining energy on regret would do him no good. He could see from his peripherals that the hand that lay firm on his shoulder was not covered. He strained to hear a heartbeat, but there was none to be traced from the man behind him and he began to wonder if he should be afraid. The man behind him was old enough and strong enough to withstand the sun, even if it was just a quick jaunt out in the light. It meant he was an elder and infinitely stronger than Clayton.

His fears were not quelled when they moved farther from the slums and the lower city into the upper city. They were moving toward the main square on the opposite side of where the castle and the barracks where Lady Esmy would have been staying. Instead they passed more wooden houses which made way to wider streets paved in stone rather than packed dirt. The buildings began to change as well, gone were the plain houses and shops, instead structures of brick began to line the street. Each house they passed seemed bigger than the last and soon walls and gates shielded them from his view. They were crossing into the homes of the noble class.

They turned left at the end of the road only to be faced with a long street which held only one large house at the end. The hand on his shoulder tightened and Clayton continued forward keenly aware that he might very well be walking to his demise. While he had no idea who his captor might be or whom it was he was meant to be meeting he was at least sure that it had nothing to do with his former House. Lord Tory had been the diplomat appointed by Namyt'tkas and while the man had dressed with the pretense that he was both rich and quite important, even Clayton could see through the pompous air to the truth. Lord Tory was no more important in this city than Lady Esmy would have been and she had come from a disgraced House. While Namyt'tkas was both rich and influential in their own right they did not have mansions within the walls of House Faegon. Only the Lords of Faegon themselves were allowed such luxuries though there had been rumors that each King and Queen had their own residences within the capitol, but Clayton was not important enough to know if that was true. It seemed very unlikely that he was being taken to see his own former King and thus it meant that the person who orchestrated this might be completely unknown to him.

There were two guards at the gate, both women, who looked at him with passive steel eyes. They bowed to the man behind him and allowed them through without complaint. Clayton could hear their heartbeats and was sorely tempted by the thought of a meal, but the gleam of their weapons from the ever rising sun was enough of a warning. The creak of the heavy iron gate opening inward refocused his attention to the manor that lay before him. There was a carriage already waiting for them just inside the wall. It seemed silly, but when Clayton saw the distance they would have to travel to reach the manor he was thankful for the heavy velvet curtains that obstructed the widows. The door was already open and a footman stood beside it with the stairs already retracted. Clayton felt the shove of the man behind him and he climbed into the small compartment. His companion followed after him and he was greeted with his first sight of the man who had so easily cornered him.

He had already known that the man was older though the lack of lines on his face was deceiving. He sat straight with perfect posture. The white shirt he wore was pressed to perfection with not a single wrinkle visible over his black overcoat. It was hardly winter and the ensemble seemed ridiculous to the young vampire, but the upper class had queer ways which he would never understand. The man had an angular face with a pointed chin and sharp looking cheeks. The most piercing feature were his moss eyes, though they were partially obstructed by a long, dark fringe.

"I don't suppose you're inclined to share you name," Clayton spoke hoping to sound more confident than he felt.

"Save your questions for Lady Sedalia."

The door closed with a slam and the carriage began its journey to the front of the manor. Clayton tried not to allow the silence to affect him. He knew that whomever lived in the manor ahead of them would be part of the noble class so the title did not surprise him, though what they could want from him was a more concerning question. He had nothing to offer, but the name of a woman who belonged to a House nearly as disgraced as he was. This dramatic show of power seemed a waste to be spent on the likes of him, but maybe that was the point. They were trying to intimidate him and it was working.

The silent ride came to a halt all too quickly and the door was opened to reveal the same footman holding a delicate lace parasol. It looked more decorative than practical, but it shielded most of the light well enough that Clayton was not too put out when he felt his companion yank at his hood to reveal his face fully.

"You will be escorted to a washroom where you will make yourself presentable for the Lady Sedalia. There you will find new clothes and enough blood to keep your bloodlust at bay. If the Lady Sedalia deems you worthy after you see her you will be given more."

Clayton was guided directly through the front entrance of the home toward the back and up a servant's staircase. He was being ushered around like his mere presence was disturbing to the occupants, but the promise of a meal after being hungry for so long was enough for him to ignore the treatment.

As promised he was shown to a washroom that was obviously meant for the servants. It was no larger than it needed to be, having just the bare essentials. There was a plain tub in the center of the room already filled with hot water. They had been expecting him. He knew he should feel more panicked at the realization, but the bowl of blood that sat on the battered wooden chest stole all of his attention and he ran to the gift using the rest of his strength. He fell to his knees before the chest and lifted the bowl to his parted lips nearly spilling some of the contents in the process. The blood was not fresh, it was mixed with the preservative that kept it from drying which left a sour taste in his mouth, but he didn't care. With each drawn in gulp he felt his senses returning to him. He hadn't noticed how terribly his head had hurt before, but when the pain began to subside he realized that he was able to string together more than one thought at a time without pain. The more he drank the more he felt the grime from his days on the streets sitting on his skin despite the quick job he had done of wiping himself with his dirty clothes. When he tipped the bowl to drain it of the last few drops he began to feel the shame from stealing the clothing on his body. By the time he dropped the empty bowl he began to feel the panic that had been missing when he fully realized his current situation.

He had allowed himself to forsake his principles because of a lack of food, he should have been stronger than that. Looking around wildly, Clayton considered the possibility of escape. He could return the clothing he wore, though they would be dirty and impossible to sell now, and he could return to the slums and humor the pretty human that had made his poor excuse for a home her own. He thought all of these things while licking the blood from his fangs, aching for another drink. He would get another drink, though, if he did as he was told. He was no stranger to taking orders and it seemed that this was to be no different. He could wash himself and meet this Lady Sedalia, thank her for the bath and the clothes and hope for one more meal before taking off back to the slums to find penance for his actions. With his mind made, Clayton made quick work of washing. The bath was a luxury he hadn't realized how much he'd missed, but there was little time to enjoy it. It took longer than he'd liked to scrub his body clean and rinse the dust and grime from his hair and by the time he was done the water was cold and black.

The towel that was left felt softer than any he had used before and he took extra time in drying himself, not knowing when he might feel such pleasure again. The clothes that they had laid out were plain, but they were still nicer than those provided by the trainers for himself and his troop. He slipped on the clothes and laced the pants and boots with steady hands. He might be horribly outmatched by the vampires in the manor, but he was thinking clearly again for the first time in a week and he knew that he had nothing to fear, not truly. They would not have wasted their time to feed and clothe him just to kill him. He would have to hold on to that hope in order to survive the day.

There was a well dressed footman on the other side of the door when Clayton stepped back out into the small hall. He was younger than the one who had led him here, but he didn't look like someone who could easily be overtaken and Clayton tamped down the thoughts of escape. He would see this farce through and then, if he was forced to, he would find a way out of the situation with minimal violence. He might not know who these people were, but he was sure that they were at least decent people. There was no honor in hurting those who offered you help, even if they had threatened him to get him here.

They made the walk from the plain servants quarters back into the main house in utter silence. It seemed like most of the staff had already turned in for the morning and the halls were completely devoid of any other people. They passed through an unimpressive door which led into another hallway that stood in stark contrast to the one they had come from. The walls were papered with what appeared to be gold leaf by the way the candles in their wall sconces reflected off of them. There were heavy velvet curtains which looked very similar to the ones in the carriage covering what Clayton would only assume were impossibly large windows. There was a table sitting against the wall which appeared to hold a marble bust, though Clayton had no idea who the man it was meant to resemble was. They continued down the hall, passing other busts and various pieces of art in the form of vases and odd sculptures.

A set of large wooden double doors sat at the end of the hall and upon further inspection, Clayton found that it was decorated in carvings of a forest scene with all manner of creatures peering out from behind the trees. The doors opened before he could take the time to discern if the animal on the bottom left was a large fox or possibly a small wolf.

Inside the room was just as elegantly furnished as Clayton had come to expect. They were standing in what could only be considered a small library. The walls were lined with shelves which looked to be bursting with books. There were two rows of additional bookcases with a path in the center leading to what appeared to be a space left open for an assortment of chairs and desks. There was a fire pit in the dead center of the room which was surrounded by two circular seating arrangements both making up one half of the circle. On one side sat a woman who might have stepped out of one of her many books that lay around her.

Even from a distance Clayton could not deny her beauty. She sat facing them, her emerald eyes calculating as they swept up and down Clayton's form. She wore her fire red hair gathered high at the crown of her head, the tips of the tail brushing against her bare shoulders. She wore an evening gown of gold that clung to her figure and pooled about her feet. Her eyes were lined with coal in the fashion that must be popular with the nobles, but was mesmerizing to him as he had never seen a woman's eyes look so bold before.

"Come in, sit," she spoke with a calm voice that reminded him of Lenore's. It brought him pleasure and pain until he felt like each step forward was a stab to his heart.

"You are in the presence of the Lady Sedalia, a Lady of the great King Zentarion's court and a member of the High Council."

"M'Lady." Clayton stumbled into a sloppy bow at the full mention of her title. She might not be a member of the royal family, but she was very nearly one by her rank. He could fathom even less of what they might want from him now.

"You are scaring the childe," she brushed aside Clayton's poor showing to chide her servant instead. "You may go. I no longer have need of you." The footman bowed out without even sparing him a glance before politely seeing himself out of the room. "Now childe, sit. There is no need for such panic."

Clayton took the seat across from her all the while training his eyes away from her. "Yes, M'Lady."

"There is no need for such formalities, look at me." Their eyes met and a small smile crossed her face. "Much better. Now you must be wondering why you were brought here. I am a little ashamed to say that my men have been watching you. I think you have something that might be of great use to me."

"What do you mean? I have nothing," Clayton said, perplexed.

"That is not true. You could have some information that I need. The girl that lives with you in the slums. Who is she?"

"I don't know. She was a working girl, the mistress of someone or other. She mentioned that he was her employer and that he was a nobleman, nothing more. Why are you asking about her? What use could you have of such information?"

"The mistress of a nobleman? Did she mention who her employer was?" Her interest was piqued and she ignored his questions which only served to annoy him, washing away any residual fear he might have felt.

"No, I never thought to ask. Why is that important?"

"Because, childe, coin is not the only form of currency in this world. There is much to gain from having the right information," she spoke in the same tone that one might reserve for a particularly slow child.

"That hardly seems honorable."

"Honorable? Was the way that spineless Lord Tory banished you honorable?"

Anger rose in Clayton and before he could think to watch his words he spoke freely. "How do you know about that?"

"Oh, Clayton banished brother of Namyt'tkas, I already told you. Information is a currency all of its own." Her smile had an edge to it this time and Clayton took a moment to consider just what kind of trouble he might have gotten himself into. "I know how this must all sound, but trust that I come to you from an honorable place. That woman is believed to have once worked for a man who the King of Kings holds in high regard. It was brought to my attention that he might be seeking ways to undermine King Zentarion and bring on a coup the likes of which this empire has never seen before. I don't wish you to think that we are trying to force you into this, but I need information from that whore and you are the one who can get it for me. Of course we won't ask you do this as a work of charity for the Crown. We will provide you meals and a place to live once you've completed this task."

Clayton took a moment to regard the woman before him. If the words she spoke were true than he would undoubtedly go back to the slums to gather information for her. He would do anything to keep their great King safe. Despite his banishment he owed his life to the Crown and he could still clear his good name. This would be the perfect opportunity to make up for any past mistakes and finally support himself without relying on anyone else. That, of course, depended on if this woman spoke the truth.

"I'll do it."

"Of course you will, I expected nothing less from a childe brought up by the noble House Namyt'tkas. Honor is your shield, is it not?"

It seems in poor taste to refuse now and Clayton only saw one option. "It is, Lady Sedalia and I am honored to be the shield you choose."

.

CASSANDRA

Delicate white silk sheets draped around Cassandra's bed and they did little to ward out sunlight. She was old enough that the tickling rays of daylight did little, but irritate her fair skin and she enjoyed the warmth that sunk into her bones. Her page was another story. Sunlight was fatal to him, as he was still very young, and when he spent the morning in her bed the heavy drapes around her windows were drawn tight to keep him from burning. On those mornings candles lit the room, scattered about to leave playful shadows on the wall and on their bodies as they made love behind the safety of her chamber door.

True to her word, Cassandra was much more cautious with her infidelity than her idiotic husband. Leon was only allowed into her room if she was sure that no one would need her. Usually Logan took court, unless there was a matter of great importance and when he was busy doing whatever it was that Kings do, she could open the hidden hall to her bedchamber and allow the page access.

Leon was with her then watching her carefully as her mind wandered. It was late into the day; the two had been awake for hours contenting themselves to wild lovemaking rather than sleep. Cassandra found little enjoyment in the act with one as inexperienced as Leon, but her young lover was easy to convince after she put some time into him and it was a sacrifice that she was willing to make. If Logan was brazen enough to sleep with a prisoner during the night when the castle was awake, then she would have to try harder to make Leon ready for her needs.

"What troubles you, my Queen?" The boy was always sweet after sex. In some ways he reminded her so shockingly of Logan that she felt an ache in her heart to have that back. The emotion was fleeting. She was far from sentimental and it was often in the dark, while Leon slept at her side that Cassandra wondered what kept her from putting her foot down when

Logan defied her.

"Nothing, my pet. Sleep now while we have the chance." Cassandra watched as the boy listened, trusting her completely in a way that Logan hadn't done in decades or possibly longer. Maybe it was that which she missed more than anything. Logan had trusted her with all of himself, just as her lover before him had, but of course that had ended poorly as well.

Cassandra would never admit that those betrayals still stung. She'd been a decent woman once. Before the fighting and the war she'd belonged to a house and to her King. She had given everything she had to that house and her everything had not been enough. She had lost something too precious to her and there had been no restitution for her loss. Cassandra banished the horrible memories from her mind, reminding herself that centuries had passed. She was better where she was, a Queen as she was always meant to be. Leon stirred in his sleep, rolling away from her and freeing her arms. Suddenly restless, Cassandra slid from the bed, forsaking a robe and walking to the balcony in the nude. No one would be awake to see her and she honestly didn't care if they did.

The sun was just beginning to set when she stepped out. It's warmth lit up her skin and made her moan. How she missed the days where she could run in the sunlight without a care. She never gave up the opportunity to stand in the light of day, even if she could only do so for a short while before it became too much to bare.

Cassandra let her eyes fall shut as the light breeze carried her away. She did her best to let her mind go blank, hoping that if she stood there long enough all of the answers to life's questions would come to her. As it always did, standing in the sun brought thoughts of her past to the forefront of her mind. She had been human once, though it was long ago, and she had loved the sun. More importantly she had loved spending time in the sun with her Michael. She didn't often let her thoughts travel to that place, but when they did she always felt herself wishing for more. That had been a time when love had filled her life. Love had blinded her. When she lost Michael she knew that such emotions no longer had a place in her life. They would be her downfall and she would not allow all of her hard work to be unraveled so easily. She had forgotten that along the way, somehow, and had paid the price of loss once more when Gareth had thrown her aside.

A soft knock at her chamber door drew her from her thoughts and brought her away from the warmth of the sun. She took the first silk robe she passed and slipped it on, not bothering to tie it up. The knocking became more urgent as she got closer and she knew her small moment of peace was over.

"My Queen, my apologies." Lord Wynn stood, bowed at the waist. "May I?"

Cassandra stepped aside to let him in. He made his way to the table in the corner without even sparing a glance to the sleeping page. The candles from their morning together were still scattered around the room and Cassandra took her time gathering them and moving them closer to where Wynn sat. It wasn't until she was done and the corner was lit up that Wynn looked toward the shadowed figure in her bed.

"I think this conversation best be had without an audience." Of course the slippery man was right. She might trust Leon more than Logan, but she still trusted them little and less than her secret keeper. Of her secret keeper she trusted only as far as she could pay him and in recent years that amount seemed to be dwindling.

"Leon, my pet, it is time to wake." Cassandra put herself between the man of lies and her page. "You must go for now, I will call on you later."

Leon woke slowly; tired from the short nap she'd allowed him. He moved into her touch, stretching to follow her retreating hand. In him she found a need to protect, something she believed she must have felt for Logan though she could hardly remember now. The last time she had felt so fiercely protective had been much too long ago. That need had been her driving factor to start the Cause to begin with, but much had happened since then and sometimes she forgot what she was fighting for.

Leon rose from the bed and kissed her with a passion she could never remember having for him. He never noticed, or maybe he never cared. Leon was the type of boy to see opportunity and never scrounge it. He would stand by her side so long as she left space for him to if only to further his own agenda. It was how all creatures were. She waited for him to slip out through the secret entrance, making note of his uncertain look toward Wynn. She knew the boy didn't trust him and Cassandra hardly blamed him.

"My Queen, we mustn't dally about any longer. There are important matters at hand." Lord Wynn whispered from his seat, his voice sliding down her spine and making her shiver.

"What news have you of the false queen Reagan?" Cassandra knew better than to play games with the master game maker. He had ways that she would never understand and getting right to the point with him would rid her of him sooner.

"What cause do you have to fear her? I have no news of the bitch. I have news of Faegon." She wanted to push him further, but she knew where to draw the line. Only Logan knew the full truth and the reason why she feared Lunaries more than any other house and she saw no reason to alert Wynn of her concerns.

"I care little of what the pretenders think. They have no hope to fight the revolution we will bring down on them." Logan often called it ignorance and pride that kept her from investigating the so-called King of vampires closer. She in turn let him do as he saw fit. A long leash was still a leash.

"If I may, My Queen, you should be very cautious with them." He leveled her with a knowing look that made her want to strangle him. Of all of her councilors he questioned her the most.

"Get to the point, Wynn, I have little time for your games."

"Would you have more time for them if I told you that my games placed a spy in their midst? Decker is still alive, my spies saw him being dragged to the dungeons." The knowing smirk made her fear for a moment that he knew more than he ought to. Knowing things that should never be known was part of his job, but his job also had a line which he was never to cross.

"Impossible. Vestera took care of him."

"But did she see him die?" Cassandra knew when she was being played for information. From Logan it was irritating, but avoidable. When it was Leon who tried to manipulate her it was cute, sad that he would think his charm could work. When Wynn pried it was dangerous. Cassandra was already being attacked on all sides; she did not need to be fighting on the home-front too.

"Careful, Lord Wynn. I look to you for council, but you are bordering on treason."

"My apologies." The smirk never left his dour face and Cassandra suppressed the sudden need to tear it from his face.

"I wish not for your apologies, but for your report. What did the traitor have to say to that fool Pa'ari?"

"He was not taken up to him, your majesty. He was taken to the High Council to see Zentarion personally."

"It makes little matter which feeble king he saw, what of his actions. Did he tell them anything vital?"

"Alas I know not. My spy was forced from the room before they took him into questioning. He seemed reluctant to talk, but the human he was with vowed to bring him to justice."

"Humans are all alike. Well, then I see no issue. Tell your spy to do better next time. We employ him to gather information, not be sent from rooms before anything happens."

"Of course, My Queen."

"Leave me now, report back when you have actual information of value."

"I believe we have found another valuable spy in Faegon. My men intend to report his progress to me." Wynn offered the news up as if it were a treasure.

"I said actual information. Come, this talk is tiresome." Cassandra dismissed him with the wave of her hand. "And please send my meal up, would you?"

Wynn saw himself out and Cassandra began to ready herself for the day. Logan was overseeing court as there was nothing of import to discuss and she knew that Leon would be asleep in his chambers until she called him. Still, a Queen had duties. She was needed on the training grounds to insure the new recruits were being taught properly. The last time she sent rogues out to canvas none of them had come back. The damn fools had been picked off like rats by the bounty hunters sent out from Faegon and this time Cassandra had to make sure that they would not suffer such an embarrassment again. She was also needed in the lower dungeons. There were two, one for vampires that needed to be questioned and one for humans who acted as meals for those living within her walls. The rogues preferred to hunt, as was their right as superior beings, but some could not, like herself and Logan and so the lower dungeons housed their fresh blood stores. There had been another fight between the guards and she would have to see what they had in their stores and if there needed to be another hunting party.

While she did own the pretty silks and wonderful dresses expected of any queen, Cassandra saved those for when she took court. It was more common to see her in her traveling leathers with her hair pulled back in a tight knot. Practicality was more important to her than her composure and those who lived under her rule knew better than to comment on her dress. She was heading a rebellion; she would have time to look the part of Queen when the fighting was done. She made fast work of dressing and took her meal with little fuss. The girl they sent was young. She looked no older than Cassandra had been when she was turned. She stood in the center of the room trembling. While taking the blood from the hunted tasted sweeter, any human filled with fear was intoxicating.

Cassandra would normally take her time draining her meals, but she had too much to attend to. She pulled the girl to her with enough force to make her sob. Her arm was thin and shaking so violently that Cassandra was sure it would break under the power of her teeth. She was pleasantly surprised when the human tried to put up a fight, but it did not last long. She drank from her arm greedily. The older you were the more blood it took to sustain you and keep you feeling and looking young. After her latest mission she felt like her age for the first time and it infuriated her. She could not afford to be weak and she took her anger out on the girl, tearing her arm apart until she lay crumpled on the floor and Cassandra had eaten her fill. Wiping her mouth off on a linen rag placed on the table, Cassandra dropped it on the dead girl's face.

"I want my room spotless when I return." Cassandra commanded as soon as she left her chambers. The servant who stood waiting nodded furiously; bowing so low she swore he would hit his head. "You must be new, I don't care how low you bow or how courteous you are. If you do your job then you have nothing to fear." The man hurried off without looking up. Satisfied that her room would at least be rid of the filth when she returned.

"They are expecting you in the training ground, your grace." Lady Vestera was waiting for her at the bottom of the steps that lead to the main hall. She looked worried, but otherwise unimpaired and Cassandra chose to ignore the urgency in her voice. Ves was loyal and never once gave Cassandra reason to question her as such, but she often overreacted and would believe that a problem existed where none could be found.

"I see. Have you made sure the riots at the dungeon have been quelled?"

"Lord Jarrod did, while you slept." The side-eye that she gave her could not be ignored.

"If you have something to say, say it Lady Vestera. It would do you no good to keep it in."

"Of course, My Queen. There were some issues at the dungeons; I wanted to inform you right away, but Lord Jarrod forbid it. I went to see Leon to tell him, I knew he would get a message to you without him knowing, but he wasn't in his room."

"I see, I am sure Leon had his reasons for being out. Is that all? You act as if something horrible has occurred."

"If you say so, My Queen. I just worry knowing how close you are to the childe and what he might be doing during the day while we all sleep."

"That is certainly none of your business, though if it makes you feel better I will have a word with him."

"It would. I would feel much better if you did. I just want you to be safe." The woman's earnest eyes may have seemed endearing to another, but Cassandra only saw the exuberance and as weakness. How was is that she was surrounded by so many useless subjects?

"I am always safe, now stop your senseless worries. What were the issues you spoke of?"

"The prisoner I brought back has been reported to be receiving a constant visitor. It seems she has been moved to a more comfortable room and the guards are frequently dismissed from their duties."

Vestera might believe her words were subtle, but Cassandra knew exactly what the woman was implying. She knew that Logan had been going to see the huntress every night, though she hadn't known that he had moved her. Cassandra often took the corridors that led between the main castle and her own quarters that intersected the royal chambers and she wondered for a moment if the huntress had heard any of the private conversations she'd had while taking that path. She tamped down on any fear the thought might cause her, determined to investigate her concerns at a later time.

"I see, well I will investigate those claims. Were there any other issues?"

"No, My Queen. Though I still worry about that boy—"

"Enough of this talk," she said putting an end to the conversation.

Cassandra walked with Ves in silence. The girl was over cautious to a fault and yet she had suspicions about Leon. She would have to limit the boy's time in her chambers until she knew what to do with Logan.

"I will be returning to the dungeons. Do you wish to have someone accompany you after you finish in the training grounds?" Despite her ferocity in the battle, the vampire always seemed a childe in the presences of her queen. It was a trait Cassandra might have found endearing once, but now it was simply exhausting. She already had Leon to worry over her every move. It often occurred to her that her council cared more for pleasing her than for winning the war.

"No. This is my castle Lady Vestera I have no need for guards within her walls." Dismissing the offer with little other thought, the queen pointedly ignored the hope she had heard in the request.

"I thought you might like a companion, your grace." Vestera hid her emotions well, but there was no masking the hurt evident by her queen's words.

"That is unnecessary, I will see you down in the dungeons." Cassandra watched as the girl walked away, defeated. She meant well, just as Leon did, but both were too young to see the bigger picture unfolding around them. They were at war and it was only the strong that Cassandra would bring with her to the end. Logan was strong, but too dangerous and while Leon was weaker than even Logan had been as a childe he was easier to manipulate. If she were to live through to the end of her own war she would have dispose of Logan soon.

The sound of steel on steel rang out in the training grounds and brought her from her thoughts. While they were vampires with speed and strength on their sides, Cassandra had been clear with her commanding officers that all of her fighters would need to be trained in the art of swordplay and knife work. The ancient council and their decrepit King all believed that using such weapons was pointless when they had fangs and claws. Of course most vampires had daggers on their person as more of a last resort, but when it came to those that fought for the Crown, the entire emphasis was put on their own strength. Cassandra had seen first hand what the strength of a vampire could do, but in the end there was no sense in completely disregarding an entire type of warfare based on pride.

Lord Jarod stood at the front of the field while the newest recruits were pitted against their trained warriors to gage their strengths and weaknesses. "I assume all is well, Your Grace."

"Yes, I had heard that there was some disquiet in the dungeons."

"Yes, but I have seen to it. It was nothing more than a few guards who forgot their place."

"I assume that when you say you have seen to it, you mean you have deposed of the traitors."

"On the contrary, Your Grace, I made sure to have them locked up. I thought you might want to speak to them yourself. They have interesting things to say."

Even if Cassandra was never sure of Jarod's true allegiances, he had the sense to never air her secrets out in front of her people for which she was glad. He had more sense than most of the people she surrounded herself and she wondered for a fleeting moment if he was correct in assuming that everyone in the House besides themselves were complete idiots.

"Thank you, I will make sure to see to them soon. How are the trainings going?"

"As well as can be expected. They are no warriors, but they are learning and those who don't will be dealt with."

"Good. This revolution is taking longer than I would have hopped. I think it's long past the time which we should be reminding those idiots of the empire that they should be living in fear of us,"

"Of course, Your Grace. I will see to it that this lot turns out better than the last."

"I would sure hope so, for all of our sakes."

Cassandra took another look around the yard, not feeling remotely impressed by any of them. She had waited far too long for her revenge as it was, she was not going to let a bunch of sorry excuses for vampires ruin her plans. Lord Wynn would have to step up and his spies would need to deliver soon if they all expected to stay employed and alive. She would have to put out word to her spies throughout the forest. The time was coming to put her plans into motion and she had to be sure that everything was perfectly set in place. Cassandra was going to bring this empire down even if she had to do all of the work by herself.

ARTHUR

Arthur wasn't entirely sure that he was actually awake when it happened. The sounds of birds in the distance were too quiet and the air was too still. The ground beneath him was soft, softer than the hard ground he had been sitting on, he knew when he opened his eyes he would not be in the abandoned village. He'd fallen asleep on his watch, something only a child would do. His wounds had been the cause, of course. Had he not been so badly injured he would have been able to keep himself awake without an issue. The gentle call of the birds was like a lullaby and it distracted him from his thoughts. They were the same calls that he had heard in his childhood and it reminded him of lazy summer mornings with Ivan and Mary Rose or candle-lit nights with Elizabeth. He screwed his eyes even tighter as he allowed his memories to take over and cloud the reality that he was bound to face when he opened them. Elizabeth would have known what to do in this situation. She would have known how to handle their daughter and it would have never come to this. The thought that she was the reason it all happened had always danced in his subconscious and he pushed the hateful words away. She had been the one to take their daughter into the forest. She had been the one who didn't return and left him with the sole responsibility of raising their daughter. It had been Elizabeth's irresponsibility that had landed them in this nightmare. Would her presence in their daughter's life actually have been beneficial? He had loved her the moment that she'd happened into his life, but that love had made him blind.

He had forsaken his parents, his duties, Mary Rose even to be with her and she repaid that devotion by running into danger with a young Natalya. He had always wanted to ask her why she had done it. Would he have the opportunity to ask her when his time came? He wondered then if he was dead. If he opened his eyes and turned would he see her? The sudden thought nearly brought him to tears. He wouldn't know what to do if that were the case. He had waited too long to see his love again, but it wasn't the right time. He still had Natalya to think of.

Natalya. This wouldn't have happened if it weren't for her curious nature, the same nature that Elizabeth had passed down to her. She truly was a mix of both of her parents and Arthur was not sure that she had received the best traits. He could admit to himself that he had a lot to do with her running away, but he couldn't think of that now. Now all he had to do was hope that when he did open his eyes he would still be alive and well. He needed to find his daughter, and with Art's help that might just be possible.

Art. The thought made Arthur's eyes fly open. The place looked like a wash of color at first and it took more than a minute for him to blink his vision back into place. When he was finally able to focus he turned to his left and was both disappointed and relieved to find himself in a bed alone. If he were dead then his Elizabeth would be there waiting for him, he was sure of it, so he was alive and he could still save Natalya. It seemed his mind was getting carried away, fueled by adrenaline. He had more immediate, pressing concerns; before he could find his daughter he would have to figure out where he was. From his vantage point he could see that he was in a single room home. The bed was against the wall in the farthest corner from the door. He could see a small kitchen area with a cook fire and a table and two chairs. There was another bed in the opposite corner that looked to be the same size as the bed he lay in. The room itself couldn't have been much bigger than the ground floor of Emeline and Art's home and yet there was no upper level. Even more unsettling was that fact that from what Arthur could tell that he was completely alone. Someone had to have brought him to this place though nobody was with him now. He kept still, hoping that he might be able to hear movement outside of the hut, but it became obvious after a few minutes that he was completely alone.

When Arthur tried to move he expected pain to shoot up his arm, but instead he only felt a dull ache. He knew his injuries had been severe and he dared not hope that he had already healed from them. *How much time has passed? How long have I been asleep?* Memories of the attack flew to the forefront of his mind as he tried to make sense of the situation. How did he come to this place, and more importantly where was this place? Had he been brought there by a kind soul or someone with a darker purpose? Arthur forced his mind to slow. He would not be able to help anyone if he didn't take control of the situation. Arthur was able to peel the heavy covers off of his body with ease, something he was thankful for. The movement caused him to realize that his wounds were stilled bound, though now he wore fresh bandages. It seemed that they were more a precaution as their pure white color told of closed wounds which undoubtedly lay underneath. The thought that they healed too quickly was not enough to distract the man from his main focus; finding Art and more importantly finding the girls. He pushed up from the bed with his good arm, not willing to push his body and possibly re-injuring himself, swinging his legs over the edge of the bed until his feet hit solid ground. He noticed then that his feet were bare. His boots were sitting against the bedpost cleaned of the blood and dirt that had been caked into the soles. Wincing, he did his best to pull them back on, it seemed that he wasn't quite as healed as his has originally thought. Gingerly, he rotated his arm, carefully watching for movement in his surroundings. He could not conceive what kind of person would find him in the woods and bring him here, but even the small niceties he had been given did not calm his racing thoughts.

There were no obvious weapons lying near his grasp. He noticed instantly that all of his carefully hidden weapons on his person were gone and he shuddered to think just how intimately familiar his captor must have become with his body. He refused to believe that he had been taken out of kindness; he just could not believe that such a thing existed in a world where his wife had been ripped from his life. He stumbled to the center of the room his large hand grasping at a chair, the closest piece of furniture, before it collapsed under his weight. In his hurry to find Art he had risen to his feet much too fast and his head screamed in protest. The room was moving of its own accord again and he took big gulps of air to steady it once more. The sound of the chair hitting the floor must have called back the owners of the hut because before he could bring himself back onto his feet two pairs of strong arms were lifting him up.

The urge to fight was overwhelming and Arthur gave into it without question. His eyes were screwed tight to keep the spinning from making him dizzy, but he still put all of his weight into trying to throw off the two men, for they had to be men with the size of the hands on him and strength behind them. He was able to turn and propel his knee into one of the men's solar plexus and it caught him off guard. Arthur was able to force his eyes open enough to see him go down. The man was young his dark hair looked like a mop on his head and there were absolutely no lines on his face. His eyes were a startling bright blue, but the most concerning part were the sharp, protruding fang-like teeth. Arthur jumped back in surprise when he realized that the men holding him must be monsters just like the thing that had attacked them in the forest. He fell back into the second man, tripping over his own feet in his haste. The struggle didn't last much longer than that. He was already weak and the two of them were much stronger than he could have hoped to fight off even at full strength.

"We're not trying to hurt you." The thing in front of him growled. He stepped back and allowed the other man to take over, clearly through with struggling.

"Why should I believe you, monster?" Arthur spat and kicked out, knowing that it would do no good, but he needed to try. He could not back down; it would go against everything he believed in.

"Would a monster have taken you in and cared for your wounds?" The predatory gaze backed with impossibly sharp fangs did nothing to put Arthur at ease.

"He's obviously afraid, Thomas, antagonizing him will do us no good." The voice from behind him was far softer. He sounded old, but when Arthur wiggled his body enough to see over his shoulder he was met with another infuriatingly young looking face. Whatever the creatures were he had yet to see one that looked older than their mid-twenties. Arthur stared into the dark brown eyes and felt suddenly calm. He couldn't look away from those eyes and his body went limp completely under the strange man's control. His whole body felt sluggish and it finally occurred to him that his sudden change in mood was unnatural. He tried to fight through the veil that was wrapping around his mind, it was like wading through a swamp and he fought with all of the strength he had left in his body.

"Is the human fighting off your magic?" Thomas sounded confused, but Arthur could barely focus to see.

"Strange, I didn't think he held any magic, but it seems I was wrong." The soothing voice of the other man was the last thing that Arthur heard before exhaustion took over and his vision went black.

Arthur was not surprised to find himself back in the same bed the second time that he woke up. He was equally unsurprised to find restraints keeping him from moving from the soft surface. Unlike the first time that he woke there were many sounds filling the hut. The first he heard was the sound of a crackling fire. The smell of stew surprised him; he had forgotten just how hungry he was. His stomach agreed and it let out a large growl. The smooth chuckle from beside him startled Arthur and the hunter in him hated himself for his weakness.

"You are an interesting one." The brown eyes searched his, but the unnatural force that had altered his feelings before never came. "My name is Antony, you met my friend, Thomas."

"I wasn't aware monsters had friends." Arthur replied without thinking. He was being held against his will and he knew that antagonizing his captors was less than smart, but old ways were hard to fight and arguing was a habit of his older than time.

"Vampire. Thomas is a vampire, I am human, see?" He showed his teeth, blunt and non-threatening. "Vampires are not all monsters, the rogues are brutal, true, but they are like us, not all good, not all bad."

"I find that hard to believe." He fought against the restraints. "How can I be sure you're human? You look like the rest of them, ageless."

"That would be the magic in him." Thomas supplied the answer as he poured out two bowls of soup. "He's not very powerful, but powerful enough. I'm surprised you were able to fight him off. I didn't sense any spark around you." He handed Antony the first bowl and Arthur watched as the man ate it slowly. Antony took the first two gulps before carefully guiding the spoon and pressing it against his tightly closed lips.

"It's not poisoned. If we wanted you dead, we wouldn't be wasting our time caring for your wounds and feeding you."

Arthur watched the other human closely. He thought himself a decent judge of character and he saw no threat in him. Slowly he parted his lips and accepted the peace offering. The soup was hot and burned his tongue, but after the initial shock, his taste buds came to life with the strong flavor of fresh carrots and chicken. The onions were soft and easy to swallow. It wasn't until the third spoonful when he was ready to actually chew that he realized that Antony had deliberately kept back the chicken so he couldn't choke. They sat in silence as Arthur drained the contents of the bowl in the same slow fashion. It was only after he had emptied it that Antony sat back taking his own bowl from the vampire.

"If you agree not to fight, I would be happy to untie you." Thomas spoke from the foot of the bed. Arthur eyed him warily, but eventually nodded. "I knew you could be reasonable."

"That's quite enough." Antony sighed and began to undo the ropes himself. "You will have to excuse my friend. He was young when he was bitten."

"Bitten?" Arthur was genuinely confused then.

"It's how vampires are made." Thomas spoke again though his mocking tone was gone. "You might know a lot about fighting us, but you don't know much about us at all, do you?"

"I care little about you or your kind unless it helps me find my daughter and her friends. There was a boy with me. What have you done with him?"

"When we found you there was no boy. You were terribly wounded and we took you here to clean you up. I suppose we didn't look very hard for another person, but Thomas would have known if there had been someone else there."

"Known how?" Arthur sat carefully, watching the two men as if they were about to pounce on him for moving.

"Your heartbeat. Vampires feed off of blood and the sound of a pumping heart is what keeps us alive."

"That's sick." The man's stomach rolled at the thought of the vampire sinking his hands into him made him want to vomit.

"It's no worse than consuming the flesh of other animals. Vampires who belong to the Crown, the civil ones, do not drink from unwilling humans. It is the most sacred of our laws. The monsters, as you call them, that attacked you are part of a rebellion party that calls themselves the Rogues. They believe that their strength gives them the right to take what they will from anyone in their way; human or vampire."

"You don't sound like you agree with them," Arthur watched the vampire carefully for any tells.

"I prefer not to take sides."

"Thomas is not really in line with the Crown, they have their own evils that cannot be overlooked, but we both despise the rogues. He takes his meals from me and we protect each other. It is a fair deal that neither of us has ever seen to break from," Antony spoke to cut any mounting tension between the two.

"If you would take our help we could help you find the ones you are looking for," Thomas offered and Arthur knew he had to weigh his options. He didn't trust the two, but running away from the hut while he was obviously outmanned was not possible. He would have to work with them, for a time, before he would be able to get away on his own. If the two were able to even help just a little he might just see his daughter again.

"How would you be able to help?"

"The easiest way would be for us to see your memories. Vampires can drink the blood of a human and see into their memories. It takes a lot of power and Thomas is young so there is no guarantee that it would work, but then we would know who we were looking for."

"Absolutely not."

"I wouldn't have to drink it from the source, it can be done as long as the blood is fresh." Thomas didn't look happy at the idea, but his willingness to accommodate struck Arthur as odd. He was not used to others going out of their way to help anyone without gain, but for the second time in as many months he was faced with someone who seemed to have no reason to give him aid and yet it was being freely given. "You don't have to decide now, but the fresher the memory the easier it is for me to read it. As it is, you've already been unconscious nearly a full moon's turn so I might not be able to gain much."

Arthur's blood ran cold at Thomas' words. "I've been here a month?"

"Yes, it was necessary to keep you asleep to speed up the healing process." Antony looked genuinely remorseful and it was his own shock combined with the unwanted pity that kept Arthur from properly reacting. "You should get some rest, you've made great progress so far, but those wounds won't heal on their own." The two moved away from the bed and back out of the house to talk. Arthur lay back down, only just realizing how tired he had become. The adrenaline in his system was finally beginning to fade away and his limbs felt heavier than he could move on his own. His eyes were closed before he settled back into the bed, sleeping easily for the first time in days.

COHEN

There was a draft in the small classroom which mattered little to the vampires, but the human students were obviously affected. They were just about to begin a lesson in vampiric history and Cohen could already tell that it would be difficult if he wasn't able to keep his student's focus. The castle was of an old design, more aesthetically pleasing than practical. It had beautiful architectural features like the large arched windows, though the wooden shutters that had been fitted for them had long since deteriorated, which let in the cold air with nothing to stop it. The human students were shifting in their chairs, obviously doing what they could to protect themselves from the chill.

"This castle once belonged to the human Kingdom known as Solara, though that was many centuries ago. There is a fireplace in every room to combat the chill from the many windows, though many of them remain unlit. Vampires do not get cold, but many find the warmth comforting. It's a reminder of the days when we were human and it is not uncommon for fires to be lit even if there are no humans in the area."

"So why is there no fire lit here?" Natalya glared from her seat. She had a cloak pulled tight around her body and she looked tired. She had been with them for a little over two months and she was still adjusting to their opposite sleeping patterns. She had attended classes for the first time at the beginning of the week, but this was her first history lesson. Cohen often found her at ease when they had the rare occasion to speak without audience, but as soon as the girl was faced with interacting with others in the House she would act out. Cohen wondered how much of her aggression was just an act, a feeble attempt at protecting herself from possibly becoming comfortable in her new home.

"We will light the fire soon, Lord Nirosh will arrive with the firewood and we will wait for him to begin the lesson."

The girl seemed satisfied enough with his answer because she had turned to speak to Emeline. The girls had become nearly inseparable since they had been reunited days before and Cohen was glad to see both girls starting to become comfortable in their new surroundings. Behind the two girls sat a young boy named Jasper. He was a human who lived in the castle, his father was one of the human ambassadors and a personal guard of Cohen's and his mother was Reagan's own seamstress and personal handmaid. He had every intent of taking the bite when he came of age and was taking the classes more as a refresher as he was already very familiar with the vampires, their history, and what the House's expectation of him would be once he received the gift. Sitting with Jasper was another human boy named Lysander who was also looking to take the bite. He was from one of the villages that sat on Lunaries' boundaries so he knew enough about the vampires and their rules, but he benefited from formal lessons just as much as the girls.

Cohen was pulled from his musings when Nirosh entered with an arm full of firewood and soon the two had a roaring fire set. When the color began to rise on Natalya's cheeks once more and the tight grip she had on her cloak loosened until it hung loose around her shoulders, Cohen relaxed. Nirosh had asked him to assist with the lessons as it was normally his duty to teach the subject as the oldest member of Lunaries and Cohen was happy to sit back and allow the man to start. He knew that Natalya had been struggling with her lessons, but when he had been her teacher for law and policies others had been surprised to see how well behaved she had been. Reagan had hoped that with his presence the girl might calm enough to actually be receptive to the information they were trying to give her. Cohen hadn't put much stock in the idea that he was the reason that the girl was beginning to relax and accept her situation, but there was no denying that he felt a bond growing between himself and the spitfire of a human and he was interested to see just how far that bond could be pushed.

"We left off of our last lesson talking about the original Vampire Houses. Who can tell me of the five that still exist which ones were original to the first empire?"

"Houses Faegon, Tryali, and Adrastos." Lysander answered. He was the youngest of the group, but he retained information well and was able to recite it back as if he were reading it from the page.

"Yes, but technically Namytar was one of the original Houses, though they have joined with Tkasar," Jasper added.

"That is true, but they would not have existed if they hadn't agreed to the merger," Nirosh amended and Cohen was impressed with how much they knew.

"What about House Rayne? They were an original House and there is talk that they are returning," Lysander asked. Since he had been from their borders he would have known more of the Forest gossip than those who lived in the castle. It didn't surprise Cohen that the boy had heard about the rise of the rogue's house.

"That is considerably different. House Rayne fell. It was decimated and all members of it scattered through the empire. The rogues who rally under the name now have no right to it." Nirosh spoke with a clear tone that said they were not going to have this discussion.

"What happened to House Rayne?" Natalya spoke and Cohen saw the opportunity to answer before it got out of hand. Nirosh was infinitely patient, but Cohen had seen first hand that Natalya took great enjoyment in pushing at everyone around her to learn what made them snap. He wondered if she realized she was doing it or if it was just a part of her stubborn nature, but it mattered not which was true.

"House Rayne was once the seat of the Great King Zentarion. There was a coup that spurred on the greatest civil war of our people. There were many casualties and it was the reason that Namytar and Tkasar merged. It was also the reason that King Pa'ari was forced to share his home and land with King Zentarion."

"Careful, Lord Cohen, you tread dangerously close to treason." Nirosh cautioned and Cohen held back a response. Nirosh meant well, but the words he spoke were true. King Pa'ari had been forced to allow the Great King into his home and had essentially relinquished his power. "It was meant to be a temporary situation, but that was in the year 862 and as I'm sure you are well aware we are nearing the year 1503 in a just about two moon's turns."

"Why would he not take his own seat again?" Emeline asked. She hardly spoke in her lessons and it had been agreed upon by all that when she did speak it was best to encourage her. Nirosh seemed ready to argue, but Cohen chose to indulge her.

"There is a prophecy that many say is all fool's whispers, but King Zentarion has made it clear that he believes in it."

"The age of Vampires will fall when six Houses stand alone," Jasper recited. He was the only one who had grown up in the castle walls and Cohen was not surprised that he had heard the words before.

"Yes, he will not build his own seat now, not where there are five vampires Houses."

"But if House Rayne is starting to rise again wouldn't it be smart of him to build his own seat once more? Then there would be seven Houses."

"If House Rayne were to rise it would be more likely that King Zentarion orders them demolished again. House Rayne was corrupt when he sat on the throne there and I for one have little in regard to high hopes when it comes to the character of those who take its throne now."

"That is quite enough, we are here for a history lesson not a debate in theory and politics." Nirosh smoothly took control of the discussion again and Cohen was happy to fall back into the shadows. He never favored the histories of their people. He had always been far more concerned in their future and while there was much to learn from the past there was no point to learning from it if they refused to take any action.

"As we were discussing earlier, the three Houses who remain from the first empire are Faegon, Tryali, and Adrastos. Of the three only Tryali is ruled by their original Queen. It can also be said that King Zentarion is the original King of Kings though as we have already covered he is not sitting on his original throne. He has been the King since, what many would argue, the beginning of time. I find that doubtful, myself, but there is no other vampire older or as old as he is so there is little point in debating the fact."

"Since then the Houses and territories have changed immensely. Only Tryali has stayed in mostly the same place with very little changes. This is not very surprising as they are the most unmoved House. Their own words are *we wait for the shadow*. They are a house who believe in allowing the world around them to change while they remain mostly the same. They only emerge from their territory on the demands of King Zentarion and even then they do not like it. They believe that the golden age of vampires has still not come to pass and they intend to wait in the shadows until it has come so they may rejoice in their perfect world."

"You don't sound like you believe that will happen." Natalya spoke, her tone more subdued than Cohen was accustomed to and she looked somber for once instead of angry.

"If you had seen half of what I have then you would know that there is no such thing as a perfect world."

The classroom fell in into a deathly silence then and a seriousness overtook them. Even the spirit that Cohen had become to associate with Natalya had been doused and she watched the elder vampire with carefully guarded eyes. It was true that Nirosh was one of the oldest vampires alive in their part of the empire, but there were many vampires who were still older than him. Of course in Tryali there were elders who had even more years and knowledge behind them, but to Lunaries Nirosh was the authority in all of the House histories. It could be said that what he had to teach was biased as the accountings were derived from his own experiences, but he was a professional. This was one of the few times that Cohen had ever seen the man's own feelings overshadow the importance of recounting the facts and the man was more than a little concerned with where the lesson was heading.

"That being said we can learn a lot from our history, can we not?" Cohen did his best to steer the conversation which earned him a pointed look.

"This is true, but politics is your department and not why we're here."

"That is also true," Cohen conceded. Natalya looked like she was about to protest and he swiftly cut in. "We can continue this conversation on politics in our next lesson, I'm sure Lord Nirosh has much to teach you and we are quickly losing moonlight."

The rest of the lesson carried on smoothly and Cohen was quite pleased at the lack of interruption, especially from Natalya. The girl meant well from what he gathered during their few interactions, but it was obvious that she had either been granted far too many freedoms and felt she could question everything they told her or that she had never been given such freedom before and was learning to take advantage of it. He had already planned to escort her back to her room after, but now he felt that he had a justifiable reason. He could talk politics with the girl, it would be nice to have someone of a like mind in the castle who wasn't honor bound to simply agree with everything he said. He knew full well that Reagan expected him to keep his eye on the girl and this seemed the best way to do so while still gaining from the interactions. He was no one's chaperon, there was too much to do to keep the House in working order, but at least if he engaged her in worthwhile conversation he could work out some of the many theories and ideas he had about the empire and where it might be heading.

"That will be all for tonight. Emeline would you please stay behind? The rest of you may go." Nirosh spoke and Cohen watched as the two girls bid each other good morrow. When they had first been reunited it seemed like it would be impossible to keep them apart, but once Natalya realized that she would be able to see Emeline more frequently once their training had concluded and they had more time for themselves she had relented and it had been easier to convince her away from the girl's side.

"Miss Natalya, would you mind company on the way to your quarters?" Cohen gave her a small smile to let her know that the offer was just an offer. He had learned very quickly that she did not take kindly to orders and even less so to anything that sounded like a manipulation.

"That would be acceptable," Natalya responded with a cheeky smile. Cohen extended his arm to her like she was a Lady and she took it with confidence. She kept stride with him as they left the room, their silence falling around them comfortably like a heavy quilt.

Natalya had made it clear that she did not trust anyone in Lunaries. She had kept quiet for most of her first meetings with anyone outside of her maid Freya and surprisingly Cohen himself and she did her best to remain silent in the halls. Cohen kept his thoughts to himself as he guided them to her quarters. He could respect her wishes and he enjoyed the silence. There were times when the noise around the House drove him mad. He, like his Queen, understood what it took to lead a successful vampire House, but he did not relish in it. He was her heir and would take on the mantel of rule if ever the day came, but he rather enjoyed the quiet moments he was granted when he was allowed them.

"The nights have gotten cooler, I fear the weather won't hold much longer."

"Are you cold in your room? I will have more firewood taken to you before the night is through."

"Thank you, I would really appreciate it," Natalya responded with a bright smile. It was the first time he had ever seen the girl look so happy. The expression smoothed out the lines that seemed to be etched into her face and she finally looked like the young girl that she was. He would not mind whatever work it took to put that expression on her face again.

"Besides the cold, how are you enjoying your stay?"

Natalya shot him an amused look at the word stay, but continued on without complaint. "I admit it has been much better than I had expected."

"And what did you expect?"

"Not this." She smiled again and this time the indulgence was clear in her eyes.

"Okay." Two could play at this game and he let the conversation end there. They were nearly at Natalya's quarters and would have time to speak freely once safely inside.

Lilliana was standing guard at Natalya's door just as she was when Cohen had collected her for her lesson earlier that night. The redhead bowed before Cohen, "M'lord, Miss Natalya."

"Lilliana, thank you, that will be all for the night."

"Of course, M'Lord, Miss Natalya." She bowed out again, but not before sharing a sly smile with the girl on his arm. It seemed that Natalya was becoming friendly with more than himself and Freya though Cohen was not sure how comfortable their shared glances made him. Reagan had warned him of the growing protective feelings he had developed toward the girl, but he hadn't seen the issue.

"You and she seem awfully friendly."

"She keeps me company when Freya is with your Queen. Is that a problem?" It was a carefully poised question and Cohen knew better than to test her.

"Of course not, I am just happy to see you settling in to your home."

"It is your home, not mine. I agreed to stay to learn your customs and to keep an eye on Emeline, no more."

They were safely in her chambers then and it was obvious that the girl was comfortable enough to speak freely in her own space. Natalya's bluntness had surprised him when she had first begun to speak to him in more than one word answers. He had mistook it for blatant disrespect at first, but she spoke that way to anyone she deemed worthy of more than a few clipped words and he soon realized it was just how she spoke.

"Do you truly plan on leaving? If you intend to watch after your friend, when will you determine that it is alright for you to leave without her?" It had been tiring to explain to Natalya repetitively that Emeline was safer with them, her own people, and while she had reluctantly agreed that it seemed unlikely that Emeline would leave Lunaries or their world, she made no mention of her own plans.

"One can live in a place without it becoming their home," Natalya spoke carefully and the smile left her eyes.

They were treading on dangerous territory and Cohen knew better than to continue. "You seemed engaged in the conversation today. Your other teachers have told me that they worry about you because you don't often participate."

"Today's conversation was interesting. They often aren't very interesting." Natalya shrugged and began to move around her room tidying up the minimal mess that she had made which Freya had yet to attend to.

"That can't be true, I know that Lady Arinessa is teaching a class on inter house politics and general vampire decorum. That class must be interesting."

"Lady Arinessa is a massive flirt and when she does anything that isn't flirting then she just seems horribly out of place. She might be a good Mistress of Whispers, but she is a terrible teacher."

"Well I wouldn't let her hear that, she rather enjoys teaching. She's always believed she had a flare for it," Cohen laughed, though he knew what Natalya said to be true. He had sat in on a class of her's before and it had been a sight to see, but for a girl like Natalya it would have seemed tired and a bit overdone.

"I have the notion that she believes that she has more talents than she does."

"That's rather unfair as you don't really know her. She is an asset to Queen Reagan and the House, but that is neither here nor there. How has your stay been, truly? Queen Reagan has been asking about you and I fear I don't know what to report."

"If she is so interested she can come to me, could she not?" Natalya had finished undoing and refolding the bedding twice and had moved the items on her vanity three times before settling back against the cushions on her bed. He had been standing by the armchair which sat in front of the fire, but once she stopped fidgeting he took the opportunity to take a seat himself.

"She is busy, but she does want to come to see you soon. Are you comfortable in your rooms? Is there anything you might be missing?"

Natalya looked thoughtful for a moment and Cohen was impressed that she didn't have a clipped remark ready on her tongue. "I would not say comfortable, but I am adapting, I suppose. Freya has been kind and I do enjoy her company I know I will miss her when Lady Reagan sees fit to call her back into her sides. I would like to see Emeline more. I also miss the sun."

"Freya will be with you for as long as you wish so have no fear that she might be taken from you. As for Emeline, she is doing well, much better since she was first reborn. When she is not attending classes she spends most of her days sleeping to regain energy. She should be strong enough in a week or so to see you more often. As for the sun, it might be a problem for our younger vampires, but I could take you to the inner gardens one morning, if you wish."

"You can go out into the sun?"

"Remember what I taught you last week? Vampires cannot withstand the sun as it dries our skin and body. We get horrible rashes and become dehydrated quickly and especially newly bitten vampires can die from very little sun exposure. The older you are the more of a tolerance your body has to the effects, though even someone like Nirosh would have to rest and drink more than the regular meal to regain strength from prolonged time in the sun."

"Would you really expose yourself to that for me?" The awe in her voice was well hidden by the cautious, guarded look on her face, but Cohen had long since learned to study others to understand their moods and motives. There was a reason that Reagan trusted him beyond all others.

"Of course. I would not be able to stay out all day because I do have a House to help care for, but if you'd like I would be happy to take you to the gardens for a few hours soon."

The happy smile he had seen on her face from earlier was back and Cohen felt elated to have been that one who put it there. Reagan had been becoming increasingly worried about the girl and he would finally be able to report good news to his Queen. Natalya was a tough girl, but she was still a child. There were plenty of reasons for her mistrust of him and his people, but she was slowly beginning to accept him, which only gave him hope that she would learn to embrace the House and the rest of their world.

CODY

Despite the well crafted security measures Cody was able to keep a reasonably leveled head while plotting his escape. From his poor calculations he could assume that it had nearly been two months since he had been thrown in the cells and just over a two weeks since he had seen Decker being taken to the farthest cells. His wounds had all but healed, thankfully without infection, and he had little else to gauge the passage of time with. Since then he had only seen their guards feed the old vampire twice, but no one had gone past their cells. Unless they had fed Decker while Cody slipped in and out of sleep, Cody feared there wouldn't be a man to save, even if he managed the impossible. In the little time he had that wasn't spent worrying about his former captive, Cody spent his time adjusting to the ambient magic. He had mastered keeping a measured level of calm and panic as to keep the guards from checking on him. It seemed the vampires were so reliant on the magic working that he was mostly left alone except for when they brought his food.

The guards had only fed him three times since the day that he had seen them dragging Decker past his cell. If they had noticed that his wounds were mostly healing and the color was beginning to return to his skin they hardly cared. It was unthinkable that a mere human could escape the maximum security cells in Faegon, even the elder vampire who lay in his cell across from him had seemed to lose interest in the man. Cody was more than use to being underestimated and was rather thankful that Gwendolyn had taught him to use it to gain leverage. The disadvantage to being seen a weak human was that those around him tended to doubt his ability to survive and often would hover around him to make sure he would be okay. He knew the guards would be by with food soon, under the guise of checking on him again, which didn't give him much time to put his plan into action.

Knowing that he would need to act quickly, Cody began to set his plan into motion. He had created a decent sized patch with the moss he had managed to forage from the walls of his cell. There was nothing particularly sharp in his cell with which to cut himself and his wounds had managed to heal nicely enough that it would have been just as hard to reopen them as it would be to cut himself again. He grabbed for any small rock that might be sharp in his cell, but found none that would do. He refused to allow himself to panic, there was little time left and this was his only chance. He saw little choice other than to bite into his own flesh, choosing a spot in the meat of his arm. Cody underestimated just how much force it would take his dull human teeth to break skin and he almost wished he hadn't tried. By the time he was able to get enough blood soaked into the patch, the old vampire had woken up and his attention was fully on Cody. His eyes were black as night and his fangs already protruded from his open mouth. This was the only opportunity that Cody was going to get to escape and there was no use in allowing self doubt to get in the way.

Using his training to his advantage, Cody wrapped the soaked blood pack in the ripped portion of his shirt. The soft fabric made little noise as it arced through the air between the bars of Cody's cell. He watched as it soared across the hall seemingly undetected as he prayed to any deity that would listen that it would land its mark. It would seem that he was too far in the depths of hell for a deity to answer, however, and the carefully wrapped pack bounced from the bar across the hall causing it to land feet from the bars. Defeat tasted like bile to Cody's tongue. All of his hopes had been resting on that blood giving strength to his only ally. He realized too late that it wasn't only defeat that burned at his throat, but actual bile was crawling up his raw throat expelling itself on the stone inside and outside of his cell. The feeling of defeat poisoned him to the point where he actually felt physically ill. In his surprise he failed to see that the old vampire had braved the consequences of touching the iron bars to snatch at the offered gift until his scrambling was successful and he pulled the delicious treat into his cell.

The vampire drank the blood noisily and the moans of pleasure that left his lips, combined with the sounds and smell of his retching, seemed to call the attention of the guards. Cody watched as if from outside his own body as the other prisoner sucked greedily at the fresh blood. Having seen the old, dried blood that the vampire was normally given Cody had to assume it was the first fresh meal he had received since being imprisoned. The hunter didn't have long to consider the ramifications of feeding the vampire before the guards were upon them. They were yelling something, but Cody couldn't understand them as his full attention was on the transformation happening before him. It was known that drinking blood kept a vampire from aging. It was believed that the blood hydrated them so they never visibly aged even when centuries passed. Cody knew all of this, yet he had never witnessed an aged vampire regain their youth before. He watched in awe as every wrinkle on the vampire's face disappeared with each gulp. Where an old man had once been a young, strong vampire stood. His eyes were no longer cloudy, but sharp. They had looked black before, but now there was no mistaking the flecks of green and gold as they danced wildly in the dim light. The magic holding the vampire in seemed to have little effect on him now that he was brought back to life and he easily ripped at the cell doors, the sizzling of his flesh on the heating bars the only indication that the magic was even still in play.

An alarm that resonated like war drums vibrated through the air as the two guards in the hall turned their attention from Cody to the very real threat that was forcing its way out of his cell. The older of the two guards thrust his sun spear into the opening of the cell, but unlike before, the vampire deflected the weapon as if it were merely harmless steel. In a flurry of movement too fast for human eyes to track the vampire captive took control of the sun spear, notably without need for a glove, and turned it on its owner. The guard crumpled to his knees, ugly red blisters webbing from the deep cut in his chest. The other guard tried to stand his ground, but he fared worse than his partner, dying as soon as the metal touched his skin.

The vampire elder emerged from his cell a different man. Even covered in filth, he managed to hold himself regally, as if he were entertaining a congregation of his own people instead of emerging from captivity. He shed his tattered rags and took the trousers from the first guard and the shirt from the second as the first guard had a sizable hole in his tunic from the damage of the sun spear. It wasn't until he was newly clothed that he did turn to address Cody.

"The name's Osmond, formerly of House Lunaries, if such a house exists anymore." The vampire said by way of greeting as he picked up the keys to Cody's cell from the second guard. It seemed a bit ridiculous to be let from his cell by key from the man who just forcibly ripped himself out of his own, but Cody ignored it for sake of returning the pleasantry.

"Cody Gilhart of the free people, though how free we are I suddenly doubt." Once he was fully in the hall Cody realized quickly that they were not in fact in a maze. The door that he had been dragged through originally was to his left and much closer than he dared believe.

"The magic is strong when you are under its spell, but quite simple when you step outside of its grasp." Osmond explained, a grimace mixed of pride and disgust fell over his features reminding Cody of how he'd once looked.

"How do you know all of this? How does it work?"

"There is little time for that, Cody Gilhart of the free people. You care for the vampire at the end of this hall, no? Now would be the time to set him free and run. More guards will be here soon."

Cody mentally cursed himself for so suddenly forgetting Decker.

"Thank you," Cody smiled gratefully before racing to the end of the hall with the keys. Without the magic skewing his vision it became obvious that there were only ten cells in the row and there was a straight path from one side of the hall to the other. Cody made his way to the end of the row to find Decker hidden in the very last cell. He was curled up in a tight ball at the back wall. When Cody was close enough to listen he realized that the rogue was quietly sobbing.

"Decker?"

Cody let himself into the cramped cell noting it was even smaller than the one he'd been given. The rogue perked at the sound of his voice. His eyes were still swollen to the point where seeing was beyond question. Cody moved into his space and moved his already injured arm forward and Decker met him halfway. The vampire greedily latched onto the offered food. Cody was already feeling weak from his earlier blood loss and Decker drinking from him like he'd never have a meal again was not helping. He was so consumed with feeding that he was not doing whatever it was that a vampire needed to do to make the drinking pleasurable for their partner. Cody squeezed his eyes to block out the pain, keeping his complaints at bay.

"Slow down, you're going to take too much if you're not careful." Cody chided and Decker relented, sucking on his arm at a slower rate. The various wounds that littered Decker's body were beginning to heal. Cody was relieved to see him healing, but he couldn't hold up much longer. When Decker could open his eyes entirely he let go of Cody's arm, licking at the wound to seal it. At last, the pain was replaced with hot, searing pleasure, but it didn't last long enough for Cody to enjoy it.

"Thank you," Decker rasped, his voice hoarse from screaming.

"More guards are just outside the door, you're going to need to get out of here." Osmond yelled from outside forcing Cody back into action.

Decker was healing quickly and was able to stand without help, which was lucky since Cody was beginning to feel a little lightheaded. Decker looped his arm around Cody's midsection and fully supported his sagging weight. When they arrived in the hall the rogue was fully supporting him.

"There is a trap door in the cell across from you, it will lead you down underground further, but it comes out on the other side of Faegon's walls." Osmond called, though his head was turned as he knocked out another guard.

"Why should we trust you?" Decker sneered, his eyes glowing purple.

"Because I am going to hold the guards off and it's your only choice," Osmond sounded exasperated despite battling two guards at once.

Just as the words fell from his lips, the far door banged open once more. This time the noise sounded distorted again. The guards were obviously in control of the magic once more and they would have to leave fast if they hoped to escape. The first guard that came through the door tried to fight off Osmond, but he was cut down just as easily as the rest.

While the guards were obviously groomed to be the strongest warriors the crown had, Osmond was ten times stronger. He easily held off the next five guards to swarm him and Cody knew then that this was their only hope to escape. Fumbling with the keys Cody tried and failed five times to get the cell in front of them open. On the sixth try Decker snatched from his hands sliding the correct key into place before pulling the human in with him.

"If you'd just let me take the lead-" Decker began to complain as he kicked aside grime and dust to reveal a trapdoor.

"That was pure luck if I've ever seen it." Cody replied finding it easy to fall into the banter that had existed between he and Gwyn.

"Always full of surprises." Decker smirked before rushing Cody down the hole into pure darkness. They fell together, though Decker never let his hands leave Cody. They tumbled down uneven dirt walls, bouncing off of the narrow drop and each other until they landed on the cold ground. The sounds of the vicious fight was suddenly far behind them as they lay in a pile in silence. "I knew this was a trap." Decker growled as he picked himself from the ground.

"Shut up and feel around the walls for a pathway." Cody hissed, moving as quickly as his body would allow in a circle until he crashed into the rogue. "If we just stop, we could let our eyes adjust."

"You mean your eyes," Decker snarked back.

"Our eyes, unless vampires can suddenly see perfectly in the dark and you're fumbling around for fun," Cody replied evenly. His head was still spinning and he was sure the spots in his vision were not actually there.

"We're stuck down here." Decker bemoaned which only exaggerated the throbbing in Cody's head. He didn't bother to reply this time and instead prodded the solid mass in front of him until he felt Decker begin to move in the direction that Cody was sure they hadn't tried yet. "Just imagine what they'll do to us once they've found us!" The rest of his complaints fell short as he fell forward into the mouth of a passageway.

"You were saying?" Cody teased. Decker mumbled some choice words while doing his best to gain his bearings and the hunter used the time to take the lead.

He walked with his hands in front of himself leading with his dominant foot in order to toe his way carefully down the dark passage. It took a few minutes, but soon he heard Decker following behind him and Cody let himself relax minutely. They were nowhere near in the clear, but at least Decker was following his lead again. He might not be in the best shape, but Decker was back to normal, if his attitude was anything to go by, and Cody found that he'd rather missed the constant, if not half-hearted, complaints.

"I don't hear anyone following us." Decker said by way of truce and Cody was glad that the vampire could not see the grin slowly forming on his face.

"No, but that's no reason to slow down."

They worked in relative silence after that. Decker kept his remaining thoughts to himself and Cody contented himself with dreaming of fresh air and moonlight to keep him from succumbing to his exhaustion. The ambient magic from the cells couldn't reach them in the tunnels, but Cody still found that he was shaking off its effects. He still had no way of tracking time and it seemed as if they were walking without any sign of stopping. The spots in his vision were returning with a vengeance and the hunter knew it wouldn't be long before he would need to stop and rest. Decker seemed to sense his weariness because he had moved closer at some point in the journey and had placed a gentle hand on his shoulder.

"Are you going to make it?" Cody thought Decker had been trying for a teasing tone, but there was no denying the worry behind it.

"Yes." Despite his affirmation, there was no end in sight for the tunnel and Cody was beginning to fear that they were dooming themselves. Osmond would not be able to hold off all of the guards and before long the tunnel they were in would be flooded with vampires. The rough walls were hardly neatly packed and Cody feared that every dip he felt could be a well placed trap, but he continued on. If Decker could act without nerves then Cody would have to as well. It felt as if they had been walking for hours with no change in climate or setting before Cody's hand came in painful contact with something solid. He cried out in pain, but only a small noise escaped his mouth as Decker slapped a hand over it while simultaneously shoving him to the side to protect him from any possible danger.

"It appears to be stone, possibly a door." Decker whispered after a moment of inspection. "Are you alright?"

"I'll be fine," Cody grimaced as he did his best to shake out the ache in his hand. "Will you be able to move it on your own? I'm afraid I won't be much help."

"That depends on if I can't find a latch first."

Cody stood back to allow Decker space to work. He could just barely make out the outline of the vampire and the door that possibly stood between them and freedom. He waited as patiently as possible as the rogue ran his hands up and down the stone looking for any sign of a handle or lever. Personally Cody believed that such a find would be too good to be true, but he kept his thoughts to himself. It wasn't like him to doubt that they would make it out of a difficult situation, but if he had learned anything from his time with Decker it was that the vampire seemed to have a knack for being in the wrong place at the wrong time which generally resulted in a lot more pain than necessary.

When it seemed that no progress could be made Cody opened his mouth to comment, but the click of a lock moving out of place echoed through the quiet pass. With one strong shove Decker was able to move the door just a crack, flooding the hall with moonlight. Reassured by the first sign of natural light in what must have been a month or more, Cody joined Decker to push the door the rest of the way open. Together they were able to move the stone just enough to allow them to both slip past.

True to Osmond's words they emerged from the underground passage to face the woods. There were no camps around and when Cody turned to look at where the tunnel was connected to he was surprised to see that the door was part of the outer wall of Faegon. It had vines growing over the nondescript slab of stone and they had been lucky enough that the small amount that they had moved it hadn't caused any of the vines to snap. As Cody continued to inspect the well hidden door, he noticed the tops of Faegon's tallest towers could be seen in the distance, but they were certainly closer to the slums than the city proper. Even if they had to pass through a camp or two on their way to the open territory they would blend in easily with the rest of the poorest of Faegon's subjects.

The second thing that Cody noticed was the considerable cold temperature. It had been the end of summer when he had set out to find Decker and unless they were experiencing an unseasonably cold night, much more time had passed than Cody had originally thought. There was no time to be concerned with that though, and Cody tamped down on the impending panic and focused at the task at hand, getting to safety.

It took considerably less time to move the door back into place and soon the two escaped convicts found themselves racing through the forest as quickly and quietly as they could. Decker kept looking back at Cody as if to ensure that the human hadn't strayed too far behind, but the hunter kept pace with him with little trouble. Despite being injured and more than a little famished, Cody had trained in similar conditions for such an event. Of course he had never really believed Gwyn when she'd told him that there might come a time that they found themselves on the wrong side of a cell. She had insisted on him learning to escape nearly any situation. He longed to have Gwyn with them then if only to hear her tell him just how right she had been. His thoughts served as a good distraction and it wasn't until a comfortable distance was set between them and the capitol that they slowed and Cody realized just how hungry he was.

"Where to now, my captor, or should I say rescuer?" Decker asked with an edge of smugness that made Cody question why he'd taken the vampire along.

"First to find some food. Then I'm not sure, Lunaries I guess?"

"The house of the fallen? Why there?" Decker seemed genuinely interested then and all trace of his smug attitude dissipated.

"Osmond, the vampire that helped us get free was from there. We can bring them news of his whereabouts at least."

"Always the noble one, I see. What makes you think they will welcome us with open arms?"

"Nothing, but their arms will be more welcoming than the ones we left behind." Cody reminded and Decker conceded the point.

"Lunaries it is then."

"Food first." Cody reiterated and Decker rolled his eyes.

"Yes, yes. Feed the human and then the filthy vampire lives to see another meal, no?"

Cody couldn't help but laugh at the theatrics. He could see right through the vampire's act. It was in the way he kept looking over his shoulder as he walked as if to reassure himself that the human was still with him. Every noise around them set him on edge and his stance would tense, he would look over to Cody quickly before continuing on. He moved closer to Cody slowly like the hunter was an animal he was trying not to spook. He might pretend like he could leave Cody behind at any time and not be affected, but the hunter knew better.

"Of course. Feed me and you could even chase me down for the blood, wouldn't that make you feel better?" Cody did laugh then at the scowl on the rogue's face. Despite his better judgment, Cody had saved the traitor to the Crown and yet he found no reason that it wasn't the smartest decision he could have made.

REAGAN

Reagan enjoyed nothing more than to take her rounds alone. There was something comforting about taking in the sights and sounds of her people without the constant presence of one of her council members. Her people also seemed more at ease when she wasn't flanked by her escorts and that worried the queen. They were more likely to approach her when she was alone. She never knew if it was out of fear of bothering her companions or out of fear of them, but either left an uneasy feeling of self doubt in the pit of her stomach. She wanted to be the type of queen that surrounded herself with people whom her subjects found easy to approach. She had heard stories that King Pa'ari of House Faegon held a court so well esteemed that speaking to anyone of them was good as speaking to Pa'ari himself. Any one of his men or women were well trusted and well liked. Reagan was sure he had no such issues amongst his own people as she did with hers.

The main issue seemed to stem from her lover and her heir. When she had Anya or even Cohen beside her it was painfully obvious that her people acted differently. Too many of her subjects were afraid of Anya's wrath and even more felt that Cohen was Reagan's pet and would report anything and everything he saw back to her. It made her uncomfortable to watch how those that she cared deeply for were regarded by the ones they were all meant to be protecting. These assessments were not entirely wrong, either and it pained her to think that she had done a poor job in casting the roles of her closest advisors. It was too late to undo any harm now. She could not lead her house without them, but often times she wondered if Lunaries and its people benefited from the company she kept.

When it came to Anya, Reagan knew she was too soft. Cohen reminded her of this every time she made an error at court. It was like a scab that would never heal between them as he continued to pick her apart and Reagan was left with the scars. At first she had believed it was jealousy. Cohen was her youngest sibling. Even when they were human he had stuck by her side through everything. Before they had been reborn he had been the main reason she had become an old maid instead of getting married. He had warded off any suitor who dared darken their doorstep and before long she accepted that her duty in life would be to protect her youngest sibling. She had worried about him then and even centuries later she still worried about him the same way. Anya would never understand because Reagan could never tell her about their past. There were too many secrets regarding their lives before she had become the heir and Queen to House Lunaries and they had to be kept. Anya might never know the full story, but Cohen had lived through it with her. He knew her better than any other and he had warned her to keep her distance from the troubled girl, but she had never wanted to listen.

It was becoming startlingly obvious that Cohen might have always been right. In the past decade Anya had become even more difficult to handle. She openly argued with the opinions of the Council. Just this past spring turns past she had suggested that they send men to House Adrastos' door after reports of their Queen pushing their boundaries and encroaching on Lunaries' territory. It was a problem that needed to be addressed, but she had been suggesting an act of war which would not bode well for their small army. They were nowhere near the force that Adrastos was and they were also in a much lower standing with King Zentarion, which meant that any punishment would come down on them, even if Adrastos had started the ordeal by stealing land. She was an embarrassment to Reagan's name and if it weren't for her love for the girl she would have turned her aside to save her reputation with her people long ago.

It wasn't as if Reagan had been blind to the trouble Anya could cause. She had known, even in the beginning, that Anya would be a handful. She had been out on a hunt when she had stumbled upon the girl, alone and scared, in Mordin Forest. Even then she had been fierce. She had been from the West, unlike the girls under their protection now. She had known full well what vampires were and even that Reagan was a Queen. She had been left without a home or a family after a rogue attack and Reagan had instantly taken to her. The moment her blue eyes roamed the human's form she knew that she had to have her. There had always been something that drew her to the girl and while Cohen had thought it the cause of magic, time had proven that her fascination with the girl was more primal.

Anya had refused her and the bite at first. The fights they use to have were legendary and Reagan had learned quickly that she was going to be a project that had to be treated with a delicate touch. She persuaded Anya to live as her personal handmaiden and made it very clear that she would be given the gift of rebirth by Reagan herself anytime she desired. Anya had told her nearly every night that she would never take the bite, but her words did not deter the vampire. Reagan had continued to allow the girl to stay close to her side and she did her best to groom her for the role of a paramour without Anya even knowing. It had taken a few years, but after that time even Anya could not deny the connection between them and she had agreed to take the bite in a private, formal ceremony. Anya had even gone so far as to ink the skin around her right wrist with a colorful cobra, the same snake constricted around Reagan's right leg over her round buttocks and ended with its head on her hip, as a sign of her loyalty to her. Cohen had borne witness to the rites and had given them his blessing even though Reagan knew that he had no desire to share his sister with the woman.

Whispers in the hall brought the queen back to the present and she did her best to push her own fears aside in order to focus on the words around her. She was in the heart of the Royal Tower, where Emeline and other important members of their house were taken to be schooled in the rules and traditions of their great house. Cohen was still escorting Natalya between her rooms and her classes personally. She had ordered him to do so until they were sure that Emeline was well enough to spend more time out of her own rooms and that the stubborn girl's presence would not be too much for her to handle. There were other reasons of course; Natalya would have been free to roam the halls of the House had she been easier to trust. She was stubborn and full of fire, something that Cohen seemed to enjoy and Reagan had used that to her advantage. He was easy to convince to stay by the girl and thus keep tabs on the curious human. It had been just about two months since the girls had come to them and from what she had heard Emeline was adapting well, but she had yet to see to either of the girls personally.

"Your Grace." One of Cohen's personal advisors bowed to her as she passed and Reagan stopped to talk.

"How are you this evening, Galvin?" She knew everyone in the royal service by name. It was important to her to show her people that she appreciated all of them. They had chosen her over Cassandra, at least the few that remained since the old days, and she could never let them feel that they had made the wrong choice.

"I am doing well, as always, Your Grace." The man blushed under the attention. He was tall, with almost a head over the Queen and yet he bent his body low as a sign of respect. When his cobalt blue eyes did meet hers there was warmth in them that Reagan had always admired.

"Very good. I hear that your son is doing well in his lessons. I know Nicolette is very proud." Nicolette was a petite woman in comparison to her husband. She worked as a seamstress, providing the queen's wardrobe personally and Reagan had always been fond of her out of all of her personal servants. She had recently begun to double as a handmaid when

Freya went to Natalya's aid.

"He is, Your Grace. We are both very proud. It is good of you to ask. Jasper would take the bite sooner if the rules allowed it." There was no law against turning children, but Reagan believed in the preservation of youth and would not allow a child to be reborn until they became of age unless injury or illness forced them to take action quicker.

"Tell Jasper that I eagerly await the day as I will be honored to give him the bite personally."

"Your Grace, the honor would be ours. Nicolette will be overjoyed to hear of this. You could not possibly understand what this means to our family." The man bowed again and Reagan smiled at his obvious surprise.

It was a high honor to be turned by a member of the royal party, much less a queen. In the vampire houses you were considered a member of nobility if bitten by another of the royal party. A member of their respective royal party had turned the lords and ladies of every house. If a King or Queen bit you were automatically indoctrinated into the royal court. Cohen always spoke highly of Galvin and his son; he had personally asked Reagan if she would grant him permission to turn the boy himself. A King or Queen had to approve of every rebirth in their House. Reagan had agreed to allow Cohen to bring Jasper into the ranks of their noble class, but she had always known that she wanted to do them the honor herself. If Jasper were made part of the royal party he would be solidifying not only his standing in the House, but also the standings of his parents.

"Go tell her now, I'm sure that Cohen has no need of you for the rest of the night." Reagan dismissed the ecstatic man and continued on her way. She hardly made it a few steps before she was approached by another human.

"Good evening Your Grace," Eldridge, the head of the agriculture department bowed before her. "The crops have been gathered for the season. The weather held well and we have enough in our stores for the winter."

"Very good, how about the cattle? Do you know if there is enough milk and meat for the humans within the walls?"

"I believe so, I will speak to Alma personally and have a report for you by dusk." Alma was a tough human woman who oversaw the livestock and butchery. She had been in the position since her father retired nearly three decades ago. It was thanks to her and Eldridge that the human's of the house were well fed and looked after.

"That will do nicely, thank you Eldridge."

Reagan continued through the halls enjoying the quiet of predawn. She missed the days when she wandered through the halls without a purpose or a care. She loved speaking to her people, but there was something to be said for moments of solitude.

"There have been more reports from the scouts," Lord Basil swooped by to flank her side. He kept his face and voice passive, though the steel in his eyes made Reagan weary. "It is not terribly urgent. I've left them for you in the Council room."

"Have them moved to my study and insure that no other eyes see them before me."

"As you wish, Your Grace. Do you wish to have company?"

"No, you may go, thank you." Reagan knew that the man only offered to be polite. There was no love lost between the two, though he was invaluable as a strategist and Reagan valued his opinion.

Reagan saw to other members of the court as she made her way to the classrooms. She could not often find the time to speak with her subjects, but when she did she made sure to make a day of it. She learned of a new baby being born to one of the cooks and the joining of one of the common vampires to her long time lover, a noble vampire, which some found to be a joy and others a scandal. She spoke to officials and common folk, humans and vampires until she felt as if she could have solved all of the problems in their community if she just spent more time with her people. When she finally reached the classrooms that she had been journeying to her heart felt heavy.

"Emeline is working on her strength and coordination in the small training room." Nirosh said by way of greeting when Reagan swept through the classroom door. He was dressed casually in his workout garb, something the queen noticed instantly.

"Do you often sit in on these lessons, or were you expecting me?" Reagan doubted that the Captain of the Guard was keeping tabs on her and rather suspected that he was overseeing Emeline's training personally. She had heard from Cohen that Nirosh seemed to care personally for the girl and Reagan wanted to investigate the nature of those feelings in person.

"We both know the answer to that question. Playing stupid was never your strength, Rae." Nirosh was too polite to roll his eyes, but it was clear in his tone. She loved the pet name that he had given her when she had first been reborn and she had treasured it every time he had called her by it. Even now as she was his queen, Nirosh made it a point to remind her that he had known her for too long to listen to any political garbage that she felt the need to spew to protect her image. "You came to check on the girl?"

"I know that Emeline is doing well, your reports and Cohen's are enough to satisfy that curiosity. I came down to check on you." Reagan took a seat in one of the classroom chairs and Nirosh perched himself on the desk, looking down on her in a familiar gesture. It made her feel like a childe again, though it was not an unwelcome feeling. Nirosh had been a mentor to her when she had first come to Lunaries and he was one of the few people whom she allowed to treat her so casually behind closed doors.

"Why would you feel the need to check on me?"

"Now who is the one playing stupid?" Reagan smiled despite his scowl and she brushed his annoyance aside. "We have both known the other too long, my friend. I am concerned by your concern."

"I feel nothing untoward of the girl!" Nirosh stood, his voice rising as his body twisted to face away from her, hiding the rage she knew would be there.

"Oh, old friend. You know I would never believe such things." Reagan moved to place a gentle hand on the man's arm. "She reminds you of your daughter, does she not?"

"She does." The stoic and strong man had never once shown her such emotion and Reagan felt overcome by the trust he must place in her. She angled her body so her small frame covered as much of him as possible. He had comforted her in much the same way when she had been a childe, she felt honored to be able to return it in kind. "I miss her still, centuries have past and I have never forgotten her."

It had been long since Reagan had been human. She could hardly say she remembered what her own parents had been like. Some days she found it hard to remember her other brother and it had been even less time since she had seen him. She felt guilt at the thought that Nirosh who had been a vampire for centuries longer than she, could still remember his human daughter better than she did her own family. It seemed more likely that he did not remember her and that he was imprinting his emotions and needs on this young childe and Reagan could not honestly decide which she felt was more heart wrenching.

The torrent of emotions swept through the man as quickly as they came and when he pulled away he looked completely unaffected. The blonde found herself wishing she could help him the same way he had done for her.

"I would like to see her practice, if you would be so kind to escort me." Nirosh would see through her ruse, no doubt. She needed no escort, she knew full well the way to the practice rooms, but it would do the man a world of good to see the girl with whom made him feel slightly closer to his own daughter.

"Nothing would please me more, Rea." He held his arm out for her, guiding her through the halls as if it were his place. Nirosh would have made a great King for Lunaries. Reagan had even considered him as a possible companion for herself, though they had never had that kind of relationship. She had always assumed she would marry for the good of her House, but when Anya had come into her life she had chosen against the wishes of her advisors and followed her heart. Had she never met Anya, Reagan easily could see how tying herself to Nirosh would have been the logical move. He would have said no, at least she always felt that he would have. He hated politics, but loved being the man to help maintain the status quo. A union between them would have certainly upset the order which Nirosh dedicated his life to defending. In another life they would have made a smart political pair, but musing over what would never be held no advantages for her or the House.

"Natalya is progressing as well, but it is slow progress. Perhaps you could work with her too." Reagan made light conversation, though she knew there was no point. Nirosh would not take a personal interest in the difficult human girl. They were both too stubborn to work well together, but it never hurt to try.

"From the words I hear whispered you should keep a close eye on that one. Darius has taken an interest in her, no? I have also heard rumors that your very own Cohen has been to see her more than is necessary."

"I don't appreciate what you are implying. Cohen visits her often on my request. As for Darius, we both know what he sees in her. She fought his aura manipulation and yet she shows no sign of magic within her. She is a curious case."

"You are always looking for a project, Rea. Be sure that fixing this one does not lead to the same disaster your last endeavor did." Of course he was speaking of Anya. In private she may have fallen for the bait, but in the open castle she knew ignoring it was the better course of action.

"I haven't the slightest idea to what you could be referring to." She said firmly and put the conversation to its end.

They entered the smaller practice room to the sound of a body hitting the mat hard. Darius was standing over Emeline as the girl slowly got back up to her feet. She looked determined more than pained and Reagan and Nirosh took to the shadows to further watch her progress. Darius held out his hand and she took it, using his strength to pull herself and simultaneously pull him down to her level. She was fast, but he was faster and before she could drag him down with her she had her back pressed against his chest with his fangs pressed into her shoulder.

"Well done, Emeline." Nirosh spoke as he moved out of the shadows like a proud father.

"She is progressing well, Your Grace. She excels at her practical lessons and her combat training is getting better as you can see."

"Very good. I believe her training is done for the day, no?"

"As you wish, Your Grace." Darius moved to wrap up the lesson while Nirosh was showing Emeline defensive stances to help avoid being taken down so easily. Reagan swept from the room when she was sure that it would go unnoticed.

The halls were less crowded the closer it got to daybreak. According to Cohen, Natalya had mostly adjusted to sleeping during the day, but both he and Freya admitted that she would occasionally stay up to watch the sun rise. Reagan hadn't had much time to check on the girl and she suddenly found herself with a little bit of time. Cohen was elsewhere dealing with an argument that had taken place in the lower villages. It was a bit below his station, but she felt that distancing her heir and the human would do them both some good. It was true that she had wanted him to stay to close to her, but she was beginning to fear that they might be too close. She knew that rumors were circulating about the pair. Nirosh's concern was not the first she had heard, but it was the first that had been brought to her personally. She didn't believe that Cohen could have feelings for the girl, but she hoped that surprising the girl with a visit would reveal more than whispered words could.

A young vampire was walking in the hall, toward her and took her from her troubled thoughts. He stoped a respectable distance from her before bowing and flashing his eyes. The warm brown was briefly replaced with a warm honey. He was one of Islara's boys. "Your Grace."

"Good evening, my childe. I hope that you are having a pleasant evening." Reagan had asked Islara to have one of her children look into her suspicions of a traitor in their midsts. She had instructed her handmaiden to give as little information as possible, though she trusted that the woman would put her best person to the task.

"I have. I've gone for a stroll just outside our walls. It's always so peaceful there. I often find that being alone can really help clear the mind."

"That is does, but of course it can be dangerous outside our walls, please do take care." Reagan thought sis did a decent job of hiding her relief. She had doubted Anya when she had said she followed Darius out of the walls and as much as she wanted to trust and believe in her lover, she had also desperately wanted her to be wrong.

"I will, Your Grace. You have a good night now." The boy bowed once more before turning and returning back to the main castle, away from the Royal tower.

Reagan walked to rest of the way to Natalya's chambers feeling more carefree than she had in some time. It seemed that not much could bring down her spirit, but she found herself proven wrong when she arrived at the girl's door. Lilliana was not at her post when Reagan arrived. Rational thought out won panic and she paused at the door to listen for the heartbeats of the girl and Freya, but could only hear one heartbeat beyond the heavy wood door. No longer able to keep it at bay, panic coursed through her at the thought of the girl being left alone while under her protection. Reagan jumped to action, pushing in the door with all of her strength; the bang of wood on stone echoed in her ears and made the two occupants of the room jump apart.

Natalya was sitting on her bed, arms crossed over her drawn in knees. At the loud noise she fought her fight or flight response and curled into her body further before jumping up and reaching for weapons that weren't there. Cohen was also in the room, leaning against the bedpost. When the queen flew into the room he moved to stand before the girl, his eyes glowing and his fangs present. Natalya clung to his back and one of his hands moved behind him to tangle in her shirt. If Reagan had any doubts about the affection that her second in command felt for Natalya they disappeared.

"There is no need for such theatrics, Your Grace." Cohen snapped and moved to sit on the bed while Natalya fell into his side, glaring at the queen.

"There was no need to rid her of guards or Freya and you're meant to be in the lower village." Reagan countered, feeling like they were just their normal selves again, not Queen and her heir.

"I took care of it already. The cook's daughter was found sneaking into the stables. They thought she was stealing, but she was just *visiting* the stable boy. It was simple and dealt with in a matter of moments. I almost wonder why you sent me," Cohen laughed despite his pointed look. The tension was gone from his stance as he looked from Natalya to Reagan and back again. "She reminds me of you."

"I couldn't possibly understand why." Reagan resisted the urge to roll her eyes, it would be unbecoming and she still had a reputation to uphold.

"Why are you here?" Natalya spoke up, completely disregarding any titles and staring down Reagan.

"I came to check on you, Natalya. I wanted to make sure that you were comfortable with your accommodations."

"I am," Natalya responded and Cohen nudged her before she rolled her eyes and continued, "Your Grace."

"Reagan will do in private, Natalya."

"Thank you, Your Grace." Cohen's smug look over her shoulder made Reagan laugh lightly. Of course he would be proud to watch the girl get smart with her.

"No need to thank me, my dear. I see you are already being looked after, though, so I will bid you both good day." Reagan nodded to both giving Cohen a pointed look. "Call for Freya when you leave, I expect that you will retire to your own quarters tonight and meet with me at sunset."

"As you command, Your Grace." Cohen nodded, though the smirk never left his face.

Reagan couldn't help but wonder if the dread that Cohen had felt when she had met Anya felt anything like what ate at her as she closed the door glancing back at her baby brother and the young human that sat beside him.

ARTHUR

The rising sun was a welcome feeling on Arthur's skin. It was a cool morning, which was to be expected as the harvest season had certainly ended and winter would soon be upon them. The small garden that the human and vampire pair kept was already gathered for the winter. There hadn't been much to do when Arthur had finally been well enough to help, but he had done what he could to contribute. It felt odd to him that he had spent the harvest working on two different plots of land that weren't even his own, but hard work was hard work no matter where it was done. He hadn't had to do so much physical labor in a very long time and his sore muscles protested with every move. He knew he would have to slow down soon, no matter how much he loathed the thought. Relaxation was foreign to him and it was difficult to have nothing to occupy his time with. Even when his tired body protested his mind screamed to be free and on the move. He had all but fully healed, the thin scar and slight twinge in his shoulder was the only evidence of his injuries. Antony's magic had greatly helped in his quick healing, but he wasn't young anymore and he knew it would be some time still until he could move without his body protesting.

Allowing his body the proper time to mend itself was difficult for Arthur. He had wanted to go find Art the moment that he had been able to move without aid, but Thomas had been the one to speak to his rationality. He was in no shape to find Art and while Thomas and Antony were more than happy to see him to full health they would not leave the protection of their home. It was something that the men had argued about more than once. Even now the human felt irritation eat at him knowing that there were two able-bodied men who could aid him in his search, but would not because of their political beliefs.

"I thought I would find you here," Antony spoke softly as he walked toward him with a steaming cup of tea in hand. "The crops are all in this year earlier than usual. I have you to thank for that."

"You found me and took care of me. I would have been in your debt otherwise." Arthur liked Antony's company even if he did not quite agree with his life choices. Thomas wasn't as terrible as he assumed all the monsters were, but he still couldn't understand how the human beside him slept comfortably at night while the vampire shared his quarters.

"It's still quite cold, why don't you come back in and I can make us some food?"

"I'd rather stay out here, thank you."

"Thomas means you no harm, I'm sure you know that." Antony had done his best to keep him and Thomas apart when possible. He had been thoughtful enough to never leave the two alone in the small house and had even gone so far as making Thomas hunt for his food while Arthur was with them. The first time he had watched Antony bleed into a cup for him he had nearly been sick.

"I find that very doubtful." The vampire wasn't the only cause for his discomfort. Arthur wasn't so much worried about being in the hut with Thomas as he was uncomfortable when Antony treated him like Mary Rose had. He could deal with Thomas and his hostility, that was a normal, masculine emotion, but Antony was a mystery which he couldn't quite understand.

"You do not mean that." Antony chided in the way that reminded him of his mother. She had used the same tone whenever he'd tried to lie to her. She never believed him either.

"I do not belong here. I must find my daughter and the others and return to our home. There is no place in Mordin Forest for a man like me."

"I'm not so sure about that," Antony sighed sounding sad. Arthur had no notion of how to respond and so he stayed silent. "Be that as it may, we do not mind you staying with us, but you know that we cannot aid you once you leave."

"I know that he'd rather not travel through the territory of his people for his own reasons, but I don't understand what is keeping you in this place. There seems to me no credible reason why you would be confined to this house and property." Arthur wasn't sure how much help someone like Antony would be, but even Art had proven helpful at points in their journey.

"I will not leave him," Antony gazed past him completely focused on something that Arthur could not see. "We are a single human and vampire with no alliances. It would be dangerous for either of us to go out there."

"How much do alliances truly protect you though? His kind doesn't seem the type to abide by something as civil as alliances. They hunt and drink blood. How could such savage people be developed enough to understand and implant order?"

"Are you being ignorant intentionally? I have explained this to you before, but I suppose I can explain it once more." Antony paused as if to dare Arthur to stop him and carried on only after a moment of silence. "There are two types of vampires like we told you before, I suppose Thomas would be a third kind, but of course he enjoys being difficult. Simply put there are vampires that have a code of sorts. They live in an actual kingdom-like structure with miniature kingdoms or Houses as they call them all under the rule of one great king. He calls himself the King of Kings, it's a bit narcissistic, but he's also the oldest vampire still living so I suppose he is allowed to grant himself the right. The rest of them are rogues. They defy the rules and laws of the Crown. Now we don't necessarily agree with all of the laws, but we can appreciate the order and peace they are meant to instill. We are certainly nothing compared to the rogues. We live on this land with the agreement to stay out of the Crown's way. If soldiers from the Crown come by we feed them and if it is a small party we shelter them. If we hear word of rogues we tell the next Crown soldiers who pass through. They don't bother us and we don't bother them. They hate us, I think. They think we're weak for not taking a side, but we've lived this way for decades and it's done us just fine."

It pained Arthur to think that he might have something in common with the monsters, but he agreed that the two who swore no alliances did sound weak. "Whatever, they're all savages to me."

"And you are entitled to your beliefs, no matter how misguided they might be. We will not leave this property to help, but we can help if Thomas samples some of your blood. Until you are well enough to go out alone I would take the time to think about your options. Now I am about to make our breakfast, come in soon or it will be cold."

Arthur watched the man go with a sour expression on his face. Loath as he was to admit it, he was hungry. He eyed the trees around himself wearily before turning in toward the house. He hated watching Antony putter about in the kitchen, but it would be foolish to turn down food. Cooking was a woman's job, something he had little concern with learning. In Ash they'd had a cook and maid who had kept up the house while Natalya had taken her lessons or trained with him. He had little physical work to tend to as the head of a moderately well to do household. He had become accustomed to running his late wife's estate. There had been no shame in keeping the books for her family's modest farmstead and he'd had enough to pay a few farmers to tend to the land as well as the maid and cook. He'd worked hard in his youth it had seemed like earned status at the time. Of course now he was a simple farmer again, bartering his labor for shelter and even that had gone to plot rather quickly.

The tea in his mug had gone cold and he'd hardly drank any of it. The chill in the air seemed to settle in his bones and Arthur knew that he would have to turn in soon and face the odd men. They had opened their doors to him and yet he could hardly bare to look at them. A noise from the trees to the west of the property caught his attention and seemed a good reason as any to stay out longer. There was nothing in sight and Arthur stood, waiting for whatever critter would emerge. His stomach turned as he wondered idly if the unseen animal would see its fate by the fangs of one of the monsters that dwelled within Mordin Forest. He wondered if maybe it would be Thomas who caught it and drained it of its blood.

The noise returned, this time to the South west, whatever it was, it was moving almost in a circling motion. The noise continued and Arthur began to wonder if it wasn't an animal at all, but a monster like the one that had attacked him and Art. The noises settled after a moment and the silence returned as if it had never left. The ceramic cup in his hand was ice cold and his stomach complained to remind him that he hadn't eaten yet and if he'd been on the farm still it would nearly be time for his second meal of the day. Odd noises were normal for the forest as he had learned and there was no reason to worry further. With one last look around, Arthur was resigned to his fate as he let himself back into the small home.

Antony was busy cooking for their morning meal as Thomas lay asleep in the bed that Arthur was not using during his stay. Antony obviously was not as accustomed to sleeping during the night as the bags under his eyes attested to, but the man had made it clear that he would not be leaving Arthur alone with the vampire. Arthur wasn't sure if it was the man being kind or if it was for self-preservation, but the quiet man never complained about the upset to his sleep cycle.

Arthur took a seat at the table while he watched Antony work. He contemplated telling him about the odd feeling he'd had outside, but he brushed it off.

"Eat and then rest, you need more sleep if you hope for the wounds to heal soon."

A loaf of warm bread with thinly cut honey glazed boar and eggs sat on his plate and Arthur greedily devoured his food. The bread was better than the hard loafs that Emeline made, which reminded him of the early days of his marriage to Elizabeth. She had also been terrible at cooking, having grown up in the castle, but they'd had the best cook in Ash and they'd enjoyed meals like the one before him on lazy mornings after she'd lost her first child. Those had been the days when he'd thought that he could live with her just like that and never feel like he'd missed out on anything in life. He'd not been wrong.

The boar was succulent and he ripped the bread apart to drag it through the grease and honey pooling at the bottom of his dish. He took a moment to savor the feeling of the food settling in his empty stomach before looking up to find another fresh cup of tea waiting for him. Antony was busy cleaning up in the wake of meal preparation. His own food sat on the table, uneaten, as he moved about silently leaving Arthur to his food and thoughts.

"Thank you." Arthur muttered. His stomach was full and the hot tea warmed his bones.

"Eat and then sleep. You can thank me by resting and then helping me out in the yard later. The harvest might be over, but there is still much to be done before the first snow."

The food was gone quickly and Arthur found himself settled back into the comfortable bed. He was feeling better than before, but it was still exhausting to be up and moving for more than a few hours at a time though he was sure that whatever was in the tea that Antony was giving him contributed to that, but his body was healing faster than he could have hoped without his help and he couldn't find a reason to complain about the forced rest. He watched Antony from his place in bed as the man finally settled to eat alone. Arthur couldn't understand the sudden sadness he felt upon seeing that, but sleep overtook him before he could analyze the arbitrary emotion.

Arthur woke up to a sudden jolt to someone shaking his arm roughly.

"Get up! Get up!" Thomas hissed in his ear. The remnants of the sunlight was peeking out from under the drawn shades. He'd slept through most of the day. "There's a rogue outside, just beyond our gate."

"Do you have a weapon? What do I do?" Arthur scrambled to get up and find something to protect himself with. The two had taken his weapons when he'd first arrived and now he wished that they had at least returned one of them to him.

"All you need to do is watch." Thomas replied as he move toward the door. He wasn't like the monsters that Arthur had seen who could only move by night. He could withstand the sun to an extent and he stood beside Antony at the door with ease.

"We can handle this, but you should see the monsters as you call them and understand that they are different from what Thomas is." Antony spoke with his normal soft voice, though his eyes were trained on whatever awaited them outside. "Come here."

Arthur found himself obeying without complaint. It occurred to him then that the thing he had heard in the woods earlier that day could be the same thing that was stalking them outside in the yard. He stood next to the other human.

"He's sick, it's partially the sun, but it also looks like he hasn't fed in days." Thomas spoke and it sent a chill up Arthur's spine. "He probably heard your heartbeats and braved the sun for a meal. He is desperate."

"What will you do with him?" Arthur asked as the grotesque creature came into view at the gate to their property. It hardly looked human, bright red patches covered his skin and dirt matted his hair. His eyes were completely dilated and nearly glowing in the setting sun. They were an odd shade of green that was so pale it nearly looked white.

"You might have had magic to resist my aura spells, but this poor creature will certainly not."

It was the only warning that Arthur got before the rogue began to shriek in agony. The birds that had been nesting nearby flew away in a furious flock. Arthur watched, horrified, as Antony simply stood and watched his face blank and void of emotion. He heard Thomas move behind him with a grim look on his face. He was just as put off by Antony's display and he turned away from the tortured rogue, unable to bare it.

"Antony is messing with his natural aura. It's the energy that surrounds all living things, even vampires. He can manipulate how you feel. You might remember that from when he put you back to sleep when you first came to us." It seemed talking about it detached the vampire from the sick manipulation of power before him and his face relaxed back into a passive stare. "This time he's using that sick vampire's aura to inflict pain. He's making his body's energy feel as if there is something attacking him while keeping him paralyzed. Naturally his body is trying to fight back so through all of that agony he is also feeling the pressure of Antony's magic restraining him and his own natural reaction to fight it."

"That's disturbing." Arthur grimaced, looking away at last.

"It's a warning." Antony spoke again, releasing the sorry excuse for a man from his grasp. "He will run from here and tell any rogue he sees to do the same. The next soldiers who pass will hear of it and then a party of them will come out to deal with the rest. I told you once before. We fight no wars, we only mean to survive."

Antony waited until the creature was gone before turning and moving back into the hut without another word. Suddenly the small home felt too oppressive and Arthur had to get away from his mounting panic.

"Be careful out there." Thomas warned, eyeing him for a moment longer before turning to follow Antony back inside.

There was a wooden bench on the edge of the property that sat just inside the gate. It was far enough away from the strange duo, but still within the protection that they extended to him. Antony had, until then, seemed like a harmless, weak man, but watching him hurt that creature without even moving was terrifying. Arthur had known that magic existed. Everyone who lived in the outer villages was tested for it before their tenth birthday. If they did display any magical talents they were sent to the capitol where they were supposedly trained. Arthur had never been to the capitol and no one who had left had ever returned so he couldn't say what happened to them. He had only ever seen children with odd abilities; like the boy who had lived just down the road, who had dreamt about the fire in the village center which killed twenty people, the week before it happened. He had been an odd boy and after the fire his entire family had packed their things and moved, presumably to Magdus, but Arthur had never been convinced of such. He had always thought that they had gotten rid of the boy and his terrifying power and been too ashamed by him to return to their home.

He had never heard of aura magic, but he lacked any other explanation for what he had just seen, or for the reason why he would suddenly fall asleep even if he hadn't been very tired. It still confused him when Antony suggested that he had magic of his own. He had been tested just as the other children had been and they hadn't found anything particularly significant about him. He had been relieved of course, he didn't want any abilities or talents that made him different. He was quite fine living a normal life. How was it that the normalcy of his childhood had led to this very moment?

He heard a noise to his right and he turned in time to see Thomas joining him. "You might hate me, and while I don't understand it I can accept that, but I hope you at least understand that no harm will come to you while you stay with us. My people are a varied people, just as humans are. There are the good and the bad, I suppose I would consider myself to fall somewhere in between."

Arthur wasn't quite sure how to respond so instead he turned away to stare back out into the woods. The sun had nearly set and Thomas stretched out as if he was going to settle back for a while. It seemed ignoring him was not going to work and Arthur gave in. "One of your people took my wife and now they've surely taken my daughter and her friends. How do I forgive that and look past it?"

"You don't. You go out there and find them, but fighting us won't help. We are here and willing to help you, but you have to allow us."

Arthur didn't know if he had the words to respond and so he didn't. He was content to silence and Thomas remained for a moment longer before speaking again.

"You are welcome here as long as you need, but remember that when you leave this place you leave our protection behind. We will not risk our lives for you or your friends," after a pause he added, "you would do the same."

Thomas stood to leave him alone, not bothering to continue the conversation. He was right, he would not have helped if the roles had been reversed. He wouldn't have even opened the door to a stranger, much less take one in who had been passed out in the ruins of an old village. He could not expect the two who had done more than he would to give him anymore. He would have to heal quickly and go back out into the forest looking for his daughter and the other two. Moments of weakness when he relied on others had to be put to a stop, there was no use in waiting for the universe to look upon him favorably, he would make his own fate.

The sun had finally set and it startled Arthur how cold it had become. He had slept through most of the day and he was completely refreshed. Antony would be exhausted and would try to stay awake to make sure he and Thomas wouldn't kill each other. Arthur wondered when it had come to this, a grown man needing to keep watch so he didn't try to harm another grown man. Thomas might be a creature of the night, a vampire as he called himself, but he was still a man with thoughts and emotions. Arthur wondered at what point in his life he'd come to believe that anything different than him must be dangerous and therefore eliminated. It could probably be traced back to the day that Elizabeth had been taken from him and his young daughter had returned from a trip into the woods covered in blood that was not her own with vacant eyes. He had seen the worst in everyone and everything that might pose a threat to his small family since that day. Is that what had led him to this moment?

Thomas was right he had to get his daughter back. He had to find Emeline and Art and bring them home. He might never find out what happened to Elizabeth, but bringing home their daughter would have to be his closure. He would complete this last journey and then it would be time to put Mordin Forest and the things that lived within the trees behind him for good.

NATALYA

A cool breeze wafted through the large open window and Natalya drank it in like water. Training and lessons kept her busy so Cohen had yet to bring her to the royal gardens, but it was a beautiful night and she hoped he might have the time soon. The breeze was picking up and it did wonders to cool her down from her workout: it got caught in the large sleeves of her night robe and snaked through the silk, chilling her body. She imagined it was as gentle as a lover's caress, though she was too young yet to know what that might feel like. She leaned out the window as far as she dared to feel the wind in her hair. It was still short, but since she had come to Lunaries it had managed to grow over an inch and it brushed against her shoulders. Her father would have made her cut it; he could have complained about it getting in the way of her training. She found she rather liked it, and the freedom she felt, every time the curls danced along her skin. Another large gust of wind pushed her hair from her face and a laugh escaped her as the large sleeves of the robe pushed up her arms until they tangled with her hair in her face. The soft, purple robe had been a gift from Reagan. It had been the first expensive garment the queen had been given as a sign of her royal status after taking the bite and she had given it to Natalya in the hopes that it would give her some comfort while she made the toughest decision of her young life.

Eventually Natalya would have to choose if she was going to call Lunaries home and if so, did she want to take the bite. It wasn't necessary for her to take it, Freya and the other humans she had met throughout the castle were proof of that, but Reagan had made it clear that she had hopes that rebirth was in her future. This only mattered if she chose to stay. If she did not then she would have to find her way home, she could not ask her new friends to leave the protection of their House to assist her. She could not bare the thought of harm befalling one of them due to her. The fact that she had grown to care so much for these people made the thought of leaving even more difficult. Her father was the only other person she had to care for and her life with him had left a lot to be desired. He was her father and her only family, but he had cost her the promise of a better life. He had destroyed her chance of a decent marriage and had driven her out of her mind until rebelling had seemed the only option. She loved her father, truly she did, but living with him had been taxing on her patients. Staying in the vampire house would mean taking control of her own fate for the first time in her life. The thought was attractive to say the least.

Leaving Lunaries and her new friends was not an option, Natalya wasn't sure if it ever had been. She had come this far because she refused to leave Emeline and that had not changed. She still felt strongly about her decision and Emeline was the closest thing she had to family, the only family she wanted to have. If she took the bite as the vampires called it she would be able to truly call her a sister.

Of course she had to consider that becoming a vampire meant becoming the very thing that had taken her mother from her. In all of her time since her mother's disappearance she couldn't remember what had really happened that day, but her father had told her that she had described a monster with a human's body the only time she talked about it. She knew without a doubt that a vampire, a rogue as her lessons had taught her, had taken her mother from her. If she became a vampire would she become a rogue one day? She knew they had all been human at one point, what drove them to become mad men? Cohen assured her that would never happen to her. He had been bitten four centuries ago and he was every bit a sane, respectable man, but still she wondered if she did turn into one of those things would there be someone ready to stop her?

She had other worries to trouble her besides her impending decision. Her sleep was being plagued by the images that played behind her eyes. Natalya knew without a doubt that not all of her dreams were dreams. Sometimes when she closed her eyes and her body started to rest her mind would take her through her memories. They were not merely dreams, of that she was certain. The colors were always a bit sharper, her senses stronger as she relived moments from her short life until she woke in a sweat, confused and drained. Ever since she was a small child she would have memory dreams as her mother used to call them. They had become less frequent after her mother's disappearance, but now they returned until she was having them at least once a week.

Her mother had been the only person who knew about her abilities. She never had to explain why it must be kept a secret. Even at a young age Natalya had known that having magic was more of a curse than a blessing. Anyone showing even the smallest amount of magic, especially from the lower class was seen as dangerous because they were not able to afford a proper teacher. They were sent to Magdus, usually by scared family members, and never heard from again. With her mother's family's banishment from the capitol there would have been even more scrutiny if anyone had discovered that she had magic. Not even her father could be trusted. Her mother kept her secret because she herself had been a fully fledged seer. She had told Natalya of her own training from the palace and how it had helped her hone her skills. Because of this she was able to teach her daughter a little about the craft. Her mother had been able to block her own visions, she said that the art form caused more trouble than it was worth and she agreed to teach Natalya with the hopes that she too would choose to block out the visions. It was why her father could never be told. They were considered dangerous and he was not one to take kindly to magic users. It had been a miracle when the government officials had confirmed her as negative for the possibility of magic. With her mother's disappearance no one else had known. The lack of guidance and the obvious weakness of her abilities meant that she never experienced more than the odd dream-memory from her past. She'd nearly forgotten that she'd had such dreams until they began to plague her again for the first time in years. Before coming to Lunaries she used to pass them off as a childish game, nothing more than playing pretend.

Ever since she came to Lunaries the dreams were more frequent. She would wake from restless days, the bitter taste of her less than ideal childhood fresh in her mouth. Despite her obviously magical hosts she dared not tell a soul of her abilities. There were no seers that she had met and Darius' aura magic made her feel very uneasy. Cohen had reassured her that the man meant no harm, that her imperviousness to his brand of magic simply intrigued him, but his words did little to calm her.

She came away from the window and lay back on her bed. She had been training with Emeline and the boys in one of the practice rooms for hours until Emeline had left feeling drained and Natalya had begged off citing her own tiredness in silent support of her friend. She only realized how exhausted she really was when she fell into the silk sheets. As soon as Natalya closed her eyes and allowed sleep to claim her she knew she was viewing a memory.

The dirty stone walls of Lunaries' dungeons looked just as harsh as she remembered them to be. She'd been to them only once, when she had been acting particularly difficult a week into her arrival and Cohen had threatened her with a cell. The threat had been empty, of course, but it had scared her straight for a few days. There was a draft much as there had been when Cohen had escorted her back to the room she now occupied. She turned, knowing that Cohen would be waiting for her, but when she looked, no one was there. Confused, she began down the hall to where she remembered the guards were standing that day, but instead there stood an older man. His clothes were plain, made of a non-dyed cotton. He lacked any age lines around his glassy, green eyes but Natalya knew she was in the presence of an Elder. His sandy hair was unkempt, as if he had been running his hands through it, yet he looked much too proper to do such a thing.

"They're gone." The words spilled from her mouth before she knew she would speak them. It was as if she was not in her own body and instead was watching another's memory through their eyes. She vaguely remembered her mother telling her that it was possible to see other's memories instead of her own, but she had never experienced it before now.

"Yes, all of them. We haven't been able to find the guards. I fear Augustus has taken them. If they were willing accomplices then I fear for all of us." He spoke the words with the air of a man who was not often wrong and Natalya felt fear that was not her own in the pit of her stomach.

"What of Cohen? He had this watch did he not?" Panic mixed with the fear that was not her own. If this was truly another's memory then she knew that Cohen was fine, she'd been with him just the night before and that was enough to calm her own nerves. The man before her stepped aside and Natalya felt as her body moved out of the dungeon and into the hall.

She noticed instantly that something was very different about the castle. The hall looked the same as it did in her time, except there were rich tapestries on the walls that were foreign to her. They were made of bright colors, though purple seemed to be the most prominent. A few even had the House Lunaries' crest that she recognized from the flags that hung on the castle's walls.

"Fret not, he must have attempted to warn the others because he was found near the gates. He was unconscious, but alive."

"Take me to him." Natalya watched as they made their way through the back of the castle toward the passage that Cohen himself had taken her through. It was a route through the inner parts of the castle reserved for use by the royal class only. There was a large lake hidden by trees which were completely bare of leaves. Cohen had promised to take her here, but they still hadn't found the time. It was a quiet sanctuary away from the hustle of life in a castle, but in this person's memory its emptiness brought dread. When they passed the water this time, Natalya was shocked to see not her own reflection, but Reagan's. The woman who looked back at her appeared younger than Natalya remembered her to be. It was hard to judge age with vampires, but there was an air of naivety about her that Natalya associated with her own knowledge of this world. She was even wearing the same robe that Natalya was wearing. It looked newer in the memory and Natalya wondered how long before this moment Reagan had taken the bite.

"He will be fine, my dear. I worry more for you, if I may speak the truth."

"You are my King, Gareth, you may speak however you see fit." Reagan spoke with a hint of sarcasm. Natalya was amazed to hear her composed Queen act in anyway that wasn't perfectly poised. She had been a childe once too, it seemed, and Natalya found the thought comforting.

"And you will be Lunaries' Queen when I am gone, you deserve the same respect." He chided and Natalya felt much like she did when her own father was chiding her, but the emotions were not her's.

"Prey that day never comes."

"And yet there will be a day. I have a feeling that we have not seen the last of Augustus." He sounded tired and a fondness that Reagan must have felt drew her to take his arm in her own.

"Have you spoken to Lady Cassandra? I thought she and Augustus were close."

"I have thought of that, yes. I will speak to her on the morrow. Right now I have a kingdom to calm down and you have a brother to see to."

"Let me go with you. I know you love her, but she is still mad that I took her place as your heir. I could not bear the thought of you confronting her alone."

"She feels no such way, my dear, and if what you fear were true don't you think you would be the last person to help me deliver such a horrible truth?"

"Then perhaps take Logan? She seems to care for him and I trust him."

"As you wish, my dear, now go, I will speak with you again soon." The King leaned down to kiss Reagan on the forehead, both of his large hands cradling her small head. He let her go gingerly before turning and retracing their steps back into the castle while Reagan was left to go to the gate.

Natalya woke with a start. Sweat poured over her body as she took a moment to gather her bearings. She quickly noted that she wasn't alone and Reagan, the star of her dream-memory sat in the chair normally occupied by Cohen.

"You have magic in you." It was a statement and Natalya waited for Reagan to continue. She was still too busy processing her dream to argue with the queen. "It's not a lot, but I think you already know that."

"I was tested as a child. They said I had none." The response came too slow and even to her own ears Natalya knew that she hardly believed their diagnosis.

"But they were wrong. Your mother had it so you must too." Reagan said as if she were speaking about well known facts and not well kept secrets.

"How do you know that my mother had magic?" Natalya felt the anger before the confusion. She was much like her father in that way. Anger was her first emotion. Even as a child her mother always said that it would be her undoing.

"You described your father to Cohen as a stubborn man who hates magic and hated our kind more. Magic, especially the kind of a seer is passed down in families. If it wasn't your father it must have been your mother, or am I wrong?" It was not a satisfactory answer to say the least, but Natalya was too tired to argue.

"No, you are not wrong."

"Tell me about your dreams." The question threw Natalya and for once she didn't have a smart comeback. "I know you have them, the guards hear you cry out in your sleep. What is it you see?"

"Today? I saw you." When Reagan made no move to respond she continued. "You're not surprised are you? I was, I've never had a dream-memory about anyone else but myself."

"They are called visions, Natalya. If you were trained you would know that they could happen when you are close to someone or if you are in contact with something belonging to them. One day, with training, you could learn to control it. You could even learn to look for specific memories and even possibly see glimpses of the future."

"You gave me this robe on purpose." Natalya felt betrayed at once, used by someone she was beginning to trust.

"I was testing a theory. What did you see?" Reagan seemed not to care that she used her. She knew from her lessons with Cohen that vampires could sense base emotions. She must know how the girl was feeling.

"I'm not sure. You were younger, I think. Some prisoners had escaped or maybe some man named Augustus set them free? You were walking with King Gareth and you told him to talk to a Lady Cassandra with someone named Logan. You said you trusted him."

"That was a terrible day. I was right to mistrust Cassandra, but I was wrong to trust Logan. We lost a lot that day. I did personally, but as a House we lost our King and half of our people to Cassandra and her madness."

"I'm sorry." It hardly seemed sufficient, but Natalya was at a loss as to how to respond.

"As am I, for tricking you that is. I just wanted you to understand that I don't want you to take the bite because of some sick desire you imagine comes with being one of us. I hoped you would see not only that day, but also the days after. I want you to be one of us because to me that means being of a family. Emeline and Cohen care for you and those that we care for need to be kept safe. You are a strong girl and I believe that you would not only make a great vampire, but I also selfishly hope you will be an asset to us in this war. I need more people I can trust, Natalya, and Cohen says you can be trusted. Let me offer you the best gift that I can, let me give you the bite and all of the training I have to offer. All I ask is you help me keep my House safe."

The Queen's honesty struck something in Natalya and she wondered for the first time what the consequences of taking the bite would be when the advantages were suddenly so obvious. "Do I still have time to think?"

"Of course, in the meantime, I will send for Cohen, I'm sure you would like to see him."

"I would, thank you." Worry tightened in her stomach when she remembered the vision. Logically she knew that he was fine, what she had seen had happened long in the past, but it would be nice to see him with her own eyes just to confirm that her fears were unfounded.

"I will make sure he clears the rest of his night. The sunrise is breathtaking in the inner gardens this time of year." If Reagan remembered the day Natalya's vision had taken place on then she would have remembered that a scared heir had stood in that very garden on what might have been the worst night of her life. Natalya wondered if any happy memories had been made in what was meant to be sacred ground since then.

"Okay," Natalya stood from the bed and allowed Reagan to embrace her. Outside of the eyes of the public, Reagan was not shy to show her fondness. "Did you want your robe back? It did its job."

"No, you keep it. It was a gift from my King and now it is my gift for you. Remember that no matter what you choose you will always have a role here in my House."

"Thank you, Your Grace." Natalya smirked and was glad to see Reagan smiling kindly back.

"Enough with that, let me get Freya and she can help get you ready."

Reagan left and Natalya flew to her wardrobe. They had given her many pretty dresses and even slacks and lovely tunics to wear, but she hardly saw an occasion to wear them since she only left her room for lessons. Suddenly the prospect of wearing anything she wished without having to worry about training made her want to try on the role of a royal. If she took the bite from a Queen she would be part of the royal party. The idea was appealing. Of course becoming stronger and being able to protect herself and her family was even more enticing. Emeline was progressing well despite the perilous start and it helped sway Natalya's decision.

A sharp knock on the door hailed Freya's entrance and Natalya made quick work picking out an outfit and laying it out for her handmaiden to help her dress. She had chosen sleek, black leather pants with a flowing white tunic. The tunic was embroidered with yellow and pink flowers on the trim with laces pulling up the back so it hugged at her curves. Freya helped her into the trousers first being careful to smooth out any lines before tying them up the back. There was a mirror in the corner and Natalya admired the shape of her body as she held her arms up for Freya to help her into the tunic. When the laces were pulled tight it revealed her modest curves making her feel like a woman instead of a child.

"Is it normal for vampires to dress so provocatively?" It was an innocent enough question as she had noted that Anya did not seem shy in her attire and even Reagan showed more skin than Natalya was accustomed to seeing women reveal in the villages. Freya seemed to understand her confusion and laughed lightly before pulling at the front of her tunic until the fabric rearranged and allowed her a touch more modesty.

"You will find things here are very different from in the human villages. Vampires are not shy about things like sex and sexuality. They cannot have children like we can and so the act of having sex is purely for pleasure. Because of this attracting a partner is much more about physical attributes and less about things such as land and title."

"Why do you dress modestly then?" Natalya asked without realizing how rude her statement might sound.

"I have no wish nor need to attract a partner. I loved a man, he was a vampire, but he died on a scouting trip."

"I'm terribly sorry."

"No need, Miss Natalya. I would have had to take the bite to be with him anyway, it's a taboo for humans and vampires to be lovers and I have never wanted their life for myself. Some think it was best the way it happened. I would have eventually died and he would have lived on, loving me and never having truly had me."

"That's terribly sad." Natalya looked at the girl through the mirror and she returned her frown with a small smile.

"Yes, well maybe you will take the bite and fall in love and you will tell me all about your love."

"I'm not so sure if that is in my future. Besides you are still young, you can love again, right?" Natalya allowed the girl to guide her to the vanity to clip back her short hair. She handed her a set of flower pins made of colored crystals that matched her shirt.

"You're right I am. Now Lord Cohen should be here any moment. Is he the man you're dressing for? If it isn't too bold of me to ask."

"No, that's alright," Natalya laughed. "I think I'm just dressing for me," she looked over her form in the mirror once more. "It is the first time I've been allowed to."

"Well then I think you've done a marvelous job. Go on now, I think I hear Lord Cohen." True to her word another knock happened at her door and Freya went to answer it for her. Cohen entered as soon as the door was open, dressed in the clothes of the guardsmen. He wore a black leather vest over a white cotton tunic. The Lunaries' house crest was embroidered into his chest. His black leather slacks clung to the well-defined muscles, catching Natalya's eyes instantly. When she realized how obviously she was staring she averted her eyes and blushed only to find Cohen smirking openly.

"You look quite lovely this evening, Miss Natalya."

"As do you, Lord Cohen." Natalya responded with the air of a girl who couldn't be bothered that she'd just been caught drooling over the man and he only laughed harder. He needn't know that she stared a moment longer just to confirm that he was there and well. There was no sense in worrying him over the past.

"Indeed. Are you ready for our walk? I was told to clear my evening and something about a sunset?"

"Yes that sounds lovely. The breeze felt wonderful earlier and I'd love a chance for some fresh air." If he was going to put on an act for her sake then she could play to the same tune. "I do love our walks and you did promise to show me the gardens and lake in the morning sun."

"Then to the lake we shall go." Cohen held his arm out to her, all trace of mockery having left his face. Natalya met his genuine smile with one of her own and graciously took his arm. "Good evening Miss Freya."

"M'lord, Miss Natalya." The handmaiden bowed and turned back into the room to freshen the sheets.

"You know she's laughing at us right now." Cohen mock whispered when the two made it halfway down the hall.

"Would you not too if you were her?" Natalya smiled feeling happier and lighter now that she was freely walking the grounds. She could easily grow accustomed to life in Lunaries and it seemed her decision to stay was getting easier by the day.

"You speak the truth, Miss Natalya how wise of such a young lady."

"How cheeky of an old man," Natalya snarked back.

"I am only four centuries old, I'll have you know. I might be considered an elder by our people's standards, but there are vampires much older than I, so I suppose that means I mustn't be too old." Cohen dropped his arm, letting hers go in favor of guiding her with his hand on her lower back. A group of noble men passed throwing them chiding looks for causing such noise.

"How old until you lose your sense of humor?" Natalya asked, brow raised and Cohen broke into a fit of laughter again.

"Oh Miss Natalya I do so wish you take the bite, I think this place could liven up a bit with your cheek." He led her from the hall further into the castle until they were at the entrance of the royal garden.

"I think I could come to love this place, truly." Natalya whispered, turning until she was looking up into his beautiful, cerulean eyes.

"You have no idea how glad it makes me to hear you say that, Natalya." His smile was warm and just for a moment Natalya forgot all of her reasons to not take the bite and live with Cohen, and Reagan in their kingdom forever. "But there is still time to think of such things, now all you should be thinking about is the sun on your face in a few hours."

"I think I can handle that," Natalya responded before turning to look to the lake, "but first I'll race you to the lake!" Her laughter rang through the quiet garden and for the first time in a terribly long time the royal gardens were alight with happiness and pure joy.

GWYNDOLYN

Morning found Gwyndolyn seated in the only chair in her cell, gently tracing the faint scars on her arm. They were nearly gone, though they still stung with the memory when her fingers grazed the faint lines. Logan hadn't seemed phased by the decoration that his wife had graced her with and neglected in mentioning the slow pace in which she was healing. The rogue queen was certainly older than the huntress and she had dug deep into her skin, clearly making a statement which the unfaithful king stared down on every visit. The only acknowledgement he made of her condition was the new room she had found herself in the day after the incident. She had been moved from the dirty cell that Cassandra had tortured her, to a much nicer one, though the state of the accommodations hardly mattered to her. There was a large bed that sat in the center which took up most of the room. It was draped with fine silks and gilded in gold. There was a desk with half burned candles and parchment that disintegrated at the touch. The ink bottles were mostly empty, littered about as if someone had actually sat in prison once, writing their days away. Bookshelves were filed with the histories of people who no longer graced the earth and Kingdoms that ceased to exist. The castle had once belonged to humans and their ancient books still lay about the chamber. The spines were cracked and each page had to be turned delicately to insure they would not crumble, but Gwyn was no stranger to needing to be gentle.

Despite the niceties, there was still no denying it was meant to be a prison as the iron bars in place of a door often reminded her. When the castle had last been inhabited by humans these quarters would have been suited for a royal captive. Gwyn was by no means royalty, but it had been on the orders of King Logan himself and so it was done. She was surprised that the room hadn't been cleared of the books as they could hold valuable information in them, but the layer of dust on every surface proved that no one had touched any of them in some time. Though she hadn't been in the room very long, she had already begun to sort the books in chronological order, being careful with each tomb. She had thought it would take weeks, expecting to be visited by the demented queen and her minions, but she couldn't be further from the truth. Logan obviously favored her and he wasn't shy about it. He had given very strict orders that she was to be left alone and his people either respected him enough or were scared of him enough that they listened. The only person Gwyn had seen since Cassandra had carved her name into her had been Logan himself. He had come to her nearly every morning for the past two and a half months and Gwyn had come to rely on his presence to count the passage of time.

Today was no different. Gwyn stopped tracing the fading letters on her arm and allowed her eyes to focus back on the page before her. She had managed to keep a few candles from her visits with Logan and was able to gain just enough light to read by. She had just finished ordering the books chronologically to the best of her ability and was starting with what she believed to be the first book. *The Complete History of King Unus of Solara.*

She had known that the humans who no longer acknowledged their existence once lived within Mordin Forest, that had been basic history in her training, but she hadn't known that they had called House Rayne home. She wondered why such a significant detail had been omitted, but she knew that King Zentarion would have had his reasons. There weren't many vampires still alive who would have known such things and she was sure that the Great King would have at least known from stories if he hadn't quite been reborn yet. She had no way of knowing if these details would be important, but it seemed useful to learn what she could. Her thoughts were interrupted by the heavy iron door of the dungeon scraping open. Only Logan had come to visit her since her arrival and Gwyn mentally prepared herself to greet him. It had been so long since she had to be anyone besides the bounty hunter it took her a minute to close off her mind and become someone else. She was surprised when instead of the king's voice she heard the voice of a different man.

"The whore is sure to be a problem, we should get rid of her as soon as possible." The slimy voice of Lord Wynn sent chills down her spine, but Gwyn held still hoping that they would take the path through the dungeons and out the other entrance which would avoid her cell.

"Not so fast. She could have her uses yet." The second voice was clearly the queen. Her voice was hushed, but even Gwyn could tell she was hardly worried about Gwyn or her relationship with the king.

"What possible uses could you mean? She will only keep Logan distracted from your page for so long. He is bound to forget her soon and then what? She does not know enough about our enemy to serve any purpose. There is nothing to gain from keeping the king occupied with the tart."

"That's where you're wrong. It bothers me little what Logan thinks of my page. He would never bring my affair into the light when he has her. He might pretend that she is only there to fill his physical urges, but I know him far too well. He cares for her; he would never stay until moonlight for her if he felt no comfort in her presence. If our people knew that he cared for Faegon's little bitch they will turn on him. She will help prove just how far Logan has strayed from our cause. Once we can prove that he no longer cares for the plight of our people it will be easy to use her presence to convince the people who still favor him that he is a traitor. Then we can be rid of both of them."

"Are you certain that this will work? You cannot afford the repercussions of our people sympathizing with him." Lord Wynn warned and Gwyn heard the annoyance in the Queen's tone.

"Even if that doesn't convince them, the bitch's true identity will help." Gwyn held back her gasp at the words. There was no way that this would be queen could know all that she implied.

"What could you mean by that? Is the whore not really a bounty hunter from the false crown?"

"She is and yet she is worse than that…" the voices faded as the pair continued down the hall and through the doors that lead back to the main dungeons.

For the first time since her capture, Gwyndolyn felt true fear. Even Cody had no knowledge of her true role to the Crown and she had very strict instructions to keep it that way. There was no way that Cassandra knew who and what she was. The vampire was smart and old enough that she might have heard rumors, rumors of the vampires trained by Faegon to withstand all imaginable torture in the most creative of ways, but those were merely rumors. If Wynn, the keeper of secrets had no knowledge of her true identity then she could at least hope that she was safe. Her identity as a bounty hunter was only a single part of her role to the King of Kings. Taken from her home as a small child, her parents had sold her to House Faegon to put food on the table and she hadn't looked back since.

Stories were told of the legendary soldiers of King Zentarion's secret army. In the days of old, when the Empire was at war with itself it was said that King Zentarion had spent centuries creating the perfect soldiers. They were loyal only to him and they could withstand any torture and turn down any bribe. They were perfect and terrifying. They were said to blend in with the rest of his men, known only to each other and their King in a sort of high order of soldiers and spies. Of course the need for such well groomed spies was supposedly long gone. The men and women of the Magni Havardr Order were no more than a legend. They existed in the deepest level of King Zentarion's legion and were meant to be unmatched by any other in wit, strength, and honor. Gwyn was one of the three that graduated from her original class of ten. The other seven were killed either during training or at the end for their failure. When she'd last bothered to check, the other two were doing well, one was a member of King Zentarion's own honor guard while the other lived and worked in the barracks, waiting for the time when their King would call them to arms in his name.

Gwyn had never seen her placement as a bounty hunter as punishment, but she knew that others in her order who had taken the task in the centuries past had certainly assumed the post a slight. As a bounty hunter she was allowed outside the gates of Faegon and to explore their Empire and report back her findings to the High Council and to the King of Kings himself. She had been rather honored by her placement and had chosen to make the best of her position. Those who belonged to the Magni Havardr Order were meant to lay low and were never supposed to gain any form of notoriety, but Gwyn had found that building her reputation only increased her likelihood of being sent out on another mission, which in turn meant more useful information for the Crown. She certainly hadn't intended on being captured by the false queen Cassandra, but she would take the opportunity for what it was. She was taken from her thoughts by the sound of the dungeon doors opening again. She didn't have the time to push her thoughts behind her well constructed mental wall before Logan let himself into her cell and it was obvious that he saw her anxiety in her face.

"What troubles you, my dear?" The soft tone scared her, there was a possibility that Cassandra had known she would be listening and it was all a trap.

"I heard whispers in the night." She had to take a chance. Even if it was a trap, she could prove that she could be trusted. Even if she didn't know the game she could still try to play.

"Oh? And what did these whispers say that has you so tense?" His words were coy, easy as if he already knew what she would say. He walked fully into her cell and wrapped his arms around her, either to provide comfort or to trap her, Gwyn knew not.

"Nothing, just rumors." She turned in his arms to stop further questions with a kiss. The distraction seemed to work and they moved as one as Gwyn stood from her seat and pushed him onto his back on the bed. She used her own weight to press him down into the mattress, keeping his focus on her instead of their conversation.

"Are you going to tell me what you're trying to distract me from?" The laughter in his voice made it clear that he wasn't upset with her attempts and Gwyn chose to take that as a sign to continue.

"No. Is that alright?" He hadn't forced her hand yet and she still needed time to think.

"For now? Yes. But you will need to tell me soon." He sealed the response with a kiss. She had time; time enough to form a plan and possibly even discover just how much Cassandra knew so she could report back to her King. "You are thinking too deeply," Logan whispered between kisses and Gwyn realized she hadn't been responding to his advances.

"I just worry about you when you leave me." Gwyn knew how to speak to people with a large ego, particularly men. There had been many of those types within the King of King's court who had all made it clear that they thought themselves better than her. Logan had never voiced such thoughts, but most royalty looked down on others especially the lower class.

"I did not know I would be missed." Logan's smile spoke otherwise, as if he had hoped that she would yearn for him in his absence. She would not be surprised if he had expected her to waste away without his attention. She hated to portray herself in such a way, she was hardly weak, but if it meant learning more about this man or the mysterious House Rayne than it would be worth the effort.

"There is nothing else for me to look forward to. You are the only comfort I have here." The words left her lips just as she had practiced in her mind. She hadn't needed to be anyone other than Gwyndolyn the bounty hunter for so long that it felt odd to put on other identities. There had been a time when she would have known to start with flattery without their tryst going on so long before employing it. She was losing her edge.

"Now Gwyndolyn, we both know that you are not the damsel in distress type. You needn't lie to get my attention. You need only ask and I would happily give you what you seek." Instead of looking offended at her attempt the man only looked amused. It was infuriating, but allowing him to believe he had the upper hand on her served its purpose and Gwyn knew she would have to tolerate his ego if she hoped to get out alive.

"Is that so? You have been gone many days in a row, I had thought you might have forgotten me," Gwyn spoke openly without the sweet and demure tone she had been trying on. There was no point in continuing the lie if both parties knew it was all an act.

"Thought, but not feared? Your words deceive your actions, I wonder if you are more than the simple bounty hunter as your reputation made you out to be." Again his expression betrayed his words. He clearly thought he knew something about her and that did not sit well with her at all.

"Reputation?" It was genuinely the first time Gwyn had heard Logan act as if he might have known more about before their meeting and the surprise in her voice was easy to employ.

"Don't try to act modest. I knew that we had Faegon's leading female bounty hunter in our midsts before you had even woken up in that dreadful cell. Vestera had been rather pleased with herself for bringing you in. You have been causing us quite some trouble, killing our people and bringing in the rest to your king. Of course Cassandra thought that I was ignorant to your identity. She made quite the fuss recently about who you really were. She had insisted I stay away from you until she had time to speak with me. Naturally she was none too pleased that her little secret was not really secret, but she has always thought herself the most clever in every room. ”

Gwyn wondered if his words were just another trick. She knew that Logan wasn't much older than she and he would have most likely been taught that the Magni Havardr Order was just a legend, but Cassandra was even older than both of them. She could have been alive when the Order was more widely known. It was very possible that she had asked Logan to lie to her to study her reaction.

Distracting him would have to work. She was out of options and quickly backing herself into a corner. "Surely she must know that she cannot be the most clever in the room when you are with her."

"I cannot say that I know what you are trying to distract me from, my dear, but it has been too many days since I have had your body and I don't wish to waste anymore time on tired talk."

"You know that you may always have my body so long as you have me here, but may I ask one request?" Gwyndolyn did her best to sound earnest, he might not believe her when she tried to act like a damsel in distress, but pretending that she needed him for safety in Cassandra's castle wasn't a far cry from the truth so laying on a little more emotion might go unnoticed as a ruse.

"You may ask, but you know that I cannot set you free. That would upset my wife quite a bit more than merely sleeping with you. She would surely hurt you then and I'm afraid I have grown very fond of you."

"I would never ask that of you," Gwyn gave him a reassuring smile. "Will you stay with me, until nightfall?"

"My dear I will stay with you until you ask me to leave if it pleased you." Logan said in such a sweet voice that Gwyn nearly believed him.

"And what of Cassandra? Your wife expects you by her side when your House is awake and watching, no?"

"No need to worry. I am her husband and her King, not one of her mindless subjects," Logan spoke dismissively and Gwyn was surprised to hear how little he obviously thought of his people. "No, I am more curious as to how you know that she is displeased with me."

There was no sense in lying, but telling the truth meant admitting that she had heard the conversation between the queen and her master of whispers. She didn't know if Logan was merely playing a role with her to gain more information for his house or if he genuinely cared as little as he acted, but she could not risk finding out. She would have to bide her time before making a decision on just how useful his alliance might be to her eventual escape.

"I thought you might not answer. Well if you are done talking then I see no reason to continue."

Gwyn knew that Logan was accustomed to her allowing him to take control, though it did not mean that he did not allow her to set the pace from time to time. He was a generous lover considering his personality and position, but it wasn't very often that she tried to assert her dominance from the start. She moved with ease as she put her strength in every action, pinning the king to her bed as if he belonged there. Logan seemed entirely unsurprised by her actions, but he allowed her to take the lead without complaint. She had given this body pleasure more times than she could count and yet he acted as if he was touch-starved each morning that he came undone with her. It was intoxicating to be wanted so fiercely and Gwyn wondered if he was simply acting a part or if she really did have such a staunch hold over the man.

Logan moaned and Gwyn came back to the moment to find her hands enveloping his firm manhood. He was an elder and while she suspected she was holder, he clearly thought himself the aggressor of the two, but Gwyn was a huntress with training. Even is Logan was acting as if he was simply letting her take control, Gwyn was sure that she could overpower him if it really came to that. His eyes were glowing the same pale blue that they always were and his fangs were protruding so she knew that he did not mind. Gwyn took a moment to puzzle at his eyes. She had allowed him to drink from her in the past, but it had always been while they were joined and she had never bothered to look at his eyes. She had always assumed that Cassandra had turned him, but it seemed she was wrong. His sire was dead and he was his own master. While it helped to explain why the rogue queen didn't have as much of a hold over the man it raised more questions.

"Was your plan to take over, simply to make me wait?" Logan asked while trying to sound coy. Gwyn could tell he was studying her though, and she quickly came back to the moment.

It was the wrong time to reflect on her newest revelation. "Of course not, Your Grace."

The whispered words released the rest of the tension from his muscles and Logan relaxed into her touch. Gwyn moved over his body as if it was hers to claim and Logan seemed more than happy to allow her. He tracked her every movement with lust-hooded eyes, but he made no movements to stop her.

Though she loved the thought of teasing Logan until he took control, Gwyn was trying to prove a point and she knew that he would soon grow tired of her gentle caresses and feather-light kisses. She braced her hands on his chest, splayed out over him to give herself leverage as she lifted her hips just high enough to feel him press against her most intimate place. She shifted and sank down on him, relishing the strangled noises that escaped Logan's open mouth. His eyes were closed and Gwyn took that moment to put the next part of her plan to work. Logan had always taken his meal from her, but she had never done the same with him. He had made sure to bring her blood, but he had never offered her his own neck. It was a risk to take blood from him without asking first, but Gwyn thought that the worst he would do would be to throw her from him and leave in a fit of anger, he had already proven that his soft spot for her prevented him from actually hurting her. Even if he did leave her in a rage, she had confidence that he would come back.

Gwyn let her fangs push against her gums until they descended past her bottom lip. Logan's eyes were still shut tight and Gwyn moved until her hair draped over his face and body, biting hard into his shoulder. Logan's reaction was instant. The noise that left his lip was unlike any Gwyn had heard him make before and she found herself on her back before she could process what had happened. Logan's own fangs were in her shoulder at the same time and he used the advantage he had from above her to rock into her at a bruising pace. Pure pleasure overwhelmed Gwyn, until all she could focus on was Logan, the mere ability to think of anything else was stripped from her as she allowed her base needs to take the forefront. She was no longer a bounty hunter and he was no longer her mark, her very being seemed to begin and end at all the points where they were connected.

"Gwyndolyn," he growled in her ear which surprised her enough that she came back to the world around her and she let go of his shoulder.

The open wound bled for a moment before she licked it closed. Logan had already taken care of the bite that he had created in her shoulder. They had both eaten recently and biting him had never been about the feeding. Gwyn allowed him to hold her tightly to his own body as he buried his face into her neck simply breathing her in. Gwyn knew that he would not last long from past experience and she was not surprised when he groaned his release into her after a few more thrusts. Her biting him hadn't quite resulted the way she had expected, but she was certainly not disappointed.

"You are just full of surprises." Logan laughed when he recovered as he pulled back from her enough to settle into the bed.

Gwyn rolled into his open arms and settled her head on his chest. "I have never drank from a king before, but you've brought me such pleasure I thought it only fair to return the favor."

"Indeed." Logan pulled her closer and placed a gentle kiss to her hair. After a moment he seemed to remember his place and he moved back just a fraction, his grip on her loosening so slightly that Gwyn was nearly sure she had imagined it.

"I thought you said you would stay," Gwyn whispered.

There was a pause, long enough that she feared he might not answer. "I will, if you still wish it."

"I do." It would not hurt to feed into his ego and she didn't mind the company, the more time she spent with him the more she would learn.

"Then I will stay." The arms around her shoulders tightened once more and another kiss landed on the crown of her head. "Cassandra is out of the castle for a while again and there is little else that could keep me from you and even she could not if she dared try. Without her insistence, her subjects wouldn't even bother to come looking for me."

"Her subjects?" It was the second time he had alluded that the people of House Rayne belonged solely to Cassandra that night. The High Council had always suspected that Cassandra was in control, despite Logan's very public image as the rule of the rogues, but Gwyn had not really believed those theories until now.

Logan was suddenly very quiet and Gwyn wondered if he'd realized just what he'd implied.

"Our subjects," Logan corrected himself, though they both knew it was too late. "Why are we speaking of such dull things?"

"What else is there to speak about?"

"You could tell me more about you."

"Well you seem to believe that you know a lot about me already," Gwyn countered.

"I know you are a woman reborn to House Faegon. You are a bounty hunter employed by the Crown and you have been making our lives quite a bit more complicated." There was no malice in his words. If Gwyn hadn't known better she would have thought his tone teasing. "But I don't know much more."

"There isn't much more to tell." Gwyn sighed. She would have to tell him a little about her life, Logan was persistent. "I was raised inside the walls of Faegon in an orphanage. I took the bite as soon as I could and I started to train to be a soldier not long after. I didn't make it, but when I had been training I made friends with a few of the bounty hunters who were based out of Faegon. I started to join them on their hunts and then I suppose you know the rest."

"What caused you to be raised in an orphanage?"

"I lost my parents at a young age." Gwyn figured that it wasn't lying, necessarily. She had lost her parents the day that they sold her to Faegon. That was the day that she decided that she had no parents, no family. "It wasn't a bad place to grow up."

"That is so sad. I cannot imagine what that must have been like. I lived with my family until I was reborn." Logan turned on his side and pulled her impossibly closer. Gwyn took a moment to study his face. She wondered if the worried look marring his face was genuine.

"Why did you choose to take the bite?" Gwyn asked hoping to change the tone of the conversation.

"I didn't," his tone was cold and it was clear that he was not going to discus the topic further with her.

"I'm so sorry, that's terrible." Gwyn moved until she was leaning fully on Logan's chest. No matter what he might be, she knew that he was not lying about this. Their eyes met and Gwyn knew then that she cared about this man, even if she shouldn't. The bite was a gift, but it also was a choice. Taking that choice from someone was cruel and the worst type of evil that Gwyn could imagine. She wondered for a moment why Logan surrounded himself with rogues when they had been known to turn unwilling humans, but she did not dare ask,

Gwyn leaned down slowly, allowing Logan enough time to stop her, but he seemed content to allow her to take the lead again. Her dark hair fell around Logan's face like a blanket and his eyes fluttered closed as their lips touched. They had shared rough kisses during sex before, but this was different. Gwyn knew that the tenderness she put into the kiss was not fake, she felt truly terrible for what had been done to him and if he read it as her falling deeper for him than that could only be used to her advantage. Logan drew back from the kiss not long after and Gwyn rearranged her body to drape against his own. For the first time since he had come to her bed, the two lay in a comfortable silence, stalling the game they had been playing even if only for a moment.

CODY

If any deity existed, Cody knew it was due to them that he and Decker had managed to escape from Faegon and remain undetected. With every village they passed and every night that came and went he found that the tight ball of tension in his chest began to lessen until it was nearly easy to breath again. The more time that passed the more space they put between themselves and the secret passage they had crawled from. It felt odd to leave the place he had called home knowing he might never return, it was not how he had imagined his legacy as a hunter would end. He hadn't thought much on the consequences of turning his back on Faegon then, but over a week with little food and even less sleep put his choices in startling perspective. He'd turned his back against everything he'd known the moment he had dared to speak against King Zentarion and yet he wouldn't change his defense of the justice system he had believed in. It was that very same justice system that had horribly failed him when he most needed it. Before he would have thought that anyone who attempted to escape prison deserved whatever befell them after, but now he wasn't so sure. With a loose plan and no means to see it through, he and Decker were relying on each other and luck to see them safely to Lunaries. There had been no time to think about what might happen after the cells. He hadn't been sure that there would be an after the cells to speak of. He hadn't dared to hope.

Hope still seemed to have little place in the hunter's heart despite having lived there for most of his life. Gwyn had always told him that hope was for fools and children. He had never asked her which she thought him to be. Now, it seemed, he would never have the chance. When he wasn't thinking about Gwyn, he was thinking about the current predicament. Cody allowed his mind to wander and consider what might have been if only he had been allowed to speak to King Pa'ari; would he have been sent to the dungeons? What if instead, they hadn't been attacked by the false queen Cassandra's follower? Even further still, would trouble have still found him if they hadn't taken the bounty marked dangerous which had sat on the hunter's board looking for any fool who thought themselves skilled enough? Cody had no doubt that one such bounty with his name was now tacked to the board. The reason for his fugitive status lay feet away from him sound asleep, not a care given to the crisis that the young bounty hunter now found himself in.

This wouldn't have happened if Gwyn hadn't died.

Of course Cody hoped that Gwyn was still alive. He could still hear her stern commands if he only closed his eyes, but there seemed little hope left in the world. He had escaped against all odds which might be the last miracle the powers that be could grant him. It seemed pointless to think that such a feat had been accomplished and that Gwyn was alive. It was impossible. All that was left of his partner was the pendant that hung around his neck and their final bounty who walked beside him as an equal, fugitives in the eyes of Faegon and the Crown.

Decker had been mostly silent during their journey since the escape. Either the man understood that Cody was in no mood or he simply lacked the energy to fight with him. They were sleeping in shifts, though Cody could not bring himself to trust the rogue, even with everything they had been through. It almost felt like admitting that he could rely on him was disrespecting Gwyn's memory. He was honestly spending most nights awake, not able to allow his guard down, which slowed his already slowly healing wounds. He would need to stop and get real rest soon, but he had no idea when that would be possible. Decker lacked the same reservations about him or he had learned to sleep in questionable places from his life on the run and he mostly slept straight through Cody's watches. He was envious of the rogue.

"You're worrying so loud I can hardly sleep." Decker snarked without even opening his eyes.

"I've never known you to have trouble sleeping. Perhaps you are the one worrying." It felt more like second nature to respond to Decker with his own wit, though he had little energy to add any heat behind it.

"We've hardly spent any time in each other's company, I doubt you know me enough to make that assessment." This time his eyes were open, but they were glazed by sleep. "Unless you'd like to get to know me better and I'd understand that, of course, but I'd have to decline. I try my best not to associate with your type."

"What is that? Human?" There was no love lost between them, but it still hurt to hear the vampire say those words. He had come to think that the man at least respected him from his whispered words about Cody's character and his efforts to bring him to justice. His words should not have stung and yet they did.

"No." The pause that followed made Cody believe that Decker had finally fallen asleep. "You are too good, Cody Gilhart. No one of your nature should pay someone like me any mind."

The hunter found that he had no words with which to respond. It was better left alone. Decker surely assumed that he had not been heard. It would have been best if he hadn't. Every time the hunter thought that he understood the mysterious vampire, he did or said something else to surprise him. It was unsettling realizing that everything you assumed to be true about a person might not be so. It was even more disconcerting to think that he might have been judging Decker by the many rogues that he had come in contact with. Surely when he had first laid eyes on the rogue that had been the case.

When they had first met he had been nothing but another mark. The man had been vile and hard to handle, but he was just like the others. Most rogues that Cody had the misfortune of interacting with hadn't been alive for very long, but in the short time he had encountered them he felt confident that he knew what they were like. They all acted as if he, as a human, was hardly worth their time. They had treated him as if he hadn't even been there, focusing on Gwyn or acting as if he were a weak child that needed to be taught a lesson. Decker was different. Sure, he had a mouth on him, but he was intelligent and had learned quickly that with a well placed word he could crack even Gwyn's carefully placed mask. Despite the fact that he was obviously smarter than most of their marks, Cody had n't initially thought that he would be different from the immoral swine that they were tasked to hunt. That had changed the moment he had saved the vampire's life.

Decker had shown him a softer side since the attack by Vestera and even though he did his best to hide it, Cody knew that the vampire was starting to become accustomed to having the human with him. He knew that Decker was being sincere when he had whispered those heart-wrenching words in Zentarion's hall. *You are truly one of a kind, Cody Gilhart. It was good to know you in the short time that I did.* The words were haunting to think about now. Decker had thought that he was going to die and those were the last words he had chosen to impart on Cody. You could learn a lot about a man in his dying moments. Cody had to believe that it meant something even if he didn't know what. If Gwyn were there she would know.

It had been a hard few months without his partner by his side. Gwyn had been his foundation for so long that without her he found it difficult to cement his place in life. She had always been the one to guide him and remind him of who he was. She was supportive and always pointed out how much he had overcome to be this man; the type of man that was worthy of aiding and protecting her. Without her to shield him from the cruelty of those in the empire he was like a child without his mother. Not only had he had lost protection, but he had also lost his best friend. It was made worse by the fact that he hadn't even realized just how much she had been protecting him all this time. He had been thrown in jail because his partner, who apparently was more like his nursemaid, was not there to speak for him. He had worked ten years for the Crown and they thanked him by accusing him of treason and leaving him for dead. Had he taken the bite one of the many times it had been offered to him this would not have happened.

Obviously not everyone in the empire treated humans as inferiors. Most of the vampires that Cody met were good people. King Pa'ari's court was made of kind people who spoke to Cody like an equal. He enjoyed the few times he had been called to the castle on the request of Faegon's true King. Pa'ari was a fair man with warm brown eyes that had seen more lifetimes than Cody could imagine. He had ruled Faegon peacefully for nearly eight centuries and there wasn't a soul alive who would utter a slander about the man. He and his wife, Queen Kristianna were often seen walking in the bazaar, speaking directly to their people and hearing their subject's concerns. They were loved by all and treated both their human and vampire subjects with the same respect and gentle kindness. This directly contrasted with what Cody knew of the supposed Great King Zentarion.

Cody could not understand how a man like Zentarion could sit on top of a throne in the same House as Pa'ari and not have his seat challenged. It seemed that his only devoted supporters were the members of the High Council, a group of vampires who were meant to be representatives from every vampire house, though they had all held their positions for so long that their true allegiances were to Zentarion. Some even spoke for houses that had since fallen and been forgotten. Of course he only knew this much about the mysterious Great King and his advisors because of Gwyn. Besides the day which he had been accused of treason, Cody had never been allowed so close to the old vampire. Now he could understand why Gwyn had never brought him when she gave their reports.

The wind swept through the trees and took scores of leaves with it, taking Cody from his thoughts. The brittle leaves brushed against his face and crumpled, littering through his hair bringing Cody's focus back to the journey before them. It was getting colder and the days were getting shorter. There was a storm brewing, he could feel the moisture in the air. They would have to find better shelter soon if they had any hope of keeping dry and waiting out the impending rain. They were in a thinly settled part of the forest where the thick tree trunks stood apart, proudly stretching out towards one another without ever touching. The trees received plenty of sunlight and had grown strong and tall, but with the harvest long since over, any cover they might have had under the canopy of trees was dashed by the falling leaves. Cody hadn't wanted to stop here, but Decker had complained and even the hunter had to admit that his feet had been tired. But now that the air had changed and Cody could nearly taste the rain he cursed that he had listened to the vampire.

It started as a simple misting. The gentle touch of moisture soaked into Cody's messy hair and powdered his skin, sending shivers down his spine. The air was cooling as the sun disappeared behind dark clouds. It should have been sunny for a few hours more, but the storm came in fast blanketing the sky. They had very little in ways of provisions so the hunter was hard pressed to cover what they had as best he could. There were small bunches of berries and nuts that he had foraged for as well as jerky that they had traded for at the last village. They hadn't had much and Cody had hated trading the plain silver ring that had once been his father's, but the food he had received had lasted him the last three days and he had to protect the scraps he had left.

"What's going on?" Decker's sleep-ridden voice shocked Cody from his scramble to protect his food.

"Nothing, just rain." Cody did his best to calm his racing heart. There was no sense in getting upset over a little water.

Decker leveled him with a doubtful gaze before blinking and looking up toward the sky. The rain was getting heavier. It wouldn't be long before they were soaked to the bone, though that did not matter to the vampire. For Cody it would be devastating to fall ill now.

"We should go." Decker was up and on his feet before Cody could respond. The rogue had gotten very little rest and yet he looked refreshed. Cody felt irrational anger swell in his chest as he watched the agile vampire gather their meager belongings with ease. "Are you coming or what?"

"Where are we going?" Cody stood gingerly to follow. Exhaustion was catching up to him and the wounds he'd sustained from being imprisoned were slow to heal. He hadn't looked forward to sitting out in the open in the rain, but he also wasn't looking forward to move his aching body.

"You're going to need shelter and rest. I can watch for the rest of the day." The vampire moved toward the East in the same direction that they had been moving since their escape. Neither had been to Lunaries before, but they knew it lay the farthest east out of the five houses. They would walk until the trees disappeared before stopping if it meant that they were safe from the reaches of Faegon.

He was too tired to argue any longer. "Okay."

Cody felt his body move forward before he really acknowledged that he was going to follow along with Decker's plan. With heavy steps he continued after the vampire, pushing away his reservations in favor of focusing on the task at hand. The dirt beneath them was quickly turning into mud. The squelch of his shoes was unsettling and it reminded him that since the attack he had been forced to wear the same attire. The holes in his shoes were allowing the cold, wet earth to cake in between his toes. The soles of his feet were already stained black. Cody couldn't remember the last time that he'd had a proper bath. They'd stopped by a stream of running water the first night, but it was too close to the castle walls and they hadn't risked stopping to clean up. Cody wondered for a moment if this awful storm might get him clean before the squelch of the ground beneath his feet brought him back to himself. He would be dirtier by the end of this, he was certain.

The rain got heavier as they continued. Mud clung to them and splashed up their legs making their movements loud and slow. "There doesn't seem to be any shelter. We should stop and wait it out."

"We're going to push on for at least another hour. If we can get you out of the rain and dried up it will make the rest of our journey easier." Decker didn't even bother to look back as he pushed the heavy brush aside slicking the water from his eyes as he kept moving. Cody watched as dirt streaks ran down the vampire's pale skin. The water was picking up debris as it tracked down his face and below his tattered shirt. It looked like war paint decorating pale skin and Cody wondered what he must look like. He probably looked like a drowned rat.

The patter of rain filled the air between them again. The silence struck Cody as reminiscent of his time on the road with Gwyn. But this wasn't companionable silence between two friends, this was silence born of tension. Before the air between them had been filled with jabs and taunts, but Cody found himself intrigued by the vampire. This side of Decker was quiet and a commanding force, a personality type that Cody was more than accustomed to as Gwyn had always been the leader and he the follower. Before the cells, Decker had been loud. He had spoken constantly to garner reactions and had especially enjoyed pushing Cody in an attempt to find his limit. Now that they were on the run the rogue was different. Every move he made was deliberate and his words were well placed. This was a side of him that the hunter didn't know what to do with. The old Decker he could handle, but this person was a mystery.

"We should try to find a village. We need more provisions and new clothes," Cody nearly shouted over the noise of the storm.

"We have nothing to trade with. There would be no reason to find a village." Decker's tone was dismissive and his pace never wavered.

"I still have Gwyn's necklace. There were times where it served as our payment for a meal or a bed. Many would give freely to aid someone sent from the Crown," Cody reasoned which caused Decker to stop and face him.

"You know that won't work otherwise you would have tried that already."

He was right. If he had thought showing Gwyn's pendant would have gotten them the needed provisions at their last stop he would have loved to use that power. "We were too close to Faegon then. We could have been noticed. Out here the people would know the significance of our place in

Faegon's populace, but they wouldn't know of our escape. It would be safer."

"They might not know that two dangerous fugitives escaped from Faegon, but we look more like thieves than men of the Great House Faegon the richest vampire house in the kingdom."

Cody hated that Decker was right. "Then what would you suggest?"

Decker never answered. The silence was nearly as oppressive as the storm. Cody was forced to strain to keep up with the vampire as they made their way to an unknown destination. He was using the last of his strength to plow through the tumultuous terrain. Cody struggled to keep his limbs mobile as the large, heavy drops of rain assaulting his eyes did little to help. He tried to cover his eyes to keep the storm at bay and the shift in his posture set his body off balance, causing him to tip forward. The small cloth he had been carrying with his limited food supply slipped from his fingers and the meager provisions tumbled into the mud. He began to scramble for the round berries and nuts, but he knew had to choose between saving himself or saving the food. He tried to pick himself back up from his frantic searching, but the ground was fast approaching his weary body. Cody's instincts kicked in and he did his best to brace himself for the impact, but Decker was in his space cushioning him from the fall before he hit the ground.

"I've got you."

Decker looped his arm under Cody's shoulder blades to support his entire weight. The hunter might have felt ashamed at how quickly he melted into the touch, but he was too tired to care. It was slow going, but the vampire was a strong and steady presence for which Cody was thankful. Fatigue had settled into his bones and Cody felt worse as he slid further with each step. Decker patiently held on to him as they continued, not once complaining or commenting on the hunter's dependence. Nearly an hour passed in the same fashion before he was sure that his legs were going to give out. Pride was not an emotion that Cody had ever felt enslaved to and he wasn't about to start, but he felt a slight pang of something akin to it in that moment. Before he was able to complain and request that they stop, Decker's sure strides came to a halt.

"Okay, we should stop now."

They stopped at a grouping of trees that were near enough to each other that their outstretched limbs touched and formed a flimsy covering. Decker pulled Cody along until the two were under the canopy where the force of the water was slowed by the dying foliage. A week or two more and all the trees would be barren. They were lucky to still have shelter.

Decker ducked back out into the open air and began to strip off his outer jacket and flimsy tunic shirt before throwing them over the branches above Cody's head. The cloth was thin and would have done little to keep in warmth, but it helped bridge the gaps between the missing leaves and block out a little more water. It wasn't perfect. Cody could still feel as droplets traveled down the leaves and fell on him in an arbitrary rhythm, but it was better than he could hope for.

From his huddled position between the largest tree's roots Cody could see Decker looking from left to right as if he was scanning the forest around them. Cody could hardly see anything through the deluge, but he knew the vampire's eyes were much sharper than his own. From his vantage point all he could see was the lone, shirtless vampire quickly becoming drenched. The hunter had never realized just how small the rogue was. He wasn't as well built as many of the vampires Cody had encountered. Vampires don't build muscle mass like humans, though they did train to keep their reflexes sharp. Many humans he had known had been well muscled before they took the bite and becoming a vampire had only enhanced what had already been there. The hunter imagined that Decker had suffered from malnutrition both as a human and possibly even as a vampire. When he did drink Cody's blood he cherished it like it was the last meal he would have in quite some time and while the situations did look dire, eating like he did was a learned habit. It was a feeling that Cody had learned to tamp down in his time with Gwyn. Food had been hard to come by as a child, but ten years working with one of the best huntresses in the kingdom had taught him well and had kept his belly full. Had no one been there for Decker to ensure that the next meal always came? Cody wondered, not for the first time, what kind of life this man had led and what had caused him to become a rogue.

Scars littered Decker's skin, something that must have been caused when Decker was still a human. Some seemed thin, only visible at the right angle, but there were other deeper ones. The ones that spanned his ribs and stomach made the hunter's stomach turn. When he turned his back, Cody noticed large scars in a sloppy lattice patterns decorating his skin. Cody had never had a belt taken to his back as a child, but there were fathers in his village who had preferred the punishment for their own children. The marks on Decker's back were distinct, almost as if they had never been given time to heal before he was lashed again. Cody's heart ached for the child that had lived through that life. He wondered again when the rogue had been turned. He looked to be no more than twenty, but he was not a young vampire. Those hazel eyes had seen more than Cody could even imagine. Decker turned to face him again and their eyes locked. For a moment, Cody forgot that this man before him had been a mark once. They were connected now in a way that the hunter had only ever felt once before.

"Stay here." Decker was out of Cody's line of vision before he could respond. The moment, if there had been one, was gone and Cody was left feeling numb.

He was not alone for long. Before he had time to allow self doubt and anxiety crawl back through his skin and into his head, Decker was back with a fist full of nuts and berries while a dead rabbit hung from the belt on his waist. Dry wood would be impossible to find, but before Cody could ask about the kill, Decker handed him his own food and sunk his teeth into the dead animal.

"You could take my blood, I know you must prefer human blood." Rogues believed that drinking human blood was their right and having to substitute with animals was dirty and below their station.

"When you've had to depend on every meal as if it was your last as I have, you learn quickly that any blood is good blood if it is the difference between life and death." Decker paused before continuing. "If I took any more blood from you now it would be the death of you."

Cody didn't respond and chose to focus his remaining energy on sucking the juice from the berries and the meat from the nuts.. The rain created a subtle beat to their silent meal and hunter and vampire took what they could from the small pickings they had.

"Sleep now, I'll keep watch," Decker slid out from their shelter before looking back at him. "And really sleep this time, I know you must not like having to trust me, but if we're going to make it to Lunaries alive then you'll need to get some rest and let those wounds heal."

Cody watched the vampire walk into the storm before sliding back into the roots that would serve as his bed for the night. It was not the most comfortable accommodations, but it was also not the worst by far. He wondered a moment on why Decker hadn't asked for his trust. He half expected the rogue to demand it, but he hadn't. Instead he had openly accepted that Cody did not trust him and seemed resigned to the fact. Cody wondered why that it was due to that resignation that he found his trust in the vampire sealed before slipping into an easy sleep.

ARTHUR

It never ceased to amaze Arthur how easily the human body could adjust to a routine. It had been ten days since he had watched Antony use his strange brand of magic and he had learned to adapt their habits after accepting his fate. He was already sleeping during the day and rising with the moon as if it was natural and he found that the light of moon was just as rejuvenating as the warmth of the sun. Despite his earlier objections, living with a vampire was nowhere near as difficult as he'd feared, loathed as he was to admit it. Since his time with Thomas in the front yard, he had been forced to see the vampire as a man, just as all men have good and bad within them, Thomas was the same. He had no issues seeing the potential for bad, but there was good too that he could not ignore. He would even go so far as to admit, if only to himself, that there were some things that he admired about the vampire. Thomas hunted for their food, occasionally taking Antony or Arthur with him depending on how big the game he intended on catching was. He was clearly the provider of the two, though Antony had made it very clear that he was not without talents. Arthur found that the two times he had been chosen to venture out with Thomas had been the most gratifying times since his acceptance of his current situation.

There was always something to be said about the simplicity of being on a hunt. When he was a child, Arthur had often gone into the woods with Ivan and the other boys of their village to hunt big game. They had never needed to bring in meat, as their little farming village had provided enough food for all, but the sport had given the boys the opportunity to feel like men and it was one of Arthur's fondest memories. Hunting with Thomas was a lot like hunting with Ivan and yet it was very different. The vampire was skilled in ways that Arthur could never hope to be as a human. His strength and speed rivaled any that Arthur had ever witnessed before, yet he no longer feared the man. He knew that Thomas would not harm him. The vampire had senses that Arthur could only dream of. He also knew the importance of involving Arthur when he was able to. Since coming to the two men, Arthur hadn't much opportunity to exercise or hone his tracking skills and the vampire was very eager to assist. Arthur wondered if it was because Antony was obviously not the type to enjoy the physicality of killing, but it would have been rude to ask.

Thomas also went as far as accommodating him by rarely drinking blood from his partner in his presence. Instead, he would take blood from the animals, though he claimed that it tasted different and entirely unpleasant. It was a courtesy that the human didn't expect and he appreciated it even more because of the surprise.

As for Antony, he spent most of his time caring for the house and checking that their defenses still stood. There had been a time when Antony's weakness made Arthur uncomfortable, but now he knew better. The strange human had strength so great that he only exercised it when necessary. Arthur wasn't sure if he had felt fear or respect when he had learned the man's true powers, but he wasn't sure if it truly mattered. Antony never allowed Arthur's discomfort to color his treatment of the hunter. He undoubtedly knew it was there, his magic made it so he could understand and manipulate auras and emotions and yet he treated Arthur well and never shied from the confusion and disgust he must convey while watching the man perform the tasks often meant for the woman of the house.

Arthur looked over to Antony as the man cut up the supper from the night before to make breakfast. He would stop every so often to look at the door, but when Thomas did not enter he returned to his task. It was a humble living, but Arthur supposed it would have been enough for him if he had been forced to live it. Thomas was already on the hunt, this time alone. They had gone out together the night before to catch a deer so today he would be out more for the exercise and the joy of the chase than for any actual food. He wished that the vampire had asked him along for company, but he had undoubtedly held him back on both of their hunts and he was sure the creature enjoyed being able to exercise his full strength and speed without needing to worry about a lone human getting in the way. Antony had also expressed the desire to have him stay and help prepare the meal, something that Arthur had only grudgingly agreed to which left the two in a tense silence.

The vegetables that lay before him were fresh and raw. They came from the small harvest that had been pulled in before he had arrived and bright radishes and healthy carrot stocks littered the table waiting for him to cut them up. There had been cooks in Ash to care for him and Natalya and even as a child his mother and sister had always tended to the meals. Arthur hadn't the slightest idea how he was meant to cut up the vegetables, his first carrot lay in a sorry pile, the experimental cuts leaving bits of uneven shapes in a heap. He vaguely remembered hearing Emeline tell Natalya that even cuts were necessary for even cooking and he was positive that his horribly mangled carrots would not be going into their breakfast.

Arthur let his knife fall from his hands with a sigh. He was not made for this kind of life. He was a man of action once and even that seemed like a lifetime ago. On his late wife's property he had been a relatively successful head of the estate. There hadn't been much left for him to care for, but he had staffed the small farms well and he had seen to it that Natalya was courted by respectable families. There hadn't been much in their lives in Ash, but it had been enough. Now all he could hope for was to find Natalya and bring her home, though he knew not how he would accomplish such an impossible task. He was still unwilling to allow Thomas to drink his blood, even if he were the one to prick himself and if he bled into a cup, though they told him it could aid in finding his daughter. The idea still sat uneasily in his gut. Every day that he sat around not making a decision was one more day away from his little girl, but it took a lot for him to push aside a lifetime or prejudice to accept that Antony used magic, accepting vampires and the fact that some could be good, honest people would take time. He knew that Thomas meant him no harm now, but what would happen when the vampire sampled his blood? Could he trust that it would not drive the man to insanity and cause him to attack Arthur for more?

"Thomas should be back soon and then we can add whatever he's found to the meal." It sounded to Arthur as if the man was trying to assure himself that the vampire would be back and less about creating conversation, but he grunted in response. "It's lucky that you found the deer yesterday, we should have enough provisions for you to rest up and heal before the first snow falls. You'll want to be out there looking for your daughter before then, I imagine."

"Yes, I would. Thank you again for your hospitality." Arthur took up his knife again, posing to help once more. "I know you two must sacrifice a lot for me to be here."

"Nonsense. We live this life knowing that helping people passing through comes along with it." Antony brushed him aside. He stopped to look at the door again before returning to his task.

Antony was normally a silent companion, but Arthur found that he spoke out loud often if there was something troubling his mind and normally those thoughts concerned Thomas. When the vampire was home and in his sights a different side of the human came out. When they were together, both men seemed comfortable in silence for which Arthur was eternally grateful. They moved around each other in a way that reminded Arthur of the comfort that had existed in his and Elizabeth's marriage, another oddity about the pair that made him uncomfortable.

"It must be hard to allow strangers into your home, especially those who know so little about this world and it's culture."

"There are not many who manage to wander out here who know nothing of vampires and of magic, so I would have to say that you are a first, but it is still no hardship." Antony had stopped his work to turn and face Arthur. His expression was odd, as if he was trying to understand what the man was trying to imply with his words. He held his gaze a moment longer before turning back to the cooktop.

"You mentioned before that many come to stay here, but there is little room enough to accommodate the three of us, why not build more on your land to allow for the travelers that pass through?"

"We make do with what we have, if we add on anymore the Crown will take it as an invitation to send more men and women our way and that is not a notion that we're looking to put into their minds. Besides we normally only accommodate those who understand our lifestyle."

"I hope I am not imposing so much that you feel you have to change your way of life just because I am here. I would not judge you for how you chose to live your life," Arthur said the words more out of courtesy than honesty.

"Truly? You seem to me a man full of judgment."

"I'm sorry?" Arthur was surprised by the resentment he heard in the other man's words.

"You forget, I read and manipulate auras. I know how our relationship makes you uncomfortable. We will keep the arraignment as it is and once you are healed and able to go on your way our lives will return to normal. There is no harm in how things are now."

"Okay." Thoroughly embarrassed, Arthur let the subject drop and the two finished preparing their meal in silence. When Thomas returned shortly after he gracefully ignored whatever tension remained in the small home.

"I heard scouts in the distance while I was out. They'll be on us any time now. Are we going to tell them about the rogue?" Thomas broke the silence first, throwing a meaningful look at Antony across from him.

"Why wouldn't you? Isn't that part of you deal?" Arthur asked curious and Antony tensed beside him.

"Not entirely."

"What he means is, we are supposed to capture them, not let them go. The Crown fears we will draw unwanted attention upon ourselves that way and then they could lose a valuable source of information." Thomas spat, clearly as unhappy with the thought as Arthur felt.

"We have told them before we do not serve them so they cannot ask anymore from us then what we give them. If they want someone to live out here and clean up the forest then they will just have to place their men out here to do it themselves." Antony spoke and it was clear that it was the end of the conversation.

Thomas, knowing better than to push his partner, turned to focus on Arthur instead. "It would be best for you to stay inside when the scouts arrive. They will ask questions about you, no doubt, but they have no right to impose themselves and that is exactly what they'll do given the opportunity."

Not knowing much about vampire politics, Arthur simply nodded. He had no understanding of their culture and he had no desire to start learning. It would suit him just fine to be left in the house.

The meal passed in a tense silence. The hunter had to assume that it wasn't out of the ordinary for scouts to come to their door, but by the way both men were wordlessly communicating neither was excited at the prospect to play host to these vampires. When the meal was done, Thomas took care of their tableware as he always did. Despite not eating, Thomas did the washing up after all of their meals. While he was occupied, Antony moved about the small cabin arming himself with a slender silver dagger and a heavy sword. Arthur knew that the weapons were purely for posturing, the man had strong and twisted magic that would aid him more than steel or silver could.

"Stay in the cabin, we will be back when the party is gone." Thomas instructed as he looked to his human partner once more before turning for the door.

Arthur didn't want to join them, but he resented being told to stay in like a child. He ignored the anger that growled in his chest and took a seat on his borrowed bed. The sun wasn't set to rise for a few hours yet, though he hoped he would not be confined to the cabin for that long. He had nothing to gauge how long it might take and the same restless energy from being excluded from the hunt returned. He resisted the urge to pace, he was older, more controlled than that. If it had been Natalya in his place she might have give in and followed the men out. Knowing that his own daughter's rash actions had been the reason he was stuck in the forest surrounded by creatures called vampires was enough to cool his rage and keep him in place.

The minutes passed and before long Arthur was sure it had been hours. The scouts were still out in the yard, if he concentrated he could hear the murmur of voices, and it seemed odd that their unwelcome visit was stretching out. Years of being mostly on his own with only his daughter to keep him company left Arthur very aware of his surroundings. When things didn't feel quite right he learned it was better to follow his gut than to ignore it and endanger himself or his daughter. Arthur knew that he couldn't sit by not knowing what was happening just outside the door any longer. He went for his weapons first, not foolish enough to face an undetermined number of vampires without his effects. Since the incident with the rogue the two had allowed him his daggers back and they were stored below his bed. He went to them, making quick work to stow them all on his person. He might be only human with no magic, no matter what Antony might have said about his latent abilities, but he would be damned if he didn't attempt to prove that he was still a capable hunter. He was careful to leave only a single dagger showing before he left the small home to join the two.

"Who is this? I told you I heard another heartbeat in the house." The leader of the scouts was a female. She was beautiful, with long brown hair tied up high atop her head. She was darker than Arthur expected vampires to be, knowing their reaction to sunlight and yet she looked almost human with the glow of her skin. Her eyes were a queer shade of green and her fangs were clearly showing as a sign of a threat. "You're holding out on us, Thomas."

"I told you he's just passing through. Now about the rogue..." Thomas clearly positioned himself between the woman and Arthur. At first the hunter resented him for believing he needed protecting, but one look from the strange vampire and he thought better of commenting.

"Yes, the rogue your pet failed to catch, again." The woman barely afforded Antony a glance. He briefly wondered if this woman had ever seen what Antony was capable of.

"His name is, Antony, Libba. You know he is my partner and not my pet." Thomas's words were just sharp enough that his polite tone was effected.

"Why don't you remind her again, Thomas? It's not like she's understood every other time." Antony growled and all eyes fell on the human.

"Don't play any of your tricks, pet. The adults are talking here." Libba sneered and Thomas' fangs grew.

"We are nearly of an age Libba, you are being more petty than usual. Queen Quanna tightening her leash?" The snarky jibe surprised Arthur and it seemed to offset the woman as well.

"You will not speak my Lady's name, human. We divert from the point. You know better than to let the rogues go." Her gaze returned to Thomas as if the two humans didn't exist and the blood in Arthur's veins began to boil.

"I believe you are the one who diverted it, no? But to answer your question, we have never agreed to kill them or take them prisoner. Take your news back to your Queen and be gone. You have overstayed your welcome this time Libba."

"I will stay as long as I wish, you filthy excuse for a vampire. If I wanted to I would march you back to my Queen and watch her skin you both for pelts."

"I'd like to see you try." Thomas sneered and all of the scouts showed their fangs. Arthur was quick to draw his dagger and Libba rushed forward to knock it from his hand.

"You would let a human stay who doesn't know the rules of your arraignment?" With her face contorted by her fangs, the female vampire was not nearly as pretty and Arthur felt his blood run cold at the sinister look in her eyes. "Silly human, these two cowards agreed to never draw steel against us. That agreement was to be extended by all those on this property and now you've gone and ruined their little treaty. Burn the place down."

"What?" Arthur shouted, sure that he had heard her wrong. "She can't be speaking the truth." He turned to protest to Thomas and Antony, but both men looked grim as they watched the scouts around them crawling about the property.

"She is, I told you to stay inside," Thomas hissed, his fangs making his words hard to understand.

"How was I meant to know you'd made such a horrible bargain?"

"You have no right to judge us, we made this work for decades before you came and destroyed it all," Antony's quiet words stung more than Arthur thought possible. Dread began to fill him as he realized how serious the situation was.

"This is absurd. I had no idea of their arraignment. You can't punish them for that." Arthur did his best to reason with the unmoving Libba.

"Well you were the one who broke the rule so perhaps you should pay the price." The glee in her voice sent shivers down Arthur's spine.

"Let him go Libba. This is ridiculous! Let him go and take your dogs off my land. Tell your Queen that she's lucky we continue to follow her rules." Thomas snarled and Antony began to work his magic on some of the scouts who were collecting kindling for the fire.

"Lucky? Oh Thomas you know nothing of luck. You can keep the human if you wish, I know how much you love them, and instead you can lose your home and be denounced by Queen Quanna in the name of the Crown."

"No! Leave them be and take me to see this queen of yours." Arthur could not allow the two men to sacrifice more for him. He was well as he would ever be and staying with them would not only jeopardize them, but he could gain no more answers about Art or Natalya's whereabouts. It was possible, however slim the chances, that he could gain more information from this Queen Quanna or from her scouts. She would undoubtedly have more resources and if he bargained well he might just be able to use them.

"See? We have a sensible one here. Come on men, there will be no fire today. We have a prisoner to take back to our Queen."

"Libba give him back, this is ridiculous!" Antony tried to reason, but Arthur's fate had been sealed.

"Forget me. It must be this way. Let things go back to the way they were before, just like you said they would be." Arthur demanded with as much power as he could muster as Libba dragged him through the gate and into the forest.

"I swear by King Zentarion I will find you Libba and I will end you!" Thomas screamed from the yard while Antony held him back.

"There is no need to shout, dear Thomas, you know just where to find me. I await your attempt beside my Queen at Adrastos. Please do come by for a visit." She cackled and pulled Arthur along until another scout handed her a noose like leash, which she slipped around his neck. Another vampire bound his arms behind him too quickly for him to rect. "Just remember, the harder you pull the more you hurt yourself." Libba sang, pulling on the leather strap to demonstrate. "Make sure you strip him of all of his weapons."

Arthur felt the leather digging into his skin, but he refused to submit. He would rather die than be taken away by the hands of a woman, monster or otherwise.

"I can respect a man with the will to fight, but stubbornness will get you killed," Libba chided before twisting him closer. The cool tip of a blade was pushed into his side and Arthur knew that she wasn't putting up a front. This woman would kill him if he resisted.

Willing to live another day, if only to see his daughter one more time, Arthur allowed her to pull him along slowly. He held in his rage as her men made quick work of all of his weapons, stripping him until he was left in only his thin cotton tunic and trousers. With both his hope and dignity lying behind him in the small cottage Arthur allowed the awful woman to pull on his collar without fighting.

"Don't worry, my pet. Our Queen is merciful to men like you. You will make a great slave for our House. I promise it is the most mercy you will see for a long time." He was sure that her tone was meant to be soothing, but she had fallen quite short of the mark.

Arthur had to keep back the bile threatening to escape him as he was made to walk. With so many monsters surrounding him he had no chance of escape. Fighting back now would be suicide. He would have to bide his time, but there would be an opportunity to escape and if there wasn't one offered to him he would create one. He wouldn't be the only slave in their House if the woman's words were anything to go by, hopefully he could find like-minded people to help him get free so he might find his little girl. *I will find you Natalya, I promise. Even if it takes until my last dying breath, I will come for you.*

CLAYTON

Lady Sedalia's ornate library was just as breathtaking as it had been the first day that he had entered it, but Clayton couldn't find the beauty in his surroundings when he knew what he would be facing. He had been in this very spot multiple times since he had first spoken to his Lady and he continued to fail her. With nothing to report he dreaded her disappointed eyes and sharp tongue. There was no fire roaring in the pit as there had been the first day and Clayton missed the warmth. It would have been a simple comfort and he hadn't even been afford that. He longed for the days when he felt emotions other than fear and the festering numbness that washed through his blood. He hoped then that the soft fabric of the expensive couch would absorb him. He knew he would not be so lucky.

He had been left alone with his anxiety in the expansive library. The same footman saw him from the door to the library during every visit and his smug looks only grew as Clayton's own worthlessness became indisputable. This time had been no different. At first he'd loved the thought of the man's face when he brought their Lady the information she sought, but doubt had carved a place in Clayton's heart. Now even the childe doubted himself in what he had originally believed to be a simple task.

"Clayton." Lady Sedalia glided into the room from the farthest door. She was wrapped in a navy garment that draped over her slender frame. The sleeves were made of a sheer fabric in the same color and were slit open from her shoulders, allowing the pale skin of her strong arms to be revealed as she moved. The skirt was cut short in the front near the middle of her creamy calves, but flowed behind her as the train slid across the ground. She wore her hair down in a mane of curls that framed her face. She looked regal and less than pleased.

"Lady Sedalia." Clayton had jumped from his seat when she entered the room and he bowed low, only righting himself when she took her customary seat across from him. "I came as soon as I received your summons."

"You come with news, I hope." Her words were clear and he knew that it would cost him dearly to displease her.

"No, M'Lady, I have not, but I am close!" A month and a half prior he might have balked at pleading to anyone, much less a noblewoman that he did not know, but that had been before this same woman had bathed and fed him with high quality blood. He knew now what he stood to lose and he would not have that taken away from him.

"You were close last week, the week before that, and so on. Tell me, Clayton, was I wrong about you? I thought that you, a fallen brother of House Namyt'tkas, were wrongfully banished. I thought that I could place my trust in you as Lord Tory had been a fool to toss you aside. Tell me, Clayton, was I the fool?"

"Of course not, M'Lady. You were right to trust me!"

"'Then why have you not brought me any results?" In the time that he had known her, Sedalia had remained calm even in his continued failure. Her sharp moss eyes had never flashed in bloodlust and he had never seen her fangs. Now, though, her irises began to change from their warm green and were becoming tinged with red. If the stories were to be believed only one vampire sire had red eyes. He was in the presence of one of King Zentarion's own children and that frightened him beyond measure.

"It is all her fault. The girl, Eva, is very secretive. She is more than willing to gossip about her former Lady, but she never speaks of her Lord. She is very careful, I know that she is hiding something, Please give me more time."

"We are vampires and time might be a trivial thing to us, but we speak of the safety of our Great King and of his Kingdom. Do you suggest that your own shortcomings are more important than the security of our society?"

"Absolutely not." Clayton spoke passionately and his vigor calmed his Lady.

"Good. Then I expect results. You will not receive another meal from me until you can provide valuable information. Now go."

Clayton didn't wait for further instructions as he rose from his seat and bowed low before fleeing from the room. The footman was not waiting for him outside of the library as he customarily was and the man was glad. He could not face another person looking at him with disappointment or disgust that night and he made his way to the front of the lavish house with ease.

It was a cool night which suited him just fine. Many of the humans who did conduct their business at night were no doubt holed up in their homes, warding away the beginning of winter chill which meant the streets were less crowded than when he had made his way to give his report.

Returning to the slums knowing that he must complete this task or risk losing Lady Sedalia's favor was more daunting than his mission to come to Faegon had been. Even in his darkest hours while training to become a vampire he had never felt so disheartened. He had come back from his first meeting with Lady Sedalia expecting that his task would be easy and that he would be in a comfortable bed, well fed and clothed within days and yet he was still living with the whore nearly two moon's turns later. It would seem that life had yet again proven that he couldn't expect a favorable outcome. His life in Misery had been deplorable and his training after had been grueling, but this was torture. For the first time Clayton felt simultaneously in control of his own destiny and helplessly at bay to fate. He was the reason that he was being denied food, but it was not his fault that his tent mate was withholding so much from him. He felt as if he was being forced to gain information for a woman of which he was still not convinced of her true character, but he also wanted to believe the words she said were true. He needed to believe that the work he was doing was for the good of the kingdom and for the protection of the Great King. He had to or else he was working for a Lady of questionable morals while living in a shack with a human whore. How far he had come since his life in Misery.

Eva, as the girl was called, was interested in the gossip of the slums more than she was in talking about her previous employer. When Clayton tried to engage her in conversations about her life before she had met him she would get incredibly quiet and excuse herself from their hovel. When she did spend time in his presence she spoke to him on end about useless things like the winter fashion that was sure to arrive in the castle and how the girl two huts down was seeing two men, had become pregnant and both men thought themselves the father. He hated to listen to her prattle on, but he forced himself to pay attention in the event that she let slip anything of use. She never did.

Clayton waited until he was safely away from the richest part of the city before slipping into an empty ally to turn his cloak. One of the first things he had been given by his noble benefactor had been a cloak with two sides. One side was made of a pitch fabric that was surely the most extravagant thing he had ever owned. It allowed him to blend in with the upper city crowd that he passed on every visit to his lady. The other side was made of much poorer fabric and was deliberately torn in places, allowing him to look like every other poor bastard in the slums. When he was sure that he looked no different from any vagrant wandering the streets of the middle city, Clayton slid back out onto the main street and back toward the slums.

It was as he passed the public gardens that he heard a melodious voice that could belong to none other than Eva. Afraid that she might notice him, Clayton slid back into the shadows while trying to find her. Humans and vampires alike passed the small alleyway that he had hidden himself into, but none were Eva. The throng of the crowd was too thick to pick out her particular scent and he was just about to give up when the movement of shiny black hair caught his eye. The head bobbed past him and into the public gardens, though he could not be sure if it was her. He slid from his hiding spot to follow the figure. Whomever she was, she was doing a haphazard job of weaving around people. If her intent was to confuse someone from following her she was doing a poor job and Clayton easily kept pace with her. When she finally came to a stop, Clayton was able to see her face. While there was no doubt that it was Eva, he hardly recognized her. She was clean for the first time since she had come to him looking for shelter. Her raven hair was shining in the moonlight and it sat in a plait that started at her scalp and wove down her head until it ended in a tail that was delicately placed over her shoulder. Her dress was not nearly as expensive as the purple number she had worn into the slums, but she had traded in her rags for a simple cerulean dress that clung to her figure. She was dressed well, but not as well as the man by her side. It was obvious to Clayton that they were together, though the man who stood at her arm made a decent attempt of acting like they were not deliberately there together. He was dressed in plain trousers and a simple coat, though they were made of richer fabrics. He did his best to keep his face shielded and act as inconspicuous as possible, but the man stood out amongst the rest of the less affluent crowd.

There was always a lot of people both human and vampire in the public gardens and it was simple enough for Clayton to blend with the crowd to move closer to the odd pair. The gardens were built in the middle of the city purposefully as it was the most accessible area and Faegon's king had built it so his people would have a place of beauty to relax no matter their social class. There were maids admiring flowers while beggars used the public faculties that were smartly hidden behind a grove of the most fragrant plants. A lord stood speaking to another man who must have been in the middle class while men and women of varying classes mingled about.

"Lord Malcolm, it is good to see you!"

"Lord Malcolm! How is your wife, Lady Rebecca? Well I hope!"

Pleasantries were called out to the man with Eva which caused the pair a great deal of discomfort, though Clayton was sure that he was the only soul who noticed. He finally had a name to report back at least, though he doubted it would be enough to buy himself back into Lady Sedalia's good graces. She would surely already know his name and was simply testing his abilities.

"This was too public a meeting," Lord Malcolm spoke so quietly that his lips hardly moved and Clayton had to strain to hear him. He was close now, so close that had Eva been a vampire she might have been able to sense him by his familiar scent. As it was he was sure that she would see him if he was not careful.

"We could have met at your home." The girl's response was cheeky, though it was clipped. It seemed even the daft girl knew how inappropriate that would have been.

"You said you had news, well out with it then."

"I would have thought you'd been happy to see me, do I not at least get a kiss?" The pout was evident in her voice and Clayton was surprised that the Lord didn't strike her for her insolence.

"Don't test me, girl. I sent you to the slums for a reason. Now do you have news for me?"

"I do, I have made contact with the man you seek. He desires a private audience."

Clayton was surprised to know that Lord Malcolm had sent Eva to the slums himself. He had thought that the girl's story had been true, that she had been sent there by his wife Lady Rebecca because of an illicit relationship that had existed between the two. The stiff way with which the man handled her was evidence enough that there was no relationship between the two and Clayton wondered what he could possibly need her in the slums for. Lady Sedalia seemed to think that he was contacting people who meant to do harm to King Zentarion and to the Crown. Was Eva really smarter than she seemed and was she Lord Malcolm's go between?

"You have? When and where does he wish to speak?" Her statement had piqued his interest and any cutting remarks that had been poised to spill from his lips had been replaced with thinly veiled excitement.

"Tonight at Adelina's."

Outrage bloomed on the aristocrat's face. "You could not give me more warning girl?"

"You were the one who insisted on secrecy," her tone left no room for argument and it seemed even the lord knew better. Clayton wondered what kind of woman Eva was if she could command respect like that from a lord.

"Too right. This meeting has lingered for too long. Change back into those hideous rags and run back to the slums before someone has noticed you've gone."

"No one will have missed me. The sad vampire I share my quarter's with has been gone all night, I'm sure he won't even be back when I return."

"That may be, but it is not worth the risk." Lord Malcolm said by way of farewell. Seeing that she was dismissed, Eva slid away from the man and into the shadows. At least the girl wasn't expecting Clayton to be there when she returned which gave him the opportunity to follow her employer. He was not thrilled to be returning to the tavern where he had been banished from his old home, but he had no choice.

Clayton was careful to let Lord Malcolm pass him before making his own way out of the public gardens. He stalked the man like he had been trained, keeping to the shadows and never letting him out of his sight. It seemed the man himself knew a bit about moving through shadows as well. Despite how well he stood out in the gardens, Malcolm masterfully wove through the streets that lead them to Adelina's without being noticed by any of his peers. It seemed like Clayton may have underestimated just who he was dealing with.

The sign for Adelina's could be seen above the crowd with its faded and chipping paint. Clayton felt his heart stop and fall into his stomach. He had been very careful to avoid the entire block that surrounded the tavern, but it seemed that he would have to stare down more than one failure tonight.

It was loud in the tavern as it was pique time for their clientele. Nearly all of the tables were full, but that hardly seemed to bother Malcolm as he made his way straight to the bar. Clayton watched from the door, pretending to look for a seat while he tracked the man's every movement. After a few quiet words with the same beauty that had worked the bar the last time he was there, Malcolm turned and took a seat at the empty table in the back corner, his eyes sweeping over the room, passing over Clayton without even seeing him. It was a risk to stay and be caught, but not turning up with information was even more dangerous. He made his way to the bar as casually as he could. The solid weight of coins in his pocket were a welcome feeling. He hadn't delivered anything to Lady Sedalia, but she had insisted that he take the coin incase he needed it in his mission. After the last time he had refused the coin of another he liked to think that he had learned a lesson in allowing pride to cloud his better judgement.

"What are you having dearie?" Clayton was momentarily hypnotized by warm chocolate eyes before he realized he had made it to the front of the bar.

"Do you have any blood from Delnori?" The queer mountain town was known for its magic folk and bizarre customs. He had heard from his former trainers that the blood farmed from them was the most exotic of any blood in the kingdom and in the lands beyond.

"Yes, but that will cost you." The doubt on her pretty face made Clayton realize that he was still dressed in his rags.

"Oh, okay, then I'll just take whatever I can get with a few zentarions." He pulled three coins from his pocket. He could come back to drink his riches away when he completed his mission. There was no sense in drawing unwanted attention to himself.

"Wait, don't I know you?" The barkeep passed him his cup and took his coins with a swift hand.

"No, I've just come to town." He took his drink and turned away to find a seat, but not before he heard her speak to him again.

"That's odd, maybe you just have one of those faces."

"Yeah. Maybe." His words were whispered, but he was sure the woman had heard him. He had to find a place to hole up while he and Malcolm awaited the mysterious man.

"Looking for a place t' stop and rest?" A booming voice caught Clayton's attention. Unfortunately it also caught the attention of many of the tavern's patrons. A quick glance to the corner told him that his mark had become curious too.

"Thank you, friend." Clayton dropped his hood to appear less like a threat. The smile on his lips was far from genuine, but the burly man who had called out to him seemed not to notice and the table was in front of the corner table. He would be a fool not to take the opportunity.

"We ain't friends yet, but that don't mean we can't be." The jolly voice was accompanied by shining hazel eyes set in a large, blockish face. His stature matched his tone and the man looked like he could easily out-lift every man and woman in the bar and still have strength to push a plow or carry lumber. The straw-like strands that sat limp on his head gave the otherwise large man a boyish look. He was a human, and an inebriated one at that if the timber of his words was anything to go by. "The name's 'ector, though most people just call me Toro on an account of me size."

"Nice to meet you, Toro. You can call me Clay." Clayton took his seat positioning himself between the corner table and the door. He wanted to get a good view of the person walking, any conversation he might overhear would not require a visual and he knew that Lady Sedalia would be sampling his blood to view his memories later.

"Well Clay, welcome to me 'umble table. I come down 'ere every week and drink away me earnings."

"Sounds like a dream." If Toro understood that his statement was sarcasm, he didn't say and the big man laughed heartily.

"It tis, Clay. No wife t' 'ound me and no children t' feed. It tis the dream. What do you dream of?"

It seemed too personal a question to ask a complete stranger, but Clayton knew that it would be impolite not responding. "I suppose I dream of the same things that any man would dream of. I wish to have a home of my own, a kind and caring woman in my bed, and enough wealth to support my needs."

"Aye," Toro nodded sagely and lifted his glass. "T' simple pleasures."

It seemed an appropriate toast considering his current lifestyle and Clayton lifted his own glass, careful not to spill any of the cheap blood in his goblet. "To simple pleasures."

Clayton took his eyes off his raised goblet long enough to notice that a man in rich, deep red clothes had swept in through the door. He looked like any other nobleman, though there was something in his eyes that made the vampire's fangs itch to descend. There was a dangerous aura about this man despite his thin frame. He was balding and had he not been a vampire he would have certainly lost what little dark strands that he had left. He had an air about him that commanded attention and yet he slid across the tavern in such a way that many avoided his gaze or simply didn't seem to notice him. Clayton forced his eyes away from the man before he was caught staring and tipped his goblet back, hoping that he was not already compromised.

He was not surprised when the strange man slid past him and sat with Lord Malcolm.

"Lord Malcolm." His voice was slick like oil and Clayton forced his body to stay stiff, keeping the involuntary shudder at bay.

"You seem to know my name, but I do not know yours," Malcolm spoke the way any noble who expected to have his way would.

"You may call me Lord Wynn."

"Lord? Of what House?" Malcolm sounded offended and Clayton imagined that he was. As a Lord of House Faegon he would know all of the Lords and Ladies of both Pa'ari and Zentarion's courts.

"Aren't we eager?" The man took a break before continuing. Clayton couldn't see with his back to the interaction, but he imagined that both men were watching the other carefully, appraising each other.

"So Clay, what brings ya t' Faegon? If this ain't yer 'ome, where ya from?" Toro asked loudly, as was in his nature, drowning out this Wynn character's response. Clayton cursed his loud companion.

"I was once a human of the Deadlands, but I am a drifter now. I have no home, though I have heard that there are opportunities for people like me within Faegon's great walls."

"Tis true, I have me a small shop where I sell garments down in the lower city. If ya need a place t' start, I could use the help."

"Thank you, if I find that I need to earn a coin or two I will come find you." Clayton was doing his best to split his attention, but he had never had to speak and listen simultaneously and he found the practice difficult.

Clayton was able to hone in just in time to hear Wynn speak again. "I believe you will make a fortunate ally to my Lady, Lord Malcolm. I will speak to her about your intent and I will return with her response."

"And when will I get to meet the Lady Cassandra?" Malcolm was impatient, it was obvious that Wynn was not impressed.

"In due time. My Lady will arrange a meeting if we see that you are truly dedicated to the Cause." With those final words, Clayton heard the scrape of the chair being pushed back from the table and he felt as the chair's back hit his own. Wynn was standing to leave and he had missed most of the conversation.

"Well Clay, I must be off, I cannot leave the stall unattended for long. Some rascal stole from me jus' a month or so past. It's odd though, I found the clothing laundered with the coin to pay at me booth the next day."

Clayton felt as his stomach dropped. This was the man he had stolen from. He had taken when he had no means to purchase the garments and he had known that Lady Sedalia had ordered the things returned and paid for, but he had never thought he would be faced with his crimes so literally.

"That is horrible," he heard himself utter as his mind began to spin.

"Nah, I'm sure it was some poor soul. That's what 'appens when you 'ave a business so close to the slums. Still I do alright for me self."

"It sounds like you do," Clayton nodded, but his mind was racing. Had Toro really not known it was him?

"Well, 'nough about that. I ought t' go. 'Ave a good night Clay, 'opefully we meet again."

Clayton just nodded in a way that did not offend the big man and he sat, too shocked to move as he watched Toro leave, not even bothering to turn and follow Lord Malcolm when he vacated his table moments later. Clayton was a good man, or so he had thought, so how had he come to spying and stealing? When had he become someone that he no longer recognized?

CASSANDRA

The sun was blazing high in the sky and yet Cassandra could not sleep. Leon was in his own chambers for the first time in a fortnight, though she dare not think his absence was the cause of her insomnia. She'd had half a mind to wake him, at least she would not be suffering alone, but she had dismissed the thought as quickly as it came. She was Queen Cassandra of House Rayne, the leader of the rogue vampires and the puppet master in an elaborate scheme that would bring the empire to its knees. She did not need anyone to stand by her side in the moonlight. She did not need anyone to keep her warm during the day.

She might not need anyone, but she was still not finding any sleep. Frustrated, Cassandra rose from her silk sheets and made her way toward the balcony. The plush settee her servants had moved out for her when she had first claimed the chambers as her own was already warm from the sun's light. There were few vampires still alive who could stay out in the sun all day without any ill effects, only the oldest of their kind could spend a full summer's day in the light. Cassandra was one of those elders, only a handful of the vampires in her own court could do the same. Logan could stand the sun for a few hours and in the beginning he would spend mornings on the balcony with her. They would lay out on the settee as she rested her head on his chest, enjoying the simple pleasures of his body. He couldn't stay with her all day, but he used to stay. Now she basked in the glow of the sun alone. It was better this way.

Cassandra slid onto the sun warmed seat and stretched her legs out until her feet dangled off the edge. She had left her robe inside so she could feel the heat on her cold flesh. Vampires were not affected by temperature, but Cassandra had always found something intoxicating about sitting in the sun. She had done it to test herself when she was younger. Her former house once had a lovely garden in the center that her former King had loved. He had taken her there many times in the beginning, before everything had gone sour. Before that bitch had come and ruined it all. There was no point in dwelling on the past and even less of a reason to ruin the sunlight thinking about the horrible girl and all she had stripped from her.

In the sunlight Cassandra was able to see all of the small marks that littered her body. They spoke of a time long ago when she had been a scared child. She had been the middle of seven children. Her older siblings hadn't cared much for her and she hadn't been strong enough to protect her younger siblings from their father's wrath. The most that she could do was take their lashings for them, but when she had been old enough to marry away she had been forced to leave her siblings to her father. The marks now served as a reminder of those that she'd failed. When her sire had given her the gift of the bite she had chosen to ink her skin to cover her scars. The first tattoo she had taken was a small serpent, the sigil of the first House Rayne, whose colors had faded, but its body was still visible as it slid around her ankle. It had been the House she had been born to and it had once given her pride to wear that mark. Her sire had also been from House Rayne, a nobleman name Michael and it had been her love for him that found her second tattoo added to her body. Their words were represented in curly script on her left rib; *Pride, Strength, Tradition.*

The words of House Lunaries was the next one to follow. *What must be done will be* decorated her right rib, mocking her and reminding her. Of all of the houses she had served, Lunaries was the house that she had loved the most and had been hurt by even more. If she really thought about it she lived by her former houses' words even now. Her fourth tattoo had been for another lover, the late Lunarian king. He had wanted to see his mark on her skin and she had seen no reason to deny him. When she was young and naive, the thought had thrilled her. They had never married, but she had never had reason to doubt his love and dedication to her, not until the bitch had come and taken it all away. He had once been a member of the noble House Namytar. She had their words inked on her skin when they had announced that she would be his heir. *Death before dishonor* was prominent against her left breast. She had never gotten a tattoo for Logan. It was something he had noticed and mentioned, only once. Cassandra was done living her life for men who only saw her as a means to an end. She had never explained that to him, but she thought she probably did not need to. Logan had known her better than Michael or Gareth ever had and that alone was a disturbing thought.

The warmth of the sun was lulling her to sleep and Cassandra allowed her heavy lids to shut. It was past mid-morning and she would have very little time to sleep now, but the queen didn't care. One of her guards would wake her when she was needed, if they dared, and in the end what did it mean to be queen if you couldn't sleep in and allow your people to handle themselves for an evening? Mind made, Cassandra did her best to let the many stressors keeping rest at bay melt away. The heat from the sun was nearly too much to bare before long, but she was too tired and too stubborn to move. She was given very few opportunities to enjoy solitude and returning to her chambers felt like an invitation for the annoyances of her House to invade her space. A breeze from the east carried over the balcony and rushed past her ears, masking the morning sounds of animals in the yard below. It cooled her skin and carried her consciousness with it until she was asleep.

Naturally, sleep left her just as quickly as it had come when moments later a shadow fell over her blocking out the warmth. Cassandra's eyes flew open as she prepared herself to tell off whomever had so rudely disturbed her, but she found all remarks die on her lips as she was faced with the smirking figure of her husband looking down on her.

"What are you doing here?" Aggravation was a familiar emotion when in Logan's presence and he hardly looked affected by her attitude.

"Well I heard that Leon was actually found in his rooms this morning, so I thought you might be lonely." There was mischief in Logan's eyes and Cassandra felt a strong need to knock it from his face.

"Even if I were, why would I feel better with you?" She was tired and even more so from his childish words. Sometimes she truly wondered what had possessed her to choose this man to stand beside her.

"My Lady! Your words sting," Logan chided as he swooped down and sat on the edge of the settee. He was dressed in casual sleep pants with an open robe partially covering his bare chest. He looked divine and he knew it. Cassandra cursed that his ego was well placed.

Logan nudged at her bare side with his knee until Cassandra moved to allow him space. She knew from experience that Logan was stubborn, possibly more so than she was, and would not leave now that he was here. She was not surprised when he slid his arm around her shoulder and forced her head to pillow on his chest. It was not uncomfortable being with him, it never had been. There had been a time when this had been normal. They had truly been lovers once, when Logan was still young and naive and Cassandra had seen a purpose for him in her plans. They occasionally still took pleasure from the other, but now he was just another obstacle.

"What are you playing at, Logan?" Cassandra asked though she hardly expected a reply. She nearly thought she wasn't going to receive one as time continued to stretch and only the morning stirrings filled the air.

"What are we doing, Cassy?"

"I've told you not to call me that." Cassandra looked up at the man through the shield of her hair. "And we're lying in the sun, what do you mean what are we doing?"

"Don't be obtuse. I meant with this rebellion. What are we doing, Cassandra? What is the point in the end?" Logan was gently running his hands through her hair, digging into her scalp in a way that used to sooth her. Now it just served to irritate her.

"You are spending too much time with the huntress."

"You are deflecting." Logan growled, applying more pressure with his fingers the more agitated he became.

"You have never questioned me before." Cassandra sighed before pushing away from Logan and his moving hands. "This empire is being run by fools."

"I have never argued that." Logan sat up, pushing her closer to the edge of the small settee.

Cassandra sighed and stood to put some distance between them. "So we take out the pillars. We have people in all of the influential Houses."

"And House Lunaries? They're not influential and yet you seem fascinated with tearing them apart."

The rogue Queen turned to face her husband with a critical eye. His face was passive, his eyes blank. He uttered their old House name like it meant nothing to him despite everything that had happened to them there. She couldn't believe he was truly unaffected, this was obviously another game to him. He loved to push her, but this was going too far.

"She took my lover. She took my throne and my home. Destroying them while winning this war is a prize I deserve. You should understand considering what she did to you."

"We agreed we'd never speak about that," Logan responded, though his usual anger was gone and instead he sounded tired. "We are living in the past, Cassy, we should be focusing on the future."

"A future that would be brighter without your sister in it."

Logan stood from his lounging position to stand in her space in the span of a second. She had never feared the man before, but there was something in his eyes that made doubt plant a seed in her mind. His eyes burned blue and his fangs descended, sharp and seeking blood. He was furious and it showed in his tight posture and cold stare.

"She stopped being my sister the day she allowed your former king to turn me. I should be dead now and I only remain here because I thought this war was meant to end the corrupt system that allows monsters to turn innocents without proper restitution!"

"We are still working toward the same goals." Cassandra did her best to pacify him not willing to back down, but also not looking for this altercation to end in bloodshed. She might not be ashamed of her own nudity, but the thought of one of the servants having to drag her dead, naked body from the balcony gave her pause.

"Are we? We seem to be doing whatever it is that you want. Do you even remember the reason I agreed to join you?"

Of course Cassandra did, his reasons were so intertwined with her own it would have been impossible for her to forget. Logan's village had been attacked centuries ago by the rogue vampires of that time. They were a much wilder people than those that Cassandra commanded now and they certainly hadn't been organized under any one leader. Cassandra hadn't been there to witness the carnage, but she had been waiting at Lunaries' gate to welcome her king home. Gareth had come back covered in blood with three new children in the arms of his guard. She hadn't learned their names for days later. Reagan was the eldest of the three and the sister to the two boys, Logan and Cohen. Logan had been on death's door when Gareth had given him the bite on the insistence of Reagan. When he had first woken up from his rebirth he had been angry, lashing out at everyone including his own siblings. He had gotten close enough to nearly kill Reagan once, blaming her for turning him into the monsters that had taken his parents and their entire village. Though the younger boy was blameless, Logan seemed just as displeased with Cohen for agreeing with her and allowing it to happen. It had been decided to keep the relationship between the three a secret for the safety of Reagan and Cohen. Not many had known the full story to begin with and Logan hadn't talked to anyone for nearly six months so it wasn't a very hard thing to cover up. It was helped by the fact that after his initial lash out, Logan hadn't spoken a word about the incident.

By then Lunaries had been exiled by the High Council and the people were more concerned with their futures than the fact that three strangers who had darkened their doorstep might be related. It had also been Gareth's idea to keep the reason for their exile from the people and only the men and women who had joined him that fateful day and Cassandra, his paramour and then heir to his throne, had any inkling of the truth. Of course taking away the security that was the backing of the High Council and empire was not the first thing that Reagan had taken from Cassandra. She slowly began to take her king's time and his attention. Before long Cassandra was stripped of her status as heir to House Lunaries as the smiling blonde did her best to sound contrite while accepting the crown. She had sworn that she hadn't asked for the honor, that Gareth had insisted, but Cassandra had known better. She might have had her doubts about Gareth before, but the night of the announcement had been the moment when she realized the she had lost the man forever.

It had also been the first night she had spoken to Logan. She had come to him full of anger and determination. He'd heard her out, allowing to her complain about the injustice of it all without offering a word of his own. She stood before him feeling empty and raw and he hadn't responded, instead he had allowed her to speak her peace and had just watched on, only mildly interested. She had left his room that night feeling as if there was no one there to support her, but Logan had surprised her by seeking her out the next night. He spoke about wanting to see reform happen where the turning of an innocent human would be atoned for by the perpetrator no matter their role in the empire. By all rights King Gareth should have been killed for his crime, but his entire house had been punished instead. That had been the beginning.

"Yes, I remember why you agreed to support me."

"Oh, I'm glad you remember." Logan scoffed. "There was a time when you cared too, I suppose I was wrong to assume that I ever meant anything to you. You've only ever been concerned about yourself."

She might have cared once, but the ability had been burned out of her. All that was left was a hollowness that had long since been filled with rage. Now when she saw the anger in his eyes it fueled her own instead of igniting sympathy. This was why she had chosen him to stand beside her. She had forgotten, but his own unbridled rage served to remind her. Logan was a dangerous bedfellow but he could be an even more destructive enemy and it would be wise for her to remember that.

"What matters to me is bringing this corrupt empire to its knees and removing the weak that keep us from true greatness. I know that is something we have always agreed on." The sun was beginning its descent and Cassandra had no desire to continue this conversation. She had a meeting with her Council scheduled soon, and it wouldn't do to sleep through the meeting, especially with her supposed husband questioning her every move in attendance. "It is late and there are pressing matters to discuss later, rest up now while you can."

"We can rest when this war is over." Logan sighed, his anger leaving just as swiftly as it had come. His shoulders sagged allowing his robe to fall forward and cover most of his exposed skin. "I'll see you later, Cassandra."

The queen watched as he turned his back to her and slid back into her bedchamber. The soft sound of the heavy wood door sliding open and then shutting felt like an explosion to her senses. She and Logan rarely fought. You would need to actually speak to a person in order to fight with them and now she had caused the chasm that was already growing between them to widen. She would have to tread carefully with him if she didn't want an attempted coup on her hands.

Her fatigue would have to wait. Logan's impassioned speech awoke a part of herself that she hadn't realized she had slowly let die out. She needed to be more aggressive if she planned on seeing the transformations in the empire that she had envisioned. She couldn't wait around any longer for things to fall into place she would have to act now. Lord Wynn, while not the most trustworthy of her Council, would have to be relied upon if she wanted results without Logan assisting her. She would have to find the man without her husband learning of it, something that would end in a much larger confrontation than their little spat this morning.

Cassandra moved about her room, quickly dressing to search for Lord Wynn. Had Leon stayed the day he would have gone to find the man for her, but the worrying conversation she'd just had with Logan wouldn't have taken place and the vampire was glad that it had. She swept back inside, blindly reaching for the nearest dressing gown, before slipping the deep burgundy cloth around her slender frame. She knotted the ties at her hip not bothering to correct the dangerously low dip of the front. Her hair was next, still a mess from lying out in the sun. She ran a comb through the tangles; every snag brought a growl to her lips and she gave in, throwing the comb down on her vanity with enough force to dent the wood. A scrap of cloth was produced from under the mess of glittering hair pieces and the woman made quick work of securing her brunette locks at the nape of neck. She was just going out to long enough find a servant to ask for Lord Wynn and then come back to her chambers anyway, she needn't look perfect.

The guard who she had dismissed from her door prior to attempting to sleep was nowhere to be seen. Cassandra was almost disappointed that he hadn't stayed. She would have enjoyed yelling at someone who didn't yell back and then she wouldn't be forced to look for anyone to find the master of whispers for her. The corridor leading to her bedchamber was long and only housed her own quarters. There was a sitting room and a small council room as well as a lavish washroom all reserved for her own personal use and she hardly had guards posted this far into the castle. She was one of the oldest and most powerful vampires in Mordin Forest. Only Lord Jarrod rivaled her age in their House and she had little to fear from him or any other.

Other than Logan.

She shook the thought from her mind, imagining as it fled from her ears and evaporated in the chilly night air. It would not do to let those thoughts cloud her judgement.

There was a servant standing at the mouth of the corridor. She was young, physically no older than sixteen, though Cassandra knew that it had to be near a century since her rebirth. She was plain, with flat brown hair and even duller brown eyes. She was short, nearly of a height with Cassandra's shoulders and she looked bored. When she sensed Cassandra approaching she suddenly came to life, standing taller and looking much more aware of her surroundings. When her queen stopped before her the girl curtsied low and flashed her sire's eyes. They turned a bright and blinding blue before becoming their regular dirt color. She was one of Logan's.

"Send for my handmaiden." She would have to get another to get Lord Wynn, Logan would undoubtedly have this wretch report to him later and she couldn't have that.

"Of course, Your Grace. I will send for her immediately." The girl curtsied again before fleeing for the main castle.

Satisfied that she still inspired fear in at least some of her subjects, Cassandra made her way back to her rooms. As soon as the door shut behind her, the fatigue she had felt on the balcony returned. She would have time enough to rest before Logan's girl found her handmaiden and she could count on her own girl to be smart enough to get Wynn for her. She never called upon her unless she needed her for official business and she certainly never relied on her to help get dressed or primped for any reason. Making up her mind, Cassandra slid out of her robe and sank into her welcoming bed. Her heavy lids slid closed and she allowed the tension in her shoulders to relax.

Sleep would not come, however, no matter how much she willed it. Her mind was alive with thoughts of Logan and Gareth. She hadn't allowed herself much time to dwell on the past, but Logan questioning her intentions had opened the door to thoughts and insecurities that she hadn't allowed herself to consider since she had walked out of Lunacies covered in her former lover's blood. She had truly believed in Gareth and she had thought that he had loved her just as much in turn. Of course he hadn't. Just like Logan had never loved her and equally like the superficial connection she had with Leon would shatter one day. There was no one she could trust with her heart, but herself.

The door opened without a knock which meant either Logan had returned to continue their argument or Wynn hadn't taken nearly as long as she had hoped he would.

"Are you well, My Lady?" Lord Wynn's smooth voice ran over her skin and Cassandra had to force herself not to shiver. She would not show weakness now, especially not in front of this dangerous man.

"I am quite well, should I not be allowed to rest while I await my lazy servants to pass along a message?" Cassandra stood from her reclined position, not surprised when she felt Wynn's eyes roam her naked form.

"They were quite efficient today, I believe, but I'm sure you didn't call on me to discuss the deteriorating quality of good help." Done with his unnecessary inspection of her body, Wynn moved from the middle of the room to the small table and chairs set just in front of the large window that opened to the balcony. The sun was setting and there would be little point to settle outside when they would need candles lit within the hour.

"You are too right. I called you here because I am concerned about Logan." Cassandra slid the robe back on though she left it open, knowing that a distracted Wynn would give her more information and she wasn't ashamed of using what she must to gain much needed intelligence.

"What has our great King gone and done to upset you now?" Wynn had the audacity to sound almost gleeful, but Cassandra let it go. He was more useful to her spilling information than the satisfaction of berating him would bring to her.

"He is has grown far too close to Faegon's huntress."

"Careful, Your Grace, jealousy is not a very becoming color on you." Cassandra scoffed and resisted the urge to do something childish like throw something at the man. "Don't be daft. He is planning something with the girl. We need to move fast if we intend to actually start a war while Logan is at least partially under my control."

At this statement the man seemed to become genuinely interested and gave up his hopeless attempt to disrobe her with his eyes alone. "What is it that you fear about him? You are his elder. You are more powerful and the people support you."

Even Wynn didn't know everything about Logan and his ties to the queen of Lunaries. It was a well guarded secret, one that she had kept for so long, she feared what might happen if it came out. She couldn't comprehend the consequences of the truth coming to light and she'd rather not test it either.

"What of your people in Faegon? Are we in position in the other houses?"

Wynn took mercy on her and allowed the conversation to divert. "Our operatives in House Adrastos are in place as well as those in Lunaries, but you knew that already. I've just arrived from Faegon myself with a tiny morsel to report. There are a few loyal to us in Zentarion's camp, but Pa'ari is proving more difficult as we expected."

"Without Pa'ari's fall this revolution will stop before it even starts. Don't tease me, Wynn, tell me what you know."

"I spoke to a man who seems very interested in learning more about you. I don't think we can turn him to our side, he seems too noble for that, but I do think we can convince him that he could be allowed into your good graces. Of course him inquiring so much about you and our house will put him in a tough spot should Pa'ari or his men discover it."

"Unless Pa'ari knows this war is coming and is trying to send a spy into our house."

"I have another plan for just that reason. I should have the man turned out of his home and stripped of his title quickly enough. That should allow doubt and panic to start to seep through Faegon's streets."

"Then get it done fast, I tire of waiting."

"As you wish, Your Grace. Is that all?"

Cassandra was tempted to ask the man to spy on Logan for her, but she wasn't sure if he could be trusted. In all actuality she was sure that he could not be trusted. "No, that will be all for now. Needless to say this conversation never happened. I will see you at our meeting later tonight."

"Of course, Your Grace." Wynn stood and bowed his way out.

Despite all of the people she surrounded herself with, and all those who claimed that they were loyal to her and only her, Cassandra was entirely alone. She just had to convince herself that she enjoyed it better this way.

REAGAN

There was a fire already crackling in her bedchamber when Reagan swept in after another trying meeting. She slammed the door behind her, even more displeased when the action did little to dampen the stress that had build up in her stiff shoulders. Her Council meant well, but there were too many strong personalities amongst her most trusted advisors and she wondered what had possessed her to appoint many of them to seats of power. Despite missing two of the strongest personalities in the Council from the meeting, Reagan still felt as if they had been there. Anya and Cohen had been noticeably absent and she was not surprised to find one of them sitting in her chair by the hearth. She was surprised, however, when she saw who it was.

"I hope you didn't miss me too much, sister dear," Cohen looked over his shoulder at her, smirk set squarely on his face, "but I promise it was for a good reason."

"Prey tell why my chief advisor and confidant thought his presence was better served elsewhere." Reagan slid her outer robes from her slim shoulders. The hunter green silk pooled on the floor by her bed in a heap. She would see to it later, or more likely Islara would when she came to turn down the sheets. She was left in loose silk pants and a matching top. The wide legs of the pants swam around her mimicking a full skirt while the shirt clung to her curves. She slid into the chair opposite Cohen, making obvious strides to rearrange her silks waiting for his response.

"Treating me like your subject, especially in private, has never worked, Rea. What's really bothering you?" His smirk had faded and concern clouded his face.

"What shouldn't bother me? Sometimes I wonder if returning to the Crown was the best for our people. I shudder to think what would become of us outside of their protection, but then I wonder if how we are being treated now is any better." It wasn't the only worry on her mind, it was actually far from it, but she didn't see a reason to waste time dredging up every minuscule concern that weighed on her. There seemed to be a never-ending string of thoughts that kept her from sleep and drove her mad. The actions of her lover were chief among them, Natalya's decision came as a close second. Neither of these things seemed appropriate to discuss with her brother.

"Trying to understand the whims of Faegon would drive anyone mad. What is truly on your mind? Do you forget that I still know you best of all?" The hurt look on Cohen's face reminded Reagan of the days when they had still been human. She had loved both of her brothers, but Cohen had always been her favorite. Her mother had worried that she would spend her life caring for her baby brother instead of for a husband and she hadn't been entirely wrong. Her mother had always feared that Reagan would hide behind her dedication to her siblings and never learn to live her own life. She had always thought that driving out all others to protect her own heart would be Reagan's downfall, so Reagan had taken a risk to trust her heart when she'd met Anya, in her mother's honor. Now it seemed she had made the wrong choice. Anya would never understand her as Cohen did. Her mother had been right to fear that she would never commit to a lover because of her dedication to her brother, but it seemed that Reagan had also been correct in believing that she could be punished if she'd tried.

"Do you ever miss the days when it was just the three of us?" Reagan need not explain what she meant. Since the day that they'd lost their brother she had never spoken his name. His loss had been too much to bare, but even worse so was the knowledge that if it had been Cohen, Reagan would have truly given up all will to live.

"No, we were weak then. Maybe not you, but we were. His weakness brought his downfall and I would much rather remember a time when I was strong enough to protect you as you have always done for me."

"I have never expected you to protect me, I've never needed it. That was my job. It still is now." Reagan soothed, rising from her chair to perch beside him. She pulled him closer to her, as she had when he was a baby and their mother had been too sick to care for him. He had been a small baby, he'd come too early and both he and their mother had almost died for the trouble. She had promised to them then that she would spend her life protecting Cohen, even if it meant forsaking the life that was expected of her. "Enough of this, what news did you have for me?"

"I spoke with Natalya, she wants to take the bite." Cohen smiled with such joy that Reagan almost pushed him to speak more. She knew the two were getting close and the thought of her baby brother falling for the young human filled her with dread. The obvious age difference between the pair might be frowned upon by some, but she knew what it felt like to know the human you cared for was willing to take the bite. It was the same way she felt when Anya had made her choice. Natalya reminded her a lot of her paramour, it was one of the reasons she felt the relationship forming between the human and her brother would end in disaster.

"That is good news. When will she be ready?" There would be time still to play the role of a worried older sister and pressure Cohen for news of his growing feelings for the girl later. Her responsibilities as Queen came first.

"Nirosh and Darius would know for sure, but the next full moon seems like a good time. She will be seventeen by then, a woman by her people's standards and certainly old enough to take the bite by ours. It would be wise for her to become reborn soon. Things are starting to change in the forest, Rea, I can feel it." A dark look passed his face.

"The Council feels the same. I expect a messenger from Faegon any time now."

"Have the scouts seen something?" Cohen was genuinely surprised and Reagan found herself wishing that he had been at the meeting. She wasn't looking forward to having this conversation again.

"No, but you are correct in thinking things are changing. Cassandra is getting bolder and I know that it will be a short time before Faegon begins to call soldiers to bear arms. I fear if we comply and send our best we will be horribly outnumbered if an attack were to come to our doors, but I fear more what denying them would do."

"Pray that it will not happen sweet sister, there is nothing to fear now. A call to arms would hurt the House, but not be detrimental. Nirosh would not be obligated to comply with the call and he would stay, as would I. It is inevitable that Darius should leave, but we have strong soldiers, some too young to be called and yet they would make a great defense."

"I hope your confidence is justified."

"You know your people as well as I do. Do you mean to say they are weaker than I've described?"

"No, but there is unrest in the castle. I know there are those that would like to see me gone and another take the throne. At times I wonder if that would be best."

"All of your worries must be addling your brain if you truly believe that." Cohen scoffed to show just how little truth he felt was in her words.

"If only our people were as loyal as you." Reagan mused, standing to pace before the fire. "There is some truth to the whispers, however. I should be out there. It has been too long since the Kings and Queens of this forest were able to roam their lands without fear. I cannot stand being confined by these walls much longer. I want to meet these rogues head on, to bring an end to this long war."

"Why must you act as if ending the war is your duty? You act as if you were responsible."

"And if I were?" She forgot how little he knew of the time before the war, before she had come into the throne and her role in causing the unrest in their House. She had shielded him from it then and now she had no one to confide her deepest guilt with.

"Oh Rea, it wasn't your fault that Gareth loved you more." Reagan gasped and stopped her pacing mid-step, spinning around to face her brother. "Do you honestly think I never knew? I was a childe, Rea, not an idiot. Everyone saw how he looked at you."

"He never loved me in the way that she feared. He was like a father to us, nothing more." They were words she used to repeat to help herself sleep at night.

"That was how you felt, yes, but he loved you, more than he ever loved her. His guilt over his feelings for you was why he took the power of being his predecessor from her to you. I'm sure he felt that if he gave you everything he thought you deserved it would make up for the fact that he was much too old to take you, a childe, into his bed."

"Your words are lies." Reagan felt the tears fall from her eyes, but made no move to wipe them away. Cohen came to her then, wrapping her in a tight hug and taking care of her tears on his own.

"Oh Rea, you are a wonderful sister and Queen, so pure of heart, but you never saw him for what he was. He was a good man, and maybe even a good King, but he was selfish. He stripped Cassandra of everything she was and gave it all to you for his own needs. You did not turn her into the woman that she is, he did. He did all of those things, you never asked for it. You certainly are not to blame for Cassandra, her actions, and especially for what she did to our brother. None of that has ever been your fault."

A knock at the door interrupted any response Reagan might have made and she pulled away from Cohen to freshen up at her vanity. Cohen walked to the door in silence, giving his queen the time she needed to pull herself together. When he was sure that she would be comfortable entertaining whomever was at the door, he opened it himself, surprised to find Kris, the captain of the scouts, at the door.

"Pardon the interruption, My Lord, but one of our scouts has returned with troubling news. I know the Council has already disbanded for the night, but I think it's best we reconvene."

"Any important news from Mordin should be shared with all of our people. Send word that there will be a meeting in the throne room, I will be there soon." Reagan commanded from Cohen's side. Her robes were fastened again and she looked just as regal as she had when she'd come in from her last meeting.

"Yes, Your Grace, I will to see to it that it is done." Kris bowed and exited the room with haste.

"Cohen please fetch Natalya, I believe this would be a good time to also announce to the House that she is soon to become their newest sister."

"As you wish, Your Grace. Shall I escort her and return to walk with you?"

"There is no need for you to accompany me. I am safe within these walls." Reagan dismissed him and he bowed himself out of the room.

Reagan walked to her wardrobe to stop in front of her full length mirror, her attire giving her pause. While many other leaders might have worn richer dress to give audience to their people Reagan often felt more comfortable in plainer clothing. She wanted her people to see her as an equal to them. After considering herself a moment longer, she straightened out her clothes in the mirror, foregoing the robes which were now certainly wrinkled. Satisfied, she left her bedchamber for the short walk to the throne room.

She opted to travel through the service corridors instead of taking the longer route through the castle. It would allow her to save on time and also to check in on some of her people she didn't always have the opportunity to see. There was a long hallway that had an access point at the end of the Royal Tower. When the castle was once part of the human kingdom it would have been essential for the servants to have unobtrusive access to their sovereign. Now it served as a mere shortcut through the kitchens to the main castle. Despite the vampire's lack of a need for a kitchen, Reagan had made sure that her builders had taken special care to make the space useable for her human subjects. It was important to insure that all of the humans living within their walls were taken care of just as well as the vampires were and Reagan took pride in the lavish kitchen she had redone for her people. They were always busy and many of her subjects stopped their work to bow to their queen. Normally she would take the time to speak to them, to learn of how their families both within and outside of her walls were, but there was no time. It seemed that many were already aware of the important meeting taking place and there were hardly any people working when she passed through. After the kitchens was the blood bank where the food for the vampires was kept. Reagan sorely wished she had time to partake in a meal of her own, it had been too long since her last feeding and even longer since she'd taken time to hunt. For those vampires that wanted a good chase before their feeding they were allowed to prowl Mordin for animal prey, so long as they returned the carcass to the kitchens for the humans to have a meal from it as well. The thought was immediately appealing and Reagan made note to ask Cohen to join her for a hunt later that night.

When Reagan made her way up to the small audience chamber behind the throne room she could already hear the low buzz of a crowd forming. Anya and Darius were sitting waiting for her while she could hear Kris and Nirosh just on the other side of the wall, already waiting for her on the dais. As soon as they saw her Anya flanked to her right and Darius to her left, they escorted her through the door and to her throne. The first thing she noticed was the sound of her subjects whispering about the latest news from Mordin. Reagan liked to think that she was an involved leader and that she was connected to her people on an emotional level and not just superficially. She hoped that she was right and no matter the news they were about to receive, that her people would continue to support her. They waited for Cohen to return with Natalya, leaving her to stand beside Emeline just at the foot of the dais while he joined her at the throne, before she motioned for Kris to bring forth the scout and begin.

"Your Grace, I have just returned from our borders on the far West. There was a disturbing lack of animals there. I thought it was because of rogues, but when I went to see if there were any in our area I found vampires sent from the Crown instead. They did not see me, or at least I don't believe they did. They were speaking about King Zentarion sending messengers to the outer Houses." Of the five vampire Houses only two of them were ever referred to as the outer houses. Lunaries and Tryali were the least likely to follow the King of Kings blindly into war and it was obvious that he was well aware of that fact.

"Messengers from Faegon should not be a surprise. We know the Crown is keeping a close eye over their territory. The threat from the rogues is a very real concern and if they believe that bringing in all of the Houses is essential than we must agree to their terms." Reagan was not one to pander to other Kings, but she knew where her place was in the empire at large. There was no point in fighting against the Crown when there was a real war to fight.

"There was more, Your Grace. They also said there would be a royal visit following the messenger if the Houses were not responding to the King's liking." The announcement brought on a low roar from her subjects.

"You know we will be forced to host a visit. No matter if we conform to their rule, the High Council will still judge our House by the failings of the previous King." Darius whispered, he let out a pained grunt with the heel of Kris' boot met his foot.

"Whatever his failings were, it is not up to us to judge," Reagan replied quietly to her head guardsman before addressing the hall at large. "We will meet these guests with open arms, it is time we stop hiding from the Crown and their High Council. We as a House no longer need fear the reign of Faegon; they clearly intend to keep their eye on us, we must allow them to do so. We might not agree with their ways, but aligning with the Crown affords protection from the self-proclaimed rogue queen and her rebellion." Reagan stood, her tone leaving no room for misunderstanding or argument.

"Queen Reagan has spoken on this matter. Beginning immediately we must prepare the castle for our visitors." Cohen spoke, walking up the steps of the dais with Natalya trailing right behind him. "This is not all we have to discuss tonight. We have the honor of introducing you to someone who will soon be your newest sister." Cohen opened his arms wide to showcase Natalya to the room. "Many of you have already met Miss Natalya. Please join me in welcoming Natalya, once of the village Ash from the human kingdom Solara, into House Lunaries as one of our sisters."

Reagan noticed how Emeline and Nirosh seemed to be clapping the loudest while Cohen was positively beaming. The only member on the dais that seemed to be unhappy by the announcement was Anya. Natalya, for her part, seemed pleased by the attention, though the slight color on her cheeks showed that she still wasn't accustomed to it. It was something she would no doubt learn to handle in time as her position as a noble and a royal would put her constantly under the public eye. Reagan had no doubt that she would rise well to the occasion.

"I would also like to announce that Natalya will not only be joining our House and even taking the precious gift that is the Bite, but I will be doing her the honor. Kneel now to honor Lady Natalya." Reagan watched, pleased as the hall was brought to their knees. Both Natalya and Anya seemed surprised by her words, but Cohen only looked at her with gratitude. When all but she and Anya had knelt to their newest noblewoman she took Natalya's hand and pulled the girl up to stand by her side.

"All rise in the name of Lady Natalya and Queen Reagan, protector of House Lunaries. What must be done will be." Cohen spoke from his position on the floor, only rising when he finished, turning to face his sister's people. Kris left the dais to tend to the scout while the rest of Reagan's council moved to the small chamber. Reagan could see Anya fuming to her left and she knew that she was about to pay dearly for announcing Natalya's role without telling her lover first.

"Are you sure welcoming this royal party is in the best interest of the House?" Darius began as soon as the door closed. "We may have finally stabilized, but we are in no shape to host Faegon."

"We have no other choice. There is a bigger war out there to fight." Nirosh spoke, ever the reasonable one. "If we begin to rebuild the old royal quarters now there might be time to have them set up properly."

"Where will we get the builders and the supplies? We are being stretched thin as it is. We could call on some of the nearby villages for help, but even then we will not have enough time." Samuel, their Chief Builder, scowled. He and Nirosh were the oldest vampires in the House and they never saw eye to eye on any matter.

"What is it that you suggest?" Nirosh leveled him with a hard gaze. Reagan could feel the pressure building at her temples. The only way to make this meeting worse would be if the fury in Anya's eyes finally bubbled over and she unleashed her anger over whichever subject was currently bothering her.

"I suggest that we stop arguing, there are bigger matters at hand to tend to." Cohen tried to pacify the situation, but it seemed that it only added to the surmounting tension.

"Exactly. For once I agree with you, we should be talking about

Reagan's sudden decision to add to the Royal Party without consulting anyone in it! You shouldn't be the one to turn her, Your Grace. That is too high an honor for the likes of that spoiled brat." Anya spoke her dark eyes falling on her Queen. The room went instantly silent.

"You know better than to speak out of turn." Reagan's answer was cold, her face turned away from the rest of her advisors. She knew without looking that Cohen would no doubt be readying himself for a fight with her paramour. "Leave us. I do not require anything more that Anya cannot see to."

The room cleared quickly. When Reagan was in a sour enough mood to snap at Anya every vampire within the house knew better than to oppose her. The sound of the door closing echoed off the stone walls and Reagan finally turned to face the younger vampire. Anya stood in the middle of the room, her head bowed. She was a strong willed person so her obedience to Reagan always came as a shock to the queen. She stepped away from the council table and made her way silently, stopping right in front of her, raising her chin with a single finger.

"You are right, My Lady, I spoke out of turn it won't happen again." Anya spoke first, her eyes defiant, but her tone submissive.

They held each other's gaze, Anya's determined eyes flickering blue for no more than a second before turning back to their natural obsidian. It was Reagan's mark, the one that forever deemed Anya as her own. Even with that, Anya tried her best to assert dominance over her queen. It never worked, but she also never stopped trying.

"I'm sorry, my childe. You know I always value your opinion." Reagan let her hand fall, but they continued their contest of wills. Eventually Anya looked away. "You know why the girl is important. Faegon would be very interested in Elizabeth's daughter."

"I thought you never wanted to speak of that day again. I don't know what that seer said to you, but after she died you told me never to mention her name again."

"I know, but it might be time to talk about that night, just not yet."

"Well if you think Faegon might be interested in her we should act fast. You can't hide what you know about her from the High Council anymore, they're going to bring you in like they did to Gareth." At the mention of her old master Reagan's eyes turned cold.

"You know nothing of Gareth, don't speak about things that you have no understanding of." Reagan growled, her words muffled by her fangs.

Anya stepped back in fear, dropping down to her knees before her Queen. The air in the room dropped to a chilling level and Reagan's fangs became predominant to show her dominance. A creature of gentle nature, Reagan only showed her fangs to feed, hardly ever to assert her place as queen. Anya was right to fear her Lady just as she was undoubtedly right about the High Council. That knowledge alone kept Reagan from unleashing her fury on her lover.

"You are dismissed." Anya took to her feet and fled from the room, ice blue eyes following her movements with a predatory edge. It was nearly dawn and the urge to eat could no longer be contained. Reagan made her way through the halls with ease; every vampire she passed bowed reflexively in her wake. Normally when Reagan's need to feed was so great that she actually left the castle walls to find a meal Cohen and Anya would accompany her, but she was too agitated to have guards. Tonight she would hunt alone.

GWYNDOLYN

Since Logan had admitted to the circumstances of his rebirth Gwyndolyn had found herself at a standstill. It had been easy to seduce the king before, when she thought he was just as committed to the cause as his wife. She hadn't had to think of him as a scared boy who had been forced into a life he had never chosen. There had seemed to be no harm in tricking him for her own benefit when she had seen him as her enemy, but now she was less sure. Now, she had to face these feelings of doubt before they threatened to undo all of her hard work. He was a mark, a source of invaluable information, a means to an end, she could not afford for him to be anymore. Despite this, she knew that this strange man was slowly working his way past her walls. He was playing her just as she was meant to be playing him, except he was doing a much better job. Was it possible that his story had been nothing more than an elaborate lie?

Gwyn wondered how his circumstances might have taken him on the path to becoming part of the rogue rebellion, much less the king. The rogues were a group of people who were notorious for turning humans against their will; it was one of the many reasons they were hunted by the Crown. Logan hated the vampire that turned him, so how could he sit atop a throne in front of subjects who committed the same crime that had been done to him? Having to live through being turned against one's will surely would not inspire one to condone the same treatment of others. He must have chosen to live for a reason. It was obvious that he truly resented being given the bite, she was half surprised that he hadn't taken his own life after the ordeal. Gwyn could not imagine not wanting to be a vampire, but she could understand being forced to live as someone you were not. She lived a life where she was forced to act a part to everyone around her. Arguably she was in a very different position, but she could at least understand his struggles more than most.

When Gwyn had trained to become one of King Zentarion's spies she had gone through decades of mental and physical conditioning. They had beat her and starved her to make her stronger, but she had also had the support of her fellow trainees to keep her sane. Logan didn't seem to have anyone like that. From the short interactions she saw between him and others within the castle it was obvious that he was truly alone. She could not imagine what her mental state would be had she not had others to lean on and to heal with. If she knew more about what had happened to Logan she might even be able to help heal the gaping wound that being reborn had left behind. She was not surprised that she cared enough to want to help. He reminded her so much of herself and that hurt. She wanted to ask him more about his past, but she didn't know what door within herself that line of questioning might open. If she saw Logan as an equal who deserved her sympathy she just might not be able to turn him into the Crown when she was finally able to escape this place. It wasn't worth the risk, but her curiosity had been inflamed and it was hard to quell. Would he even answer?

There were other things that she could talk to him about. She could mention the things that she had heard Cassandra say when the queen thought that no one would overhear. She had only heard that one conversation. The inconsistent guards outside of her door started to become more consistent with time and she had a fleeting worry that it was because the woman had known somehow, but when she did not appear to interrogate her, Gwyn allowed her fears to subside, if only slightly. That one moment of pure luck had been enough though. She thought about that conversation often when she was alone. The fact that queen was looking to rid herself of Logan was interesting and useful. Logan would be easier to sway with that information, but it was obvious that Cassandra also knew something more about her and she did not want to admit that to Logan. There had been a close call with the man before, but she knew that the king had no idea of her true position within King Zentarion's court. He would not risk visiting her so often if he knew her true abilities. She had to insure that he never found out. What would he do with that information?

It had been ten days since the last time the blond king had come to her. Ten days in which she had been left to pace her drafty cell with only her silent guards to keep her company and the loneliness was starting to become draining. She longed to hear another voice, to see the world outside of her cell, and feel the cool autumn air on her face. More than anything she was hungry.

"Do you know when I might get my next meal?" Gwyn asked the empty air. Her guards didn't even turn to acknowledge her, just as she had suspected. "I'm hungry and I'd rather like to see Logan again."

"*King* Logan will return if he deems you worthy." The female guard spoke without turning. From behind, her mousy hair looked poorly kept.

Gwyn was brought water to bathe at least three times a week and even still she managed to look cleaner than the deplorable creature before her.

"Don't talk to the prisoners, Lydia." The man beside her chided. He was older than the girl, though neither of them were very old. Both vampires were easily only a few decades reborn. She was an elder and in another life that would have commanded all the respect necessary to have her set free, but Cassandra's vampires had no sense of respect.

"And you will refrain from disciplining my guards, Sander," the commanding tone of their king brought both guards to full attention.

"Of course, Your Majesty. My apologies." Sander bowed and flashed his sire's eyes. They were the sickening purple that Gwyn had expected. When the girl bowed and did the same, she was surprised to see that her eyes flashed blue. She was one of Logan's girls. Gwyn took a moment to ponder if the man had purposefully stationed one of his girls with her knowing that the other man was his wife's.

"Lydia would you see to it that hot bath water and fresh blood are brought to our guest immediately?" Logan said it in a much softer voice then he had spoken to Sander with, though there was no doubt that it was a command. Lydia would face dire consequences for not following his orders exactly.

"Yes, m'lord. I would be happy to insure your guest is seen to." Both guards bowed out again before Logan let himself into her cell.

"You had much too much enjoyment out of that." Gwyn chided though the smile was not absent from her face.

"As did you." Logan smirked, moving in for a deep kiss. "Sometimes I wonder what kind of pair we might make together."

Gwyn wondered if she was simply imagining the unheard "*if we ruled this house together*" or if the pointed look she was getting meant exactly that. "Will I have you to myself for long?"

"How long would you have me for?" Logan stood before her with her face between his hands once more as if he might kiss her again. His blue eyes bore into her own and all of the raw confidence that he normally exuded melted until he looked at her with a different intensity.

The moment was destroyed when a clang at her cell door announced the arrival of servants carrying the large bathtub and buckets of hot water. Gwyn regretted needing to part from Logan as the hard, guarded look that normally shield his eyes fell back in place. The huntresses hoped that when they found themselves alone once more that she might be able to draw those deeper emotions out of him.

The servants made quick work of setting up the bathtub before excusing themselves respectfully under Logan's hawk like gaze. Logan had never been there while she bathed before and the servants who normally tended to her needs would often bring dirty water and old blood. It seemed this time she would be treated to the expectations that Logan held for her.

Being the bed warmer for a king certainly had its advantages.

"Come my dear," Logan motioned for her to disrobe and enter the hot water.

Suddenly Gwyn felt herself having reservations. Sleeping with Logan was easy and pleasurable. It was intimate and yet not. It was just another act that she would commit just as she had in the past to seduce information out of clueless men and women. Allowing Logan to wash and care for her seemed very different. This spoke of a new level of intimacy, bordering on affection. The pair were already treading on a fine line and this could very well be her undoing.

"Are you sure you wouldn't mind? I can bathe on my own I wouldn't ask you to assist with what would be a servant's work."

"No servant should do the things to you that I wish to do." Logan's charming smile was back, but the intensity that they had shared earlier was gone. This Logan was easy to deal with and it made Gwyn relax. She knew that she could work with him when he was acting the part of a charming, selfish king.

"Only if you are sure, Your Majesty," she threw in the title because she knew how he would react. Predictably his eyes clouded in lust and Gwyn found her clothes shredded before she could react. Her body was sinking into the warm water by the guidance of strong hands as she allowed him full access to her body. Despite his urgency he was gentler with her than she expected which left the bounty huntress rather disappointed. "Oh you can be rougher than that, Your Majesty."

"Be careful what you wish for," he growled through fangs. Lust sparked a heat in Gwyn that only urged her on.

"I am not a delicate flower. I'm not sure what women you may have been with in the past, but I can take a little pain with my pleasure. In fact I rather enjoy it," Gwyn nipped at every inch of the king that she could reach and the man held on to her fiercely. This Logan she could handle and pushing him could only benefit her.

"Do not tempt me woman," he pushed her back into the water. "Let me clean you first before I grant that request."

Logan's hands roamed over her skin taking special care to wash her. He used his skilled fingers to dig into her muscles to relax her sore body until she was purring under their ministrations. He always took care to touch and taste her completely when he took his pleasure from her and yet she felt as if he was touching her for the first time. He worked his way down her back first, stopping at her hips before turning her so he could give the same attention to her chest and stomach. He had her gasping and begging before he had even reached the water's surface. There was more clean water beside them and he paused to use it to rinse through her hair and the surface rose until it just lapped at her breasts. Logan continued to work her up by scrubbing at her scalp and neck. Gwyn had never been touched in this way before. Not a single part of her regretted that she might feel this way for the first time by Logan's hands.

When surely there was no more dirt in her hair, Logan turned back to her body, cupping at her breasts again, pulling filthy sounds from her mouth that had Gwyn blushing despite all that they had already done. The confident smirk was back, but Gwyn was too wound up to comment. She should have cursed that Logan knew it too, but instead she cursed because he was taking his time with her. She hadn't been merely goading him when she said she could be handled less gently. She had hoped that he would listen so she might prove to him once more that she could be his equal.

If Logan knew what she wanted he certainly didn't act like it. He continued to move slowly, taking her apart with his hands under the pretenses of washing her. If she were in her right mind, Gwyn might think it interesting how selfless it was of him to give her such pleasure without seeking his own, but she was not, in fact, in her right mind. She had never felt fingers slid between her legs in this way before. Of course she washed herself and she was not naive to what a man and even a woman might be capable of, but not even any of her female lovers had been so bold to slide their fingers so deep into her she just might burst from it. Logan seemed not in the least bit bothered by her obvious surprise and he leaned in to kiss at her pronounced collarbone, nipping his way down to her heaving chest. The combined sensations of his hot mouth and talented fingers found Gwyn screaming Logan's name with a surprised shout.

"Has no one ever done this for you before?" Logan asked as if awed. He moved to pull his fingers from her and Gwyn complained at the loss. "What a shame. A beautiful woman like you should be worshiped."

Gwyn wasn't sure how to respond to such an affectionate statement. Thankfully, Logan saved her from having to as he leaned in and kissed her sweetly. The touch of his lips so gently on hers set another fire in her belly and Gwyn reached out for him, the water from her bath sloshing out of the tub and soaking his clothes. "Oh I am so sorry, Your Majesty."

"You don't sound very sorry," Logan tried for stern, but her hands had found his manhood and the breathy quality of his voice made the delivery fall a bit short.

"But I am, would you allow me to show you?" Gwyn moved to drag him in, but Logan employed his strength to keep her from bringing him into the tub with her.

"You said you were hungry earlier, why don't you eat first and get your strength up?"

"I can eat after you're gone," Gwyn brushed off his concern easily.

"No, I don't want you to neglect your own needs. I told you I will stay as long as you wish. Come."

It wasn't as if Gwyn had to give him permission, Logan had already lifted her up and wrapped her in a large towel. He dried her with the same gentle attention he had given to washing her and Gwyn shivered at the memory. It was the most care that anyone had ever treated her with and the bounty huntress couldn't stop the warmth that filled her. When he was satisfied, he sat her at the small table that stood ill used to the far side of her cell. There was a goblet of the freshest blood she had been given while a prisoner to House Rayne, save the blood she had drawn from Logan himself, and she savored the flavor as she sipped it slowly. He let her eat without filling the silence with pointless talk. He knew her enough to respect her desire for quiet and instead spent his time looking at her as if he was categorizing her every detail, should he forget her when she was gone from his life. Gwyn refused to consider what circumstances she might find herself in should Logan no longer be her benefactor.

"There is unrest in the castle." Logan spoke when she set the goblet down, his eyes closed off and yet his words were very forthcoming. "I would not speak ill of my queen, but I also am taking precautions to insure that your door is always guarded by one of my own children."

"Why are you telling me this?" Gwyn was curious more than anything, Logan did not seem the type of man who felt the need to justify his actions.

"You are a smart woman, Gwyndolyn, and you no doubt saw that display of power by Sander, Cassandra's man. Lydia is an insolent brat, I will admit that, but she is loyal to me and would not allow any harm to come to you as she has been instructed to."

"You seem to put a lot of trust in the girl. She is still young yet, I would be better off defending myself if it were to come to it," Gwyn stated more as an observation than a criticism.

"That is true and I pray it never comes to that, but it soothes my own anxieties to know that you are being guarded by one of my own." It was an honest statement and that surprised her.

"What is it that you fear that would cause you to put a guard at my door?"

Logan paused much longer than Gwyn had anticipated. He seemed to be searching for the best answer in her eyes; it was incredibly unnerving. "What was it that you had held back from me, Gwyn? Do not think I had forgotten."

It seemed to matter not that she had asked her question first. Logan was expecting an answer from her and she had a hard time divining a reason not to tell him. He had his suspicions that she was more than just a simple bounty hunter, maybe giving him part of the truth would buy her enough trust to turn him from Cassandra.

"Would you prefer I show you? You may sample my blood for the memory, if you'd prefer."

Logan looked genuinely surprised at her offer. "You would allow me such an intimate thing? You surely know that I can easily identify a doctored memory. There would be no way to lie to me."

"I know, that is why I suggested it." Gwyn did her best not to sound like she was speaking to a child. Offending the delicate sensibilities of a king would not grant her any favors. "I don't want you to have any room for doubt."

The king watched her for a moment and Gwyn was sure he would find fault in her plan. "Come here, then, I would be very interested in what you heard."

Gwyn stood on steadier legs than she thought she possessed. She left the towel behind as she made her way slowly toward the imposing vampire. Even in casual evening pants and a loose tunic still damp from her bathwater, Logan held the air of royalty about him. The hunger in his eyes could be due to many things and Gwyn focused on the task at hand. In order for him to see the memory that she wanted him to have access to she would have to focus on it completely while he drank from her blood. It was a delicate art and often resulted in embarrassing situations when the giver of the memory was not skilled enough or lost focus easily. Gwyn had trained to give her memories to the High Council since she was a childe and was one of the most consistent with the art that Faegon had trained. She had her worries when it came to Logan, but the reward she could gain from its success would outweigh the risks.

She slid into his lap with the confidence of a woman who belonged there. Her side rested against his broad chest and she leaned until her head rested on the edge of his shoulder, making herself comfortable while granting him full access to her neck. He didn't have to draw the blood from her this way, but Logan had already acknowledged how intimate it would be and she did not want to break the spell that had fallen over them. She did not trust him, not truly, but he would have to believe that she did.

"Are you sure?"

Gwyn found it oddly touching that he might ask her permission when she had already given it and even if she hadn't, he could easily overpower her in this position and that had been the point. "Yes."

At first the fangs descending into her skin lit fires of passion in her blood. She controlled the base emotion, doing her best to keep her immediate thoughts from escaping. Flashes of Logan's skin pressed against her own fled through her consciousness and she could feel the smirk of lips drawing her blood and memories from her. It was enough to jolt her mind back to the task at hand and she carefully began to focus on the night that she had overheard Cassandra and Wynn.

"It bothers me little what Logan thinks of my page. He would never bring my affair into the light when he has her. He might pretend that she is only there to fill his physical urges, but I know him far too well. He cares for her; he would never stay until moonlight for her if he felt no comfort in her presence. If our people knew that he cared for Faegon's little bitch they would turn on him. She will help prove just how far Logan has strayed from our cause. Once we can prove that he no longer cares for the plight of

our people it will be easy to use her presence to convince the people who still favor him that he is a traitor. Then we can be rid of both of them."

Gwyn felt Logan tense beneath her and she held on to his arms to keep him from moving. She wanted him to see the rest of the memory.

"Are you certain that this will work? You cannot afford the repercussions of our people sympathizing with him."

"Even if that doesn't convince them, the bitch's true identity will help."

"What could you mean by that? Is the whore not really a bounty hunter from the false crown?"

"She is and yet she is worse than that…"

Gwyn relaxed her grip as the memory and the voices faded and Logan took a moment to extract his fangs from her neck, lapping at the puncture holes so they closed instantly. Gwyn was old enough that they would have healed nearly as quick, but the king was not in a mood to be reminded of that.

"What did she mean that you are more than a bounty hunter?" Logan was still as a windless night and his voice was even. He was doing a remarkable job hiding his anger, but Gwyn felt as it radiated from him and wrapped around her until it was nearly suffocating.

"I have not lied to you, Logan, but I did not tell you the full truth either. I was recruited to be in the King of King's royal guard. I was trained by the best in his regime and in the end I was given the dishonor of being placed in the bounty hunter's barracks instead of by the King's side."

"The king? Not your king?" Logan was smart and had understood her words and their meaning. She could still salvage this mission if he thought she was not quite as loyal to the empire as originally believed.

"How could he be my king after he tossed me aside without reason? You said yourself that you have heard of my reputation. My skills and accomplishments make most soldiers look like little puppets and yet I was left to rot in the barracks while my brothers and sisters who had trained with me still remain by the king's side." Gwyn channeled all the bitter feelings that had consumed her when she was first assigned the bounty hunter job in the hopes that Logan would not see past the half truth to find the lie.

"Indeed." He was drawing into himself and Gwyn knew that she had lost his attention for the night. As if responding to that very thought, Logan moved to pick her up and off his lap, gently putting her into his now vacant chair before standing. "I have things to attend to. This is troubling news and I fear what my paranoid wife might do should she continue to orchestrate this farce any longer."

"You said you would stay." Gwyn pouted. There was no way for her to control the happenings outside her cell and she could not guess at what Longan might do now. The thought was terrifying.

"I know, and I am not angry with you, please do not mistake me. I will be back, I promise." The king leaned down to give her a parting kiss almost as an afterthought. She missed the connection they had just shared. He had never treated her so kindly before then. For the first time, it felt as if he was leaving behind a true lover and not a mark. When had that shift happened?

"I understand, but please don't leave me too long this time. I grow worried what Cassandra might do in your absence."

"You needn't worry about her, my dear, I will take care of everything." With those words, Logan left her cell.

A draft from the main castle seeped in when the heavy doors that separated the dungeons from the main castle were opened and Gwyn found herself shivering despite her immunity to temperature shifts. She had to trust that she had done the right thing. She had to believe that Logan would return and she would be one step closer to getting free. If only the repressive feeling of doubt in her chest could be ebbed away by positive thoughts.

NATALYA

Since arriving at Lunaries, Natalya had learned to take the constant changes in her environment in stride. She had, until their banishment from Ash, lived a very strict routine under her father's careful guidance. Having to adjust to a new life in Sylvine had seemed an impossible task and upon arriving in a completely different world, Natalya had thought that she would never learn to adapt. Of course she had been wrong on both fronts. Becoming comfortable on Rosewood Farm had been possible due to Emeline's kind nature. Knowing that Emeline needed her in this foreign land made her prioritize her anxiety and before she knew it, the transition was effortless. She had come to enjoy having scheduled classes as well as training and time with Cohen in the gardens. She also enjoyed the small freedoms she had been granted since she had announced that Lunaries would be her home. Now that it was obvious that she could be trusted, she no longer found a companion assigned to her at all hours. She could wander about the castle freely and found that the Lunarian people were warm and welcoming despite the fact that she was a stranger joining their ranks. She had grown accustomed to the Lords and Ladies even, though she did not yet know how to feel about becoming part of the royal party.

When she had walked into her lesson and realized that they had a different instructor than she had anticipated she let the startling change go without the normal anxieties. Normally Nirosh or Cohen would teach them and on a few occasions, Reagan would have the time to school them, but at the odd times when the House needed their royal court, Holland was there to take over. She was petite, smaller even than Natalya, and yet the strength she possessed was something to respect and fear. She was one of the guards-women that was assigned to Reagan's personal guard and was also the next in line to take over for Darius, should the need ever arise. She had taught them once before and Natalya had really enjoyed her lesson.

"Today we are going to talk about etiquette. There are going to be a few things that might seem odd to you at first, but there are reasons for our practices." Holland began the lesson. The boys who were normally with them were not in attendance since they had grown up in and around the House and were already accustomed to the manners expected of them. Emeline and Natalya sat in on this lesson as neither had any knowledge of vampires much less their customs before their unfortunate encounter with the rogue who had turned Emeline.

"There is a lot to cover, but we are going start with something simple. As you already know, vampires feed on blood. It is against our laws to draw blood from an unwilling human, this of course is common courtesy. It is also seen as in poor taste to drink blood straight from the source. In this case, the source is in reference to the donor. In polite society, a willing human donor would donate their blood to a bank where it would be stored until a vampire was ready to feed. In some special circumstances a vampire will have a designated donor. They might choose their source due to a bond between the two. Also some vampires will have a preference to a donor due to the taste of their blood. Even in these cases they will have the donor bleed into a cup before consuming their meal."

Emeline was dutifully taking notes as always, but Natalya was simply listening to the lecture. She wondered why it was so against the rules to drink from a source, but Emeline didn't seem to find the practice questionable and so she let it go. There would be time later to ask Cohen who would undoubtedly answer all of her questions without tiring. The rest of the lesson passed in the same fashion, Holland continued to explain different rules that were not necessarily laws, but more unspoken expectations and Natalya found herself excited for the end of the lesson. It wasn't nearly as interesting as history or practical trainings.

"You are doing splendid, Emeline. And you Natalya, you are taking to our people's history quickly. You will make a fine vampire." Holland praised them as they wrapped up their lessons for the night.

"Thank you, Lady Holland." Emeline curtsied with a grace that Natalya only hoped would come to her with the bite. She was more than able to handle her body when she practiced or fought, but there was something captivating in the way that Emeline and the rest of the vampires moved that she envied.

"It is just Holly, here Emeline." There was laughter behind her pretty green eyes, born from her telling the girl the very same thing since she had first met them.

"Yes, thank you Holly." Natalya smiled gratefully, not bothering to try and curtsy less she made a fool of herself.

"You are well on your way to your rebirth, the court is excited to invite you to our ranks." The words were meant to fill her with cheer and yet Natalya only felt uncertainty well beneath her skin. "I for one cannot wait for the day."

"But wait we must," Cohen's warm voice startled the girl and she was saved from the unwanted praise. She instantly felt at ease as the Lord moved into the room. "Miss Natalya, a word?"

"Yes, m'lord." Natalya hardly hid the joy from her voice as she did her best to politely curtsy to her teacher, only faltering slightly before threading her hand through the offered arm.

They strode from the room toward the gardens and to their favorite spot. Despite not being one of the royal class Natalya had found the secluded gardens to be a second home. Cohen was quieter than she was accustomed to and she let the silence envelope them until they were sitting beneath the tree that she had come to think of as their own. He drew her body into his, cradling her against his side with a strong arm pressing her to his side. It was not unusual for them to sit together in such fashion yet this time the action seemed more intimate than before.

"Are you having second thoughts about taking the bite? I heard your displeasure at Lady Holland's' words." The words sounded like screams after the silence and Natalya felt her heart quicken and the air stolen from her lungs.

"It's not the bite I'm afraid of."

"Then what is it you fear?" Cohen turned to face her, forcing her chin up with a finger until she was looking him in the eyes.

"When I take the bite, after my lessons are over, you will have no reason to spend time with me. You will return to your duties and then where will I be?" She was horrified when she felt hot tears slide down her cheek, but the thought of losing this time with Cohen was enough for her to forget her pride.

"Oh, Natalya, you silly girl." Cohen smothered her fears with one of his kind smiles. He rid her of her tears, using both arms to pull her into his chest completely. "You are important to me, not just because you are taking the lessons and taking the bite. I've known since I first met you that there was something special about you that I would never be able to let go. It's rather selfish of me to take your time like I do, but I would not stop just because you no longer need my help."

"What do you mean, something special about me?" Natalya should feel ashamed at how openly she begged for praise, but being with Cohen always made her mind foggy and she often forgot herself.

"You are brave in the face of fear. You stood up for your friend against all odds and were able to work through your perceptions of my people to make sure she was safe. You are a remarkable girl and I would be an idiot to walk away from that because of something as simple as you learning everything I have to teach you. Besides, taking the bite does not mean the training ends. We still need to find a place for you in the castle, a job if you will, so you needn't worry about how to fill your days."

Natalya let the words sink in as she pushed deeper into his embrace. She was safe there with him and it was obvious that whatever it was that she felt for him he felt the same. She would not lose this thing between them after her lessons were complete and the relief was enough to make a fresh wave of tears burst from her eyes. For his part, Cohen continued to hold her and maintained his silence, simply being a comforting presence.

"Thank you." Natalya spoke again when she was sure she could without crying once more. Cohen merely smiled, letting her go to sit back against the tree and soak in the moonlight. Natalya missed his presence immediately and moved to relax back into him again. "Where will I sleep after I take the bite?"

"In the same chambers you currently reside, if you wish. We did not move you closer to us as a punishment; we wanted you to feel that you could come to us night or day if necessary. You will truly be part of the royal party with Queen Reagan's bite and it would still be appropriate for you to reside within the Queen's tower."

"And what of Emeline? She told me she was nearer the servant's quarters. Is there nothing that can be done for her? It is not her fault she was turned by a rogue."

"This is true. It is by the rules of our people, but not necessarily the way that our Queen wishes to rule. You might have noticed that our Queen fears not the wrath of the Crown and we, in many ways, live apart from their rule, but things such as classist ideals are hard to break. We are a fairly young House, though Lunaries has existed as long as Faegon, the people here are younger than most and yet they still believe in the social system enforced from the Elders."

"Why are the vampires here so young? Lord Nirosh seems to be the oldest person here."

"He is. He is all that is left of the old Lunaries, but I believe this is a subject best left for your history lessons." Cohen obviously did not want to speak of the past, but Natalya could not help her curiosity. No one ever mentioned the time before Reagan had taken the crown, it was almost as if that time was a dark pit that no one wanted to fall back into.

"I very much doubt we will ever cover the topic. Lord Nirosh is the only one I have ever heard allude to that time and even then he does not speak so willingly." Natalya chose not to mention her dream-memory to Cohen. If their Queen had seen it best not to tell him of her gift then Natalya was not one to go against her wishes. She knew very little about the time before their Queen and from what she saw in that memory they were not the best of times to have lived through.

"Queen Reagan will teach you, if she deems it necessary. I regret that I must part from you now, however." Cohen moved to stand and Natalya slipped her hands around his arm to keep him in place.

Panic welled in Natalya's chest. She had never meant for her curiosity to drive Cohen away. It always seemed that he was one of the few who accepted her tireless questions with a smile and did his best to answer them to her satisfaction. She could not push him away. "Was it what I said?"

"No, my sweet girl. Fear not, I am merely hungry." Natalya did not let go, confused by his rush.

"Why can you not take my blood?" Natalya could not understand how he hadn't seen such an obvious solution, himself.

"For starters there is no vessel for you to bleed into," Cohen said, his tone halting and unlike his normally friendly demeanor. Natalya should have taken it as a hint and stopped her questions, but she found she could not help herself.

"That shouldn't be a problem, you can drink directly from me. I do not mind." For a moment, Cohen's eyes began to glow, the tips of his fangs just present over his lip. The look went as quickly as it came and he gently removed himself from her grasp.

"You know not of what you offer. In your lessons you have learned that we drink from blood banks or animals, it would not be proper"

"That does not bother me," Natalya insisted. "I do not understand the negative connotation."

"I am truly sorry, Natalya, but I must go." Cohen pulled away with more force. "I have never made habit of taking blood straight from a human and I do not wish to start with you, and just before you take the bite yourself. I promise I will come for you later and we can continue our talk?" He must have seen the hurt look in her eyes because even though she did not respond, he knew he would not be seeing her again that night. "I see, I mean no offense, Miss Natalya, perhaps when you become one of us you will understand."

He left her there alone to sit with her anger and fear. She could not understand how he could so easily turn away the gift of her blood when it was something that she offered less easily and only to him. It hurt to know that he did not care for her as much as she originally thought. She knew that many vampires, especially those of the royal class, would only take their blood from a specific human donor. She had hoped that Cohen would take her as his donor while she still had human blood to give, but it would seem that he preferred another.

It made no sense, but Natalya was mad at the thought of Cohen with another woman. They had nearly just met, considering Cohen's age for he was certainly much older than she, but it made her blood boil to think of another sharing his affection and even possibly his bed. Since she had come to Lunaries he never gave any indication that he was involved in a relationship. It didn't seem possible with how much time he spent with the Council and also with training her and the others. The rest of his free time was spent with her, there didn't seem like there would be enough time in the night for him to be with another. So that meant that he refused her, not because of another woman claiming his heart, but because he had his heart to give and he did not deem Natalya worthy. That angered her even more.

So consumed by her thoughts, it took Natalya by surprise when she found herself standing at the door of her chambers. Many of the humans would be taking their meal in the dining hall and yet she felt too sick and raw to consume anything. She pushed her door open with much more force than was necessary and was surprised to find Freya hard at work to tidy her room.

"Beggin' your pardon Miss, I did not expect you for some time." Natalya waved off her apology and sluggishly made her way to her bed, sinking into the mattress and burying her face into the pillows. "What's the matter, Miss Natalya?" The bed dipped with her handmaiden's weight and soon small hands carded through her short hair. It felt wonderful and Natalya took a moment to melt into the touch before answering.

"Cohen hates me." She knew she sounded like a petulant child, but she could not help it. When it came to Cohen all her senses seemed to leave her and she was left fawning over him like all the girls in her village that she had scoffed at.

"That's absurd. Lord Cohen adores you. What happened, maybe I can help you understand." Freya moved until she was lying beside her, drawing Natalya's face out of her pillows and onto her stomach. Natalya lay in that position in silence, until a gentle tap on her forehead reminded her that the girl was waiting for her response.

"Cohen left me in the gardens to go take blood."

"I'm sorry, I'm not sure I understand the problem." Freya said gently and her careful handling of the situation made Natalya both ashamed by her emotions and annoyed with the girl for babying her.

"I offered him my blood and he turned me down as if I didn't understand the connotations. I know that human blood is a gift, but I am willing to give it to him!"

"Oh dear, okay. You must have gone over this in your classes already, but I'm sure Holland grazed over the details, she is wonderful, but she does often overlook the more important facts. To them, it seems obvious, but they forget that their customs are new to you and other humans who did not grow up around them. There are no laws that state that a vampire cannot take blood from a human, this is true, but it is seen as taboo. You see, when a vampire bites and drinks they have a specific aphrodisiac that they give off, essentially they bring pleasure to their host which dulls the natural panic one might feel if their very life force was being drawn from them. The aphrodisiac is addictive, or so I've heard, and it often leads to a twisted and dependent relationship between the human and the vampire. While this may be a more common practice in the villages and outside the castle walls, it would not do to have a member of the royal party to be seen in an illicit relationship with a human, especially one who will be taking the bite soon."

"Wait, if he were to take blood from me, from my body, it would insinuate a sexual relationship?" This was the first that Natalya had ever heard of it. Holland certainly had not mentioned such things in their lessons earlier in the night. Suddenly Cohen's reaction, which seemed odd and exaggerated before seemed to make at least a bit more sense.

"Exactly. Do you understand now why Cohen could not take blood from you?" Freya looked at her with earnest eyes and Natalya felt that she had to agree even if it wasn't true, if only to put her handmaiden at ease.

"Yes, I do." Natalya wasn't sure that she was ready for a sexual relationship with anyone, though she was technically of marrying age. She wondered if Cohen was hesitant because she was human and much younger, or if it was his position as the heir to the throne that stopped him from succumbing to the temptation that she had offered him. She dated not think it was because he did not want that type of relationship with her. She was not blind, she saw the way he looked at her when she had offered.

"Good. Now you must be starving. Rest a bit and I will fetch you your supper." Freya helped her rearrange the bedding until Natalya was comfortably nestled in her bed and left quietly for the kitchens.

Only in the security of her empty room would Natalya allow herself to be honest about the news she had just received. She understood why Cohen refused her blood now. He had appearances to keep up of course. He hadn't seemed unwilling if the change of his eyes had meant anything. If he had not been the Queen's right hand was it possible that he would have given in to his urges and taken her blood right there? Natalya knew that she wanted him to, even if that meant entering a more intimate relationship with the man. She might not be sure if she was ready for such a thing, but she had no doubt in her mind that when she was it would be with Cohen that she wished to pursue intimacy. He made her feel safe in a way that she had never allowed another person to make her feel. Not even her betrothed, Edward, had managed to become so close to her and she had known him since they were children. The only person whom had ever been close to was her father and Natalya was not entirely sure she had every truly felt safe while in his presence. She knew that he meant well, but even when he was trying to make her feel safe she had always known that she would have to rely on her own skills, should the occasion call for it. Cohen made her feel like she could relax without worrying about the consequences.

It should worry Natalya that she felt so strongly for him in such a short time. She had barely known him for long, just three months, but there was something about him that she could never quite get out of her head. Every time she left his side she wanted to be back with him. It *should* scare her, but instead it only fueled her desire to be with him even more. For the first time in her life she felt that there was someone with which she would happily spend the rest of her days. She hadn't even felt that way about

Edward, though she had never expected to.. She had always accepted that she would need to marry due to her duty to her family, and in recent years as a reason to escape her father. Since coming to Lunaries it had been freeing to know that she didn't have to marry someone just because she needed to foster a good connection for her family. She hadn't anticipated having feelings for someone and yet here she was, pining after a man much older and stronger than she. It might have felt constricting, having these emotions, but instead it felt gratifying. She wanted to be with Cohen for selfish reasons fueled by her emotions and not based on anyone else's needs. The only thing that seemed to stand in the way of her feelings for the vampire was the differences of race and soon that would no longer be an obstacle. Of course, he would have to reciprocate her feelings, but she knew that if he didn't yet that in time she would be able to show him how.

Satisfied that Cohen did not in fact hate her, Natalya was able to finally put her worries to rest. She closed her eyes and remembered the heat she had seen in Cohen's eyes when she had offered her blood to him. She was confident that he wanted her. He had to, he had very nearly taken her blood and had only kept himself from doing so by leaving her side. She wondered what he might have said to her after, if she had allowed him to seek her out after feeding, but Natalya was glad she had dissuaded him. Hopefully that would make him reconsider her offer. She had to show him that she was not a clueless little girl and that she knew exactly what she wanted. She wanted him and she would be damned if she didn't get him.

CODY

The forest was silent. It was as if a spell had been placed over the land. It seemed impossible that there were no animals about, scavenging for food to store before the impending winter. Even the wind seemed barred from the uneven path that the pair crossed. The hunter was not sure he had ever felt the large, boisterous forest so still. It unsettled Cody and yet he knew that he had to push on. He was lost and he felt ashamed knowing so. He was meant to be a skilled hunter whose primary hunting grounds were the very forest that he and his captive turned escape partner were wondering. They were farther east than he and Gwyn would normally travel and that did not help. By his rough calculations, Cody was sure that they were on the far edge of House Adrastos' land, but he couldn't be sure. For the first time since his childhood every tree looked the same. The snarled trunks should have appeared unique and yet Cody was sure he had seen the grouping of trees at least twice before. Even the leaves that decorated the forest floor seemed to be in patterns that the hunter had encountered recently. The canopy overhead blocked out nearly all of the sunlight, which was an advantage to Decker, but meant that Cody needed to be creative about finding his bearings.

Even if he had the sun to guide him, Cody wasn't sure how much good it would do. Between the lack of food and rest, he knew his body was quickly approaching its limit. The rain storm had brought with it a persistent cough that he hadn't been able to shake and he knew Decker had been watching him carefully, though he had yet to comment.

The two had actually spoken very little since the storm that had brought their journey to a crashing halt and the passage through Faegon's territory had come and gone without any other incidents. Before long they would be in no man's territory. It wouldn't be safe to travel the gray ares between the house of warriors and House Lunaries, but there was little choice. They would have to pass through it to get to their final destination, but Cody wasn't certain if they were still going in the right direction. East would have been easier to track if he could actually see the sky, but moving in the open sunlight would bring on a whole new bout of problems, ones that they could not risk.

"We're lost." Decker commented more to himself than to Cody. Since he had done his best to keep Cody from getting stuck out in the rain, he had become more agreeable. He even allowed Cody to take the lead without any complaints and took directions without arguing. "We should stop for a rest and to catch our bearings. We're both tired and I think I've seen this tree before."

"Are you sure? At this point all of the trees look the same." Cody groused, frustrated both with himself and with their timing. They should have reached Lunaries already and he was starting to lose hope that they would make it at all.

"I'm sure I know this part of the forest better than you do." Decker pointed out simply. In the past it might have been a taunt or even an excuse for the rogue to pick a fight, but Cody knew that the rogue was trying to be helpful. Still, the hunter was tired and the mind numbing repetition of walking, night in and night out, made him irritable.

"I used to live near the forest. I grew up climbing these trees." The comeback sounded pathetic even to his ears.

"If I didn't know better I would say you were looking to fight with me." A bit of the old Decker came out then and it seemed that they were about to fall back into the annoying banter of cutting remarks and underhanded insults. This time, however, it would be entirely Cody's own fault. That did nothing to calm the uncharacteristic irritability that was stewing in Cody's mind.

"Good thing you don't know better." Cody pushed his body further. He knew that they needed to stop and rest, but doing so would be admitting that they were truly lost and he couldn't bring himself to do that. Cody felt a hand on his arm and he spun around to be met with sharp violet eyes.

"Come on, I think I know you well enough by now to know that you need to stop and rest. We can fight over nothing if it would help pass the time, but I'm not going to let that get in the way of making sure you are okay." The words were sincere and Cody was sure that he meant it even if he wasn't sure how much empathy Decker was capable of. The knowledge that he could recall such a deep emotion, for one who seemed too far gone for something so human, was overwhelming to Cody. He shook the rogue's hand off of his shoulder, ignoring the growing feeling of home he was beginning to associate with the man. "Don't believe me if you don't want to, but I see no reason for you to make yourself sick. If we are smart, we can make it to Lunaries within a few moon's turns. We are well beyond

Faegon's grasp out here. Besides, you have saved me many times now and that is not something that I take lightly."

Cody really did need to stop and rest. He turned to face Decker, trying to process the words he was sure he had heard and the movement caused his vision to swim. Decker's words caused an onslaught of emotions that were contributing to his worsening vision and he refused to waste more energy trying to categorize them. He felt as his body swayed and he began to fall to the ground. This was surely not the first time he had involuntarily fell while in Decker's presence, though this was the first time he was prepared for the strong arms to catch him. Even prepared for the rogue to keep him from harm's way, he was nearly knocked breathless when strong arms wrapped around him and pulled him against an equally strong chest. It was clearly his delirium that caused his body to relax into the now familiar embrace. He was not in his right mind and that was why he felt safer in these arms, there could be no other explanation.

"I told you we needed to stop, honestly." Decker's voice was near chiding. "Rest and food is what you need, come on."

"Can't move," Cody complained, leaning into him further, accepting that he had pushed his body to its limit and there was no going on from there.

"Don't pass out on me now, Cody Gilhart! Don't you dare leave me!" The panic in Decker's voice seeped into Cody's pores and further clouded his already fading mind.

I don't want to leave you. Decker, please make it stop. The cold arms seemed to pull him deeper into the abyss. Suddenly the thought of fighting to stay awake held no appeal. He had spent the better part of two weeks fighting against his body to put as much distance between them and Faegon and it was finally time for him to give in. *Maybe I could just rest a moment and when I wake we can continue.*

There was a fire crackling nearby when Cody woke up. The smell of burning wood was heavenly and he was reluctant to open his eyes and face the world around him. He wondered if he might be able to rest a bit longer, but he knew that they were still far from safety without knowing where he was, he could not rest. Slowly he began to open his eyes, blinking until his surroundings came into focus. The shadows from the flames licked against the uneven stone walls and it took Cody a full minute to realize that he was in a cave. The floor below him was hard and cold, though the packed dirt made a better bed than the rocks would have. His nose was clogged with the smell of moss and dying grass, which seemed to be haphazardly woven and thrown over his body. He scanned the cave once more before his eyes landed on Decker who was sitting beside him, opposite of the fire.

"You need to stop passing out on me, it's no less terrify every time." The vampire was staring in the fire, as if looking at Cody would be admitting weakness. Cody nodded at first before realizing that the man could not see it.

"I'm sorry." His throat hurt as soon as he spoke his first words. Speaking had obviously been a mistake and he was left in a fit of dry hacking coughs. Suddenly, Decker was in his line of vision, hovering far closer into his personal space than Cody anticipated. His mind was still sluggish, not quite recovered from passing out, and his body reacted to the intrusion by overcompensating and he reeled back, instantly feeling both dizzy and nauseous. It took a moment for him to realize that Decker was offering him water from a rock, chiseled into a makeshift cup. The bounty hunter drank greedily, not at all embarrassed when some of the water dribbled down his chin.

"If you drink it too fast you will be sick," Decker chided before pulling the rock back, giving him a critical look.

"Thank you." Cody was careful to whisper the words, mindful of his sore throat.

Decker regarded him for a moment before nodding, though it seemed that the motion was more for his own benefit. Satisfied that Cody wasn't about to die on him, the vampire moved back to give him space. When he spoke again it was entirely off topic and Cody found himself struggling to keep up.

"I used to weave myself blankets out of whatever I could find, back when I was human. I'm surprised I still know how to." Decker was sitting against the wall again the distance in stark contrast with the compassion with which he freely gave the hunter. The words made no sense and yet Cody felt that he could quench his thirst from them. Cody was rather tired of being weak and relying on Decker to care for him, but it seemed that each time it happened the vampire warmed to him a bit more.

"I'm glad you do." Somehow the statement seemed to say too much and too little. He felt both stifled and exposed, but Decker seemed not to notice his sudden discomfort.

"As am I. Rest now, I'm going to see if I still remember how to cook. Otherwise you'll be having raw rabbit for supper."

Cody missed his companion as soon as he stood and moved toward the fire and promised meal. Cody wanted to call out to him to ask to be moved toward the warmth, but he didn't. He didn't know if he wanted to be nearer to the fire or to the vampire and not knowing his own desires was not something that Cody was familiar with. Living in the forest with Gwyn left little room for Cody to be unsure of anything. He relied on his instincts to keep himself and his partner safe, but ever since he failed Gwyn, Cody felt as if he didn't even know himself anymore. If he couldn't keep her safe than how could he trust his instinct to keep himself safe?

"I can hear you thinking from here. If you keep that up you'll hurt yourself further, then where will we be?" It was a familiar taunt. Cody didn't need to look up to see the smirk on the vampire's face. He'd already grown so use to him that he could read his emotions through his words. "I don't care if you share, but maybe talking will help."

"I don't know if I can talk to you about this," Cody spoke honestly. He didn't realize how the words might sound, but the look of hurt on Decker's face made it clear that he had made a mistake.

"I know that asking you to trust me will never work, but I thought that after all we've been through you might learn to trust me even a little."

"I do trust you," Cody whispered, not sure what else to say. It was true that he trusted the vampire, more than he had ever expected that he could, but he was upset because of the feelings that he was starting to have for him. He couldn't possibly talk to Decker about it when he was the problem.

"It doesn't seem like it, but I suppose it doesn't really matter." It was obvious that Decker did not want to be having this conversation and, even as he spoke, it felt like he was trying to back out of the impending confrontation. Neither of them were comfortable talking about their emotions and the rogue clearly regretted bring it up.

"It does matter," Cody reasoned, moving to sit up so he could look the rogue in the eye. He hoped that he might see the sincerity he was trying to portray and allow Cody a graceful out so he might end this conversation with at least some of his pride intact. "I do trust you, but right now I'm not sure how I can put my worries into words."

"You could try."

"I could, yes, but when they involve you I'm afraid you're not the best person to have this discussion with," Cody explained, frustrated.

"Your worries involve me? How? I am abiding by your rules, I have kept you from further injury and from falling ill. I haven't done a single thing to make you feel uncomfortable and I am still here. How could this be about me?" The darkness in the rogue's eyes hurt Cody, knowing he had put it there.

"I know you've done all those things! I'm upset because you have exceeded all of my expectations and I'm not sure how that should make me feel! I should hate you because you're a rogue and yet I find that you are doing exactly as you said. You haven't left me, you have done more than you needed to in order to see to my safety and health and I know it's not just because I am your only chance at freedom! I could live with all of this if it wasn't causing me to develop confusing feelings about you!" Cody felt much better having gotten his thoughts off his chest, but the confusion on Decker's face sobered him quickly.

"Feelings? What do you mean by that?" The Decker from before might have asked him to bait him further, but Cody knew that this version of the rogue before him wasn't the same man.

"Please, don't make me say it."

"Why? Are you ashamed because I am a vampire? Is it because I'm a rogue?"

The question lingered between them and Cody hung his head.

"You can finish cooking your own meal then." Decker threw down the stick he was using as a poker and effortlessly jumped to his feet. He was already out of the cave by the time Cody was able to scramble to his sore feet.

"Wait! Where are you going?" Cody stumbled to go after him, but he was still weak and he knew that he wouldn't be able to keep up with the vampire.

"Hunting. It's about time I find some prey. Bigots' blood tastes horrid." Decker shot him one more disparaging look before melting into the darkness of Mordin Forest.

Cody waited for Decker to be far enough out of earshot before giving a swift kick to the nearest rock. He regretted the action as pain seared through him and he crumpled to the hard, cold ground. Decker hadn't been wrong. He had grown up being taught that relationships between humans and vampires were forbidden. It had more to do with the fact that a vampire could accidentally bleed their lover dry in the heat of passion and thus it was considered dangerous to mix feeding with pleasure. Cody might have been able to overlook that fact. He was strong willed and trained in ways that most humans were not. Had she ever been interested in him, there would have been a time that Cody would have agreed to an intimate relationship with Gwyn, but the opportunity had never arisen. Gwyn would never have been interested in him and in the end Cody was glad that they had kept things professional between them. Decker was right about his being a rogue bothering Cody. There was no sense lying to himself about it. He would have to find a way to sort out his confused mind and find a way to bring the almost friendly atmosphere back between them. Lying on the ground in the mouth of the cave wasn't going to do him any good, however. Mad at himself more than anything, he pulled himself closer to the fire and his overcooked rabbit. Even with its near-charcoaled skin, it smelled wonderful and the hunter knew he would have to apologize to Decker when he returned.

It seemed the moss blanket served a dual purpose and Cody sat on it while licking the grease from his fingers. He always preferred eating in the wild to the fancy dinners that Gwyn would force him to accompany her to at the castle. She hated the formalities even more than he did, but when you were invited to sit with nobles you did not refuse. Here, with no one watching, Cody greedily cracked the rabbit bones, reveling in the hot meat as it hit his tongue. It felt as if it had been a lifetime since he had hot food and he devoured it like an animal.

When he was through, his food sitting happily in his stomach, a thought occurred to him. What if Decker did not return? Despite his own earlier statement, Decker did not actually need him. He was out hunting for food and if he still believed in the ways of the rogues then he would not need Cody for redemption. Cassandra might have put a bounty on his head, but he could easily join up in another rogue camp. There were hundreds of them hidden in the forest and despite what she might think, the queen of the false House Rayne did not speak for all of them. Even if that didn't work he could even continue to live alone. It would be harder with both Faegon and Rayne looking for him, but he believed Decker could outwit them and stay undetected if it was truly his wish. The thought made his food roll in his stomach. He would have to find Decker himself, and soon, but he wasn't in any state to wander Mordin Forest alone.

Loud footsteps near the mouth of the cave caught Cody's attention instantly. Before he could account for his own actions he was on his feet and reaching for the nearest weapon, which happened to be a stick from the cook fire. Decker's hunched figure flew by him in a blur, shoving the few supplies they had into their poorly constructed pack.

"Put that down you fool! It will do nothing against them!" Decker shouted as he finally slowed enough so that Cody could clearly see his movements.

"Who? What is happening?" Cody tossed the stick back into the fire and moved to help the vampire, their earlier fight forgotten.

"Vampires, I saw them while I was heading back, they might have seen me, I can't be sure." Decker seemed satisfied that he had everything that they needed before pulling Cody toward the mouth of the cave.

"Vampires? What house?" Cody pulled back, he was no match for the vampire in his current condition and he doubted that he could talk their way out of a confrontation. Decker turned to look at him fully, his eyes their sickly shade of purple indicating to Cody that there was no more time to reason with the vampire.

"Does it look like it matters? We have to go. Your humanity will cost us this time. If you were a vampire we would not be in this mess."

"I'm sorry."

"If we survive this then we are having a conversation about what just happened, for now I accept your apology. Right now we run."

Cody was too stunned by Decker's words to argue and he allowed himself to be dragged from the cave. It took him longer than he would care to admit to get his footing and begin to run. The cave wasn't very deep and they were at its mouth before long. There, they were greeted with steep stones that were haphazardly placed like steps. Cody hardly had the time to consider that Decker had carried his unconscious body up the same, treacherous terrain, before the same vampire was pulling him down the makeshift path. The steps wound in a circle, until they reached the base of the small cliff. There were large rocks at the base, hiding them and the path, almost a if they had been deliberately placed there. He had no idea where they were and he had to rely solely on his companion for direction. Keeping pace with Decker was excruciating. The vampire still needed to pull him along, but he did his best to keep up. Even over his own labored breathing, Cody could hear their pursuers. It seemed they were more focused on capturing them than they were with needing to hide their presence and Cody was thankful for all of the training Gwyn had given him. There would be no way for them to outrun the vampires, but if he was smart, Cody just might be able to fight his way out of being captured. All thoughts of fighting were stripped from Cody's mind as a blur of color swept past him and a woman seemed to materialize in front of him, forcing him to stop or to collide with her.

"Halt! In the name of Queen Quanna of the great House Adrastos! Leader of the brave and true! Pray tell, what is your business in these woods?" She was pretty, too pretty to look like much of a fighter, but Cody knew better than to judge a vampire by their looks. Her hair was pulled into an elegant knot on the top of her head. Her skin was darker than most vampires Cody had seen before and it took her exposed fangs and glowing green eyes to confirm her race.

"We will tell you our purpose when you tell us yours." Decker spoke through his fangs, not bothering to back down from the obvious threat. Cody could count at least four other vampires surrounding them and he knew to count on at least half a dozen more just out of his sight in the trees. They were outnumbered.

"Careful, rogue. I would separate your head from your shoulders for your insolence, but I have my orders." The pretty vampire spoke to Decker only, ignoring Cody despite the fact that he had very nearly slammed into her moments before.

"And those are?" Cody knew that as soon as they admitted defeat and willingly followed this woman all opportunities for answers would be lost.

"To take the rogue who consorts with the rogue Logan and whatever companions he might keep to our Queen." Her inhuman green eyes fell on him then and Cody felt the disgust in her sneer like a slap.

"He's not my companion, he's a bounty hunter sent to take me to Faegon." Decker was attempting to inch forward to stand before Cody, offering him what little cover he could.

"Your actions betray your words, rogue. Besides Faegon is due west and you are heading east. Do not take me for a fool. You seek refuge with the people of Lunaries, the betrayers. Come now and we will spare you any pain except that seen fit by the Queen." The feral glint in her eyes spoke volumes on what she wished her queen would allow her to do to them and Cody did not see a reason to test her.

"That's comforting." Decker whispered and Cody nudged him to be quiet.

"If we go with you, you will see to it that we are taken to your Queen in a humane manner. We will not be chained nor will we be imprisoned. If you will allow me, I would gladly show you my credentials as a bounty hunter for King Pa'ari and King Zentarion."

"Keep your credentials, you have my word. Guards see to it that our prisoners are not harmed. We make haste for home." The woman turned away from them and they were flanked by the other four men and women that had come out of the shadows with her.

"Aye My Lady!" The four chorused and it surprised Cody that they could even speak for how quietly they seemed to follow the woman. The vampires beside them fell into place and more slipped out of the shadows to form a ring around the two of them. Cody knew that there was no way to escape and he turned to Decker prepared to face his anger. Instead he was surprised to see the rogue calm, his face no longer changed by the bloodlust. He seemed resigned to their fate just as Cody was.

There was no way they would be able to have the conversation that Decker had promised, but Cody had already made his decision. Before meeting Decker, the vampires loyal to the Crown had simply treated him with little interest, but seeing how they were willing to resort to such cruelty at the mere sight of a rogue made him reconsider the character of the company that he had kept. He reached out slowly to take Decker's hand in his, hoping that the vampire would understand it for what it was. He wasn't doubting the feelings he had for Decker any longer, if this was the last chance he had to prove that, he was not squandering.

"If it is any consolation, I have been feeling the same way." Decker let the words hang between them, their eyes locked, before a rough shove from behind pushed them toward their new destination.

"Enough talk. Save your breath for Queen Quanna and the justice that awaits you."

The feeling of hopelessness was fast becoming a constant friend to Cody, but Decker's hand squeezing his own was like a burst of hope that he desperately needed. He couldn't afford to make an enemy of his only friend. He let the four soldiers around them guide them along, focusing instead on the hand in his own. He might have lost just about everything else in his life, but he was not going to allow anyone to take this away from him.

CLAYTON

Clayton lay back on his small cot in the tiny hut, blessedly alone. Eva was visiting one of the many women that she gossiped with, or at least that was what she'd claimed. She could be with her mysterious lord for all the vampire knew, but he found that he couldn't be bothered enough to care. He was much more interested in the scroll that lay rolled in his lap, one that he would not have been able to read if she were puttering about and looking over his shoulder. The Lady Sedalia had sent word to him, though it was not her seal in the wax. She would not be foolish enough to place her name on anything that could be confidential and possibly fall into the wrong hands. Despite this, Clayton had known exactly whom had sent him such cryptic correspondence. He opened the scroll again and reread the words for nearly the tenth time since receiving it.

My Dearest,
I fear that our time together might be coming to a close. Our shared interests are becoming
dangerous and we may need to take to Mordin Forest if we intend to see this through. I
know that you will meet me. It is with that in mind that I ask for you to leave your
reservations behind and seek me out tonight.
Yours Always

It was a code, of course. There was no one who would write sweet words to him. Their shared interests was Lord Malcolm of course and it seemed that he would be meeting someone in Mordin Forest. Clayton wished that the letter had included a time and place, but he knew that would be much too much of a risk. He did think it interesting that she asked him to leave all of his reservations behind, that particular line caught his eyes with every repeat read. He couldn't deny that he was still unsure of what he was doing, working for Lady Sedalia. He had been generously

rewarded for his first useful piece of information and he had thought to turn away then, to take his money and begin to make an honest living, but something had stopped him. Spying, no matter the justification was not what Clayton considered a good man's work and yet he had not left.

Of course he had been reminded many times that his findings could very well help stop the impending war and that seemed a noble enough reason to continue. House Namyt'tkas had trained him so he might be ready to fight for them and for their King should the time come, but if he continued his work he could assist in ending the conflict before it even started. He could save Lenore and his other friends from having to fight in a war. With that in mind, Clayton rose from the lumpy cot, stretching to work the cricks from his back before reaching for his cloak. Eva wouldn't care that he wasn't there whenever she did return. If she was with Lord Malcolm she would no doubt be back soon so her employer could slip into Mordin Forest to meet another mysterious player in this exceedingly convoluted game. Since partially overhearing the introduction of the curious Lord Wynn to Eva's employer, he had caught the man out and speaking to other characters of questionable intentions, but Eva was never with him. He was glad that the girl was staying out of most of the trouble, he shuddered to think what horrors might befall her if she became tangled in this mess.

Clayton made his way out of the hut bundled in his cloak with the rags facing out, covering the nicer side so not to attract unwanted attention. With the money he had been paid, he had managed to purchase new shoes and a few articles of clothing, but he had been sure to buy cheaper fabrics and dull colors to blend in with the rest of his fellows in the slums. He carried a very minimal amount of coins with him for fear of being robbed while the rest of the money was hidden in Mordin Forest not very far from the city gates. The space was as safe as he could find and he had scouted many spots to be sure. He spent as much time exploring through the trees as he was allowed. Lady Sedalia's demands consumed most of his time and he hardly had any time to himself. When he was able to, he spent time exercising and training in the ways that he had learned with Lenore and the rest of their troop to keep himself in shape. He might not be a soldier any longer, but there was no sense in letting those skills go to waste. Because of his frequent jaunts through the gates in the slums, the guards didn't question as he walked up to them to be allowed out of the protection of Faegon.

"Remember to return before the gate closes for the night," One of the regular guards, Petros, said by way of greeting, as he always did and Clayton nodded.

"If you see any good game bring it in for us, yeah?" Tasia, his female counterpart teased. They were usually the ones who stood guard and they were always curious about what he did when he left the protection of the

city.

"He does not have the time to hunt, Tasia, he is meeting a lover," Petros answered in jest. His eyes were filled with mirth and Clayton was not sure if it was because he thought himself funny or that he thought Clayton having a lover was funny.

"He could have a lover inside the walls, there is no sense in going through such trouble to see someone. I told you, he is going to hunt. No one could ever be as gentle as you, not genuinely," she teased, but Clayton still heard the uncertainty in her voice.

"I would think Faegon's guards would spend more time watching over the gate than gossiping," Clayton responded as he passed, not bothering to stop and have a proper conversation with the two. Tasia's words were ludicrous, of course. She had no idea who he was or what he had been trained to be. He ignored both of their continued comments as he did every night and he passed through the thick stone wall, beyond the large heavy wood and iron doors, and into the welcoming expanse of trees. He always felt his spirit lift when he was no longer surrounded by so many people and sounds. His village had been small and training with his troop had kept him from experiencing crowds. He found Faegon's staggering population extremely overwhelming. The only common factor between his various residences was their proximity to a forest.

He always loved getting lost amongst the trees. They never asked him questions that he did not know how to answer, they never expected anything from him, but people always did. He had never felt like he belonged, no matter where he lived. Nothing ever compared to the way he felt when surrounded by wildlife. He could be quiet for hours and no one demanded to know why. There were no strange glances or hovering friends with good intentions. He had thought that Lenore had been different, that she had understood him, but he had been horribly wrong. Now he found himself tied to another woman, though she was nothing like his sweet Lenore. Working for a noble lady of the ancient House Faegon was the opposite of what he had expected for himself. With Lady Sedalia he was expected to always look immaculate as well as perform on a level that he wasn't sure was physically possible. Every meeting he was expected to have news or there would be serious consequences. In Mordin Forest there were no expectations to fail and people to disappoint.

Clayton found himself horribly tempted to run just then. He could leave this life behind him and start over. He wasn't anyone, not really, there was no reason that he couldn't live on his own in one of the five houses' outer villages. It would be safest to live on Adrastos' land or even the strange, secluded House Tryali's land as he would be known to Houses Lunaries, Faegon, and Namyt'tkas. He might never have the life he had always dreamed of, but it would be a life on his own terms and that was more than he had now.

He pushed the thoughts aside just as quickly as they had come to him. He had a job to do, one that he had committed to and he would not go against his word. His honor was all that he had left and he would be damned if he allowed his own cowardice to take that from him. He was wasting time. Shaking the thoughts from his head, Clayton pushed on. As a skilled tracker he was able to easily spot Lord Malcolm's light steps in the damp dirt. There had been rain just the day before which left the earth soft and easy to imprint upon. Luck was on his side as he carefully picked out the footprints, knowing the grooves from the man's expensive shoes by sight.

He was not disappointed in the man's own precautions and was impressed to find that he had doubled back many times to elude any unwanted companions and even his very steps seemed lighter and harder to track the father into the forest he went. Just when Clayton was beginning to feel tired, he heard the whisper of voices and his spirits rose. There was no reason to be this deep in the forest unless you were up to something foul. There were perfectly reasonable and private places to conduct your business within Faegon's walls and Clayton knew that whomever Malcolm was meeting would be connected to the depraved rogues.

In the beginning, Clayton had held out hope that Malcolm was a good man. He had thought that possibly he was trying to learn more about the rogues to report back to his King, but after the increasing number of interactions between the Lord and various shady looking characters Clayton began to lose faith. Just last week he had come across Malcolm speaking to a stern looking man who might have passed for a noble of House Faegon had he not looked extremely uncomfortable in his surroundings. Unlike Malcolm, not a single person seemed to know him or greet him with any familiarity and Clayton had been sure that someone would ask who he was and what business he had in Faegon for how inconspicuous he had made himself. That day he had heard as they spoke in vague words about the security of the castle and who was part of King Pa'ari's personal staff. It sounded mostly innocent enough, but he had been following Malcolm long enough to know that he was a very well respected man of Pa'ari's court and any information he was willing to give to the other side should be considered valuable and dangerous. He had been rewarded handsomely after that particular discovery. He had brought what seemed like damning proof that this man was working for Cassandra, but Sedalia had cautioned him not to become overly presumptuous. It would not do to act as if they had won when there was still no true proof that he was defecting to House Rayne.

Clayton pulled himself from his musing to focus on the hushed tones just a stone's throw away. He could just make out the familiar figure of his mark standing with a girl he had never seen before. She was petite, slender to the point where it seemed a good wind might take her away. Her long

brunette hair hung about her like a cloak, her own clothes very plain, sensible for travel. She wore trousers of a pitch fabric and a laced bodice of a similar fashion over a clay colored tunic. Her eyes burned a queer lilac and Clayton knew then who stood before him. It was rumored that Cassandra was one of a rear bloodline that had been graced with inhuman purple eyes. From the lands bordering the Deadlands to Lunaries it was known that the false queen turned very few of her own children and when she did it was for a good reason. Sedalia had warned him of these vampires as, should he find his path crossed with them, there would be one in particular not to be trifled with. She was called Vestera and spent more time in a state of bloodlust, proudly showing off her Sire's mark, then not. She would be the most wild and the most treacherous to have to face alone. She would indiscriminately kill for her queen, even if it was one of their own. Clayton did not enjoy the thought that his mark might be speaking with this woman that he had secretly feared.

"My Queen is very interested in the information you claim to have for her." The woman spoke with a tone the dared defiance. She leaned against the trunk of a very old looking tree, her arms folded as if she were bored. Her relaxed stance did little to fool Clayton, he knew she would be ready to attack or defend herself in a moments notice and he watched as her fingers hovered and twitched over what he could only assume were concealed weapons.

"You do not believe that I have what you seek?" Malcolm's response was cold and he seemed to be bothered very little by her posturing. "Why waste your time on me, then?"

"Because, if you do help us with the Cause then I can stand beside my Queen at the end of the carnage, a Lady of the new world. If you are lying, she just might let me tear you apart and that would be nearly just as satisfying." If she had not already had her fangs drawn, Clayton knew that she would then. She seemed the type to enjoy a bit of the dramatics. He instantly felt tired of her.

"Threatening me doesn't seem very wise."

Clayton agreed with the man, though he knew that this woman would not play by his rules. It seemed he would be stuck watching the two orally spar until they exhausted themselves and then the real work could be done. Settling down for a long wait, Clayton briefly amused himself with the hope that this interaction would at least supply him with enough information to call an end to his job. He had more than enough coin to keep him afloat and Toro's offer to join him was an open invitation. It would not be glamorous to work as a shopkeeper's assistant, but it would be honest and would fill his belly.

"It matters little what you think. You will provide us with what we seek or you will find that disappointing House Rayne is the last thing you do."

"You are nothing more than a stupid little girl if you think that your

petty words would motivate me to help you. No, I do this because I believe change needs to come about and no other ruler has the capacity to see it through."

Not at all bothered by Malcolm's words, the woman continued on as if he hadn't just insulted her intelligence. "You have given us names and loose plans on how one might sneak into the castle and have access to Pa'ari and his wife, I will admit those are helpful things, but you could have just as easily given us false plans. You could have been told to give use these instructions by the man himself. How am I to know that you really intend on taking up arms for House Rayne?"

"If my word is not enough, I am not sure what more I can do to prove it to you. If you would allow me an audience with Queen Cassandra I am sure I can convince her just how real my intentions are." The cold way the man had treated Eva and this woman seemed a thing of the past and the warm, smooth way his voice sounded then was nearly enough to convince Clayton. "It is high time that this empire is ruled by a sensible individual, someone who understands that times are changing. We cannot simply sit back and hide in our castles, behind our walls, until the end of time. The humans in the Deadlands keep entering our borders in hordes to escape the horrors that come from the mountain. We cannot sustain ourselves by protecting those miserable wretches. The humans on the other side of our borders are nearly as bad. They might not acknowledge that we exist, but what happens when they decide to push their borders further west? It won't be much longer until we are overrun by humans. This fate must be culled at all costs."

It was an impassioned speech that seemed enough to change the woman's mind.

"I might have been wrong about you," she conceded. "I will tell Queen Cassandra of my findings when I return to her side. Will you be content receiving her answer by raven? I fear there might not be the time to send out another scout."

"Time? What is happening?"

Lilac eyes watched the man critically for a moment longer than necessary. "There are other matters that my Queen must attend to. If she deems you worthy she might just include you in them."

It wasn't likely that he would learn any more tonight and Clayton knew that the conversation was nearing its end. He took his focus from the two in front of him, calculating an escape so he could return to the slums at a reasonable hour without being caught by his mark. He should have enough to report and not be chastised. If he was lucky he might even be able to meet Toro at the pub before turning in. He could just see the pride in his Lady's eyes at his newest discovery. Clayton was so enthralled by his fantasy that he was thoroughly caught off guard by sudden shouts coming from behind him. He turned to see the cause of the commotion and was shocked

to see both vampires surrounded by a crazed looking bunch.

The circle that had formed around the two was made of dirty men and women wearing pitiful rags for clothes. Clayton couldn't be sure if they were from Faegon's slums or if they were rogues, but he knew that he could not afford to be caught by them. The elder vampires currently in their sights were strong enough to fight them, but Clayton knew that he would be no match against them if more than a few deemed him important enough to bother with.

"Let us pass and no harm will come to you." Malcolm spoke first, eyeing the group wearily.

"I think we'd rather not, thank you very much," The largest of the group answered. He looked to be the healthiest of them, his eyes only slightly tinged with pink and his body slim rather than skeletal. They were a mix of humans and vampires and they all seemed to answer to him. As if to show just how much of a hive mind that they functioned on, the rest laughed and nodded along, seemingly too stupid to see the danger they were in. Even with a group of ten, well nourished and armed, they would not stand a chance against the two elder vampires.

"Who are you lot, do you know not who you stand before?" Malcolm tried again. The woman next to him remained curiously silent and seemed rather undisturbed by the unwelcome company.

"Does it matter? You're a Lord of some lofty castle. And you a Lady most likely of the same House. You both live in towers above people like us. What I am more interested in is what you might be doing so far away from your protective walls." The leader spoke in a tone that suggested that he knew he would never receive and answer and he wasn't concerned.

"State your names and alliances." Malcolm spoke, commanding respect and expecting them to listen.

"I will if you will," the leader's leer sent Clayton's skin crawling.

"I see," the woman pursed her lips, her lilac eyes narrowed. "I am Lady Vestera of House Rayne, child to Queen Cassandra of House Rayne."

All eyes fell to Malcolm and the man tensed before responding. "I am Lord Malcolm formerly of House Faegon, child to Lady Gemma of House Faegon. I am a servant of Queen Cassandra of House Rayne."

"Rogue scum." The leader spat and the murmured agreement felt like an echo in the small space.

"And you? Do you belong to a house? Do they care for you like they proclaim to?" Lady Vestera sneered.

"We are free men and woman. We answer only to ourselves. We do not put our faith in the rich that care not about the poor, but rather in their own self image." The group moved in closer as if by one mind. Clayton watched wearily, not brave enough to attempt to intervene. "I'm sure your Great House wouldn't miss you."

The free men and women descended on the nobles like a wave of

filth. From his spot, Clayton could hardly see beyond the dirt clouding the scuffling group. He could hear the screams and the impact of skin hitting skin. Petrified, Clayton sat as still as the trees, his body rooted in its place, keeping him from finding safety. He screwed his eyes tight, clasping his hands over his ears. He was suddenly transported back to when he was a child and the bigger children would pick on his only friend Karl. He would run when they came out. He would hide and cry while Karl took a massive beating and then he would hide from Karl until the boy had healed and he could look his unmarred face straight on without feeling the gnawing guilt in his soul.

It had been a joke when he left for Namyt'tkas. He hadn't been brave or honorable. He had to fight hard against his inner demons before he could face men like Urien and protect those who were weaker like Lenore. It was all for naught. He had been kicked out from his only home and made to be a second rate spy for a woman he knew little to nothing about. He would be ashamed of himself, but he was too busy allowing the panic to rage through his body that he couldn't be bothered with a second emotion.

Tell me, Clayton, was I wrong about you? I thought that you, a fallen brother of House Namyt'tkas, were wrongfully banished. I thought that I could place my trust in you as Lord Tory had been a fool to toss you aside. Tell me, Clayton, was I the fool?

Lady Sedalia's words rang in his head and spurred the man to action. He was stronger than he was before. He would not allow himself to succumb to childish habits. Slowly he forced the panic back, blinking until his heavy lids opened completely and he was faced with the same whirlwind of movement that he had been before. There was a moment when he thought he saw Lady Vestera slip out of the brawl, clothes tattered, before slinking back into the forest, but Clayton knew that it must have been a trick of the light.

A sharp cry rang out from the cloud of movement and suddenly the forest fell deathly silent. Clayton dared to stand, forcing himself to draw up to his full height so he might gain a better vantage point. There were eleven bodies scattered about the clearing. They were all cut and bruised badly and the sight made the vampire sick. The strong scent of blood wasn't even enough to whet his appetite as he watched dead, humorless eyes stare back at him. The ten men and women who had caused he ambush lay with their limbs twisted at odd angles. One notably was impaled by a large branch and nailed to one of the trees. The leader was in the middle, his claws sunk deep into the throat of Lord Malcolm. The lord lay in a heap, his fine clothes torn until the looked nearly as old as the rags on his attacker's backs. His eyes were wide, looking right at Clayton as if to accuse the boy for not coming to his aid.

Clayton could not stand there a moment longer. With unsteady legs, he did his best to banish the sight from his mind, knowing that he would have to revisit this scene to report to Lady Sedalia. He felt faint suddenly and he

leaned on the nearest tree. He could not remember the last time he'd fed and yet he found himself coughing up blood, his vision swimming as his body protested under the stress. He could not disappoint his lady by losing himself in the forest. Clayton took one last look at the carnage behind him, committing every detail to memory. He could only hope that this would be enough for his Lady. He knew then that he would take whatever coin she gave him and slip away in the night. He was not an honorable man. He had never been and he had been a fool to believe otherwise.

GWYNDOLYN

Logan had become increasingly withdrawn over the following days since Gwyn had shown him the memory. He had come back, as he had promised, but was much more reserved. All of the bravado that he had shown her before was gone and she was starting to see the real Logan for the first time. He was morose, sometimes coming to her just to lie with her, no words exchanged. Some nights he took his pleasure from her and left, almost as if he were simply acting out the motions, but mentally he was far off, just outside her reach. The only constant that Gwyn could rely on was that there were always two guards at her door. She wasn't always able to tell for certain, but she knew that one belonged to Cassandra and the other to Logan. It felt as if the couple was playing an elaborate game where Gwyn was the winning piece and neither wanted the other to have access to her without the other knowing.

Cassandra hadn't come by, of course. After her first failed attempt to pull the truth from her, she had left her well enough alone. She might have planned to have Logan seduce the desired answers from her, but it should have been obvious by now that such a plan would never be seen to fruition. Cassandra was losing the last tethers that held Logan to her and Gwyn wasn't even sure if the woman knew it.

Logan, for his part, didn't seem to care much about the ever changing world around him. Gwyn had been very patient with him, giving him time and space to come to terms with the demons that seemed to be haunting him. She knew now that he had never wanted this life. It had always been assumed by the High Council that he was in every way an equal partner of Cassandra's and thus equally as liable for the devastation that their attacks had wrought across the empire. Gwyn's findings would not only shatter that presumption, but it would also call into question just how much Logan could be held accountable for.

These questions were best left for the High Council and the King. Gwyn was not a trained tactician and she had no right to voice her opinion to anyone beyond her own subconscious. She was trained to fight for the empire and bring in information on their enemies. In rare cases she was entrusted to bring in the very enemies that sought to bring an end to the only way of life she knew, as was in the case with Decker. She had failed that mission, letting Vestera take her and leaving her human companion behind. She did not think about Cody often for she feared that if she did it would make his inevitable death too real to bare.

"You are relieved." Logan's voice brought Gwyn from her thoughts as she watched the guards, at this point accustomed to his rude dismissal, bow to their King before retreating without argument. "Gwyndolyn, my apologies. I did not mean to leave you for so long. There were things that I needed to tend to."

Gwyn hid her surprise at his words. He was smiling gently and it didn't look strained. She was curious as to why he looked so happy, but she managed to keep her questions to herself. He was in a good mood, there was no sense in ruining it. "I am just happy to see you, m'lord."

Logan swept into her room and instantly embraced her. It was so reminiscent of the days before that she could nearly be convinced that she had never told the man about the deception of his wife. "You look troubled my dear, tell me what can I do to ease your mind?"

"I am only troubled when you are not by my side. Your presence brings me all that I need to ease my fears." Gwyn was a master at telling men what they wanted to hear. She did it so often she hardly realized before the lies tumbled from her lips.

"Come now, there is no need to act with me. There is something on your mind. I was not here for you before, but I am now and I promise I will not leave you so suddenly again. You can tell me whatever it is and I promise I will fix it."

Gwyn paused weighing her options. She could not lie to the king, but she could tell partial truths. She would have to tell him something that was the least damaging to keep his attention. "I am worried about my partner. A human who was in my charge at the time that Vestera attacked me. I fear the worst has happened to him, but I have no way of truly knowing."

"A human, you say? Vestera only brought you back with her. This human, what was he to you?" Accusations were absent from his words, but he looked at her with such unbridled hurt that Gwyn wondered if he did truly care for her.

"He was like a son to me. I found him when he was but a boy and I trained him into a fine young man. I know that he could survive without me, but I was thrown unconscious before I could see what became of him." She would not hide this from Logan. He had already come to trust her and she had to be at least partially honest with him. He had told her

about his past and she had rewarded him with a half truth. This was something she could give to him and not fear the consequences.

"If he was truly like a child to you then I can understand your distress. I know not what happened to this boy, but I will do my best to find out for you." Logan held her just a touch tighter then before releasing her and moving them to sit back in her bed. "Now tell me, is that the only thing that troubles you? I know that this arrangement is less than ideal, but I still value your comfort."

Gwyn did not doubt his sincerity. "I worry about you, if we are being entirely honest. Since I showed you what I heard you've been distant. Before it seemed like you might trust me and-" She paused, allowing him to think her words had gotten ahead of her, though that was far from the truth. "Of course you needn't share with me. You are a king and I understand that you have no obligation to humor me."

"Nonsense. There is more reason to humor you, as you say, than there is to give the same attention to half of my court." Logan watched her with a critical eye. "Come here."

Gwyn crawled up her bed toward him, allowing him to pull her into his body as soon as he could reach. "What are you planning?"

If Logan thought her question was too bold he didn't say. "It seems my wife is looking to replace me with her page. She forgets that while there are many here who are loyal only to her, I have a force of my own who would defy her if I asked. She ought to be more careful, but caution has never been one of her strong suits."

"Will you challenge her? What would that mean for your house?" It seemed that her questions were beginning to hit a nerve because Logan turned her so she could look him in the eyes before speaking.

"You are awfully curious," he said while he watched her a moment more. "It has been a long time since you have left this cell, has it not? How would you like a stroll through our gardens? They aren't as lovely as the ones in Faegon, but they are a sight better than these gray walls."

Gwyn nodded, allowing him to change the subject. She had to be careful not to push him and to let him believe he remained in control. He would only give her information when he was ready and pushing him would only make turning him against Cassandra and their house harder. He was also promising her the chance to see more of the castle which would certainly be helpful if she ever hoped to escape.

"Won't the queen object if she saw me strolling through her halls?"

"You need not worry about her. She and her pet Vestera are out of the castle and the rest of her council will omit this from their report to her when bribed." Logan was entirely unconcerned and Gwyn kept her thoughts to herself.

"What will I wear? Surely you don't expect me to walk around in this." She motioned to her robe which was stretched and ripped due to his

enthusiasm. She might not care what his subjects thought, but Logan did have a reputation to keep.

"Oh yes, I nearly forgot." Logan untangled himself from her, moving to the door to her cell and disappearing for mere moments before returning with a bundle of black cloth in his hands. "I had this made for you should there come a time that we put this cell behind us. If it were up to me, you would be moved into my wing as a guest, but my wife might take offense to that."

Gwyn reached out for the cloth, holding it out until the fabric unraveled into a beautiful dress. She must have gasped because Logan was laughing quietly beside her before he was moving to disrobe her. Gwyn let him move her around until the stunning dress was draped around her body and the rags she had been wearing were left in a heap on the ground. She sorely wished there was a mirror in her cell for the first time as she wanted nothing more than to see herself. The top of the dress was held up by a single ribbon tied behind her neck, the cloth covering her breasts did little else and were she human she might be bothered by the draft as it tickled her exposed sides and back. There was another ribbon tied at her back, helping keep the dress secured on her person. There was a panel of fabric that covered her slim stomach, but left her hips well exposed. The top of the skirt was embellished with shimmering jewels and gold embroidery that looked like an alternating sun and moon pattern. The skirt itself was full and heavy, but a generous slit on both sides allowed her room to move freely and showed her legs at certain angles when she moved.

"You look stunning." Logan smiled fully for the first time since she had shared her memories with him and Gwyn felt her heart ache. This man had been through too much deceit in his life and she was just adding to it. "Come, let's tame that hair of yours and then explore the castle. I'm sure there is plenty of trouble we can find before my dear wife returns."

Gwyn felt herself be guided to one of the chairs and sat down while Logan ran his fingers through her tangled hair. He produced a comb from the small pouch that he had been carrying with the dress and he took the time to tease every knot from her hair without pulling or ripping it.

"I had a sister, when I was human, and a brother. Our mother died when we were young and she took care of us like we were her own children. On the few occasions she would allow herself to enjoy a night without us, I would help her with her hair. We were too poor for her to hire a girl to help with those sorts of things."

Gwyn felt touched that the stoic man might share something so deeply personal, but she feared that speaking now would break the spell that had fallen around them and she stayed silent. Instead she allowed him to braid her long hair, creating a crown atop her head before securing it with pins of matching suns and moons. Gwyn felt like a proper lady when Logan stepped back and admired his work.

"Thank you," Gwyn stood and took his offered arm.

"You are most welcome." Logan led them from the room and Gwyn fought the impulse to look back around her cell. She would be returning to it soon. She almost felt scared leaving the security that it held, but she was a huntress, one of the Magni Havardr, the most accomplished fighter of her age and she would not allow herself to fear a few rogues in their den.

The two left the cell behind and walked through the empty corridor that led to the dungeon's main entrance. She was the only prisoner being held here, though she knew that in the darker dungeons below there were bound to be more unfortunate souls. The guard that stood watch didn't even give them a second glance as Logan led her through, both walking with command and grace. Gwyn was sure that part of the reason she had been ignored was due to her attire. She might not be able to see the full ensemble, but she knew she would have blended in easily with the royals in Faegon in such a dress.

The part of the castle they were in was eerily silent and there seemed to be very few servants around. The ones that they did pass walked with their heads bowed, not daring to look up at Logan or bother with his companion. She saw just how easy it would be to walk freely with him when Cassandra and her ever loyal pet Vestera were away. Gwyn thought a moment for the trouble they might cause if they crossed paths with Leon, but she trusted Logan to deal with that should the situation arise. Her only goals were to map as much of the castle in her mind as possible and learn more information from Logan. Besides, if Leon caused her any trouble it would be easy and satisfying to kill the brat, if only to see the look on Cassandra's face.

Flames in sconces lit their path. The light bounced off the dark walls and were stalled by the heavy velvet curtains that hung on the walls. Unlike the ornate tapestries of House Faegon, they were plain and certainly covering real windows if the signs of sun bleaching on the edges were anything to judge by. House Rayne was once the seat of King Zentarion and in its prime it would have been the example of culture and beauty. Since it's fall, and Cassandra's assumption to the throne, it seemed that little had been done to preserve the opulence that had once been. Gwyndolyn hadn't been alive during that time, so she could only use the stories she had heard to compare to, but she was sure that this was nowhere near the way things had been when King Zentarion had called House Rayne his home.

The dark hallways led way to even more desolate surroundings as Logan led them through the ill used servant's quarters. It was a short walk from there to a partially formed archway that led outside. They walked in the light of a half formed moon down an unmarked dirt path. The trees that surrounded them still held on to their colored leaves, though the ground was decorated with orange, red and yellow. It was obvious that the grounds were not cared for as dangerous roots had grown through the

walkway, making it easy to lose one's footing. Logan expertly guided them through the maze, showing just how often he must visit this particular part of the castle.

"There is a small lake this way. Few benches have survived since the time when this garden was a focal point of the castle, but there is one just by the lake which allows for a wonderful view of the sky." Logan motioned off toward the right before taking her off of the main path. Gwyn had trusted the man thus far, there seemed little reason to stop now.

"Do you always have company when you visit here?" Gwyn tried for a casual tone, but the teasing look he sent her said she had missed her mark.

"No, I hardly ever take anyone with me this far into the garden. Why? Do you wish to be the only woman I spend my time with?"

"I just wanted to know how many people knew of this spot. It wouldn't do to be seen by half your House, now would it?"

Logan shook his head with a chuckle, but he did not answer. Instead he lead her the rest of the way in silence, until the large expanse of trees turned into a wide clearing. True to his word there was a small lake with a few lone stones lying about which may have been benches at one point. There was a single bench still intact that sat near the water and in perfect position to watch the sky. Logan sat back, gently pulling Gwyn to settle in his arms before tilting his head up as if to soak in the moon's light.

"Thank you for trusting me with this place." Gwyn smiled, taking a moment to just soak in the smells of the lake. She couldn't remember the last time she had been outside of her cell and it felt freeing to sit in the open moonlight without needing to fear if she might be caught.

"You might find this strange, but I trust very few people in my own court and yet I find trusting you is becoming easier with each passing day."

"Is it possible that it is because I am one of the few people here who does not wish to see you dead?" Gwyn asked seriously.

"Cassandra doesn't want me dead," Logan chided. "She just wants the people who are loyal to me. She can do that without killing me. Our people are of a deceiving nature. They all turned their backs on houses that they called their own once. Every single one of them chose to put down their arms for other Kings and Queens for whatever reason. I have no illusions that my people would remain mine if Cassandra really put her mind into betraying me."

Gwyn thought his easy dismissal of Cassandra and her intentions naive, but she did not respond. Kings always thought that they were right. Logan might not have been raised a royal, and he certainly had never been trained to become one, but he had the same mentality as any royal she had known. Insulting him would do her no good.

"As you say, Your Majesty."

Light footsteps and hushed words kept Logan from answering. Both vampires turned toward the path, but the trees were dense enough that they

were not able to see who was approaching. Gwyn shifted silently closer to Logan, closing her eyes to heighten her other senses. There were two sets of steps, one of a small figure and another slightly heavier, though both were being careful to be quiet. They spoke in hushed tones, but as the path wound closer to the lake, their words began to become more clear.

"You must wait until our Queen returns. Taking such rash action will not please her," Wynn's oily voice set Gwyn on edge and she shifted even closer to Logan.

"It's not rash, Cassandra herself has said that we need to rid ourselves of him. She may never have said it, but we both know that she means to kill the man before this war is over." Leon spoke with passion.

"Sh! You know not who may hear you," Wynn chided.

"Who do you fear? Logan is in the cells with his Faegon whore. He cares more for her than his own people. Not killing him seems an act of treason, does it not?"

"You are too bold for such a young childe. I would caution you to remember your place."

"I know my place, it is beside my queen. Where is yours?"

"Don't be a brat. I am loyal to *our* queen just as you are. Keep your murderous intent at bay at least until she comes home. She will want to see him dead for herself, you cannot deny her that."

The voices began to fade back into hushed whispers as the pair traveled on down the path leading back toward the castle. Gwyn waited until the whispers faded before opening her eyes to face Logan. She expected raw anger. She thought she would find blazing blue eyes and sharp fangs. Instead when she gathered the courage to look up at Logan's face she found blank acceptance. His eyes dulled in defeat and his proud shoulders sagged as he did his best to hide within himself.

"I'm sorry," Gwyn spoke as she cupped his face, hoping her touch might ground him and give him strength.

"You were right." All traces of the assured man she had come to know finally vanished. The last of his walls that she had tried so hard to break down crumbled and a sad, broken man was left in its wake.

"I am so, so sorry. I didn't want to be right." They sat in silence with Logan's face in Gwyn's shaking hands. There were no words left to be said, nothing left to be done. Reality was staring them in the face and there was no room left for Logan to deny what Cassandra intended to do with him. "What do we do now?"

"Now?" Logan sighed and pulled back from her touch. He sighed deeply once more and sat up straight, his regal mask falling back into place. All traces of the heartache and betrayal were gone and Gwyn found herself lucky to not be Logan's enemy as a hard set gaze came across his face. "Now we go to war."

REAGAN

The normally calm castle was alive with noise. True to the scout's word the messenger from House Faegon had passed through into their border bringing news of a member of Faegon's royal family arriving with word from the Crown. The castle seemed to have woken from its never-ending sleep as maids took to clearing out the empty halls. It would not do for the messenger to report back to the King of Kings that the once great house Lunaries was not ready at a moment's notice to host him or anyone from the royal party. No one from the capitol had visited them since their pardoning ceremony, but they were still one of the five great houses and preparedness was expected of them.

There were humans and vampires alike running through the halls. Everyone was doing their part to prepare for the guest. Rooms that were hardly used were being aired out and linens were being freshened from stores that Reagan wasn't even sure she had known existed. There were few humans able to give blood on such short notice, though they had no lack of willing parties. Many of their people were already weak from providing for the house as it was and those who were allowed to give more were held in high regard. The donors were tended to by Reagan and her men personally, not a single one of them wanted for anything. Nirosh was working with Emeline to insure that those who gave such a sacrifice were well fed and had proper rest between donations. While Natalya was denied the ability to donate blood due to her up and coming rebirth, she did her best to help where she could, finally showing a true willingness to be part of the House rather than just a passive member.

"Your Majesty?" Nicolette called the Queen from her thoughts.

"I'm sorry, where were we?" Reagan turned from her spot on the balcony overlooking her private gardens to face her handmaid.

"We were discussing what you wished to wear to greet our royal

visitor."

Nicolette and her husband had been in her employment since they had been very young. She had watched them grow into the incredibly wonderful and influential members of her court and she'd even had the privilege to watch their son grow. Because of their shared history, Nicolette was never afraid to be honest with her queen. In the private quarters, away from prying eyes she treated Reagan as more of an equal. Her long standing history with the Queen was never more evident than when she turned Reagan back on task. She was never shy and was always comfortable making her presence and opinion known. Her honesty humbled Reagan and reminded her that her role was to the people, not the other way around.

"Yes, we were. What would you like to dress me in today?" She trusted Nicolette above all others, both as her friend and as her personal seamstress. Nicolette herself created many of her finer garments and she always knew her Queen's taste to the point where she became the only one allowed to fashion her formal attire.

"I believe this would be appropriate." She indicated to the dress, which hung from the wardrobe door. It was a beautiful sky blue dress that brought out the color of Reagan's eyes. The shift was done in a soft bleached linen that gave her just enough modesty as to not feel like she was on display. It was formal enough as to not offend the royal visitor, but not so rich that it made her feel out of place in her own humble court.

"That will do splendidly." Reagan smiled, running her fingers over the delicate needlepoint work done in gold that framed the wide sleeves and generous skirts well.

With Nicolette's assistance they laced her bodice, tying her into the underskirt before arranging the shift to accent her narrow waist and modest bosom. She never believed in dressing provocatively to gain an advantage, but she knew that many spoke of her beauty and putting on a pretty face could not hurt her people's status more than what already had been done. Her hair was parted and braided in two sections until they joined into one large braid at the base of her scalp. When Nicolette was done she pulled the tail to the side, weaving strands of jeweled gold chains until her blonde hair shined in the firelight. It was not often that Reagan dressed in attire appropriate for a royal. She never felt that creating such a separation between her and her people had any benefit, but it felt right to see herself represented as the Queen that her people knew her to be.

"You have outdone yourself as always," Reagan smiled, ready to face what felt like impending doom.

"Thank you, Your Majesty."

Reagan saw herself out of her chambers, strangely alone despite the occasion. Anya was in the small audience hall making final preparations for their guests, while Cohen was tending to Natalya, ensuring that she was dressed appropriately and was aware of what was expected of her as an

impending member of the Royal class. Nirosh, she assumed, was with Emeline much for the same reasons. While neither girl was technically part of the royal party they would both be in attendance and positioned near the dais. Natalya would be taking the bite soon and so it was appropriate for her to be present for such an audience. While Emeline was not in the same situation, Nirosh had unofficially adopted her and that meant that she would be allowed many luxuries that would not normally be afforded to her as long as she was under his protection. Reagan rather thought letting the girls stand together was a good idea. They were in many ways sisters going through what must be a difficult and undoubtedly life-altering situation since their introduction to vampires. It was good for them to have each other to whether the obstacles together and Reagan was more than happy to allow them any comfort that she could.

The halls near her chambers were mostly empty, but the farther the queen traveled into the heart of her castle the more of her subjects she encountered. Reagan could not stand the unrest she smelled in the air as she entered the last corridor leading to the smaller audience hall. Her people were frightened, as they had every right to be. The watchmen said that the royal and his honor guard would be upon their door before the night was through. Lady Arinessa, Lord Basil, Lord Nirosh, Kris and Darius would remain present with her during the treating, though Anya and Cohen would remain guard at the door during the proceedings, a fact that had not gone so well with her lover. The two stood guard at the door then, which meant that everyone else in her court had already arrived. They would walk with her to greet the party at the gate and lead them back into the castle.

"Are you sure about this?" Cohen asked as soon as she met them. "I should be in there with you. Anya can stand watch on her own."

"I will not be left alone to watch. I should be in there as I belong at my Queen's side." The look that exchanged between the two was more annoyed than hostile and Reagan knew that the anxiety was overpowering their senses.

"I believe that as the chosen heir I am more entitled to being with our Queen and yet I ask to sit in on this audience not because I feel insecure about my position, but because of my genuine concern for our Queen."

"How dare you propose that I care not for her safety." Anya growled and Reagan could not help, but let her amusement show. The laugh that escaped her lips shocked even her, resulting her smile growing.

"How very like you to take pleasure in our pain." Cohen teased, all thoughts of arguing with Anya gone. His hand came up to cup her face in a show of intimacy before he remembered where they were and dropped it.

"Regardless, we agreed on this arraignment and it is final. I will be fine," Reagan reached for his hand to squeeze it gently before releasing it when Anya let out a pained noise beside her. Reagan smiled ruefully at her paramour before kissing her softly on the lips. "There is no need to worry,

everything will go as planned."

"If you are sure, my Queen," Cohen sighed. "We must get going if we wish to meet them at the gate."

"I still protest, my Queen. I belong in there by your side," Anya demanded. The tender look left Reagan's eyes as she leveled her lover with a warning gaze. She could not help, but wonder when the girl had become so bold as to defy her openly and frequently.

"I will only tell you once more, the decision is final." It pained her to have to reprimand her lover, especially in front of another, but she must remember her place.

"As you command." The bow was simply a courtesy. Anya graced her queen with a cold stare.

"Anya, I do this out of my love for you, stay out of that room and protect me as only you and Cohen are capable." She held out her arm for Anya to take to soften the blow of her words and the girl took it without argument. Reagan felt her relax, her entire stance loosening at the physical contact with her Queen. Guilt rose as Reagan realized it had been far too long since she had spent time with her lover. She silently vowed to rectify that as soon as they were done hosting Faegon's men.

The trio walked to the castle entrance in silence. Cohen trailed steps behind them and Anya seemed to grow happier being in her company. That happiness did not last as they came to the gate, many of the castle guards already stationed and waiting for their Queen's orders. Anya and Reagan stood at the top of the stairs while Cohen took his place just a step below to Reagan's right. The messenger had made it to the castle first and was already being shown to a room with a hot bath waiting. Reagan did not have to wait long before their royal visitor arrived with four men and women making up his honor guard. The honor guard was made up of vampires younger than Reagan, though the queen could nearly smell the power that radiated from them. It would not surprise the her if they were members of the elite guard that was rumored to have been trained for the King of Kings himself.

"Speak your name and purpose before the fair and just Queen Reagan of House Lunaries." Cohen commanded when the five vampires lined themselves at the bottom of the steps.

"It is my honor to present to you Brae, Gillian, Nolan, and Anraí all members of King Zentarion's personal honor guard. I am Lord Paden, born of King Zentarion, third in line for the seat of the great Kingdom."

Paden was a tall man with a square jaw and hypnotic cerulean eyes. He wore his hair in a well groomed, short fashion that was becoming popular in the capitol, but had not quite made it to the outer Houses. Brae and Nolan looked like they might have been true siblings. They were both petite though Nolan at least appeared fit enough to be reliable in a fight. They both had olive skin and chocolate eyes so dark they nearly looked black.

Gillian was taller than both of them though she looked more like a Lady than a fighter. Her long hair was swept into an intricate braid accented with charms of gold. She was pale as the moon and her blonde hair shone in the light like the sun. She had wide, hazel eyes that looked inquisitively around with the exuberance of a child. The final guard Anraí seemed to be the oldest of the four. He hung farther back and Reagan found his passive stare the most concerning. She knew she would have to keep an eye on all of them while she hosted them.

"Lord Paden, I gladly welcome you and your men and women into my home. Please see to it that all of your needs are met during your stay. If it should please you I will have your guards brought to their chambers and we may retire to my audience hall and speak further." Reagan smiled graciously to her guests. She had little tastes for such formality, but she had no issues pandering to those who put such stock in titles rather than character.

"A Queen unafraid to start with business, your forwardness is refreshing, Your Majesty," Paden stepped forward and ascended the stairs until he stood just below Cohen. "I shall follow your lead."

"Lord Paden, this is Lord Cohen, heir to House Lunaries. Lady Anya is my paramour and one of the best hunters in these parts." Reagan gestured to her companions before turning back into the castle.

"It is a pleasure to meet you both," Paden bowed in what seemed like forced politeness, though Reagan did not comment. "I am afraid this is not a social call however."

"That is a shame. You come to us at a wonderful time. I had hoped that you would have the time to enjoy the gardens. There is a beautiful tree within my personal gardens, which leaves turn a wonderful deep red this time of year." Reagan knew the man was not fooled by her gesture, but it would not do to be called rude in the face of one of Zentarion's own children and heirs.

"You are kind to offer, Your Majesty."

"May I be frank, Lord Paden?" When she saw the man nod Regan continued on, remembering his compliment to her forwardness just moments ago. "What is it that brings you to House Lunaries if this is not a social call?"

"Well, there are things I would prefer to speak about behind closed doors, but I can tell you that a new bounty has been requested by King Zentarion directly. He seeks the capture of two men who plot against the Crown. One is a human, a former human liaison who turned his back on the Crown when his vampire partner was killed by a companion of the rogue Logan. The second is a vampire, believed to also be a confidant of the rogue."

"And you think you might find them out here? We have heard of no such men." Reagan was truly baffled by such news, they had never been informed of bounties before. Other Houses were allowed to send their own

hunters to turn in bounties on their behalf to Faegon for money and esteem, but House Lunaries was not one of them.

"Your's is not the only House I am visiting. We have other stops to make before I return to my King's side. If we are to catch these dangerous men, would it not make sense to inform every House in the empire?"

"You are too right," Reagan conceded. There was no sense in causing a scene over something so trivial. "Where do you venture from here if you do not mind my asking?"

"House Namyt'Tkas, Your Majesty. We are doing a tour of the land before returning,"

"And does that tour include House Tryali?"

"It is part of the Kingdom, is it not?" If Paden had not intended to be rude, then he failed in his attempt. He seemed not to notice nor care that his attitude might be off putting and Reagan feared for what this audience with him could bring.

"You are correct, how silly of me," Reagan spoke with barely concealed sarcasm. She saw Anya smirk on her other side while she could only imagine the look Cohen must be throwing their unwanted guest. They arrived at the audience hall in time to save the small party from any more forced conversation and Cohen and Anya opened the doors for the two before bowing out and taking their stations for the meeting.

Reagan had chosen the small audience chamber instead of the council chambers to give herself a clear air of superiority. It was obvious now that her decision was the right one for how heavily Lord Paden seemed to put weight on titles. Reagan settled herself at the top of the dais while Darius and Kris stood at her sides. Nirosh stood with the girls and various other members of her council and noble class arraigned themselves throughout the small area.

"We have the honor to be graced by the presence of Lord Paden of House Faegon." Reagan spoke when she settled into her seat, enjoying the annoyed look that crossed the man's face when she omitted his many other titles. "You may speak openly here, Lord Paden. You find yourself amongst valued and trusted members of this House."

"Your Majesty," Paden bowed low in front of all present in a show of respect. Reagan suspected he only did so to compose his anger at her obvious slight, though there was no way to be sure. "I have traveled here in the name of our great King to insure House Lunaries' ability and willingness to protect its borders and the borders of the Kingdom against enemies such as the self-named rogues led by the traitors Logan and Cassandra, formerly of House Lunaries."

"Formerly is correct. We have done our part over the last two centuries, even when the Crown did not see it fit to include us in their ranks. I see no reason our abilities, as you so delicately put it, would be called into question. We are a House that has rebuilt through a time of

immense heartache and we will continue to strengthen as a people under the rule of King Zentarion." Reagan would have to be cautious with her parlance in such company, but she would not stand by and let an outsider speak so cruelly of her home and her people.

"That might be, but there are reports of rogues in your woods. We have word that one such criminal turned an innocent and you took her in. You know very well of the rules regarding such acts."

"You may speak frankly with me, Lord Paden. You believe that because the late King Gareth took in a childe bitten against his will over two centuries ago that I would make the same mistakes as he? The very childe you speak of is amongst us now. She is a capable young woman who is more than happy to defend this House, her House, in the war against the rogues that forced this life on her. You speak of past mistakes and yet all I see here is a promising future."

"You would show such disrespect to our laws? I would take care for one word from me and our Great King might see it fit to place a more capable ruler on your throne."

"You will not come into my home and threaten me!" Reagan said, doing her best to keep her bloodlust at bay. She did not raise her voice, there was no need as only a fool would have overlooked the power in her words. "Our dear sister Emeline was attacked outside our borders and it was with my blessing that she was let into our home. We had no hand in turning her and the rogue that brutalized her was killed for her crimes. You expect that I would just leave a mere childe in the woods without protection? Or are you suggesting that I should have killed her instead. What crime have I committed?"

"Very well, Your Majesty, you leave me no choice. For the blatant ignorance you show in this matter you must report to Faegon to answer for your actions in front of King Zentarion before the next full moon." A thunderous uproar filled the room at the decree. Reagan had never felt anger quite like she did then and she had lived through many terrible things in her lifetime. It took her standing to command the room's attention, effectively cutting through the mounting noise.

"I will heed your summons, but know this. You and your men and women are no longer welcome within these castle walls. You will regret making an enemy of this house, yet, Lord Paden. You may tell the King that he will see me within the designated time. Guards, see this man and his companions out." Darius and his men instantly surrounded Paden and shepherded them from the hall. The remaining guards quickly ushered all others out that were not part of the Royal Council

"Your Majesty, shall we retire to the council room?" Kris asked, worry clear on her face.

"No, Anya and Cohen are all I require. They shall report to the small council room immediately," Reagan ordered. She did not wait to make sure

that the word was passed along as she exited through the back door. She knew her actions had only made her people's precarious relationship with Faegon all the more strained, but she wouldn't allow Paden or the crown to make a fool of her.

The short walk to the small council room was enough for Reagan to calm her raging anger and when she took her seat she felt she would be ready to handle whatever her two most trusted subjects had to say. She was not disappointed when they entered moments later, Anya throwing the doors open so harshly that Reagan thought that the heavy doors would fly from their hinges.

"You cannot seriously be accepting that summons!"

"You will calm down and sit down so we can speak like adults." Reagan waited for them to follow her command before continuing. "I will be accepting it and I will be going alone." Reagan tried for diplomatic, though she should know better. Diplomacy never worked with Anya and it certainly would not begin to do so now.

"You cannot go and you certainly are not going alone. It's not safe! The Crown wants you out of the way to put someone easily manipulated in your place!"

"That is absurd! Lord Paden was just making idle threats. They would never ignore that I am the heir. Whatever they might be, they take their laws seriously," Cohen chided, "though Anya is right. It would not be safe to go alone."

"They could ignore the line of succession and claim it was for the betterment of the realm, no one would argue," Anya shot back and Reagan felt as the situation quickly spiraled out of her control. Anytime that the two of them joined on a united front usually meant that Reagan would have to fight a long and hard battle for them to see it her way.

"Cohen is right, Anya, no harm will come to me if I follow this summons. There would be greater harm to our people and to me if I did not. I will not be going entirely alone, I will take Darius to be sure, but you two must remain here." Anya might not see reason, but Reagan was their Queen and she would have to try to persuade her before reminding her that in the end, her opinion would not sway her ultimate actions.

"Darius? Why would you take him over me? You can't honestly tell me that you wouldn't be safer here with your people. Anything could happen when you're outside these walls! Think Reagan, if you died out there what would we do? What would I do?" Anya yelled, her words echoed through the council room.

"Anya," Cohen tried, his hand moving to rest on her shoulder, but the woman moved too fast.

"Don't you dare," she hissed. Her fangs were bared and her eyes clouded blue.

"Anya," Reagan warned from her seat at the head of the council table.

She rubbed a delicate hand over her own face, her eyes just as stormy as her paramour's though her fangs were not present. "I know the dangers, but I have been called by the High Council. They will send an army if I don't reply. Would you have me endanger my people if I could spare them? We are already weak in numbers. We can't afford an attack! Darius is the most obvious choice. As the Captain of the Guard he will be more than capable of protecting me. Cohen is the heir and must stay to rule in my place, you know this. I need you to stay with him to insure that the castle is seen to while I'm gone. I will come back when this is over. You must believe I will."

"How can you know that for certain? I can't afford to lose you!" The broken sound made Reagan's passive gaze break. She stood and moved to stand behind the woman in a single motion.

"You will never lose me." Her words were quiet, but they sounded like waves crashing to her own ears.

"I will take my leave now, My Lady." Cohen bowed respectively to the two before making a swift exit from the room. Reagan was grateful that he had more tact than Anya and knew when to leave them be. She would have to speak with him later, but now her lover needed her and she had put the woman aside too often, all for the sake of their people. She could not continue to hide from this.

"You can't promise me you won't die." Anya's words were so quiet Reagan could hardly hear them even in such close proximity. It seemed the two were battling to see who would move first and still they stayed frozen, inches apart.

"I know." Anya let go first and sagged against her queen. Reagan caught her with the ease of a woman so in tune with her lover that she needed no warning to anticipate her movements. She wrapped her strong arms around Anya and took all of her weight until the woman was no longer supporting herself. "What must be done will be."

"Don't quote that rubbish to me." Anya bit back and tried to pull away, though Reagan would not let go. She had never let go of her love before and she was not about to do so now.

"But it is the truth." Reagan brushed the short brown curls from Anya's neck, resting her chin there so her cheek pressed against the other's. "You know I would never leave you, not if it could be avoided. I must do what is right for the people, our people. The House is too weak for me to be a fool and turn down the summons."

"Let me go in your place. You and Cohen belong here," Anya pleaded, doing her best not to cry. Reagan knew that she was desperate if she was willing to go and leave Reagan alone with Cohen.

"I belong where my people need me."

"They need you here." Anya tried one last time, this time her battle with her emotions ended and she began to sob.

"No, they don't. Neither do you."

Reagan drew Anya further into her arms and she held her cradled to her chest. It was late enough that not many people would be wandering the corridors. She could count on her personal guardsmen and women to remain discreet as she carried her sobbing lover to their chambers. She had neglected her both out of selfishness and childishness and now she was paying the price. No matter the final outcome of her summons with King Zentarion and the Crown she would still have a home to return to and if she wanted to have friendly faces to greet her she would have to repair some of the wounds that she had caused. Her fractured relationship with Anya was not the only problem that faced her, but it had to be the most important. In the small time she had left, before she was forced to leave, she would have to show the woman just how much she was willing to work things out with her when she returned.

COHEN

Two nights had passed since Cohen had last seen his sister. Since her very public scene with Lord Paden, Reagan had spent her time locked in her chambers with her paramour. She had sent word to him the night before to ask for privacy and discretion while she dealt with the wildfire that her relationship had become. Cohen hadn't been happy with the orders, but he respected his sister too much to question her. He could not understand why the impudent child deserved more attention than the queen's people, but that was not for him to judge. Instead, it fell on him to care for the House just as he would have to do in Reagan's absence. He would never admit it, but he was happy for the practice. He had no experience ruling over an ancient vampire House, in fact he had no practice being in control of much of anything without his sister there to help.

Still he would need to stay and do his best to keep Lunaries afloat while Reagan was gone. It made sense that he would need to remain at the castle while his sister was away. He was the heir to her throne and the only person Reagan trusted their people's wellbeing to. Cohen would have been lying if he said that he did not wish to accompany her to the capitol, but he also saw no reason in burdening her further by arguing the point. She already had Anya by her side for that, he would have to remain the reasonable party.

"Lord Cohen." Holland bowed as he passed her in the halls of the royal quarters.

"Holland, walk with me." Cohen paused so she could fall into step with him as he continued his pass through the corridors.

Reagan did these rounds nightly to make sure her people saw her face and could easily voice their concerns. It had not gone unnoticed that for the past two nights it had been her heir to speak to the people. Still, the nightly operations ran as smoothly as could be expected. The tension that was in

the air in the early days of Cohen's introduction to Lunaries was back. The people were on edge after Lord Paden and his men openly threatened their queen. They feared what would happen if Reagan was taken in chains at the gates of Faegon and they feared for their own wellbeing without their beloved queen to protect them. The people were loyal to his sister, he only hoped that they would be more loyal to Reagan than they were to Gareth.

"There is something troubling you." Holland's soft voice called him back to reality.

"There is much and yet there is no sense in mulling it over now. Tell me, how do the people fair. I am afraid I haven't the skills our Queen possesses when it comes to being aware of the many whispers that carry through these walls."

"They are worried, no doubt, but they trust that she is doing the right thing. They love her, something that will forever work in her favor."

The sentiment made the growing knot in his chest lessen until he was sure that he might actually sleep for the first time since he learned his sister was being forced from their home, from him. "That is good. I feared that those who adore our Queen might be disturbed by the company she keeps."

Holland shot him with a warning filled gaze. She seemed to pause longer than necessary before responding, her words short and deliberate. "Who our Queen chooses to share her bed with is not your concern and certainly not the concern of the people. You are her heir. Act with the decorum befitting your role."

Thoroughly chastised, Cohen bowed his head. "You are right, as always. I oft think your talents are wasted with the guard. You protect our Queen well, but I wonder if you would do better on the Council."

"Now you are just speaking nonsense." Holland's laugh was as light and pretty as bells and her dark expression had melted away. "Come now, let us talk of happier things. Lady Natalya is doing very well."

Since her appointment to the royal party would be eminent, Reagan had encouraged her people to start to grant her the titles and respect that would soon rightfully belong to the young girl. "That she is. She has been a blessing in these tough times."

"Oh yes, our Queen has told me what kind of blessing she has been." The coy smile was verging on vulturous and it infuriated him.

"What do you mean by that?" Cohen could not help the cold tone as he felt the need to protect the girl from whatever harmful things Holland might say.

Instead of answering, the petite woman rolled her eyes before blowing the blonde fringe from her face. She watched him carefully with perceptive green orbs. When it became obvious that she was not going to be forthcoming, Cohen sighed and held out his arm, intending to lead her to a more private location where the guards woman might be more open. Holland only paused for a moment before accepting his arm.

"When will the Queen be available again? Lady Natalya has been asking for her."

"Really? Did she say why?" Natalya was always asking after him. She had only mentioned his sister a few times while they conversed, but she had never asked for her that he was aware.

"She said it was something to do with a prior conversation that they'd shared. A private one."

Cohen could only think of one or two occasions when Natalya had been alone with Reagan. He wondered what they might have discussed that had her asking after the woman. Natalya was private, so her resistance in telling Holland the nature of the conversation was not shocking, but it still worried him.

"Our Queen requested privacy while handling a delicate matter. She will make herself available when she is ready." He might as well have just admitted he didn't know when she would return by the way his companion stared at him. Holland, like many of those close to the queen, had long since become comfortable enough that they saw no issue with speaking frankly to Her Majesty and the rest of the royal party. Cohen often found it refreshing, but Holland's judgement was bordering on treason. "You will remember with whom you are accompanying, Holland."

"Yes, M'lord." Unlike Anya who would have spoken with defiance lacing her voice, Holland had the decency to act sorry, though he highly doubt she felt it. "If that is all you need, I have duties to attend."

He would not be getting answers from her tonight and it reminded him to keep his temper in check. How Reagan managed it all, he might never know. "Yes, thank you. Tell Darius that I want Lilliana stationed outside Natalya's door during Queen Reagan's absence. One can never be too careful."

He couldn't resist another jab at Anya and Holland saw it in her own best interest not to point it out this time. She merely nodded, removing her hand from the crook of his elbow and bowed out, heading back the way they had come. If Reagan's concerns about his and Natalya's relationship were so fierce that she was making comments to Holland then he must confront his sister directly, or be more discreet with his intentions.

No longer in the mood to deal with politics or nosy subjects, Cohen began to make his way to see the girl who commandeered most of his waking and sleeping thoughts. Lessons would have already concluded for the night and Nirosh had been spending an increasing amount of time with Emeline, though Cohen had no idea what they got up to in the man's private quarters. Whatever it was, it was certainly none of his business. Reagan had once told him that the elder vampire saw flashes of his late daughter, one of his own flesh and blood before he had taken the bite, whom he had never quite laid to rest in his heart, in the girl. He genuinely hoped that having Emeline there would bring some joy to the man. Of all

those that belonged to the ancient House, he was one that had seen the most misfortune.

Lord Nirosh had once been a Lord of the human Kingdom Solara and had lost his wife and daughter by the hands of vagrants who had mistook him for a crooked noble of which whom their land had been forcibly taken for. Instead of seeking retribution he had silently agreed to retire to the castle where he had taken on the role of advisor to the then human King Tristan. He was part of the hunting party that saw the King's close friend Lord Gareth struck down by a rogue vampire. It had been Nirosh's task to see Lord Gareth to safety and then accompany him back to the castle when he was fully healed. Of course Lord Gareth had been given the bite and had chosen to remain within Mordin Forest destroying his assignment. Nirosh had attempted to return to Sylvine, the then capital of Solara, but had been turned away by King Tristan himself, who mourned the loss of his dearest friend and blamed Nirosh for not forcing sense into the man's head. That had been the last that Nirosh had seen of his old home before being exiled to Mordin Forest. That tragedy was the first seed planted in the anti-vampire movement that caused the ignorant humans to deny their existence entirely and effectively ended a treaty laid down by the first vampire King and the Solarians.

Nirosh deserved to be happy, but so did Cohen and he would be damned if he let his sister keep him from it.

Cohen found Natalya in her room as he had expected, though Freya was nowhere to be seen. It was for the best as he hadn't really fancied having the handmaiden as an audience for this encounter. Since he had fled Natalya in the garden the two had only seen each other once, the day of Lord Paden's visit and that had only been long enough for him to escort her to the hall and he had yet to amend the pain he had no doubt caused the girl.

Natalya was standing by the large bay window in her bedroom. The moon was high in the sky and its pale light washed over her olive skin and played off of her curls. Her hair had grown since she had arrived to them over three months before and then were carried off her back by the gentle breeze. While dresses were customary, the women of Lunaries were allowed to dress in any fashion they saw fit, Anya being a primary example as she could be found in pants more often than skirts and Natalya looked every bit the tomboy she had been when she had come to them in soft slacks and a loose tunic. Cohen would always find her beautiful in pretty dresses and silks, but she was even more breathtaking as she stood comfortable in her own skin.

"I hope I am not disturbing you, Lady Natalya."

The girl turned to look at him. Nothing about her stance suggested that she was surprised by his presence and he wondered just how sharp her senses were due to her unusual upbringing. "Not at all, I always enjoy your

company."

The words caused enormous guilt to weigh in Cohen's heart. "I should have come sooner."

"I understand why you didn't. I'm sorry I made you uncomfortable." Cohen hated the sad look on her face; it had no business there and he had caused it.

"That's okay I know you didn't intend to." He spoke softly and moved further into the room as if he were walking toward an animal that he didn't want to spook.

The shy, quiet girl before him disappeared and an annoyed look crossed her face. The girl he had known before, the stubborn one who hid her gentler side to not get hurt, was staring him down. "Just to be clear, Freya explained the connotation of my offer to you and I do not regret making it. I only regret how it made you feel."

Cohen was stunned. "You are still very young, Natalya. You can't know if you want this or not."

"Don't be absurd." Natalya actually laughed, striking him with an incredulous look. When he didn't answer, she rolled her eyes and continued. "I understand that things are done differently here. I have studied your customs and I know that children are considered such until a much older age than in Solara. I never told you, but had I stayed in my home village I would be well on my way to being married by now. I had a suitor and his family were the best prospects that I'd had. His family had the money and servants that mine did not, but my mother's name still held influence and we had a large estate that was falling into disrepair because our lack of resources. It was a good match. He and I were to be wed next spring."

"Wed? But you're still a child!" The thought of another man spending his time with his Natalya made him sick, but the knowledge that she was so young and expected to be a woman grown made him feel all the worse.

"I'm hardly a child in my people's standards. I'll be seventeen in less than a month, that's old, you have to understand. I would nearly be considered a spinster by the time the wedding came." Natalya moved to sit by the fire, being drawn to it by the chill of the night air. Cohen watched her act blasé in the face of this enormous reveal and he wasn't sure how he was meant to feel any longer.

"Regardless, you are not there any longer. You have a whole new life here. There is no need to think about such things. You are no longer required to get married and you have time to learn and grow, there is no need to-"

"To what? I like you, something I thought you knew. I'm not asking to marry you, I know full well that I no longer have to become involved with someone because of duty. I'm not telling you this because I am trying to follow a path I left behind. I am telling you because for the first time in my life I have the freedom to choose something for myself and I choose to

explore this thing, whatever it is, with you."

There seemed to be no suitable way to respond to such an honest declaration. Cohen had been terrified that girl wouldn't have understood what she had offered to him by baring her neck. He worried that when she found out she might feel obligated to be with him, or worse that she may confuse her own feelings and seek him out only to realize that he was far too old for her. He had allowed his own worries to plague him until he could no longer sleep, but not once did he consider that this strong, wonderful human girl might truly care for him in the same way that he was coming to care for her. It seemed that Natalya would continue to surprise him, even when he was sure that he might know her better than anyone else in this world.

Natalya, it seemed, was done waiting for him to respond and soon he found himself being crowded by her small form. His senses were assaulted as the scent of her engulfed him. He was accustomed to having her close to him, it wasn't odd to find them huddled close out in the gardens or sparing in the practice rooms. He was so accustomed to her that he wasn't in the least bit surprised when he felt her arms rise up until she was cradling his face in her hands. She stared at him, into his very soul, with her warm brown eyes as if to ask for his permission. In all of the ways he imagined this moment he had never considered that Natalya might be the initiator. He nearly laughed at himself, he should have known, but he didn't want to spoil the moment. Instead he nodded so slightly that he feared that she might not notice. His fears were quelled when soft lips met his own.

Natalya smelled like fresh packed dirt and a roaring hearth fire. She was breathtaking both as a fighter and as a lady. She spoke with the assertion of a wise woman who had never doubted herself. He had expected her to taste bold and earthy as everything else about her seemed to be, but he was surprised to find her lips sweet and subdued. He longed to chase the teasing hints of honey and lavender, her favorite brew of tea, and he found that he could easily lose himself in her very essence and the thought didn't cause an ounce of fear.

The moment passed and Cohen found himself stripped bare under the girl's watchful gaze. "Was that okay? I don't want to force you into this if you're not interested."

This time Cohen did laugh. "I should be the one asking you that." He reached out to pull her close, overjoyed when she relaxed into him instead of pushing him away. "Don't ever doubt that I care about you. I want this, I want you, at least for as long as you will have me."

"Good." The grin she was giving him was contagious and all of the past anxieties he had about this confrontation faded until all he felt was pure joy. "Now I assume you've come to see me for more than serious conversation and a kiss,"

"I have, regrettably," he leaned in to steal another short kiss, relishing

in the luxury, before continuing. "I heard that you were looking to speak to Reagan."

"Oh, that. Yes I had asked after her to Holland, I didn't know she would come looking for you." Despite the intimate moment they had just shared, Natalya still did not seem keen on telling him what she needed the queen for and the thought disappointed him.

"Is there something that I can help with?"

The girl seemed at war with herself for a moment. She looked conflicted, but her eyes did not seem to see him, instead she was engrossed in whatever battle she seemed to be waging in her own mind. "I'm not sure. It pertains to something private that the queen and I have discussed. I am not sure that she would want me to share this with you."

"Reagan and I are very close. I am her heir after all, I am sure she would not mind, she trusts me with all else." Cohen did his best to hide the pain he felt knowing that Natalya and Reagan were holding something back from him.

"Alright, you might want to take a seat, though." Cohen was weary to hear what she had to say, but took at seat by the hearth, willing his wild emotions to settle. "I need to discuss with our queen about the most recent vision I had. I am a seer and she has been doing her best to help me navigate the art."

Of all of the things that Natalya could have told him, Cohen found himself shocked by the news. "You're a seer? Have you always know this or is this something you've just discovered?"

"Yes. I've known nearly my entire life." Natalya was very calm, it was obvious that she hadn't just discovered this gift, for it certainly was. Cohen did not believe in the school of thought that magic was too dangerous to be utilized. Of course magic in the wrong hands could be dangerous, but having a trained seer in the House would be a great advantage.

"What does Reagan have to do with your visions? Is something going to happen to her?"

"No, well I am not sure. I am not a very gifted seer, I can only really see the past, at least that is all I have ever seen. Theoretically, at least according to some of the old books that are left in the library, I could train to see things that are happening at the same time or even the future, but right now all I can see are past happenings in my dreams."

"What did you see that has you so upset?"

"I'm honestly not sure. I want to speak to her first, if that is quite alright."

"Of course." Cohen held his hand out and Natalya took it instantly, falling into his lap as if she had done so many times before. "I will send word for her as soon as I leave here."

"I suppose it could wait a bit longer," she agreed, her entire demeanor lighting as she settled deeper into his embrace.

This time Cohen was fully prepared for the kiss and he took his time to enjoy the feeling of soft lips on his own. Natalya was by no means experienced, but she was confident and passionate and it wasn't as if he had much experience of his own either. He had never had a serious lover before or after taking the bite, though there had been a woman here or there that had graced his bed. That had been before Reagan had become queen and he her heir. Since then he had done everything to keep his reputation pure. He had never felt that he was denying himself anything, there had never been anyone who he could see himself seriously wanting to court. He had been happy with his position in the House and had never felt that there was a need to seek out a partner, but after having met Natalya he wondered if he could truly live the rest of his life without knowing every last thing about the amazing girl in his lap.

His thoughts and eager kissing were interrupted by a frantic knock on the door.

With a soft curse, Cohen detangled himself from Natalya's arms. "Unfortunately I must get that."

"Very unfortunate," Natalya agreed, pressing one more kiss to his lips before sweeping for the door. She opened the door with the air of an annoyed Lady and Cohen thought that she would grow into her new role rather well. "What seems to be the problem?"

"I am looking for Lord Cohen, Lady Natalya. Queen Reagan seeks an audience with him." Jasper stood at the door looking rather flushed. Cohen wondered if Natalya looked at all disheveled, that she might give away what they were doing, but his fears were soothed by her next words.

"You don't have to use my title, Jasper. Honestly you are going to be granted the same honor, stop acting like I'm suddenly a different person. I'll make sure that Cohen goes to our Queen at once, there is no need for you wait on him."

"Of course, Lady—" the boy winced when he was leveled with a dark glare. "Natalya. Of course Natalya."

Cohen waited for the boy to run off before gently chastising the girl. "There is no need to be so harsh on him. Jasper is a good lad."

"He is, he is also more interested in Emeline than I think is necessary."

Ah, the heart of the matter. Sometimes Cohen wondered if Natalya remembered that Emeline was her elder and did not need her to protect her virtue. She had been married once, of course, she was a woman grown and could easily handle the likes of Jasper.

"Well that is something I will leave you and Emeline to discuss. I am afraid I must be off." Cohen regretted having to leave, but knew that it would be impossible to stay.

"Don't forget to tell Reagan that I need to speak to her." Natalya reminded him unnecessarily. She knew he couldn't forget so she must have been stalling him. Cohen thought, for just a moment, about delaying with

Reagan and walking back into Natalya's room. Maybe in another life that would have been possible.

"Of course." He watched as the girl took a step closer into his space before pausing. The door was still open and while there was no one in the vicinity, they should still exercise caution. It seemed the normally rash girl understood that.

"I will be seeing you soon, then?"

He could not stand the doubt filled look on her pretty face and after a quick sweep of the hall he leaned in for a short, searing kiss. "Yes I will see you soon, I promise."

Cohen stepped out of Natalya's reach before she could continue the kiss. It would not do to be caught in her embrace in the middle of the open door all while leaving their queen waiting. With one last chaste kiss, Cohen parted from the girl, moving swiftly into the hallway and way from any more temptation. He didn't dare look back, for fear that we wouldn't be able to leave a second time.

It wasn't a very long walk to Reagan's chambers. Thankfully they had moved Natalya to the royal quarters early in her stay, which meant that he was already very close to the queen's personal suite. He dreaded having to confront his sister about keeping secrets from him, especially those regarding Natalya, but it had to be done. When he reached his sister's door he had to resist a childish urge not to knock. Knowing that Anya was more than likely still in the room quelled the desire.

"Come in," Reagan called sounding much more at ease than the last time they had spoke.

"You wished to speak to me," Cohen said by way of greeting, granting Anya a curt nod, just polite enough to avoid being berated.

"Yes, thank you for arriving so swiftly, Cohen. You may leave us, Anya." Reagan and the girl shared a look that held more passion than anger before Anya left the room. It seemed that whatever the two had done for two solid nights alone had been a good start at repairing their broken relationship.

"Things are going well, I take it," Cohen took to Anya's vacated seat at the small table. It was laden with papers that had come from the council room and the sight of them filled him with a tiredness that tending to the politics of commanding a house in Zentarion's empire always caused him. The official summons from the Crown lay chief among them and Cohen repressed the instincts that encouraged him to burn the thing. It would do little else then assuage his anger and he doubted Reagan would appreciate it.

"They are, not nearly as well as they are with you and Natalya so I hear." The look Reagan gave him was all big sister and any trace of the poised queen left the room.

"She is looking to speak to you, if that is what you are asking, otherwise I haven't any idea what you mean." Cohen couldn't help but feel

forced on the defensive.

Reagan didn't seem the least bit surprised by his words, if anything she seemed insulted. "Don't play stupid with me, Cohen, it never worked when we were children, it's certainly not going to work now."

"I honestly don't know what you have heard, but I do know that you have been speaking to Holland, a touch insulting if I might add."

"That woman needs to learn to keep secrets to herself," Reagan sighed, though she didn't sound terribly put out. "I know you and the girl are growing close, I just worry about you."

"You worry that she will be like Anya, something you will never admit, but she is not, so there is no need to fear." Getting the dig in felt good, even if he immediately regretted it.

"Don't speak about Anya that way. She might annoy you, but if you expect any amount of respect from her than it wouldn't hurt for you to allow her the same courtesy."

"Speaking of secrets," Cohen countered to steer the conversation back on even ground. It was a proven fact that he and Reagan could argue for any given length of time about her paramour, but he had more important things to discuss. "When were you going to tell me that Natalya is a seer?"

"That was never my secret to tell." Reagan answered smoothly and suddenly the queen was back, her voice all diplomatic brooking no arguments. "I told her that she should be careful who she tells, I never suggested to her that she should or should not tell any individual. You cannot blame me if she did not trust you enough to tell you."

"That's cold, sister. She is looking to you for guidance and she seems afraid by something she has seen." Cohen sneered, shocked that the same woman who had raised him to be a good person would stoop so low.

"Then I should see to her immediately." Reagan stood, ending the conversation effectively. "You, on the other hand might want to reduce your visits to her. She is still young and has no idea what she may or may not want." She paused for a moment, her tone softening just enough that it might have sounded sincere if it did not come at the hilt of her cruel words. "I just don't want to see you hurt at the end of this."

Cohen wasn't sure that he could trust those kind eyes and for the first time in his life, he wasn't convinced that his big sister would be able to make everything better. "At what cost are you willing to protect me?"

For just a moment, it looked like Reagan might respond, but she disappointed him. "I must find Natalya to discuss her vision. You can see yourself out, I am sure."

Without a moment more, Reagan stood and let herself out of the room leaving Cohen alone, confused and upset. He wasn't sure when his sister began to take her role as a queen more seriously than she took her role as his protective older sister, but he wasn't happy with it. It wasn't that he enjoyed her constantly meddling in his business, but he had never once

doubted that he was the most important thing in her life; now he wasn't sure and it was a disturbing thought. For the first time in the centuries since he had taken he bite on his sister's insistence, Cohen wondered if it was possible that they had lived too long. He had never thought before that they might forget their humanity and become a mere shell of what they had been, but now he found the possibility entirely too likely for his comfort. He might not have the time to speak to Reagan about his fears now, but he was going to make damn sure that when she returned that they carve out time to have a serious discussion. He resented the reach of her influence on his life and he wondered just how far was too far for the queen in her to be interfering with his personal matters. She had always taken off her political mask with him, but if she was no longer able to do so then he was afraid for her soul.

NATALYA

Natalya stood in the open doorway in a daze. She had finally gotten Cohen to herself after their disastrous fight and she was able to show him that she wasn't a confused child. She was a woman grown and knew very well what she wanted from him. She cursed that they had been interrupted, but it was the nature of his position as the heir. She would never, should never come before the House, something she had given quite a lot of thought about, before confronting him. There might have been a time when that would not have been enough, when she would have needed to be the center of any man's universe, but after spending time with the vampires and coming to learn her place in their world she found that she didn't need a man to validate her. She rather enjoyed Cohen's company simply because he made her happy and that feeling was the most freeing thing she had ever felt.

Realizing that she must look like a fool standing in her open door with a lovestruck expression on her face, Natalya shook the butterflies off and moved further into the corridor. There was no reason for her to remain stuck in her room. She was not confined there like a prisoner and it was about time she acted like a Lady who belonged to House Lunaries. She hadn't wandered much on her own. She always surrounded by Cohen, or a guard, and even if she never truly minded their company it was often stifling. Normally Lilliana was the guard on duty outside her door and so she would accompany Natalya, though occasionally Freya would have some time in her day to simply trail her to the small royal library and back. She never felt unsafe in the halls, but she had never felt much like she belonged. Since Reagan had announced that she intended to personally give Natalya the gift of the bite, the girl found that the atmosphere surrounding her had changed. It seemed that with the queen's endorsement, the people were ready to accept her into their ranks.

It would be nice to take a stroll and the night was warmer than it had

been in a week. Natalya made her way from her room to the entrance of the royal gardens with ease. She passed very few people as it was already nearly dawn and many of the vampires were preparing for the night. The humans who did remain awake during the day would be rising soon to stand guard and keep watch over the castle. Of the humans of Lunaries, Natalya knew very few of them. She had adapted her sleeping to fit to her classes rather early on and of the humans that were awake during the night, she had only met her two peers and Galvin, Jasper's father. Even Nicolette, Jasper's mother had never crossed her path in the time since she had come to them. Natalya wondered a moment on just how isolated from the rest of the people she had been before brushing her worries aside. Since she had arrived to Lunaries her life had been in a constant state of motion. With her classes and her time spent with Cohen it was no wonder that she knew very little people outside of the close circle of teachers and the Council.

Natalya wandered from the Royal Tower out toward the gardens, a place that was quickly feeling like a second home. The flowers that had been fading when she had arrived were gone and the leaves were bright in their colorful hues. There were workers raking them in throughout the garden and each passed to bow to Natalya, offering a polite "m'lady" before returning to their work. Natalya continued on to her and Cohen's favorite spot before settling down. Reagan would know to find her here when she and Cohen were done speaking and she still had the troubling images she had seen in her dream to consider before facing the queen.

Natalya leaned back into the tree that she had come to think of her as own as she allowed the memories to play in her mind's eye.

She had been witnessing a memory of Reagan's again. She had learned to divine whose eyes she saw through without needing the aid of a reflective surface after two weeks straight of memory dreams. Now she was able to simply know in the same way that she knew they were memories and not works of fiction. Reagan had been sitting in the council room with Lord Nirosh, both being vampires making it impossible to discover when this particular moment had occurred.

"You are finally ready to tell me what happened to you in the outer villages?" Nirosh spoke, though Natalya had the distinct feeling that it was not actually a question.

"You are not to repeat a word of this, of course," Reagan had spoken in the tone that Natalya had learned to recognize as her queen voice. She hardly used it, especially not with her loyal Council members, and it had been surprising to hear it then.

"That should never need to be said, you are stalling, Rea. Stop this foolishness and tell me what happened." Nirosh spoke every bit like the exasperated father figure that he was and Natalya could still remember the warmth that had spread through Reagan in that moment. Their queen genuinely loved and valued Nirosh's opinion and it calmed the vampire's

nerves to know that he would remain at her side, no matter the situation.

"There was a woman who was badly hurt. She had been attacked by a rogue," Reagan spoke carefully as if this information itself was the secret.

"They are getting more bold by the day, we must report this to the Crown." Nirosh spoke firmly, but Reagan would not be swayed.

"We cannot." Her words were firm and brook no argument, though the Master of Arms was not deterred by it.

"Why? We are already in a precarious position. They would not be happy to find that we are not reporting to them as is expected."

"The woman, she was a human seer, she refused the bite and I was forced to watch her die."

"That still does not explain why you want to keep this a secret from the Crown."

"But this does," Reagan spoke, pulling a gold pendant and chain from her robes. This was the part of the memory that Natalya had played over in her mind again and again. The pendant had been a golden sun encircled by two snakes, the symbol of Solara. Natalya had seen that pendant in her dreams before, it had belonged to her mother. "This woman told me an interesting story, one that I do not believe should be told to the Crown. She told me that she was from the land beyond our borders, from the human Kingdom Solara. She was in the forest with her young daughter searching for her son. She had fled her lover and married another man. She told me that she had once been the lover to the Solarian King and had birthed a son. Her husband never knew the baby survived and she had taken him to the woods to allow fate to set his destiny. She had visions that he was still alive and would one day sit upon a grand throne. She had been searching with her daughter, but they had been attacked. She made me promise to find her son and her daughter and set right the wrongs she had committed to both her children."

"What does this have to do with the Crown?"

"The throne that she described, it was not of the Solarian Kingdom, it was of House Faegon, I am sure of it."

Natalya had woken up then, confused and furious with Reagan for hiding something so important from her. She didn't have proof that this was about her mother of course, but too many of the details fit. She had never known that her mother had another child, but she did remember going into the woods with her mother often. She had never been told why, but she had always known even at her young age that they were looking for something. Was it possible that she really did have an older half brother? Was there truly a lost bastard child of the Solarian King running about Mordin Forest who would later ascend to Faegon's throne? Had her father not truly known that his wife had birthed a healthy baby or had he turned a blind eye and allowed her to leave him behind and continue on with their lives?

There were so many questions running through her mind and she knew that Reagan would more than likely not have all of the answers. The only woman who did had been dead for nearly eight years.

Natalya allowed her mind to wander through the vision once more. The conversation had played in her mind repeatedly since she had first heard it, but there was one detail that she could not forget. Her mother's pendant, the very one she remembered glittering in the sun while they played in the fields when she was a small child, was somewhere in this very castle. She had never seen the pendant on the queen, but she knew that the woman would have kept it. She was a sentimental woman, but furthermore it would be proof of the exchange. Natalya remembered her mother explaining to her when she was a child that it was a special pendant, given only to the King of Solara and his family. She had never understood how her mother had come by one as they were obviously not kin to the royal family, but now Natalya had a fairly strong suspicion. Reagan would hold onto that pendant, if for no other reason, because it was of value and an heirloom of a boy that the queen suspected would one day become the King of House Faegon.

"Is there room for another?" Reagan's sweet voice pulled Natalya from her musings.

"Of course, Your Majesty." Natalya scrambled to stand and nearly fell on her face. She could never quite understand how she could be so graceful when fighting and yet so careless normally.

Instead of berating her, Reagan laughed lightly, shaking her head. "There is no need for such formalities. The gardens are clear for now, we are alone and able to speak freely."

Natalya wondered how long it had taken the queen to clear the garden and how long she had been with her before she noticed. She was letting her guard down and as much as she trusted those close to her in her new home, that was no excuse to let her training go to waste. "I had another vision about you."

"I see, no wasting time with you is there?" Reagan soothed the question with one of her gentle smiles that made Natalya miss her mother with such a strong ache she thought she might choke on it. "Cohen told me that you seemed very troubled by this vision. What exactly happened?"

"You were speaking to Lord Nirosh about a seer who you found in the outer villages. You never said her name, but I know it was my mother."

The calm demeanor that the queen wore fell and she looked startled. "You were never meant to see that."

"So you were keeping that information from me intentionally?" Natalya couldn't help that her voice began to rise as her temper went with it. How dare this woman pretend to care for her and then deliberately withhold vital information about her family and past.

"No, not exactly. I was planning on telling you everything. I was

waiting for you to take the bite and began to learn the art of memory reading through blood. It would have been easier to just show you the moment that I shared with your mother than it would have been for you to see that memory. I am truly sorry, Natalya."

"You were going to tell me?" Natalya whispered, hating that she sounded like a child, but far too hopeful to feel like anything other than one.

"Of course, I would never keep something like this from you. I wanted you to see that moment for yourself, though. Your mother was badly hurt and I struggled with allowing you to see her like that, but her voice was strong, even to the end, and the fire in her was so reminiscent of the one I see in you. I wanted you to have the gift of seeing her one more time." Reagan sighed, seeming to steel herself for the conversation. "She told me your name, and you looked so much like her that when I first laid eyes on you. I knew then who you were. Since then I have had to bare this secret. I truly am sorry."

"Why didn't you save her?" It mattered little to her that Reagan had hid this from her, not when the more important question was why was her mother not waiting in the halls of Lunaries for her.

"She refused to take the bite and our laws are firm. You know that this House fell from grace for turning an innocent against their will, even though it was for a good reason. I could not make that mistake again."

"Why wouldn't she want to stay? She had me and my father. And a son." The realization that she had a half brother, someone who shared her mother's blood and was the kin of a King rocked Natalya to her core. "I have a brother."

"Your mother, Elizabeth, explained everything to me. I wanted you to learn the story from her own words, but I remember them all as if they were yesterday, if you do not want to wait."

"Tell me." Natalya demanded.

"Elizabeth was the daughter of a noble man and woman. Your grandfather was one of the masters of the royal library in Magdus. He was a great historian and tactician and was a personal advisor to the king. Your grandmother was one of the queen's ladies in waiting. She was her companion and confidant. Your mother was their only child and a dear friend of the then prince. They had grown up together from birth. The prince was only five years older than her and was already promised to a princess from another kingdom to unite them in a treaty to support trade between the two. Your mother was very gifted with the sight. She trained at the temple in Magdus and had even taken the rite of passed to become a High Priestess, which is quite the honor. She would have sworn off all relations upon her induction, but she disobeyed her masters and sought a relationship with the then prince. She became pregnant and confessed everything to her mother in hopes that she might persuade the queen to

allow the two to wed."

"Your grandmother was scandalized and immediately told the queen, agreeing that it would be for the best for the three of them to leave the kingdom. She promised the queen that they would never tell the child their true parentage and they would never dare attempt to usurp the throne. The queen agreed that they would be allowed to live out their lives in a far away village, so long as they kept their word. On top of their banishment, your mother was stripped of her title of High Priestess of the Sight and much of her power was taken from her in a what I assume was a painful ritual. Your mother was able to tell the prince of his unborn child before she was forced to flee, but she was never able to write him that she'd had a son, your grandmother forbade it. She then met your father, who fell in love with her the moment that they had met. Your mother was still early in the pregnancy and she had tried to fend off his advances. When it became obvious that he would not be dissuaded she told him the truth. He promised to still love her, no matter the circumstances she was in and they agreed to wed. Elizabeth agreed to marry him because she had never thought that another man might agree to have her, knowing her affair, though she still loved the prince until her dying day."

"Are you saying my mother never loved my father?" Her father loved her mother so fiercely she refused to believe it was true. She had very little memories of her parents interactions from when she was young, but she did not believe she had imagined the loving look in her mother's eyes when she looked at her father.

"Of course not. She grew to love him, but in the beginning it would have been a marriage of convenience for her. They wed before the baby was born and your father was out on a hunt with your grandfather when the baby came. Your grandmother persuaded your mother to leave the baby in the woods and tell your father that she had lost it. She told your mother that once your father saw a baby in her arms that was not his he would resent it and her, in time."

"That's absurd! My father loved her so dearly. I know that would never have happened." She had never met her grandmother, her maternal grandparents had died when she was just a baby during a particularly harsh winter. Now she was glad, she could not imagine that she would have liked the woman much.

"I'm sure he would have. Your grandmother was afraid that with the child being a boy, your father might persuade him to take his birthright as an heir to the throne. If the baby had been a girl, I'm sure you would have been raised with an older sister."

Natalya tried to imagine what that would have been like, but she couldn't. "So my mother had visions of her son, my half brother, sitting on top of a throne and she decided to take her small child into the woods to search for him?" It sounded insane and yet she had gone into the woods

with her mother every opportunity that they'd had.

"Your mother just wanted to find her son and have you meet him, hopefully bring him back to have the family that she had always wanted. She only mentioned the throne because in her visions he seemed to be in his late twenties which was impossible at the time that we had spoken. She told me that your brother was born four years before you and you were only eight at the time."

"So that vision won't come true for nearly a decade more. He must only be twenty-one now and you said that he was in his late twenties in the vision she had?"

"Yes, though these things are not set in stone. Visions of the future can change based on the actions of many. It was just one possible future that your mother saw and she knew that. She wanted me to find her son to tell him who he was, that his mother did love him, and if possible to reunite the two of you."

"This is insane."

"It is a lot to take in, you must know that I never intended for you to find out this way," Reagan soothed.

Natalya had to remind herself that yelling at Reagan and throwing a tantrum would not get her what she wanted. She wanted more answers, but she would need to get better at controlling her visions first. If she had something of her mother's she might just have a chance. "Wait. What happened to my mother's necklace?"

"Nirosh has it. I asked him to keep it safe for me in case anything were to happen to me. He was instructed to tell Cohen about my encounter only if necessary. Your mother wanted it to go to your brother and while I feel there is no harm in you having it until we find him, I fear what visions you may have if you come in contact with it. You have been having very strong and frequent visions about my past since wearing my robe and we do not have any deep personal connection. The experience could be overwhelming."

It made sense and yet Natalya was not satisfied with the answer. "I want it back, it belongs to me more than anyone else in this house."

"You are right. When I return from my summons, after you take the bite, we will actively look for a teacher for you so you may learn better control. Then you may have your mother's necklace."

"Fine." Natalya knew she sounded petulant, but she did not care.

"This is for your own good, do you understand that? The visions you might have when you wear the necklace will be stronger than the ones you have now, I don't want to see you hurt by your own gift."

"I said fine," Natalya grunted, well beyond ready to move to another topic. "What do you need from me while you are gone? Everyone else in the house seems to have a job or task, but I'm not sure what you would have me do in your absence."

"Just continue your classes. I know you and the others are training hard and when I do return you and Jasper will be welcomed into the House reborn. Until that time just continue to excel as you have. While I am gone Cohen will need to take on the many jobs that I normally do for him. That being said he will be very busy and I expect that you will allow him to do his work and not keep him from his duty to the House."

"What exactly is that supposed to mean?" Natalya asked, not bothering to hide the anger from her voice. She refused to be seen as just a distraction for Cohen and she liked it even less that Reagan seemed to think that she did her heir's job for him. "I can assure you that if Cohen chooses to spend time with me that is entirely up to him. He is a grown man and will do whatever it is that he pleases no matter my opinion or influence."

"It is true that he is a man grown and can make his own choices, but I see the way he looks at you. If you care about him you will allow him do his duty to this house and will allow him to do so without needless distractions. I know that you two care for each other, but you are young and pose a distraction for him when he is needed more by his people."

"Our people, or am I not really part of this house?" The fury that was brewing in the girl was beginning to bubble over and she stood to put some distance between herself and the queen.

"Don't be a child, you know that is not what I meant." Reagan looked up at her from her seat with all of the grace a queen could posses. Natalya knew the look was meant to make her cower and submit to her, but she was not that kind of girl.

"Then what do you mean, Your Majesty?"

"You are young and there is so much of the world that you have yet to see. Cohen is a man, to be sure, but he is still very much like a child and he has no notion of what it means to be in a committed relationship. The two of you are fumbling around in something you do not understand and I will not watch this House suffer for it."

The truth of the matter was out and yet it did little to assuage Natalya. "I am not Anya."

"Don't you dare speak of things that you do not understand." Reagan rose to stand over her then and Natalya wondered if she had pushed the queen too far.

"I understand far more than you give me credit for." Natalya took another step back, though the vampire's speed greatly outmatched her own and Reagan could have her in her gasps with ease if she truly wanted to. "I have not told you all of my visions that I have seen. I know that you protect Cohen because he is your little brother, I know that you feel like you failed him in some way and that this is some misguided attempted to do right by him, but you are wrong. I do care about him, more than you do if this little conversation is indication of anything. Next time you think to hide things from me or from him remember my *gift* and that I have more control than

you think."

With those final words, Natalya swept from the gardens, doing her best to control her shaking hands and racing heart. She was so angry that she didn't think for a single minute that turning her back on the queen was not smart, but she was lucky that Reagan had no interest in attacking her, or even pursuing her.

Absolutely crippled by anger, Natalya stalked back into the castle in search of Cohen. Reagan was proving to be of little help and she needed someone she could trust to help her sort through the many questions these new revelations had brought.

REAGAN

The royal bedchambers had never been in quite such disarray before. Reagan was scheduled to leave for the journey to Faegon with Darius just after sunset and she had only just completed packing. She had excused Islara and Nicolette from the job, hoping to give them a rest which she sorely regretted. Instead of preparing for the journey ahead, she had used it as an excuse to spend more time with her lover. Anya was sleeping in their bed, having been tired from their daytime activities. Reagan had kept her promise to herself and done her best to shower her paramour with as much love and affection as was possible in the short time since her announced trip. If her passionate lover had caught on to the distraction technique, she had not complained and now Reagan's lack of preparedness was the price to pay for her efforts. If she was also using this as an excuse to avoid fighting with Cohen and Natalya, then that was no one's business, but her own.

The girl was beautiful in sleep. The worry lines that often marred her face were smooth as if they had never been there. When she was not awake and worrying over every single detail out of her own control, she looked as young as the first day Reagan had laid eyes on her. If it were possible, she had been even more aggressive back then, the decades had mellowed her, even if it hardly seemed that way. Reagan had always told her that she was lucky to have taken the bite; the slowing of age helped combat the lines that would have surely made permanent residence on her face otherwise. She moved closer to Anya as if to join her again in the spacious bed, but she stopped short before she could follow through. If she did, she was likely to forgo her obligations and that was something she, and her house, could not afford.

Turning her back from the tempting sight, Reagan slid on a simple cloak over her traveling clothes, preparing for her journey. Faegon was just

over two week's distance from Lunaries on foot without straining herself or her younger companion and she did not have the luxury of a drawn carriage or multiple guards to carry her things, as many of the other vampire royals no doubt were accustomed to. She would be forced to carry her meager belongings and she had done her best to pack light. If she were any other ruler she might have struggled with the task of paring down her clothes and necessities to just one pack, but Reagan's reign had been thrust upon her amidst a coup so she had never been afforded such a comfortable lifestyle. There had always been more important places to focus her attention rather than using her title to live in luxury. As a result she preferred to run her castle with a much more relaxed atmosphere than her predecessors.

Gently, she brushed her fingers along Anya's cheek, pressing a kiss to her temple before slipping from the room. Anya would chide her upon her return, but the queen knew that waking her sleeping lover would only end in an argument, or possibly another round of lovemaking, and she had time for neither.

The few servants and various other folk who were up at such an early hour bowed to their queen as she passed. Another time would have found Reagan stopping to speak with each of them in turn, but there were more pressing matters to attend.

"Your Majesty," a familiar voice called and Reagan paused to allow Nicolette to join her.

"I do wish I could stop to talk, Nicolette, but I must be going."

"I know, Your Majesty, I just wanted to give you a gift before you left. I am honestly glad that I found you in time." The woman produced a beautifully made gray vest. It was simple, made of comfortable fabric with small gold details accenting the pockets and lapel.

"It is beautiful," Reagan smiled, carefully taking it into her hands and pulling it to her chest.

"It is magical, Your Majesty. The thread was made by a sorcerer. I had it purchased at the last market I was able to attend. It has protective properties, which shield the wearer from most weapons and even some basic poisons. I have not had an occasion to use it, but now seemed the best time to put it to the test."

"That is very thoughtful of you." Reagan knew that her people cared for her, but seeing that they truly loved her as their queen assured her that any past wrongdoings on her part were for the best. Whatever she had been before she had taken on the weight of a crown had allowed her to be the type of ruler who was loved and respected by her people. "I will wear it with pride."

Nicolette curtsied before her queen before excusing herself to her duties. With Reagan leaving and Cohen acting as King until her return, Nicolette was set in charge of all of the royal maids and servants. She was

well suited for the task and Reagan had no doubt that she was leaving her home in very good hands. Reagan watched her handmaid go as she slid the gift into her pack. No doubt she would need it in the weeks to come, but for now she was safe amongst her people.

Reagan walked through the halls as if it would be her last time. She had no illusions about the state that her House was in. The Crown was not happy with them and her prompt dismissal of their messenger would only worsen their standing. She doubted that she would see these walls in the next decade or so, if ever. It would not surprise her if upon her arrival she were taken in chains and held without trial until she was long forgotten. She was not sure her advisors were up to the task of ruling without her, but they might have to be. It would not do to dwell on her fate when she was meant to keep a calm face in front of her people and Reagan pushed the lingering doubt from her mind.

Cohen was waiting for her by the gate, surprisingly alone. The smile on his face was forced and she wondered for a moment if Anya had been right and that she should have chosen to stay. A Queen must be a woman of her word, however, and it was far too late to change her mind now. The rest of the castle was giving them a blessedly private moment and Darius seemed to be absent as well, she would be wise to take advantage of it.

"I know why you must go and yet my heart aches to see you leave." Cohen greeted her with an uncustomary embrace. His lips brushed her cheek and Reagan took the opportunity to inhale his scent. It was filled with old memories from their past and made her long for those simpler times.

"I know, but I must leave now, lest I make this departure harder on either of us."

Cohen watched her a moment longer, before seeming to come to a decision. He drew his emotions in, hiding the sorrow from his face. "What would you have me do in your absence?"

"The old West Wing has been needing to be rebuilt for some time. While I hope not to return with Faegon royals at my heel, I fear that there are very few ways for my meeting with the High Council to go. It might be wise to prepare for unwanted guests. Otherwise I expect you to be the fair and just King that I know you will be in my absence."

"Of course, Rae. I will await your return every night as I am sure your people will join me in doing so." Cohen did a fair job of keeping his controlled façade, but she knew him too well to fall for it. She hated to bring any of her people pain, Cohen most of all, but she could not allow selfish desires to get in the way of her duty.

"I know, I wish it didn't have to be this way. If you could also keep an eye on Natalya. She should keep up with all of her training. Her abilities are far more vast than I believe she is aware of and I do not wish to see her squander them." She thought to warn him off the girl again, but refrained. There was no need to cause a fight, not now.

"I will. She will be my top priority, second only to the House." Cohen watched her with careful eyes, treading around the topic of any further involvement with the girl. They were dangerously close to breaking the professional act and falling into the roles of quarreling siblings and she did not want to leave her brother this way.

"Enough of this, where is Darius?"

At the sound of his name, the vampire materialized from the shadows near the end of the corridor, looking as if he had just happened upon them. Reagan was not as easily fooled and she knew that the man had heard at least the end of their conversation. She knew that Darius was intrigued by their human charge because of the raw magic that seemed to glow around her and Reagan was glad that she would be taking him with her. She had no fear that Darius would harm the girl, but his advances were inappropriate and she knew that he, on many occasions, had made her uncomfortable.

"Are you ready to set forth, Your Majesty?" Darius asked, his face betraying nothing.

Cohen had the grace not to mention the strange entrance and Reagan let her guard slide down once more. Being under the careful watch of Faegon had made her paranoid. She could not afford to doubt her true allies when her people's place under the Great King Zentarion was under question.

"It is best to leave before the rest of the castle wakes, Your Majesty." Cohen slid back into his polite façade with ease. Even with those they trusted, they did their best to keep a mask on around each other. Only Nirosh knew the true nature of their relationship and subsequently the real story of the fall of Lunaries and Reagan's rise into power. It was best kept that way.

"Thank You, Lord Cohen. Keep our people safe until my return."

"What must be done will be." Cohen replied with the ancient words of their people.

Darius moved to open the door and Reagan walked out of her home into the pale light of the moon. She dared not turn back to look upon what she was leaving as the dread from earlier returned. No matter how much she tried to reassure herself that she would be back in little time she felt that she would never see her home again.

"There is no need to worry, Your Majesty. You will see your people again soon." Darius soothed, always perceptive with his abilities. She felt as he tried to alter her aura in an attempt to calm her.

"Thank you, Darius, but I am quite fine. I am not in need of your services, as of yet." Reagan knew that quelling the fear in her heart would only cause it to blindside her later. She was never in favor of hiding her emotions and she would not allow the man to change that now. Darius did not respond, but she did feel his magic receding and the dull ache returned,

making itself at home in her chest.

Despite the great distance between Lunaries and Faegon there were very few villages between the two Houses of neutral standing. Those that pledged their allegiance to any other vampire House would most likely close their doors to a foreign and disgraced queen. Reagan did not allow herself much pride and yet she would not allow them to suffer wasted time by begging or battering to stay within village walls that rather see their backs. It meant that the two would be forced to look for safe places to rest within Mordin Forest to insure that they would not be taken surprise by rogues.

Darius was the perfect member of her court to take with her because of his past involvement with the false queen. It was also, no doubt, why both Anya and Cohen found themselves united in trying to persuade her to choose another travel companion. Cohen had never showed mistrust of the man before, but even he had confided his doubts to her just the night before. Reagan had been just as dismissive of Cohen's words as she had always been of Anya's. Her lover feared the man because of his ties to Cassandra, which while valid, seemed a moot point as he had been dutifully serving House Lunaries for nearly five decades and she had never once seen a reason to doubt him. Cohen's fear was the man's age. Darius was still a childe in many rights, but he was smart and strong. He was the leader of her personal guard for a reason. If he was good enough to protect her in her home, he was good enough to protect her outside of it as well.

His former ties to Cassandra and her ilk were possibly a more troublesome topic, but Reagan saw no reason for him to be loyal to the fake queen or her swine of followers. He had been turned by Cassandra herself, against his will. When they'd first come upon him he had narrowly escaped the woman's wrath and he was more than vocal about his distaste of the woman. If she had learned anything from her own life experiences, when turned against your will you would do anything to fight against the ones who wronged you. He was strong and driven, using his anger toward Cassandra to fuel him until he rose through Lunaries' ranks. Making him the commander of her guard had seemed obvious as a way to reward him for his efforts while also putting him in a position where Reagan could easily keep an eye on him. In the decades that had passed since his appointment, the queen saw no reason to distrust him and thus dismissed the accusations of her paramour and heir as nothing, but paranoia.

"Your Majesty." Darius said, pulling Reagan from her deep thoughts.

"I fear that titles are dangerous in these woods. Until we are safe in Faegon it would be wise to just use each other's names." They were still well within Lunaries' land. While there weren't very many villages surrounding the once great house, a few still remained. It wouldn't have been out of place to run into someone where they were, though Reagan did not want to take the chance of assuming anyone in these parts was a friend. The rogues had become increasingly persistent under Cassandra's lead and she had no

doubt that they lurked in every corner of the empire. She would have been surprised if the woman didn't do her best to plant spies in every part of the forest.

"Yes, Your—I'm sorry, Reagan," Darius fumbled with his words and Reagan did her best to hide her smile. He was so young and it wasn't often that she was given reminders of that fact. Within the castle walls he had the mantle of his title to uphold and so he had always acted twice his age. Reagan had often wondered if it was to prove to those around him that he was mature and capable enough for his responsibility or if it was to convince himself. "I just wanted to thank you for the honor of accompanying you. I know there was opposition from the others."

"You have no need to thank me, Darius. You earned the position you are in now by proving your loyalty and strength to me. It is I who should be honored. I would not worry about the whispers in the castle. There will always be fear within our walls, it is the unfortunate nature of our standing within the empire, one that I fear might have just worsened by my actions, but the words of scared children do not always reflect the truth within their hearts. Often when the veil is lifted and the reason for the fear is gone, those same children open themselves up to reason."

"If you are sure." Darius, for his part, sounded far from sure. Reagan wondered how it came to be that her people had grown to distrust so easily and forgive less so. She had once thought her House an accepting and open environment, but now she was less sure.

"I am. You will see. This trip to the capitol is less than ideal, both in timing and reasoning, but there will be good to come of it. Now, enough of that talk. Let us enjoy the peaceful journey in the forest. It's not often that either of us has the time so simply appreciate our surroundings."

They fell into a comfortable silence and Reagan allowed herself to follow her own advice and enjoy the scenery around them. Since the loss of Gareth and her assent to the throne, she hardly left the castle grounds without the need to follow a tight schedule. It was not safe, even for a trained vampire, to wander in the King's land due to their banishment and when she did have a need to leave her own protective walls it was often done with a large group which kept her from appreciating the beauty that surrounded them. It was only in recent decades that she'd had the freedom to leave the castle to hunt, and even then she'd only ever been out once or twice without her guards or Anya and Cohen in tow. Even with her paramour or her heir, there had been incessant chatter that inevitably turned to bickering. Darius blessedly enjoyed silence more than most of her usual companions and she found she enjoyed the comfort his presence brought her.

This journey with Darius was also one of the first in which she left the lands surrounding Lunaries since her appointment as queen. Even when Gareth had been King, she had stuck close to their walls. It hadn't been safe

to wander, what with the banishment and horrible unrest amongst the Lunarian people. Because of this, she had never really been able to learn the forest that her castle lay within. Many of her people, those who had stayed due to their loyalty to Gareth, or those recently born into their ranks would have been at the same disadvantage as she. Thus the captain of her guard became the obvious choice to accompany her. Darius knew the woods far better than most, being that he was not from Lunaries originally, and he led their journey with ease. He passed each tree as if they were landmarks, though Reagan could hardly tell the difference between those of the same family.

There was a chill in the air. Winter had begun, though they'd yet to see the first snowfall. It would be a new year soon, though Reagan dared not hope that she would be back in the safety of her own castle to see it in. The trees closest to the castle had already lost their leaves and it was no surprise to Reagan that Mordin Forest had seen the same treatment. Bare, gnarled branches stretched out to snag them, but Darius wove their path with a simple grace and Reagan allowed herself more time to simply observe. The moon was high in the sky by now. It was not quite full yet, but the light it gave was a calming presence for that the queen was glad. Moonlight, though not as bright as the sun, could still be harsh and Reagan feared that had she the proper light, she would slow their journey to simply take in the forest around them. Though she would not admit it, she knew in her heart that she would not see this forest again. There was no doubt in her mind that Zentarion would see her thrown in a cell, the fate of her beloved home left to hang in the balance. The perceived wrongdoings of her predecessor compounded with her own inability to turn her back on Emeline had jeopardized everything she had worked so hard to build and yet she did not regret taking in the girls.

As if he could read her very thoughts, Darius carefully broke the spell of silence between them. "You did the right thing with Emeline and Natalya, even if the Crown doesn't see it, I do. Your people do."

"It means a lot to hear that," Reagan admitted. She might not regret her decision, but she had feared that her people would never forgive her.

"Not to say that there is gossip around the training grounds, but the men and women do talk as they practice and all I have ever heard is praise for your leadership. There is something to be said of a woman who does what she knows in her heart to be right, even in the face of ridicule from the Crown."

Reagan smirked as Darius' words, knowing that he might sense the change in her mood, but thankful he could not see her face. Even in the most well trained armies there was gossip, she had no doubt, and her people were no different. When they were given so little freedoms, constricted to the castle grounds and tight radius of trees surrounding, it was wonder that gossip was kept as generally well hidden as it was.

"People talk, Darius, there is no harm in it, but I am glad that what you have heard has been good. I do not think our people could survive another civil war."

The topic had taken a dark turn, as most things involving Lunaries' history did and the pair fell back to their own thoughts. Darius was leading them through the thickly settled no-man's-land with ease. They were nearing the border to Adrastos and Reagan wondered briefly if it would be wise to travel deep into Queen Quanna's land and attempt to find shelter. Stopping needlessly would slow their journey, but starting a fight on her people's border with a queen held in high regard with the King of Kings would not be wise.

"We should attempt to make for camp soon. I think it wise to push through Adrastos' territory in one go, if possible."

Darius nodded without response, slowing his strict pace to being searching for shelter. The issue with traveling in winter was bare trees made for terrible cover and neither had packed a proper tent, both agreeing that looking for natural lodging to blend into their surrounds was more practical.

A suitable camp did not present itself until the sun had begun to creep up into the sky. Reagan could feel its warmth as the trees above them basked in it and she longed to truly feel the sun again. She should be old enough to stand under it long enough to feel its touch soak into her bones, but the forced seclusion had caused her not to grow immunity to it like many of the elder vampires. She would last longer than Darius, however, and she would not risk the man's safety for her own whims.

Luck appeared to be on their side just then. The winding path that they were following began a slow incline before he branched off to two roads. One began to descend in altitude again, taking them well into Adrastos' lands. The other continued to climb for a bit before it rounded behind a large boulder. Darius quickly slid behind the natural pass, motioning for her to wait while he investigated the possible shelter.

"We may rest here for the morning, the boulder is well positioned before a natural enclosure. It wouldn't hold more than the two of us and it made up of other, like-sized rocks. It looks like moss has grown up and over them and it is naturally obstructing the sun." Darius spoke as he turned to allow her to pass first.

The enclosure was just as the man had said. It was just deep enough that the two would be able to lie down without fearing that their feet might be exposed at the opening. They were hidden from the path, at least, and Reagan had grown to be a light sleeper, with some small modifications she could be sure that if anyone attempted to sneak up on them that she would wake before they got close.

While Reagan surveyed the small enclosure, Darius began to set down his pack. They had brought sleeping mats and a small supply of blood with

them. They would be hunting for most of their food, but Nirosh had insisted that it would be wise to bring some. Reagan was more than glad at his urging as she rested her tired feet and took her meal.

"I think it wise if we find some small branches and twigs to weave into small tiles. If we hide them under the leaves around the path to this little hiding spot, the noise of any intruder will be enough to wake me and keep it so neither of us has to stay up all day on guard."

"That would be wise," Darius nodded while stopping his vile. "You stay and relax, I will bring us the supplies."

Reagan could not find it in herself to argue. She should be ashamed at how tired she felt, but she'd hardly been able to get any rest in the days leading up to her departure. Between spending time with her paramour and seeing to the castle, it was a wonder she'd found time to sleep at all. Luckily, Darius returned shortly, his arms filled with twigs and the two worked on weaving them into shapes that were meant to resemble squares, though with how stiff her fingers were becoming and how heavy her eyelids were, Reagan found it rather lucky that any of hers held together.

"Rest now, Your Majesty," Darius said and Regan lacked the energy to correct him. "I'll set the traps and be back in a moment."

Reagan gave in to her exhaustion and curled up into her half unpacked bedroll, imagining that she was in her soft bed, holding Anya to her, instead of on the cold, dirt packed floor with only the sounds of the slowly waking woods to keep her comfort.

CASSANDRA

Lord Wynn and Lady Ves were sitting at the council table when Cassandra swept into the room, anger blowing through her hair and making her heels sound like a whip being cracked. Both of her advisors stood at her arrival, wary of her apparent anger. Cassandra ignored them and the table entirely to take residence by the large open window. There was a nice breeze coming in and Cassandra wished, not for the first time, that it would take all of her troubles with it.

"Your Majesty," Lord Wynn began to speak, but was promptly stopped by Lady Ves' heel in his foot. The sound of her hissing and his grunt was indication that the two were beginning to bicker. Sometimes Cassandra wondered exactly what she had done to deserve these idiots as her Councilmen and women, but then she remembered that she had hand picked them. It was just impossible to find good help it seemed.

"Where is Logan?" Cassandra demanded, ignoring the childish struggle happening between the two. Perhaps if she continued to ignore them it would end and she wouldn't have to discipline two full grown adults, elder vampires no less, for acting like babies.

"I cannot be certain, would you like me to call for him, Your Majesty?" Lady Ves answered.

Cassandra turned to face them in time to see the girl straighten herself and her attire, confusion evident in her face. Cassandra hardly ever called on Logan, not since Leon had become a fixture in her bed, but the page would not be able to help her now. Despite whatever her feelings were for her heir she could not keep the latest news from him.

"If I did not wish to see him then why would I ask his location?" Cassandra growled, spinning to face the two, her fangs evident through her sneer.

"Of course, Your Majesty. My apologies, Your Majesty." Lady Ves

scrambled toward the door and out of her wrath.

"We can come back from this, it is truly just a minor setback," Lord Wynn tried to speak again, but Cassandra was well beyond her limits with the man. He was just as liable as Vestera in this mess. Seeing the man's fake sympathy made her sick.

"Tell me that your other schemes in Faegon have not fallen apart."

"Of course not, Your Majesty, this may have altered our plans, but it has by no means destroyed them."

"For your's and Vestera's sake I would hope so," Cassandra growled. She knew she had slipped into bloodlust and she must look insane, but she was far too enraged to care about decorum.

Logan chose then to enter the room, effectively stopping the undoubtedly scathing comment from Wynn, a very meek looking Lady Vestera on his heels. Lord Jarrod materialized behind her moments later and Cassandra wondered just how far word of her failure had traveled through the castle.

"We are losing this war before it has properly begun and it is all due to your sheer incompetence," Cassandra snapped and all eyes fell on the petite girl before her.

"I did my best, but we were overrun. Malcolm was older than me yet even he could not get the upper hand. The Free Folk are becoming more bold."

"I do *not* want to hear your excuses. Do you think that maybe had you stayed and assisted him we would still have a source close to Pa'ari? You have always said you would go to any length to see the Cause through, but I suddenly find reason to doubt you. You allowed Decker to fall into the hands of the arrogant King of Kings and now you have let this mission fail. Tell me why I shouldn't just see to your death now."

"Your majesty, she is just a childe," Lord Jarrod spoke, though there was no love lost between him and Ves. Cassandra could not fathom why he might come to her aid.

"So you are suggesting that it is my fault that I assigned her and she simply wasn't ready?" The Queen rounded on the oldest vampire of her house.

"What Jarrod means is—"

"I do not want to hear your excuses, Wynn." Cassandra shouted and a sudden silence fell over the small council.

"My Lords, My Lady, I believe it best to see yourselves out. I would like a word with my wife alone." Logan spoke, his tone even, though his eyes glowed their eerie blue and he made it clear that his suggestion was an order.

Jarrod and Vestera left first, though the girl fled and the elder vampire did so at a subdued pace, as if to defy his King's orders. For once, Wynn seemed to understand his place in the Queen's court and he left without

argument, inclining his head toward Cassandra and Logan in turn before retreating to his shadows. Cassandra watched him leave all too aware that the man might have motives of his own to allow their source to die when he did. He was a man of whispers and lies and he never once fooled her into believing that he was loyal to her and not to his own personal agenda. He would have known about the movements of the Free Folk in that part of the forest and had deliberately not informed anyone.

"I would keep a closer eye on that man," Logan spoke the very thing that she had been thinking. He might not always agree with her, but they had always shared the belief that Wynn could only be trusted so long as they were the highest bidder. "I would also not take that tone with our people, you seek to unite them under one force yet you treat them as inferiors and that only increases the divide."

"Do not lecture me on politics," Cassandra growled, shifting her focus and anger on her husband, "and never undermine me like that again."

"Of course, dear wife, how silly of me. I must have gotten swept up in the moment." The smirk on his lips made the queen want to hurt him, but she knew she had to reign in her bloodlust for now. She could not afford to lose Logan's loyalty and his people not yet.

"Wynn might believe that he is my only spy in these halls, but we both know that I am not stupid enough to not employ men of my own." Cassandra watched her husband carefully, but he showed no signs that something might be amiss.

"I would never think for a minute that you were stupid." The coy smile was teasing, but there was a coolness in his eyes she wasn't sure if she had ever seen before. She would have to analyze that later when her carefully constructed rebellion was not falling apart before her very eyes.

"Enough with the flattery. I did not bring you here to nauseate me with fake kindness." Cassandra took a deep breath to calm herself, allowing her fangs to recede so she might have a moderately level headed conversation with Logan. "There is word from our brothers and sisters in the forest. Faegon has a messenger on the move."

"And they have not stopped them because?" Interest sparked for a moment before the bored facade fell back into place.

"It is Paden, the third in line for Zentarion's false crown. His honor guard is made up of the four strongest vampires in Zentarion's employment."

"They let a royal member move about the forest with only four guards?"

"That is not the true problem here. They have already been to Lunaries, it seems. If the word is true, Reagan will be leaving the security of her castle to journey to Faegon to answer for crimes against the High Council and Crown."

"How can we be sure that this word you received is to be trusted?

Who told you these things?"

Logan still reacted poorly at the mention of the false Queen, his very own sister. He, like Cassandra, could not forgive her and Gareth for their shared past misgivings, but he could never muster the same anger that she felt. He was weak for allowing such sentiments to influence his judgement of her. He would never admit it, but the only way to truly gain vengeance for what had been done to him was to kill Reagan. He claimed that the reason he wouldn't kill her was because he still believed in political reform and she needed to be taken to trial, not made an example of by assassination. He feared it would turn her into a martyr, but Cassandra knew better. Despite all that he had seen, Logan was still a naive boy when it came to the ways of the world. He was soft and ultimately it was what convinced Cassandra that his uses to her and her plans were nearing their end.

"That is for me to be concerned with, not you. You will have to go out and meet her and whatever poor excuse for a guardsman she brings with her. You know as well as I that Reagan will not take a full honor guard. She has always been too confident in her own strength to admit the need for help." The comment struck a cord as she intended and Logan's frown turned into a dark scowl. "Do you not agree with me? You know that I am right, do you not?"

"I will not go after her. She is a nuisance to be sure, but I will not harm her." Logan stood his ground well. It was something that Cassandra had appreciated about him most when they had been the black sheep of Lunaries. He had always stuck by her side then, though she could hardly remember the boy that he had been as she looked at the man he had become. Now his stubbornness was more than a small inconvenience.

"Enough. Your weakness sickens me. If you will not go after her then I will be forced to do so. I hope you remember your place in my absence." Cassandra sneered and walked forward into his space. She might not be of the same height as him, but she was a force to be reckoned with and it was high time that Logan remembered that. Her eyes were glowing and her fangs ached to retreat as she kept her bloodlust at bay. If she let herself go now she was afraid she just might kill the man and she still had uses for him yet.

"My place?" Logan did not back down from her close proximity and instead crowded forward so they were just inches from each other. "I thought my place was always by your side, but it has become increasingly obvious that you would rather surround yourselves by zealots and idiots! Vestera only follows you because she loves you, I know that you know this, you are too smart not to see that. Wynn is a slippery man who has no alliances, but his own. Leon is ambitious and would kill you to take your place just as quickly as he would sell you out to the Crown if it would raise his station. And Jarod? We know nothing about the man besides what thin

lies he tells us."

His presence was becoming claustrophobic and Cassandra worried that she was losing control. She took a step back to put some distance between them, but her fangs did fully descend this time and her stance was stiff, ready for a fight. "And you? You once agreed with me that Zentarion needed to be tried for his crimes. I think we have more than proved that corruption is running rampant in this empire. When did you decide that cutting off the head of the snake was enough? I thought we had agreed that demolishing the infrastructure was the only way to insure that this world was built the way it needed to be."

"I was young, and angry. You are allowing rage from a centuries old slight to bring our very world down to its knees. Neither of us has any experience or knowledge on how to help it rise from the ashes after. You will destroy us all." His words were exasperated and tired, the anger seemed to bleed from him. That would not do, Cassandra could handle anger, but this resignation mixed with pity was more than she could stomach.

"I will burn this empire to the ground if need be. And in the end I will be the one sitting atop the throne as I watch my world reborn. I thought you would be there with me, but clearly I misjudged your commitment to the Cause. I have no time to deal with your foolishness now, but when I return I swear to you it will be with your sister's head and then I will give you one chance, and only one chance, to prove to me that you are still loyal to me."

The threat was open and Cassandra rather enjoyed the wide-eyed look she was receiving from her husband. When it was evident that he had no response planned to her very real ultimatum, she swept past him and out of the room, not willing to waste another moment on the man. There was no time left to argue. If she were to leave in order to hunt down and kill Reagan she would need to take precautions to insure that all of the hard work she had put into maintaining this rebellion was not undone in her absence. The influence of the huntress whore on her husband was becoming more and more evident by the day. While her spies had yet to turn up evidence of unrest in her ranks she knew that Logan was no idiot. He, unlike Wynn, would conduct his operations throughout her people subtly. She knew not whom she could trust and the anxiety would cause her to make a mistake that could lead to her losing control. The time to play with Leon was done. She would need to test him to see if he was capable of becoming more than just her page. She would need someone to see that order was kept while she waged her war against the people who stripped her life from her and Logan was no longer an option.

The servants passing through the corridor leading to her quarters quickly fled from her path. Before long the entire area would be clear just as Cassandra preferred it. Even before the fall of her once beloved House Lunaries she had loved her solitude. People were always complicated. You

could never control their actions and control was something that Cassandra needed to feel sane. Her first love had always chided her when she became inconsolable when even the smallest thing had not gone her way. She ought to have learned after her second love, but it seemed she had fallen into a similar cycle. She had grown accustomed to the life of being a King's wife. She was his Queen in all, but the name, and had even been the heir to his crown until the wretched whore Reagan had come into their lives and ruined it all. Logan might not understand why the fake queen needed to be struck down, but Cassandra would never forgive her for the wrong she had done to her. Mostly she would never forgive herself for allowing something as trivial as love to cloud her judgement, but she would not think on that now.

Cassandra was brought out of her dark thoughts by a troubling sight. The door to her private study stood just slightly ajar alerting her to another's presence. The servants knew to keep out of this room and only came to tidy it on her command and even still only when Cassandra was present. There were very few allowed within the chamber without her explicit permission and she had left many of them in the wake of her fury, surely they would not be foolish enough to seek her out now. She felt the anger already resting deep in her bones rise to the surface again and she felt her fangs pierce into her lip before she realized she had given into her bloodlust for a second time in the same night. Taking a steadying breath, she pushed the door open with a rough shove, hoping to show the intruder just how much trouble they would find themselves in when she caught them. The echo of the heavy wooden door hitting the stone rang in her ears and she nearly winced at the noise before composing herself. There was no one sitting at the table stationed in the center of the room, though the books she had left there earlier had been touched. Some had been moved, closed and pushed to the side while others were open to pages she knew were not of her own choosing.

She walked past the books noting that one was open to a map of the forest as it stood in a time before even she had been reborn. It was inked with an unnecessary flourish, far too garish for her tastes. The Houses illustrated on the page were nearly all extinct or relocated throughout Mordin Forest, reminding Cassandra of the empire's sordid past. The many villages and keeps between the original vampire strongholds were all but gone and Cassandra took a moment to pause over the strange groups of human and vampire dwellings that no longer existed before righting herself in search for the intruder.

The study's walls were lined with bookcases that seemed to touch the high ceilings. There were bookcases throughout the open space creating corridors, which would look like a labyrinth to anyone not accustomed to roaming the many titles for knowledge and pleasure. Cassandra had made sure that comfortable chairs were placed throughout the room, between her

favorite stacks of books, and it was one near the histories detailing the ancient ogre wars that she found the culprit.

"Lady Cassandra, I wondered how long it would be before your arrival. There are some very interesting tomes here." Lord Jarrod looked quite cocky sprawled in one of her favorite chairs. He was lounging back as if it were his library that she had found him in and she noticed that he had one tome open on the table beside him.

"As it would happen this is my study, so yes I was aware of the nature of these tomes. That one that you are so barbarically damaging is older than you and I combined." Cassandra swept in and scooped it up as if it were fragile as an infant before sliding it back into its place.

"That is a fair point, Your Majesty. Both points, I might add." The man spoke as if they were discussing the weather and not the shameful disrespect that he was showing to the only known recorded histories of their people. Jarod acted like a man of high breeding and class, but he was just a boy who played at things that he did no understand.

"What is it that you want, Jarrod? You know better than to pester me, especially here. Speak your mind or be gone." Cassandra was tired and all she wanted was to sink into her favorite chair that was being occupied by the smug bastard, and pretend that the world outside the doors of her study did not exist.

"I am here to tell you that leaving this castle to chase after the false queen will only end in your own despair." He had the decency to say these words with a grave tone, the bored looks from before were replaced with a serious stare.

"Are you a seer now and I was failed to be informed? I find it doubtful you possess the intelligence to come to this conclusion on your own." It seemed everyone in her court saw fit to test her today. Jarod was nearing her limits of patience and he was about to find himself in a poor state, the ancient books surrounding them be damned.

"As it were I am not a seer, just a man who is willing to open is eyes to see everything that happens in his surroundings. You might believe that your seat here is secure and in no need of defense, but I warn you that you could not be more wrong."

"Are you threatening me? I see no evidence of this supposed treason you speak of so I can only conclude that it is you who intends to mastermind it and I find that doubtful." Cassandra had to dig deep within herself to bury her rage at his words, willing the rising bloodlust to retreat. It would not do to kill one of her advisors, not when she already planned on killing Logan when he refused to commit to her plans to cripple the empire and reform it to her standards. It would be bad form to kill half of her council on the eve of her glorious war.

"How could it be me? I believe you just insulted my intelligence. If I am as stupid as you believe then any attempt at treason from me will surely

fail and yet I am neither stupid nor am I the one attempting to unseat you." His frank tone was infuriating.

"Enough, be gone now before I have you thrown into a cell."

Lord Jarrod rose to his feet, mocking her with a bow so low it seemed his nose might touch the ground. "I do hope that your knowledge is as vast as your confidence, Your Majesty. I would hate to see the disappointed look on your face when my warning comes to pass. If you still do not believe me then ask Lord Wynn why he has not reported these whispers to you and you might find that you know who the true puppet master is here."

"GET OUT!" Cassandra shouted, picking up the nearest object, a heavy silver candlestick and hurling it at the pompous vampire's head. He ducked it with little effort and strode from the room as if he hadn't a care in the world.

Lord Jarrod had always been the most reserved of her advisors. Until this point he had been loyal to her and she had never had cause to question that. He was quiet, gave advise where he thought it necessary, and had always been just a little too cocky for her liking, but harmless. Was it possible that she was such a poor judge of character? She had once thought Logan a sound partner to assist her in this rebellion and she was clearly very wrong about him. She had been the pretty face to turn his head and his mind when he was young, but now another pretty face was playing the same game and he just as easily fell for it once again. Was it possible that everything he had said about her other chosen companions was true? She immediately brushed the passing thought aside. Self-doubt had never served her well and there would be no good in traveling down that road now. She had always stuck by her actions and this time was no different. She had proclaimed, quite loudly and adamantly, that she would journey to take out the insipid girl who had forced her into the life she now lived and she would not let her people see her as weak for not following through.

The words that Lord Jarrod spoke rang in her head causing her temple to pulse and throb. She knew before he had broken into her study that leaving her kingdom and people in the hands of Logan would be a mistake, but it seemed that her fears of Wynn's questionable intentions were just. She would have to make sure that he was kept watch over while she was gone as well. It would seem that she would need both Lady Ves and Leon to keep the traitors from undoing everything she had worked for.

The thought that there might not be a threat, that Lord Jarrod was just scaring her with his misguided advice as he had been known to do in the past was not lost on the queen. She could not expose anyone as a traitor without further proof, though she would not have time to do so before her journey. She would have to leave knowing that everything was not in her control and instead it was put in the trust of her advisor and her page. She was not entirely sure which was worse, the advisor whom Cassandra was sure loved her more than a subject should love her queen or, a boy who was

only warming her bed to gain power of his own. Trusting them would be easier than trusting her husband or any of her other sworn subjects, a disturbing thought to be sure.

Cassandra sank into the plush seat before her, pulling one of her favorite tomes off of the shelf that was just within reach. She might not be fighting ogres, but she hoped that another thumb through of stories of times long since past would shed light on the precarious situation she now found herself in. Even if she had to sit in that very spot until the sun shown through the study windows, Cassandra would look for any answer that did not end in her own undoing.

CLAYTON

The sun was just beginning to set beyond the thin curtains that hung in the large windows of one of Lady Sedalia's guest bedrooms. Clayton lay behind their protection, ignoring the voice in his head telling him that if he was awake he should be up and moving, not lazing about. It was still early and no one was expecting to see him for a few hours so he allowed himself some indulgence. The mattress was easily the softest he had ever felt and the smooth silk sheets slid over his skin, pulling him into their embrace until it was nearly impossible to separate himself from them. He turned on his side, pushing his face into the soft pillow to inhale the clean scent. The white silk contrasted beautifully with the dark mahogany of the bed and the gold embroidery glittered in the fading sun. The curtains that surrounded the bed were sheer, but blocked out most of the harmful rays that poured through the open window. Clayton was happy to be able to feel the warmth on his skin without the accompanying burn.

The rest of the room was just as lavish, though he hadn't had enough time to investigate it before he had crawled into the bed the day before, bone tired and in shock. He had moved through the forest and snuck back into the city without being detected, though he honestly couldn't be sure how. He hadn't even considered returning to the slums as he allowed his leadened feet take him to his lady's house. Sedalia hadn't been home when he had first arrived and the doorman had seen him to this very guest room and had shut the door behind him without comment. Clayton shuddered to think what he might look like and he was very glad that he hadn't been forced to report to the radiant lady of Faegon in such a state.

Dusk was nearing an end and a polite knock on the door pulled the man from his thoughts. Clayton called out to allow them entrance, not willing to deny himself the comfort of the bed just yet, no matter what his manners might dictate. A petite girl of no more than nine or ten entered,

her eyes downcast. She was human with dark skin and even darker eyes. She had her hair put back in a tight knot and her clothes were just as plain and practical.

"M'lady requested that I check on you, sir. She is wondering if you might be awake and if you would like a bath before seeking audience with her in the dining hall." She spoke with a gentle voice and Clayton wondered for a moment on who this girl might be and what had brought her to this position, but the answers to these questions mattered very little and he pushed the thoughts aside.

"I would be pleased for a bath and meal, if the Lady Sedalia does not oppose to being made to wait. I fear I have no clothing, however, and I would need far nicer clothes than these to see our Lady."

"Of course, new clothes will be provided, shall I fetch the bath then and return with clothing?" Her eyes were still downcast as they had been their entire interaction and it made Clayton profoundly sad. He pitied this creature who would never know any other station than the meek one in which she found herself. He had been lucky to climb from his place as a child even if he did fall a few rungs down the ladder; he was still in a much better position than where he was born.

"Thank you." The girl seemed surprised by the words and she blushed before bowing out of the room in a rush.

There was no sense in pretending that he might fall back asleep, knowing full well that Sedalia would be expecting him soon, so Clayton reluctantly rose from his warm bed. He had hung his cloak in the empty wardrobe the night before, carefully facing the rich fabric out. The rags, even if just for decoration, had no place in a room so luxurious. His dirty tunic and pants had been next to go, left in a neat, folded pile on the seat of the vanity. It seemed a servant had taken them in the night as they sat where he left them newly laundered. After insuring the small amount of coin he had arrived with was tucked in the pant pocket still, Clayton took the time to explore his room.

The large bed he had occupied sat on a raised platform against the farthest wall from the door. The wardrobe and vanity stood against the wall just off the platform and were carved from the same wood as the bed, contrasting beautifully with the soft colors of the fabrics in the room. A plush settee of a warm peach was positioned in front of an unlit fireplace that sat proudly across from the bed. Matching armchairs framed the settee to give seating for three, though Clayton was unsure when he would ever make use of such a design.

The last wall was monopolized by large arches that led to a balcony. The arches were thoughtfully draped by the same sheer fabric that canopied the bed, filtering out the harmful sun without preventing the soothing warmth that it brought. Of course Clayton never worried about feeling cold, not since the gift of the bite had taken such simple discomforts from

his body, but he still enjoyed the caress of the sun's warmth. It reminded him of his training days and spending time with Lenore by the lake when everyone else was asleep. He thought to walk out and explore the balcony as the sun had very nearly set, and there would be no harm in spending a few moments in the light, but another knock on the door signaled a brigade of servants arriving with a bath and hot water so he could be ready to see the lady of the manor.

Clayton made quick work of sliding into the hot bath. He took his time to make sure that the stink of the slums was washed away with it, bathing the dirt and grime from his skin and hair, though he knew that even after a thorough cleaning it would be difficult to rid himself of the stench. Even as a child in a poor village he had always made sure to stay clean and presentable, but the smell could never be helped. He had been made fun of as a child for scrubbing his skin until he was red and for washing his clothes until the cloth became thin and threadbare. He could never explain why, but it had always been important to him to appear respectable. He had been told that he was reaching above his station and living in a fantasy. He had shown them all when he grabbed the attention of the recruiters from Namyt'tkas. Disgust was all he felt when he remembered the smirk he wore the day he had left his home. He was suddenly very glad that no one from his old village would know the shame he faced when he was stripped of his title and home. He could not bare the thought that even the most unfortunate of souls would pity him.

He washed his despair away with his thoughts and rest of the dirt from his body before donning the bathrobe that had been laid out for him. It wasn't hard to imagine for a moment that this life could be his. If he continued to work for Lady Sedalia he would never rise in the ranks, but he would be allowed a more than comfortable life. He could use his earnings to purchase a nice home and a few servants. He could settle down and possibly even find a wife. It was all being offered to him now and all he would have to do was not turn tail and give up just because the mission was proving more difficult than he had originally thought. Even forsaking his morals and continuing to spy, though it went against everything he had once believed, seemed a reasonable choice when Clayton lay back on the comfortable mattress. Many honorable men had little to show for their hard work, but many more despicable characters profited off of unsavory dealings. If he could help bring some of these people to justice as he had been trying to do with Lord Malcolm than he would be doing enough good to counterbalance the bad he was committing.

The same meek serving girl returned with a stack of clean clothes, the blush still coloring her cheeks. "The others will return for the tub, there is fresh blood waiting for you in the informal dining hall, Lady Sedalia is expecting you there."

"Will you escort me to the informal dining hall? I have only ever been

to the library," Clayton took the bundle of cloth from her then, inspecting the rich fabric.

"Of course, I will wait in the hall."

"There is no need." Clayton walked the short distance to the corner which housed a screen which he could change behind. He put the clothes down on a small table, carefully removing the robe and hanging it on the edge of the screen. "What is your name, child?"

"I beg your pardon?" He could not see her face, but he could imagine the blush deepening as she stuttered in surprise.

"I said what is your name. I certainly can't call you girl, now can I?"

"M'lady has instructed me never to speak to our visitors, Sir."

"Well I am no mere visitor, I also work for our Lady. She would not object to you speaking with me when we both live to serve her, would she?"

The girl seemed to mull this logic over and Clayton took the time to sort through the clothing he had been given. The fabrics were heavy and very rich. Dyed in dark, bold colors he noted the elaborate embroidery that decorated the many pieces. Even the undergarments felt nicer than any he had ever worn and Clayton slid them on with care. The pants were cut to his exact figure and he wondered for a moment how they had gotten his measurements, but he knew questioning the reach and knowledge of Lady Sedalia was pointless. He laced the brown pants and slid on a hunter green tunic. A padded vest was next which matched the pants, but was sewn in a quilted pattern which added texture to his ensemble. There was nice eggplant jacket that slid over the outfit and was clasped with a gold brooch and chain shaped like a shield. It was the sigil of Namyt'tkas and he felt a sudden pang of loss at the sight. He would not be allowed to wear the brooch outside of these walls, he had no right to bear their sigil, but he appreciated the gesture.

Clayton had nearly forgotten that the girl was still in the room and he was shaken from his thoughts by her quiet voice. "My name is Elise, Sir."

"Well, Elise, how do I look?" Clayton walked out from behind the privacy screen and turned slowly with his arms thrown wide to show her the entire outfit.

"You look very respectable, Sir." Elise still looked incredibly uncomfortable, but she was looking at him instead of the floor at least and he considered that progress.

"I hope you genuinely believe that and are not just saying kind words. I could look like a fool and what would Lady Sedalia say then?"

The girl looked horrified at the suggestion and Clayton wondered, too late, if he had upset the girl. Interacting with others was never a gift of his. "I would never allow you to meet m'lady if you did not appear presentable."

"There is no need to worry, Elise, I meant no harm I was only teasing." Clayton reassured, but the blank look on the girl's face made it evident that she was not accustomed to any type of humor. He again felt

pity for the poor creature.

"Oh," she spoke slowly as if she was not sure how to proceed. "If you are ready, I will take you to the dining hall."

Realizing that he was not going to get any more of a reaction, Clayton nodded and stepped into place next to the girl as she held the door for him. His instincts screamed that he should be holding the door for her, but he clamped down on them. He would have to be careful with this girl, he might not believe her old enough for this type of work, but stirring rebellion in the hearts of his peers would not please his Lady. He did wonder, if only for a moment, where the girl's parents might be and what horrors must have befallen them that their daughter would need to work to help provide. He briefly entertained taking the girl under his wing when he purchased his own home. He could send her to school and help insure that she received a good education in all of the necessary skills to become a good homemaker or even a cook. Any job would hold higher esteem then being the message runner for a rich noble lady. It would be in poor form to take his employer's servants, though, and he chose to believe that when she was older, Elise would have other opportunities in Sedalia's house.

"We are here, Sir." Elise motioned to a closed door accented in silver, with a doorknob made of the largest sparkling gem he had ever seen.

"My name is Clayton, I am no lord or sir. You may use my given name if we are to be seeing each other as often as I believe we are."

"Of course, Sir," Elise stammered, coloring again when she realized her mistake. "Clayton, my apologies."

"There is no need, but if you could be available after Lady Sedalia and I are through, I am not entirely certain that I could find my way back to my room."

"I will be waiting for you here when you are through."

"Thank you, Elise." Clayton grasped the glittering purple gem firmly, pausing long enough to collect himself, before letting himself into the room.

The informal dining hall seemed far from relaxed to Clayton, but he couldn't say that he had been in enough dining halls to make that assessment. There was a long table set up in the middle of the room which was clearly the focal point. It could easily sit twenty people and each place was laid out as if they were expecting company at that very moment. Beautiful clear crystal goblets were on display and rose colored napkins were folded into beautiful flowers and nestled in each. Empty pitchers were stationed throughout the long table, presumably for blood given from humans with different diets or from different regions. He had heard that there were rich vampires that would keep humans who were only allowed certain foods so that their blood held differed pallets of flavor, but until seeing the over indulgence in Faegon, he had never believed such tales.

The room was lit by a large chandelier also made of clear crystal and

lit with more candles than Clayton had ever seen at once, bathing the room in shimmering light. There was also a large hearth, which was not lit, at the center of the farthest wall. There were modest sized windows lining the back wall framed by plain rose curtains to match the rest of the room, the only thing that didn't seem extravagant about the entire decor.

Another servant was waiting for him, though Lady Sedalia was nowhere to be seen. He silently pulled out a chair to the left of the head seat. Clayton took the seat, surprised when the man pushed it in and removed the napkin before tucking it into his shirt gently.

"Lady Sedalia will be along shortly, she thanks you for your patients. While you wait she has asked that I take your order and prepare your meal." The man was older if his graying hair and the lines on his face were any indication. Clayton imagined that he had spent most of his life serving his lady and was not at all offended by the confused look he was undoubtedly giving him.

"Order?" Clayton wondered if he was showing his peasant upbringing.

"Yes. We have fresh blood that was freely given hours ago or we have more exotic flavors stored from various regions. Lady Sedalia has informed me that I should retrieve anything that you desire."

"Is there any blood from Delnori?" This could be his only opportunity to try it, depending on how long he was meant to keep his cover for and he was not going to squander the opportunity.

"I am sure there is a bottle in the storeroom." With those final words, the man bowed and left the room.

He was not left alone for long, it seemed as soon as the doors had shut, they were being opened again, this time by yet another servant, though Clayton hadn't noticed if he had seen this one before because his focus was entirely taken by his employer.

Sedalia looked magnificent as always. Today she wore a high collared dress of a sheer black fabric with a short gold shift underneath. There was a slit in the fabric at her chest, showing off her breast deliberately, though Clayton certainly was not complaining at the sight. The dress gathered at her slim waist before flaring out and pooling around her feet which were clad in glittering gold sandals.

"Clayton! I had heard you arrived in a rough state last night. I am glad to see you doing well. I feared for you when I sent our last correspondence, but I hope that we have gained much useful knowledge for the Crown." Her words were cheerful, but there was no mistaking the underlying cold tone. She would not be pleased if his information was not up to her standards.

"I have much to report, but I am afraid that not all of it is good." He was nervous, but he hoped that it did not show. He could not afford to show weakness to his employer.

"I understand, we will not wait for our meal then. Come forward so I

may see your memories." Sedalia beckoned him closer.

Clayton was nervous. He had no training in the art of sharing memories and he knew that his strong emotions toward the night could taint the memory itself if he was not careful. He moved from his seat to kneel before the woman, praying that he would not embarrass himself. "How would you have me?"

"Your wrist." Lady Sedalia held out her hand expectantly not allowing him to back out. She seemed to sense his hesitation and her pretty face was clouded with disappointment. "There is no sense in hiding anything from me. I will learn of what happened last night no matter if you show me, but I prefer that I learn it from your memories so I may see exactly what happened."

Clayton pulled back the jacket sleeve and lifted his wrist, willing his anxiety to dissipate. "The images may be disturbing."

"I assure you I have seen horrors the likes of which you will never witness in your lifetime." Clayton took one more moment to collect his thoughts before nodding to show that he was ready. "So we begin."

Images from the night before flashed before Clayton's eyes almost as if Sedalia was pulling the thoughts for him just as quickly as she was drawing his blood. He was forced to relive the horror as Sedalia heard the conversation between Vestera and Malcolm for the first time. He was not proud that he had so little visual evidence of the attack, but he held on, knowing that the worst was yet to come. When the dust settled and eleven bodies were left to greet them, Clayton felt the fangs in his wrist detract and he was alone in his mind once more. The silence was unnerving.

"I should have done more to save him."

"He was a traitor to his king and to the Crown. There would have been no sense in endangering yourself for the likes of him." Sedalia spoke dismissively of the encounter as if eleven people had not just died. "The only shame is that he died now, before we could interrogate him for his crimes. Still, he might have told these rogues something of value, this will need to be reported to the rest of the High Council."

"Will you be able to share this memory with them?" He hated the thought that he might have relive his own failure in front of the rest of the High Council. He knew that Sedalia cared not if Malcolm lived, but he was sure that not everyone would share her sentiment.

"Of course not. You will have to present all of your findings to them. They know not that I have employed you to gather this information, we as the High Council are meant to play a much more passive role in the everyday lives of the people in the empire. It would be wise if you present this information without mentioning that we have any affiliation."

"That seems horribly deceitful." Clayton paused at her words, feeling extremely uncomfortable at the thought of lying to the most powerful people in the empire.

"There is not always a place for truth and honesty in a realistic world. These dangers you have helped uncover would have gone unnoticed had I not employed you. Could you imagine, had you not learned that Malcolm was feeding information to the rogues? We would never had known that our King's security was at risk. What is one small lie in the face of saving our very way of life from being destroyed by spoiled children who seek only to leave our world in ruins?"

"Of course you are right, Lady Sedalia." Clayton knew that there was no arguing with Lady Sedalia when she had her mind set on a goal. He was better off simply agreeing with her and accepting his fate than he would be arguing with her any longer. She did have a point, though, he could at least concede that. He would lie to the High Council if it meant giving them crucial information about the rogues and their sources. He could not allow his sensibilities to stop him from doing his duty. It was up to him to keep the King of Kings, and all of his people, safe from the rogues.

"That's a good boy." Sedalia smiled down on him, though her fangs were still protruding and it gave her a nearly sinister edge. "Oh good, our meal is here. Take your seat, Clayton, we are not savages."

Clayton stood and took his seat, the excitement of trying out the rich blood no longer as strong. He took his full glass with steady hands, though internally he was trembling with fear. The first sip tasted like ash and he did his best to calm his nerves so he might enjoy the blood.

"This is delicious," he complimented, hoping the words did not sound as hollow as they felt.

"Good, consider this just your first taste of the great things yet to come for you."

Clayton let the words sink into his skin as he sipped the most expensive meal he had ever had, dreading whatever other great things might be in store for him.

REAGAN

Being away from home, and from all the things that Reagan loved, was difficult enough without the constant stress of being a near fugitive in the King of King's forest weighing on her heart. She and Darius were well out of Namyt'tkas' boarder and even the trees looked richer as they slowly made their way to the capitol. Old, thick trunks lined the well groomed road. Faces were carved in many, the eye sockets dug so deep that they nearly appeared endless. Lesser beings whispered that the King of Kings held the power to see through the many eyes, ever watching his subjects and upholding the laws of his empire, but Reagan knew better. The eyes were merely a shallow scare tactic, one that might inspire a reaction from another, but certainly not from the Queen of House Lunaries. Her companion, however, seemed quite weary if his constant shifting looks were any indication.

"The eyes in the trees are harmless. There is no need to fear them and we are losing time," Reagan chided. She normally prided herself in her controlled temper, but even she had her limits.

"It is not the trees I worry about." Darius spoke, though Regan was not certain that the words were meant for her. "But you are right, we mustn't lose moonlight. We'll be well into Faegon's land soon and despite our House's standing we would be safer to find camp in the heart of Pa'ari's land than on its edge."

The man had a point and Reagan conceded that focusing their energy on walking was a better use of it than attempting to decipher her guardsman's cryptic words. Though Reagan did not wish to think that Queen Quanna or King Titus would harm her, they were her equals only surpassed by King Zentarion himself, she refused to allow hubris to be her downfall. Quanna was ruthless. It was known that she would follow Zentarion's word to her grave, but if given a long enough leash she would

raze the forest of all rogues and any who were suspected of being rogue sympathizers. Her bloodlust might only be rivaled by Cassandra and Zentarion and she was not someone that Reagan wished to meet in Mordin Forest without a full honor guard. Quanna was one of the oldest vampires alive, not including Zentarion or his High Council. She would have been the oldest out of all the Kings and Queens if it weren't for Tryali and their cowardly avoidance of any confrontation. Titus was even more of a stranger to Reagan. He had been appointed his position by King Zentarion the day he had forced the two great houses to merge as one. The Kings of Namytar and Tkasar here slain on the battlefield of the first Great War and Zentarion had called on his power as King of all to refuse the throne to both of their heirs. Instead, he had provided coveted seats on his High Council as substitute. It seemed nothing more than pity to Reagan, but there had never been news of dissent within Zentarion's ranks, so Reagan assumed that neither vampire saw it as a slight. It might have seemed like a safe assumption that being hand picked by Zentarion would make Titus his loyal servant, and thus keeping Reagan safe in this land, but there was no such thing as being safe, not in the times they were living in and she was glad to be out of both monarch's territory.

"Something is troubling you, do you wish for my assistance?" Darius was cautious with his words. She had already had to tell him more than once on their journey that she had no need of his aid to manage her emotions. He meant well, Reagan was sure of it, but his instance was becoming tiresome.

"I'm not troubled, merely sick for home and wishing for an end to our journey."

"I miss Lunaries as well, I am quite looking forward to a fresh meal and a soft bed." They had long since run out of the meager rations that they had packed and they kept their hunting to a minimum. Catching big game would have drawn unwanted attention and slowed them down. The pair had been left to settle for smaller creatures, often going a night or two before finding enough blood to fill their bellies.

"I would not dare to hope for a warm welcome upon our arrival. Had we been summoned by King Pa'ari than I would dare to dream, but it seems more realistic to lessen our expectations."

"You do not believe that we would be mistreated, not truly? I understand the gravity of our summons, but certainly we would be treated as guests. Even if your title was not enough to command respect, the King of Kings would still hear our story and seek to find justice." His words were impassioned and it was then that Reagan remembered just how young Darius truly was.

"I am afraid you are naive if you truly believe that."

Darius paused then, stopping mid step to turn and face her. There was a queer look to his eyes, but his words were what genuinely concerned the

queen. "May I ask you a question? It is quite a touch more personal than what I'd consider appropriate."

"You know you are always able to ask me questions," Reagan replied, curious as to what the normally reserved man considered so personal as to warrant such a disclaimer.

"I know I may ask you, but will you answer it?" He did not dare ask if she would try lying to him, but the uncertainty was there in his eyes. It would have been foolish, of course. Reagan knew that she would not be able to lie to him, his aura magic was strong enough that he could tell a lie just as easily as if she had a heartbeat to gauge by.

"That depends entirely on what the question is."

Darius seemed to think carefully then, composing his words in his mind before daring to speak them out loud. "Why do you mistrust King Zentarion so?"

The answer was easy and yet Reagan wasn't sure how to respond. There was too much hidden about her past, about Lunaries' past, and to tell Darius the answer to his question truthfully would only bring more questions to the surface.

"You must understand that much happened to our House and to our people long before you came to me. It is not safe to speak these words here." Reagan turned to look about them and noticed then that a small opening in the canopy above them had given way to the night sky. It was a full moon, and while that might have been considered a good omen by those superstitious enough to believe such things, it was a blood moon that looked down on them. The dark red glow seemed to wash over everything it touched and dread began to eat at the queen. "We must keep moving, there isn't much time and I fear that the King of Kings will not take kindly to us being any later than we already are."

Darius seemed to take a moment longer before nodding and following her lead. While Reagan had not been to the capitol in many centuries, she knew that they were nearing the outskirts of House Faegon's land. She could very nearly taste the magic in the air with every step. There was no proper temple in House Lunaries as there were so few people who lived within her walls who could use any magical art, but House Faegon was known to house a temple for every school of magic. She had thought about sending Natalya more than once, it would do the girl good to be taught by a High Priest or Priestess with the gift of Sight, but it wasn't safe to send her so far. She had privately confided her thoughts to Cohen and he had agreed with her to keep the girl close. Now she doubted that it was because he had agreed with her and instead had selfishly agreed to keep the girl close to himself. She would have to keep an eye on the pair when she returned home.

If I ever return home.

The ominous glow of the moon hung right above their heads as the

road cleared and made way to a stone path, the first indicator that they were entering the main road to House Faegon. There were no guards posted at the entrance. The small, festering feeling of dread was quickly blooming and Reagan was sure that she was no longer imaging the eyes that she felt all around her. She had told Darius that the trees were merely a decoration and she wholeheartedly believed that. She was more worried about the very real eyes belonging to spies for Cassandra that could be lurking in the distance.

"What really caused the fall of our House?" Darius' question caught her by surprise and Reagan was ashamed to admit that she was startled by it and by the proximity of her guardsman. Darius was now in stride with her, his elbow just nearly brushing hers in a way that would certainly not be considered appropriate, had they been back home.

"That is something taught to each and every youth and new member to House Lunaries." Reagan did her best to sound flippant, but even to her own ears she sounded caged, like a startled animal.

"With all due respect, I know that you are hiding something from me, from the House." Darius looked sideways to her then, his expression unreadable. The blank stare was so foreign on his face that Reagan very nearly took a step back, but stopped herself before she showed such a weakness.

"That is a particularly long story." Stalling would do nothing. They were alone, or at least seemingly alone, and there would be no way for her to escape the inevitable. All the words of doubt that Anya had loudly thrown at her since they had found Darius were suddenly seeming quite believable. He had no use for such information, not if he were truly loyal to her and her people. She had refused to believe that the young, scared boy that they had found, turned by Cassandra herself and then left to rot, was really working for the wretched woman. Every nurturing bone in her body had told her to trust him and lift him up. Now she wondered, far too late, if she had been wrong.

"We have the rest of the journey for you to tell it." The blank mask finally cracked and there was a gleam in the man's eyes that Reagan found deeply unsettling.

"Why do you want this information?" She hardly thought that the man would admit it so freely if he was working for Cassandra, but there seemed to be nothing to lose at this point.

"You are stalling and it is tiresome." Darius stopped his confident jaunt and turned to face her. His back was to the road leading back home, forcing her to stand in front of him on the open road just on the edge of House Faegon's borders.

"I suppose you will not wait until we are on safer ground?" The stern look she received nearly caused the queen to strike her subject, but she was not that kind of woman and certainly not that kind of ruler, no matter if

this man was not truly loyal to her. "You must understand that this secret has been heavily guarded, not just by myself but by those close to me. To tell you would put the lives of hundreds, if not thousands at risk."

"Go on, you will not talk your way out of this. I will have the truth from you."

Reagan glared at the man then. She could possibly overpower him, but she doubted that he was alone. It seemed that the eyes she had felt on her over the past night and day of travel were not her imagination. As if to prove her right, noises from the trees around them signaled the arrival of twelve men and women. Each had their fangs protruding and each had deep brown, glowing eyes. She knew those eyes well as they were staring at her now, waiting for her to continue.

"It all began before I took the bite, when I was human. I lived in a small village on the edge of Mordin Forest with my two younger brothers. Our village was attacked by a band of rogues, rare for that time since they did not normally hunt in groups. The older of my brothers had been bitten, but not turned. My brothers were all I had; I could not lose him so I begged the nearest vampire to do something. I had no knowledge of the laws that bound this society and I am lucky that it was King Gareth that I had found. He turned my brother, forcing him to drink his blood knowing what it would do to Lunaries, but choosing to do the right thing despite it."

"My youngest brother and I took the bite not long after, but the damage had already been done. The High Council had heard and we were banished. My brother, who I begged to be turned, resented the gift, something he confided in anyone who might listen. He was an outcast, but I was being well integrated into the house. Over time, Gareth took a liking to me and began to train me under the guise of wanting me to be the commander of his guardsmen. Even I had no way of knowing that he truly wanted to rename me as his heir."

"Despicable," Darius spat and his bitten children mumbled their agreement until it felt like a dull roar was escalating around them. Reagan knew that she wouldn't have the time to reach her weapons, but it seemed that Darius was genuinely engaged in her story and so she did her best to subtly set her feet, stealing herself for the attack she knew would come.

"The day that he announced that his former heir and lover, Cassandra, would become the commander of the guard, and I his true heir I knew that there would be a steep price to pay for his actions. I loved Gareth as I would a father and I did not even realize his attraction to me until that moment. I begged Cassandra to believe me, but the damage had been done. Her and my brother had suddenly become close, something I hadn't noticed. I feared what poison she poured into my brother's head and I began to gather my own allies within the castle. I knew even then that before long it would turn to civil war. I was lucky in that my youngest brother understood my plight, he knew that I had not intended for any of it

to happen. On the day of the coup I lost my King and my brother."

"Who were your brothers?" Darius asked, though by the look on his face he had already figured it out.

"The youngest you know, Cohen has stuck by my side through all of our hardships." Reagan spoke, her voice just above a whisper, though she knew that she could not hide from the truth any longer.

"And your other brother? You speak as if he has died." Darius' words were careful, as if he was trying to trap her in a lie, though Reagan hardly saw the point. She had not lied yet and she would not now.

"He is alive, I'm sure. I have not seen him or spoken his name since the day he left through the castle gates with Cassandra. His name was Logan. She was jealous of me and took him from me. She cares little for him or for anyone that is not herself and she will turn on him. I only wish that I might reach him before then. I have to believe that he is smarter than that. I refuse to believe that a wretched bitch like her could really win in the end."

A noise from the trees caught Reagan's attention, though she noted the look of surprise that passed Darius' face. She should not have been surprised to see Cassandra emerge from the shadows. She looked more regal than Reagan thought she had a right to. Dressed in fine black leather travel pants with a small matching vest that did little to hide her feminine curves or the words that lay inked on her chest. Her hair was swept back into a long braid that twisted on top of her head. House Rayne was further from Faegon than Lunaries was and yet she looked as if she had just stepped from a royal carriage.

"My, my. I would love to say that the centuries have been kind to you, but that would be a cruel lie." Cassandra sneered, her eyes traveling Reagan's body with unabashed distaste. "This wasn't the plan, Darius, but I can overlook that since you so kindly brought her to me. You can send your pets away now, and let your elder handle this."

Instead of signaling them to step aside, Darius motioned in a way that was familiar to Reagan and she was easily flanked on all sides. She had seen Darius use the same motion in training her guardsmen and for a fleeting moment Reagan hoped that she had been wrong and that her companion had truly been loyal to her all along.

"I don't think so," Darius stepped in front of his children to face his sire. "You see, I've learned some interesting things that you've kept from me and I believe it's time you give me some answers."

"Oh my pet, what makes you think you can demand anything of me? Has your time with this cowardly false queen made you go soft?"

Rage like Reagan had never felt before coursed through her. Any rational thought flew from her mind and she pushed past Darius' children and the man himself as easily as one might move through water.

"Those are bold words for a woman who tore her House apart simply

because of her pride." Reagan hissed, lunging forward to meet the woman.

Cassandra was quick to join her and their bodies met in a clash so strong that the force threw them apart. Cassandra landed on her feet with ease, but Reagan fell to the ground, the lack of training becoming evident as her body protested when she jumped to her feet. Darius and the twelve vampires who had come to his aid were nowhere to be seen and Reagan knew that this would have to be a fight that she won alone. A blur of brown hair was the only warning that Reagan got before she was being roughly shoved into the nearest tree. She scratched at Cassandra, her claws meeting with anything within her reach and she felt more than a little satisfied when she heard the rogue hiss in pain.

"I knew you would let Darius in. It was always in your nature to take what didn't belong to you. You wouldn't be able to resist taking him in. I might have been the one to turn him, but do you know who decided to send him to you? Logan was the one who chose him out of all of our other children. Even after all these years he knows how to get to you still."

The words stung and Reagan felt the fight leave her. There would have been a time that she would not have believed Cassandra's words. She and Logan had not been close since they had been human, but she knew that he had loved her, at least at one point. Too much time and far too much pain had happened since then and Reagan found herself beginning to doubt everything she had thought she'd known.

"And even if that were the case? Does that make you any less wrong for the evil you caused?" Reagan bit back, realizing that she was allowing Cassandra to play games with her head.

"What evils? You took my love from me, my crown. I didn't do anything but open Logan's eyes to the corrupt woman that you try so hard to pretend not to be! You cost me everything, I hardly see my fault in the matter." Cassandra's normally beautiful face was contorted in rage.

"I didn't do anything! I was a child!" Reagan reached for weapons that were not there and settled for her claws and teeth.

"You were hardly a child. You knew exactly what you were doing!" Cassandra whipped out a dagger and slashed at Reagan's body, cutting her loose tunic in the process revealing pale skin. "You are just a whore who never deserved anything that was given to her."

"I never touched him, not once. He loved me and I never once knew that until it was too late." Reagan sobbed as she felt the kiss of the sunspear against her stomach.

"That just makes it worse!" Cassandra screamed while she spun them around. She had her pinned to the ground in her fury, the dagger close to her neck. "You had it all and you didn't even appreciate it!"

"I will not be ignored!" Darius cried from the sidelines and Reagan resisted the urge to turn to look at him, using the interruption to kick her leg up, catching Cassandra's calf and causing her to teeter until she fell to

the side. Darius swooped down on her then and Cassandra flung him off of her with ease, sending him flying into the air. He landed with a sickening thud.

"See, even those who used to serve you no longer wish to partake in your war." Reagan taunted and rushed to pick up the forgotten dagger. Darius' men had since scattered and they were the only ones left on the stone road. Cassandra's cold laugh caused her to pause and the opening was all that the wicked woman needed to have her pinned down once more.

"It matters not. Darius will wake to see your dead corpse and he will know that he is not welcome in my home. The sight of your body will be the only memory proof that he'll need to stay in your idiot brother's good graces. I only regret that you won't live long enough to see the fall of your House, but killing you now is too sweet to pass up."

Reagan struggled against her confines, but it was no use, Cassandra was a vampire trained for war, over three centuries her senior, and Reagan had spent her rule sitting atop a crumbling throne. She would never see her House again, never lay eyes on her brother or kiss her paramour. She would never feel the sun or know the joy of watching Natalya grow to be the wonderful vampire that she knew she would be. A single tear fell down her cheek as she felt the kiss of the sunspear on her throat once more.

"I am so sorry." Reagan choked out as the pain from the dagger became too much. The act of speaking had just pushed the blade in deeper and a sudden, searing pain coursed through her body. For a moment the blade was removed and she thought that Cassandra might have finally found some mercy, but all such hopes were dashed when the blade came slashing down on her throat, opening her up to the sensation of fire. If she was screaming she could not hear it with the roaring in her ears. Her vision went next as a white light blinded her. The smell and taste of blood overpowered the strong scents of the forest until it clogged her nostrils and became so much that it was as if she could hardly smell at all, her tongue heavy and useless as her sense of taste faded away too. Her sense of touch was the last to go and as her body crumbled into the ground the numbness in her bones faded until she felt nothing.

CONSUMED BY SHADOWS

SIONANN

A light autumn breeze was wafting the smells of fresh bread and produce through the middle city streets causing Queen Sionann of Solara to pause and regret skipping her morning meal. She ignored as her stomach protested and she prayed that their meeting would not take long. They were nearing their destination and yet the crowded streets seemed to exist only to disprove her. The streets were full of merchants and their customers going about their business, though many stopped their shopping to speak kind words to their Queen. On any other day, she would not have hesitated to stop and talk with her people, but there were more urgent matters to attend to and the longer she was kept from the castle, the more suspicious her husband would become.

"Make way, make way," Charles, a member of her personal guard called ahead as he and the few men she had allowed to accompany her did their best to part the sea of people before them.

"We should be there soon, Your Majesty." Alanna, Sionann's personal advisor and oldest friend, said. The queen wasn't sure if she was assuring herself or if the words were meant for her, but smiled, however tight lipped at the woman and continued on the path.

The sun was high in the sky, though it would be dark before long as was normal this close to winter. They had been blessed with a mild harvest and the sun shone bright on her orange hair bringing out the natural strands of blonde and gold. Being a fair-skinned lass with hair the color of fire always set her aside in her husband's land and she had almost thought to cover her customary curls in a dark hood, but Alanna had warned against it. It would not do to hide from her people, no matter the occasion for her jaunt, and she had been hard-pressed to agree. She was not favored by the public at large and any excuse for them to criticize her would only bring undue stress on herself and the King. The people of Solara, specifically

those from Magdus, the capitol, were always weary of her. Her being from the main continent had much to do with it, as many of the nobility she spent time with had grown to care for her as a person, but it would not have fared well for her, had she been discovered bundled beneath dark robes in the middle of the day.

In contrast, Alanna looked much like many of the woman from the Solarian kingdom. Her long, dark hair was gathered in the intricate updos that were popular for women of nobility in their region. Her skin was still light, though nowhere near as fair as the queen's, and she did have evidence of sun on the bridge of her nose and the tops of her cheeks. Had she been born to a lower class family her skin would have been truly sun kissed and freckles may have even decorated her skin. It was more than just her physical attributes, however, that made her blend in better in Magdus. Because the island was so much smaller than the main continent it was as if it was its own world entirely. Sionann would never put her concerns to words, but she never felt like she belonged amongst these people. Even the streets around the castle, the very same ones she had traveled through over the past ten years, still seemed odd to her and she never left without a guard or a companion so as to not get lost within her own city.

The winding cobblestone streets seems to stretch on for miles, though Sionann knew that was just the slow pace in which they walked. The city temple was strategically placed at the center of Magdus, allowing for all people no matter their station easy access to the comfort it provided. It was not uncommon for her to travel to the temple, especially just after the harvest, to give thanks for the bounty that was collected for the year, but today she had more urgent matters.

"Your contact is aware of our requests?" Sionann asked her companion faking little interest, though internally she was abuzz with nerves.

"Yes, I received word from them just last night. All will go according to plan." Alanna replied, her cool blue eyes showed no emotion and the queen hoped the same could be said for her own.

"Make way, make way!" Charles called again from the front of their small party. The grand archways of the temple were within sight and the crowd was beginning to lessen. Services were held at sunup for the lower class and again at midday for the middle class. There were night services held for special occasions, most notably for the end of harvest and also when winter's frost broke and the vegetation began to sprout once more. The temple was always open to those looking for comfort or to pray to the great God Surya and the wonderful Goddess Luna, for both sun and moon have light by which to guide their children. Sionann would need more than a guiding light to find her way, but she had faith that her wait was over and her prayers answered.

Sionann and Alanna were the only two of their group to take the stairs

that led to the temple doors. It was sacrilegious to bring weapons beyond the temple doors and they would have no need of escorts beyond them. The queen took her heavy, navy skirts into her hands, lifting them so her slippered feet could mount the steps with ease as her companion did the same. They were similarly dressed in less regal attire as was common for strolls through the city. The dainty tiara that sat atop her curls was the only thing that set her aside from her advisor and the jewels reflected off of the high sun and littered the steps before them with round, bright dots.

Large, oak doors stood open for the pair and they were greeted with the earthy smell of sandalwood and vanilla. The high windows outfitted in stained glass causing the reflection of her tiara to become lost as the floor of the temple lay decorated with shards of color. It was much more lavish than any temple Sionann had known back in her own home, but she had grown accustomed to its unique charm. She and Alanna moved through the main hall with ease. If she hadn't been in such a hurry, she would have stopped to light a candle for those she had lost, but there was no time and she hoped that Alanna would forgive her for not stopping to pay their respects. There would be time for that later, once the meeting was done and the less time they lingered the better.

From the main hall there were three doors. The one to the left lead to the private dorms belonging to the priests and priestesses that lived in and maintained the temple. Straight ahead lead to the large hall where services were held. The door to the right was where she and her companion were headed and the women moved as one toward the small, private prayer rooms. Doors as large and impressive as the main temple doors made way to a long, dark hall. Along both sides stood tall, proud archways that each led to the private areas. Heavy velvet curtains that acted both as sight and sound barriers hung in each archway. When the rooms were not in use, the curtains were gathered to the side and held by gold tassels and bound to the wall. There were many open rooms, not surprising due to the hour, but Alanna guided them to the back of the hall to the farthest room on the right. The purple curtain was hiding the occupant of the prayer room, but that did not dissuade her.

"Who comes to seek the path to eternal light from the God Surya and his sister Goddess Luna?" A voice from beyond the curtain called and startled the queen. There would have been no way for the person inside to know that they had been standing there, yet they spoke as soon as they had stopped in front of the archway.

"It is your humble servants who seek light and guidance from you, Surya and also from your sister Luna. We come with open minds and hearts and accept your teachings, whatever they may be." Alanna responded and Sionann waited with bated breath. The words from behind the curtain had been the traditional words spoken by the priest or priestess during services, but Alanna's response had been a modified one that she had never heard

before.

"Welcome, then my humble servants, you may enter," the voice answered and Alanna reached forward, entering the room before her queen to insure her safety.

Candles were lit and dispersed amongst the prayer room in no discernible pattern and it took Sionann a minute to adjust to the extreme change in light. In the middle of the room sat a rich, red rug as was customary, though the woman who sat at its center looked out of place. Those dedicated to the temple and its teachings wore plain robes bleached of all color. While it was considered appropriate for the temples to be done in glittering gold and gems, it was expected of those who cared for it to present themselves as simply and demurely as possible as to not offend the God and Goddess. It was obvious that this woman who they came to meet was not of the temple or even of the same faith. Her dark hair was held back in intricate braids with a thin silver chain woven throughout. She wore robes that covered her from head to toe, though the pale pink fabric was sheer and revealed the curves of her body with ease. Her dress was made of fabric in a similar color and it allowed for her arms and neck to be shown, revealing ink drawings permanently tattooed on her skin. She had flowers that appeared to grow from the top of her chest and up to her collar before traveling down her arms. They stopped around her upper arms on both sides. From her seated position, Sionann could see her bare calves. She may have been more scandalized by the sight had she not been more focused on the dead flower petals that were inked there.

"Queen Sionann of the Kingdom Solara, I present you with High Priestess Tash, former student of High Priest Stepan the Great Healer." Alanna made the introductions, seemingly unfazed by the girl's state of dress, or rather undress.

"Your Majesty," the girl, for surely she looked no older than a girl of sixteen, took to her feet and curtsied low. "I have been told that you seek guidance for your son, the prince."

"It is not guidance I am looking for, I seek a cure for my son's ailments," Sionann's voice was firm, not seeing a need to speak around the reason for this secret meeting. Time was a precious thing and she was not sure if she trusted this girl to be of any assistance.

"Right to the point, I can appreciate that," Tash's smile was forward, though not unkind. "I assume that you have exhausted all other known methods before seeking me out?"

"Every healer and physician in the city has been through the castle doors and my son is still sick, do you know how to cure him, or am I wasting my time?" Sionann was not one to become upset so quickly but this girl made her weary and the farce of medicine men and woman coming and going from her home had gone on long enough. "He should be coming of age soon and he is not yet well enough to take his birthright as heir to the

throne. I will not see my husband's legacy end without using all resources at my disposal."

"I meant no offense, Your Majesty. I was merely surprised by the message that came from Alanna and also from this choice of venue. It was not difficult to gain access to, per-say, but you must know that a woman of my abilities is not welcomed in these walls."

"A woman of your abilities is even less welcomed into the castle walls," Sionann replied, not bothering to comment on the girls' discomfort. It mattered not to her if the men and women of the Faith were unhappy with a priestess of magic in their presence, no less one of Stepan's own student. Her husband, the King, would have been even less happy to have hosted her in their home and so this venue had been set. "I may be the Queen, but my King's word is law. It is no secret that he detests magic and all those who wield it, but I, as a mother, cannot sit by and watch my baby die. Can you save my son or not?"

"I would have to see him to be sure, could you arrange for that?"

Sionann hesitated. It was one thing to risk being caught speaking to this girl, it would be an entirely different risk to bring her into the castle. There was no way to move the prince, Phalen was too weak to move outside of his room.

"I know your concerns, Your Majesty, but I trust Tash. Her training speaks for itself, but she has gained many of those flower petals from curing members of my own family." Alanna spoke up, her eyes downcast as if she was afraid to speak out of turn.

"I don't understand what you mean by that." Sionann admitted, not ashamed that everything about this girl and her tattoos was foreign to her. Back on the main continent there had been very few people born with the gift of magic. It had been said that the origin of it all was from a place called Delnori which was located in a harsh mountain range, well beyond Solara's borders. When she had sailed the Great Sea and wed King Quincy she had learned quickly that the man barely tolerated magic and its use, though she had never learned why.

"These petals are a physical representation of my successes and failures. When a person chooses to train in their art they are awarded with a tattoo. I chose the tiger lily because I loved the vibrance of their petals. For every person I helped heal I gained a single, live petal."

"And the dead petals? Do they represent your failures?"

If the girl was embarrassed, she didn't show it and she merely nodded. "Yes, these were nearly all gained in training, but they serve as a reminder to me as well. Not every person is meant to be saved and to have life there must also be death."

It was not the response she expected, but she found that she was still satisfied by it. "I can get you into the castle undetected, but you will need to be dressed more... *appropriately*."

"This is the customary garb for a prestress or priest of magic. It is important for those who wish to seek our help to see our capabilities. But I understand how it may look in the halls of a proper castle. You will not need to worry about providing me with clothing. I will come when convenient in the proper attire of a medicine woman. I assume you sought me out in secret because myself and my kind are not welcomed in the castle."

"I will let your insolence go this one time because I need you to cure my son, but you will, under no circumstances, speak to me in such a way again. Are we clear?"

"Yes, Your Majesty."

"Alanna will reach out to you as she did today to let you know when you are expected at the castle." There was nothing left to say to the girl and Sionann turned to her closest confidant. "Let us return to the castle. I am sure our prolonged absence will have been noted by now."

"Your Majesty, Lady Alanna," Tash curtsied to both.

Alanna pushed back the curtain and allowed her to pass through first. The two fell in stride together as they walked back to the main hall. They stopped before a row of candles and Alanna reached out first to light one.

"For my love, may Luna guide you in the afterlife," she whispered as she lit the white pillar candle for her late husband. He had passed two winters ago and the woman had never really been the same.

"For my son, may Luna guide you in the afterlife," Sionann took the freshly lit candle that Alanna had just replaced to light her own. Before Phalen had been born she had been pregnant with another son, he would have been her first son. She had lost the baby and thus her pregnancy with Phalen had become even more precious.

"Thank you, Your Majesty. We did not have to stop to light the candles."

Sionann reached out to grasp her hand. She may be a Queen, but death saw no favoritism and in his eyes all people were equal. "We must always stop to remember those we have lost. To have life there must also be death."

If Alanna recognized the words from Tash's statement earlier she did not say and she simply nodded. "This is true, now we must return to the castle, the King will wonder where you have gone."

"We will just have to tell him that we took our time to pray, he will not see any fault in that." Sionann took the lead from the glitzy hall back into the afternoon sun. Charles and her small guard staff stood waiting for them at a respectable distance before moving to flank them at all sides.

"There was a messenger from the castle just a moment ago, he said it was urgent, but I didn't feel it appropriate to disturb you or Lady Alanna in such a sacred place, Your Majesty."

"Thank you Charles, we will make haste for the castle then, please take

us through the quickest route."

"Of course, Your Majesty." Charles took up the front once more, calling out to the people to clear the streets and make way for their queen.

Now that they were back under the strong glare of the sun, Sionann had a moment to consider the consequences of what she had just done. Quincy, her husband—the King, had never once told her why he detested magic so, though the maids in the castle had loose lips and she gathered that it had something to do with a girl who had lived in the castle walls before. If the rumors were to be believed, she had committed an egregious crime against her husband when he had still been the prince and Quincy had never forgiven her. It seemed drastic to her that her husband, a genuinely kind and forgiving man, would denounce all magic all based on the wrongdoings of one girl, but he would never tell her what happened and there was no sense in wasting time trying to solve the mystery. Sionann knew that Quincy would be furious with her when he found out that she had sought the help of a High Priestess, but there were no other options.

"Prince Phalen will be alright, I know Surya and Luna will hear our prayers," Alanna reassured her and the queen did not have the heart to disagree.

"Thank you, Lady Alanna, I do hope you are correct." The two continued on in silence as Charles cleared the path for them. Sionann wondered, if only for a moment, if she was truly making the correct choice before banishing the thought. High Priestess Tash would heal her son. There was no doubt in her mind.

ABOUT THE AUTHOR

Melissa A Geary is a Massachusetts native who began writing *The Shadows Series* in college. When she is not writing she enjoys time spent with her husband Tom and their puppy Memphis. To learn more about Melissa and her work, visit www.melissaageary.com.

37168077R00258

Made in the USA
Middletown, DE
22 February 2019